Ghosts of the past, horrors of the present

Your name is Walter Roland.

You are a reporter.

Your job is to search out and to reveal the truth.

In today's Germany, that job is not popular.

But when a terrified woman's accusations and a man's hideously slain corpse open your eyes to a conspiracy that extends from the highest levels of wealth and power to the deepest depths of depravity, you cannot turn away...

... even if it kills you....

Also by Simmel and available from Popular Library:

THE BERLIN CONNECTION

THE MONTE CRISTO COVER-UP

THE CAIN CONSPIRACY

THE CAESAR CODE

DOUBLE AGENT—TRIPLE CROSS

I CONFESS

THE AFFAIR OF NINA B.

THE WIND AND THE RAIN

THE SIBYL CIPHER

THE
TRAITOR BLITZ

Simmel

Translated from the German by Catherine Hutter

FAWCETT POPULAR LIBRARY • NEW YORK

THE TRAITOR BLITZ

Original German title: *DER STOFF, AUS DEM DIE TRAEUME SIND*

Published by Fawcett Popular Library, a unit of CBS Publications, the Consumer Publishing Division of CBS Inc., by arrangement with Droemersche Verlagsanstalt Th. Knaur Nachf.

ISBN: 0-445-04512-4

Printed in the United States of America

First Fawcett Popular Library printing: January 1980

10 9 8 7 6 5 4 3 2 1

This book is dedicated to the man who in this novel is called Bertie.

1

Research

1

"So now my friends will kill this person," said Fräulein Louise. Outside her window I could see the old chestnut trees, their glistening branches bare. It was raining hard. "They will kill this person," Fräulein Louise repeated, smiling happily. "Nothing can stop him."

"Have they finally found out who it is?" I asked.

"Not yet."

"I see."

"And so," she said, "it could be a man or a woman." Her face bore an expression of boundless confidence. "It could be a young person, an old person, a foreigner, a German...."

Her name was Gottschalk, Fräulein Louise Gottschalk. She spoke with a slight Czech accent. She came from Reichenberg—Liberec today—in what was the Sudetenland in Hitler's time. Her hair was snow white. She was sixty-two years old and had been a social worker with juveniles for forty-two years.

"Does he or she have a brother?" she went on. "A sister, a father, a mother? Any relatives? Perhaps. On the other hand, this person may have nobody. What profession? Any profession or none. Anything is possible."

"I see."

"Where is this person's home? Or is he or she fleeing? What is his name—or hers, if it is a woman? My friends don't know the answer to any of this. After all, they've never seen the person."

"I know. And still you're sure?"

"Absolutely sure. Do you want to know why? Because I outwitted them."

"Outwitted them?"

"Yes. I discussed it with them until they were just as determined as I am. After all, they can't let someone who has done something wicked go on being wicked. Because of him. *Because of him!*" she repeated. "You understand, Herr Roland?"

"Yes."

"Pretty smart of me, wasn't it?"

"Very."

"So that's what they promised me. And my friends can do anything. There's nothing on earth they can't do. That's why I know they'll find this person and save him! Oh, you can't imagine how happy I am!"

"Yes, I can."

"When they have caught him and he has been saved—that will be the most wonderful day of my life!" She laughed like a child anticipating Christmas morning.

I have never known anyone kinder than Louise Gottschalk. Not until I met her did I learn to appreciate what they really meant—all those conceptions that have become senseless or perverted by unscrupulous misuse: tolerance, belief in goodness, loyalty, reliability, love, courage, and the tireless efforts to make others feel safe and at peace.

Fräulein Louise's friends are: an American advertising man from New York's Madison Avenue; a Dutch publisher of textbooks from Groningen; a German pickle-factory owner from Seelze, near Hannover; a Russian circus clown from Leningrad; a Czech architect from Brunn; a Polish mathematics professor from Warsaw University; a German savings-bank employee from Bad Homburg; a Ukrainian peasant from Petrikova, near the Dnieper River; a French court reporter from Lyon; a Norwegian cook from Christiansand, in the southernmost part of Norway, near Cape Lindesnes; and a German philosophy student from Rondorf, near Cologne.

Fräulein Louise's friends come from various regions, and their characters, experiences, likes and dislikes, opinions and degrees of education are very different, too. They have only one thing in common—they have all been dead for ten years.

2

He heard seven shots, then he heard his father's voice. It seemed to come from far away. The shots didn't frighten him. He had heard too many since coming here; besides, there was shooting going on in his dream, but his father's voice woke him.

"You must get up, Karel," said his father.

He was standing beside the bed in which his son had slept; his smile was reassuring. He was a tall, thin man with a broad, high forehead, and he had beautiful hands. That evening the expression on his tired face was somber. "I've spoken to people in the village," he said. "They change the guards at midnight. While that's going on, the channel is unguarded for five minutes. That's when we can cross."

"What if they don't change the guards?" asked Karel.

"They change the guards every night," said his father, "and every night people manage to get across. Did you get some sleep?"

"Yes."

Karel stretched. He had left Prague with his father about fifty hours ago. They had been fleeing that long. It had been difficult to get out of the city. They had made complicated detours on crowded streetcars, on a truck and on foot, to avoid the foreign soldiers, their tank barriers and controls. Finally they had hopped a train and had ridden for a long time in an empty cattle car.

Karel's father knew they were looking for him. In the early morning hours of August 21, as soon as he had heard the news, he had known what would happen to him. They were looking for him to arrest him. This was logical and inevitable. He wasn't angry with those who were looking for him. They had to do it, just as he had had to do what he had done.

The fact that they were looking for him had made him cautious. He had thought over every step carefully, and everything had gone well so far. They had almost reached the Bavarian border. Only two more kilometers and they would be safe. But these last two kilometers were the most dangerous of all. That was why Karel's father had insisted that his son get some sleep, here in his grandmother's house. His father's mother. Only his friends knew where his mother lived and none of them would betray him.

The old woman lived alone on the outskirts of the village, where she ran a small stationary store. When there were any newspapers, she sold them, too; but for two days now there hadn't been any. Karel and his father had come to her because she lived near a section of the border that wasn't supposed to be too closely guarded; one could cross more easily here.

"What's the time?" asked Karel.

11

"Ten o'clock," said his father, laying a hand on his son's forehead. "You're hot. Do you have a fever?"

"No. I'm sure I don't." He shook his head. "I'm only hot because of the lion."

"What lion?"

"On Wenzelsplatz. In my dream. There were a lot of lions, and even more rabbits. But the lions had guns and the rabbits couldn't get away. The lions shot at the rabbits and every time one of them fell down."

"Poor rabbits!"

"No, no. Nothing happened to the rabbits. Every time a lion shot, a *lion* fell down. Wasn't that strange?"

"Very strange," said his father.

"Seven lions shot and all seven fell down and that's when you woke me up." Karel threw back the quilt and jumped naked out of his grandmother's high bed. He was eleven years old. His body was strong, long-legged and tanned, his eyes were big and as black as his short hair, which shone in the light of a nearby lamp. Karel was a serious boy; he read a lot. His teachers had nothing but praise for him. He had lived with his father in a big apartment in an old house on Jerusalemska Street. If you leaned out of the window, you could see the beautiful trees and blossoming shrubs and flowers of Vrchlickeho-sady Park and the small pond in the middle. When he had been a little boy, Karel had gone for walks in the park with his mother. He could remember it very well. His mother had asked her husband for a divorce and had moved to West Germany with another man just before Karel's fifth birthday. They had never received a letter from her.

When Karel's father had got him out of bed in the early morning hours of August 21, packed two suitcases and hurried out of the house with his son, first to hide in the apartment of friends, Karel had seen tanks with machine guns in the park between the roses, carnations, and dahlias. Men in strange uniforms had sat in the turrets, looking bewildered and sad. Karel had waved to them, and quite a few had waved back.

Karel's father pointed to a chair beside the bed. "I've put out your things," he said, and Karel could see his blue suit, the one he was only allowed to wear on Sundays. "We've got to wear our best things," said his father, who was also wearing a dark blue suit, a white shirt, and a blue tie embroidered with tiny silver elephants. Two shots could be heard outside, in rapid succession. "We may lose our suitcases or have to leave them behind."

"Oh, that's why we're all dressed up," said Karel. "I see." His father crossed over to the window, pushed the calico curtain aside a little and looked out at the village street, lying empty in the moonlight. "Damn the moon!" he muttered, looking up at the honey-colored orb afloat in a dark sky full of stars. "I had so hoped it would be cloudy."

"Yes," said Karel. "That would have been better. Would you please help me with my tie?" He was a polite child. As he raised his chin so that his father could knot his tie, he asked, "But we're taking your trumpet, aren't we?" Now he sounded excited. "You're going to need it over there."

"Of course," said his father, his fingers awkward as he leaned down to fix his son's tie. "We're taking both suitcases and the trumpet."

Karel's father was a musician. For three years now he had been playing the trumpet he was about to carry from his native Republic of Czechoslovakia across the border to the Republic of West Germany, the so-called Bundesrepublik. It was a very good trumpet. Karel had often played it, too. The boy was very musical. Until the night of August 20, Karel's father had played in the EST Bar. It was one of the most elegant nightclubs in Prague and was part of the prestigious Esplanade Hotel on Washingtonova Street, next to Vrchlickeho-sady Park and not far from their apartment on Jerusalemska Street.

"I'll carry the suitcases," said Karel's father, "and you carry the case with the trumpet."

"Oh, yes!" Karel was radiant. He worshiped his father because he was such a great artist and could play the trumpet so beautifully. Karel wanted to be a musician when he grew up; he had made up his mind about that. Whenever his father had practiced, Karel had sat on the floor at his feet, listening. But with the coming of spring, Karel hadn't been able to listen to his father practicing any more. A lot of strangers and some men and women he knew came to their apartment and talked agitatedly with his father and with each other for hours. They spoke of "freedom," of "the dawn of a new day," of "the future"—all very beautiful things, Karel decided. And then there was the evening when Karel was terribly proud of his father. *Svaz spisovatelu*, the Author's League, had invited other cultural groups to join in a panel discussion on television. It had lasted several hours, and among famous men and women—those pictures and names Karel had seen in the paper—there on the television screen in

13

their living room, he saw his father again and again, and heard what he had to say. And he had had a lot to say. Karel couldn't understand all of it, but he was sure that what his father said was good and wise, and he couldn't stop watching. The debate lasted until 3:30 in the morning (the television station had set no time limit), and it wouldn't have been exaggerating to say that practically every adult in the country had been listening and crying for joy and clapping at the screen, applauding those men and women who were saying what millions had wanted to say, had dreamed of for such a long time.

It was one of the things Karel couldn't understand, that because of his father's appearance on this television program, they had had to leave their apartment when the foreign soldiers came, and hide in the home of friends, and now had to flee the country in the middle of the night. But that was what his father had told him. The broadcast was the reason.

Since he couldn't understand any of it, the boy began asking questions again.

"If you hadn't talked so much about freedom and a new era, the soldiers wouldn't have come after us, would they?"

"No. I guess in that case they would have stayed in their barracks."

"And we could have gone on living in Jerusalemska Street."

"Yes."

The boy gave the matter some thought. "I don't care," he said finally. "What you said was wonderful. Next day everybody at school envied me." He thought again, and then went on. "I bet they're still envying me. And what you and the others said is still beautiful. I never heard anything like it. Honestly! My friends' parents and everybody else I spoke to felt the same way about it. And a thing can't be beautiful one minute and not beautiful the next, can it?"

"No."

"And you see," said Karel, frowning, "that's why I can't understand why you have to run away because of it, and why they want to lock you up. Why do they want to lock you up?"

"Because what I said didn't please everybody," said his father.

"The foreign soldiers didn't like it?"

"Oh ... the foreign soldiers—"

"What about them?"

"They only obey orders."

"So the ones who give the orders weren't pleased?"

"They don't dare be pleased."

14

"Are those people very powerful?"

"Very powerful, yes—and then, again, quite powerless."

"Now I really don't understand," said Karel.

"Let me try to explain," said his father. "In their hearts, many of those who give the soldiers orders liked what we said, just as much as you and your friends and millions of people in our country did. And they're just as unhappy about it as the soldiers were in the park."

"So they're not wicked."

"No. They're not wicked. But they daren't admit that they liked what we said, and they daren't allow us to say things like that, or think or write them . . . because if they did, something terrible could happen."

"What?" asked Karel.

"Their people might get rid of them just as we got rid of our powerful ones. That's why those people who are so powerful are not really powerful at all. Now do you understand?"

"No." Karel frowned, and as if trying to excuse his ignorance, he added, "That's politics, isn't it?"

"Yes," said his father.

"That's why I can't understand it," said Karel.

Somewhere behind the little moonlit houses, far away across the fields in which the corn already stood high, they could hear the *rat-tat-tat* of an automatic weapon. "They're shooting again," said Karel.

"But not as often as this afternoon," said his father. "Come. Grandmother's waiting in the kitchen."

They left the dingy old-fashioned bedroom with its nineteenth-century furniture. Karel's father glanced for a moment at the picture over the bed, a lithograph of Jesus and his Apostles at the Garden of Gethsemane. The Apostles were asleep and Jesus was standing in front of them, the only one awake. He was speaking, His hand raised. At the bottom of the picture, in Czech, were the words, "Watch and pray, that ye enter not into temptation: The spirit indeed is willing, but the flesh is weak." And in the left-hand corner, in very small letters, in English: Printed by Samuel Levy and Sons, Charlottenburg (Berlin) 1909.

Outside, in the moonlight, the automatic was still *rat-tat-tatting*, dogs howled, then all was still again. And in the year 1909, immortalized on a lithograph by Samuel Levy and Sons in Berlin-Charlottenburg, the Savior was still preaching to his sleeping Apostles. It was 10:14 P.M. on August 27, 1968—a Tuesday.

15

3

"Radio Free Europe. We have just broadcast the news for our Czechoslovakian listeners." The voice ending the newscast came through the loudspeaker, followed by a recording of the *Fidelio* overture.

The old radio stood in a corner of the smoky kitchen, and it was playing so softly it was barely audible. Karel's grandmother had her ear pressed against the speaker. Now she switched to the Prague station and turned the radio off. Stooped over, she walked to the stove, on which a big pot was simmering. Her face had grown smaller with age, and her ability to stand up straight had diminished. Often she wished her time to die had come, but death kept her waiting. "There you are!" she said as Karel and his father walked into the kitchen. She picked up a ladle and began to fill three soup plates. "Lentil soup," she said, "and I put in a few slices of smoked pork."

"Was it fat?" Karel sounded anxious as he sat down at the table beside the stove.

"It wasn't fat, dear heart," said his grandmother. She always called him "dear heart." "It was just as lean as it could be."

"That's good," said her grandson.

Outside there were shots again. Karel tied a big napkin around his neck, waited for the others to start, then began to spoon up his soup. "It's very good, Grandmother," he said. "Couldn't be leaner."

After four spoonfuls of soup, Karel's grandmother said, "Radio Free Europe just said that the United Nations is in session day and night because of us."

"That's good of them," said her son.

"The Americans are furious."

"Of course. And after the newscast they played Beethoven."

"I'm not sure. It sounded like Beethoven."

"Of course it was Beethoven."

"How do you know?" asked Karel.

"When something happens like what's just happened to us, the station always plays Beethoven after the news. The Fifth Symphony or the *Fidelio* Overture."

"*Fidelio* is beautiful; so is the Fifth Symphony," said Karel. "Everything Beethoven wrote was beautiful, wasn't it?"

"Yes," said his father, passing a hand across his son's hair.

"We should resist and not lose heart," said his grandmother. "We are a heroic people. That's what they said."

"Sure, sure," said her son, eating his soup.

"And they are going to help us."

"Of course they are. Just the way they helped the Hungarians when it happened there."

"No. This time they're really going to do something about it. The Americans are going to demand that the Russians get out of our country and out of all the other countries they've occupied."

"Like hell they will!" said her son. "The Americans least of all! The Russians told them exactly what they were going to do so that the American people wouldn't panic and think the Third World War had started. They told the Americans that they had to occupy our country—it had become a necessity—but that was all they intended to do. And the Americans said: If that's all you're going to do—all right!"

"I don't understand," said his mother, looking frightened and old. "How do you know all this?"

"Our people found out about it in Prague. It's a conspiracy between the Great Powers. But of course in the West they have to pretend to be horrified. And that goddamned station still dares to offer us hope and urges us to resist! Just as they did when Hungary was occupied, and before that during the rebellions in East Germany and Poland."

His outburst was followed by silence, then Karel asked, "Are the Americans and the Russians the strongest countries on earth?"

"Yes," said his father. "And we belong with the small and the weak."

Karel thought for a moment, then he said, "We should be glad about that."

"Glad? Why?"

"Because if we were as strong as they are, we would have to lie now, like the Americans, and be afraid, like the Russians. I mean, you said a while ago that they were unhappy, and that they had to give their orders because they were afraid." Suddenly the boy looked confused. "Or am I wrong?"

"No, you're right," said his father, "and now finish your soup."

"You're a wise boy," said his grandmother.

"No, I'm not. But I'd like to be." He was sitting up straight, his left hand on his left knee, eating his soup with his right hand. A well-mannered boy.

"How am I going to know that you got across safely?" asked the old woman. "How am I to know nothing's happened to you?"

"Nothing's going to happen to us," said her son.

"I know. But still—I'd like to be sure. You are my last son, and Karel is my only grandchild. I have no one in the world but you two."

"We're taking the trumpet with us," said her son. "When we get to the other side, I'll play a tune you know. The border is near. You'll hear it."

"I can play the trumpet, too, Grandmother."

"Really, dear heart?"

"Yes!" Karel nodded proudly. "I can play 'Skoda lasky' and 'Kde domov muj' and 'Pluji lodi do Triany' and 'Strangers in the Night,' and other pieces, but those are the ones I know best."

"Play 'Strangers in the Night,'" the old woman told her son. "That's such an old song. I didn't know it was popular again. It was my Andrey's favorite—God rest his soul—and I love it, too. Will you play it, my son?"

"Yes, Mother."

Suddenly the old woman put down her spoon and covered her wrinkled old face with her red, calloused hands. Karel looked at her, startled, his father bowed his head.

"Is she so sad because we're going away?" Karel asked softly. His father nodded.

"But we can't stay here," Karel whispered.

"And that is why she is sad," said his father.

4

They left at 11:15. The old woman had calmed down. She kissed Karel and her son and made the sign of the cross on their foreheads. Her son kissed his mother's hand. "Farewell, Mother." Then he picked up the two suitcases, a large and a smaller one, and Karel took the case with the trumpet in it.

They left the house by the back door that led to the small vegetable garden with its few fruit trees, walking side by side in the moonlight, which lit up the landscape in ghostly fashion. They walked slowly through the garden, past the beds, under the fruit trees, and finally climbed over the low fence that separated the grandmother's small plot from a field path.

When they had left the village behind them, Karel and his father walked Indian file across the fields, listening for any sound. The corn hadn't been cut yet, and it hid Karel almost completely. It reached to his father's waist. As they crossed a path, Karel could see lights in the distance. "Are they on the other side?" he whispered.

"Yes," answered his father. "We're almost at the canal." He whispered, "If they discover us, throw yourself on the ground and don't move. If they yell at you to get up, hands up, you do it. You do everything they say, understand?"

"Yes."

"But if I say 'run,' then you run! No matter what happens or what they yell. Always in the direction of the lights over there. You run, no matter what I may be doing. When I say 'run,' you run!"

"Yes, Father."

They had come to the end of the cornfield, which bordered on a narrow strip of woodland. Here tall pine trees stood side by side, and the earth was carpeted with pine needles that muffled the sound of their steps. They walked slowly over the soft carpet, looking cautiously from side to side, as Karel's father led the way from tree to tree. Once a branch snapped under his feet. For a few seconds they stood motionless, then slowly moved on.

Beyond the trees they could see the silhouette of a primitively constructed watchtower. The high scaffolding, with its rectangular platform at the top, looked ugly. It was about half a kilometer away from where they were standing, at the edge of the wood.

Karel's father lay down on the pine needles, Karel stretched out beside him. The earth was warm and smelled of pine. Karel whispered, "Are there guards on the tower?"

"No," whispered his father. "They told me in the village— there's nobody on the tower. The guards are with their tanks, scattered all over the place, and their tanks are camouflaged." He looked at his wristwatch. "Eleven minutes to midnight," he said. "We must wait."

Karel nodded. He lay flat on his stomach, breathing in the wonderful aroma of the pine needles. How simple it all was. They had the wood behind them and there, in front of them, lay the canal.

It was five meters wide, and its black water flowed sluggishly in a straight line from north to south. The first fugitives had swum it; now somebody had laid the trunk of a pine tree across it where the moonlight couldn't penetrate. About one meter above the log there was a thin wire which one could hang onto if one wanted to cross on the log. They must have cut down one of the pines in the wood and dragged it to the water across the ten meters of flatland that lay in between, where the earth sloped slightly down the canal.

"You cross first," Karel's father whispered. "The log will only hold one person at a time, and I'll see that it doesn't roll."

"But what if I fall into the water? I can't swim."

"You won't fall into the water. Do you see the wire?" It was glistening in the moonlight. "Hang onto it. Leave the trumpet here if you feel safer without it. I can manage it, too."

"With two suitcases? No, I'll take the trumpet." Karel's hand tightened around the leather handle of the case. After that they were silent. Karel's father never took his eyes off his wristwatch. At last they heard the sound of the motor, soft at first, then louder, then it stopped. At the same moment the church bell in the village chimed the midnight hour. "They're on time," Karel's father whispered.

"They're changing the guards now?"

"Yes." Karel's father looked once more from side to side, then he slapped Karel gently on the shoulder. "And now—*run!*"

Karel ran, stooped low, across the damp, grassy earth to the water and the pine log. Two heartbeats later, Karel's father was running behind him with the suitcases. As Karel scrambled onto the log, his father put down the suitcases and sat on the end of the log, which was above the water. Karel held the case in his left hand; with his right he clutched the cold smooth wire. Slowly he balanced his way across the water. "That's the way to do it," whispered his father.

The log rolled a little. Karel slipped and for a moment it looked as if he were going to slide off, but he caught himself. The sweat was running down his face and his teeth were chattering with excitement. He had reached the middle of the log. One more step. Another . . . Karel was panting. The log grew thinner.

Karel looked straight ahead. *Don't look down!*

Only a meter and a half separated him from the other side, one meter . . . *don't look down!* The log began to roll again; Karel slipped, caught himself. Two more steps. He jumped and landed on the ground. Clutching the handle of the case he ran, stooped low as he had run before, across the grass which was just as broad and wet here, to the trees that were here, too, and crouched behind one of them. A pine-needle carpet and pines all around him. Just like on the other side, but fewer trees.

He could see his father step onto the log, the large suitcase in his left hand, the small one under his left arm. With his right hand he was holding onto the wire, just as Karel had done, only he moved much faster than Karel. A few steps only, and his father had reached the middle of the log. One step past the middle and two searchlights flared up on the watchtower, their light passing swiftly along the length of the canal until Karel's father was trapped in their rays. He stopped as if frozen to the spot. Karel stifled a scream.

The searchlight blinded his father. He teetered back and forth on the log, trying to shift his head into the dark so that he could see. Horrified, Karel thought: So there *are* guards on the tower! So the people in the village lied! No, he thought, they couldn't have done that. They were good compatriots. They simply hadn't known. . . . Or *was* it a trap? The information was all wrong.

A hoarse voice was shouting through a bullhorn, "Come back or we'll shoot!"

Karel was lying flat on his stomach, staring at his father. The hoarse voice boomed again, "Come back or we'll shoot!"

In his efforts to stay on top of the log, Karel's father went through the most grotesque contortions. His body bent forward and back, he let go of the suitcases and they fell into the water with a splash. And then the automatics began firing at the man struggling in the light. "Run!" yelled Karel's father. "Run, Karel, run!"

The shots that hit him pitched him into the water. The automatics went on firing, their bullets hitting the water now, spitting up little fountains as in a heavy rain, and they hit Karel's father again and again. His body, face down, began to float downstream.

One searchlight followed his course, the other covered the bank on the other side, to the edge of the wood where Karel was lying. Suddenly he came to life, jumped to his feet, and began to run as fast as he could across the carpet of pine neddles, faster than he had ever run in his life. He stumbled over a root, got up, ran on, his heart pounding. He slipped on the pine needles but still he kept running, zigzagging between the trees. He came to a field. Twice he fell on the hard earth. Then he reached a path with fruit trees growing on either side. Behind him, far away, in the direction of the canal, he could hear men's voices. They brought him to his senses. He sank down on the earth, panting, and looked up at the moon. The case with the trumpet lay behind him. He thought of his father, whom he had forgotten completely while he had been running. Now he screamed as loud as he could, "Father!" And over and over again, "Father!"

There was no answer.

Violent sobs racked his body. He began to crawl around on all fours like an animal, and screamed again, "Father! Father!" He stood up, swaying, and pressed his hands against his eyes. They hurt because he was screaming so loudly. Everything was spinning around him. All he could think of was: Father is dead. They shot him. My father is dead. They shot him. Still he screamed, "Father! I'm here! Father! Father! Come to me!"

His father didn't answer. On the other side of the canal dogs were barking, soldiers were cursing. Karel screamed again. Then he could feel his stomach heave and vomited. "Father ... Father ... Father...." He was whimpering now, then he was silent.

Perhaps his father wasn't dead. Perhaps he had managed to reach land and was looking for Karel in the silvery light. Perhaps he couldn't hear him....

The boy sprang to his feet. If his voice couldn't carry far enough, the trumpet certainly could. His father had said so. He had promised to play a song for his mother. If Karel played the trumpet, surely his father would hear it. He felt so dizzy, he kept falling as he ran back to the case that was lying behind him on the path. His hands were trembling as he opened it. Now his father would be able to find him—if he could just play long enough! Karel cried and laughed as he lifted the shining instrument to his mouth with both hands. He lost his balance, fell, and got up again. "Father," he whispered, "wait just a minute."

He leaned against an apple tree whose branches hung down, laden with fruit. He dug his feet into the earth to steady himself, then lifted the trumpet to his lips and began to play. Karel didn't get every note right, but the song was clearly recognizable— "Strangers in the Night," loud and filled with longing. Karel thought: Father will hear me and find me. It was a trick he was playing on them. He's smart. He pretended that they'd hit him and let himself fall into the water and swam to the other side. Yes, that's what happened. That's really what happened.

"Listen!" said Sergeant Heinz Subireit, who was patroling the Bundesrepublik border in a jeep about two kilometers away from Karel. With him was his friend, Squad Leader Heinrich Felden.

"'Love Out of Nowhere,'" said Felden, who was driving.

"Somebody's gone crazy," said Subireit. "Blowing a trumpet out here!"

"*. . . Where have I seen those eyes . . .*" Felden sang softly.

"*. . . that warm smile that lights up the dark corners of my lonely soul?*" Karel was playing. Come to me, Father! Please come! I'm so afraid!

"*. . . Is this our first encounter . . .*" sang Squad Leader Felden.

"Oh, shut up!" said Sergeant Subireit. "Get going. It's got to be somewhere over there. Let's see what's going on."

"*or were we lovers in some distant former life?*" played Karel, the tears running down his cheeks. Father's alive! He's coming! Now he hears me. Yes, yes, he hears me. . . .

The song of the trumpet rose up from the indifferent earth into the indifferent sky, with its moon and its cold, endlessly faraway stars. It blew across the land. The soldiers who were pulling Karel's dead father out of the water heard it; so did Karel's grandmother in her little kitchen. She knelt down in front of the stove—it wasn't easy for her to kneel—and folded her hands and prayed, "Thank you, Almighty God, for saving my son and grandson."

She could still hear the trumpet playing, and she knelt on the kitchen floor and cried with happiness.

5

"So he went on playing, the poor boy," said Fräulein Gottschalk, "until the border guards found him."

It was about 3:30 P.M. on November 12, 1968. A bright autumnal sun was shining in a brilliantly blue sky. It was unusually warm for the middle of November. Exactly eleven weeks and approximately a thousand kilometers lay between the flight of the boy, Karel, and his father across the Czech-Bavarian border in the early morning hours of August 28, and this day and place in North Germany, a desolate area between Hamburg and Bremen, where my friend Bert Engelhardt and I met Fräulein Louise for the first time.

Engelhardt was a big, heavyset man, fifty-six years old, with very light eyes and hair and the rosy face of a young man. His life had been so adventurous and filled with so much danger that nothing, absolutely nothing, could shake him anymore. What do I mean, 'shake him'? I should have said 'touch him.' He had a big heart, a blithe spirit, and nerves of steel. They were what kept him young. Nobody could have guessed his age. He smiled a lot, sincerely, ingratiatingly, but he also smiled when he was annoyed. His forehead was bandaged. The bandage had been changed the night before. He needed it to protect the wound he had received seventy-two hours ago in Chicago.

Bertie had been a news photographer since 1938. His first job had been with the *Berliner Illustrierte*. He had lost count long ago of how many times he had flown around the world since then, to political conferences, murder trials, interviews with film stars, millionaires, and Nobel Prize winners; to leper camps; to the smuggler's island of Macao and the stinking slums of Calcutta. He had traveled deep into the interior of Tibet, China, Brazil, Mexico; he had filmed documentaries of the gold mines in South America, the green hills of Borneo, the icy wastes of Antarctica; he had crossed the length and breadth of Canada and been involved in every war. And there hadn't exactly been a dearth of wars during Bertie's career. He had won many international honors, and an exhibition of his best photos was right now traveling all over the world, like Bertie. He had been wounded several times in the many big and little wars and minor skirmishes he had covered, once severely, in the Second World War we started, wounded in his right leg. He still walked with a slight limp.

I, Walter Roland, was thirty-six years old when we got ourselves involved in the strange, sweet, and gruesome series of events I am about to describe—a time when Bertie looked so much younger than he was, and I so much older. Oh, yes, I was tall, but gaunt. I didn't have Bertie's remarkably healthy color. I was sallow. There were dark circles around my brown eyes, which always looked tired. My brown hair had turned white over the temples and was streaked with gray. I had no appetite, whatever that may have been worth. I chain-smoked, so I was told. It was probably true, judging by the way I felt. And lived. Too much work, too many women, too many cigarettes, and too much booze. The latter above everything else. For years now I hadn't been able to function in any capacity without whiskey. If I didn't have a bottle in reserve, I got claustrophobia. I always carried a silver flask with me. Sometimes I'd turn white as a sheet and feel as if I was passing out. Horrible. But a few swallows and I was back to normal. If you can call being totally dependent on alcohol normal.

I was a journalist. Top reporter on the staff of the illustrated weekly, *Blitz*. Fourteen years now. Bertie had been part of the show for eighteen years. Two aces, both of us. I don't want to indulge in self-praise—there isn't anything to be proud of, anyway—but we were ace reporters in that cesspool. Exclusive contracts. Bertie was the highest-paid reporter in Germany, I was the highest-paid writer. You know *Blitz*—one of the three biggest illustrated weeklies in the Bundesrepublik.

At the beginning things weren't all that bad. I didn't drink or whore around so much, but then everything at *Blitz* changed, and I changed right along with it. Not Bertie. He remained the same normal, reliable, good-natured, and courageous colleague he'd always been. I was the one who fell apart.

Because I had so much money, I became a snob who had to have his suits, shirts, even his shoes made to measure; who drove the craziest cars, lived in a luxurious penthouse, and drank only

Chivas Regal, the most expensive whiskey in the world. Nothing else would do. And the broads had to be top-drawer, too, and cost a fortune.

Lately I'd been practically anesthetizing myself with women, whiskey, and roulette. This was because what I had to write for *Blitz* during the last years had been enough to make one puke. There were times—fortunately, not too many—when I simply couldn't work at all but stayed in bed, took Valium and stronger stuff to sleep through a whole day and night, sometimes two days and two nights, because suddenly I'd had it. I was finished, unable to cope with the horrible feeling of weakness, panic, and helplessness. At times like that I couldn't breathe, my heart acted up, I felt dizzy and couldn't think straight. And I was afraid. No idea of what. Of death? That among other things, but not mainly. I have no idea what to name this form of fear. Maybe you've felt it, too.

My liver wasn't functioning properly, other vital organs weren't either—all because of the life I was leading. That was why I had my jackal. That was what I called my condition when it became acute, because then I had the distinct feeling that a jackal was circling around me, coming closer and closer until he was leaning over me, and I almost choked over the putrid stench of his breath.

Attacks like these could last two days, but then I was back in circulation, more or less, and had to make up for lost time, full speed ahead—which, to my surprise, always turned out to be possible: something I was proud of. When I got going like that, I would work night and day and come up with more than any of our team of writers. If a time came when I couldn't, I'd change my way of life. Another one of my screwy ideas. I saw a doctor only when it was absolutely necessary, because I knew exactly what he'd say. If I went on living like this I wouldn't see forty. They'd been telling me that for four years now, every one of them, all very fine human beings *and* doctors. To be treated with respect.

The publishing house and editorial offices of *Blitz* were in Frankfurt. You may want to know why they sent Bertie and me, their highest-paid employees, into this desolate area. There was a reason for it, of course, and you'll soon see why, when I get around to describing *Blitz* in greater detail. Anyway, here we were and had just met Fräulein Louise and hadn't the faintest idea of what lay ahead of us. She was still telling us about the boy.

"He defended himself like a maniac," she continued. "Didn't want to move from the spot, was sure his father was still alive and would come to him. He fought with the soldiers," Fräulein Louise went on. "He kicked them, scratched them, bit them. He wasn't in his right mind at the time."

"So what did they do with him?" I asked.

I was sitting opposite Fräulein Louise, straddled back to front on a chair, my elbows on the backrest. Far away I could sense the jackal, but no sweat. My flask was in my hip pocket. I took good care of myself.

"They were scared. They sent for an ambulance and a doctor. He gave the child an injection that calmed him. Then they were able to transport him." Strange, to find someone way up here in North Germany with a Czech accent.

"So where did they take him?" I asked, putting out my Gauloise on a tin ashtray. I smoked only black French cigarettes. One of the pads I always carried with me was lying beside the ashtray. I could write shorthand fast and well. And my memory hadn't failed me yet. Quite a few pages were already filled because I'd seen so many interesting things since our arrival. I hadn't written down anything I'd heard. For that I had a cassette recorder, which I also took with me everywhere. It was standing on the desk. I always had a lot of cassettes with me and used the recorder whenever I was doing research. It had been on ever since we had met Fräulein Louise.

"Where they took him? Well, here and there and finally to a clinic in Munich. In a state of shock. He was in the hospital six weeks, my poor little boy, then they sent him here."

"So he's been here five weeks?"

"Yes. And he'll be staying longer."

"How much longer?"

"As long as I can manage it. I don't want him sent to a home. We're still looking for his mother. She's supposed to be living somewhere in West Germany. He doesn't have anyone else. Since he's been here he's talked about his mother all the time. It's a wicked world we're living in, gentlemen, especially for the children. It's been like that ever since I started working with children, and it wasn't any better before. That's why I decided to become a social worker. It isn't the children's fault that the world is such a wicked place."

"How long have you been a social worker?"

"Since 1924."

"What?"

"Yes. That surprises you, doesn't it? Forty-four years. Nearly my whole life and always with children. I began working when I was eighteen. Those were bad times, too, right after the inflation. I worked in Vienna first. Twentieth district. What misery! People were starving, nobody had money. Nothing but filth and poverty. So much poverty! The first thing we did was establish a clinic for children. I went begging to the various agencies for money for my children. Ran my feet off. Things didn't get better. Then there was the World Depression in 1929. Things got even worse. That was the time when they—" She stopped abruptly.

"When they what?"

She didn't answer.

"What's the matter?"

"Nothing," she said hastily. "So...after 1929, things got worse. There was unemployment. It looked as if half Austria was unemployed. Until Hitler came. That's why he had it so easy. Because he promised work and bread."

"Yes," I said. "And what did you do when Hitler came?"

"Nothing changed for me. I went on working with my children, and anyway, the war came soon after that. And all through the war I looked after my children. When things got very bad, we were moved out into the country—of all places, to my native land! Not far from Reichenberg. January 1945. That's when we had to move. Two hundred and fifty children and only three of us. I had them through snow and ice, to Munich. We stopped in a camp outside the city because it was safer. I got all of them through, except three. They died of exposure. It was so cold." She was staring straight ahead, her face a mask of grief. "It was so terribly cold...."

Fräulein Gottschalk—"Call me Fräulein Louise," she had said when we had been introduced—was of medium height and gave the impression of being worn out from overwork. She was painfully thin. Her white hair had a silvery glint, and she wore it combed straight back with a knot at the nape of her neck. Her eyes were blue and their expression was unbelievably kind, which was the impression given by her whole face—delicate, narrow, pale, with wide, bloodless lips. She still had all her teeth, good strong teeth. She had on a gray skirt and an old brown cardigan over a white blouse, and she was wearing ankle boots to give support to her swollen legs. "It's not easy for me, all the walking I have to do. I've got water, you know, in my feet. Not that I'm complaining. I've had to run all my life. They do all right by me, really, my feet do...."

"And then?" I asked, putting out my cigarette and lighting the next one with my lighter, eighteen-carat gold, naturally. "Then the Americans came to Bavaria, didn't they?"

Fräulein Louise was looking at me, but her gaze seemed to come from far away. "Yes. Friendly people. Good people. They gave me food and clothes for my children and coal for our barracks. The Russians were friendly, too," she added hastily. "Their tanks caught up with us on our flight, and they threw food down to us, and blankets. And they found some horse carts for me. If it hadn't been for the Russians, we'd never have made it to the friendly Amis. Funny, isn't it? War and death and destruction, and people were bad; but when things were worst of all, our enemies helped my children—the Russians, too, in spite of everything that had happened to them. Yes, yes...." She sighed. And the recorder was picking up every word.

"Well, after that I cared for the children under the Amis, in Bavaria, until they divided everything up into zones, and there was the blockade, and so many people came over from the Russian Zone—children, too. And that was when they sent us up here."

"In 1948?" I dropped my cigarette in my astonishment. "You mean to say you've been here twenty years?"

"Twenty years. Yes, sir. A third of my life. It was a camp for young people, up to eighteen, just as it is today. Families couldn't always flee together, you know. There were children alone, parents alone. Hundreds of thousands came streaming in in those days. Millions! And so many young people. Oh, dear God, sometimes we didn't know which way to turn. After the uprising of June 1953, we never got any rest at all! We worked day and night. We were filled to the rafters, and it's a big camp. You've seen it. And I always had the children. We could fill a whole city with the children I've taken care of and protected since 1924."

"And you're still doing it."

"I'll do it until I die," said Fräulein Louise. "I don't care what children. I don't care what color they are or what their religion is or where they come from. And I don't care what government I work under. I'll work under any government that lets me look after my children." She smiled at me, a little uncertainly; her lips were trembling.

Bertie let me do the talking. He was busy in his fashion. He

29

had brought along two cameras, a Nikon-F and a Hasselblad—both with incredibly fast lenses. With them Bertie could shoot in a room without a flash. He took pictures of Fräulein Louise while I talked to her. Human interest. If anything was to come of the story, that's what we needed—human interest. And Fräulein Louise was giving us plenty.

"But since they put up the Wall," I said, "things must have quieted down. Not many people can get past it."

"Not from the Zone," said Fräulein Louise. "Before the Wall there were twenty-four camps for refugees in the Bundesrepublik. Now only a few are left. Friedland and Zirndorf, near Nürnberg—they're the famous ones. And this one here in Neurode, for young people and children. And we've become quite international! Didn't I say it was a wicked world? People are still afraid. Will there be war? Revolution? A dictatorship? Will we have to flee again? You've just seen it happen! Czechoslovakia! And before that—East Germany! And Greece." She laughed softly. "You won't believe this, but I had five little Vietnamese here six months ago. No, no . . . there can be no rest, there can be no peace, and I must go on looking after my children, the poor little things. During the last months, of course, they've been mostly Czechs."

"Children from your native land."

"Yes, sir. They have translators here. You saw them. But you can always make yourself understood with children. And since I speak Czech, they let me have the Czech children. I take care of them, especially poor Karel."

"He's your favorite?"

"They're all my angels," said Fräulein Louise. "I have no favorites. But Karel is so helpless and still so shocked and afraid. Right now he needs special attention."

Karel was in the next room; only a thin wall separated us from him. I had seen the boy; so had Bertie, when we had walked into Fräulein Louise's office. The door to the next room had been open. We could see that it was furnished like a living room, with a braided rug, a wardrobe, a bookshelf, a bed, a floor lamp, a radio on a bedside table, and on the wall six pictures painted by children. Fräulein Louise had said these were her rooms—this was where she lived.

Karel had been sitting on a stool in the middle of the room when we entered, the brass trumpet on his knees. His good blue suit had been cleaned and pressed, his shoes were polished. He looked very small, sitting with his face to the wall, his back turned to us, a tragic sight in his motionless despair.

"Walter!" said Bertie. "We've got something here." And he got his Nikon-F ready for action. Karel turned around when he heard us coming. He was very pale. Outside, children were playing in the mild sunshine. They were dancing to the music that was coming over the loudspeakers. The voice of a man was singing, "*Such a day! Such a beautiful day as today should never end....*"

We walked up to Karel. Fräulein Louise had told us his name. He looked at us, but he didn't move. A squadron of jets flew low over the camp. The noise was horrendous. It made me nervous and I inhaled the smoke from my cigarette deep and fast. Starfighters were passing overhead, a formation every twenty minutes.

Karel didn't show any reaction to the jets either. Not even his eyelids twitched. It was as if he had died sitting up.

"Hello, Karel," I said.

No response.

"He doesn't understand much German," said Fräulein Louise, excusing the child, which was absurd and touching at the same time. She offered the boy a piece of chocolate, she spoke to him in Czech, he shook his head. "He doesn't want it." Fräulein Louise sighed. "And it's milk chocolate. With nuts. Sometimes he likes it. But he hadn't got over it yet. That's what I keep telling everybody when they say I shouldn't show any favoritism—he shouldn't be sitting here all day. But he wants to. He says here he isn't afraid."

"Of what?"

"That they'll start shooting again."

"Who should start shooting again?"

"I don't know. He's very confused. He's afraid they'll shoot at him the way they shot at his father. Here, he says, nothing can happen to him, so he's here most of the time. I work in the next room. I leave the door open and he's quiet. But of course he has to eat and sleep with the other children, in their barracks." She leaned over the boy. He looked up and gave her a wan smile. It was a dreadful smile, the saddest smile I have ever seen. Worse than the worst tears. Fräulein Louise spoke Czech again. She pointed to us. Karel turned his head and looked at us. The smile died on his lips and he turned his back on us again.

"I told him you gentlemen were from a big illustrated magazine," Fräulein Louise explained, "and that you're writing a story about the camp and taking pictures." And Bertie was doing just that, of Karel and his trumpet, from every possible angle. He managed to get in front of the boy, too. Bertie knew his job. Small children and little animals, naked girls and pictures of accidents, as gory as possible—*that* was what people wanted to see. It made them lascivious. It stirred them sexually. Sex appeal. Human appeal. The big shit—that was our profession!

"It's a very important magazine, isn't it?" asked Fräulein Louise.

"Yes," I said.

"How big is it?" she wanted to know.

"Circulation of one point nine million a week."

Bertie was still taking pictures of Karel. He had stretched out on the floor and was focusing on the boy from below. Karel paid no attention to him. "According to reliable statistics," I went on, "every copy is read by at least five people, which gives us approximately nine million readers." I was reeling this off as usual, and that was when Fräulein Louise did it for the first time.

She cocked her head sideways a little, her eyes looked far away, and she said softly but clearly, as if what she was saying was not for our ears, "Come hither. I will show unto thee the judgment of the great whore that sitteth upon many waters, with whom the kings of the earth have committed fornication, and the inhabitants of the earth have been made drunk with the wine of her fornication. . . .' That's how it is, isn't it? What do you say?"

She was looking across my shoulder, and now she seemed to be listening, her lips parted. I must admit it shook me! They were strange words to come from her lips and under the circumstances made no sense. Who had come into the room and was standing behind me? I turned quickly.

Nobody had entered the room. Nobody was standing behind me.

Fräulein Louise had used the first person plural, *Ihr*, as if addressing more than one person. It was grotesque. As a matter of fact, it was crazy! She was speaking to people I couldn't see! Nonsense—to people who weren't there! I looked at her again.

She was still standing with her head cocked a little to one side as if listening, then she said softly, "They will quarrel with the Lamb, but you say the Lamb is invincible. You're quite sure of that?"

"Who's quite sure of what?"

Suddenly her eyes were clear again, seeing us as if she had just awakened from a deep sleep. "Quite sure of what?" she said slowly.

"The Lamb."

"What Lamb?"

"That's what I'm asking you. You spoke about a Lamb, and about other things. You said—" But she had stepped up to me and now she interrupted me, her face red. "I didn't say anything!"

"But you did!"

"No!" she cried excitedly and at the same time—or so it seemed to me—embarrassed and frightened.

"I heard you, too," said Bertie, still on the floor taking pictures. He said it smiling, amiable and guileless. He was so concentrated on Karel, he hadn't noticed the change that had come over Fräulein Louise and wasn't aware of the strangeness of what she had said.

"You couldn't have heard anything!" cried Fräulein Louise. "Either of you! We only hear earthly voices. Now please come to the office with me. I don't want the boy to get excited. Before I show you the rest of the camp, I'll make us some coffee and tell you what the poor child has experienced."

She walked ahead of us, clumsy on her swollen legs. Bertie got up and we looked at each other across the benumbed boy. Bertie was smiling as he watched Fräulein Louise leave the room, and he tapped his forehead with his finger, and right then I had the strong feeling—it struck me like lightning—that things were not all that simple as far as Fräulein Gottschalk was concerned. It wasn't a clear-cut case of bats in the belfry. There was more to it, a lot more. I had the facts, which I could write in a way that suited my almighty paper, to thank it for my high-paying job, but I also had to give my instincts some of the credit. Because at that moment I felt clearly that I was on the track of something that would lead eventually to strange, and, in plain language, terrific revelations! At the same time I felt dizzy. My jackal was turning in, still far away but circling closer. I took my flask out of my pocket, unscrewed the top, took one drink of Chivas and a second, just to be on the safe side.

"You're going to kill yourself with that stuff," said Bertie.

"Sure, sure," I said, puffing away on my Gauloise. But the jackal was gone and I no longer felt sick and dizzy.

"What's the matter, gentlemen?" said Fräulein Louise. "Aren't you coming?"

"Yes, yes, we're coming."

Bertie followed her into her office, but I stayed behind for a moment, staring at the wardrobe to which Fräulein Louise had been talking as if more than one person had been standing in front of it. It was an ugly plywood wardrobe, not even varnished, a cheap piece of furniture. And I stood there staring at it like an idiot.

But that was how it all began, what was to become the story of a lifetime in no time at all, the greatest story I had ever written: about a morass of lies and deceit, down to the last determined criminal and betrayer, about idealists, liars, bums, and ordinary murderers, about complacent administrators and false witnesses; a morass of immeasurable injustice and brutal murder, of thievery—spiritual and material—of mass brainwashing, perpetrated with incredible finesse; of mass betrayal and blackmail and of plans that exploded mercilessly and disastrously over the heads of their devisers. This is where it all began, in front of a cheap plywood wardrobe that wasn't even varnished.

6

In her office, as water heated on a hot plate, Fräulein Louise told us Karel's story. When she was done, the loudspeakers were still playing music outside and the afternoon sun was slanting brightly into the dusty room. Fräulein Louise's hair was pure, finely spun silver now. We could hear the voices of children playing and young people arguing in many languages. Something occurred to me. "Fräulein Gottschalk—"

"Louise, please," she said. "Fräulein Louise. Everybody calls me that."

"Fräulein Louise. . . . All the other social workers live in those two white barracks over there, don't they?"

Bertie sat down beside me and listened. He had finished taking pictures, or so he thought. . . . And so did I!

"That's right," said Fräulein Louise, "and it's because the other social workers here don't like me. A lot of people here don't like me." She added defiantly, "I don't like them, either!"

"None of them?"

"Most of them. There are a few I'm fond of. Good people. Herr Kuschke, for instance. He drives the camp bus. And Dr. Schiemann. He's our doctor here. And Pastor Demel. He's the Protestant pastor. And Reverend Father Hinkel. He's the Catholic priest. So them I like. Especially Pastor Demel. Perhaps because I'm Protestant, too. No," she said quickly, "not because of that but because he's an exceptionally good man. Reverend Father is a good man, too, but I just happen to have a better relationship with the Pastor."

"But those are Christian ministers," I said. "There must be children here who are not Christian."

"Of course there are. It's very confusing. The Turkish children are Muhammadans, the Greeks are Orthodox, and so on. And then those little Vietnamese children. But the holy gentlemen are so kind. They know there's only one God in heaven, so they are good to all the children and look after them, regardless of their religion. That's why I like them."

"And the children like you?" asked Bertie.

Fräulein Louise smiled happily. "Of course they do! They are the joy of my life! Children haven't learned to be wicked yet, like their elders."

"Have you always lived alone here because you don't get along with the other social workers?"

Fräulein Louise looked upset. "No," she said. "At first I lived over there with them. I had my own room and didn't pay much attention to the other women. I lived there for twenty years, until five weeks ago."

"Five weeks?"

"Yes. Until Karel came. That was the day I moved over here."

"But why?"

"Because—" Fräulein Louise hesitated. "Oh, there was all sorts of gossip and a big quarrel . . . but that wouldn't interest you."

"But it does," I said.

"All right, then," Fräulein Louise said reluctantly. "The other social workers complained about me."

"What could they possibly have—"

"They—they said I behaved funnily."

"Funnily?"

"Not funnily like fun. Oddly. That's what they said. Especially the Hitzinger woman. She can't stand me. Now, she's a bad person. She often gets angry with the children. You can't

35

imagine how upset I get about it. A woman like that shouldn't be working with children. But she was at the bottom of it all!" Now she was talking fast. "She got the others all stirred up about me and now nobody likes me." She leaned across the desk, her voice low and confidential. "Believe it or not, there's a conspiracy against me."

"No!" I said.

"About what?" asked Bertie.

"They want to get rid of me." Fräulein Louise's voice was soft and troubled. "They want me to go away, away from my children. Can you imagine that? What would I do without my children?"

"What sort of a conspiracy?" I asked. "After all, it must be based on something."

"Well, yes, I suppose it is. The Hitzinger woman and the lies she tells about me. Dreadful things. Things her friend Reiter told her. She isn't here anymore, but Hitzinger is. And now they want to get rid of me, all of them. Even Dr. Schall. He's the director. They want to retire me. And I'm only sixty-two!"

Fräulein Louise passed a hand across her eyes and swallowed hard. "I can't sleep anymore. I'm so scared. Every morning I feel sick. I tremble because I'm afraid I'll get the letter, the blue one, and nobody helps me! I'm all alone, and all of them are against me!"

Softly at first, then louder, I could hear the shrill whine of another jet squadron. The whine changed to a thunderous roar, the windows rattled. I thought the planes would pass directly over the barracks, and they did. I could see them through the windows—three Starfighters flying low, then banking to the right and up into the clear sky again.

I cursed loudly, none of which could be heard above the roar of the planes. Now I said nervously to Fräulein Louise, "I don't see how you can stand it."

"I don't hear it anymore," she said. "On the other side of the moor there's an air base. They always fly a lot when the weather's good." She was looking at me seriously. "As I just said, nobody helps me."

"I heard you."

"Not a soul." Suddenly she seemed to have an idea. "A man like you, Herr Roland, must have a lot of influence."

"What do you mean?"

"Well, you work for an important magazine. You've written

books. Pastor Demel told me all about it when you called and said you were coming to see us."

"I wrote them ten years ago. Trash. Both of them."

"Pastor Demel liked them." Fräulein Louise was persistent. "I can't read very much. It makes my eyes smart. But Pastor Demel said—"

"Please stop!" I said, sounding more vehement than I intended, and there he was again, though still far away—the jackal. "I don't want to know what the pastor said. They were garbage, one worse than the other!"

"Why are you suddenly so angry?" Fräulein Louise looked startled.

I pulled myself together. Mention of the two books I had written before joining *Blitz* had reminded me of that time, and of everything that had happened since. Bertie knew what was going on inside me. He looked worried. He wasn't smiling now.

My smile, I was sure, was a grimace. "I'm sorry, Fräulein Louise. It wasn't directed against you. It's just that—right now—" But it was stronger than I. "... Not good—sorry," I stammered, drew my flask out of my pocket, unscrewed the top, grinning feebly at Fräulein Louise, who still looked startled. I didn't care. The jackal. Mention of the two books I'd written had done it. The years ... all those wasted years ...

I drank. "My stomach's easily upset," I explained.

But Fräulein Louise was not to be deflected from what was on her mind. "Well, then, that's all right, if you didn't mean it, Herr Roland," she said. "And you, too, Herr Engelhardt—you must know a lot of people. Important people! Rich people! Rich people are so powerful. Perhaps one of them could help me. *I must stay with my children!*"

Bertie looked embarrassed. He shook his head, his light hair flopping over his bandage. I said, "Fräulein Louise, we're only reporters."

"Famous reporters!"

"We go where we're sent," I went on, ignoring her interruption. "We take pictures and write what's expected of us. We do know a lot of people, and some are famous and rich, but they wouldn't do anything for you, Fräulein Louise. We're there for them, not they for us. We drive or fly wherever we're told. We drove to this camp on assignment. But I'm afraid we can't do a thing for you." I noticed that I was still holding the flask in my hand and that Fräulein Louise was looking at it, and I finished rather lamely, "Would you like some?" I held it out to her. "In your coffee?"

"Is it cognac?"

"No. Whiskey."

"Ugh! I drank whiskey once, by mistake. Tastes like medicine." She shook herself. "No, thank you, Herr Roland. The coffee—oh dear! The water must be boiling!"

She got up and walked over to the hot plate, frowned, stuck her finger in the water and cried, "It's cold! Ice cold!" She lifted the pot and passed her hand over the plate. "It's cold, too!"

Bertie had picked up his Nikon-F again. She didn't notice. She was too preoccupied with the malfunctioning hot plate. "Look at that! No wonder the water doesn't get hot! The coil's broken. One of them must have borrowed it again! What nerve! When they know I'm so dependent on my coffee. They don't want to live with me, but they'll borrow my hot plate! No, by God, I'm not going to put up with it! It's a crying shame! I'm going to report it to the director."

And then it happened again, without warning. From one moment to the next. She stopped her tirade in the middle of a sentence and stood still, head cocked to one side, looking across my shoulder, her eyes far away, her lips parted, listening, obviously listening, three seconds, four . . . and Bertie photographed her. She didn't notice it any more than Karel had noticed it a short while before. She stood there, frozen to the spot, listening to a voice—or voices—we couldn't hear. I turned around. Not a living soul.

I turned around again. Now Fräulein Louise was speaking, softly and not very clearly: "Humbly—yes.. And peacefully. Very well. Your people gave us bread and *schmalz*, I know. And they gave us the good army rations. You were such a rich army, and the Russians were so poor. They didn't have enough to eat, and yet—and the blankets. Although it was so cold. That was during the big storm. I remember it so well. . . ."

This time it hit Bertie, too. He went on photographing, but he had stopped smiling. I got up. I realized it wasn't the right thing to do, but I acted instinctively. I put out my cigarette and said in a loud voice, "Fräulein Louise!"

Her eyes fluttered. She noticed that Bertie was taking pictures and sank down in her chair. "You have no right to do that, sir. Give me the film."

"Sorry, but—"

"Please!"

"No," I said angrily. "Not until you tell us to whom you were talking and what it all means."

Fräulein Louise buried her face in her hands. Bertie went on shooting. She didn't move. After a while she said, "And now . . . if you publish pictures of me, then—then it's all over." At that moment there was a scream from the next room, a horrible, long drawn-out, tortured scream. It wasn't human. It sounded like an animal wounded and dying.

Fräulein Louise forgot about what had just been troubling her, forgot her swollen legs, and ran into the living room next door, Bertie and I close behind her. Karel was standing in the middle of the room, his eyes open wide, his face distorted and white. Saliva was running out of his mouth and he was screaming like an animal. It was a horrible sight. Only Bertie seemed delighted. "Great stuff!" He was smiling again, and taking pictures, and Karel never stopped screaming.

Fräulein Louise ran up to him and yelled at him in Czech. He yelled back at her, broken sentences, broken words, also in Czech. The trumpet had fallen on the floor. Then he clutched his throat, his voice rattled, and he fell like a stone. There he lay, his limbs twisted, motionless.

"The song!" cried Fräulein Louise, and Bertie and I understood. We could hear it, too. "Strangers in the Night" on the loudspeaker outside. Slowly the trumpet solo began.

"He heard his song." Fräulein's voice was a whisper. "He thought his father had come and they were going to kill him. Is he—what's happened to him?"

I hurried over to the boy and knelt down beside him. "He's fainted," I said.

"We must get him to bed," cried Fräulein Louise. "Can one of you put him on my bed? I'll call Dr. Schiemann."

She hurried back into her office. I was about to lift the boy when Bertie stopped me. "Just a minute." He was still smiling. "Step aside. I want a few shots of him lying there. I'll do it in color. Make a good full page. A real tearjerker." He put a film in the Hasselblad.

We could hear Fräulein Louise telephoning. She was screaming, "Turn off the music! I'm telling you . . . turn off the music! . . . Because I'm telling you to. I'll explain why later. No! It *must* be turned off! Thank you." And the music stopped abruptly.

There was an eerie silence, then children's voices outside again, and Fräulein Louise in her office, dialing another number. "Hello? This is Fräulein Louise. I have to speak to the doctor. Who is this? Oh . . . Sister Rita. . . . Not already? Jesus, Maria, and Joseph! No, no. I understand." And Bertie was taking pictures.

He was quite right. It was a tearjerker. People are moved to tears when they see a picture like that. Manna from heaven for the masses! Especially women.

And from the next room, "Yes, yes, I understand. Ask him to call the minute he can. Please!"

"That's it," said Bertie. "I'll put the boy on the bed and open the window. He'll come to in no time."

He was the gentlest person in the world, but when it was a question of work, he lost all sensitivity. "Give me a hand," he said.

I did.

A small table stood beside the bed, on it a lamp, an alarm clock, a vial of sleeping pills, and an open book. As we laid Karel on his side (so that he wouldn't swallow his tongue), I glanced at the book. There were passages underlined in red. I closed the book, keeping a finger between the open pages. Shakespeare, *Collected Works*, Volume III. So she did read. In spite of her eyes which smarted when she read. I opened the book again. *The Tempest*, Act IV, Scene 1. Prospero: "Our revels now are ended. These, our actors, as I foretold you, were all spirits and are melted into air, into thin air. . . ."

I didn't get any farther because Fräulein Louise was standing behind us. "How is he?"

I put the book on the table as surreptitiously as possible. "He's all right. He'll come to in a minute." I opened the window. Bertie picked up a blanket that lay folded at the end of the bed and covered the boy with it. "Where's the doctor?"

"With Panagiotopulos, the Greek girl."

"What's the matter with her?"

"She's in labor. But much too early. I'm worried about her."

Karel moved a little and groaned. Fräulein Louise sat down on the edge of the bed and stroked his thin face and spoke to him tenderly in Czech. He nodded weakly, then closed his eyes again.

"It's really helping him—the fresh air," said Fräulein Louise. "He's better."

The phone rang. Fräulein Louise hurried into her office. I followed her. Bertie stayed with Karel, whose eyes were open again, wide. The boy was trembling. Bertie still had work to do. . . .

40

When I got back into the office, Fräulein Louise was already on the phone. "Central? Yes? What is it? . . .Oh, I see. A telegram for Hromatka." I listened, feeling more strongly all the time that I had entered another world. "How did it come this time?" Fräulein Louise was asking, her tone grim. "Pilsen via Leipzig. All right, all right. But who's died this time? Her mother? Is that so. Well, she's not to be told a word about it. Do the Catholics know already? . . .Good. They'll take care of it. Thank you," and she hung up.

I asked, "Whose mother is dying?"

"In all probability, nobody's," said Fräulein Louise.

"But you just said—"

"Our young people here get phony telegrams all the time," she explained. "East Germany started it; now they're all doing it."

"Why?"

"To get the children back. An emergency. Somebody's dying—a mother, an aunt, an older sister, a brother—"

"Or a father?"

"No. Never a father," Fräulein Louise explained. "He's the one they really want."

"I don't understand."

"It's quite simple. The father is usually the first one to escape, then the children, then the mother. If it's a big family, they can't all escape at once. The children of doctors or scientists or men who were politically involved are mostly the ones who get the telegrams. We used to give the children the telegrams right away, and that was a mistake. It resulted in a lot of disasters. Now we always check first to see if the message is true."

"How do you do that?"

"Oh, the churches hold together. Everywhere. They have their people and means of communication and they can check the message fast. But the children, once they knew, were impatient. They couldn't wait and ran away. Hop, hop, back to their native land. And ended in jail. So then what did the father do? He went back, too!"

"Some system!"

"Well, yes," said Fräulein Louise. "On the other hand, take East Germany. So many doctors have left the DDR the results have been catastrophic. Do you think it's right for a doctor to abandon his patients? The people are poor—they talk about justice and injustice and don't know what they're talking about. Everything is worldly, nothing is important. But the living can't grasp that. Those who suffer will be heard, but those who are

41

satiated will never see God. You know, I haven't tried to pass judgment for a long time, but I must protect the children. The children are innocent. Whatever man does, the children must not be allowed to suffer!" Her last words were interrupted by a loud noise outside. "*Now* what's happened?"

We hurried to the window. At the entrance to the camp, quite some distance away, I could see a crowd milling around in the light of the setting sun. Several camp guards—older men in plain, drab uniforms—and more conspicuously, a beefy-looking fellow in overalls, a very fat man in a gray coat, and a girl with black hair. Children were shouting, men were cursing; the beefy fellow in overalls tore the club out of the hand of one of the guards, who stood by helplessly as the beefy fellow beat the fat man in the gray coat to the ground. The girl was screaming hysterically, but I couldn't understand a word she was saying. Bertie limped to the door as fast as he could. "It's a madhouse!" he cried delightedly, then he went outside, running across the cement walk and the brown weed-strewn ground, one of his cameras in his hand. Fräulein Louise's voice broke as she screamed, "Indigo! Indigo! Irina Indigo!"

It was evidently the girl's name, because she turned and looked in our direction.

"Come here!" yelled Fräulein Louise. "Come here at once!"

"No!" the girl yelled back. "I want out! I want out!" And she started to run.

"Pastor Demel!" screamed Fräulein Louise, and a young man in a black suit, whom I hadn't noticed before, grabbed the girl whose name was Irina Indigo by the arm.

Meanwhile the fat man had scrambled to his feet and broken loose from the beefy fellow. He kicked the latter in the stomach and tried desperately to reach the camp gate. He shoved two men who tried to stop him aside, and struck a third in the face. The beefy one caught up with him, grabbed him from behind and clubbed him again. The fat man collapsed. The beefy fellow yanked him to his feet. "Herr Kuschke!" Fräulein Louise screamed wildly.

The beefy fellow—Herr Kuschke, evidently— turned around, and with a Berlin accent you could cut with a knife, yelled, "It's okay, Fräulein Louise. Everything's all right."

"Bring Indigo to me, Herr Pastor!" cried Fräulein Louise to the man in the black suit. "And the man, too!"

"No, no!" screamed the girl whose name was Irina Indigo.

The pastor, whom Fräulein Louise had designated as one of the good men she counted as a friend, dragged the protesting girl to our barracks. Kuschke, also a friend of Fräulein Louise's and counted by her among the good, had the fat man by the collar and one of his arms twisted behind his back. You could see the fat man didn't like it. The whole group approached the barracks, and Bertie took pictures furiously.

7

Frankfurt. Kassel. Göttingen. Hannover. Bremen. 466 kilometers on the autobahn. A hop for a Lamborghini 400 GT. That was my car—a white 3.93 lter V-12 with 9:1 compression ratio and brake horsepower of 330 at 6500 RPM. Twin carburetors. 80-liter gas tank. Top speed: 250 km. an hour. A two-seater. All under the heading, Snob!

To go back for a moment—Bertie and I had left Frankfurt for Neurode at 7:00 A.M. His stuff was in a duffel bag, mine was in a large leather suitcase, and my suits were on hangers in the back. We didn't know how long we'd be gone, so I'd taken along three bottles of Chivas and filled my flask.

Bertie had slept all the way to Bremen. He had just returned from overseas the day before. I let him sleep. It was a strange thing, but in my car I always felt first-rate. For instance, I didn't have a drop to drink all the way to Bremen. Didn't need it. In the hotel I had two double whiskeys, but actually only because I felt so good.

It was foggy on the autobahn, once we had inched our way out of the chaos of Frankfurt. Everything came floating toward us and passed us by as in a nightmare, as if in another world. There . . . I've written it again!

At about 8:30 the fog cleared. The sun shone and I stepped on the gas. Still, we didn't get to our hotel in Bremen until 12:30. The Park Hotel, naturally, since there was nothing better. The secretaries in the editorial office knew what they had to order for me—everything deluxe. It had taken me a while to impress my firm with the fact that I worked best in the most luxurious

43

surroundings available, but now they knew. This was a must, especially when I was writing about human misery, which both of us were hoping to find in Neurode. Sells well, human misery. In this case Publisher Herford had something special in mind, and that was why two ultra-pros like us had been chosen to go to Neurode.

After a quick lunch at the Park Hotel, we drove on. We wanted the advantage of daylight as long as possible, for picture taking. Besides, something told me we should hurry, and this "something" had never yet given me a bum steer.

After Zeven the road was a mess. No shoulder, potholes, right-angle curves, and things got worse until it wasn't much better than a dirt road. On both sides of the road gorse and other thorny bushes were growing, and stumps of osier willows reared up, and many bulrushes. About half a kilometer ahead of us the moor began and didn't seem to want to end. Wild areas of brown heather, everything else had finished blooming and was rotting. Here and there you could see water, brown or black. And you could smell it. It smelled good. But the landscape grew increasingly dreary. In many places peat had been cut and piled high. There were black and white birches, bare black alders, and gnarled willows.

Three villages—you could barely call them that—a handful of houses, rather, each smaller than the other. A church, a grocery store, an inn . . . and we were out on the desolate moor again. I couldn't drive faster than fifteen kilometers. The car lurched from one hole to the other.

"And this is the road on which they transport the children," said Bertie, who had taken a few shots of the area. "I feel sorry for the camp driver, with a bus on a road like this! That camp's going to be there forever, I'd say, the way things look. They could at least build a road on it!"

Again a cluster of houses, and the moor on our left, behind bushes and reeds. "That prickly stuff is juniper," said Bertie. He was interested in nature; I wasn't. "This strip of land down to the moor is still part of the coastal plain; that's the sandy landscape on our right, an eruption of the Ice Age. It's higher than the moor and runs all around it. This happens to be a high moor."

"So what else is new?" I asked, driving as cautiously as I could, so as not to damage the car. I had a very spiritual relationship with my car. There weren't many people of whom I could say that.

Bertie warmed up to his topic. He explained about lower moors that formed where there were open expanses of water, and the flora of the high moors. There were many interesting plants besides erica; insectivorous plants, for instance—he was obviously enjoying filling me in on every detail—different species of sundew, two kinds of bladderwort and some butterwort. I took his word for it. Once he had wanted to be a naturalist; I had wanted to be a lawyer. Neither of us had stuck it out.

"Where there's peat, you're usually on a high moor, and a high moor rises more slowly than a lower moor."

Not as far as I could see. In some places ground fog hid the landscape, and the sun glanced off it in misty rays. Never in my life had I seen such desolation. "A high moor is shaped like an hourglass," Bertie went on. "Where there's a lot of rain and high humidity and the earth is poor and acid, you'll find peat. And peat builds up the moor. Sphagnum is present in..."

I watched out for potholes and Bertie told about the delicate peat-bog plants, how ramified they were, how highly leafed. "They die very gradually, from the bottom, but they keep growing at the top because a tiny branch under the crown develops into a stem that is just as strong as the mother stem and in the end becomes independent. Peat moss stores the water it needs to survive, can store it for ages. Peat soaks up water like a sponge...."

"Look," I said. "Isn't this strange?"

"What?"

"For over a kilometer now, I haven't seen any peat, only moor and water and tree stumps. Don't they cut peat any more here?"

"They evidently got as much peat out of this area as they could," said my friend. "There's nothing much more, probably, except corpses."

"What kind of corpses?"

"People who fell in and couldn't get out again. Haven't you ever heard of moor corpses?"

"Maybe. Can't remember. So what about them?"

"They don't decompose!"

"You mean they look exactly as they did in life?"

"The moor corpses that have been found did. Totally preserved. Even their clothes. In Sweden they've got one from the Bronze Age."

"But how can that be?"

"The acids in the soil act as a preservative and prevent disintegration," said Bertie.

That was the first time we mentioned moor corpses, and it's why I've reconstructed Bertie's description of the moor in such detail. Yes, that's when we talked about corpses for the first time, in the weak noon sunlight of a beautiful November day, on the miserable road that led to Neurode. And had no idea of what lay ahead of us. Alders and birches rose high and bare into the blue sky above us.

8

Neurode showed up after a sharp curve and consisted of about a dozen houses. Here the earth was covered with a fine, brick-red dust. We passed two inns and a few stores, then we were on our execrable road again. A sign with weathered letters read: To The Youth Camp—1 km.

We got that kilometer behind us, too. The area was so eerie, I told Bertie, "If I was driving through here at night and had to take a leak, I wouldn't get out. I'd pee in my pants."

"You're right," said Bertie. "It's dangerous as hell on the edge of the moor. And to walk across it . . . man! You sink into the waterlogged moss, the water glitters in the moonlight, will-o-the-wisps beckon you away from the path into impenetrable depths, down, down. . . ."

"Oh, shut up!" I said. "There it is. Next to the signpost."

I turned sharp left. The moor was much farther back here; the sandy earth seemed to have pushed it aside with what looked like a broad sandbar. In front of us, and surrounded by the moor on three of its four sides, lay the Youth Camp Neurode. A short, broad road—asphalt, no less!—led to the entrance.

Bertie whistled between his teeth; I, too, was surprised. The camp was enormous. I hadn't imagined it would be nearly so large. There were big free areas between barracks, countless barracks; and the whole thing resembled a concentration camp, with its wire fence, barbed wire at the top that bent inward and high poles with searchlights, which of course weren't turned on now. The asphalt ended at a very wide, locked gate. A small gate next to it was open. Directly beyond it there was a barracks, obviously for guards. But the most astonishing thing was that on the area in front of the entrance, cars were parked in the brown heather, at least two dozen. Expensive cars. Big cars. Mercedes. Diplomats. Buicks. Fords. A lot of American cars.

"What's going on here?" I said, parking my Lamborghini beside an Oldsmobile. We got out, Bertie with his cameras, the pockets of his leather jacket bulging with film. I had my recorder and pad, and we walked up to the entrance.

The owners of the cars, male and female, were standing beside the fence that surrounded the camp. Many of the women were wearing fur coats—leopard, mink, Persian lamb; elegant ladies, rings glittering on their hands. Most of the men were wearing dark suits, white shirts, classy ties, a few wore homburgs. A first-night audience! Outside the fence. On the inside were the young people, boys and girls from about fifteen to eighteen. Some of them were also dressed well (remnants of their flight?), others had on training suits, pullovers, and jeans or simple clothes.

A lively discussion was going on between the two groups. The ladies and gentlemen were being persuasive, they gestured with their hands, they were excited. The young people listened. I wanted to listen, too, but as soon as I approached, all conversation ceased and everybody looked at me suspiciously. Among the men I could see quite a few questionable types, in spite of their elegant dress. And on the other side of the fence I saw blond girls, redheads, girls with black hair—a sensational sight, all in all. And Bertie took pictures. A man turned around suddenly, saw that Bertie was going to take his picture, threw his arms up to his face, and yelled, "Get the hell out of here or I'll knock your block off!"

"Nice people," said Bertie.

"What *is* going on here?"

"Let's find out," said Bertie.

We walked through the small gate which had a sign over it—No Admittance Without Permit!—and we had a camp guard on our necks before we'd taken three steps. "Good day, gentlemen. Where do you want to go?" An elderly, sickly fellow.

I showed him my press card, Bertie showed his. I had informed the camp director, Dr. Horst Schall, that we were coming, and he had given us permission to visit, interview whomever we liked, and take pictures. The guard looked us over sharply, then checked our identification cards again while I told him that we were expected. He nodded. "You're here because of the Czech children."

"Mainly, yes. But we're interested in other things, too."

He said, "Follow me," and walked on ahead to the barracks nearest the gate where three more guards were seated. They greeted us after we greeted them. All three were well over fifty. One of them was telephoning. They were very polite. One of them asked us to be seated—somebody would come and show us through the camp. Six minutes later Fräulein Louise Gottschalk appeared.

"*Grüss Gott*, gentlemen," she said smiling.

We introduced ourselves, she told us her name. "Because the gentlemen are interested mainly in the Czech children, I have been sent to show you around. Because I'm the one who looks after the Czech children." She laughed, a short angry laugh. "That's why I'm here. Otherwise they would certainly have sent someone else. Please come with me. I'll show you the camp first." Her last words were almost unintelligible because the first squadron of jets we were to experience flew overhead, so low that the earth seemed to tremble.

9

In the course of the next two hours, Fräulein Louise showed us the camp—not all of it, but enough to give us the general idea. She explained how it functioned. It was supported and run by the Red Cross, the Inner Mission, the Catholic and Protestant churches, and by the Labor Welfare Board. Subsidies were provided in Bonn. "Not enough," said Fräulein Louise, "Not enough."

Light music was playing over loudspeakers. We saw young people and children of all nations. The little ones were playing with a social worker or alone. The older ones moved to and from the various administrative barracks or walked, talking earnestly, up and down the cracked cement walks, which were lined by bare birch trees and black alders.

All the barracks were the same—long, low, and built of wood. They seemed to have been painted recently, but when you went inside you could see how old they were. There was a smell of many years, of many people, the sort of smell you can't get rid of, despite the fact that everything was scrubbed clean. I noticed that there was a camp for girls and one for boys. We saw recreation rooms, dormitories, triple bunk beds, mess halls. Everything was orderly. There were a few flowers and photos of film stars and pin-up girls on the walls, some pictures painted by the inmates. Where the little ones were housed there were toys.

Yes, everything was in good order, yet it reeked of despair and poverty, of homelessness, of wet clothing and a great, pervading sadness. A veil of melancholy lay over the entire camp. Weathered names in Gothic lettering were inscribed beside the entrances of barracks: East Prussia, Memel, West Prussia, Danzig, Posen, Königsberg, Stettin, Upper Silesia, Mark Brandenburg, Saxony, Thuringia, Mecklenburg. Under the names somebody had painted the shields of the various provinces or cities—a long time ago, apparently, because the colors were faded by the weather. Many of the barracks bore names like this, names of the regions that had been surrendered by the Soviet Union or Poland or East Germany after the war. Children from Poland and East Germany lived in them, but also young people from many other countries.

We met a lot of girls. There seemed to be more girls than boys in the camp, or did it just seem that way to me because so many of them were beautiful? For the most part they were serious; very few smiled at us. The boys seemed less reticent. Everybody greeted us politely.

There was a fairly large wooden church with a tower consisting of four columns at each corner so that you could see through it to the bell inside. It was cold in the church. Bertie took a picture of a little boy kneeling in front of the altar, fast asleep.

Fräulein Louise hurried on ahead of us, explaining everything as she went along. She told us what an Emergency Admission Procedure was and took us to see the county representative responsible for it. A Czech and an interpreter were with him. An emergency admission was a complicated business that took a long time and demanded a lot of paper work, but that was the way it had to be, said Fräulein Louise Gottschalk. She took us to the branch office of the Labor Bureau, to the Delousing Center, and to the infirmary, where every new inmate was taken at once for a thorough medical checkup. She took us to the office of the Security Police, where two men from the Internal Security Department were sitting at desks talking to a Spaniard and a Greek. The men spoke both languages. When we came in, they immediately stopped talking. Both men were taciturn. Bertie wasn't allowed to take pictures.

One of the men was called Wilhelm Rogge, the other Albert Klein. Klein was big and fat, Rogge was thin and wore thick glasses. I spoke Spanish and asked if I could listen to the conversation with the Spanish boy. Rogge said no, that was out of the question.

"When you've finished looking around," said Klein, "would you please leave us? We're very busy."

"Now look here—" I said.

"*Please*," said Klein.

There was nothing to be got out of Security. I could understand that such precaution was necessary and said as much. The gentlemen Rogge and Klein smiled politely and noncommittally.

Fräulein Louise took us to the Caritas Center, to the Welfare Department, to the office of the camp psychologist. She showed us the two white barracks where the social workers lived, the big communal kitchen where girls in blue aprons were peeling potatoes, the doctors' barracks. The doctors weren't there, but we could see that the place was well equipped; in one room there was even an operating table. Fräulein Louise showed us the central telephone office. A pretty girl was sitting in front of an old switchboard, plugging in connections. Her name was Vera Gründlich and I flirted with her briefly.

We wanted to talk to adults, young people, and children. Fräulein Louise got us two interpreters who spoke all the languages spoken at the camp. We let the children and young people tell us why they had fled. Always for political reasons. The recorder picked up everything. I held the microphone in my hand.

"It's not always political," Fräulein Louise whispered to me. "Very often it's for quite different reasons, but that's what they have to say so that they'll be recognized as political refugees, you understand?"

Two hours later Fräulein Louise said she wanted to show us where she worked. We walked across the heather to a barracks in the rear of the camp. "There we are," said Fräulein Louise.

We passed a tall flagpole imbedded in a big cracked cement block. This must once have been a parade ground. I asked, "How old is the camp?"

Fräulein Louise didn't answer. I asked again. Again she didn't seem to hear.

"How much money can you spend per person daily?"

"Two marks fifty," she replied promptly. So this was a question she was willing to answer. "That's for clothing, bed and board, pocket money, heating in the winter—everything! Not much, is it?"

"No." Bertie was smiling. "Not much."

"The adults in the other two camps also got only two marks fifty a day, but my children got ten pfennigs more." *My children*, she said. . . .

Two marks fifty per person. And sixty kilometers from here, Bertie and I had had two rooms with bath in the Park Hotel for eighty-five marks a day each. Just for the room. Not quite sixty kilometers away. . . .

We had reached Fräulein Louise's barracks. Almost directly behind it, I could see a row of black alders, growing close together, and behind them the high barbed-wire fence and the searchlights on their poles. "Does the camp end there?" I asked.

"Yes," she said. "Back there."

"And what lies beyond the fence?"

Again she didn't answer. I repeated my question. No reply. Then I could see for myself. Beyond the fence lay the eerie, endless moor, great areas of which were already obscured by fog.

10

The door of Fräulein Louise's office flew open. "Okay! In you go!" growled driver Kuschke, his usually good-natured face grim. With the help of a shaky old camp guard he shoved in the fat man who was wearing a light blue suit under his gray coat, a pink shirt, and a wild tie, and who reeked of a sickly sweet perfume. He spoke in a high sing-song voice and made a flabby and effeminate, but sly and thoroughly unpleasant impression.

51

"You're going to be sorry for this!" he whined. "I have friends in Hamburg. In the administration! Wait till they hear what goes on in this place!"

"Shut up!" said Kuschke, and to Fräulein Louise, "Here's the fat slob. And we've brought Indigo, too. Was going to bolt with the bastard."

The girl whose name was Irina Indigo came into the room, led by Pastor Demel. She was hysterical with rage. The young pastor, who wore a black tie and his hair in a crew cut, was trying to calm her down, without success. She screamed at Fräulein Louise, "I can't stand it here! Not another minute! I've got to get out of here!"

Bertie was standing beside me, taking pictures with the Hasselblad. "Who's the fat one?" he whispered.

"No idea."

"I know him."

"You *do?*"

"I know him." Bertie was staring at the fat man. "I know him, goddamn it! But I can't place him." He scratched his head above the bandage.

Meanwhile Fräulein Louise had pounced on the girl. She was extraordinarily sharp with her, considering how pleasant she had been until now. But then I remembered her outburst over the damaged hot plate. Apparently she gave in to such rages.

"Fräulein Indigo, you know better than that. Haven't I told you you can't leave the camp without permission and a pass?"

Irina Indigo had black hair. She wore it pageboy cut. She had dark eyes that were flashing now, full red lips, and very white skin. She was tall, slender, and wore flat shoes, a light blue jumper, a skirt to her knees, and a matching coat. She had long silky lashes. Her Czech accent was barely noticeable.

"I must get out! I must get to my fiancé! I've said so a dozen times. *I've got to get to him!*" She pointed to the fat man. "This gentleman was going to take me to him. In his car."

"That's what you get for trying to help somebody," said the fat man, rubbing his sore head.

Kuschke lifted his free arm as if he wanted to strike again, but the fat man ducked. "Don't you dare!" Then he noticed that Bertie was staring at him. "And what's the matter with you?"

"I know you," said Bertie.

"That's what *you* think," said the fat man.

"But I do," said Bertie.

"You can kiss my ass!" said the fat man. Kuschke wrenched the arm behind his back higher, and the fat man bellowed with pain.

Fräulein Louise walked up to him belligerently, a female animal protecting her young. "What are you doing here? Do you have a pass?"

"He doesn't have a thing," said the guard, looking embarrassed.

"If he doesn't have a pass, how did he get in?" asked Fräulein Louise.

The camp guard's face reddened.

"Well?" said Fräulein Louise.

"It's our fault," was the camp guard's embarrassed reply. "The game. Germany-Albania."

"*What?*"

"Soccer, Fräulein Louise. On television. A lot of the young ones were watching, too."

"Well . . . that is unbelievable!" said Fräulein Louise. "That's what happens when people have nothing but amusement on their minds and don't attend to their duties."

"Yes," the tired camp guard admitted unhappily.

"All four of you watching television?"

"All four of us. Yes, Fräulein Louise. That's when he must have got in."

"That's a nice state of affairs!" raged Fräulein Louise. "Meanwhile anything can happen!"

"We're sorry, Fräulein Louise. Nothing's ever happened before."

"Aha!" Kuschke had frisked the fat man. He sounded triumphant. "There we are!" He pulled a pistol out of the fat man's belt and handed it to the guard. "A Walther 7.65." He released the clip. "Loaded."

Kuschke found two more clips in the left pants pocket of the fat man who smelled to high heaven of musk. "Christ! A whole arsenal!"

"Do you have a gun permit?" asked the guard.

"Of course," said the fat man.

"Where?"

"In Hamburg. Do you think I carry it around with me?"

"But the gun—yes," said Kuschke. "We're confiscating the pistol."

The fat man whirled around. "You're not confiscating

53

anything!" he shrieked in his high-pitched voice. "What you're doing here is absolutely illegal!"

"Shut your big mouth!" Kuschke said quietly. He was a strong man with huge hands. "Or you'll hit the wall and won't get up again."

Irina Indigo had looked startled when Kuschke had found the pistol. Now she stood there helplessly, not saying a word, and avoided looking at Fräulein Louise. Bertie walked around the fat man, eyeing him from all sides, frowning. He was obviously trying to remember where he had seen the man before. I smiled at the girl. She didn't seem to notice.

"Identification!" barked the guard.

"What for?"

"One more shitty question like that and I'll flatten you!" said Kuschke.

The fat man handed over his passport. The guard walked over to Fräulein Louise's desk and began to take notes. Suddenly Irina Indigo cried out, "This gentleman came into the camp because I waved at him!" Bertie took a picture of the fat man.

"You can't do that!" he shouted. "Not to me!" And he went for Bertie. I took a flying leap across the office, punched the guy in the ribs, then in the stomach. Gasping for breath, he collapsed in a chair. Bertie took pictures. Action pictures.

Now the girl screamed at me. "What do you think you're doing? Who are you?"

"Okay, honey." I lit a cigarette. "You and I will have a little talk in a minute." I looked at Bertie. "All right?"

"First-rate," said Bertie, and took two more pictures of the fat man.

As I said before, I have an instinct for people. And for events. Now I had what I call hunting fever. At first I'd thought we'd drawn a blank by coming to this miserable place, but since Fräulein Louise had spoken to her invisible audience, everything had changed. I went over to the guard who was taking notes. "What's the man's name?"

"Karl Concon."

"Concon..." Bertie repeated the name. "Concon...."

"His profession is hotelier."

"Hotelier!" said Kuschke scornfully. "A brothel on the Reeperbahn's more like it. Excuse me, Fräulein Louise, but isn't it a filthy mess? They come to us in droves, the bastards. They promise the little bitches a co-op apartment and two thousand marks a month, guaranteed! And what do they get? Gonorrhea!"

"Herr Concon didn't promise me anything," cried Irina Indigo. She looked furious.

Bertie slapped his forehead. "Now I know who you are! I never forget a face! You were on trial. 1956—no, 1957. I was there. We had a story on it in *Blitz*."

"You're soft in the head," said Concon and laughed, but it was a shaky laugh.

"In Hamburg," said Bertie. "A picture story."

"What was he being tried for? Who is he?" I asked.

"A slob," said Bertie. "A big fat slob. A fag. Not that I have anything against fags."

"Neither do I," I said. "God knows, I've got lots of gay friends. Make very good friends."

"Sure," said Bertie. "But not this guy. This guy doesn't know how to be a good friend. This fag blackmails fags. Among others, a quite important German officer. That's why he was in court."

"For blackmail?" asked the pastor.

"No. For treason."

"I wasn't convicted," Concon cried angrily, rubbing his sore head again.

"Because of insufficient evidence," said Bertie.

"Treason? Blackmail?" Fräulein Louise was beside herself.

"Right," said Bertie. "Treason and blackmail. Herr Concon, you've grown considerably fatter since then. Take down all the information, Walter—passport number, date of issue. Let's do our research properly."

"I need the information, too," said Fräulein Louise.

The pastor gave her a strange look, but he didn't say anything. Fräulein Louise picked up a pad and pencil and walked over to the guard who was copying the information. I heard a click. The cassette had run out. I put in a new one fast and went and stood beside Fräulein Louise and recorded all the data on Concon's passport. Bertie was right. Assignments like Neurode were usually given to our researchers. When something had happened or was suspect, they went out with their cameras or took along a photographer and collected all the necessary material, then I or some lesser light wrote it up. This time things were different. I was doing the research. Herr Karl Concon was born in 1927, on May 13, and was therefore forty-one years old.

Fräulein Louise told the unhappy camp guard, "Hang onto the man and call the police in Zeven. They're to come and get him."

"Yes, Fräulein Louise."

"You can't hold me!" cried Concon, and collapsed. He was evidently badly hurt.

"Sure we can hold you!" Kuschke rubbed his big hands.

"I'm telling you, you can't hold me, you pigs!" Concon was screaming.

"We're going to bring charges against you," said Fräulein Louise.

"Don't make me laugh! For what?"

"For entering the camp without a permit. For disturbing the peace. For trying to kidnap a young girl," said Fräulein Louise.

"I never—"

"You didn't?" Kuschke, with his almost unintelligible Mecklenburg accent. "We dreamed it all, maybe?"

"And we shall also examine what Herr Engelhardt told us about you."

"You asshole!" Concon to Bertie, who was smiling.

"Please, please, Fräulein Louise, let me at least call my fiancé!" begged Irina Indigo.

"Impossible!" said Fräulein Louise.

"Why don't you let the girl call him?" I asked.

"I've begged and begged, and the answer's always no!" the girl pleaded.

"Because it's forbidden," said Fräulein Louise. "If we permitted it, they'd all be calling. We can't allow it. Two marks fifty each is all we get for every one of them."

I said, "I'll pay for the call."

"You?"

"Yes. I have to call my editor, too."

Fräulein Louise hesitated.

"Please—"

The phone rang. Fräulein Louise took the call. "Gottschalk. . . . . Yes, *Herr Doktor*. All right. We'll come right over." She hung up. "It's a girl," she said.

She walked over to the door of her living room and opened it. Kuschke and I followed her. The driver said, "I'm glad. The Panagiotopulos girl was so afraid it was going to be a boy and he'd have to be a soldier in the next war."

We looked into the living room. Karel was sitting on Fräulein Louise's bed, pale, his hair disheveled. The trumpet was still lying at his feet. Fräulein Louise walked up to him.

"We're going to see the doctor," she said. "He's too busy to come to us. Do you think you can walk?" The boy nodded and got up, swaying a little. Fräulein Louise supported him. Bertie shoved me aside and took pictures.

Fräulein Louise led the boy through her office, saying as she passed Irina Indigo, "Since Herr Roland is willing to pay, you may call. But don't try to get out of here again!"

"I won't, I won't, Fräulein Louise." Suddenly she looked happy. "If I can just talk to him—"

"Are you through?" Fräulein Louise asked the camp guard.

"Yes!" The guard put his notebook and Concon's pistol in his pocket. "Let's go," he said to Concon, trying to sound energetic and firm, the poor old fellow. "And don't try anything or you'll get more of the same."

"And I'm here, too," said Kuschke.

"I'll go with them," said Bertie.

"Okay," I said. "When the police come, call me."

"Will do."

As he left the room, Concon hissed, "I'll speak to the mayor in Hamburg about this, and you'll be fired! Every one of you! And for this sort of thing we're paying taxes!"

Fräulein Louise had almost reached the front door when Karel turned and without a word walked back into the other room. He came out again right away. He had gone to get his trumpet. He was holding the gleaming instrument in his little hand. He didn't say a word but walked slowly, cautiously, like a blind child. He saw us and bowed, like the little gentleman he was. "See you later, Karel," I said.

"I'll go with you," said Pastor Demel. But Fräulein Louise had something else on her mind. "Please, Herr Pastor . . . I can manage the boy by myself, but my hot plate—the coil is broken again. You're so clever, you fixed it once. Would you take a look at it again?"

"I'll be glad to," said Pastor Demel.

"Thank you," said Fräulein Louise, and the door closed behind her and Karel. The pastor looked at the hot plate, took a big pocket knife with a lot of different blades and tools on it out of his pocket and began to work on the coil.

Irina Indigo looked at me. Her eyes were dark and they were sad again. I looked at her. We were standing at least two meters apart, but our gaze held.

A fresh squadron of Starfighters came roaring out of the sky, louder and louder, and again the windows rattled. I waited for my nerves to react. They didn't. For the first time I remained absolutely calm as the planes passed overhead. I looked for my jackal. He wasn't there. The roar of the engines grew less and faded away altogether. Irina Indigo and I were still looking at each other.

11

I remembered that I was a wreck of a man, a lush but a hard-working reporter who was onto something that showed promise, not a playboy who could lay a beautiful, helpless young girl, certainly not before he had helped her, so I pulled myself together and asked, "What's his number?"

"When I was fleeing, I used it as a prayer. Hamburg 2-2068-54."

"Does he have an apartment in Hamburg?" Pastor Demel was sitting on the desk now.

"No. That's the apartment of his best friend in the Bundesrepublik. Rolf Michelsen. They've known each other for years. Herr Michelsen lives on a street called Eppendorfer Baum. Number 187." My recorder took notes. "Herr Michelsen took in my fiancé. That was agreed upon long before he fled. Herr Michelsen often visited Jan in Prague."

"Jan?"

"Jan Bilka. That's my fiancé's name."

"What does he do, this Herr Michelsen?"

"I don't know. I don't know him personally. Jan used to talk about him, but he couldn't tell me everything. Jan was a very important official in the Ministry of Defense, so there were many things he couldn't talk about."

Suddenly I felt hot. "Of course not. You said in the Ministry of Defense?"

58

"Yes," said Irina. "Can we put through the call now?"

"Right away," I said, and walked over to the phone. "If he was a top official in the Defense Ministry, he must have been at least thirty."

"Thirty-two," said Irina. "Why are you looking at me like that? I'm eighteen. So what!"

"Nothing," I said.

"I'm studying psychology," she said. "He had an apartment; I had one on the top floor in the same house. A sublet. We've known each other for two years. Satisfied?"

I nodded and dialed the first number that came to me—nine—and, lo and behold, got central. I recognized the voice. "Is that pretty Fräulein Vera?" I said. "This is Roland, Fräulein Vera. Yes, I was the one who came in to see you a while ago. Please get me—" I looked at Irina.

"Hamburg 2-2068-54."

"Hamburg 2-2068-54," I repeated. "I'll be coming by to pay for the call. Fräulein Louise gave her permission. Thank you, Fräulein Vera." I gave Irina the receiver. "Hello!" She sounded breathless. And then, after a pause. "Yes, of course. I understand." And to us, "It'll take a while to make the connection. I'm to wait."

"Fine."

"You are Herr Walter Roland?" asked Pastor Demel. He was looking at me curiously.

"I am." I sounded unfriendly, which had not been my intention, but suddenly I felt miserable.

He introduced himself. "Paul Demel."

"Pleased to meet you," I said curtly, and to Irina: "When did your fiancé escape?"

"Almost three months ago. On August twenty-first." She was holding the receiver to her ear.

"Fräulein Louise told me you were coming." Pastor Demel was smiling. "I'm very pleased to meet you personally. I have a lot of questions to ask you."

"You're the man who liked my books," I said, and there he was again, the miserable animal, my jackal.

"Yes. I especially liked *The Infinite Sky*."

"And I suppose you want to know why I'm not writing any more novels."

"Among other things," he said amiably.

"Because I can't write any more books!" I said, trying

59

desperately to control my feeling of harassment, without entirely succeeding. "That's why! All I can do now barely manages to come under the heading of journalism. I'm a reporter."

"I find that hard to believe. I think you proved—"

"I proved *nothing!*" I cried. "Please, Herr Pastor!"

"You just became discouraged too soon," he said.

"And I was hungry!" But I was thankful he didn't know the name I was writing under now. My profession was riddled with gossip, and a lot of people knew I was writing under another name. But Pastor Demel was apparently not one of them. I would have been ashamed to face this young priest if he had known who stood before him besides Walter Roland.

"You're a reporter?" asked Irina. She sounded afraid.

"As you just heard," I said. "Does that bother you?"

"No, of course not." She laughed, but it didn't ring true. "Why should it bother me?"

"It bothers a lot of people," I said, "especially when I want to write about them."

"Well, there's nothing—Hello? Yes?" She listened. "I see," she said, then, "thank you," and put down the receiver. "The number is busy. The operator's going to try again."

"Patience," I told her.

"Yes, yes. I know."

"Why did you flee?" I asked.

"Because of him."

"What do you mean?"

"When they found out that he'd fled, they came to see me. The State Police. Czech and Soviet. They held me for two days and questioned me for hours, day and night."

"What did they want to know?"

"Everything about my fiancé."

"What sort of things, for instance?"

"What department he'd worked in. What files he'd been in charge of. His position, his private life, our affair. They were interested in everything. But there was very little I could tell them. I didn't know what department Jan had worked in, nor what his position was, nor what files he had access to. I realized then that I really knew very little about him, and that shocked me. Can you understand that?"

"Perfectly. Go on."

"They didn't believe me. They let me go but they kept coming back. Every day. My landlady got terribly nervous and wanted me to move out, but she was afraid. Terribly afraid. So was I."

"You didn't give them the Hamburg address or the name of his German friend, did you?"

She said indignantly, "Of course not!"

"It was just a question. Don't get mad. And then what?"

"Then they called me back for more questioning. It took days. Always the same questions, but different officials. They wouldn't let me go back to the university, but I wasn't supposed to leave Prague either. I had to report to the police station nearest me twice a day. And the questioning went on and on."

"They must have been extremely interested in your fiancé," said Pastor Demel.

"Yes," said Irina. "But why?"

The pastor and I looked at each other but didn't say anything. "Then," Irina went on, "last week, on Thursday, all Jan's friends and colleagues were arrested, at the same time. Oh, I forgot to say, I was constantly confronted with these people during the questionings. I knew a few, most of them by name only, but some I didn't know at all, not even their names. But I knew when they were arrested."

"How did you know?"

"I got a telephone call. Anonymous. I don't know who it was, but after that I got away as fast as I could. I was terrified. I couldn't stand any more. I was sure that next thing, they'd come and get me. I wanted only one thing—to get to Hamburg, to Jan."

"And now you're safe, absolutely safe, so calm down, please."

"Yes, you must calm down," said Pastor Demel, and then, obviously to distract me, he said, "Look, the coil has been flattened. Somebody must have hit it with a hammer." He looked straight at me. "All right, not another word about your books. Would you give me a hand here? The thing keeps slipping."

I went over and held onto the hot plate while he tried to interlock the broken parts. "Never mind, I'll have to take the thing apart or I'll never be able to fix it." He snapped a corkscrew out of a slot in his pocket knife, and went on working. "But may I give you a piece of advice, *Reporter* Roland?"

"Please do."

"Very well. You're interested in the Czech children. Naturally. They're very topical. But while you're at it, take a look at the fine ladies and gentlemen outside, the pimps and madams in those Cadillacs and Lincolns, coming to get our girls."

"To get our girls?" Irina was looking at him wide-eyed, and I thought how innocent she looked, and then I thought how a lot of girls I'd seen here looked like that—refined, beautiful, and very very innocent. And Irina had had an affair for two years with a much older man. . . .

"They want them for their cabarets," said Pastor Demel. "Strippers, bar girls, or for the street. A few years later the poor things come back, broken, finished—more often than not, sick. We help wherever we can, but once they're out of the camp, they can do what they like. And those who have been here a long time are let go anyway."

"How long have you been here?" I asked Irina.

"Since yesterday."

"That's much too short a time," said Pastor Demel. "You can't possibly have been to all the offices yet—the Labor Bureau, Security, and all the rest. And before you've been through all these formalities, you can't leave. But after that the boys and girls your age may leave, and what do they do? They go the village, to the Skull and Crossbones Tavern."

"Where?"

"The Skull and Crossbones Tavern. The children from East Germany gave it the name."

"Why?"

"Oh, years ago they found human bones in the area. You can imagine the excitement that created in the camp. The peasants told us that during the Nazi era executions took place where the tavern now stands. They don't like to talk about it. We had quite a time getting it out of them. Well, there you are. They come to an agreement with the girls here at the fence, then they wait for them in the Skull and Crossbones, and off they go. This Herr Concon was certainly in a hurry to get hold of you."

"Yes," I agreed. "It's very odd." I still felt hot. "So why don't you lock up the camp and let nobody out?"

"That would be illegal," said Demel. "Restriction of freedom. Besides, those types out there at the fence would get their girls after we'd found work for them through our labor bureau and closed our files. So there isn't any point in shutting off the area in front of the camp. They'd just wait for the girls in Zeven or catch them on their way there."

"What sort of people are there out there, anyway," I asked, "besides the crooks from the Reeperbahn? The ladies, for instance."

"You live in the West, don't you?" he asked. "Do you have a maid?"

62

"A cleaning woman," I said, "twice a week."

"Well, then you're lucky," he said.

"Why doesn't the call come?" Irina's voice was a whisper. She paced up and down, biting her lip.

"There are no more servants," said Pastor Demel, "but here at the camp you can hire as many as you like. You don't have to promise a room with a bath and television and a fur coat for Christmas. They're thrilled if one of those fine ladies will bail them out and go through all the red tape with the authorities for them."

"Where do they come from?" I asked.

"Düsseldorf, Cologne, Frankfurt, Hamburg, Munich—surprised, aren't you? Yes, from so far away. The fine ladies from the Bundesrepublik," he went on. "But they're not looking only for servants. A lot of them are in business—hosiery, fashions, pharmaceutical products. They want assembly-line workers. The men, too—mining, electronics, dock workers: everything from pasta to steel. Germany needs workers. The boys make a deal at the fence, and off they go. Or the press! Forgive me, Herr Roland, but I'll bet you that at least two men from the press are out there at the fence."

"What could they possibly want?"

"Newsboys. Subscription salesmen. Even the poorest students won't do it today with the pay they offer. But our boys will do anything. So that gives you some idea of the circus we're running here."

The telephone rang. Irina rushed to answer it. "Hello? Hello? Jan?" Then her face fell with disappointment. "Oh . . . I see. Yes. Thank you." She hung up and turned to me. "It's still busy."

Suddenly, and this time totally unexpectedly, there he was, close to me—the jackal. I got up. I sat down again. I got up again.

"There!" said Pastor Demel. "You let go and it snapped out."

"I'm sorry."

"What's the matter with you?" He was looking at me. "You don't look right. Your lips are blue."

I didn't care anymore. I got out my flask, unscrewed the top, and held it out to the pastor. "Would you like some whiskey?"

"No, thank you," he said. "Never during the day. Bad for my nerves."

I drank.

"Sometimes I feel dizzy," I said. "It comes over me just like that. And sick." I drank again. "I find it terribly depressing here. For instance, your Fräulein Louise. Is she—?"

"You're going to ask if she's mentally sound." He looked down at the hot plate. "I think it'll hold. Now all I have to do is get the two coils—"

"Herr Pastor!"

"Yes?"

"She's strange. She listens and there's no one there. She talks and there's no one there."

"Yes." He sighed. "It's a great pity. Such a good woman. A valuable woman. How she loves her children! But, unfortunately, people keep talking about her behavior and provoking her. They really should retire her; and, in all honesty, I can't put in a word for her. But when it happens, when she has to leave her children . . . it'll be the end of her. She'll hang herself. No . . . she'll walk out onto the moor."

"But who *is* she listening to? And talking to?"

"Her friends."

"What friends?"

"Well . . . ," said Pastor Paul Demel, "her dead."

12

June 5, 1968, late afternoon. A Wednesday. Almost twelve weeks to a day after Karel's father had floated slowly downstream, shot by a guard. Fräulein Louise was standing far out on the moor on a firm little mound, and eleven figures were standing around her, forming a circle. She was talking to them excitedly, wringing her hands, waving them in the air, pacing back and forth as much as the space permitted. The wind swept wisps of fog across her and the figures; every now and then they disappeared from view. There was a full moon, its silver light diffused by the fog hovering over the moor. Small pools of water glistened in its light. The sounds of the nocturnal moor were eerie, its voices ghostly. Vast stretches of swamp grass gurgled, and in the distance the long, sad whistle of a locomotive faded into the night.

The fog floated away and Fräulein Louise became visible again, her white hair gleaming in the moonlight, surrounded by eleven figures. A meeting of ghosts.

The young woman who had been watching her for fifteen minutes shuddered. Her name was Hilde Reiter, and she was standing on the broad base of a cracked concrete pillar at the east end of the camp. Here the fence made a ninety-degree turn around the pillar from east to south.

Hilde Reiter had arrived at this spot in haste and great fear. She was wearing a coat and carrying a large suitcase. It was her intention to escape from the camp, for which she had a very good reason. Hilde Reiter knew that the camp director would take her to the police in the morning. That was why she had come here, to this cracked pillar. For fifteen minutes now she had been trying with all her might to topple it and drag the barbed-wire fence down with it. It was the only spot in the camp where one could have any hope of escaping.

Hilde Reiter was in a state of panic. If she couldn't get away, they would arrest her, make her stand trial, lock her up. The young woman hurled herself against the pillar and shook it until she was exhausted. The pillar remained upright. Hilde Reiter wasn't strong enough. Desperate, weeping tears of rage, she straightened up and caught sight of Fräulein Louise on the moor. I'm going crazy, she thought. I've gone out of my mind! How did the old bitch get out there? Nobody can walk on the moor.

She was shivering, although the night was warm, a warm night in what had been a rainy spring until now, the beginning of June. In fact, so far the whole year had been damp, with rain almost every day. The desolate moor was therefore swampier than ever and impossible to navigate on foot. The drainage ditches were filled to overflowing, their banks on both sides had crumbled and disappeared in the water. Scattered areas of high ground seemed to be floating. Old osier willows were growing on them, looking like crippled humans with their gnarled crowns, wild juniper around them, splintered moor pines, and birches everywhere, tall and thin.

Hilde Reiter clung to the pillar or she would have fallen off the base on which she was standing. Fascinated, her eyes wide, she watched Fräulein Louise talking excitedly to the eleven figures. "*Dong-ka-chunk . . . oong-ka-chunk,*" croaked the bittern. With the first cry the bird breathed deep, with the second it exhaled.

Hilde Reiter had been working at the camp for two years. She had come to Neurode because her friend, Gertrude Hitzinger, who had been a social worker in Neurode for three years, had written to her that the work was light and easy, with plenty of free time. Hilde Reiter was thirty-three years old. She was a handsome woman, but her expression was stern, and she had her peculiarities. It took Fräulein Louise a while to find out what they were—a year and a half, in fact. That was when Fräulein Louise caught her beating a small boy. Hilde Reiter had pulled down the boy's pants and was thrashing him on his bare behind with a bamboo switch. The boy was screaming. Fräulein Louise, who had suspected something of the sort for some time, was watching from behind a tree. Hilde Reiter said to the child, "You screamed. All right, then, you get three more. Every time you scream, three more."

The result was an uproar. Fräulein Louise was beside herself. Away with this sadist! She must leave the camp! Ranting and raving, she went to the camp director with Hilde Reiter. Dr. Horst Schall warned the woman: One more incident like this and she would have to go. Fräulein Louise said, "I'll keep an eye on her, Herr Doktor. You can depend on me."

Keep an eye on her? It drove Hilde Reiter up the wall. So now she was going to be spied on, every step she took watched by this old bitch who didn't have all her marbles, who talked into thin air and heard voices . . . because sometimes she'd stand there in the middle of a conversation, her mouth open, and definitely be listening to what some invisible nobody was saying. And this nut was going to keep an eye on her?

She turned the tables. She and her friend, Gertrude Hitzinger, began to spy on Fräulein Louise, and they did it so cleverly that she never noticed. Again and again they were able to report Fräulein Louise's strange behavior to the camp director. He had known Fräulein Louise for years as a faithful worker, ready to lay down her life for her children if necessary. So he did nothing about the reports. Once, when he was talking to Fräulein Louise and she was in good spirits, he mentioned the invisible people.

"Me? Talk to people who aren't there?" she cried. "I never heard of such a thing! I never did such a thing! Never! It's a lie, a horrible lie! And I know where you heard it! From Hilde Reiter and her friend, Hitzinger!"

When Hilde Reiter saw that she was getting nowhere with her reports, her hatred for Fräulein Louise grew. She and her friend went on spying on Fräulein Louise. They discovered that she left the camp frequently and no one knew where she went. The two women followed her. Usually she walked along the sandy road in the direction of the village, through the village, then between high reeds and bushes and—was suddenly gone! Disappeared! Every time!

Hilde Reiter and Gertrude Hitzinger told the other social workers about it. At the time, Fräulein Louise was still living with them, and their words fell on willing ears. None of the other social workers really liked Fräulein Louise. She was too blunt, too harsh, too suspicious and odd. She gave all her love to the children; there was nothing left, not even sympathy, for anyone else. She didn't take any interest in the petty intrigues of the other social workers; she hadn't made friends with any of them. So all of them were only too ready to believe Hilde Reiter and Gertrude Hitzinger. Fräulein Louise was given two nicknames: "the kook" was one, "the witch" the second. And the tension between her and the others grew. Dr. Horst Schall was unhappy; things couldn't continue like this. He tried to smooth things over. It didn't work. He talked to Fräulein Louise. In vain.

"Lies! It's a pack of lies, *Herr Doktor*, I assure you," she cried, turning pale, then a fiery red.

In the first week of June, Hilde Reiter couldn't control herself again: A pretty, dark-haired, wild young boy from Greece was brought to the camp. He was fourteen. He broke a window with a football. The sun was shining, all the children were outdoors. Hilde Reiter took the boy to her room, told him to take off his pants, took a ruler, and so that she would not get dirty—so she said—she pulled her skirt up to her crotch. The boy had to lie face down across Hilde's bare thighs. He didn't utter a sound as she hit him. Her breathing became labored, she felt a pulsation in the pit of her stomach, her blood felt hot. She didn't notice the door of her room opening slowly. Now she was panting. When she looked up, her eyes veiled with excitement, it was too late. Camp director Dr. Schall was standing in her room.

He didn't say much. "You are dismissed. You are suspended from all duties immediately. I shall report you. Tomorrow we will go to the police at Zeven. Until then you may not leave the camp."

13

"Still busy," said Irina Indigo, putting down the receiver. She was terribly upset. She hadn't felt the slightest interest in what the pastor was saying. All she could think of was hearing the voice of her fiancé.

"Must be a long conversation," I said curtly, because I was absolutely fascinated by Pastor Demel's story, "or several long conversations. The operator will keep trying. You'll just have to be patient."

Irina shrugged and sat down. "Go on, Herr Pastor," I said, "go on, please."

14

"Gertrude! Gertrude! Wake up!" Hilde Reiter was kneeling at her friend's bedside, shaking her. Gertrude Hitzinger woke up slowly. "For God's sake . . . yes, yes—who wants—what is it?"

Hilde Reiter spoke so fast the words were almost unintelligible. Suddenly Gertrude Hitzinger was wide awake. "And the old bitch is still out on the moor?"

"Yes. I'm telling you—yes."

"But she can't be! There's no path out to it! That's impossible!"

"But she *is* out there! And there are people with her! And she's talking to them!"

"Men?" Gertrude Hitzinger's eyes narrowed.

"They look like men. Yes, they are men!" cried Hilde Reiter, and as she said it, she really believed it. Men! Of course those had been men standing around the old witch! If she was going to be punished, she'd see to it that the old bitch got thrown out, too.

Gertrude Hitzinger got out of bed, put on a coat and shoes and said, "The others have to see this, too. Wake them, Hilde! Hurry!"

A few minutes later a group of eight women was hurrying across the former parade ground, Hilde Reiter leading them. The moon was very bright now, the fog had lifted. The women crowded around the fence by the pillar. "Where is she?" asked Gertrude Hitzinger, peering out across the moor. "I don't see her!"

None of the women could see Fräulein Louise.

"But she was there!" cried Hilde Reiter. "She was there! On that mound!"

"Where?"

"On which one?"

"There are a lot of them!"

"That one over there, the one with the willows. No, not that one. More to the right. Next to that stunted pine. Can't you see her?"

"I can see the pine, but not the old witch."

"Then she must have gone away."

"Gone away? How could she do that? Through the swamp? Across the water? You're crazy!"

"It's impossible. Look—the sand ends here, just a few meters beyond the fence the moor begins, and in you go!"

They were all talking at once.

"She couldn't have walked on the swamp."

"There's no path!"

"But I've told you over and over again—Gertrude and I have followed her, and she always disappears after she's walked through the village," cried Hilde Reiter. "I swear it's true. She was out there and she was talking to men. I saw it! With my own eyes! Let God strike me blind if I'm not telling the truth!"

An hour later Fräulein Louise came back to the camp. The guard on duty waved a greeting from his barracks as she opened the small gate with her key and locked it again, nodded at him, and hobbled off. When she entered her room and turned on the light, she found eight women waiting for her.

"What's going on here?" she asked, startled.

"That's what we want to know," said Gertrude Hitzinger. "It's one-thirty. Where were you?"

"I—I—" Fräulein Louise was breathless. "I couldn't sleep so ... I went for a walk."

"In the middle of the night?"

"Yes."

"Where?"

"What do you mean, 'where?'"

"Where did you walk? In the camp?"

"Yes," Fräulein Louise said hesitantly. "In the camp."

"That's not true!" cried Hilde Reiter. "We told the guard to call us when you came back from outside, and he did. You were not in the camp, Fräulein Louise. Where did you go?"

She didn't answer.

"Where?" Gertrude Hitzinger demanded.

"That's none of your business," Fräulein Louise cried angrily.

"And if you don't get out of my room at once, all of you, I'll call Dr. Schall."

"We've already called him," said Gertrude Hitzinger, grinning maliciously. "And he wants to see you at eight in the morning."

Fräulein Louise sank down on her bed. "Oh, dear God," she whispered. "Dear God!"

15

"Fräulein Louise," said Pastor Demel, "we've always understood each other, haven't we? We're friends, aren't we?"

"Well, of course, Herr Pastor," said Louise Gottschalk.

She was sitting opposite him in his study. She was calm, completely controlled, and smiling innocently.

"You mustn't be afraid," said the pastor.

"I'm not afraid."

"Coffee?"

"Yes, please."

Demel took a pot of steaming coffee from a hot plate and filled two cups that were standing on the table. Then he lit a cigarette.

"Oh, but this is good," said Fräulein Louise. "Just what I wanted—a cup of coffee."

"Help yourself to milk. Sugar? One or two pieces?"

"Three, please."

Demel sat down again. "Fräulein Louise," he said, "I have to ask you something."

"Go right ahead, Herr Pastor. My, but this is good coffee! Anyone would give their eyeteeth for a cup of coffee like this."

"Hilde Reiter isn't with us any longer, so you don't have to be afraid of her anymore."

"I was never afraid of her, a deranged person who beats children. I'm not afraid of anything, Herr Pastor."

"That's good. But is it really true?"

"It's really true, Herr Pastor."

"But then why didn't you want to tell Dr. Schall where you were last night? Perhaps you're afraid of Dr. Schall?"

"It wasn't right of me to say I'm not afraid of anything," said Fräulein Louise. "There are things I'm afraid of."

"What?"

"Of some people. Those who don't understand me. I was afraid Dr. Schall wouldn't understand me. And that he wouldn't let me stay with my children if I told him everything." She bowed her head.

"And that's why you wouldn't answer him?"

Fräulein Louise nodded.

"But if I tell you that Dr. Schall has asked me to speak to you because we know each other better, and if I tell you that he considers you one of the most valuable employees of the camp, and that he has no intention whatsoever of dismissing you, for the simple reason that you've done nothing wrong—will you tell me where you were last night?"

"Did he really say that? That he thinks I'm one of the most valuable employees and that he won't dismiss me?"

"He did, Fräulein Louise. That's exactly what he said. So now will you tell me?"

She raised her head and her big blue eyes were filled with confidence and relief. "Of course I will, Herr Pastor. I'll be glad to. I'll tell you anything you want to know because you'll understand. We're friends and I know you wish me well."

"So where were you?" asked Pastor Demel.

"I was on the moor," said Fräulein Louise. "Way out. That's where I always go to see my friends. You see, Herr Pastor, I still have friends, better friends than most people."

"Who are they?"

"Well," said Fräulein Louise, "there's the Russian soldier from the tank corps. He drove a tank. And the American pilot. He flew a bomber. Then there's a Czech radio operator. He fought in the British Army. And a Polish soldier. He was with the artillery. And there's the Ukrainian who had to work in a labor camp, and a German SS leader, and a Norwegian Communist, and a German—he's a Jehovah's Witness. Then there's the French soldier—he was in the infantry—and a Dutch socialist and a German from the Reichs Labor Corps. . . . Let's see now. Is that all of them? One, two, three . . . eleven. Yes, eleven in all. That's right. They've all had their troubles; sometimes they tell me about them. The French one had asthma. Dreadful asthma. Of course he doesn't have it anymore."

16

There was silence for a while in the pastor's room. Fräulein Louise finished her coffee, smiled happily and asked, "Could I have another cup, please? It's such good coffee."

"Of course, right away," said Pastor Demel as he fetched the coffee pot, still in a slight state of shock. While he was refilling Fräulein Louise's cup he said, "That's a lot of friends you have out there, and from such different countries."

"Thank you," said Fräulein Louise. "I'll help myself to milk. And may I have three lumps of sugar again? Yes, from so many countries. And they're all different ages. The Reichs Labor Corps man is the youngest; he's only twenty-three—not quite twenty-three. He died in 1935." She drank her coffee noisily. "Did you know that this camp was here then?"

"No."

"It's been here since 1934! That's the way it is. When they build a camp with barracks in Germany, it's here to stay. And there's always someone to imprison in it. Let me tell you all about it. First it was a camp for the Reichs Labor Corps. They were supposed to drain the moor. They didn't stay long—only till 1937. Then it became a camp for political prisoners, Germans first, later on from other countries, too—the countries Germany conquered. A concentration camp. Yes, Herr Pastor, that's how the German Jehovah's Witness got here, the poor fellow, and the Norwegian Communist and the Dutch socialist. They all died here and are buried in the moor. Yes, yes, Herr Pastor, don't look so surprised. You have no idea how many dead there are, lying out there on the moor. Hundreds! The moor is full of dead. It suited the Nazis very well that the moor was here. It made things so simple for them."

"I'm sure it did," said Demel. He noticed that his cigarette had burned down to his fingers and hastily put it out.

"Well," Fräulein Louise went on, "after the politicals, they used the camp for prisoners of war, and they came from all over the place. The Czech—my compatriot—the Frenchman, the

72

Pole, the Russian . . . and they sent people here from other camps. Neurode is so big, as you know. And they died here, too—the prisoners of war I mentioned. Then when all the camps got so overcrowded that they didn't know where to put the poor wretches, the Nazis divided this camp and made two camps of it. They filled one half with forced labor groups. That's how the Ukrainian got here. He died of pneumonia. And then, at the end of the war, they brought pilots here who had been shot down. They were kept in the other area at the end of the camp, English and American pilots. That's how my Ami got here."

"And died here?" Paul Demel asked softly. Outside they could hear children laughing.

"And died here. And the war was scarcely over when the British came, and *they* took over the camp. They liked the loneliness and decided it was the ideal place for the Nazi big shots and the SS men. That's how my SS leader got here. Yes . . . for three years it was a camp for Nazis; then came the Blockade and the first refugees from East Germany. The Germans took over again and tore down the watchtowers and de-electrified the barbed wire. They painted the barracks, planted a few flowers so that it would look brighter, and in no time the camp was full again, this time with children and young people. And that's where we're at today, one can say 'thankfully,' Herr Pastor. No, this camp hasn't stood empty since the day it was built!" The thought made Fräulein Louise laugh.

"So your friends are all lying dead in the moor," said Pastor Demel, looking bewildered, but he did manage a smile.

"That's what I've been telling you." Fräulein Louise nodded brightly. She seemed to find everything she had told perfectly natural and reasonable.

Pastor Demel decided to look through Fräulein Louise's file and see if she had ever been under psychiatric care. "How do you know all this about the camp?" he asked.

"The older peasants told me. They remember it all."

"And for how long have you visited your friends in the moor?"

"Well, I'd say about two years now. But before that, three years ago, they spoke to me and introduced themselves and told me who they had been before they died."

"But then you only heard their voices."

"That's right. Only their voices. But I soon could tell to whom each voice belonged. Like today. They're often with me when I'm working. Or at night. Especially at night. The voices, I mean.

73

I can't see them in the camp, not even today. You see, in the camp they're invisible."

"I see," said Pastor Demel. "But they speak to you and sometimes you answer them."

"That's right, Herr Pastor."

"Right now—I mean at this moment, is one of your friends here in the room?"

Fräulein Louise cocked her head to one side, listened for a moment, her eyes with a faraway look. Then she nodded. "Yes, Herr Pastor. The Frenchman and the Ukrainian. I had to wait for them to tell me that it would be all right to let you know. They say it's all right. They approve of my telling you everything. And why not? You're a good man, they say, who will understand."

"Well, now—"

"Yes, yes," cried Fräulein Louise, with another swallow of her coffee. She looked happy; Pastor Demel had never seen her look so happy. "And so," Louise Gottschalk went on, "two years ago the student came to me one night. He's my favorite. When I see him, it breaks my heart."

"For joy?"

"For joy and sorrow, too. Both at the same time. I don't know why. When I see him, it seems as if I see my whole life, just the way it was, the poor, thin little fellow. I know it sounds stupid, but I'm just a stupid old woman. You understand, don't you, Herr Pastor?"

Paul Demel nodded and thought how lonely a person had to be to create people out of sheer imagination.

"So he came to me—the student did—and asked me why I didn't come to visit him and his comrades, the way they visited me."

"He wanted you to visit them on the moor?"

"Yes. On the moor. That was the evening I saw him in the camp for the first time. Strange, wasn't it? He was wearing his work clothes, overalls and boots. He's not tall and so terribly thin. My God, how his shoulder blades stick out! Probably never had enough to eat. But smart! Did I say already that he was my favorite?"

"Yes."

"I like all of them, very much, but I like the student best."

"So where were you supposed to meet them?" the pastor asked uneasily.

"On the mound with the eleven osier willows growing on it.

You know the place I mean. It's pretty far out on the moor."

"But there's no path leading to it. Nobody can get out there! It's all swamp."

"That's what you think, Herr Pastor." Fräulein Louise laughed. "There is a path. There are paths on every moor. Usually only the peasants know about them, the ones that go out in the winter to cut rushes for the floors of the stalls. Because they have very little hay here. A peasant showed me the path. You have to go through the village. Then, about fifty meters farther along, the path starts. You can hardly call it a path, it's so narrow—more like a ridge...."

A ridge, thought Demel. And she had been walking on this ridge for two years now, balancing on it, on either side of which... He forced himself to stop visualizing it. "But weren't you ever afraid, Fräulein Louise? That's terribly dangerous!"

"Not for me, Herr Pastor. Because I'm going to see my friends. They're waiting for me to join them on that little mound."

"Between the willows," said Demel.

She shook her head and smiled again. "When I get there, they aren't willows any more. They're my eleven friends. It's an illusion, you see, for those who can't see my friends. I suppose for all people. I guess they also see nothing but the willows when I'm out there. Those willows are my friends. The trees disappear while we're standing there."

"But Hilde Reiter didn't see willows," said Pastor Demel. "She saw people. Men."

Fräulein Louise had to give this some thought. "That's right," she said, sounding astonished. "So she did. Such a wicked woman, of all people. How could that have happened? *I* think she saw willows and *thought* they were men. Because she *wanted* me to be out there talking to men, so she'd have something bad to tell about me. That's what it was. Wicked people are powerful, too, Herr Pastor, you know that."

"Yes," he said, and sighed. "So out there, on the mound, you are united with your friends."

"United! That's right. Out there I'm safe. They protect me. Nothing can hurt me. That's why nothing's ever happened when I walk out on the ridge, because I know and believe so firmly that nothing can happen to me. And nothing ever will!"

"When you get there, are your friends always waiting for you?"

"All of them—yes."

"And what do they look like?"

"Well, just the way they looked when they were alive. I can sense the spirit in them, that's why I can see them clearly."

"So they are still on this earth? They haven't found peace yet?"

"No, no! Of course they have found peace, a marvelous peace, Herr Pastor. Let me explain it to you just the way they explained it to me: When a person dies, he wanders all over the earth for years after his death, because he is of this earth. And during this time he can appear to people until at last he enters another world, but he enters this other world on its lowest level."

"Level?" asked Demel.

"Yes. You have to see it like a broad stairway with many steps, Herr Pastor." Fräulein Louise was terribly excited. Her cheeks were red, her blue eyes blazing. "At the very bottom of the stairs—that is the human being. And on the very top of the stairs is the God-being. That's where the blessed are. My friends are on a step in between...."

"I see."

"Not with the saints. Not yet. But a few steps below them."

"In a preparatory stage?" said Demel, coughing as he inhaled the smoke of his cigarette.

"In a preparatory stage! Yes! That's a beautiful way of putting it. And what's so wonderful about it, Herr Pastor, is that in the stage my friends are in, there is nothing but friendship and peace, and only good can happen there."

"So all your friends must have been good people."

Fräulein Louise hesitated. "Well, no. You can't exactly say that. *Now* they are good—yes, or they would never have reached this stage. You understand?"

"I understand."

"I mean, *if all meanness hadn't fallen from them.* In the stage on which my friends live, between human-being and God-being, they can still remember the life they lived on earth—the positions they held there, their nationalities, their professions, too. The Czech, for instance—he was an architect in Brunn. The Norwegian was a cook. The Dutchman was a book publisher in Groningen. The American was an advertising man in New York, on Madison Avenue." She spoke the foreign words correctly. How can this be possible? thought Pastor Demel.

"And so on. The SS man had a pickle factory in Seelze, near Hannover. The Russian was a clown in a circus in Leningrad. The Pole was a mathematics professor at Warsaw University. The

Ukrainian was a peasant. The Frenchman was a court reporter for a newspaper in Lyon." All pronounced correctly by Fräulein Louise, who couldn't speak German without an accent.

"The Jehovah's Witness was employed at a savings bank in Bad Homburg, and the labor camp fellow, the youngest, who's been dead the longest—he was studying philosophy. He came from Rondorf, near Cologne. Would it be terribly forward if I were to ask for another cup of coffee? . . . No? . . . You are an angel, Herr Pastor."

"Go on, Fräulein Louise," said Demel.

"Well, all of them remember this, and they remember what they were like, their personalities—yes, I guess you could call it that. They still have their personalities, but—and this is the wonderful thing—they're all friends, a group of friends, because they're on a higher level. There's nothing mean where they are, no jealousy, no hatred, no aggression, no sexuality, no desire of any kind."

"No desire?"

"Of course not. How could there be? They are spirits. Desire is nothing more than a cage for the body. And without desire they can be one, just as they are one, with all those who are blessed. And I am one of them. They have taken me in and we meet on the moor and talk to each other."

"What do you talk about?" asked Demel.

"About everything that happens in the camp. My friends are very interested in that. And about my anxiety for the children. When I don't know what to do with some boy or girl, if a child is difficult or sick or has tried to run away—they advise me." Fräulein Louise cocked her head to one side, listened, nodded.

"What is it?" asked Pastor Demel.

"The Frenchman," said Fräulein Louise. "He's listening."

"I see. Where is he?"

"Standing by the window, behind you, Herr Pastor. He just said I should tell you that they never express themselves quite directly to me. They don't tell me what to do. For instance, they don't say, 'Go back to the camp and be very friendly and considerate with that naughty child—it's only naughty because it's had so many experiences'; no. They say things like, 'What you intend to do, do it soon, because you will succeed.' And then I know exactly what they mean. That's quite clear, isn't it?"

"Hm. Yes. Of course. Quite clear. Do the voices sometimes warn you, Fräulein Louise?"

"Of course they do! Often! And always in a way that I have to interpret. It's the only way they can communicate."

"Why is that?"

"Why? Because there is nothing tangible in the beyond," said Fräulein Louise. "That's perfectly understandable, isn't it, Herr Pastor?"

17

"Schizophrenic," I said.

"That's what I think," said Paul Demel, running his fingers through his short hair. "The poor woman. I told you all this because by now everybody knows it anyway. They don't want her in the social workers' barracks anymore; she's ostracized by the women and hides there. Feelings against her have become so strong that Dr. Schall is thinking seriously of retiring her. It's a real tragedy."

Irina was staring at the phone as if she could hypnotize it. "I'm going crazy," she said. "It *can't* be busy for hours! The operator's forgotten me!"

"I'm sure she hasn't." I laid a hand on the girl's shoulder. "Be patient. The call will come through soon."

"I'm sure it will," said Pastor Demel.

"You said a while ago that you were going to find out something about her past," I said to Demel, "whether she ever had to have psychiatric treatment."

"Yes," he said.

"And with what results?" I glanced at my recorder. It was working.

"She was born and brought up in Reichenberg," said Demel, pulling the cord out of the hot plate. "It's all right now. Nothing wrong with it. Yes. Her parents died when she was young. She was in a home for two years, fine character, very nice young girl, helpful and outgoing. From the age of eighteen she was a social worker in Vienna. At the age of twenty-four she was sent to the Riesengebirge in Silesia for a while, on the Czech side, not far from the White Meadow."

"What is the White Meadow?"

"A moor, like this one. You see, everything fits. But it—it get even better. In the Riesengebirge, Fräulein Louise experienced love for the first time, relatively late in life and the only experience of its kind, as far as I could find out. The young man—he was younger than she—went out on the moor one day and never came back. He died on the White Meadow. His body was never found. I wasn't able to ascertain whether it was an accident or whether the young man had suicidal tendencies."

"But he died young," I said, "long before his time. Just like—" I stopped.

"Yes, just like Fräulein Louise's friends here," said Demel, nodding. "After her stay in the Riesengebirge, there is a gap of about six months. I don't know what happened during that time."

"Perhaps the first attack of schizophrenia," I said, stroking Irina's shoulder. "Calm down, girl. The call's got to come. Any minute."

She looked up at me and tried to smile, a tortured smile.

"You may be right," said Demel. "She may have been in a sanitarium and then, when she recovered, worked as a social worker again. She has always been a social worker, and always in camps."

"Under all sorts of regimes."

"Yes," said Pastor Demel. "And her behavior seems always to have been as it is now—she was friendly and helpful, but kept to herself. Aloof with adults. The only thing she loved was children. She always gave them everything she had. She's been here twenty years now. Imagine it, Herr Roland—twenty years. You have no idea what it's like here when the fog really settles down in the winter and the snow is meters deep. Kuschke drives her to Zeven once a month. She hasn't been to Hamburg or Bremen in years. So I imagine that out of scraps of memories of the few people she has felt close to in life, and through the stories peasants have told her about the many dead in the moor—"

The telephone rang. Irina leaped to answer it. "Yes . . . yes . . . thank you . . . thank you!" To us she said, "She's making the connection."

She waited, listening; suddenly her face was filled with an expression of utter disbelief. "What's the matter?" I asked.

"I hear music," she said. "And what music! Listen!" She held the receiver to my ear and I could hear a slow, melancholy waltz, played by violins but almost inaudible because of the static.

"'Remembering,'" I said, and gave the receiver back to her.

"My favorite song," she said. "I'm old-fashioned when it comes to music." She hummed a few bars, and suddenly I realized that Irina, in spite of the profession she had chosen, in spite of her intelligence, was a helpless, lost creature. I was sure that one could lie to her easily, hurt her easily; I was sure that she believed anything a loved one told her. And she had put her faith in this man she was trying to reach, given all her love to this fiancé of hers, Jan Bilka.

"Jan loves 'Remembering,' too," said Irina, "and that I should hear it now . . . it must be a good omen, don't you think?" And then, almost immediately, she cried, "Jan!" and began to speak very fast in Czech. Pastor Demel and I watched her. Suddenly she stopped abruptly, looking angry. "Hello! Hello!" she cried. "Operator!" And she tapped the phone furiously.

"What's the matter?"

"We've been cut off!"

Fräulein Vera must have answered because Irina began to talk into the phone again, agitatedly. "Fräulein! The line went dead suddenly. We were cut off. No, no, no! We were disconnected before I tried to reach you. Please try again! Please! Yes . . . yes . . . thank you."

Irina waited. She drummed with her fingers on the desk. A pity Bertie wasn't there to take pictures. "What happened? What did you say?"

"I—I—"

"Calm down," I said, "and try to tell me what you said."

"I said, 'Jan, this is Irina. I'm in the West, in Camp Neurode. You can come and get me out. Come with your friend. . . .'"

"And then what?"

"And then the line went dead."

"Who answered the phone?"

"Jan, of course."

"Are you sure?"

"Positive!" she said angrily.

"No use getting angry with me," I said. "It isn't my fault."

"I'm sorry."

"That's all right," I said, and thought: the little boy, the schizophrenic old spinster, the escaped refugee from the Czech Defense Ministry . . . if things went on like this, we'd hit pure gold! I could sense it. I could always sense it when I was on the trail of a story. "What did your fiancé say?"

"When he answered? '2-2068-54.'"

"In German?"

"Yes."

"Nothing else?"

"Then I started to talk."

"Because you recognized his voice?"

"Yes. Of course."

"Are you *sure* it was his voice?"

"I just told you. It was Jan's voice. *His voice!*" She hadn't put the receiver down; she was holding it with both hands. Now she said, "It's ringing again."

The rays of the setting sun fell on her, blood red. I looked out of the window. The alders and birches were silhouetted black against the fiery sky in the west. "She's still ringing," said Irina, and suddenly she began to cry. "But that's impossible," she sobbed. "He just answered!"

I took the receiver from her. It was damp. I listened. The phone was ringing...ringing.... Irina was weeping. Pastor Demel went over to her. "Don't cry," he said. "Please. We'll find out what's wrong. Don't be afraid."

"But it was his voice! A minute ago he was there! Something *must* be wrong!"

"Just a minute," I said, trying not to show my excitement as I hung up. Seconds later I picked up the receiver again and got the operator. "Fräulein Vera? Roland speaking. Please don't be angry, but you don't seem to be getting an answer in Hamburg."

"I've been ringing 2-2068-54." She sounded annoyed.

"I'm sure you have. Perhaps it was a faulty connection. Would you mind trying again? Please? Do it for me!" I laughed softly. Me and my effect on women. Crazy, when you come to think of it—an old lush like me—still, I could have any woman I wanted. They told me I was charming.

"All right, Herr Roland. But I've got bigger and better things to do."

I was sure she had. "Thank you, Fräulein Vera."

"This man who was going to take me with him, is it true—was he arrested for blackmail?" Irina asked hesitantly. "Do you think he was going to kidnap me? Do you think there's some connection between him and Jan? Do you think something's happened to Jan?"

Yes. I was thinking just that. "Nonsense!" I told her. "Nobody wants to kidnap you. That bastard had something quite different

81

in mind. And what do you mean, 'something's happened to Jan'? Didn't you just hear his voice?" Pure gold, I was thinking. "They're ringing again," I said.

She tried to take the receiver from me, but I pushed her away. This time I wanted to be at the end of the wire when somebody answered. I looked at my wristwatch and let the phone ring a full three minutes, then I said, "No answer," and hung up.

Irina's lips were trembling, she was breathing hard, her voice was hoarse. "I'm afraid," she said. "Something has happened! I know it has! I know!" You can bet your sweet life on it, I thought, and said, "Try to control yourself, girl. Something seems to have gone wrong, yes, but we don't know what. It could be something harmless. There are hundreds of reasons—"

"Give me *one!*"

Oh no, I thought, and said, "Fräulein Indigo, you mustn't go to pieces. That's the most important thing right now. And I'll try to help you."

"You? Why should you want to help me?"

"Because I'm a reporter and a reporter needs stories. And we may have one here. But I can only help you if you trust me."

The telephone rang. Irina cried out. I picked up the receiver. It was Fräulein Vera. "Did you get through?" she asked.

"Unfortunately, no. But thanks a lot, anyway. I'm going to make another call in a minute, to Frankfurt."

"Very good, Herr Roland. I'm sorry about Hamburg."

I turned to Irina. "So, what about it? Will you trust me?"

"No!"

"Fräulein Indigo!" It was Pastor Demel, protesting.

"I don't trust anybody here! Why should I?" And she sat down in front of the desk, laid her head on her arms, and wept. I let her cry for a while. I knew how it would end. She had no choice. And sure enough, she soon lifted her head, sobbed some more, and said, "I didn't mean it."

"So you're willing to trust me?"

She nodded.

"Good. Now we'll make some headway." And then I began to phone.

I asked Fräulein Vera to connect me with my office in Frankfurt. I gave her the number, and the call came through right away. The voice of the girl at the other end of the wire: "*Blitz.* What can I do for you?"

I have a good memory for voices. I'd known all our operators for years. "Hello? Marion, my love? Roland speaking."

"Oh, Herr Roland!" She sounded breathless. What did I tell you?

"I'm up north. Let me speak to Herr Kramer, please."

"Right away."

"Thanks, sweetie."

Kramer's secretary came next, then I had Kramer himself on the wire. He was executive editor in charge of all copy, and a good friend of mine. I'd known him as long as I'd been with *Blitz*.

"Hello, Hem," I said.

"Hello, Walter. What's new? Laid out somewhere up there? The jackal on your trail again?"

"No, Hem."

We called him "Hem" because Paul Kramer, age fifty-six, was a dead-ringer for the great Hemingway, the same face, the eternally unkempt hair, the metal-rimmed glasses, the plaid lumberjack-type shirts he liked to wear, the wrinkled flannel pants, but most of all—his character. If there was anything that kept me upright at *Blitz*—at any rate to some extent—it was Hem. The kindest, smartest, and best editor I'd ever known, probably the best editor alive. The only man in the world whom I admired. I would have liked to be like him, but that was not possible.

"Are you in the cathouse?" he asked.

"No."

"Well, now I'm curious. Talk!"

I talked. Irina and Pastor Demel listened. I told Hem everything that had happened; when I got to Irina and her fiancé, I chose my words carefully. But Hem got the message that I was onto something big. We had evolved our own language for that sort of thing.

"Boy . . . Walter . . . if it works out—"

"Exactly."

"Stay with it."

"I intend to."

"As far as I'm concerned, you've got carte blanche. Do whatever you think's right. And keep in touch. Every hour on the hour."

"Will do."

My curt replies were making the pastor and Irina nervous. I grinned at them.

"At night, call me at home. You've got the number?"

"Yes."

"We've got to know where you are."

"Yes."

"I take it you'll try to get to Hamburg with Bertie and the girl. On the double."

"Yes."

"She's listening."

"Yes."

"I'll pass it on to Lester and Herford." Lester was editor-in-chief, Herford was our publisher.

"Hem, I need money."

"That figures." I didn't have to say what for. For years now Hem and I had understood each other with a minimum of words. "How much?"

"Fifteen thousand," I said. "I'd like it by wire. Park Hotel, Bremen. In my name. No—in Bertie's." Something had occurred to me.

"Okay. Just a minute while I tell Ruth, so we don't lose any time." Ruth was my secretary. I could hear him talking to her, then to me again, "Okay, go ahead."

"I need everything you can find on Karl Concon." I spelled the name. "There's a file on him."

"From when?"

"1957. According to Bertie. We did a picture spread on his trial. Send me the original or copies. Makes no difference."

"You want the stuff in Hamburg."

"Right. Fuhlsbüttel airport. General delivery. Bertie or I will get it. Address it to both of us. Send it airmail special delivery."

"Right away."

"And, finally, send Conny a teletype." Conny was Conrad Manners, our correspondent in Hamburg. "Tell him to get going on it right away. Just a minute." I turned to Irina. "What's the address of your Herr Michelsen?"

"The address?" For a moment my rapid-fire dialogue with Hem seemed to have stunned her. "Eppendorfer Baum 187."

I repeated the address to Hem. "Tell Conny to see if he can locate Jan Bilka. But quietly. He's only to keep an eye on him."

"I get it," said Hem. "Tread softly."

"Right. And if he finds him, he's not to let him out of his sight. Doesn't Conny have a girl he lives with? I can't remember her name."

"Edith," said Hem. "Beautiful Edith."

84

"Now I remember. Conny's to let her know where he is, at all times, until I get there. I'll go see Edith first. Conny will need a description of Bilka. I'll give you Fräulein Indigo." I handed her the receiver. "Describe your fiancé."

"Yes," she said obediently. To Hem she said, "*Grüss Gott.* I'm supposed to . . . yes. He's thirty-two years old, about one-eighty tall, blond hair cut very short . . . yes, military style. Gray eyes, a longish face, a scar on the right side of his chin. He's thin but very strong, and he's tanned. That's about all I can tell you. Just a minute," and she gave me back the receiver.

Hem said, "That should do. I'll get the teletype out to Conny right away, and you keep in touch."

"I will. 'Bye, Hem. And now connect me with Rotaug." Dr. Helmut Rotaug was head of the legal department for *Blitz*.

"I realize you can't speak freely," said Hem, and for a moment I thought I could smell his Dunhill tobacco. He smoked a pipe. "I take it you want to talk to Rotaug about the releases."

"Yes."

"I'll brief him. Then all you have to do is write down what he says. So long, Walter." There was a click on the wire as he made the connection with Rotaug. I waited and smiled at Irina, who was watching me and looking worried. I couldn't blame her. Then Rotaug was on the wire, with his low voice, which always managed somehow to sound menacing.

Rotaug was sixty years old, had been with *Blitz* since the beginning, was trusted implicitly by publisher Herford, and looked like a toad. He was shrunken and stooped, always wore black suits, white shirts, silver ties, and high stiff collars with the corners turned down, like our former financial wizard, Dr. Hjalmar Schacht, God rest his soul. He had a long, wrinkled neck, the skin of which was yellow, peppered with liver spots, and hung in folds; an oval face—cold, expressionless, and also covered with liver spots; and a completely bald head, yellow like his neck, but the skin was taut. He had almost no lashes on the lids of his small, beady eyes, and he always wore a beautiful stickpin in the knot of his tie. He had the face of a banker, a chairman of the board, a financier, and he was a genius in his field. A genius, not a human being.

Our relationship? Polite but frosty. I knew that Rotaug had told Herford years ago, "Ace reporter? Maybe. We make millions with him? All well and good. A great fellow. But mark my words, one day this great fellow is going to involve us in the biggest scandal of our publishing history." That was Dr. Helmut Rotaug, who after a polite, cool greeting, asked, "Do you have a paper and pencil?"

"Just a minute." I got out my pad and pen. "Ready."

"Do you have a typewriter with you?"

"In the car."

"Very well. The release has got to be typed, two copies. Your client gets the original, you bring us the copy. We need the place, date, then the word 'Statement,' and under that, 'I, the undersigned . . .'" and he dictated the whole, shrewd, ingenious agreement. Nobody signing it could get around it. I took it down in shorthand, a long statement; Rotaug didn't miss a trick. At last he was finished.

"So there you have the text. And don't forget to get a receipt for any money you hand out. Any more questions?"

"Thank you, no. It was very good of you, Dr. Rotaug—"

"Good-bye," he said, and hung up.

I put down the receiver and stuck the pad in my pocket. Just as I was putting the cap on my pen, a woman's voice outside screamed, "Run, Karl, run!"

We rushed to the window. What happened next took place much faster than can possibly be described. The first thing I saw was fat Karl Concon, running as fast as he could in the direction of the small open gate. Two camp guards were stumbling after him. I opened the window and heard the woman's voice again. It seemed to come from the parking lot, from a car parked there. "Karl, run! Run, Karl, run!" And Karl Concon was running.

"Those goddamn assholes!" I shouted. "How could they have let him get away?"

I vaulted over the windowsill onto the ground, and ran as fast as I could across the sandy, heather-covered ground. Outside the men and women on the other side of the fence seemed frozen to the spot. A few had ducked or thrown themselves on the ground. Nothing moved. It looked like a film strip that had suddenly stopped. Karl Concon, stooped over, zigzagged forward as fast as he could, like a hunted rabbit. Yes. It was a woman in a black Buick and she was still screaming, "Run, Karl, run!" I could see her face stuck out of the open window of the car. She had a scarf tied around her head. That was all I could make out—I was still too far away to see more—and it was then that I saw Fräulein Louise.

With Bertie at her side and holding Karel by the hand, she

came out of the infirmary, the barracks near the entrance that was painted blue with a big red cross on a white background. I ran over to them. People—children and adults—were closing in on the scene. To my astonishment I saw Karel, his trumpet in his hand, break loose from Fräulein Louise and start running toward the gate. As he ran he screamed something in Czech. All I could understand was the word "Mama!" and a shiver ran down my spine. Mama! And it all came clear. The boy's name was Karel, the fat fag's name was Karl. The boy must have thought the woman was screaming "Karel," not "Karl."

"Talks about his mother all the time, ever since he's been here," according to Fräulein Louise, and on the flight his father had told him to run when he cried, "Run, Karel, run!" And now Karel was running. . . .

Fräulein Louise began to run after him. She cried out to him in Czech, he paid no attention. I could see Bertie running, his Nikon-F in his hands. And then all hell broke loose.

A machine gun began to fire. The shots came from a Dodge parked beside the Buick. I could see the barrel sticking out of the window next to the driver's seat. The bullets hit the ground and sprayed sand into the air. They were aimed at the gate, which Concon had finally reached and run through. Whoever was shooting was trying to protect Concon and stop anyone from following him.

Both camp guards who had been chasing Concon threw themselves on the ground. Some of the shots passed through the fence, others ricocheted crazily. Bertie grabbed Fräulein Louise and pulled her down with him. Suddenly everyone inside the gate was on the ground. I was still running, but when a bullet whizzed past my ear, I threw myself down, too. Children screamed, the older people cursed and swore, and with an icy heart I could see that Karel was still running. Nothing stopped him. He was being told to run and he ran, staggering a little, and he ran directly into the next rain of fire.

I don't want to imply that the man who was shooting intended to hit the boy. Not at all. But he was determined to protect his man, whatever the price. Perhaps he thought the camp guards would return fire. He didn't know that they couldn't because their only weapon was a billy club.

It was a sight to turn your stomach when the volley hit the boy. The power of the shots entering his body made it fly at least a meter into the air and be thrown back. I saw Bertie raise himself a little and take a picture. If it came out, it would be worth a fortune.

Karel fell into the heather, his trumpet thrown some distance away. Screams. But Karel lay still. Karl Concon had reached the Buick and jumped into it. Its driver, the woman who had shouted "Run, Karl, run!", stepped on the gas; and the Buick, its tires screeching, made a wide turn and tore off. The dark Dodge, with the man who had fired the shots at the wheel, followed it. They made a right turn at the end of the short street and were gone.

Everyone was screaming and talking at once. A man in white came running out of the infirmary, obviously Dr. Schiemann. Fräulein Louise, the doctor, Bertie, and the camp guards, and twenty or thirty other people ran over to where Karel lay. I jumped to my feet and ran, too. A third guard came hobbling out of the guard room, a fourth followed him, just as halt and lame. Their two colleagues were bellowing as they tried to disperse the young camp inmates. "Get out of here—damnit—get out!" The crowd dispersed.

When I reached the small group that had collected around Karel, I bumped into Bertie, who, just as dusty as I, had the Hasselblad in his hands and was shooting like mad! "Jeeeesus!" he groaned. He wasn't smiling anymore. "What shots! And all in color!"

"Do you have enough light?"

"Sure. Lens wide open. One thirty-second!" He limped around the small group, knelt, shot between their legs. I went over to Fräulein Louise. She was swaying; I thought she'd fall. "Karel—my Karel—a tragedy—" she stammered when she saw me. "If only the man hadn't been called Karl! He thought his mother was calling to him. He was screaming, 'Yes, Mama, yes, I'm coming.' Dr. Schiemann gave him a tranquilizer. His mind wasn't quite clear. 'Yes, Mama, yes, I'm coming.' Oh, dear God in heaven, why did you let this happen?" The tears were raining down her face.

The doctor, who had been kneeling beside Karel, got up. He looked grim. "Is he—?" Fräulein Louise began to ask.

"Yes," said Dr. Schiemann. "He was killed instantly."

Fräulein Louise let out a cry and flung herself on her knees beside the boy, stroked his face, spoke to him imploringly in Czech as if she thought she could bring him back to life. The ground beside him was rapidly turning red. Fräulein Louise was kneeling in the boy's blood. She didn't notice.

"How could this have happened?" I asked one of the guards.

"The guy was perfectly quiet. We were watching him. I swear we were. But then he jumped to his feet suddenly and knocked down one of our men, kicked another."

"In the stomach," said the one who had come out hobbling. He was holding his stomach and groaning. "Full force." There were tears in his old eyes. "I was thrown back, into Eugene." He pointed to another one of the guards. "Both of us fell down, and that's when he got away."

"There were only four of us," said Eugene. "Fritz," he pointed to the guard who was standing there, panting, "was on the phone. It isn't our fault. It really isn't. We did the best we could."

"Why didn't one of you go after the cars?"

"How could we? We don't have a car." Out of a corner of my eye I could see Bertie photographing me and the tired old camp guard.

"And you don't have handcuffs either?" I asked.

He shook his head. "We're not allowed to have anything like that."

"Then you should have tied the bastard to a chair," I said. "You knew the man was dangerous."

"Who do you think you are, anyway?" said the guard who had been kicked in the stomach. "You can kiss my ass, as far as I'm concerned."

"I'm a reporter," I said, "and you'll read about this. You can depend on that."

The man who had been kicked said, "I'm sorry. I didn't mean—"

"It's all right."

"We don't know what we're saying. Nothing like this has ever happened before."

"It's all right!" I shouted. Everybody stared at me. Even the guard who had been kicked straightened up. "Back to your barracks! All of you!" he shouted. "Get going!"

His colleagues shoved those who were hesitating on their way. Finally the last of the curious left.

"Get a stretcher," said Dr. Schiemann. "Bring him to the infirmary." Then he said quickly, "No. Leave him where he is. Don't touch him. Get the police in Zeven. Tell them to get here fast."

"Yes, Herr Doktor." One of the guards ran off to the barracks.

"Step aside, please, Walter," said Bertie. He was stretched out

89

on the ground with his Hasselblad. "And you, too, Herr Doktor, please."

We stepped aside. Bertie took pictures of the dead boy with Fräulein Louise kneeling beside him, and again a squadron of Starfighters roared over us, low, very low. The ground shook, the air vibrated, and I felt sick. Then the planes were dark spots in the flaming sunset. A black cloud hung over the glow in the west; only a thin eclipse of the sun was visible, and Fräulein Louise was still kneeling in her grief. She didn't move, she didn't speak. She knelt, bowed low over the dead boy.

I took my flask out of my hip pocket and drank. And the jackal went away. He had been very close.

18

Fifteen minutes later. The day died fast here; it was almost dark. The men and women outside the fence had disappeared. Except for my Lamborghini, the parking lot was empty. The young people had withdrawn to their barracks, the small gate was closed. Fräulein Louise was still kneeling beside the dead boy.

The camp guards were waiting for the police from Zeven. They would have a long wait. There hadn't been a response yet to the first call for Concon. One of the guards was standing at the gate. *Now* they were guarding it! Nobody had dared send Fräulein Louise away.

"So how about it?" I asked Irina Indigo. We were standing pressed against a wall of one of the barracks, in the shadow, and she was staring at me wide-eyed.

"You want to take me to Hamburg?"

"Goddamn it!" I said. "What do you think I mean?" I was terribly nervous. "My friend and I will take you there. We'll help you find your fiancé. Or don't you want us to do that?"

"Of course I do. But just now somebody said no one could leave the camp."

"My friend and I will be allowed to leave once the police arrive and they have our statement. And once we're out, you'll join us."

"Where? How?"

"You heard about the cracked pillar Hilde Reiter was trying to push over when she saw Fräulein Louise on the moor. Over there." I gestured with my chin.

"But she never got out. She couldn't move the thing."

"One person alone can't, probably two can't either. But with a car we can manage it," I said, and thought: I hope!

"With a car? What car?"

"My car. The only one left on the parking lot. And we have a rope. We'll manage it. I promise you," and again thought: I hope. "It's ten to five now. The police should get here in three quarters of an hour. I'll be waiting for you at the pillar at ten."

"What about my things?"

"What do you have?"

"A big suitcase full of—"

"Leave it here. Can't be anything in it that we can't replace. You must realize by now that you haven't a chance of getting out of here normally. Not once Security starts investigating you."

"Oh, God!" she said, and clung to me suddenly. "Then you do believe all this is connected somehow with Jan."

"Yes."

"But a while ago—"

"I lied. To calm you down." I was talking fast now. I had to convince this girl. I needed her; I had to have her. And I couldn't leave the camp before ten, because first I had to send Bertie to Bremen to get our things and the money. And I had to speak to the police when they came, and get a few releases. I had a lot to do.

"It's against the law, what you're doing," said Irina. Her eyes were black, she looked terribly worried.

"Of course it is. So . . . will you be there at ten? It's your last chance to get to your fiancé, fast. And to find out what's going on in Hamburg. Yes or no."

"Yes," she whispered.

"Okay. Now go back to your barracks. Don't attract any attention. Walk in the shadows, if you can. Nobody must see that—"

"There you are!" The voice of a man.

I turned around. Tall, thin Wilhelm Rogge with the strong glasses, whom I had met in the Security Office, was standing in front of me. I cursed my stupidity. Security! Great! I should have gotten Irina out of the camp right away, right after it had happened. But how could I possibly have done that?

"Good evening, Herr Rogge," I said.

He nodded. "I've been looking for you everywhere, Fräulein Indigo. My colleague Klein, too."

"Why?" she stammered.

"Well, we want to have a talk with you," he said politely.

"Right now?"

"Yes. Right now. If we weren't so busy, we'd have had our little talk yesterday. You're at the top of the list."

"At the top of the list?"

"Well, of course. Such an important refugee with such an important fiancé. So come with me, please. Good evening, Herr Roland."

"Good evening," I said, and watched the two disappear into the twilight. Godamn it!

What now? If Irina told Rogge and his colleague what she had told the pastor and me—and what else could she do?—then God only knew what they'd do with her, much less make it possible for her to get to the fence by ten. I was beside myself with rage. Then I was quickly calm again. I had to believe in my luck. Until now I'd always been lucky in this shitty profession. Always. I had to go ahead as if nothing was wrong. I could always give up if and when I had to.

I looked across the heather to where the dead boy was lying. The fog was rolling in, covering the ground. It settled around Karel's body and Fräulein Louise, who hadn't moved from her place beside him. I hoped Bertie had seen this pietà and taken a picture of it, in spite of the fading light.

It must have been a dining hall, the barracks I was leaning against, because suddenly I could hear children's voices, praying in German, "Come, dear Jesus, be our guest, let what we're about to eat be blessed."

19

We had fastened the loop of the tow rope high up on the cracked pillar, to get as much leverage as possible. The other end was knotted to the rear axle of the Lamborghini. I had left the road just beyond the village and driven the car cautiously through the bushes and over frighteningly soft ground, up close to the fence. The Lamborghini was hidden by gorse and juniper bushes. The whole camp was lit with floodlights on high posts, and one was burning here. It was damned light, *and* a full moon in a cloudless sky. We could hear the wind rushing high above us, but no ground gale—yet.

"She's not coming," said Bertie. He was sitting beside me in the car.

"No knowing," I said. "It's now five to ten."

"She can't come. Security's got her and that's the end. Always. From here on she can't make a move without a cop."

"How do you know?"

Bertie's pessimism could get under your skin sometimes. Both of us were smoking and staring straight ahead into the camp, where nothing was moving. The police were still there. "We'll wait until eleven. She'll come. I can feel it. Bet?"

"That she'll come? That's like taking candy from a baby. No. I'm not betting. Nice mess...."

"Why nice mess?"

"Without the girl."

"We'll go to Hamburg in any case."

"Sure. But without the girl—"

"Bertie!"

"What?"

"Shut up!"

He did. Offended. He had driven from the camp to Bremen and back in record time. I had passed out the money he'd brought with him and pocketed the receipts. Then we had let the police question us again. Odd, but neither Herr Klein nor Herr Rogge from Security showed up. At last we left the camp and drove here, and here we had been sitting for the last forty minutes. I had contradicted Bertie without much conviction. I didn't think Irina was coming either. I couldn't imagine that Security would let her....

"Hello?"

Both of us sat up like a shot. My heart was beating wildly. Irina was lying flat on the ground behind the fence. She lifted one hand and waved. I got out of the car and ran crouched over the soft ground to the pillar. "Punctual," I said. She nodded.

"Stay where you are."

I had the jack handle with me. Bertie, at the wheel, looked back at us out of the window. I gave him a sign. He started the motor. Gave it gas. Cautiously, very cautiously. The car began to move slowly. It seemed to me that the Lamborghini made a hell of a lot of noise in the still night. The rope grew taut, the car jerked suddenly; if the wheels start spinning now, I thought, we're finished.

The wheels didn't spin. The car moved forward, centimeter by centimeter. The crack in the pillar began to widen on the inside, and the pillar moved a little toward the outside. I leaped to the fence, shoved the jack handle into the crack, and pushed it up with all the strength in me. The car moved forward, the crack widened a little more. The wire had a metallic, grinding sound as it began to stretch. Bertie was doing his thing marvelously. The pillar crackled, the barbed wire above it was taut now, too.

Now I did the opposite thing—I leaned on the jack handle and pushed down with all my weight. I pushed so hard that my feet left the ground and I was suspended in midair, head down, an upside-down human U. With any luck . . . if no one came . . . if no car passed, no driver saw us—goddamn the floodlight! The sweat was running down my back. I could hear a humming sound above me. The nylon rope. If it broke . . .

It didn't break. We were lucky. The pillar began to fall, slowly at first, then faster. And it dragged the fence down with it. I had to jump back to avoid the barbed wire headed my way. "Now!" I whispered, and Irina jumped to her feet. She had on a coat—no luggage. "Crawl over the fence," I told her. "It's practically on the ground. Hang onto the mesh. Slowly. Slowly now. You've almost made it." The sweat was running into my eyes. Bertie had stopped the motor. "Look out!" I said. "That's barbed wire. Step on it."

She did as I told her, clinging to the mesh fence which was still at least a meter above the ground at the top. "And now stand up and jump!"

"I'm afraid."

"Jump! I'll catch you."

"But if the barbed wire—"

"Jump!" I hissed.

She stood up, swayed for a moment, and jumped, straight into my arms. Her face struck mine. I could feel her breath, clean and sweet, like fresh milk.

"Well done!" I said. She looked at me and for the first time her sad eyes looked happy. Irina was beautiful. . . .

While she was clambering up the fence, Bertie had untied the nylon rope and put it in the trunk. Now I ran to the car with Irina. She sat between us. I drove. Two minutes later we were driving over the miserable road with its potholes, but this time I didn't spare the car. I drove as fast as I could. We were tossed back and forth.

"You didn't think I was coming, did you?" said Irina.

"No," said Bertie.

"I didn't think so, either," said Irina. "Not after the way Rogge and Klein questioned me."

"How did they question you?"

"Oh, at first they were very polite, but they wanted to know everything. Everything! Much more than you wanted to know. They were like the officials in Prague. I felt as if I was back in Prague. I was sure they'd take me away from the camp to God knows where."

"But they didn't."

"No, they didn't. The telephone rang in the next room. Rogge answered it and talked for a long time."

"What about? With whom?"

"I don't know. The door was closed. He called Klein in and they talked for a very long time. I couldn't understand a word. When they came back they were more polite than ever. It was weird! They told me I could go to my barracks. If they needed me again, they'd come and get me."

"They let you go? Just like that? No guards?" Bertie sounded astounded. He couldn't have been more astounded than I was.

"Yes. They just let me go." She was trembling. "You know what?"

"What?" I asked, trying to get the execrable road behind me as quickly as possible without breaking an axle.

"I think it all hangs together with Jan and the telephone call. I mean, they must have found out what happened in Hamburg and lost all interest in me."

"If anything happens in Hamburg," I said, "it could only make you more interesting."

"So why did they let me go? What has happened, Herr Roland? What has happened?" With her last words she grabbed my shoulder, the car slid from one pothole to another, and went into a skid. I struck Irina in the side with my right elbow and she cried out with pain. "Don't do that again!" I said. "Ever! Do you understand?"

"I'm sorry. I didn't think—"

"Okay, as long as you don't do it again. We'll soon find out what's going on in Hamburg," I said. Idiot....

20

"Where I come from nobody knows; and where I'm going everything goes.... The wind blows, the sea flows, and nobody knows...."

Fräulein Louise was putting one foot in front of the other as she spoke. Her eyes were smarting from the many tears she had shed. She felt dreadful and a furious fire was raging inside her. Left foot, right foot. Left foot, right foot. She was walking out onto the moor across a path that was barely twelve inches wide. She was breathing hard and her feet hurt. Ducks flew up ahead of her. The will-o-the-wisps she knew so well danced around her, glowed and disappeared. It was a half hour before midnight. Fräulein Louise was wearing an old black coat with a hood, and she was carrying a big bag. Out there, on the knoll, she could see figures. Her friends were waiting for her. She must not keep them waiting. They had called to her after she had gone to bed and was lying sleepless and tortured by her thoughts. They had come and spoken to her.

"We are always there for Louise..."

"Louise should come to us on the moor...."

She had risen, dressed, and set out. The guard at the entrance had greeted her as she unlocked the small gate. The guard knew where she was going.

Fräulein Louise hurried on. The bare birches were silver in the moonlight that shone at her feet. But she looked straight ahead to where her motionless friends were waiting. A swamp owl kept fluttering over her head. She's surprised, thought Fräulein Louise; she thinks I'm a juniper bush, and she can't imagine why a juniper bush can run. Yes—run. Because now Fräulein Louise was running along the path which only she and the old peasant who had told her about it knew. She hurried along in the moonlight between water holes and the deceptively floating islands of swamp grass, and for her own encouragement, she talked to herself. What she said was nothing new to her—she had known it for twenty years—but she couldn't remember where she had heard it first. Sometimes she thought her friends must have taught it to her, then again she thought of a wonderful motion picture she had seen right after the war, that had played between time and space, and decided that this poem had been recited in it and been engraved indelibly on her memory. "Under the stars, under the moon I am alone, and not alone. Past and future are always with me... in the vastness of time and space..."

A vast black area stretched out on her right, an area void of life. That was the place where there had been a fire last year, a fire that had burned and smoldered from Easter until winter. It had still glimmered under the first snow. Only the drainage ditches had prevented all the peat on the moor from burning up. Five hundred acres had been charred black, down to the sandy ground. Then the wind had come and scattered rosebay seeds over the black peat coal and they had taken root. The following spring the whole burned area was covered, at first with green; then, in the summer, buds had appeared on the long clusters and they had opened and blossomed, bright red in spite of all the rain, a rosier red where it had stopped burning later, and all this where before there had been smoke and destruction and scorched earth. Acres of wild rhododendron! Fräulein Louise had looked out of her window at this rose garden and enjoyed the sight. But now the flowering was over, and the scorched earth stretched out black and dreary again. It would take years, decades, to regenerate.

All this and what follows Fräulein Louise told me in the course of my frequent visits. I visited her often—not often enough, though, not nearly often enough. But I was writing in such a fever, with only one thing in mind—get on with it! Get it done! My knowledge of so many deadly secrets had to be put in writing, and what I wrote had to be protected. I had to be cautious. But by this time Fräulein Louise liked me, and even more important—she trusted me. "You are a good man," she said. And when I protested, she said, "Well, all right, maybe not. But you'd like to be a good man."

"Yes. That I would."

"There you are," said Fräulein Louise, and went on to tell what happened that night, and here I am, writing it down.

21

If, unlike Fräulein Louise, one didn't know that they were eleven men, one would have sworn that they were eleven osier willows standing on a knoll that rose out of the moor at the end of the path, between brush and reeds, in the mist and pale light of the moon. By the time Fräulein Louise reached them, she was breathless. The Russian greeted her first. "At last Little Mother has come. A very good evening, Louise."

"Good evening, my happy ones," said Fräulein Louise, as the others greeted her, too.

The Russian was a stocky fellow. He had on the olive-green uniform in which he had fought. He said, "It is good that Louise is with us again."

"And can you imagine how wonderful it is for me?" said Fräulein Louise.

The will-o-the-wisps flickered over the moor. The Russian had been a famous clown before the war, before he had had to become a soldier. But without the mask of makeup, he looked serious.

"You know, of course, what has happened," said Fräulein Louise, and her eleven friends nodded. "And you also know that Irina got away, probably with those two reporters. They managed to push over the pillar and it took the fence down with it. That's how she must have got out. I saw the place on my way here. And the tracks of their car. You saw it, too, didn't you?"

Again her friends nodded.

"Did you see them get away?"

"Yes, Louise," said the American. He was very tall and, like the Russian, in uniform.

"This Herr Roland, and the other one, the photographer—they're miserable sinners. They are still wholly worldly."

"But there is still hope, even for them," said the Jehovah's Witness. He had a gray-and-white-striped suit that looked like pajamas. A faded yellow stripe ran down the legs of his trousers. In one hand he held a red book.

"Is that just something you believe, or are you sure?" said Fräulein Louise.

"We still know much too little," said the Ukrainian, who was wearing a leather jacket, corduroy pants, and shabby shoes with wooden soles. His face looked like a ploughed field—so many wrinkles, so earthy and old. "Actually, we know almost nothing."

"But you believe it," said Fräulein Louise, "and believing is safer than knowing."

"Yes, we believe it," said the Pole. "But that isn't important. Louise must believe it." He spoke urgently. He too was wearing his uniform, which was incredibly shabby.

"What *you* want to do is all that matters," said the German student, the youngest of the eleven. He was wearing green overalls and dirty boots that reached up to his calf. The student was the only one who addressed Fräulein Louise with the intimate *Du*; all the others used the more formal *Sie* when they talked to her. Fräulein Louise looked at the student and again was strangely moved. He always reminded her of something in the past of her long life. She never could recall exactly what, and there was a chronic pain in this unclear memory, but it was a sweet pain.

"Our Louise wants to go to Hamburg," said the student, "as quickly as possible. She has put on her winter coat and taken her bag along because she is in such a hurry. Should she go to Hamburg? Is it in our interest?"

The others were silent.

"*Children!*" Fräulein Louise cried passionately. "Both of them were children! My poor Karel, and Irina, too. They murdered Karel and kidnapped Irina. God knows where they've taken her. I can't let this happen! I won't let it happen! I—" She was struggling for breath. "I have to find Irina, and I have to find the person who murdered my Karel. And this person has to be saved. For he has *killed!* A way must be found for Karel to forgive him and save him, and that is why this person *must leave this world!*"

The eleven were silent.

"You agree with me!" cried Fräulein Louise, who was becoming more and more agitated. "You know I'm right. You know that there is a higher justice, and that in this case there will be no higher justice unless I attend to it!"

The eleven men looked at her and said nothing.

"Talk!" Fräulein Louise begged. "Please talk! If you don't

talk, evil will triumph. Injustice and cruelty will continue to rule the world, the same injustice and cruelty you suffered until you were redeemed!"

The SS man, tall, with a long narrow face, who had once owned a pickle factory in Seelze, near Hannover, said sadly, "I didn't suffer. I brought suffering upon the innocent." He was wearing the black SS uniform with the high boots.

"But you have acknowledged it," the Dutchman said in a consoling tone. He was wearing an old civilian suit and a shirt with no collar.

"The innocent whom you made suffer have raised you to a higher sphere," said the Russian.

"I suppose so," said the SS man dolefully.

"And you lie in the moor with us," said the Pole.

"Not with you," the SS man said sadly.

Fräulein Louise knew what he meant. The Nazis had stuffed their dead in sacks, weighted them down with stones, and thrown them into the swamp, but the SS man had died while the camp had been under British jurisdiction, and the British had buried their dead in a more civilized fashion. They had chosen a place behind the camp, where the earth was firmer, and had dug the graves there and buried their dead Nazi prisoners in wooden coffins.

"You lie in the same moor," said the Russian. "You died here, like us. What difference does a sack and a few stones or a wooden coffin and a grave make? None at all."

"Where we are now," said the Ukrainian, "all people are equal."

"Then see to it that there is justice!" cried Fräulein Louise. She was getting terribly impatient.

"Justice isn't up to us," said the American.

"Why?" cried Fräulein Louise.

"Because it harms justice."

Fräulein Louise lost her temper. "Justice is harmed only when nothing's done about it!" she cried, and at that everything went dim. When she could see clearly again, the eleven men were gone and Fräulein Louise found herself surrounded by eleven stunted osier willows, all alone out on the moor.

"Oh, please!" she begged. "Please don't leave me! Come back!"

But none of the eleven came back.

Fräulein Louise fell on her knees, wrung her hands, and

whispered, "I shouted. It's my fault that they disappeared. I shouted, and when I shout they disappear."

A squadron of Starfighters on a night flight roared across the moor, their red, green, and white navigation lights blinking; but Fräulein Louise paid no attention to them. She was crouched so low that her folded hands and forehead touched the cold earth. Sobbing, she whispered, "Forgive me. Please forgive me. I won't shout again. Only please, please come back. I am so alone. I need you so. For the love of Christ, I beg of you, come back."

A slight gust of wind blew across her and to her boundless relief she heard the Dutchman say, "We are here again, Louise."

22

"Please forgive me for shouting," said Fräulein Louise, and her friends nodded.

The Czech radio operator, a little man with a funny face, wearing a British uniform, said, "Formerly, when I was in Louise's world, I often shouted. For joy. Or in anger. But as a living man to the living. You can't shout at a dead man. He has to disappear if you do. *Has to.*"

"It was only because I'm so desperate," said Fräulein Louise. "I want to see justice done. I must look for Irina. I must find little Karel's murderer. Don't you agree that this is something I've got to do?" She looked from one to the other.

The American pilot said, "When there is something one feels one has to do, it will succeed."

"It will?" Fräulein Louise was overjoyed. How strange! Before they had disappeared her friends had seemed doubtful about her going to Hamburg. Now they had apparently changed their minds.

"Yes," said the American pilot.

"But why is Little Mother in such a hurry?" the Russian wanted to know. "Time . . ." He paused, and then went on, "Time is an earthly thing. We don't recognize it anymore. In our world all things are timeless. But that which Little Mother calls time in her world is working for her. So she should not be impatient. The good thing is always victorious in the end."

"But not always in my world," Fräulein Louise said softly.

"No. Not often. But then it is victorious in our world. So what does it matter?" asked the Russian.

"It matters a lot to me," said Fräulein Louise. "I can't wait that long."

The Ukrainian peasant who had died here when it had been a forced labor camp, said, "A higher power than ours will help Louise and go with her. And any strength we can give her with our hopes and prayers shall accompany her."

"It isn't enough!" Fräulein Louise sounded desperate. "I'm all alone in the world. Do you expect me to fight the all-powerful evil on this earth all by myself?"

The SS man shook his head and said, "Louise is a brave woman. If she sets out to fight evil now, with all the strength at her command, it doesn't really matter if she succeeds or not. Don't ask for success."

"But I must!" said Fräulein Louise. "I have to! I am of this earth! I couldn't bear to fail!"

"Because you are still alive, and that is your misfortune," said the SS man.

"What do you think?" Fräulein Louise asked the Frenchman who had been court reporter in Lyon and had died here as a prisoner of war. He was wearing his old uniform, with boots and puttees, and was also quite young. He had a slightly ironic twist to his mouth. "In principle I must agree with our friends," he said. "But there's been much too much action on this earth, with evil results. It might be best to leave this thing to a higher power. We have not yet attained it, but we can sense it better than Fräulein Louise." Whereupon Fräulein Louise began to cry softly.

"I believe you," she said. "I shall soon be with you forever. I love you. But I can't understand you. Why can't I understand you, today of all days?"

"Because we are your friends," said the Jehovah's Witness in the white-and-gray-striped jacket and pants, who had once been a savings bank employee in Bad Homburg. He raised his hand with the red book. "Little Karel was torn out of an evil world and has entered our good world. What blessed fortune! Everything in life is predestined to enter into God. And if anything happens to Irina, she will be happier than she is now. Everything is following a good path, the path that has been ordained by Almighty God."

"Listen, my friend," said the Norwegian cook who had been arrested as a Communist and brought to Neurode. He was very tall, taller even than the American pilot, and he was wearing his concentration camp outfit with the red stripe of the political prisoner on his chest. "As long as people don't live together in friendship and peace, there will be oppressors and oppressed, murderers and their victims. That is why I believe Louise should take up the fight. More and more of the living are fighting for what is good."

"I agree with the cook," said the Dutch textbook publisher.

"You would do what I want to do?"

"Yes," the Norwegian cook and the Dutch publisher said simultaneously.

"You understand me!" cried Fräulein Louise with renewed hope.

"I would act, too," said the Polish artilleryman who had once studied mathematics at Warsaw University.

"You, too?" cried Fräulein Louise.

"Of course, me too," said the Pole.

"Are you a Communist?"

"I was when I was alive. And when I moved into higher spheres, I absorbed everything that was good and eternal."

"And you, Frantichek?" Fräulein Louise asked the Czech who had been an architect in Brunn. He was her compatriot and the only one she addressed by his first name. To the other she said simply *Du.*

"It really is stupid," said Frantichek, "that little boys always have to be so wild. The way they run around . . . you can tell them a hundred times to be careful. But no. It's stupid. It really is."

"Is that all you have to say?" said Fräulein Louise, not trying to hide her disappointment.

"What do you mean? Oh. I see. Of course I'd do exactly what you decide to do," said the Czech.

"And I'm for Louise, too," said the slender, frail young man from the labor camp.

"You, too?" Fräulein Louise was overjoyed. Naturally, she thought, my favorite.

"Yes, me too," said the frail young man. "Because in the course of my studies I found out that it won't get any better in this world until the philosophers are ready to act."

"And that's our opinion, too," said the Norwegian cook.

"So listen to me!" Fräulein Louise was terribly excited again. "There's something else I must tell you."

And the moor was filled with the sounds of life and death.

23

"You know," said Fräulein Louise to her dead, who were listening attentively, "that my mother died when I was very young. She was only thirty-six years old. I was her only child, and when she died I was in despair. But you know all that, don't you?"

The dead nodded.

"My father was a glass blower, a quiet man. The people in Reichenberg always used to say that he knew a lot of secrets. He and I loved my mother very much. When my father saw my despair, he spoke to me: 'Don't cry anymore, Louise. Don't be sad. Mother died too young. She didn't have time to experience or do anything that it would have been her fate to experience and do. But when a person dies before his time, his soul can return to this world and fulfill what was left unfulfilled.' Is that true?"

The dead stared at each other. They looked embarrassed.

"I'm asking you—is that true?" Fräulein Louise repeated.

The dead were silent for a long time. At last the philosophy student spoke. He said, "Yes, it is true."

The American said, "If they want to, the souls of those who died young can enter into the body of a living person."

"That's what my father said," cried Fräulein Louise. "Souls can enter the bodies of the living. And they can determine what the living person does from then on. How he thinks, how he acts."

"Louise's father wanted to console her, naturally," said the Jehovah's Witness.

"Naturally," said Fräulein Louise. "But he said a lot more. He said that Mother had only gone from us seemingly. And because she would certainly want it, her soul would return to us. *Into* us. And when we did good, when we did what was just, and when an inner voice guided us, then we would know: This was Mother's voice speaking to us. That's what my father said, and now you're telling me he was right."

She looked at her friends; they looked at her and were silent.

"All of you here," said Fräulein Louise, "died before your

time. None of you were able to fulfill what you were meant to do. Therefore, all of you—all of you can return. If you wish to."

"We don't have to return," said the Pole.

"No," said the Russian. "But Little Mother is right. Our souls can enter into the souls of the living when we believe we can lead a poor earthly creature into a better life."

Fräulein Louise folded her hands. "Believe me," she implored. "I beg of you! I am too weak and too old to see this thing through alone. I need help. Your help. There is no other. The living have hardened their hearts. All they still know is hatred and lies. The rich and the powerful, the politicians and the generals with their medals—none of them will help me. All they do is lay wreaths on graves and shake hands and embrace and kiss little children, and are liars! Every one of them! I don't care about them and they don't care about my children. They don't know the meaning of innocence! Because they don't believe in your world! Are you listening to me?"

"To every word, Louise," said the American.

"I've changed my mind," said the Ukrainian peasant. "I agree with the cook and the professor now, and the others who think as Louise does."

"You mean you believe we should really take part in this earthly event?" the Frenchman asked hesitantly.

"Yes, yes! Of course! And help me! And stand by me!" cried Fräulein Louise.

The men were silent again. A few mumbled unintelligibly.

"Louise must know that if we do it, it is dangerous," said the Frenchman. "For us and for her and for everyone concerned."

"Dangerous? If you are with me?"

"Yes. Dangerous if we are with Louise in her world," said the Frenchman. "Because our world is different, and Louise will never be able to understand us completely. No earthling can. It is really dangerous."

"But why?" cried Fräulein Louise.

"Because now we are without desire and at the same time friends. In Louise's world—what will we be like there? Will we still be friends?"

"Certainly," said the Norwegian. "All of us have learned to recognize what is good and what is evil."

"Just the same—" insisted the Frenchman.

"Return, please, I beg of you," Fräulein Louise implored.

105

"Return to this earth. You will only do good. I know. I am sure. You have been purified. You can't do anything evil anymore. Will you return? Will you?"

The men drew close together. Fräulein Louise stood apart from them. She couldn't understand what they were whispering, and she watched the moon lay a silver bridge over the moor, like a span between the realm of the living and the realm of the dead.

"So what have you decided?" she asked.

"We shall try to help you, Louise," said the American.

"But I say again—it is dangerous," said the Frenchman.

"Oh, do be quiet!" said the Norwegian cook.

"I wanted to say it once more," said the Frenchman, his mouth twisted in an ironic smile.

Fräulein Louise was terribly excited. "If you're going to help me, will you recognize each other?"

"No," said the Russian. "Because we only met in death."

"And how will you look in life?"

"We don't know yet. We can turn up in all sorts of shapes. It will depend on whom we choose as the guardian of our souls," said the student.

The Jehovah's Witness said, "And we shall exist only as long as Louise believes we exist. Once she ceases to believe, we cease to exist."

"I believe in you," cried Fräulein Louise. "You will come with me. I won't be alone when I go to Hamburg. So much will happen soon, won't it? Tomorrow, perhaps."

"Tomorrow, yes," said the Dutchman.

"In how many hours?" asked Fräulein Louise.

"Is that important?" asked the Russian. "It's always tomorrow. Little Mother should know that. Today was once tomorrow."

"I thank you! I thank you! Oh, I'm so happy!" cried Fräulein Louise, weeping tears of joy. She hurried over to her student and embraced him, and he felt rough and hard in her arms, like the bark of a tree.

2

Layout

1

The penis is hard, we have an erection; the member is about to fulfill its function. (To be continued.)

I wrote the words hastily, then took paper, carbon, and copy out of the typewriter. That was that. Eighteen pages. Sixty spaces between the vertical lines on the paper, three pages equal to a column of text. I had been told to hand in six columns, and I had managed to finish on the dot. I nearly always did. A simple question of routine. After all, I'd been in the business since 1954, the last three years as author of a series entitled: "Sex: Everything There Is to Know About It." This was the sixteenth article. Before I was through there'd be twenty-five, possibly thirty, depending on the management, their names be praised, every one of them! The articles that had preceded this one had appeared under the titles: "Do You Know How to Love?" "The Estrogen Miracle," "How to Love à Trois" (not what you're thinking, but advice to a couple who already have a child), "Why Girls Love Girls," "The Golden Pill," "Make Me Happy!" etc., etc. Never had a topic been so successful since the founding of the Bundesrepublik and a free democratic press. Right now it was *the* success story in the business. The other papers had, of course, started doing something similar right away, but so far without the same success. This was because—no false modesty, please!—they didn't have a Curt Corell. Page fifteen . . . page fourteen . . . page thirteen . . . That was my pseudonym; that was I—Walter Roland.

As already mentioned, I was fully aware that beyond our profession, quite a few people knew that Walter Roland and Curt Corell were one and the same person—not many, though. Millions were still thinking of the inspiring articles I had written once as Walter Roland, and had no idea that I was the same man who had been dishing this hogwash out to them for the last three and a half years. Once I had said there was no story on earth I couldn't write, but when the damned thing threatened to become such a riproaring success, I got cold feet and decided on a pseudonym. There were, after all, limits to what Walter Roland was willing to produce. In the meantime, Curt Corell had become far more famous than Walter Roland in his heyday. For the last three and a half years, the latter hadn't written a thing!

What I am writing now does not fit chronologically into the course of already described events—a fact you may have noticed—but I can't help it. A story like this one can't be told in any other way. Events have to be described where they can give the reader the greatest insight possible into the relationship of things. Because everything that happened was mercilessly logical.

And it's high time I explained the situation in which I found myself when we kidnapped Irina Indigo from the Neurode Youth Camp.

What I am about to describe happened a day *before* we took off for Neurode—actually almost two days before, because we left late at night—and what I am going to relate now took place in the early morning of the previous day. Only such a short time separated me from my old world!

Two and a half years ago the circulation of *Blitz* wasn't anything to brag about. It was sinking fast. The advertising department at once became hysterical—understandably. All advertising prices—which, by the way, were astronomically high—were dependent on copies sold. When that number dropped, the price of advertising had to be lowered; and the advertisements, according to a computerized imperative, had to constitute approximately half the content. Every six months there was a reconciliation of copies sold and advertising prices. The most important clients—those who bought two pages or whole pages in color—reserved their space months in advance. Therefore, when the circulation sank below a certain level, the price of advertising was affected, and there was a sackcloth and ashes mood in the editorial offices. Because now two questions arose: If the circulation figure sank further, the publisher was duty-bound to inform all advertisers immediately. If the loss reached five percent, they could ask for their money back or take credit for it. That was problem number one. Problem number two: If the number of copies sold somehow did *not* continue to sink, but recovered, the publisher couldn't ask for a penny more in advertising revenue until the next expiration date. That's the way it was three and a half years ago. The decline stopped briefly a hairline away from the ghastly low-water mark, then continued to sink and sink and sink. And the day for the issuing of the new rates was coming nearer and nearer. Then the miraculous happened. I had a brainstorm! The idea for a series on sex education and information. I wrote the first few articles, and behold! The circulation jumped. Up. And how!

"That's done it!" cried publisher Thomas Herford, tears in his eyes when he heard that *Blitz* had sold ninety thousand copies more after the fourth article by Curt Corell; and that was why the first series, which had saved the day, had to be followed by a second, and a third, and a fourth, *ad nauseam*. Nonstop! The genius of Curt Corell had made a princely prisoner of him.

Week after week, fifty-two times a year, I had to produce this repulsive material, which had become by far the most popular series in years. I had access to a whole library on the subject. Photographers and graphic artists waited eagerly for my orders, money was no object.

Facts, suggestive photos, explanations, instructions, consolation and scientific affirmation for desperate teenagers, married couples, loving couples, big and small, old and young; for the impotent, the fetishists, lesbians, hermaphrodites, homosexuals—everything was human, everything had to be understood, but first one must know about it: In short, How to Lead a Fulfilled Love Life. All this I kneaded weekly into a perfect dough without omitting even the most insignificant ingredient and always with nothing but the most serious intentions—that goes without saying—and from this dough I proceeded to bake my miraculous cake. For icing I threw in graphic illustrations, always in the best of taste, when photographs didn't suffice. According to the research department, the illustrations were especially popular. In "Make Me Happy" there was a four-color picture, a whole page, with legend—A, B, C, a, b, c, 1, 2, 3, I, II, III, and so on, all the way up to 27 and XXVII, a work of art that looked like a cross between a generalissimo's map and a painting by Dali. The penis red, the vagina blue, and the various other organs pertinent to the theme in yellow and violet—the whole thing peppered with dots, fine lines and arrows, and with the title in bright red: "How Does the Sperm Reach the Egg?" A prestigious newsmagazine thereupon baptized *Blitz* as the "Shit and Fuck Weekly." "They're envious," said Thomas Herford, shrugging it off; and a house letter promptly recommended that all editors, authors, and employees read that great book: *Envy: A Social Theory*, by Helmuth Schoeck.

The circulation of *Blitz* continued to rise and began to move perilously close to the two giants among the illustrated magazines. Herford's delight became mixed, as evidenced by what he said to his closest associates one day. I was invited to join in these conferences. "Of course I want a large circulation and highest advertising revenue possible, but I also want a circulation that doesn't get out of hand. Don't let's get too big. That would cost me millions a year and I'd soon be broke."

There was a price ceiling on advertising. One couldn't go legally beyond it; however, this might be justified by circulation. The advertising revenue covered costs only up to a point, but not if the editions became very large and one ended up with a magazine that was thick and expensive and couldn't charge more for the advertising! Then one operated at a loss. Millions in one year, according to Herford, and he was right. The order therefore was: Be as successful as possible but not *quite* as successful as possible.

Ah, me . . . pitifully, relentlessly, the life of the millionaire is threatened. . . .

2

8:20 A.M. November 1968. A Monday. A beautiful autumn morning. Pale blue sky, pallid sunshine, ground fog over the city streets. I felt hot, as usual.

Sleeves rolled up, tie loosened, a Gauloise between my lips, I was sitting at my desk, my hair still wet from the shower. My office was on the seventh floor of an ultramodern, eleven-story, steel-glass-concrete high-rise building on Frankfurt's Kaiserstrasse. The windows looked out on a courtyard, a blessing, because they were building a subway on Kaiserstrasse.

The editorial offices were on the seventh floor, photography on the floor below. A monster aquarium, this publishing house. Nearly all the walls were of glass. I could look through office after office, almost the length of the entire floor. Not a soul there yet—only the cleaning woman and me, working at my desk.

I was surrounded by empty bottles of Coke, overflowing ashtrays, books and papers that provided me with copy—the Kinsey Report, the Masters Report, good old Magnus Hirschfeld, medical journals, the *Lexicon of Erotica*, slips of paper with notes, only a few. I didn't need money. By now I had "the right approach" to the crap, as fast as I could write. I took a pencil with very soft lead and started correcting.

Erotic zones: necking, petting—OK. Clitoris—just a minute. A carat here, and in the margin, in parentheses, "tickler." I've margined hundreds of ticklers, but every tickler is a goodie.

One couldn't remind oneself often enough how important it was that a series like this should make as scientific an impression as possible, because of the public prosecutor and the censor board, to say nothing of the voluntary censorship of the illustrated weekly itself. And then the readers wanted it so much. So . . . insert!

Where was the damned book anyway? Ah, there it was! "And since the touch of the tickler results in a powerful reaction on the part of the female, the famous Hollander van Swieten, personal physician of the Austrian Empress Maria Theresa, advised her, when she consulted him because she was concerned with her lack of fertility . . ." No. First in Latin, just as it stood there, because this type of fucking, dear reader, is serious business. So: *"Praetero cenveo, vulvam Sacratissimae Majestatis ante coitum diutius esse titillandam."* Translated: "Moreover, I am of the opinion that the clitoris of your Most Holy Majesty should be titillated for quite some time before coitus."

I wrote as clearly as I could, printing the words, so that the typesetters couldn't complain again that they couldn't read my handwriting. "And the result of this good advice? The Empress gave birth to *sixteen* children!"

Things like that went over well.

I was grinning again. I'd just thought of a joke in a Frankfurt cabaret recently. A man was sitting upright on a double bed asking the girl lying beside him, "Have you read Corell this week?" Whereupon the girl, startled, stammered, "But of course! Why? Did I do something wrong?"

That, ladies and gentlemen, is fame! My deadliest enemy, editor-in-chief Gert Lester, could tell me a dozen times a week that I was slipping, the fink! I was Curt Corell, business as usual!

I drank some Coke, wiped my mouth with the back of my mind, and went on correcting. *Labia majora. Labia minora.* The love mound. Mas*u*rbation, not mas*to*rbation. Typing too fast. The soft pencil careted words that were to be inserted, indicated new paragraphs, underlines for italics, asterisks where there was to be a space. The crap read just fine!

3

Four hours earlier, at 4:30 A.M., I had awakened and looked at my wristwatch. I could wake up whenever I liked—all I had to do was decide the hour—and today I had to get up so early because I was so damned close to my deadline. I should have handed in the article for the issue on Friday. But I'd been sick on Friday. Nobody's business but mine; the only one I'd told about it was Hem. On the phone.

"I can't let you have it today, Hem."

"The jackal?"

"Yes. I'm in bed."

"Too much booze?"

"Much too much. Too many cigarettes. Can't write a line today."

"You're going to do yourself in," Hem said to me, lying in bed with my jackal.

"Nonsense! All I need is some sleep. I'll take twenty milligrams of Valium and sleep it off."

"Okay, my boy. Do your best."

"You know, Hem, it's an absolute miracle that I can still write this series. I could vomit every time I think of it."

"I can understand that. But what the hell! You've got to produce."

It was a stock phrase of this highly intellectual man. "What the hell! You've got to produce." How often Hem, grown wise and humble in our profession, had said that. Once he had wanted to be a composer. He didn't make it. He couldn't make a living with his compositions, so he played piano in bars. Then came the war. In 1946 he came home from a prisoner-of-war camp, tried composing again, again with no success. Friends helped him get a job as music editor; soon he was promoted to executive editor in charge of all copy. That was a big experiment, but in those days *Blitz* still experimented. And it worked. The man who had failed as a composer became a first-rate executive editor, who was recognized and admired in the entire profession.

"Yes, yes, I know. What the hell!" I said to Hem.

"They're going to foam at the mouth...."

"Let them! The assholes! Or let them write it themselves."

"But I'll cover up for you."

"Thanks, Hem."

"Not at all. Just being practical. If I bawled you out now and forced you to write, you'd send in some supershit, you and your jackal. When you've recovered, may I hope to have something usable?"

"I have the whole weekend."

"Don't promise anything. I know you, Walter. But Monday morning at 9:00 A.M., it's got to be on my desk or it's curtains."

My jackal was with me all Friday and Saturday, only worse. I had difficulty breathing, but it never occurred to me to call a doctor. It would pass. Sunday morning things were no better. Finally I pulled myself together, forced myself to go to a restaurant and eat, quite a lot, and just managed to get home in time to throw it all up. Which was what I had expected. But now my stomach was sensitive again, and the Chivas could help. I began to drink at three and drank all afternoon and could sense that the jackal was leaving me. Then I went out and wandered from one nightclub to the other, seven or eight in all—can't remember exactly, except that all of them had "my" bottle of Chivas. And in some stable or other I must have picked up two girls who were lying beside me Monday morning at 4:30 A.M.—a redhead on my left, a black-haired girl on my right, both of them naked and looking innocent as they slept.

I got up carefully. I didn't want to wake them. I took one last look at their beautiful bodies, then I covered them. The black-haired one was snoring softly. I noticed that I was naked, too, and looked around me, saw the girls' things scattered all over the place, the records still on the stereo, the light still on. Then I remembered everything.

I turned off the stereo. The Pathétique. Tchaikovsky. My favorite composer. I had listened to it last night while the two girls had danced a wild striptease for me. I had sat there, drinking

115

Chivas and watching the girls. I had paid them in advance, much too much as usual. And they had put on a great show and made love convulsively on my super-size bed, moaning and groaning and overdoing it for my benefit.

I don't have to write what the three of us did after that. Nobody'd print it anyway. But I made out with both of them until in the end they were whimpering, I should stop, please! And I was just as drunk as they were. But my cock was always in great shape when I was drunk. That's why I wasn't afraid of the jackal at moments like this, unless he happened to be present, and I wasn't afraid of illness or death. Death was meaningless for someone who could work like a dog and take on two girls when dead drunk and only get more and more horny. No. I was not the right type for death. Whenever the jackal had come and gone, I took two girls home with me. It was something I was doing more and more frequently lately. Always when I had had the jackal. Then I slept beautifully between their warm, firm young flesh.

In November 1958, I, Walter Roland, alias Curt Corell, was at the height of my career. I lived in a penthouse which belonged to the firm, didn't cost me a cent. A six-room apartment with every convenience known to man, on the top floor of an elegant high-rise apartment house on the Gregor-Mendel Allee, in the prestigious residential section of Lerchesberg, south of the Main River. Ultramodern decor, priceless lacquered furniture in various colors—red, orange, blue, white, lilac—because in every room the walls were painted a different color and the furniture matched. Shell chairs that swiveled; in the white bedroom a huge brown leather bed. Indirect lighting and floor lamps with colored shades. Wall-to-wall carpeting with a design of oriental bridges. A whole wall for books, the TV built in. Every room led through a glass door out onto the roof terrace, where flowers and plants bloomed in the summer; and you could bask on chaise longues or under sun umbrellas. At night you could sit outdoors and look across the entire city of Frankfurt. And all this was mine through my writing! Like the white Lamborghini 400 CT. I had brought the whores home in it. However drunk I was, I could always drive and fuck. I had money to burn, and I burned it.

In spite of my colossal salary I was constantly in debt. Two hundred thousand marks in the red. So what? They were happy to give me anything I asked for; they practically came to me, their arms open wide—take, oh, take whatever you need! (So that I wouldn't go to one of the rival houses from whom I got at least one offer a month.)

I had arrived! But I had to assure myself of it constantly. That was why I drove like a lunatic in a crazily expensive car, appeared at parties with the prettiest starlets, gave knock-out parties of my own, and stayed only in the best hotels.

I walked softly into the kitchen and put on water for coffee. I needed a lot of coffee, because now I had to work, work hard, and I was still drunk. I staggered into the black-tiled bathroom and showered for a long time, hot and cold. That helped. I could think clearly again. While I shaved, I listened to the radio. A UKW station was broadcasting the news. Bitter fighting in the Mekong Delta. A purge in Czechoslovakia, Dubcek out. An American plane hijacked to Cuba, an Israeli plane to Athens. Heavy fighting on the Israel-Jordan border, a commando raid in Syria. Bloody fighting between Protestants and Catholics in Ireland. Racial unrest in the U.S.A. Inflation, strikes, catastrophes. Nothing new. I always heard the news first thing in the morning. I had to be informed.

I left the bathroom and walked into the dressing room with its off-white closets, each with its own mirror. I put on a gray flannel suit, a white pongee shirt, a black tie, socks, low shoes. In the kitchen I made the coffee strong and drank slowly. I wasn't hungry. I looked at the sleeping girls once more, took four hundred-mark bills out of my wallet, and shoved them partway under the lamp on the bedside table. With a red felt pen I wrote on a piece of paper, "*Ciao*, my pets. This is for you. Lock the door when you leave and drop the key in the mailbox." No signature. Not even my initials. No point in getting intimate; we would never meet again.

Get on with it! Get on with it! Now I was in a hurry. I knew all the detours where they were building the subway; I drove fast through the cool, empty city streets, and I got to the office via the delivery entrance in the rear of the building. I drove my Lamborghini into the underground garage and walked upstairs to the lobby. No elevator for the few stairs. One had to do *something* for one's health!

A tall doorman in a blue gold-braided uniform opened the door to the lobby after I had rung the bell. Like everyone else who moved a finger for me, he got a lavish tip. "Good morning, Herr Kluge."

"Good morning, Herr Roland. Thank you very much."

My attaché case was full of books, papers, and notes for the article I had to write. Right now. This minute. Just then a big burly man in a creased suit, unshaven and obviously hung over,

117

carrying a flight bag full to bursting, appeared in the enormous lobby with its marble floor, marble walls, and leather armchairs and tables. He came in through the high glass door that was controlled by an electric eye. A dirty white bandage was wound around his forehead. I recognized my friend Engelhardt.

"Hi, Walter!"

"Hello, Bertie. So they got you this time."

"Nothing to it. Hit by a stone." He was smiling as usual.

Three days ago a famous Negro leader had been shot in Chicago, with resulting racial unrest. "When did you get in?"

"Half an hour ago. The others are taking the noon plane." *Blitz* had sent a whole crew to the U.S.A. "Boy, oh, boy, they're slaughtering each other in Chicago! And I've got the pictures!"

"And you're getting plenty of advertising, in all the papers."

"And space? Are we going to have enough space?"

"Nine pages!"

"Ye gods!"

"I saw the proofs of the ads. Terrific! And of course you get your credit line." I could still recall the text, in fat caps: "The Death of the Black Jesus! In order to be able to give you a nine-page report of the murder of the Negro leader, Jesus Maria Albermore, 3,562 negatives were developed, 298 pictures were received by radio, 414 telephone calls were made between Frankfurt and the U.S.A., 231 cables were exchanged, and 67,000 miles were flown. *Blitz* ace photographer Bert Engelhardt and seven reporters flew to Chicago, Los Angeles, Detroit, New York, Baltimore, and Boston. The head of the photo department interrupted his vacation in Tenerife and flew to Chicago for an exclusive interview with the widow of the murdered leader." All this when no one had any idea how many negatives had been developed, how many wires exchanged, and how many kilometers flown.

Bertie was running. "Where are you going?" I cried.

"To the darkroom. I have to develop three films!"

"I thought you'd sent it all ahead."

"Wait till you see what the boys are bringing back!"

I walked over to the two elevators. There were always people waiting in front of one of the elevators; it was for the use of minor employees and visitors. A second one, rarely used, was for the heads of departments—general manager, head of advertising and circulation, chairman of the board, president, editor-in-chief, executive editor, and, of course, the publisher. Each of these important gentlemen had his own key to this particular VIP elevator. There was no key to the other one—the Plebian Cage, as it was called—but it was never on the floor when you wanted it. The common man had to wait.

Fourteen years before, when I had had to interrupt my study of law because of lack of funds and had got a job with *Blitz* and had seen this fine system for the first time, I had wondered seriously whether I should work in such a firm. I had been highly indignant. But my indignation faded and I took the job. Six years later I was top writer and at Christmas they had festively handed me a key to the VIP elevator. I felt sick with fury and for four more years ostentatiously went right on using the Plebian Cage, which was always full and never there when you wanted it. But one day I'd had it. I'd just hit the jackpot with my sex stories and bought the Lamborghini. The goddam Plebian Cage didn't come and didn't come. So I took my pristine key out of my wallet and used the VIP elevator. The hell with it!

In the VIP elevator it smelled of perfume, and during office hours soft music played from a muted loudspeaker. At this early hour there was no music, but the perfume was there.

Seventh floor. I got out, walked to my glass office, taking three bottles of Coke out of the refrigerator on the way because I was thirsty as hell. In my office I emptied everything out of my attaché case, rolled up my sleeves, and loosened my tie and collar. Cigarette. There—all set. I inserted paper and carbon in my typewriter and looked at my wristwatch. 6:12. I began to type. The article almost wrote itself. Thus I produced my weekly ration of substitute sex for the millions who wanted it. Let them have it!

4

"Under the stars, under the moon I am alone, and not alone. Past and future are always with me . . . in the vastness of time and space. . . ."

At midnight, November 12, when Fräulein Louise, her eyes smarting with the tears she had shed, was whispering these words as she walked along the narrow path on the moor, hurrying to see her friends, I reached the bridge over the Elbe at autobahn exit Veddel, Irina and Bertie at my side. I was driving fast, 230 kilometers an hour. The car slithered from side to side on the deserted autobahn because an ice-cold gale had blown up from the northwest. It hit the Lamborghini head-on and the car shook. I held the steering wheel firmly and watched the road like a hawk. At this speed a head wind could sweep us off the highway, but I knew my car.

It was storming in Hamburg. Moored boats were dancing on the water, slates were blowing off roofs, there was the sound of metal clattering, and the wind howled. I drove along Heiden-kampsweg, through the dark suburbs of Klostertor and Borgfelde, to the Berliner-Tor-Damm. Not a soul on the streets. I knew my way around Hamburg: north across Büerweide, Steinhauerdamm, and Mühlendamm to Armgartstrasse. Then I turned left and began to drive west on Mundsburgerdamm to Schwanenwik, which was on the Aussenalster. Even that little inland sea was restless, and the lights of the big hotels on both sides of the Lombardsbrücke—the new one is called the Kennedy Bridge—sparkled in the water. Wisps of clouds flew overhead. Adolfstrasse was a crazy street, one way in different directions at different times of the day. I turned into it and stopped the car in front of No. 22A, an old, white building standing in a small garden. Several families lived in it. It was very quiet.

"Is this Eppendorfer Baum?" Irina asked excitedly. "Is this the house?"

"No," I said. "We'll drive to Eppendorfer Baum from here, but we had to come here first. This is where Conny Manners lives."

"Who?"

"Our Hamburg correspondent, remember? I called my office before you made your call and asked them to send him a teletype to get going and try to find your Jan Bilka."

"Oh, yes." But she was restless now, and impatient.

"Conny's girl friend is expecting us. She'll tell us what Conny's been able to find out, if anything. So come on."

I helped her out of the car. Bertie got out on the other side. "His friend Edith," he said, smiling. "Beautiful Edith."

The storm was howling, trees were groaning, limbs were snapping or bending low and waving back and forth, forming bizarre shadows on the asphalt. We walked through the little front garden—the low gate was open—and I rang the bell beside Conny's name. He lived on the third floor. We waited for quite a long time. Then we heard the intercom click, and out of the loudspeaker, the voice of a woman, teary and afraid. "Who is it?"

"Roland," I said. "Roland and Engelhardt and somebody else."

"Who else?" said the woman's voice, and then we could hear her sobbing.

"For God's sake, Edith!" I cried. "Let us in! I'll tell you all about it when we get upstairs."

"I want to know who the other person is."

"A young lady."

"What sort of a young lady?"

"Edith, have you been drinking?"

She sobbed again, then she said, "So you won't tell me."

"No. Not like this. Let us in. We're in a hurry, so open the door, for God's sake!"

Edith's voice, asking, "What's that name—the name you call Herr Kramer?"

"Now listen—"

"You don't know?"

"Of course I know!"

"Then tell me the name or I won't unlock the door."

"Hem," I said. "Satisfied?"

"And how old is he?"

"Damn it—"

"How old?"

"Fifty-six."

There was a whirring sound in the lock. We hurried in. I found the switch for the electric light. There was no elevator in the high, narrow stairwell, and we walked up the stairs, which were steep. One tenant to each floor. The door to Conny Manners's apartment was closed. I rang again. The door was opened a crack, as far as the chain would allow. I noticed that the front hall was dark. Then I saw the gun. A Colt .45, a small cannon! The American MPs used it. The barrel was pushed through the crack in the door. I knew Conny owned a Colt; now his girl apparently had it. We heard her trembling voice, "Go and stand by the window so I can see you. All three of you, or however many there are of you."

"Three, damn it," I said. "Edith, I've already told you that."

"Over to the window," said Edith.

The light in the hall went out. I put it on again. Then I looked at Bertie and Irina and shrugged. What else could we do? I was the first one at the window.

"All right," said Edith from behind the door. "That's you, Herr Roland. And now the others."

Irina and Bertie came and stood beside me.

"And that's Herr Engelhardt." The gun was still aimed at me. I had experienced a lot of crazy things during the last hours. Had Edith gone crazy, too? "Who is the girl?"

"Look here, Edith. This is idiotic! Open up or—"

She interrupted me. "Or what? Or nothing! I close the door and call the police."

"Edith, you're nuts!"

"I am perfectly sane," she sobbed. "Who is the girl?"

So I started to introduce them, but I couldn't remember Edith's last name. "Herwag," she said.

"Edith Herwag," I told Irina, who looked frightened. Then Edith wanted to know where Irina came from. Not until I had told the whole goddamned story—the light in the hall went out again, of course; we had to switch it on twice—was the gun barrel withdrawn, the chain removed, and the door opened. "Come in," said Edith Herwag.

She was really beautiful, a tall blond. She had worked as a model until she had moved in with Conny. He didn't want her to model anymore; he wanted to marry her. And they would marry soon, I was thinking, as I walked into the small entrance hall behind Irina and Bertie.

Edith was very pale; she swayed slightly and her green eyes were huge. She stood there, the gun aimed at my stomach, and began to cry again, and all I could think of was how easily a gun like that could go off. . . .

"What is it, Edith?" Bertie asked, smiling.

"Conny. . . ." she sobbed, and now the gun was aimed at Irina, which didn't make me feel any better.

"What about Conny?" asked Bertie, in his usual friendly way. "Has anything happened to him?"

All Edith could do was nod. And the way she nodded made my blood run cold. She still had a finger on the trigger and the safety was off.

"What's happened to him?"

She went on crying uncontrollably.

"Edith!" I cried. "Edith!"

"Leave it to me," Bertie said softly, and asked, "Did he have an accident?" Edith shook her head. Mascara was painting a grotesque tracery on her cheeks.

"No accident?"

Edith shook her head.

"So what happened?"

"Murder," said Edith Herwag.

5

Conny Manners got out of his blue Porsche 911 S and walked slowly across Eppendorfer Baum to number 187, the address we had given him, the house in which Jan Bilka was staying with his friend Rolf Michelsen. Eppendorfer Baum is a commercial street in a good neighborhood. There are stores on the ground floor of most of the houses. Conny could see that there were apartments on the floors above them. He was of medium height, slender, thirty years old, and had been with *Blitz* four years. Before that he had worked in the central office of the DPA, the German Press Agency, and before that with UP International in their Hamburg office. He was wearing a rust-brown duffel coat, no hat. He had been at home when my message for him came on the teletype. That was at ten minutes to five. Conny confirmed the message and told his friend Edith that he mightn't be back so soon but that he'd call from time to time and keep her informed. She was to take it all down and read it to me when I got there later this evening. Then Conny had driven off in his Porsche.

He hadn't taken the heavy rush-hour traffic into consideration, and he was furious because it took him almost three quarters of an hour to get to the house on Eppendorfer Baum. Actually forty-eight minutes passed between the teletype from Frankfurt and his arrival at number 187. He crossed Eppendorfer Baum at exactly 5:38 P.M. Two witnesses who saw the whole thing testified to this later. These two witnesses also saw the headlights of a parked Mercedes switched on and off three times.

This car was parked a little way down Eppendorfer Baum, and the lights were flashed just as Conny began to cross the street. At the third flash a big black car pulled out from the other side of the street. The Mercedes meanwhile moved off and passed Conny as it drove away. The black car was about as far from Conny as the Mercedes had been—approximately a hundred meters.

Conny had parked in front of a zebra stripe. He began to cross the street on it. The big black car came driving down Eppendorfer Baum. The driver shifted gears and, according to the witnesses, the car was doing at least a hundred kilometers an hour as the man at the wheel made straight for Conny. The car would have run over him while he was still on the crosswalk if Conny hadn't realized at the last moment what was happening and made a desperate jump backwards. The man at the wheel of the heavy car swerved and managed to hit Conny with his left fender. Conny was thrown into the air and came down with a thud on the crosswalk. A pool of blood quickly formed around him.

Cars stopped, people screamed and ran over to Conny. One of the two witnesses called the police from a nearby phone booth. An ambulance arrived six minutes later from the University Hospital on Martinistrasse, seven minutes later two patrol cars, eleven minutes later two cars from homicide. One of the officers in the patrol car had called them in. And behind them, finally, a car from the Accident Investigation Squad.

Conny was badly injured. The doctor in the ambulance said he would have to go into surgery immediately. They put him on a stretcher and the ambulance drove off, its siren wailing. The police stayed at the scene for an hour. They questioned both witnesses, took pictures, measurements—a routine investigation. There were some glass shards from the headlights of the fatal car. The police picked them up, together with some small flakes of paint, and put everything in plastic bags.

While the officers were still talking to the witnesses in their patrol cars, they received a call on the radio. It was very strange, one of the witnesses told Edith later. "First central called the car by its number," the witness had said, "but then the dispatcher's voice said something totally incomprehensible."

"What?" Edith had asked.

"'Capri needs a city pilot.'"

"What?"

"Just that." And the other witness had corroborated it. "That's what he said—'Capri needs a city pilot.'"

"And what did the officer say?" Edith had asked, and the first witness had told her. "The officer said, 'Cinnebar crosses the North Pole.'" The first witness had added, "I told them it wasn't an accident, it was murder." The second witness told Edith, "That's right. Both of us saw the Mercedes giving that signal with its lights, and we said so. But suddenly the officer who had been questioning us seemed uninterested. All he said was, 'A light signal . . . is that so?'"

6

"The police called just after six," said Edith Herwag.

We were sitting in Conny's living room. Edith had recovered to some extent, but she still cried a little every now and then. I had found a bottle of whiskey and made her drink some. Conny's whiskey; I didn't want to waste my Chivas.

"They told me that Conny had been hit by a car and was in the University Hospital. I drove straight there." Now she was crying again and I filled her glass half full. We didn't drink anything. We wanted to hear her story and get on with things, because now we were in more of a hurry than ever.

"Thank you," said Edith.

The Colt was lying between us on the table. Edith drank, stopped crying, and spoke in a voice that was strangely flat, almost monotone.

"I called a taxi. I was at the hospital at ten to seven. Conny was in the operating room. They told me there was no point in my waiting, but of course I waited. It took another hour. At a quarter past eight they rolled him out."

"Could you see him?"

"No. He was covered, and a doctor was walking beside him, holding up a bottle with blood in it. I could see the tube, but I couldn't see Conny's arm. I tried to walk alongside the stretcher, but the doctor said no. I began to cry. Then two men in civilian clothes took me by the arm and led me to the exit. I screamed and kicked, but they didn't say a word, just dragged me to the exit. A third man standing there told me to take a taxi home, they'd call me when I could see Conny or if his condition worsened or . . . if he—" She said nothing more.

"Who were those men?"

"I have no idea."

"Were they from the police?"

"Perhaps. I don't know. It was all so strange. The first two didn't say a word to me, and the third one just a sentence or two, and then they went away."

"Where to?"

"Back into the hospital. Of course I ran right back in a few minutes later, and a desk nurse, who evidently didn't know anything, told me that Conny was in a private recovery room on the second floor."

"Everybody goes to a recovery room after surgery," said Bertie.

"I know," said Edith. "But a *private* one? When I finally found the room, there were the two men who had led me away. They were standing at the door and told me there was nothing I could do. I should go home; they'd call me."

"Did they say *they'd* call *you*?"

Irina was sitting there as if paralyzed, watching Edith and listening to her, and the wind outside was rattling the windows.

"Yes—no—I don't know. No . . . they said the hospital would call me. And that Conny was doing all right, all things considered. That's what they told me. A doctor came along and I wanted to talk to him, but they held me back and I couldn't."

"What did they look like?"

"Oh . . . like civil servants. Very strong and middle class. They were dressed that way, too."

"Young?"

"I'd say around forty."

"Did they threaten you in any way?"

"When I said I had no intention of going home but was going to sit on a bench and wait, one of them said that if I didn't leave right away, he'd take me downstairs and put me in a taxi and tell them not to let me into the hospital again."

"But that's impossible!" cried Irina, aghast.

"That's what I would have thought," said Edith, "but it happened. I refused to go away, and he grabbed me and dragged me down to the entrance. He got a taxi and shoved me into it and gave the driver this address."

"But people in the hospital must have seen you!"

"Only doctors and nurses. The patients were in their beds and all the visitors were gone."

"And so?"

"And so nothing," said Edith. "The doctors and nurses never made a move to help me. They behaved as if they didn't even see what was going on. That was when I began to be afraid for my own life for the first time, and later even more."

"When, 'even more'?"

"After I'd talked to the two witnesses and they'd told me what they'd seen. Of course I didn't go home, not right away. I told the driver I wanted to go to Eppendorfer Baum 187 first. He should wait." She shivered.

"A little more?" I asked, reaching for Conny's whiskey.

"No, thank you. No more." Now the tears were running down her beautiful face again. "I can't stop thinking about the blood, the blood on the pavement. Somebody had spread sawdust over it, but it had seeped through, and it glittered. . . ." She threw back her head. "Then I looked for the two witnesses."

"How did you know about them?" asked Bertie.

"The first time they called, the officer mentioned two witnesses. He hadn't been briefed yet."

"Hadn't been briefed? About what?"

"Well . . . about . . . I don't know. Do you?"

Bertie shook his head; I said, "No."

"But there *must* be something going on!" cried Edith. "I mean, the way they behaved toward me—that isn't usual."

"It certainly isn't."

"There's something I'm not supposed to find out. And the officer who told me about the two witnesses—he wasn't aware of it yet. Don't you think I'm right?"

"Probably," I said. "And you found the two witnesses?"

"Of course. Or I wouldn't know what I've just told you. They told me. But they didn't get the license numbers of the two cars."

"Who are they?"

"One of them is the superintendent of number 187, the other one is an antiques dealer. His shop is in the house. They told me all about it in his apartment. The Pole was afraid they'd see me with him."

I saw Irina quiver. She said softly, "What Pole?"

127

"The super," said Edith.

"The super is a Pole?" I asked, sounding idiotic, but I was stunned; so was Irina, I could see, and I knew both us were thinking of Fräulein Louise and what Pastor Demel had told us about her friends.

"That's what I said. The super is a Pole," said Edith. "Why are you staring at me like that? The antiques dealer is a foreigner, too. French."

"A Pole and a Frenchman," said Bertie, and now he wasn't smiling. I had told him all about Fräulein Louise on the way here.

"Yes, for heaven's sake," said Edith Herwag, sounding annoyed. "A Pole and a Frenchman. Living human beings, not ghosts. I didn't make them up. You can go and see them for yourselves. Or do you think I'm hallucinating? Don't you believe me?"

"Yes. Of course we believe you."

"Then I don't know what all the fuss is about," said Edith. "They're two very nice, friendly people who happened to be standing on the street when it happened. By the way, the Frenchman isn't well; in fact, he's quite ill."

"What's wrong with him?" I asked.

"He has asthma," said Edith Herwag.

7

The Kniefall Market was situated diagonally opposite the *Blitz* publishing house. You could hear the earsplitting noise of the subway construction here, too. The Kniefall Market was famous in Frankfurt: a huge white-tiled hall with various booths selling meat, fish—live or on ice—sausage, cheese, vegetables, exotic salads, bread, jams, and liquor. The Kniefall Market sold everything, all of it top quality, and all of it cheaper than anywhere else. Fat, quick little Waldemar Kniefall had a terrific turnover. He catered parties—the most fantastic buffets—with experienced waiters and pretty waitresses. His ideas for expansion were limitless. Back behind the booths the head of the Kniefall clan (sons, daughters, his wife, and two sons-in-law worked for him—a strictly family business) had had a bar put up, with barstools, an espresso machine, rows of bottles behind it, and a few tables and chairs in front of it. Here in this quasi snack bar, housewives could sit down for coffee and have a bite while their orders were being filled. At noon, business people from the neighborhood came, had an aperitif, and ordered a sandwich or the light, fine (and cheap) hors d'oeuvre menu that wasn't fattening and didn't make you sleepy. At noon every seat was filled. But actually things went on like this more or less from noon until evening. People met here and did business here. The market had its own parking lot, to which cars had access now via Grosse Gallusstrasse and Kirchnerstrasse—you couldn't get to it anymore from Kaiserstrasse because of the subway construction. There were always people milling around in the market, there was always something going on. But early in the morning like this, the snack bar was empty. Only one man was sitting there, facing the wall, a glass on the table in front of him. Myself.

"Another one please, Fräulein Lucie."

"You've already had one double," said pretty young Fräulein Lucie from behind the bar. She sounded unhappy, but I consoled her: "Don't worry about me. I can take it."

There was a mirror on the wall in front of me, and I looked at myself with revulsion. A gray face. The eyes that had sparkled with the stimulation of writing were dimmed, the euphoria of earlier was gone. I, who only moments ago had been pounding out my article on the typewriter, cynically, triumphantly—there I sat in the dimly lit bar in the Kniefall Market, weak, bitter, deflated.

Lucie, blond, dark eyes, twenty, in a clean white smock, put another glass of whiskey and a bottle of soda in front of me on the small table. We'd known each other for quite a long time and she was a little bit in love with me. I could tell; so could everyone who saw her with me. She didn't hide it very well, although she tried.

Lucie had been working at the Kniefall Market snack bar for two years now. She came from Brandoberndorf, a small town in the Taunus district. In those two years she had had only one boy friend, a pretty fellow; all the girls were after him. He drove a yellow VW with the special delivery mail. Loved Lucie and two-timed her. Decamped with some of her money. Since then she lived by herself in the big city of Frankfurt. Not easy for a young girl.

Lucie was very worried about me. I knew what she was

thinking: Why is he always mad when he comes here? Why does he drink whiskey in the morning?

"Your whiskey, Herr Roland," mumbled Lucie.

I looked up at her, nodded, smiling—a crooked smile. At once she smiled back, but I only saw her in the mirror. I lowered my head fast, mixed my drink, and took a big swallow. And the jackal was there again. Very close.

I knew that Lucie was thinking: What's wrong with him? Mumbling to himself. Sounds as if he was swearing. Well, yes, that's exactly what I was doing.

"A shitty life," I was mumbling. "I'm a fool, a bastard! Oh, God, what a mess I've made of my life!" Then I began to think: Nothing new about that. But I'm thirty-six. Time to balance the books, no? So ... whored around, wild as hell, wasted my life, wasted my talents. I was talented once. Oh, yes. Then I used to write good things. All last year's snow....

"The hell with it!" I said aloud this time. Lucie was washing glasses and watching me. Her lower lip was trembling. "Bastard! Fink!" I said to myself this time. Ace writer. Make a fortune, spend a fortune...lucky son of a bitch!

I'd been indulging in this sort of soul-searching for seven years now, always in this cool, dim place, long before the arrival of Lucie. Another girl had been behind the counter then, and another, and another—such a lot of girls! Who could keep track of them?

The telephone behind the counter rang. Lucie took the call. "It's for you, Herr Roland."

I got up and walked over to the phone, my glass in my hand. After saying, "Roland," I finished my drink and shoved the glass across the counter with a gesture that indicated I wanted a refill, and Lucie nodded sadly. I had my bottle of Chivas here, too.

With a thick Berlin accent a woman's voice said, "Hello, Wal*tah!* They told me at your office I could get you at Kniefall."

I said, "Hello, Tutti. What's new?"

I knew Tutti through a documentary on prostitution in Frankfurt. A darling girl. Gertrude Reibeisen was her real name. She called herself Tutti because she found the name Gertrude ugly.

My old friend Tutti answered with the one word. "Leichen-müll*ah!*"

"So he's with you?"

"I'll say, he's with me. And I can't get rid of him. Every time the same *geschiss*. But this is his last performance, I'm telling you! If he shows up here once more, Max'll cut off his balls!"

"Where's Max?"

"Right here. Want to speak to him?"

"No, Tutti. I don't want to speak to Max, I want to speak to Leichenmüller."

"Oh . . . you want him. Well, he's lying on the bed and says he won't move. Says he wants more." Her voice was low as she went on. "I'm not holding this against you, Wal*tah*. It's not your fault. I'm only calling you because you said I should if Leichenmüll*ah* acted up again."

"And I'm glad you called me, Tutti. It was good of you."

"*Quatsch*, lover boy! You know I like you. Why don't you come and snuggle down in my nest some time? Listen, Wal*tah*, I've had Leichenmüll*ah* here since Friday. Max says I should shut up. Says, 'He pays, don't he?' As if money was all that mattered. Nobody thinks of my poor pussy!"

"He's been there since *Friday*?"

"Three days. Yeah. I don't have nuthin' against a few hours, but I'm beginning to feel like a hombrekker."

"A what?"

"You know, Wal*tah*. The English call it a hombrekker, don't they? A woman that breaks up marriages. A guy like that belongs with his family over the weekend, don't he? Instead of which, I've had to dish up one trick after the other. He's not a man, he's hung like a bull! To say nothing of Hänschen."

"Hänschen?"

"Yeah. My canary. He's stopped singing because I haven't had a minute to go out and get him some greens. And then he has to stay covered so long in the morning because Leichenmüll*ah*'s screwed me half dead and I don't have the strength to get up."

"Couldn't Max get the greens and uncover Hänschen?" Max was Tutti's pimp, a great fellow.

"He's jealous of the canary," said Tutti, with the accent on the *y*."

"Jealous? Of a bird? For God's sake!"

"Well, you see, I got this kinda spiritual relationship with the little creature," said Tutti. "My little bird never beats me up." I could hear a man's voice protesting. Tutti went on. "So that's the way it is. I don't care if you listen, Max, it's gotta be said. So Wal*tah*, whaddawedo? Want me to call the police?"

"No," I said, "please don't. I know a better way. Tell

Leichenmüller you've spoken to me and I told you that Lester swore on Friday—"

"Who swore on Friday?"

"Lester. Our editor-in-chief."

"Oh."

"He swore he'd fire Leichenmüller if it happened again and he didn't turn up at the office at ten."

"Is that true?" Tutti sounded horrified.

"Of course it's not true. He wouldn't do anything like that. Leichenmüller is tops in his profession. But I can't think of any other way to get him back into circulation without a scene. Fortunately, he's a very weak, reserved person."

"Not here, he ain't!"

"No, not in your bed, but everywhere else."

"And you think that'll do it?"

"I'm sure it will. But you've got to be very dramatic about this firing business. Tell him I'm terribly worried about him and have practically written him off. He'll come."

"You'd better be right, lover boy! Anyway, I'll pass the good word on to Leichenmül*lah* so that it raises his hair, not just his pecker. If somebody's had it—and God knows he's had enough—and he doesn't want to get out when he sees how pooped I am, that's something I jest can't stand. *Adschön,* Walt*ah!* If I can't get him to quit, I'll call right back. Stay where you are!"

"I'll stay right here. But you'll manage all right. *Wiedersehen,* Tutti. My best to Max."

"I'll tell him. So long, Walt*ah!*"

Tutti hung up, so did I, and with a sigh went back to my table. Lucie had brought my third whiskey double. I took a big slug. "That guy makes me want to throw up."

"Leichenmüller?" Lucie asked curiously. "Who is he? What a name!" *Leiche* meaning "corpse." But he wasn't really a *Leichen*müller, he was a *Leiden*müller, *leiden* meaning "suffering"—"no great improvement, but I felt I should clear up Lucie on the point. "His name's really Leidenmüller. Heinrich. But we call him Leichenmüller because that's what he looks like. Thin, pale, hollow cheeks, feverish eyes, and—because the devil wants it that way—the best layout man we've ever had. Another whiskey, please."

"Yes, Herr Roland," said Lucie, looking absolutely miserable.

She spilled some Chivas while filling my glass; her hand was trembling as if she was the one who was drunk. But it was only unhappiness.

"An impotent man," I said.

"Who?"

"This Leichenmüller, our top layout man. And a typical good citizen. Backbone of the nation. Married. Two children. But at irregular intervals he's overcome by a dark hunger for whores, and disappears . . . for two days, three. Always when he's needed most. He's evidently been out since Friday afternoon and our editor-in-chief is having a fit. Fortunately he prefers Tutti to any of the other girls. I mean Leichenmüller now, not Lester. A long time ago I promised Frau Leidenmüller—when I was drunk, of course—that I'd keep an eye on her husband. That's why I asked the girls or their pimps to call me when he goes crazy. Then I keep having to find new ways to threaten him, and he always comes back. In all other respects he's the nicest fellow in the world. Thank God, he's with Tutti, who knows me."

Lucie put a fresh whiskey and soda in front of me. "Don't look so mad," I said.

"I'm not mad, Herr Roland."

The jackal was going away, fading like the noise in the street. I began to feel better.

"And Leichenmüller is paid well," I continued. "There are very few of them around—exceptionally gifted graphics artists and layout men like him—and all of them are a little crazy one way or another. But Leichenmüller's really top-drawer. And now, just to make things easier for you, Fräulein Lucie, why don't you bring me my bottle?" and I gave the girl who was so much in love with me my most charming smile. "And some ice and soda, and I won't have to bother you again."

"The—the whole bottle?" she stammered.

"Yes. I won't drink it all."

"If that's what you want," said Lucie, and hurried off.

Lucie came back and put my precious bottle of Chivas down on the table in front of me with a bang. Now she *was* mad. So what! I had my bottle; I drank and looked into the mirror and grimaced with revulsion as it occurred to me that I'd been writing the crappy sex series for three and a half years. At first it had actually been fun. Then the circulation began to go up like crazy because of it, and then it wasn't fun anymore. Then it was suddenly a deadly serious thing, praised to the skies by everybody, astonishing everybody, and there was no end to it in sight!

Once, when I said I didn't want to write such shit anymore, Lester had offered me more money. Lester knew his man. I took the money and went on writing. But in the long run there was no profit in it for me. Since Lester had become the boss, I had to knock myself out all the time, with girls or whiskey or roulette. Until now I seemed able to take it, but I couldn't go on like this forever. I'd been living the last seven years in a state of constant partial anesthesia. Only two people knew why: myself and Paul Kramer, because once I had told him, "I shudder to think of the moment when I'm totally out of whiskey and girls. Can you understand that?"

"Yes, my boy. Perfectly," he had said. Fantastic man, pick of the crop.

This drinking in the morning had more than one reason. Editor-in-chief Lester had installed a so-called "research department." Here they were supposed to find out what was popular, less popular, not popular. They had wound up with a computer.

You may laugh, you may say I'm lying, but I'm not lying. It's the truth! Everything you read in *Blitz*, the pictures you look at, the style, the content, the subject matter, the color—all decoded by computer!

8

This computer was fed with the results of the research of a Public Opinion Institute. A certain Erhard Stahlhut was head of our research department, a friend of Lester's, a student of mathematics who hadn't made the grade. Incidentally, this Public Opinion Institute belonged to Lester's brother-in-law. In this way everything stayed in the family.

The computer reports—which, strangely enough, always seemed to coincide with what publisher Herford had in mind—had meanwhile become a Holy Bible for him. Dark green and the index number one hundred stood for the *ne plus ultra* in positive reaction that the computer could compute. This ideal evaluation had never been reached. My series, with ninety-two, was the top rating so far. The worst color was red, index number one. In between there were all sorts of shades from red to green, and in accordance with them, the numbers one to a hundred. Who dared to say anything against the computer? No one. But everybody cursed the damned thing.

When Stahlhut had started, he told Herford, "Anyone publishing a successful magazine must have his finger on the pulse of the masses. Polls aren't enough. Nothing should be printed unless we know as nearly as possible *and in advance* that the masses are going to accept it."

And Herford had asked, "But how are we going to find that out in advance?" And Herr Stahlhut had replied, "No problem! We have enough representatives of the masses right here in the house. The ideal audience. I suggest we have them read what we intend to print—every installment, novel, articles, everything. Let them voice their opinion. Their opinion is the voice of the people. To hell with the intellectuals. They don't have any use for our magazine anyway. Our workers, our employees—they're the ones! Let them tell us how they like it and what they don't like, *before* we print it! And let the writers write accordingly."

This pearl of an idea bowled over publisher and editor-in-chief. They were speechless with admiration. The first reading of this kind took place the following week. The audience was men because it was a male-oriented story. The next reading, a romantic novel, included women. When the material wasn't exclusively male-oriented, women were always present because it was mainly women who bought and read the illustrated magazines. And for seven years now, the house had stuck to this method. Everything was read aloud; no writer escaped, not even a foreign writer who had written a best seller for which *Blitz* had paid through the nose.

And when it was my turn?

I had always had a gift for writing for women, and this sex series was directed at women. Of course my articles were read aloud. And that was why I came over here to the Kniefall Market bar whenever I'd handed in an article. Here was where I waited while my latest production was passing through the "voice of the people" mill.

9

"That business about oral sex, that's got to be clearer," said cleaning-woman Wassler. "There's too much beating about the bush. 'Frenching' doesn't tell me a thing. I think Herr Roland should describe it more precisely. No Latin and foreign words!"

"I think he's plenty precise!" cried a young woman from the bookkeeping department.

General protest.

Frau Wassler: "He doesn't write clearly enough. He didn't in the last number. I let my husband read it, and he didn't know what Herr Roland was talking about!"

Her colleague, Reincke, who was also ill-humored, said angrily, "You're dumb, Bertha. That's what's wrong with you. Your old man understands every word; he just pretends he doesn't. He doesn't want to understand."

This shook Frau Wassler. "Do you think so? But we have four children."

"So there you are—that's why!"

The air in the conference room was blue with cigarette smoke. My judges were seated around a long conference table— cleaning woman, typists, bookkeepers, cooks, waitresses: twenty-seven girls and women in all, and a twenty-eighth at the head of the table, one of the few women editors with *Blitz*—Angela Flanders.

Angela Flanders was fifty-four, always beautifully groomed and elegantly dressed. She had been a journalist for a quarter of a century, first with a daily paper, then with an illustrated paper, for ten years now with *Blitz*. She told me all about the conference later.

The women had their coffee in front of them; many were smoking. Packs of cigarettes lay around. Every woman had a pad and pencil. They were seated according to their profession— telephone operators with telephone operators, typists with typists, and so on. Angela Flanders had tried several times to break things up, in vain. The ones who knew each other wanted to sit together.

Now Angela Flanders rapped on the table with her pencil. "Ladies, has anyone anything more to say?"

A gray, mousy little creature from the canteen kitchen raised a hesitant hand.

"Frau Eggert?"

Frau Eggert could scarcely be heard. "Well—well—" she stammered, "there's a reference...but it doesn't really come clear in this article—and after all, for us women everything depends on—"

"What are you driving at, Frau Eggert? Don't be embarrassed. We're just women among ourselves, and I don't tell a soul who said what."

Frau Eggert started again. "Well, you see—I think it should be stated clearly just once that men—that the men should stick it out—I mean, should go on until—until—"

General agreement. Angela Flanders took everything down in shorthand. Frau Eggert, encouraged by her success, went on, "Especially because in the last article we were advised to take estrogen."

Applause.

"And now a lot of us do, and you know what that does to us...."

Frau Reincke, wearing a bandanna: "Makes us give in easier, but it don't do nothing for an orgasm. Don't come no faster."

A certain liveliness now swept through the group, and Angela Flanders had trouble keeping up with the women.

A fat cook: "Haven't they found anything yet, Frau Flanders, that'll make the man last longer?"

"Of course there are ways...."

"Then the article should tell about them, give the names...."

"Yes, yes...give us the names."

"What the things are called!"

"I've made a note of it, ladies. Please go on."

A painfully thin secretary of about forty: "I've made a note here...titi—titillate the vulva...In this case he's talking about the Empress Maria Theresa. But that bit's much too short."

"That's right!" cried one of the bookkeepers.

"You see, even an Empress needed it. So women like us should have it explained properly, how this titillation's supposed to take place."

"That's right!"

More coffee poured, more cigarettes lit. Frau Reincke took

over energetically. "Speaking basically, now, Frau Flanders—yes? Not a word against Herr Roland. It's terrific that we're at last getting some real information. There can't be too much of it. But when you take a good look at this series, it's written for the men. Don't misunderstand me, please. The thing is—I'm all for the men getting a load of this kinda stuff, so's they get the general idea of what their duties to us are."

Cries of bravo.

"But!" Reincke raised a silencing hand. "*We're* the ones who read it! Our men—they may take a look at the photos when the girl don't have any clothes on, but none of them take anything Herr Roland writes to heart. I know all about that from my own lousy experiences." Applause. She raised her voice above it. "Nine years ago, when we got married, I was a virgin. Not the foggiest idea about the whole thing. Didn't get anything out of it either. And today? Nothing's changed. . . . In, out, dissatisfied."

"I beg your pardon?" Angela Flanders was confused. "What did you say?"

"You know what she means," said one of the bookkeepers. "Herr Reincke has his fun without any preliminaries, and Frau Reincke gets all excited but no satisfaction."

"I see."

"That's it!" (Frau Reincke.)

"And that's the way it is with me," cried one of the mailroom employees who had fled from the Warthegau district as a child, in 1946. "My guy keeps telling me it's my fault. The boob tells me, 'You're getting nervous, Minka, but in your case it's a delayed orgasm.'" Nervousness in the audience. "Says he knows all about it: A medical student explained it to him. Now I'm asking you, what's a 'delayed orgasm'? Either I come or I don't. And Herr Roland should explain this to us."

"That's how I feel about it," said one of the mailroom clerks. "My husband just makes things easy for himself with that sort of attitude. All he cares about is getting his. He doesn't give a damn about me. But I'm not as quick as he is. I'm no rabbit. I need time, like all the rest of us. Am I right, ladies?"

"You bet!"

"And that's why," Reincke concluded, "the whole series—you'll pardon my saying so—ain't right in its approach. It tells all the time what the man should do to make his wife happy. But does he do it? No! He don't even bother to read it, and if he does read it, he don't do it. Much too conceited for anything like that.

And that's why," Reincke went on, louder now above the applause of her colleagues, "and that's why Herr Roland should write on what we *women* should do to get our Heinis going!"

"That's right!"

"That's the way I feel about it!"

"And," Reincke went on, "then we women would know what to do to get our guys stirred up. I mean, in this series we should be told what *we* have to do, so that the men do the things Herr Roland is telling them to do. Because we've got to be the ones to get the ball rolling—titters—or nuthin's ever going to happen! Herr Roland should write about the men and how to titi—how to titillate *him!* A lot more about that. So that he can do the right thing by us when we've finally got *him* going. And that's especially important for women who've been married a long time, because it's all old stuff for them. I'm telling you, Frau Flanders, it's the older ones that read the stuff."

"You have a point there," said Angela Flanders.

A pale videotape employee said, "You're mistaken, Frau Reincke. We young married women have our problems, too. Don't think for a moment that things are so all right with us."

"You see, Frau Flanders," said Reincke, "what I said is good for all marriages, old and young."

A jolly little twenty-one-year-old, gorgeously built girl from the news department piped up. "I don't know what's the matter with all of you. Except for a few times, I've always gotten what I wanted out of it. I—"

"*You?*"

"We know all about that. You tell us every time."

"I'm good and sick of it," cried Reincke.

A secretary from the science editorial department said, "The young lady is evidently a biological miracle!"

"Ladies! Ladies!" cried Angela Flanders energetically. "Let's move on."

But Reincke was too indignant to move on. She leaned across the table and barked at the biological miracle. "So let us in on your secret!"

"It's absolutely no secret," said she coolly. "My Uwe goes on as long as I want him to, then he asks if I've had enough, and I say, 'Yes, Uwe, you can stop now,' and he does."

Reincke's jaw fell open, for a moment she was struck dumb, then she recovered and said, "How about switching for a while, Frau Schönbein?"

"That would suit you, wouldn't it?"

"Oh, the fuck with it!" cried Reincke. "I've just about had it with your miracle penis!"

Angela Flanders was afraid the women might start fighting, and she pounded on the table with her fist. "Ladies! Please!" Whereupon a young woman from personnel began to cry bitterly. "What is it? What's the matter?" stammered Flanders. "Why are you crying, Frau—"

"Westphal," sobbed the weeping young woman.

"Frau Westphal."

"Fräulein!"

"What's the matter, Fräulein Westphal?"

Still weeping, the woman stammered, "I—I can't stand any more of this. Please, may I be excused from future meetings?"

"But, why?"

"What's the matter with you?"

"These meetings are terribly interesting."

Reincke asked, "Have you ever had sex with a man?"

"With *a* man?" sobbed Westphal. "With many men! But never felt a thing. And they were all ages. But I've never had an organism."

"She means 'orgasm,'" Reincke explained benevolently, and turned to Angela Flanders. "And that's to go in, too," she said energetically.

"What's to go in, too?"

"Emotional trauma," said Reincke. She turned to the young woman from personnel. "Were you ever raped?"

"Yes," sobbed Westphal. "Brutally."

Reincke was triumphant. "You see? What did I tell you? Emotional trauma. That's got to go in. That's—"

"I've made a note of it," said Angela Flanders.

"A Russian?" asked Reincke, herself filled with dire memories.

"No . . . Ami."

"That's funny."

One of the switchboard operators raised her hand. "Yes?" said Angela Flanders.

"I've been wanting to draw your attention to this for some time, and in this last article I see that there are again a few sentences that could make you laugh. I'm saying this because last Sunday my husband was reading Herr Roland's article, and he laughed so hard that he didn't have an erection that night, and that was what the article was all about! And after I'd told him, 'This one you've got to read!'"

Now everybody was talking at once. Everybody agreed that the articles had to be absolutely serious. "Please take care of it, Frau Flanders. And there are a few places in this article that could be held up to ridicule."

A young lady from bookkeeping: "My husband read the article about the erection and he didn't laugh. It had quite the opposite effect on him."

A packer asked suspiciously, "How long have you been married?"

"Six months."

Ribald laughter.

Another packer: "Wait till you've been married eighteen years! After eighteen years ... Jeesus!"

Reincke said with emphasis, "So there you are, just as I said. The whole series had got to be turned around. We women must know what makes the *men* horny. More about what the men need, or Herr Roland's just casting pearls before the swine!"

10

By the time we arrived at Eppendorfer Baum the storm had assumed hurricane proportions. It almost threw Irina as she got out of the car. I had to hold her. She hooked her arm in mine and clung to me. I could see she was afraid, which wasn't surprising after what had happened twenty minutes before. The storm had blown away all the sawdust on the pavement and somebody had forgotten to wash away the blood.

Poor Conny. I hoped he'd pull through. The hospital hadn't called Edith while we were there and we had finally left her in her despair, with Conny's whiskey. I hoped she'd get drunk; it would soften the blow if something more were to happen to Conny, or anything else. I was expecting more disasters.

Irina and I leaned into the wind and fought our way to number 187. We were the only people on the street. My watch read 1:55. To the right of the front door I could see the window display and entrance to the antique shop, mainly pieces from the Far East, beautiful pieces. The window was lit up. *André Garnot, Antiques,* was printed on the glass door in gold lettering. To the left of the door there was a boutique, but that window was dark and I couldn't see a sign with the name of the owner, only a button with a small plate above it: Stanislav Kubinsky, Superintendent.

I rang. I waited. I rang again. Nothing stirred.

"They're asleep already," said Irina. She was very excited.

I rang again. This time I didn't take my finger off the bell. My other hand was in the pocket of my coat, holding onto a twenty-mark bill. It touched something cold. Conny's Colt .45. I had taken it away from Edith to prevent her doing anything stupid with it and because at that point I wanted a weapon. It was loaded.

We had managed to calm poor Edith down, to some extent. We had called the hospital, and a doctor on night duty had told us Conny's condition was fair, but it was still too early to say anything definite. It could be hours before that would be possible. Edith promised to let nobody in except us, and to stay home until we got back unless the hospital called her, in which case she should be sure to call back to find out if it had really been the hospital. Then we had gone off—Irina, Bertie, and I. I had driven directly to the main station, where people were still hurrying to their trains and a few drunks were sleeping on benches. There I went to the telephone booth from which you could dial Frankfurt. I had changed a lot of one-mark pieces at a ticket counter. Bertie and Irina waited outside in the car. Irina had protested. *When* were we going to drive to Eppendorfer Baum and Jan Bilka? But I had to talk to Hem, and after what had happened to Conny, I didn't feel that his phone was safe, nor his teletype.

It was hot in the booth. After getting out of the car I had unlocked the trunk and taken one of the three bottles of Chivas I always took with me, and filled my flask. Now, after dialing Hem's number, I took a couple of swigs. The booth smelled of perfume and urine. I got very hot, but I didn't get around to opening the door because just then Hem answered. He hadn't gone to bed yet, he was wide awake. I told him everything that had happened. Now Hem was caught.

"Boy, Walter, if this keeps up we have *the* story!"

"That's what I think."

The smell of urine was stronger than the perfume. I took another swallow because the smell was making me feel sick.

"I called the night editor right away, and the photo editor, and I talked to Lester and Herford. I'm sure we can fill three pages, at least three, with advance publicity and photos. You have the releases?"

"Of course." My voice rose. "And when we're ready to go, I write the story *under my name!*"

"Of course, Walter. Don't yell."

"I'm excited. This is the first story in years that I've *got* to write under my own name. I'm not letting anyone else have it!"

"Nobody else is going to get it, I promise you. So shut up! We can set up the three, perhaps four pages by noon, but we'll need Bertie's photos as soon as possible."

"I'll send him right off to Fuhlsbüttel; then the first plane can take the films. You'll have them in Frankfurt by eight."

"Good. Tell Bertie to address them to us, general delivery, Frankfurt airport. We'll send a messenger. That'll be faster. We'll need a short opening by you—one page should do it—and the captions for the photos. By ten."

"You'll have them."

"And you'll call me again if anything new comes up. I'll have the phone by my bed. And, Walter—"

"Yes?"

"Don't let the girl get away."

"I'm seeing to that."

"Where are you going to spend the night?"

"I think I'll go to the Metropole." It was Hamburg's most luxurious hotel. I always stayed there.

"Call me when you get there."

"Yes, Hem."

"Have Bertie get the files on Karl Concon to you. They must have arrived in Fuhlsbüttel a while ago."

"I'll tell him."

"Where are you off to now?"

"Michelsen. The girl wants to get to her fiancé. She's pretty frantic."

"Then drive there. But don't leave her there, not under any circumstances."

"Hm."

"What do you mean, hm?"

"How am I supposed to do that, Hem? If he's really her fiancé

143

and wants her to stay with him and she doesn't want to leave him—"

"Rot!" said Hem. "The girl's the key. I can feel it, the key to everything. We must not lose her."

"But how—?"

"You threaten her with the police. If worse comes to worst, you tell her you'll notify the police as to her whereabouts and she'll be sent back to the camp."

"That might do it."

"Of course it'll do it. Bilka will be sensible and let her go. He can see her anytime he likes. Do you have her release?"

"Not yet."

"Damn it—why not?"

"Because I haven't had a chance, damn it! The girl's a nervous wreck!"

"Don't shout!"

"You're shouting, too."

"Because I'm so excited."

"So what about me? The first story in years, the first story I can put my name under without feeling ashamed!"

"Yes, yes. But first *have* your story! Now listen to me, Walter. This is very important. Bertie surely knows a few VIPs at police headquarters in Hamburg."

"Sure. Why?"

"As soon as you've taken the girl to the hotel, one of you goes to headquarters and tells the whole story. That you're there with the girl and where you are and why..."

"But that's—"

"That's what? Crazy? It would be crazy if you didn't do it. They're looking for you ever since the girl disappeared. Do you want to wait till they nab all three of you?"

"No, of course not."

"So there you are. I think it would be best if you went to whatever man Bertie tells you to contact. He should call him first."

"And if the guy isn't there?"

"Idiot! Bertie asks to speak to him. Says it's important. Big thing! Which it is. He gets the man's private number, calls him, tells him everything. So you get a friendly reception at headquarters. You show your identification. You tell him you'll be responsible—no, you tell him that *Blitz* is willing to take the responsibility for the girl. You have power of attorney. They can

144

call the house anytime to verify. If they want security, we'll wire the money. You pay it if you have enough. But this has to be settled or you'll mess up everything. We need the police on *our* side. If you go on driving around in that car of yours, they'll get you anyway."

That was right. "That's something I hadn't thought of."

"So," said Hem. "And now something equally important. Do you have enough change?"

"Why?"

"I've been thinking about what you told me, and I want you to go at this assignment with a certain approach. In order to explain what I mean, I need time. So?"

"I have about twenty coins left."

"Good. Now . . . the main character in this story, as far as I'm concerned, is Fräulein Louise."

"Well, now—"

"Let me go on!" Hem sounded quite fierce. I'd never heard him talk so sharply. But immediately he was calm again. "Fräulein Louise. Schizophrenic, no?"

"Yes. A mental case. A woman with a sick brain."

"Aha!" said Hem. "With a sick brain. And what do you depend on in your work, Walter? On your brain. Or am I wrong?"

"I depend on what I see and hear, and on my instinct."

Hem said, "Instinct, seeing, hearing—it all hangs together with the brain, wouldn't you say? All the impressions you get."

"What are you driving at?" I asked. "Of course it all hangs together with—"

"The brain. Yes," said Hem. "And now you're in for a surprise. I'm going to tell you a few things I'm sure you never expected to hear from me. But it's my opinion, since I've done some reading on the subject, and I'd like you to share it with me on this particular assignment. You see, our brain isn't simply a switch for our responses and reactions."

"Well, well," I said.

"Well, it isn't. Ask an expert. The brain is something quite different. It's a highly intricately constructed calculator. All this talk about the electronic brain has to be taken seriously."

"Aha! You mean the brain is a computer. That old story."

"Yes. That old story," he said. "Don't forget to throw in a coin." I did so.

Meanwhile, a drama was developing in front of my booth. A little man, conventionally dressed, definitely middle class, came

145

from the direction of the stairs that led from the trains with a pretty, much younger woman, flashily dressed, on his arm. The woman's hair was black, obviously dyed, and she was wearing a mink coat. She had a coarse, exciting face. The man seemed to be crazy about her. They had just stopped to kiss—she had to bend down to him—when another woman, a faded blond, plump, wearing a cloth coat, came storming out of the booth next to mine, rushed up to the pair, and tore them apart. She yelled so loudly I could hear her in my booth with the door closed:

"So I've caught you at last, you louse! Not going to get back from Munich until tomorrow morning, is that so?"

"Magda, please!" cried the little man, looking scared to death as he stepped back.

"I've been on your trail long enough, you bastard!" screamed Magda. "And now I've got you. And your whore!"

"*What did you say?*" cried the woman in mink.

"Whore! That's what I said," cried Magda. "A filthy, miserable whore who carries on with a married man!"

A few people stopped, amused. "What's going on out there?" asked Hem.

"Two women fighting over a man. Marital tragedy. Go on, Hem."

"A computer, Walter, just as you said. And that's what you've got to keep in mind all the time as you go after this story. In this case, it's terribly important."

"So what about the computer?" I asked. "Especially since in the case of our schizophrenic friend it seems to have broken down."

The people standing around the two women were laughing and applauding, directly in front of my booth now. The little man tried to get between the two women, but they shoved him aside. "You keep out of it, you fink!" cried his wife.

"That's what I want to explain to you," said Hem. "And don't be in such a rush to say the computer's broken down. We still can only barely imagine what the brain really is, it's that intricately constructed. You can't cease to be astounded when you read what we know about it, Walter."

"Say that again, you old bag! Just you dare say that again!" cried the woman in mink, and the blond went for her screaming, "Bitch! Bitch!" and grabbed the woman in mink by her black hair. The little man stood on one side, looking absolutely miserable.

146

"And therefore it's not surprising," said Hem, "that people are constantly talking and writing about the miracle of the human brain."

"You say 'miracle' so contemptuously," I said. Another coin.

"I know."

"Why?"

"I'm just getting around to that. So . . . in the cerebrum and cerebellum, we have, roughly speaking, ten billion nerve cells, three times as many as there are human beings on this earth, and a thousand times the storage elements of a giant computer, and all this in our little skulls, connected a million times over. . . ."

The woman in mink punched Magda in the chest; Magda reeled back, her hands still gripping her rival's black hair. As she was thrown back, she took the hair with her. The woman in mink had been wearing a wig. Now her oily brown hair was exposed. Applause from the gallery!

As the woman in mink burst into tears, the wife triumphed, not exactly elegantly. "So that's what you look like, you whore!"

"In the optic nerve alone a million nerve fibers conduct the impulses to the optic center." Hem's voice. "Things must be really jolly outside your booth."

"I'll say they are!"

With a wild whoop, the whore charged and Magda went down. The two women rolled over and over on the dirty floor. The little man jumped up and down helplessly and wrung his hands.

"They're beating each other up," I said.

Hem said, "Billions of cells connected directly or indirectly by billions of nerve fibers. If you want to compare this with a computer, then we would have a skyscraper on the top of our necks instead of a head. But no—in our case a brain, weighing two and a half pounds, does it all. And that's a miracle, right? Makes a terrific impression on you, doesn't it? Makes you believe in God, no?"

"Yes."

The women had fought their way, kicking and screaming, to my booth. Magda's nose was bleeding—the whore was the stronger one. She rose, knelt beside her victim, and began punching her face. Magda yelled for help, her pitiful little husband did, too. The black wig lay in the dust. I threw another coin into the slot.

Hem said, "And now pay attention! This miracle of a brain,

147

the greatest miracle on earth—there you have my article of faith—is nothing more than a ridiculous little nothing when compared with the infinite cosmos and the idea of infinity, which none of us can grasp."

"*What?*"

The whore was punching Magda in the mouth. A few people shouted for the police. The husband was weeping.

"A ridiculous nothing—yes. And ridiculously simple when compared with infinity and the endlessness of the space in which we live, on one star among millions of stars! If you try drawing this comparison, you'll soon have to admit that this miracle, this brain of ours, explains pitifully little about any of these incomprehensible aspects of the universe and creation—in fact, can't grasp them at all!"

Two policemen came running. They tried to separate the two women, at first taking plenty of abuse themselves. The little man was screaming, "Magda . . . Lilo! Lilo . . . Magda! Stop! Please stop!"

"And why should ours, of all the planets, be the one with the most highly developed living creatures? Ha? Who says so? Wouldn't you say this was the crassest arrogance? Try to imagine any star in the Milky Way, and imagine sensible creatures on it that have brains that would make ours look primitive. The people on that star, or on any other star, may possibly have brains with a grasp so broad that they can see and *anticipate* and *relive* things of which we have no idea whatsoever, which we can't even visualize! Can you follow me?"

"Yes," I said, and threw in another coin.

One of the policemen had separated the two women. They were still fighting each other, but now only verbally. "Why are you telling me all this in the middle of the night?"

"You'll see in a minute," said Hem. "I can imagine creatures somewhere out in infinite space, with brains in which our earthly conceptions of time, I mean now the chronological passage of time—the it-was, it-will-be—don't exist! These creatures experience all creation *at the same time!* With them, Homer can exist beside Hitler, Ikhnaton beside Einstein. And those who died long ago are still alive, together with those not yet born. These people have an outlook we can never have. They can see the interrelationship of all things—they can see the past, the future, and the present, all at the same time! Thus they can detach themselves from our rationalism and materialism!"

The two women, exhausted at last, looked like tattered shrews, their clothing torn. The policemen led them away, the husband trotted behind them, docile to the end.

"Perhaps," said Hem, "perhaps schizophrenics have brains like that. Your Fräulein Louise may be one of them. What do we know about schizophrenia? Nothing much. Only that the notions of a schizoid person often include religious ideas, as in the case of Fräulein Louise."

"You're trying to tell me that what she experiences is the truth, and what I experience, what all of us are experiencing, is not?"

"It's possible, Walter. It's possible. And I want you to keep this in mind constantly while you're on this job." The crowd was dispersing. One of the policemen came running back, picked up Lilo's black wig, and ran off again. "Many mentally ill persons produce so-called philosophemes—detached philosophical propositions. This feeling of *déjà-vu*, of hindsight and foresight and clairvoyance, which evidences itself so frequently in schizophrenics, in their predictions—all this may be evidence that their brains are infinitely finer and capable of thinking on a grandiose scale, compared with the brains of us so-called normal people."

"*Donnerwetter!*" I cried. "And this from you?"

"Yes," he said, "and this from you. I think it's a case of maturing. Twenty years ago I wouldn't have thought like this either. The power of the church is over, after all the things they've done. Next year the Americans are going to try to put a man on the moon, and the Pope will see the moon on television and pray for the astronauts up there, so they say. Isn't that the bloody end?"

I threw in another coin. It was quiet now in the station. "If the Amis really manage to get on the moon and all goes well—in the face of infinity, or as observed by the brain of a creature on such a Milky Way star, a brain that may register things a billion times more accurately than ours, this American outing to the moon will mean nothing more than—than, for instance, Muller's goal against the Albanians in the soccer match this afternoon. That's all. What we do—what happens on this earth—is vanity, trivial and stupid in the eyes of the brain I can imagine and, quite possibly, in the brain of a schizophrenic person. Who can tell if her brain isn't experiencing life as it *really* is. One thing's for sure—*we don't!*"

"You're trying to tell me that since there actually is a Pole living in that house on Eppendorfer Baum, and a Frenchman with asthma, and taking into consideration that Fräulein Louise counts an asthmatic Frenchman and a Pole among her dead friends—you don't consider this pure coincidence?"

"That's exactly what I'm driving at, Walter," said Hem. The light went on. I threw in another coin. "And that's what I want you to keep in mind constantly! Don't depend too entirely on your brain alone. Deal with the possibility that everything I've just said to you *may* be valid. You know I'm not a churchgoer, but you also know that in my opinion the only thing mankind down here has created, the only positive and truly great thing, is our religions. No matter which one. I grow more sure of that all the time. And the religions are so great because they divert us from the materialism and rationalism that control our world today and leave us able to grasp only the most primitive truths. They lead us away from all this, Walter, away and *up*—who knows, someday perhaps to those creatures with the truly remarkable brains."

"Like the one in Fräulein Louise's head."

"Yes," Hem said slowly. "Like the one in Fräulein Louise's head. Perhaps. I know these are positively criminal speculations to be coming from a newspaper man who's encouraging you to go after a great story, but I simply had to tell you all this. You understand me, don't you?"

"Yes, Hem," I said. "I'll keep it in mind constantly."

"But without going overboard!" he added quickly. "Don't get me wrong. Of course Fräulein Louise is a mental case, according to our standards. And you're writing with *your* brain, for brains like yours and mine. So it would be disaster for your story if you were to portray Fräulein Louise as anything but schizophrenic, or describe her experiences as anything but those of a schizophrenic person. As visionary aberrations. What I would like is for you to manage somehow to undermine, just a little, our smug certainty that we always know how to differentiate between madness and sanity, just enough to make people give it a little thought. You understand?"

"Yes. I understand, Hem. 'Bye now. See you soon."

"Yes, see you soon, my boy," said Hem.

Walking through the waiting room, I took a liberal swallow out of my flask. I went over to my car in the big lot, which by now was completely deserted, and told Bertie to get out, with all his films. He stuck them into one of the padded envelopes we always used, and got out of the car. Irina looked at me anxiously. "I'll be right back," I told her. "I'll just see Bertie to a taxi." I didn't want to make her more nervous with what I had to tell Bertie. After all, I didn't have a release from her yet.

Bertie and I struggled against the wind to the single taxi that was parked at the entrance to the lot. As we walked along, I yelled Bertie's instructions to him. "And when you've done that, come straight to Eppendorfer Baum 187. We'll wait for you," I shouted.

"A-OK, my friend," Bertie shouted back. He was smiling as he got into the taxi. I heard him tell the driver, "To the airport," and the taxi drove off. Before I even had time to turn around I could hear Irina's scream, carried by the wind. "Herr Roland!"

I turned around and froze.

There was a man at the wheel of the Lamborghini. The headlights went on, the car backed to make the necessary turn, and I ran—no, I flew—because now I had the wind behind me. The Lamborghini made a U-turn, the driver shifted gears, and the car began to move in my direction. "Herr Roland! Herr Roland! Help!" screamed Irina.

I reached the car. The window on the driver's side was down. The man behind the wheel was blond and had on a blue sailor's cap. He tried desperately to push me away, in the course of which he briefly looked at me. He was quite evidently a sailor and he stank to high heaven of schnapps. How had this drunk got into my car? He must have done so in the few seconds it had taken to get Bertie to the taxi.

I took the Colt .45 out of my pocket and pushed the barrel against the sailor's temple and yelled, "Stop or I'll shoot." This worked: He took his foot off the gas—I had been running alongside the car, which by now was moving fairly fast. "Turn off the motor!" He did, and Irina was thrown forward against the padded dashboard. She didn't move. She must have hit her head hard and fainted.

The car stood still. Not a soul in sight. I had the Colt aimed at the man's head. "Get out!"

He didn't move.

I grabbed his sleeve in an effort to yank him out of the car, and the sleeve tore at the shoulder. I pointed the gun at his temple again and said, "Out, or I shoot!"

The door opened suddenly, knocking me back, and the man jumped out of the car. He was a giant! A monster! And he was anything but drunk. He took advantage of my surprise and struck my hand from below. I had to drop the Colt. Then he flew at me and his huge hands were around my throat. He didn't utter a word as his hands tightened. I realized it was his intention to kill me. Everything around me began to spin. I couldn't breathe. I raised my left knee and kicked the sailor as hard as I could in the genitals. He screamed and sank to his knees.

I could breathe again, saw the Colt, ran over and picked it up and tore back to the sailor. He was lying on the ground, his face distorted with pain, clutching his crotch. He tried to grab my right leg. I stepped as hard as I could on his hand, then I kicked him in the stomach. He rolled over and vomited.

At last I saw people. They had jumped out of a car that had stopped and were fighting their way to me against the wind. Three men. All I could think was: Get out of here, fast!

I ran to the Lamborghini, jumped behind the wheel, started the car, stepped on the gas pedal, and the car shot forward. Then I noticed that Irina was sitting up, holding her head.

I made the turn out of the lot on two wheels. Irina screamed. I paid no attention to her. My tires screeching, I turned into Glockengiesserwall, crossed the Lombardsbrücke to the Esplanade, and drove from there to the Stephansplatz subway station, keeping my eye on the rearview mirror. I wasn't being followed, but I couldn't shake my fear. At the subway station I turned right and drove like a madman to the Dammtor Station, up and across Theodor-Heuss Platz, a short distance on the Rothenbaumchaussee, and at last stopped the car.

"What—what happened?" Irina stammered.

"That's what I'd like to know. How did the guy get into the car?"

"Suddenly he was sitting there. Didn't say a word. I wanted to jump out, but he'd already started the car. You left the key in it. He was a drunken sailor—"

"He was no drunken sailor, not that guy!"

"So what did he want?"

"To drive away with you."

"With me? You mean kidnap me? Herr Roland . . . what's going on here?"

"I wish I knew. How's your head?"

"It hurts, but it's getting better. I passed out, didn't I?"

"Looks like it. Let's see." I switched on the light inside the car and took a look at Irina's forehead.

"Is there a bump?"

"I don't see anything." But then I did see something. A piece of material was lying on the floor between the pedals. I must have torn it out of the sailor's sleeve, I thought, as I bent down to pick it up. A rectangle, red embroidery with a blue cross appliqued across it lengthwise. The cross was outlined in white. "That—that's a flag," said Irina. "A little flag."

"Yes," I said. It looked like a sleeve emblem.

The wind was still raging outside, making a dreadful noise. "What country do you suppose it represents?"

"Norway," I said. Suddenly I had to think of what Hem had said over the phone, and I felt cold.

"Norway?" Irina whispered, her eyes wide.

"Yes," I said. "Norway," and noticed that my hands were shaking. Quick... my flask. I took a big swallow. "Me, too, please," Irina said softly. I give her the flask. She drank and looked out the window. "Norway," she whispered.

11

At last the light was turned on behind the front door. A shadow on the opaque glass, huge at first, then growing smaller as the figure neared the door. One of the glass panels opened. An old man, wearing glasses, with a fringe of thin gray hair growing around his bald head, stood framed in it.

"'Evening," he said, sounding gruff, yet at the same time afraid. This afternoon's scare was still with him, I thought.

"Good evening, Herr Kubitzky," I said. "I'm sorry that we had to awaken you. We want to see Herr Michelsen."

He was obviously startled at the name. His glasses slipped down his nose; he shoved them up again. He was wearing a thick coat over his pajamas.

"Michelsen?" he said.

"Michelsen. He lives here, doesn't he?"

"I—he—yes. He lives here."

Stanislav Kubitzky spoke with a Polish accent. His face seemed to have shrunk with fear. He was clinging to the metal window frame. "But right now—in the middle of the night—who are you, anyway?"

I handed him my press card. He looked at it. "Herr Walter Roland. Journalist. Oh, dear Jesus!"

I'd had it. I snatched the card out of his hand and shouted, "That's enough! Are you going to open up or not? If not, I'll call the police. They've been here once already today."

That did it. He opened up and let us in. It was very quiet in the hallway. After the noise of the storm outside I felt deaf. "You practically forced me to open up," Kubitzky said miserably.

"Yes."

"If you make trouble for me, I'll report it," he said.

"Sure," I said, and noticed that I was speaking much too loudly.

It was an elegant hall, with marble plaques on the walls, marble stairs, a red carpet, and an old-fashioned wooden elevator in a black iron cage, on cables.

"Where does Herr Michelsen live?"

"Third floor," said Kubitzky, and pocketed the twenty-mark note. "Thank you, sir. You can't miss it. There's only one tenant on each floor. Do you want to take the elevator?"

"Yes."

He walked over to it, opened the mesh metal door, then the sliding door, in the course of which he seemed overcome by fear again. This was one scared old man.

"But you'll tell them upstairs that I didn't want to let you in because it's so late," he begged. "Please."

"I will."

He closed the door, I pressed the button, and the elevator rattled up slowly. Kubitzky was still standing there, watching us ascend. His lips were moving as if in prayer, and I would have liked to know if he was really praying, and what for.

"What is the man afraid of?" asked Irina, who by now was pretty afraid herself.

"Afraid? That man? He isn't afraid of anything," I said. "We just woke him up. He's confused, that's all."

"He's afraid," said Irina.

"No, he's not," I said.

The elevator stopped. I got out first, Irina followed me. The elevator remained where it was. Directly opposite the elevator there was a high, wide double door, and on a brass plate the name: Michelsen. There was a peephole over the plate and

154

beside it, a bell. I rang. The light in the stairwell here didn't go out automatically after a few minutes. It burned on. I found this out when we waited a full ten minutes in front of the high door. During this time I rang again and again.

"Oh, God," said Irina, clutching my hand. "What's going on in here?"

"Nothing," I said grimly.

She hadn't noticed that the metal cover of the peephole had been pushed aside and a human eye was staring at us, a preposterously arrogant eye.

"Come on!" I shouted at the eye. "Get going and open the door, damn it!"

"Would you please express yourself in a more civilized fashion," said the man who went with the eye. His voice was preposterously arrogant, too. "How dare you come ringing at my door at this hour of the night?"

"My name is Roland," I said, forcing myself to calm down and be patient. I took out my press card again and held it up to his eye.

"Journalist?"

"Yes."

"Then please leave. I don't receive journalists at this hour."

"Are you Herr Michelsen?"

"No. So get going."

"I'll do nothing of the sort."

"Then I'll call the police."

"A good idea," I said. "I'd like to have them present anyway when I go in. Especially since you're not Herr Michelsen." He couldn't be Irina's fiancé either, or she would have reacted differently. She was standing there quietly.

"So go on," I said. "Call the police. If you don't *I'll* go downstairs and call them."

I turned to leave and at the same moment heard the door being unlocked and opened. A tall, slim man of about fifty, well-groomed, with black hair and sideburns, a long face, narrow lips and raised eyebrows, stood in the doorway. "Come in, please," he said.

A crystal chandelier was glittering behind him in the hall. The walls were covered with silk, a big Chinese vase was standing on an antique chest. "Who are you?" I asked.

"My name is Notung. Olaf Notung. I am Herr Michelsen's servant."

"Herr Michelsen's *what?*"

"Herr Michelsen's servant," he said. "Don't I speak clearly enough?"

I was astonished. So there were still people who had servants. In an apartment this was unusual. I would have liked to know what sort of a servant Olaf Notung was, what his duties were. "Are those the clothes you wear in service?" I asked.

"No, Herr Roland."

"How come you're still up? Does Herr Michelsen have guests?"

"No, Herr Roland. This is my free afternoon. I was in the city. I met friends and we went to the theater. After that we had drinks in a bar. I just came home half an hour ago." He made a polite gesture with his hand. "Please come in. You must want something. We don't have to talk in the doorway."

I let Irina go first. Notung closed the door behind us. "Shall we go into the salon?" he said, walking on ahead. Even the way he walked was arrogant.

Many doors led from the hall to other rooms. The door Notung opened led into the salon, a room the size of half a tennis court.

"Won't you sit down?" he said. "What can I give you? A drink? Coffee? Tea? Cigarettes? Let me have your coat. I'll—"

"Let's stop all this nonsense," I said.

"I beg your pardon!"

"Where are the others?"

"What others?"

"Herr Michelsen and Herr Bilka."

"I don't understand." His face was expressionless. "Don't you want to sit down?"

"No! You understand very well. I asked you something. So?" I was furious. The fellow exasperated me beyond measure.

"I'm afraid I don't understand you," said Notung. "At least not entirely. Herr Michelsen is away."

"What do you mean?" Irina sounded shocked.

"Away, *gnädiges Fräulein.*"

"Where has he gone? How long is he going to be gone? When did he leave?"

"I don't know. I mean, I don't know where he's gone or how long he is going to be away. He must have left sometime this afternoon, because when I came home, I found this note." He took a piece of paper out of his jacket pocket. In pencil, all in caps, I read, "Dear Olaf. Have to leave at once on business. Shall call tomorrow morning and let you know how long I'll be away. Best. Michelsen." The name was handwritten.

"Does he do this sort of thing often?"

"I beg your pardon?"

"I'm asking—does Herr Michelsen often take off suddenly like this?"

"Yes, he does, sir," Notung replied softly. "Herr Michelsen has a big export-import business. His office is in the Jungfernstieg. He travels a lot."

"Then we would like to speak to Herr Bilka."

"You asked for the gentleman before. That's why I said I didn't understand the question. A Herr Wilka?"

"Bilka," I said. "Jan Bilka."

"I don't know any Jan Bilka," said Notung.

"Don't talk like an idiot!" I yelled, and his eyebrows went up. "Of course you know Jan Bilka. He's a good friend of Herr Michelsen and he lives here."

"I'm dreadfully sorry," Notung said pompously, "but nobody lives here except Herr Michelsen and myself."

Irina's hand flew to her throat as she said, "Do you mean to say you've never seen Jan Bilka?"

"Not only have I never seen a Jan Bilka," said Olaf Notung, "I never even heard of him, *gnädiges Fräulein.*"

12

Irina sank down on the large couch. "I felt something like this was going to happen." Suddenly she began to tremble. I got out my flask.

"Oh, may I—?" Notung started to say.

"Don't trouble yourself," I said, and unscrewed the top of my flask. I leaned over Irina. "Have a drink," I said.

She shook her head. Her face was white, her hands were fists. I was afraid she was going to pass out. "Please," I said.

"I—I don't want to."

"You've got to!" I bent her head back a little and put the flask to her lips. She drank and began to cough. "Another one," I said. "A big one this time." She swallowed a big one and shook herself, but she stopped trembling. "But—but that isn't possible!" she cried. "Bilka lives here. I know he does."

Notung stared at her, then at me, as if he didn't know what to do next. He said, "This has to be a misunderstanding. A most regrettable one. Please, *gnädiges Fräulein*, don't cry."

"I'm not crying," Irina sobbed, the tears rolling down her cheeks. She didn't wipe them away. I handed her my handkerchief.

Notung said, "I can only repeat—nobody lives here besides Herr Michelsen and myself. Nobody ever did. I ought to know. I—"

"Stop!" I cried.

"I beg your pardon."

"You're to stop. In short, you're to shut up. Period!" I took a drink from the flask. "You're lying. You know very well—"

Raising his voice at last, he interrupted me. "I refuse to stand here and be insulted. Please leave the apartment at once!" But I went on. "You know very well that that is a lie. We spoke to Herr Bilka this afternoon, on the phone. And he was here at the time, here in this apartment."

"Impossible!"

"What's your number?" I asked.

"2-2068-54," he answered promptly.

"There you are! That was the number at which we spoke to Herr Bilka!"

"And I am telling you that is impossible. There is—there was no Herr Bilka!"

Irina jumped up. "Tell the truth! Please, please tell the truth! So much depends on it for me. Has something happened to him? Have you been told not to talk about him?"

Notung looked sincerely embarrassed. "You simply must calm down, *gnädiges Fräulein*."

"Calm down? How can I calm down?" she cried. She was trembling again. For years I hadn't felt sorry for anyone but myself. Now suddenly I felt pity for another person, honest and heartfelt pity. Irina was so vulnerable, so young and lost. I thought how the only person in her life right now who could help her was myself. And in me she had found one hell of a guy to lean on!

158

"Herr Bilka is my fiancé! Herr Michelsen is a good friend of his. He visited him often in Prague. And they had agreed that my fiancé should come here after his flight. And I heard his voice this afternoon, coming from this apartment after we had been connected with this number!"

Notung was looking at her dispassionately. To me he said softly, "Shall I call a doctor?"

"You're to keep your mouth shut!" I said.

Irina clung to me suddenly, her panic-stricken face raised to mine. She was stammering. "What do we do now? Herr Roland, please help me. Something terrible has happened to Jan. Please, Herr Roland. . . ."

I stroked her silky hair. "We must go slowly," I said, "but we'll get to the bottom of it, I promise you. But now you've got to pull yourself together."

She nodded, wiped her tears away, and let go of me. "It must be quite clear to you by now," I said, turning to Notung, "that *we* are going to be the ones to call the police."

"That's entirely up to you," Notung said coldly. "As a matter of fact, I beg you to do so. I have no intention of putting up with your insulting behavior a moment longer. *I* shall call the police and bring charges against you for disturbing the peace. I shall—"

"Quiet!" I said, and Notung could feel the barrel of the Colt against his stomach. I was so furious that I acted instinctively when I drew Conny's pistol out of my coat pocket. I realized that this might get me into trouble, but I didn't care. The whole thing stank! Irina's hysteria was the last straw. I didn't give a damn about consequences. That dog had no intention of calling the police.

Notung looked at me. He would have liked to look at me haughtily, but there was fear in his face, great fear. Not only because of the pistol aimed at his stomach, but also for another reason—I could have sworn it!

"What's the meaning of this? Are you crazy? Put that gun away or I'll call for help."

"So call for help."

Two seconds passed. Three. Five. Eight. . . . He didn't call for help. His eyes were slits now. "What do you want from me?" he asked, his voice hoarse and not in the least arrogant any more.

"Turn around," I told him, "and don't forget that I've got you covered. So don't try anything. We shall now go for a little walk."

"Where to?"

"Through the apartment." I gave him a light nudge in the back with his gun. "Get going. First back into the hall, where you'll lock the door and put on the chain." I'd noticed that the door to the outer hall had remained open.

Notung was very quiet now. He locked the door and put the chain across it as I had told him. I left the door to every room open so I would hear if someone tried to leave the apartment.

"Let's start," I said, nudging him again.

We wandered through the entire apartment, seven large rooms and several antechambers. Three bedrooms. All the rooms were decorated in the best taste. It must have cost a small fortune to furnish them. Silk wall coverings everywhere, in different colors, and all the furniture fine old antiques. "And you do all the work yourself," I asked Notung.

"We have a cleaning woman and a cook, but they don't sleep in. On Mondays they only work half a day."

"What are their names?"

"The cleaning woman's name is Marie Gernold, the cook is Elizabeth Kurz. I don't know where they live."

"Of course not," I said, "but that shouldn't be difficult to find out."

"Why do you want to find out?"

"Because they may have seen Herr Bilka."

He had nothing to say to that.

We walked from room to room. I opened drawers, went into walk-in closets. There really wasn't anybody else in the apartment. I emptied drawers on the floor, creating chaos in every room. I had told Irina to watch out for anything that might belong to her fiancé. "And if it's only a cufflink—the smallest thing is enough."

She didn't see or find anything.

In one dressing room the closet door was open. As far as I could see, two or three suits seemed to be missing.

"That's right," said Notung. "The white suitcase Herr Michelsen always uses when he flies is missing, too." I had opened a door in the wall. Behind it there was a small space with many pieces of luggage. Notung looked in a bureau. "Underwear is missing, too. And shoes," he said.

At last we had done the whole round, with no success. No Michelsen, no Bilka. Nobody but Olaf Notung. Finally we were back in the huge salon. "*Now* do you believe me?" asked Notung.

"No," I said.

"If I may be permitted to give you some good advice—"

"Keep your good advice to yourself," I said. "And don't think for a moment that I'm through. I'll be back. And I won't be alone. You can count on that, Herr Notung. And if you have any idea of traveling right now, too, I'd advise you not to do so without informing the police first about where you can be reached. Because it is my intention to go to the police at once and tell them everything that happened here." We had to report to the police—Hem had told us to—so in this case I wasn't even bluffing.

"And I shall also have a thing or two to tell the police," said Notung. But it sounded flat.

I put the gun away. We went back into the hall. Irina was managing to control herself; I could sense how hard she was trying. Notung opened the front door and we walked out into the hall. Nobody said good-bye. The door closed and I could hear it being locked on the inside. I led Irina to the elevator that was still waiting, closed the mesh gate and the sliding door, and pressed the button. The moment the elevator started rumbling down, Irina fell forward, against me. She was weeping, and it sounded as if she would never stop.

I stroked her hair and tried, mechanically, to console her, all nonsense because I hadn't the slightest idea what had happened or what was going to happen next. "Jan!" she sobbed, "Jan! They've done something to him! I know it! I know it!"

"No," I said. "I don't believe it."

Actually I didn't know what to believe. I looked across Irina's shoulder, through the elevator cage, and said, "I'll find him, Irina. I'll clear this thing up and if it's the last thing I do, I'll—"

I didn't finish the sentence, because as we were passing the first floor, I saw a man in a bright silk robe standing in front of the door of his apartment and beckoning to us.

13

André Garnot was a tall, slender man with short gray hair that stood up straight from his scalp like a brush; his face was expressive and he had beautiful eyes under bushy brows. Even in his robe he looked like an aristocrat.

The four of us were seated around a low table in Garnot's apartment—the antique dealer Garnot, the superintendent, Irina, and I. Kubitzky was still wearing his heavy winter coat over his pajamas. He was mumbling to himself in Polish, nervous and afraid, as he had behaved ever since we had met. "This was just the way we thought it would happen," Garnot said, and with a slight accent, when I had finished telling the two men everything we had experienced upstairs with Olaf Notung.

"Just the way," said the little Pole.

"What are you so afraid of?" I asked.

"Of them, up there," said Kubitzky.

"The servant?"

"The servant and this man Michelsen."

"Why are you afraid of them?"

The Frenchman explained. "Herr Michelsen is—well, shall we say, a rather strange man. And the visitors he receives are even stranger."

"Foreigners?"

"Among others," said Garnot. "But many Germans, too. At all hours. It's been upsetting Herr Kubitzky for years. And then sometimes there's shouting up there, so loud you can hear it all the way down here, sometimes in the middle of the night."

"What do they shout?"

"I don't know."

"Why don't you know, if you can hear it all the way down here?"

"They shout at each other in some foreign language or other. Herr Kubitzky and I have never been able to make out which one. It may be in several languages."

"And shots have been fired," said the superintendent, looking at me above his thick glasses.

"When?"

"Several times. Once they dragged somebody away. Two men. They had the third man between them. His legs were lifeless. They shoved him into a car and drove off."

"Didn't you notify the police?"

"Of course," said Garnot. He was holding something in his hand that looked like a silver lipstick.

"And?"

"They questioned us. Then they went upstairs; stayed there

about two hours. Came down again. Didn't say a word. Went away and didn't come back."

"I never heard of such a thing!"

"But that's the way it was," said Garnot, who suddenly looked very pale. "Next day Herr Kubitzky got a phone call. If he ever interfered again with what was going on upstairs, he would end up in a cement tub."

"In a *what?*"

"In a cement tub. The caller explained it to Herr Kubitzky. He would be stuffed into the tub, which would then be filled with cement and dropped into the Elbe. So you can imagine why Herr Kubitzky is afraid. There were several more calls in the same vein. And then, today, the business with the two cars . . . that was obviously murder."

"Are you sure?" I asked.

"Absolutely sure." Suddenly Garnot gripped his chest and groaned.

"What's the matter?" Irina was startled.

Garnot leaned back in his chair, gasping, then he lifted an arm and held the little silver object to his open mouth, and pressed the cap. There was a soft hissing sound. "Asthma," Kubitzky explained in a whisper. "The poor man has asthma. When it storms like this, it's always worse."

The little silver object was an inhaler. Garnot was struggling for breath, his face had turned purple, and his labored breathing rattled in his chest as he sprayed the vial into his mouth. We sat there motionless. The storm was still raging outside. All I could think of was: Asthma. Fräulein Louise's dead French friend . . . asthma. . . .

"You can't help him," Kubitzky said softly. "We must wait until the medicine takes effect."

It didn't take long. Two or three minutes later Garnot's face began to pale again; his breathing became less labored. He put down the spray. "Excuse me," he said. "It's this miserable storm. It affects the bronchial tubes, they clog up, then they tighten. . . ."

"So you can't really breathe," I said.

"Actually," said Garnot, "what I can't do is breathe out properly. When I breathe out, more air than normal is retained in the lungs, so, with the next breath I can't get enough air. But let's not talk about it. It's odious. I apologize. I know you're in a hurry, so I'll tell it fast. The man you are looking for, mademoiselle and monsieur, is about thirty years old?"

"Yes," said Irina.

"Tall? About five-foot-ten?"

"Yes!"

"Blond hair, cut very short—you might say, a military haircut?"

"Yes, yes, yes!" Irina jumped to her feet.

"A long face, looks very strong, tanned, with a scar on his chin."

"That's him!" cried Irina, beside herself now. "That's Jan! Jan Bilka!"

"We didn't know his name," said Kubitzky.

"How is that possible, if he was staying with Michelsen? He must have had to register with the police," I said sharply.

"Yes," said Kubitzky, biting his lip and looking embarrassed.

"Didn't Michelsen give you a registration slip for him?"

"No," said Kubitzky.

"Didn't you ask for one?"

"No. He told me he had attended to the registration."

"And you were satisfied with that?"

"Yes." Kubitzky lowered his head.

"He was afraid," Garnot explained. "After everything that had happened in Michelsen's apartment—and then he'd been told not to pay any attention to Michelsen."

"I see," I said, and to Garnot, "and you saw a man fitting this description and staying with Michelsen?"

"Yes. I saw him several times, although he stayed in the apartment most of the time."

"So he *did* live there!" cried Irina.

"Of course. We've been trying to tell you that all along."

"Since when?" I asked.

"Since the end of August," said Kubitzky. "But I implore you, don't betray me. Don't let anyone know that you have this information from me!"

"So the servant lied."

"He certainly did. This gentleman—what did you say his name was?"

"Bilka!" cried Irina, wringing her hands. "Jan Bilka!"

"This gentleman, Jan Bilka, stayed with Herr Michelsen from the end of August until today. They left the house together."

"You saw—" She could say no more.

"Sit down!" I told her, forcing her to sit down beside me.

"They left the house together, yes," said Garnot. "Herr Kubitzky saw it and I saw it."

"When did they leave?" I asked. "Before the man was knocked down by the car?"

"No," said Garnot. "After that." He was still breathing with difficulty, and we watched him anxiously. He smiled and shook his head. "It's all right. This weather is really a killer. No, as I said—afterwards, Herr Roland."

"How long afterwards?"

"Oh, quite a while," said Garnot. "The police were here in the meantime, remember?"

"They left the house at exactly 8:04," said Kubitzky. "I looked at my watch." He wiped the sweat of fear off his forehead with his handkerchief. "Three vehicles drove up. Then Herr Michelsen and this man, Jan Bilka, came down in the elevator. Both of them were carrying suitcases, Michelsen one, Bilka two. There weren't many people on the street, and I could see everything."

"So could I," said Garnot. "From the window over there. There were men in the vehicles."

"How many?"

"Nine in all," said Garnot. "They got out and stood around in the street, here and on the other side, their hands in their pockets. It looked to me as if their purpose was to prevent anything from interrupting them."

"Could you recognize the men?"

"No. They were just men wearing coats and hats. They all wore hats," said Garnot. "Michelsen and this Herr Bilka got into the middle vehicle, a big black van. It looked like a delivery truck. It was completely closed. I thought the whole thing was extremely fishy, so I wrote down the number of the van." He took a small piece of paper off the table. "Here you are."

I took the paper. The number was HH-DX 982.

"You're sure that's right?"

"Quite sure. The van was standing under the light, the other two vehicles were in the shadows. After Herr Michelsen and Herr Bilka got into the van, the men who had come along ran back to their cars and all three drove off fast."

"And the servant?"

"He really has Monday afternoon off," said Kubitzky. "The cook and cleaning woman, too. And the servant really did come home late tonight." Suddenly he slapped his forehead. "We've completely forgotten, Herr Garnot! The young woman!"

"Yes. How stupid of us," said the antique dealer. "Michelsen and Herr Bilka had a woman with them."

"What sort of a woman?"

"Blond. Very pretty. Still quite young. She moved in when Herr Bilka did, in August."

I could feel Irina's hand clutching mine; it was ice cold.

"And this young woman drove off with them, too?" Irina asked, almost inaudibly.

"Yes. Really stupid of us to have forgotten her. We're both so upset...."

"Who was this young woman?" I asked. "Do you happen to know her name?"

"No," said Garnot. "We don't know her name."

"But I met Michelsen with her one day in the hall," said Kubitzky. "I greeted them and they returned my greeting, and Herr Michelsen murmured a name I couldn't understand. But then he said something else."

"What?" cried Irina.

"He said, 'The young lady is the fiancé of the friend who is visiting me,'" Kubitzky replied.

14

"Please don't be mad, Herr Roland."

I was sitting in the snack bar of the Kniefall Market, staring straight ahead—only forty-two hours before the events described above—and I was still waiting for the editorial office to call me and tell me what those goddamned women thought of my latest article. Lucie was standing in front of me, red with embarrassment. I could see she had mustered up every bit of courage she had. "I know it's no concern of mine, but—"

"But what?" I asked Lucie.

"Why do you drink so much in the morning?" she asked, and added hastily, "I know that's your business, only—"only—and now her voice was trembling—"I worry so much about you."

"You worry about *me?*" I stared at Lucie, and suddenly I felt sorry for her. That's good, I thought. Very good. That's the first time a girl has ever said anything like that to me. The two whores, for instance, with whom I had spent the night—they weren't worried about me. They were sleeping off their hangover, and when they'd wake up, they'd turn on the radio loud and have breakfast and get themselves all dressed up. And all the others were the same. Only Lucie was worried about me! "Every time you come here, you drink and mumble to yourself, and every time you look worse and worse. What's wrong with you, Herr Roland?"

"What should be wrong with me? I feel great!"

"Herr Roland!"

I drank some more whiskey, shook myself, and suddenly it seemed to me that this young girl was the only decent person in the whole wide world! This was, of course, a result of the many whiskeys I'd drunk the night before. The whiskey was also the explanation for how I was behaving.

Everybody has a breaking point, with or without liquor, and when they reach it, they unburden themselves, not to those closest to them, but to any person who happens to be handy and sympathetic—a bartender, a taxi driver, a sleeping car conductor, or a young waitress in a market.

"All right," I said. "So I don't feel great! So actually I feel awful!" And it seemed quite natural to me that I was talking like this to Lucie with the blond hair and the dark eyes, about whom I knew nothing except that she came from Brandoberndorf.

"But why is that?" Lucie shook her head. "You earn so much money. You're famous. Everybody reads what you write—"

"*Ach!*" I interrupted her with a gesture of revulsion. "What I'm writing—that's what's killing me!"

"I don't understand." Now the girl looked startled. "If it tortures you like that, why do you write it?"

Yes—why? A good question. The answer should have been, "Because I'm much too depraved and demoralized and guilty to write anything better." But does one say things like that? No. One says, "I used to write quite different things. Better things."

"But what you're writing now isn't bad." Lucie's cheeks were pink again. "I read it." She knew my pseudonym, of course. "And all my friends read it. It's very interesting and so scientific. It teaches you a lot."

"It's crap!" I said in a low voice. "It's the most colossal crap I've ever written! But you mustn't tell anyone what I just said."

"I won't! Word of honor!" She looked terribly distressed.

"But won't you get into trouble?" I asked her. "Should you be talking to me like this?"

Lucie shook her head. "You're a steady customer. Besides, there's nothing to do right now."

"Just the same." I got up, my glass in my hand, and noticed that I was slightly drunk. "Let's talk at the bar. There we're not so conspicuous."

I walked ahead of her with the cautious step of the drinker who knows he's had enough and has to be careful. She followed me with my bottle of Chivas. I got up on a barstool and put the glass on the counter gently. "And what will you drink?"

'In the *morning*, Herr Roland?"

"You've got to drink something, anything, or I can't talk," I insisted stubbornly.

"All right, then. I'll drink a glass of tomato juice."

"With vodka. With plenty of vodka!"

"No. No vodka, please."

"Without vodka ... OK. For all I care."

I watched her get a jug of dark red tomato juice out of the refrigerator and fill a glass with it. "Well, at least put some pepper in it!"

She obediently put some pepper in it from a big wooden pepper mill.

"What was I saying?"

"That once you'd written other things, better things." She lifted her glass, toasted me, and drank. I drank Chivas.

"Yes. That's right. That's when I took the job with *Blitz*." I twisted my glass in my hand. "At the time it wasn't only the biggest but also the best German illustrated magazine. With a fine reputation. Outside Germany, too. Like *Life*...."

Lucie, who probably had never heard of *Life*, nodded.

"All thanks to Hem."

"To whom?"

"To our executive editor, Paul Kramer. We call him Hem. For years he put everything into making *Blitz* the top-ranking illustrated magazine in Germany. In those days it was an honor to be working for *Blitz*. We printed short stories by Hemingway and Somerset Maugham, novels by Jan de Hartog and Remarque, novellas by Ernst Lehmann, Irwin Shaw, Truman Capote. *Breakfast at Tiffany's*, for instance...."

"George Peppard and Audrey Hepburn." Lucie sounded breathless. "I saw the picture. Oh, but he was handsome! Do you remember how the two looked for the cat in the rain?"

"Yes."

"And the song, 'Moon River.'" Lucie began to hum it.

"For God's sake, I know the song!" I said angrily, and startled the poor girl.

"I won't say another word. Please go on." But she had distracted me. I sat there doodling in the wet circles my glass had left on the counter. Lucie was silent.

After a while and some more Chivas, I said, "This man, Hem, taught me the meaning of the word *journalism*. Once I was ready for it, he gave me the most terrific assignments—historic series, series on medicine, science." I was smiling. "The one I liked best was 'The Bee Nation.'"

"'The Bee Nation,'" Lucie repeated. "That must have been beautiful."

I held out my glass. "Another whiskey, please."

"Herr Roland!"

"*Another whiskey!*"

"My goodness, but you can look angry. I'll get it. Right away."

"Thanks, Fräulein Lucie. And then, the big criminal cases. They were my specialty. I did my own research, and I knew how."

I was sure Lucie was wondering: What the hell is research? But she nodded eagerly.

"Hem put me on every big crime case, not only in Germany—in all Europe. He sent me to Brazil. That case of the murdering nuns. I was in Rio because of it." I drank. "Yes. First there was the frantic desire to catch up with the written word, to learn, a thirst for knowledge. Then Germany began to prosper and the curiosity phase began. Big criminal cases and political scandals. Then we had the—oh, hell, let's call it the historic wave. Everybody wanted to know more about the past. What were they really like—the good old days? That resulted in our big series on kings and emperors—the Hohenzollerns, the Wittelsbachers—forty-five, sometimes fifty articles on the subject. Oh, yes!" I went on drinking, lost in the past. "And when we were really on top, came the gourmet wave. Do you remember 'It Doesn't Always Have to Be Caviar'? That fellow Simmel wrote a novel about a secret agent who was crazy about cooking, and all his recipes went into the book. We didn't publish it. *Quick* did that. But everybody got on that bandwagon, too. Pages and pages of recipes, cooking with illustrations. You can't leaf through any paper or magazine today without finding at least one or two pages of recipes."

"That's right." Lucie laughed. "And did you write them, too?"

"No. But right after the food wave came the housing wave. 'Hooray, We're Building Houses Again!' Those articles were by me, and all the other series...."

I drank again and was silent, but Lucie continued to gaze at me expectantly as I looked down at my hands and went on remembering. How Gert Lester and his crew came to *Blitz* right after the housing series, and how that was when *Blitz* began to go to the dogs, thanks to Herr Lester and Herr Thomas Herford and our wonderful research department under Herr Stahlhut. What a fight Hem had had to put up for material that was halfway decent! To prevent everything from being rewritten as sob stuff, or with a war, sex, or crime slant. What scenes! And how heroic Hem had been about it! In vain. And that was why he had resigned himself to it long ago. "What the hell! You've got to produce!"

Smut was turned out regularly to satisfy increasingly baser instincts. Shitty novels, written for the boobs in the land, sometimes by a team of as many as five authors. One man for the male dialogue, a woman for the female dialogue, a specialist for action, another for continuity and plot, another for narrative and descriptive passages, the whole thing programmed by a computer down to the smallest detail and according to the latest poll. If we happened to get hold of a really good novel, it had to be completely rewritten to meet the requirements of the *Blitz* computer. It was Lester who brought this rewriter-itis into the house. We lied and cheated the reader from page one to the end. But should I tell poor Lucie all this? My tired eyes were burning. I drank and didn't notice that some whiskey was running down my chin. I looked at Lucie broodingly.

Would my life have taken a different course if I had ever loved a girl like her, really loved? Lucie was a good girl. She might have persuaded me to oppose the powers that be, to leave when things changed at *Blitz*. Yes, a girl like Lucie might have done that for me. A girl like her would have gone to work if for a while things hadn't worked out for me. But I had never been interested in girls like Lucie, with decency written all over their faces. Now, when it was too late, I was attracted to them. I laughed softly.

"Why are you laughing?"

"Nothing."

"I don't understand you. It must have been wonderful. You

must have been a happy man...then," she said, sounding bewildered.

"I was. And I never drank in the morning. Never!"

"So what happened?" asked Lucie, totally confused.

"The circulation," I said bitterly. "The goddamn' circulation! And—and the computer!" I was whispering now, like a conspirator. "That's a secret, Fräulein Lucie—don't tell a soul, but we have a computer over there that decides everything we write. Hem can have a coronary before he dares to print anything decent today...."

"A computer?"

"A computer. With good Herr Stahlhut watching over it. And the good ladies in the house watch over me. They pass on every line I write, the darlings. They're doing it right now, and that's why I'm here."

"I know," whispered Lucie.

I doodled letters of the alphabet into the wet rings on the dark counter as I said, "They were just different times then, and they won't come back." I lit a cigarette. My hands were trembling. "That's about the size of my troubles," I said, and laughed. "All only an excuse for drinking. You know alcoholics always need an excuse. One has a dog that died, another is unhappily in love, the next man has trouble with his children. Don't shake your head, Fräulein Lucie. I'm an alcoholic. Don't get involved with me."

"You are unhappy," Lucie said softly, and now we were looking into each other's eyes.

The telephone on the bar rang. It startled both of us. Lucie answered, spoke briefly, hung up, and said hesitantly, "You're to go over."

I got up gingerly. Lucie watched me, looking miserable as I had difficulty putting on my jacket. *Donnerwetter*, but I was stoned! So what! I paid, only for the tomato juice and the soda—the Chivas was mine and paid for—and I gave Lucie much too large a tip, as I always did.

"No, Herr Holland. I can't accept that much!"

"You can," I said, and shook hands with her. "Farewell, Fräulein Lucie."

"*Auf Wiedersehen*, Herr Roland."

I walked out of the store, straight as a ramrod. I looked back once and saw tears in Fräulein Lucie's eyes. She was wiping them away and staring down at the letters I had written on the counter with the spilled whiskey—*LUCIE*—and then crossed the name

171

out twice. I turned around fast and hurried out of the store. Now, I thought, the tears will really flow.

15

Swaying a little, my hands clenched, shoulders braced like a boxer—that's how I walked back to the publishing house. The sun shone weakly. I felt hot. Shouldn't have drunk so much on top of all that whiskey last night. God, but I felt it now! Most of all in my head, which was spinning. So what! It wasn't the first time I'd gone before editor-in-chief Lester stoned.

I had to make a detour, because right here the subway contractors had dug into the very bowels of the earth. They had put up thick planks and railings, making it possible to cross from one side of the street to the other. People were pouring across them from every direction, pushing, shoving. In the depths below I could see hundreds of laborers, steel helmets on their heads, crawling around like ants, digging, drilling, handling what looked like endlessly long steel wiring, working on machines mounted on cranes, pile drivers, pneumatic drills.

I stood for a moment on one of these bridges, leaned against the railing, and looked down at the future tunnel. The shaft was supported by beams, wires ran along them, powerful mixers were disgorging cement into the future tunnel wall. On a high pedestal stood a sort of drum; around it, five Italian laborers were mixing cement and were yelling—you couldn't call it singing—in unison: "*Evviva la torre di Pisa, di Pisa—che pende—che pende e che mai non va giu!*" I grinned. I spoke Italian: "Long live the tower of Pisa, of Pisa, because it leans and leans but never falls!" It continued in a more earthy vein.

I looked down at the laborers as if all of them were my friends. Those are good people, I thought somberly. They're doing something worthwhile. They're men. Greeks, Italians, Yugoslavs, Turks, Germans—*working men!* And I? I was a parasite, a piece of shit! If only I could be a laborer—somebody who did something constructive, who created something, something useful, something that mattered!

172

"Hey, look where you're going!" yelled a passerby whom I had bumped into. I stumbled on. I didn't look down at the laborers anymore, because suddenly I felt ashamed.

16

"If this happens once more, do you hear? Once more—you're fired!"

As I got out of the VIP elevator on the seventh floor, I could hear the strident voice of our editor-in-chief, so accustomed to giving orders. "Everything has its limits! I've been patient with you long enough! Nobody is irreplaceable, and you aren't either!" Gert Lester, storming in his glass office.

His top-notch head layout man, Heinrich Leidenmüller, husband and father, occasionally pursued by dark forces, stood before him—a very thin man with big ears, wearing glasses. He kept bowing. He was pale, he hadn't shaved, and he looked wasted, as usual. Angela Flanders and Hem were also present. They were sitting to right and left of the big chrome writing desk on tubular chrome chairs.

"In my department you're not going to behave like a whore-fucker, not in my department!"

The bastard, I thought, and was filled with blind rage. The filthy fucking bastard! Letting loose like that in front of Angela Flanders. Knew very well that you could hear every word in this glass emporium. And Leidenmüller said, "Yes, sir," "I know, sir," "It won't happen again, Herr Lester!" And each time a bow! Lester was making the guy look like an ass in front of the entire department. I felt hotter and hotter. I took off my jacket and walked into the office of Lester's private secretary without knocking. "Hello, Frau Zschenderlein," I said.

Sophie Zschenderlein suffered from a kidney deficiency. She had to take cortisone, which her doctor prescribed in fairly large doses. The medication had given her the typical cortisone moon face and caused her to gain weight. She had become ill quite suddenly two years ago. Until then she had been a very attractive woman. She shouldn't have been working, and sometimes she found it very difficult to get to the office, but one had to work if one had an eleven-year-old son, was divorced, and one's husband had left the country and paid no alimony or child support. Illness and fate had made her bitter. Her whole heart now belonged to her boss. She served him with devotion. She had the feeling that here was a man who needed her, who was glad to see her, even with her distorted features. That was why Gert Lester's friends were her friends and his enemies her enemies. Like all those whose offices overlooked Kaiserstrasse, she was very nervous, suffered from headaches, was dizzy sometimes, because here, at the front of the building, the noise from the subway construction was dreadful and penetrated every office. And this had been going on for months and would continue to go on for months more.

I had already opened the door to the holy of holies when Frau Zschenderlein jumped to her feet. "But you can't go in! Can't you see—"

The booze. God bless the booze! I grinned at her drunkenly and was already in Lester's office. He gave me an icy look. "What a pleasure! Herr Roland. Our star attraction! To knock and wait until I say 'Come in' seems to go beyond you, eh, Herr Roland? Please sit down, Herr Roland." Now he was going to be ironic. "Let's not be formal. Make yourself at home."

"That's just what I'm doing, Herr Lester."

"Good, good. Just a minute, though; I still have some unfinished business here before I can devote myself to you, Herr Roland."

The unnerving noise of the construction below penetrated Lester's office, too. I smiled at Angela Flanders—a real friendship existed between us—and nodded at Hem. He looked troubled as he ran his fingers through his unkempt gray hair, then stroked his Hemingway beard. He must have been raging inside. Flanders looked depressed, too.

Hem was wearing a plaid shirt and flannel pants. He had removed his tie and jacket. He never wore a jacket when he was called into Lester's office, and he never laid aside the Dunhill pipe he always smoked and also smoked here. The smell of the tobacco was pleasant. At least *something* was pleasant!

Gert Lester (dark suit, white shirt, foulard tie) passed a hand across his short hair. His eyes narrowed, the nostrils of his eagle nose quivered. But Lester had to control himself because he needed me. So he bellowed at Leidenmüller instead. "Get back to your work! I'll cover for you once more, but it's the last time. And now get out!"

Leidenmüller was still bowing. "It will never happen again, Herr Lester!" he stammered. "Never!"

Of course it'll happen again, I thought, and they won't fire you because you're too damned good! And this super-bastard will put you through the same degrading scene every time.

"And thank you for your trust in me, Herr Lester." Leidenmüller withdrew, bowing and walking backwards, with which he bumped into me. "Oh! I beg your pardon!"

"Oh, shut up!" I mumbled. "Stop shitting in your pants in front of this fink!"

"What did you say?" asked Lester.

"Nothing worth repeating," I replied.

"But I want to know what you said."

I shrugged. Leidenmüller had meanwhile left the room. Work had come to a standstill in many of the offices; you could hear only a few typewriters. The employees up here—reporters, writers, editors, secretaries, stenos, were all looking into Lester's office.

"I told him he shouldn't shit in his pants all the time in front of you, Herr Lester," I said amiably, and bowed to Angela Flanders. "Begging your pardon, Angela."

Hem puffed on his pipe, blew a cloud of smoke into the air. Not a muscle in his face moved.

Lester began to bellow. "I never heard of such a thing! What got into you—?"

I turned back toward the door. "Where are you going?"

"Outside. Until you calm down."

Five seconds passed. We stared at each other. Finally Lester said, "Had a few drops to drink?"

"Many drops," I replied.

"Sit down!" yelled Lester.

I shrugged and sat down on a chrome chair in front of the desk. It shook unpleasantly. My jacket fell on the floor. I picked it up and laid it across my knee. Now nobody in the area was working anymore.

"So?" I said.

Lester was trying his best not to lose his cool and to control his absolute aversion to me. But somehow I always managed to unnerve him. "Has anything happened to irritate you, Herr Roland?"

"No."

"But you look as if something had."

"I do?"

"Have we hurt your feelings in any way, Herr Roland?"

"No."

"You're not very talkative today, Herr Roland. What's the matter?"

If you don't stop this shitty dialogue, I'll punch your face bloody, I thought, and right after that: I'm a lot drunker than I realized. I'd better watch it. Yes, yes, Hem, stop giving me the heavy warning signals. I get the message.

"I asked you something, Herr Roland."

"I heard you, Herr Lester."

He leaned forward. "Do you want to make trouble?"

"No, Herr Lester."

"But I get the feeling that you do."

"Then you're mistaken, Herr Lester."

"Because if it's trouble you want, you can have it. I'm in the right mood."

"I'm sorry to hear that, Herr Lester. Could we perhaps get down to business now?"

"Could we get down to business? I like that! We've *got* to get down to business, Herr Roland. There's a lot of work still to be done on your article. There were a lot of things that didn't go over at all well with the women—unfortunately, quite a few basic things, and there isn't much time. You left it to the last minute again!"

"I explained all that. I wasn't well. I had—"

"You whipped the thing up this morning. I have my informers...."

"Aha!"

"And that's what it looks like. Thrown together. I guess you think you can get away with anything, Herr Roland!"

"I don't think I'm going to put up with this, Herr Lester."

"Walter," said Hem, taking his pipe out of his mouth. "Try to behave like a normal person and not like a drunken idiot."

I nodded. Whenever Hem spoke to me I usually snapped to.

"Excuse me, Herr Lester."

"It's all right. Frau Flanders, would you please read the ladies' objections to us."

Angela Flanders took her notebook and began to read from it. Every now and then she looked at me apologetically. There

176

really were quite a lot of objections. But the basic one was that much more attention should go to the idiosyncrasies, preferences, functions, and reactions of the *man*.

Lester jiggled up and down on his chair, drummed on the desk, and looked at me malevolently. While Angela Flanders read, I grew calmer and calmer. Then I began to smile. Hem noticed it and looked worried. Angela Flanders got nervous; in fact, she looked frightened. For quite a long time there was silence in the glass office. When she finished I noticed that everyone was looking at me. "Anything else?"

"That's all, Herr Roland." Lester was drumming on the desk again. "But I'd say it suffices. We've got to turn the whole thing around, do an about-face. Should have long ago. You'll have to approach your subject matter from a totally different viewpoint. A lot of work, I know. Talk it over with Herr Kramer. Before you start on it, come and see me once more. We must let nothing get by that might endanger the success of the series. Luckily, you write fast. And now drink a lot of black coffee and sober up. The thing must be ready to go to press by 6:00 P.M. It's *your* fault. If you'd handed it in sooner . . ."

At that moment the whiskey took its toll. Suddenly, after too long a period of pressure, I couldn't go on, didn't want to go on. The noise outside seemed to grow louder; suddenly I saw the deep subway shaft again and the laborers below me and heard them singing the song about the tower of Pisa, and that did it. With my hearing, my sight, and my thoughts far away, I said, "*No!*"

"What do you mean, 'no'?" For a moment Lester seemed baffled.

"Walter!" Hem had leaped to his feet. He wanted to stop me, but I rose slowly and waved to him to be quiet. My voice was suddenly very low. "No. I am not going to rewrite the article."

"You—"

"I don't intend to rewrite anything anymore, Herr Lester," I said. "I shall never rewrite anything again. Why don't *you* rewrite it, Herr Lester?"

Editor-in-chief Lester, not as tall as Hem and I, now jumped to his feet, too. He looked a little ridiculous standing behind his huge desk, and he was screaming again. "What do you think you're doing? Insubordination! I've noticed your obstructionary attitude for some time now. Don't think I haven't. But with me, you're not going to get away with it. I've succeeded in eliminating a lot better men than you, Roland. I'll destroy you, Roland!"

"Walter!" cried Angela Flanders. "Be sensible, *please!* For my sake!"

"I am being sensible," I told her. "I'm sorry, Angela, I'm sorry, Hem, but I can't go on. I simply can't!"

"Walter! For God's sake, shut up!" cried Hem. "Do you think we enjoy what we're doing? So what? The paper's got to come out. The article has to be rewritten."

"But not by me!" I said stubbornly. "I'm drunk, I know it. But I'm not so drunk that I don't know what I'm saying. *I am not going to rewrite the article! Evviva la torre di Pisa!*"

Lester shouted, "We'll see about that! When I get through with you, you'll be this big." He demonstrated with thumb and forefinger. "You—you miserable lush!"

Lester liked to shout. Everybody in the house knew it. "As I've said once before," he bellowed, "you're slipping, Herr Roland. You're not writing as well as you used to, and I'm not alone in saying this. The analysts in the research department are saying the same thing."

"The analysts in the research department are fucking idiots!"

"That—that's—But why am I getting so excited?" yelled Lester. "It's the alcohol! Your brain's soaked with it. This last article is an outrage! And for that you get paid top rates? And when I tell you it's got to be rewritten, you refuse. Great! Just great! Herford will be delighted!"

He was shouting so loudly that everyone on the floor could hear him. A few had come out into the hall—editors, authors, secretaries, all ranged along the glass wall of Lester's office, like outside an aquarium. From there they could see and hear everything. More and more of them came over, looking curious or disturbed, startled or grinning, disturbed or delighted to see Lester getting his comeuppance for a change.

My head thrust forward, I walked slowly, very slowly, past Hem, who tried to stop me, to the desk Lester stood behind. What I said then, I who had stuck it out for fourteen years in this hellhole at the expense of my health and nerves, I who had drunk myself soft in the head—what I said then was saturated with hatred and fury against the entire industry. I spoke very softly, slowly, and clearly.

"For years I've been writing what was demanded of me, Herr Lester. Every bit of shit. Every idiocy. How we actually won at

178

Stalingrad. How the German Crown Prince, the best Crown Prince we ever had, really won at Verdun. I have rewritten and fabricated the whole unheroic history of Germany for you, obediently, docile as a little boy. What heroes I turned in for you! And the sex maniacs! The heartbreaking fates of prostitutes. The homosexual tragedies. I've written the memoirs of Nazi criminals after they left jail, because none of those brothers can write a literate German sentence!"

"Walter!" Hem came rushing over to me. "Come to your senses, please!"

I had reached the desk. Now I began to walk around it, my hands behind my back, leaning forward a little, straight up to Lester. "No," I said. "No, Hem. I have no intention of being sensible anymore. I am sorry for you and I am sorry for Angela. You were my friends. I wish you weren't here right now. I wish I could be alone with this gentleman—"

"Don't you dare start anything with me!" screamed editor-in-chief Gert Lester, pale now, his arms raised protectively in front of his chest. And the noses of the curious, gloating, horrified humans outside pressed against the glass—everyone on the floor had assembled.

"Who has raised the circulation of this paper over and over again?" I asked quietly—oh, so quietly. "I have! On your orders I transformed a decent illustrated magazine into a sewer!"

I was standing over Lester now. He took a step back, then another. "Herr Roland, I demand that you—"

"You are demanding nothing from me!"

Lester took two more steps back. The people outside, mouths agape, were watching every move, listening to every word. One girl cried out. Frau Zschenderlein came rushing into the room, bristling with indignation. "Herr Lester, what—?"

"Out!" I shouted. "Get out!" in a voice so menacing Frau Zschenderlein fled.

Lester screamed, "You rotten drunk! You dare to—"

I stood up straight for the first time, and for the first time shouted, like a crazy sergeant, *Shut your trap, you miserable specimen!* And something extraordinary happened. Lester's hands shot down to the seams of his trousers. It was as if he were about to click to military attention! Angela Flanders, her head in her hands, started to cry. Hem sank back helplessly into his chair. His pipe had gone out. Lester removed his hands from the seams of his trousers fast, but it didn't do him much good. Everybody out in the hall had seen it happen, and they'd tell everybody who hadn't.

Lester was struggling for breath. "You—you—" But I was after him. Step by step I moved forward and he moved back. In a circle at first, then in a straight line. It must have looked grotesque, but nobody laughed. The faces pressed against the glass looked like grimacing masks. And I went on chasing my boss around his office.

"What haven't we all done together, Herr Lester? We've babbled about everything from miracle drugs for cancer to blue-green vomit! We've raised fucking to a worldwide sport." I was speaking calmly again, but at this point I was in no way responsible for my actions. Disgust, degradation, grief for the years lost, all this came rushing out. "We've done our bit for the Fatherland, we two, haven't we? We should get a medal for it. The *Bundesverdienstkreuz* at least. What achievements! German orgasms are the best orgasms! Read *Blitz* and become a rutting stallion, a mare perpetually in heat! Read *Blitz*, the paper with the intellectual level of its editor-in-chief!"

"You goddamn bastard!" screamed Lester. "I'll—I'll—"

But we never found out what he intended to do, because just then the intercom in the ceiling—which was a fixture in every office and was controlled by central—tuned in on us. The indifferent voice of a young girl said, "Attention, please. Editor-in-chief Lester, Herr Kramer, Herr Roland, and Herr Engelhardt are please to come to Herr Herford's office immediately. I repeat: Editor-in-chief Lester, Herr Kramer, Herr Roland, and Herr Engelhardt, please ... to Herr Herford's office."

17

"With his fiancée ..."

"Yes."

"But I am his fiancée!"

"Then he had another fiancée."

"He already had her in Prague. Didn't you hear Herr Kubitzky say the girl spoke with a Czech accent, and Michelsen said Bilka had brought her with him?"

I had heard all right. "Sorry," I said, "but that's the way it seems to me."

"Then he must have been engaged to two women at the same time."

"Yes," I said.

I didn't have to say much; she wasn't listening, anyway. She was sitting beside me in the Lamborghini on the empty street; the wind was howling around us and shaking the car. I had started the car and turned on the heater because it had turned cold. By now it was 2:35 A.M. We were parked in front of 187 Eppendorfer Baum, waiting for Bertie, who was supposed to meet us here. The airport wasn't far away. Something must have held him up.

Irina wasn't crying anymore. She had wept at first, but now she was staring straight ahead, and her voice had a metallic ring to it. She was trying with all her remaining strength not to break down. I decided to let her talk for a while before getting down to business. She said, "But we were together two years."

"Yes," I said.

"And the other woman . . . how long has he known her? Not so long."

"I wouldn't know."

"Can a man love two women?"

"Yes."

"No!" she cried. "Not at the same time! Not truly! He loves one of them and sleeps with the other."

"Not necessarily," I said. Where was Bertie?

"But that's the way it was. He loved the other woman, but he slept with me. I was good enough for him in bed, but he fled with the other woman. She was the one he took with him, not me!"

"Did you want to go with him?"

"Of course I did," she said in that metallic voice. "But he said we couldn't leave together, that he'd send for me as soon as he'd found something in the West. He said I'd hear from him. And I waited. I waited for three months. I would have waited longer if I—"

"I know," I said.

"You don't know anything!" she cried. "Oh, forgive me! My nerves are shot. You've been so good to me. Please forgive me!"

"Sure," I said. "Of course. I can understand how you feel. He betrayed you."

"Yes."

"And went off with another girl."

"Yes." She sounded miserable.

"I'd say that no decent man would do a thing like that," I ventured, hopefully but cautiously. There were a lot of women who could go on loving a man who had treated them like that, but not Irina. Thank God, not Irina, I thought, as she suddenly cried out, "You're absolutely right! He's a pig! A pig! And I trusted him. I always believed everything he told me."

"And now he's gone away with the other girl," I said. "God knows where. He may even have left the country. And you sit here without a cent and don't know what to do. It's a bloody mess!"

Suddenly she was sobbing again. I gave her my handkerchief and she blew her nose. "Thanks."

"You see, Irina," I said as casually as possible, "I got you out of the camp and brought you here and—"

"And I'm terribly grateful, Herr Roland."

"Nonsense! You don't have to be grateful. But I'm a reporter. I'm supposed to write this story, and you play a part in it...."

"Yes, and? Oh, I know, you mean you need a release."

She was recalling my conversation with superintendent Kubitzky and antiques-dealer Garnot, in his apartment. It had been quite hectic when I had asked for a release from both of them. Kubitzky, especially, had behaved like a madman.

"Sign a release? And then you'll tell everything? I'm not crazy! That would cost me my life! No, Herr Roland. Not from me. I won't sign anything. It's unfair of you to get us to talk and then say you want to write about us!"

"Well, why did you think I was asking you all those questions?"

"It isn't honorable. No. I won't sign anything. And if you write a word about me, I'll sue!"

"Now listen to me," I said. "I can tell the police everything you just told me."

He was beside himself. "No, no!" he cried. "You wouldn't do anything so despicable!"

"But I shall have to," I said. "It's my duty. You can't forbid me to go to the police. And if I do, things will certainly start happening."

"But my life!"

"We're not in Russia!"

"No? And what about what's happened up to now?"

It went on like that for at least fifteen minutes. Then Garnot turned to Kubitzky and said, "Herr Kubitzky, I advise you to sign the release. When one knows something very wrong has happened and does nothing about it, one becomes guilty oneself. The police have our names anyway, as witnesses. We're already involved. And I trust the police. They'll protect us."

"Yes. Like the fine fellows who were here and said to pay no attention to what goes on upstairs."

"I'm not going to any of those fine fellows," I said. "I'm going to headquarters. This isn't a gangster country. You're in much more danger, Herr Kubitzky, if I *don't* go to the police and report this thing. Can't you see that?"

Kubitzky began to waver. "All right, then. But I won't take any money for it. Not a penny!"

"Neither will I," said Garnot.

I went on arguing with them for a while, but I couldn't shake them. So I got my typewriter out of the car, typed the releases, and they signed. Kubitzky's hand was shaking so hard he could scarcely write his name.

That had been a quarter of an hour ago. Now, in the car, I told Irina, "The release...yes. You can refuse. Up there I was bluffing, but now I'm being honest. If you refuse to sign, I can't do a thing. On the other hand, the press won't leave you in peace if this thing develops into anything big, which I'm afraid it will—and in that case not as my exclusive story. But you can give me exclusive rights."

"Of course I will," she said, to my immense relief. "Write it all! Write the whole story! I'll give you the release."

"Good. And I'll give you the money. Five thousand marks."

"But I don't want any money either," she said.

"Why not? It's not my money. *Blitz* is paying you, and it won't hurt them."

She shook her head.

"Well," I said. "I'll type the form and I'll put in five thousand marks. If you don't want it now, you may later."

She didn't say anything. I moved my seat back as far as possible and brought my flat little portable and my attaché case to the front. I took out carbon and paper and put the case on my knees, the typewriter on top of it, turned on the light in the car, and began to type.

Irina was watching me. I could feel it. My cigarette hung out of the corner of my mouth, the heater was humming, and I typed the text Dr. Rotaug had given me, and put in 5,000 DM as the fee. My flask was lying on the leather-upholstered dashboard. "May I?" asked Irina.

"Yes," I said. "As much as you like. There's plenty more in the trunk."

She raised the flask to her lips, leaned her head back and drank, and I stopped typing and looked at her. I saw her white throat and her profile and I thought how pretty she was. How alone and abandoned. And with me now. Probably for quite a while. If I . . .

I stopped thinking, crushed my cigarette in the ashtray, and finished typing the release. I gave her the original and the copy and my pen. She signed slowly, as if in a trance.

"The money is yours, anytime," I said. "You can have it now if you like."

"No, I don't want it," she said, while I signed.

"Maybe later."

"Maybe," she said, and began to cry again, quietly, motionlessly.

I put the attaché case and typewriter in the back of the car again, then I turned to Irina, put an arm across her shoulders, and tried to comfort her. But there really was no comfort for what had happened to her. I felt sorry for her, truly sorry, and I was very glad I had her release.

Somebody knocked on the window. Irina cried out softly. "It's not going to happen again," I said, and before I let down the window I took the Colt out of my pocket. A fat little man in a plaid coat was standing beside my car. He wore a plaid hat and was wearing a loud tie. He was grinning sheepishly. He could have been forty-five or fifty. I held the Colt concealed in my right hand and with my left hand opened the window.

"Hello," said the little fat man.

"Hello," I said.

"Sorry to disturb," he said. "Do you understand me?"

"Yes," I said. "What's the matter?"

"My name is McCormick. Richard McCormick." He spoke German with a strong accent. "Pharmacist from Los Angeles."

"Pleased to meet you," I said in English.

"Speak German, please. I like speak German. Want to learn more. Here on Europe tour, you understand?"

"Yes."

"Joe and I."

"Joe?"

"My friend. Joe Rizzaro. He pharmacist, too. We lost. Take wrong street. You understand?"

"Where's your friend?" I asked, grasping the Colt firmly.

"In car." He pointed behind mine. I turned around. A big olive-green Buick was parked in back of us. A man was sitting behind the wheel, smiling and waving to me. I had been so busy typing, I hadn't even noticed the car pulling up. Also because of the wind. And the light was on in the Lamborghini, which was why I hadn't seen the Buick's headlights. Now they were out.

"We want Reeperbahn, Sankt Pauli—you understand?" said Mr. McCormick.

"Yes."

"Well, where is?"

"You've driven too far," I said. "Much too far."

McCormick said, "We want Sankt Pauli. We want see beautiful Fräuleins. You understand what I mean?" He bowed. "Excuse me, lady."

Irina's eyes were wide, her face expressionless.

"Reeperbahn good for beautiful Fräuleins, eh?"

"Very good," I said, my finger on the trigger.

"So, how we get there?"

"You turn your car around and—" I said.

"Speak German," said McCormick. "I like speak German. So . . . turn car around." He laid a plan of the city on the window ledge, one of those folded plans, and handed me a pencil. "Please, you draw way back, mister."

"Now, listen—"

"Please. We want to see beautiful Fräuleins—you know why," and he leered at me.

I took the pencil in my left hand and said, "This is where we are. You turn around, go all the way back, as far as you can—" and got no farther. With his free hand McCormick, or whatever his name was, pressed a damp cloth against my mouth and nose. I lifted the Colt. He dropped the map and twisted my hand so that I had to drop the gun. He was very strong. I could see Irina open the door on her side and jump out. The cloth had been soaked in a repulsive, sharply pungent liquid and was very cold. I struggled for breath, but all I could breathe was the goddamned stench. The last thing I heard before everything went black were Irina's screams and after that footsteps hurrying across the pavement.

GOD GAVE ME MY MONEY.
JOHN DAVISON ROCKEFELLER 1839–1937

The words were engraved on a gold plaque which was approximately the size of a copy of *Blitz*, and had been inserted into a wall of bookshelves that reached from floor to ceiling. The walls were covered with books, colorful new editions, rare old books, leather-bound books. The shelves—all mahogany—were indirectly lighted. I knew this inner sanctum of our publisher, I had been here frequently, and every time I could have sworn that he hadn't read a dozen of the thousands of books that lined the walls. I was the last to enter; Hem, Lester and Bertie walked in ahead of me. Poor old cortisone-Zschenderlein had brewed some strong black coffee for me during my altercation with her boss, and before going upstairs I had managed to down some—hot as hell and strongly laced with lemon juice. After the second cup I had gone to the washroom and vomited, then drunk another cup on my now empty stomach. I can't say I was sober—far from it—but I wasn't dead drunk anymore. Frau Zschenderlein had said she would send up more coffee so that I could go on drinking here.

"God gave me my money"—the motto of our publisher, Thomas Herford. Like Rockefeller, Herford was a multimillionaire. And like his Titanic prototype, he was religious. A Bible, bound in pigskin, always lay open on an antique lectern, a huge volume with parchment pages and illuminated lettering.

Herford's office was enormous—six meters high, approximately a hundred and twenty square meters. King-size rugs covered the wall-to-wall carpeting. A seemingly endless table and a lot of carved chairs with hard seats and narrow carved arms, for conferences. Three corners with easy chairs, low tables in front of them. Opposite the entrance stood Herford's antique desk—papers, books, newspapers, magazines piled high on it. Four telephones—one silver, another supposed to be pure gold.

A silver intercom. To the left of the desk, a television set and a monitor that went with the computer. The monitor was turned on. The glass flickered black. But now, in green computer type, a row of letters paraded across the screen.

Thomas Herford's office, like that of his manager and head of the research department, was on the top floor, the eleventh. The window behind his desk was divided into three parts and looked like a gigantic mock-up of an airplane cockpit: one pane slanted front, the two others, slanting a little to the side, were slightly smaller. The view of the city was spectacular.

Thomas Herford rose. In the seating area beside the desk two men got up, too. I recognized turtle-necked Dr. Rotaug and Manager Oswald Seerose and, sitting between them, Grete Herford, the publisher's wife—"Mama," as he called her and as she was called by practically everyone in the house—a highly important person, because his wife's taste meant more to Herford than his own. He asked her to be present at all important meetings.

"There you are, gentlemen," said Herford, coming forward to greet us. "Terribly sorry to have to tear you away from your work, but Herford has something important to tell you." He shook hands with us, one after the other. I was the last one, and until he got around to me I took a quick look at the monitor. The green lettering had this to say:

SOUTH-GERMAN SMALL TOWN. THOSE QUESTIONED: CATHOLIC. AGE: 35–40. MAR-RIED. OWN THEIR HOME. 1–2 CHILDREN. INCOME: 1850. MIDDLE CLASS, CIVIL SER-VANTS AND EMPLOYEES. NO SELF-EMPLOYED. ALL WITH HIGH-SCHOOL DI-PLOMAS, COLLEGE OR BUSINESS SCHOOL EDUCATION. RESULT: 72% FOR BLOND, 15% FOR BRUNETTE, 3.8% FOR RED, 9.2% UNDECIDED...THOSE QUESTIONED: FE-MALE....

"What's the matter with you, Roland?" Herford's voice. I looked away from the monitor. I had almost fallen asleep standing. Sober? No. Publisher Herford was holding out his hand. "Got up with a slight hangover, eh?" he said jovially, taking my hand in his heavy paw and shaking it until it hurt. "Go on,

Roland, admit it! I'm not going to have your scalp for it. Had a shot or two while you were waiting?"

"Herr Herford, I—"

"At the Kniefall Market, as usual?"

"I have—how do you know?"

"Herford knows everything. Has his people everywhere. Ha-ha-ha! Just had a hell of a fight with Lester. Herford knows all about that, too. He has his informers, ha-ha-ha!"

He called everybody by their last names except for his *Du* friends, and he liked to refer to himself in the third person. Lester's cough sounded embarrassed. He hadn't uttered a word since the scene on the third floor. "Well, now the fight's over, right? We've got something important to discuss. Herford needs his team. Every one of them. And no shenanigans. So shake hands, the two of you, and tell each other you bear no grudges."

"No grudges? Herr Herford, it was an unqualified attack by this drunkard, and I must demand—" Lester began indignantly, but Herford interrupted him. "Be quiet, Lester!" His voice was sharp. "Don't say another word! I'm sure you're not all that innocent yourself. I know you. A good man. A very good man. Just don't know how to handle people. No feeling for it. Always have to play the superior officer. But with a creative person, that won't do." He said it without a trace of irony. "Roland is my best writer, a nervous, sensitive person. That's why he drinks. Doesn't matter as long as he writes. He's a phenomenon, our Roland!"

Lester was a coward. After Herford said this about me, he evidently decided the best thing to do would be to control his resentment. I looked at him. His face was gray. I knew he'd shut up now, but he'd have his sweet revenge in his good time.

I wasn't one iota better. I was just as yellow as Lester. I had decided to give notice or let them fire me. I had felt determined to call it quits. But I had no character, or let's say I hadn't had any for years. Nor did I have the guts to do it, since I wasn't all that stoned any longer. My brief period of rebellion was over.

"So are you going to shake hands or not?" Herford shouted.

Lester promptly stretched out his hand; I took it in mine. His felt like rubber. I said, "I do not hold a grudge against you, Herr Lester." It's the truth—that's what I said. And he said, "And I don't bear you a grudge, Herr Roland."

The words almost cost him his life. He choked on every one of them. Hem grinned at me. Bertie was grinning, too. He still had on the crumpled clothes he'd traveled in, but he'd changed his bandage. Hem had on his jacket and tie now, and he had left his pipe downstairs. And all I could think of was: Lester's revenge will come, no doubt about it. Like the amen at the end of a prayer. And I knew Lester was thinking the same thing.

"That's better!" Herford at his heartiest. He gestured in the direction of the two men and his wife. "You know them. Herford doesn't have to introduce you."

We bowed. Lester hurried over to Frau Herford and kissed her hand. Mama's makeup was pale, she looked like a corpse, and she was hideously dressed, as usual. She was wearing a sand-colored, crocheted shawl over a white woolen dress, gray stockings, and stout, flat walking shoes. A black mink coat that must have cost a small fortune was draped over the back of her chair. Her gray hair was tinted to garish violet, and she had on a brown hunter's hat with a long, curly feather. Mama's face was friendly and she had the dumb, soulful eyes of a cow.

"Coffee for our star writer?" said Dr. Rotaug. He was wearing a black suit, a silver tie, a white shirt with the obligatory high, starched Hjalmar Schacht collar, and he stared at me with his small, expressionless eyes.

"It's on the way," Lester said maliciously. "It's being sent up so that Herr Roland doesn't pass out on us."

Manager Oswald Seerose said amiably, "Head buzzing, is it? I know. The day before yesterday I was at a party. Drank everything handed to me. Mixed my drinks and regretted it."

"But you should never mix drinks," said Mama. She had a Hessian accent; and the way she looked, she could have been the mama in any television series, but *not* the wife of a prominent publisher!

"I'll never do it again, *gnädige Frau*," said Seerose. He was wearing a checked suit, was tall and thickset, and looked like a British aristocrat. He was by far the most impressive looking person in the house.

"Before we start—unfortunately, photo-editor Ziller is still on the plane, on his way back from the States, so Herford couldn't ask him to join us—but before we begin, let me read something to you from the Book of Books."

"Book of Books." That's what he said.

This wasn't new to me; it was accepted procedure. No meeting, no conference took place without the reading of some uplifting passages from the Bible at the beginning and end of every session. Mama rose to her feet and folded her hands, in the course of which her hunter's hat slipped a little to one side. She wore no jewelry. The others folded their hands, too; only Hem, Bertie, and I didn't. I stood where I could see the monitor. The green words moved across the screen:

RESULTS OF ALL POLLS: 79.6% PREFER BLONDS...17.2% BRUNETTES...3.2% RED...CONCLUSION: THE COVER GIRLS MUST BE BLOND. REPEAT: BLOND...

Herford walked over to the lectern with the Bible on it. He was a big, stocky man; behind him Mama looked like a child. He had a square head with thick, curly gray hair, a square jaw, and bushy black brows. His wife may have been dressed in poor taste, but Herford wore clothes that were almost ostentatiously elegant—a light, shiny, silver-gray suit (custom made by the best tailor in Frankfurt), a blue shirt with rounded edges on the collar, a black tie, and black shoes. A platinum clip in his tie, a platinum watch on his wrist, and a big diamond ring on the little finger of his right hand. The solitaire glittered in blazing color as Herford raised his hairy hand. With emotion he read: 'From the First Epistle of Paul the Apostle to the Corinthians, Chapter Thirteen. On charity...."

As he read, I watched the monitor to see what the green computer words were saying:

PROGRAM 24A—11: BREASTS . . . RESULTS . . . BREASTS BARE: YES—84.6% . . . BREASTS BARE TO THE NIPPLES ONLY: YES—62.3%...NIPPLES COVERED BY DRESS: YES—32% . . . COVERED BY BATHING SUIT (BIKINI BRA): YES—69.5%....

"Though I speak with the tongues of men and angels, and have not charity," Herford was reading ceremoniously, "I am become as sounding brass, or a tinkling cymbal...."

BY A BRASSIERE: YES—68.3%...COVERED BY THE HANDS: YES—85.4%...BY PLANTS (LEAVES, FLOWERS, ETC.): YES— 87.7%...DETAIL A: NIPPLE VISIBLE THROUGH COVERING: YES—92.3%....

"And though I have the gift of prophecy, and understand all mysteries, and all knowledge; and though I have all faith, so that I could remove mountains..."

...RECOGNIZABLE UNDER MATERIAL, NOT SHOWING THROUGH: YES—52.3% . . . TRANSPARENT MATERIAL: YES—68.5% . . . CRASSLY VISIBLE BEHIND FIRM MATERIAL: YES—71.5%...VISIBLE UNDER A WET MAN'S SHIRT: YES—93.7%...DETAIL B: SHAPE OF NIPPLE: POINTED AND SMALL WITH SMALL AREOLA: YES—42.4%...POINTED WITH LARGE AREOLA: YES—58.4%...LARGE AND THICK WITH SMALL AREOLA: YES—67.1%....

"...and have not charity, I am nothing. And though I bestow all my goods to feed the poor...."

...LARGE WITH LARGE AREOLA: YES— 89.9% . . . DETAIL C: COLOR OF NIPPLE: . . . PINK: YES—49.3% . . . LIGHT BROWN: YES— 55.6% . . . DARK BROWN: YES—91.3% . . . WITH A LITTLE HAIR: YES—11.3%....

"...and though I give my body to be burned, and have not charity, it profiteth me nothing. Charity suffereth long and is kind..."

...DETAIL D: SHAPE OF THE BREASTS...VIRGINAL, SMALL: YES— 45.6%...WOMANLY, MATURE AND TAUT: YES—60.3%...TAUT AND VERY LARGE: YES—95.4%....

"...charity envieth not," Herford read fervently. "Charity vaunteth not itself, is not puffed up..."

...PEARSHAPED:YES—39.6%...

"...doth not behave itself unseemly..."

191

...LIKE BUDS: YES—9.1%...

"...seeketh not her own, is not easily provoked..."

...LIKE APPLES: YES—93.4%...

"...thinketh no evil..."

DETAIL QUESTION: COLOR OF BREASTS . . . PINK: YES—87.7% . . . SUNTANNED: YES—67.8%....

"...rejoiceth not in iniquity, but rejoiceth in the truth. Amen," said Herford. "Amen," said Mama, Seerose, and Rotaug.

One of the telephones rang. "Goddamn it!" shouted our publisher angrily. "They know Herford doesn't want to be disturbed now!" He rushed over to his desk and lifted one of the innumerable receivers, the right one; he knew which phone had rung. "What is it?" he bellowed. "Didn't I say—what? Well, all right. Where? In his office? Very well." He put down the receiver and pressed a button on the silver intercom. "Herford!" He let go of the button. A humble voice in the speaker said, "I'm terribly sorry to have to disturb you, Tommy, but it's really important."

"So where's the fire, Harold?" asked Herford, leaning over the instrument and pressing a button again. Harold...that was Harold Viebrock, head of personnel, another big shot. And all of us listened silently to the following conversation:

"I'm surrounded by idiots, Tommy! Didn't we agree to fire Klefeld?"

"Yes. So? All settled? End of February young Höllering gets his job."

Young Höllering was the not-so-very-young-anymore son of our most important distributor, whom Herford evidently wanted to do a favor. Friedrich Klefeld was in the sales department, *Blitz* employee for twenty years, almost since the founding of the paper.

"I'm afraid it's not going to work out with young Höllering."

"What do you mean, isn't going to work out? Has to work out! His father's after Herford about it all the time! Herford's given his word—"

"I know. I know. I talked to Lang and Kalter about it a few days ago, told them to fire Klefeld. So he should have received his blue letter in time."

"Right."

"That's what I thought. But you know what happened?"

"What? Get on with it, Harold. Herford has guests."

"Lang and Kalter, the idiots, didn't get it out in time."

Though I speak with the tongues of men and angels and have not charity, I thought, as I saw Herford turn purple with rage and shout into the phone, "Didn't get it out in time? Are you trying to tell me that they didn't give him notice in time?"

"That's what I'm trying to say. I'm beside myself. This morning—"

"The assholes!"

"Herford, *please!*" This from Mama.

I am become as sounding brass or a tinkling cymbal....

"Idiots! That's what they are. This morning they come to me, their tails between their legs, and tell me they're terribly sorry but they forgot...."

"Terribly sorry? Goddamn them! This is one shitty mess. Klefeld has a year's notice, contractual." Herford was seething. "And we'd have paid it—if he'd agreed to get out at once and his job could have gone to young Höllering. And we wouldn't have had to worry about the Labor Court. Because Klefeld's wife is sick. He keeps coming in late. Clear violation of his contract. We would have gotten away with it if he'd taken it to court, right?"

And though I have the gift of prophecy and understood all mysteries, and all knowledge; and though I have all faith ...

"That's right, Tommy. And if we'd lost because he's been with us for such a long time and therefore can't be ditched, we could have negotiated with him, paid him something. A suit like that takes time. We could have risked it. He'd never have been able to stick it out anyway, financially."

"Of course not! His wife—the hospital payments—what does he want from us anyway? We're treating him much too well. He'll get his year's salary if he leaves. Would have been thankful to accept any settlement. With his wife's leukemia, he needs money."

"All that plasma. His insurance has refused to pay anymore."

"There you are. And we would have been well out of it. And he's old, too, isn't he? Sixty-three?"

"Sixty-one."

"Sixty-one. All right. We should have fired him long ago."

...so that I could remove mountains ...

"If we fire him next time around and are unlucky, his old lady

193

could be dead and he wouldn't need the money all that much anymore and would rather go on working...."

"Goddamn it, anyway! There must be *something* we can do."

"Herford, *please!*"

"Excuse me, Mama, but I can't help getting so excited about it. These idiots! So what can we do, Harold? Herford's got to do old Höllering the favor. You know he controls Upper Bavaria."

"I know. But you can't do a thing about it. And what's worse—"

"What's worse?"

"The head of distribution didn't know anything about our plan to fire Klefeld. We decided to keep it secret, didn't we? So yesterday they gave a party for Klefeld, collected money, bought presents—flowers, schnapps—a real blast. And they had an award printed. And the award says that the house thanks him for twenty years of devoted service and that you are looking forward to many more years of harmony and collaboration!"

"I am *what?*"

...and have not charity, it profiteth me nothing...

"Yes. Sorry, Tommy. But the document carries your signature, with our new facsimile method, you know—looks exactly like the real thing. Now nobody can fire Klefeld. Not if he goes to the Labor Board with that award."

"Shut up! I feel sick! Those cretins! If one doesn't do everything oneself... Listen, Harold—Lang and Kalter get fired today, as a precaution."

"Will do, Tommy. Was going to anyway."

"And then look through the files and find someone we can discharge now. Not an important man, of course, but young Höllering's got to get his job. His father has all Upper Bavaria! Herford will tell him he's got to work his way up, then he gets Klefeld's job."

...BREASTS BARE: YES—84.6%...

"Will do, Tommy."

"And you'll see that Klefeld gets his letter in time next time."

"Absolutely, Tommy. You can depend on it. We must just hope and pray that his old lady's still alive and he needs the money."

"Look in the files at once, so that I can place young Höllering right away, at least for the time being."

"I'll see to it. I'll call you back. 'Bye, Tommy."

"'Bye, Harold."

...NIPPLES PROTRUDING UNDER LOOSE, WET SHIRT: YES—93.7%...

Herford shut off the intercom, straightened up, and said, "I'll get ulcers before I'm through in this place, goddamn it! What a shitty mess! Well, Lang and Kalter get theirs today, that's for sure." He pulled down his vest and a jovial smile lit up his face that had been distorted with rage a moment ago. "So...that's done. As if I didn't have enough trouble! And people think Herford makes his money in his sleep."

"Envy," said Lester, helpfully.

"Yes, envy," said Mama. "Isn't envy a dreadful thing? When you think how hard Herr Herford has had to work to build up everything here." I looked at Hem, but he had chosen to look out of the window. "Take your pills," Mama was telling Herford. "You get so upset."

Herford fished a little gold box out of his vest pocket, snapped it open, and I could see a number of varicolored pills. Herford was a pill freak. He swallowed quantities of them. In his villa in Griesheim he was supposed to have a large medicine chest filled with medication. Now he took two blue capsules and swallowed them with some water, which he poured into a glass from a carafe.

"If Herford wasn't so devoted to his profession," he said, "he would have given up long ago." His profession and his millions. Hopefully Frau Klefeld would live a long time so that Herr Klefeld could be persuaded, in 1969, to leave his job immediately with a decent settlement.

"Gentlemen!" Herford had taken up his position beside the Bible lectern again, a man of honor from top to toe (Only blond pussies on the front page. German readers didn't like brunettes). I looked at him and was frankly curious about what he would say. We were seated in deep, comfortable armchairs, and Mama was looking at her husband as if he were an illuminated saint. The two were made for each other.

"Gentlemen—" Herford stopped. "*Now* what's the matter?"

A painfully plain secretary (Mama chose the secretaries for the eleventh floor) had knocked and brought in my coffee. "Oh," said Herford, with the patient smile of a shark, "for our writer. Of course, Frau Schmeidle. Just put it down beside Herr Roland."

Frau Schmeidle poured my coffee out of a large coffee pot and I added a good amount of the lemon juice out of the jug that had come with it. I was still pretty drunk, and it was high time I sobered up.

"Please excuse the interruption, Herr Herford," said Schmeidle, and hurried off again, an elderly gray mouse.

"Don't mention it," said Herford amiably. "Now drink your coffee, Roland, because you're going to be much needed."

I nodded.

"Herford asked you to come here," he went on, thumb in vest pocket, "to discuss something basic with you. Mama and I have been talking it over for months."

"Day and night," said Mama.

"And we have come to the conclusion that it is our duty to do it."

"Do what?" Rotaug asked quietly. He always spoke quietly.

"We have a democratic press in this country," said Herford, evidently moved by what he was about to say. "And Herford is proud to be able to say that *Blitz* was always in the vanguard of this democratic press. After all, a magazine with a circulation like ours has a duty to perform. Am I right?"

"Sometimes I'm afraid that Herr Herford may collapse under the burden he carries," Mama said to me, and I nodded seriously.

"*Blitz* has always fully realized its responsibilities," said Herford. "Herford can remember the Adenauer years, when communism began to spread in the unions and the SPD." (Not true!)

"At the time it was clearly our duty to prevent impulses and trends from going too far, and we held a fairly liberal course, but a little to the right." We haven't been anything but liberal, a little to the right, to this day, I thought, and glanced at Hem, who was still looking out of the window.

"Under the present coalition government, the right-radical movements are becoming increasingly powerful. And that is why—Mama and I have already outlined our idea briefly to Herr Stahlhut and asked him to make a comprehensive survey on the subject—" (Aha! I thought. So that's the scenario!) "... we feel it is our duty *now*, with the help of the powerful abuses—consider for a moment the recent growth of the NPD—to steer the people back onto the correct course."

"Herr Herford is always thinking of the people," said Mama. "So am I."

"All of us think first and foremost of the people, *gnädige Frau*," said manager Oswald Seerose.

"The voice of the people is the voice of God," Rotaug said softly, as if to himself.

"In totalitarian states the press is allowed only one opinion," said Herford. "In a democratic state it has to keep track of many opinions." He laid his hand on the Bible. "It is our sacred duty"—he really said it; he said "sacred"—"to check on these opinions and to steer them onto the right course. We have therefore decided to let *Blitz* take a left-liberal course until further notice. For the freedom of our people! For their well-being!"

I began to feel sick. The jackal was closing in. I drank my lemon coffee. I would have liked a swig of Chivas.

So Herford and Mama had suddenly found a heart for the left. Herford and the left? The devil and the good Lord? Water and fire? *God gave me my money.*

Herford was saying, his hand still on the Bible, "At the time when we made our right-liberal drive, things looked bad, and our enemies taunted us with the fact that by switching allegiance, our circulation rose—as if we had done it for that!"

"If our circulation goes up again now, with our switch to the left-liberal course, will they taunt us again?" asked Mama.

"That's something that can't be avoided," said poker-faced Dr. Rotaug. "Don't let it trouble you."

"Of course, Herr Herford doesn't let it trouble him," said Mama. Her dark mink slipped to the floor. Lester jumped up and picked it up. "Thank you, dear Herr Lester." She sighed. "The just man always has to suffer."

"True, true," said manager Oswald Seerose. "But as long as he knows he's doing the right thing, he doesn't have to defend it."

Evidently the circulation was slipping. I knew that Bertie, who hadn't spoken a word, and Hem were thinking the same thing: A change of the guard in Bonn was long overdue. Anybody who thought Herford and Mama were stupid was crazy. They had the instincts of rats who know when to leave a sinking ship. When the time to get back on it came, with their fine instincts, they'd be the first!

"Good intentions," said Herford, "don't always go together

197

with good earnings. For us they did until now. But Herford doesn't know how things will turn out when we follow the dictates of our conscience and move to the left. However, even if it does lead to higher earnings, that does not speak against the rightness and the decency of our intentions."

Suddenly I had to think of something Hem had said: "In the last analysis, the thing that causes the downfall of all ideologies is not the evil in men, but his limitations, the tragedy that man can think only on a small scale—wretchedly and narrow-mindedly."

19

"No party and no ideology," Hem had said at the time, "can afford to declare that it is propagating evil. Because most people are basically stupid, egotistic, and tactless, but not evil. That is why it would never be possible to win over a great number with a recognizably evil program. As a result, all isms and ideologies, whether Catholic, socialist, or communist, must address themselves to mankind with the well-meaning and decent maxims."

This conversation had taken place in his big apartment in which he—a widower now—lived alone. It was an old house in the Fürstenbergerstrasse, under Grüneburg Park, and outside the windows you could see the beautiful trees and lawns of the park and the high-rise buildings that had been built around it. The apartment was much too big for Hem; he didn't use all its rooms. Hem collected music scores and a big library of musicians' biographies, books on the history of music, and monographs of all the famous composers. He had the largest record collection of anyone I knew, and a very elaborate sound system. He still had his cello, and sometimes when I visited him, he played for me. His favorite modern composer was Helmuth Rahmers, a Swiss, and Hem was, of course, a member of the Helmuth Rahmers Association and owned all the composer's records.

On the day he spoke to me of the narrowness of man's thinking, Rahmer's Concerto in E Flat for violin and orchestra, composed in 1911–12, was playing on the stereo in the next room.

It wasn't a concerto in the usual sense but rather the monologue of a violin with orchestra accompaniment, with the oboe, clarinet, and horns dominant. The music resounded in the beautiful room with its Empire furniture. I sat opposite Hem, who was smoking his pipe, and listened to his favorite composer. The first movement—romanticism a la Schubert, the sound of the horn as if emananting from a magical forest. One G-flat Minor passage serene, as if the moon were rising. And the dreamy violin above all the other instruments, as if grieving for a lost love, a love long past, dispelled and blighted....

Hem was saying, "I can see it more and more clearly, my boy, how certain people use noble conceptions only to further their own ends. I don't know why so few people recognize this. The maxims serve these people but these people never serve the maxims. They should practice what they preach—'syntony,' as they say in psychiatry—but they never do. They use their so-called beliefs aggressively, to attain power, and for nothing else...."

The violin sang. An allegro tried to interrupt but was prevented from doing so by the horn. Horn and violin were united in their grief.

Hem said, "The important thing is the motive that inspires the guiding principles or faith. The motives—God help us and our civilization—were always bad. The principles were not—couldn't be; no one would have dared. Or how could the masses be inspired and made compliant and ready to make sacrifices? That, Walter, is the greatest deception ever practiced against mankind, at all times and under all regimes. Man was captured by ideas and qualities and wishful thinking, by dreams that were good, if you can forget their corrupt and criminal initiators for a moment!"

The wild emotions of the first movement were becalmed. A repeat motive came next: cautious, gentle, more controlled. And I heard Hem say, "It is grotesque, and nobody even wants to mention it, but I do: A person should be honest, loyal, brave, fair, hardened, and healthy—what could be said against that? Nothing. But the people who preach this then turn around and murder six million Jews, remove their gold teeth, make lampshades of their skin, and cause the greatest war of all time, unimaginable suffering. Doesn't this demonstrate clearly how mendacious this mentality was, how diabolical and evil? But you can't say that bravery, loyalty, daring, honesty, frankness, and the readiness to make sacrifices are bad characteristics. They are *good* characteristics!"

"You don't exclude the Nazis?" I asked. "But they were really criminals. You can't—"

"Slowly, my boy. Don't rush me. Of course they were criminals. The greatest criminals of all. But even they included good things in their programs and ideologies, *had to!* They couldn't simply say, 'We want war! We want to destroy all Jews and so and so many other nationalities!' That wouldn't have worked."

"But in their party program they already spoke of 'living space' and 'ethnic purity,' and they were openly anti-semitic."

"I know what a crazy program it is, my boy. I only want to prove to you that even the greatest criminals don't dare to step in front of the people without suffering some good and decent goals. Freedom and Bread! Work for Everybody! Law and Order!"

"And the Jews?"

"That was exceptionally hellishly planned," said Hem. "The Nazis' appeal was directed at the German people, so all they had to do was declare the Jews non-German. Whereupon the stalwart disciples of the Nordic god could do as they pleased with them."

The second movement began, hopeless and dark. An organ. Woodwinds trying to fight the darkness, and then the first violin, again as if mourning a love that no longer existed.

Hem said, "And thus you can pervert the principles of freedom together with all the rest. This is what has happened to all ideologies since the beginning of time, and is happening today in East and West. The Nazis did the exact opposite of the good things they preached. They sent their strong, brave young men to die senselessly on the battlefield so that Goering, the biggest pig of them all, could steal art treasures, and Goebbels could sleep with every film star, and Hitler, that gruesome psychopath, could rise out of a lower middle-class milieu to the rank of a god! And look at communism! I approve of their principles one hundred percent. What comes closer to religion than communism? Freedom! Equality! The brotherhood of man! The abolition of all earthly possessions! What could be more wonderful? And where are the twenty-five million who lost their lives when Stalin was purged? Or give me a more beautiful sentence than 'Love thy neighbor as thyself.' And what oppression, what horror, and the death of how many millions did the Crusades and the Inquisitions bring with them? The church is as guilty as all the rest. And in the name of God and the Cross!"

"And what about the others, the democracies?" I asked.

"Democracy is not an ideology," said Hem, "but here, too, my theory is valid. With one small qualification: when a democracy is very old and firmly established—as in England—then it is hard to destroy, even for the most corrupt. But it can be done. It's only more difficult. Take a look at America's Declaration of Independence. 'We hold these truths to be self-evident, that all men are created equal, that they are endowed by their Creator with certain inalienable Rights, that among these are Life, Liberty, and the Pursuit of Happiness.' Wonderful, isn't it? Great! All men are created equal! And what's going on with the blacks in America? To what extent have corruption, power, and crime undermined that democracy? The pursuit of happiness—Who cares a damn about the millions in need in the United States? A few hundred American families own one quarter of the wealth of this earth! The right to live? If you walk through Central Park in New York City, even in the daylight, you stand a chance of being killed. There is no criminal record in the world to equal it. What went wrong with the Kennedys' murders? With the murder of Martin Luther King? All born free and independent. And what about Vietnam? Who is slaughtering the Vietcong over there in a war that's never been declared, slaughtering them like animals, vermin that have to be destroyed, so-called subhuman elements. It's the same thing everywhere, all the time. And always has been!"

The second movement faltered, the main theme recurred, still full of hope, as opposed to the plaintiveness of the introduction. And there—a merry passage, brushing everything else aside, and as if released, violin and clarinet joined in.

"Take a look at the programs of our Catholic Party and our Social Democrats," said Hem. "How much difference is there between them? Very little. Because in our time there really can be no other programs than those demanding an improvement of our social structure—health, prosperity, security, a stable currency, and cultural development. Who would dare to say in his program, 'We're not going to give the children a new gym; we don't care if they have potbellies!' Or any party that would say, 'We approve of marijuana!' They'd be booted out of political life! So party programs have lost all meaning. They're never fulfilled. They're nothing but propaganda to keep the various groups of cold egocentrics and status-seekers in power. Listen! That's the main theme of the last movement, but it can't get through; the suffering it's trying to replace comes in so much stronger. There . . . now we're in B Minor, and what follows is like a love dialogue, you could almost write the words. Do you feel it, too? Misery and fear, and now, in the third movement, the love theme from the introduction comes in again."

Hem listened for a long time to the music of his genius; then he said, as if to himself, "In the last analysis, only a primitive type can succeed in reaching his goals, a man who isn't intelligent or mature enough to really see through the situation. And this type, once he is in power, immediately says to himself, 'In order to remain in power, I have to get rid of my political opponents. I have to fill all positions with my people and—there you have it—'compromise, and come to some sort of pseudo-agreement with the enemy, whether it be church, communism, Nazism, hawks or doves, Democrats or Republicans—if I want to stay in power.' And with this primitive procedure, no system will ever represent the interests of the good, the decent, the poor, or the little man. Only the ones in power are served. You understand?"

I nodded.

"The primitive man's outcry is. 'I must stay in power!' The party member cries, 'Yes!' The primitive man has all he can do to eliminate and liquidate those who could endanger him and with whom no phony compromise is possible. Your question just now—'What about the Jews?' Hitler and his gangster friends knew that the Jews were smarter, that an older culture lay behind them. Why do I say 'older'? Culture is enough. The Nazis had none. And they also realized that their smartness gave the Jews power. It was therefore understood that the Jews would be Hitler's most formidable enemy and that his aim would have to be to bring the Jews down if he was to survive. So he made the fight against the Jews a part of his program, and once he had the power, he destroyed them. The Catholic Church knew very well that it was threatened by enlightenment, so—away with the forces of enlightenment. Stalin knew that the intellectuals, that anyone with independent socialist ideas, was a menace to him. So—kill and destroy them! The model American democracy feared that its exploitation and corruption would be exposed. The result: the McCarthy witch-hunt. Everyone who was not for the fanatic patriots of the New World, who raised his voice in doubt, had to be persecuted, was a—"

"A communist," I said.

"Right. A communist. He had to be locked up, he shouldn't be allowed to work, he had to be eliminated. And in one way or another, every crime on this earth arises out of this stupidity, this narrow-mindedness, this inferior thinking. *Ignorance* is our misfortune, not any basic evil in mankind."

Through the open window, above the sound of the music, I could hear the laughter and cries of children playing in the park. "That's the way it is," said Hem. "That's the way it was and that's the way it always will be. Individuals or groups will abuse a correct teaching—there are so few anyway, at best the great religions, *not* those who preach them ... I don't count *them*—and use a correct teaching to further the development of their power. And the opposition movements all over the world today, who say all the things I just said, proceed blindly, pour out the baby with the bath water, and destroy the last remnants of order that are still worth anything. Inexperienced in the actualities of our condition, unthinking and revolutionary, the new prophets strike out indiscriminately at left and right, and smash everything that still manages somehow to hold the world together...."

Freedom. Hopeless. At least in the intermezzo. The violin sang blissfully; the woodwinds were joyous, too.

Hem said, "Why am I saying all this? Why do I have to think about it all the time? Because you and I are faced with this phenomenon every day."

"With *Blitz*?"

"With *Blitz*," he said sadly. "There was a time, at the beginning, a time without ideologies and maxims and computers...."

"A good time," I said. Hem nodded and puffed on his pipe. "Because we had no ideologies," he said, "no scheme, no dogmas. Today we can choose the best and cleanest theme—the minute we set it in this format of word and picture, it is corrupted. Look at your triumph! What is there to be said really against a serious series on sex?"

"Nothing," I said.

'Nothing. In our present age of communication, the theme of sex education should be welcome if—and here we go again—if the whole enterprise weren't organized so that Herr Herford and his mama might earn themselves silly...."

"And I earn myself silly."

"You and I and all of us," said Hem. "In the Bible Herford likes

to read, it says, 'Except ye repent, ye shall all likewise perish.'"
He shook his head. "We are not going to repent. No one on this
earth is going to repent. Not the little man, not the big man. And
all of us will perish."

The full orchestra tuned in once more, the violin quivered in
tragic protest, then faded away....

20

After all that had happened, I was able to talk to Fräulein Louise
just as Pastor Demel had been able to. She had learned to trust me
and knew that I meant no harm. That is why she could speak
clearly with me about her friends.

"There is one thing I don't understand," I said to Fräulein
Louise during one of my visits.

"Yes?" She smiled at me. Her hair was snow-white now; her
face, as kindly as ever, as usual wore a slightly ecstatic
expression.

"You went to visit your friends on the moor at midnight on
November twelfth?"

"Yes. So?"

"But already that afternoon, hours before your friends
promised to help you, the French antique dealer, André Garnot,
and the superintendent, Stanislav Kubitzky, were telling the
police that they had witnessed a brutal murder attempt on our
correspondent, Conrad Manners."

"Yes—so?"

"You've told me that Kubitzky and Garnot are your French
and Polish friends, returned to life in the bodies of the two living
men."

"Yes. That's right. Why? I spoke to them both later."

"That's just what I'm driving at," I said.

"What *are* you driving at, Herr Roland?"

"If Garnot and Kubitzky are really your two dead friends,
then they must have gone into action many hours *before* you
spoke to them. Long before they promised to help you. Now do
you understand what I'm driving at? That afternoon your friends

didn't know anything about your plan. How do you explain this time discrepancy?"

"Time, he says." Fräulein Louise shook her head. "Herr Roland still talks about time after I have told him so much about infinity and eternity. Look here, Herr Roland, in that other world there is no such thing as time. Time is a wholly earthly concept. And why not? How could there possibly be time in eternity and and infinity? Would you mind telling me how long a few hours are there?"

"I can't."

"You can't. And why can't you? Because if you could, there would be no infinity or eternity. Then we would be able to measure them as we measure time down here."

Fräulein Louise shook her head and leaned forward a little. "You say I met my friends around midnight on November twelfth and they promised to help me," she said. "That's putting it in an earthly way. That's too simple. That's the way we dumb living creatures express ourselves. Pardon me, please. I didn't mean 'dumb' personally; you know that. Actually, I could have met my friends a thousand years ago or a thousand years from now—it would have come to the same thing. Because since there is no time in the beyond, time has no meaning. According to our stupid conception of time, my friends can move backwards and forwards in it, and can do something long before they have promised to do it . . . or much later. I'll say it again—there is no such thing as time in the beyond, and that is why the Frenchman and the Pole could be in Hamburg in the bodies of two living men *before* I talked to them."

"So your friends acted *before* they received the impetus for their actions from you."

"Expressed in earthly terms—yes. But expressed in the language of the beyond, they of course acted only *after* they had received an impetus. Because there is nothing illogical in the universe. Do you understand now? At least a little?"

"A little," I said hesitantly, and thought of what Hem had told me that night in the booth at the Hamburg station.

"When you think about it, in our life it's not so very different."

"How do you mean that?"

"Well . . . that we feel the effect of something before it has happened. Just think about it. Have you never felt sad and didn't know why?"

"Yes, but—"

"Well, there you are! You were sad about something that hadn't happened yet, something that still had to happen. But your connection with the beyond—everybody has a connection with the beyond, a very fine one—let you sense what was going to happen, and that's why you were so sad. It was a moment in which you could see ahead. Where was time then? You see! In that moment you may even have known what was going to happen to you, but you didn't want to face it, so you thought it away. Only the sadness remained. If we poor living creatures can occasionally move between past, present, and future, you can imagine how well my friends can do it. For them there is no space and no yesterday or today—for them there is always only a tomorrow."

"Yes. Now I think I know what you mean."

"Well, at last! It's perfectly clear, isn't it?" And she laughed. "And please write all about it, about time and eternity—yes? And all about me, so that people can understand everything that happened. You have my permission. In writing."

Yes, I had her permission in writing, and Fräulein Louise had accepted the money. But in court her release wouldn't be worth the paper it was written on. But then, Fräulein Louise and I were never going to have to face an earthly court together.

21

"What did you do after you had talked this over with your friends?" I asked Fräulein Louise.

"I acted right away," she replied.

"Right away?"

"I didn't have to go back to the camp. I had my bag with me, and my identification papers and money."

"How much money?"

"A little over four thousand marks."

"*What?*"

"Well, yes. The two thousand you gave me, and my savings. I never spent anything at the camp, had everything I needed, didn't I? So I had my salary, except for what I gave away."

"Did you give a lot away?"

She laughed happily and said, "With so much poverty around me, Herr Roland? Not that I did anything extravagant, but there were the children, poor things...."

"But that you went off with four thousand marks in cash.... Wasn't that a bit risky?"

"If I'd left the money at the camp, *that* would have been risky. Even if I'd hidden it. And why? Because they spy on me all the time—the women do—and in the end they'd have found it and stolen it."

"You hid your savings?"

"Yes. And in a very good spot. But then I thought, Who knows... perhaps they'll find it after all."

"Why didn't you ever put your savings in a bank?"

"Go away with your banks!" cried Fräulein Louise. "I've never trusted them, never! I can still remember in 1929, or after 1945—what people had put in the banks was gone! That's how easy the banks made it for themselves."

"The money was worthless for those who kept it at home, too."

"Is that so? Anyway, I didn't have any savings until after 1945. But if I'd had any, I'd never have put the money in the bank. I simply don't trust them."

She was quiet for a while, then she changed the subject. "Of course I asked Pastor Demel, casually, with whom Irina had spoken on the phone; with this Herr Bilka, he told me, and that he had answered the phone, but then she hadn't been able to reach him any more. I wrote down the address of this man Bilka. And the telephone number. 2-2068-54. Right?"

"And you still remember it?" I said, astounded.

"Oh, I have a wonderful memory." She laughed again. "No. Not really. I was just showing off. Look, here's my little notebook. At the time I wrote down everything in it." She showed me the notebook, imitation leather, the kind stores give away at the end of the year. Jens Fedrup, Grocery, was printed on the spine.

"You were sure that I was taking Irina to Hamburg?"

"Of course! You'd disappeared. Irina had disappeared. She wanted to get to her fiancé. You were a reporter. I'm not stupid, Herr Roland."

"I know you're not, Fräulein Louise."

"But how to get there in the middle of the night—that *was* a problem. First I walked back a ways. I thought I'd go to the Skull and Crossbones. There are often people there late. Such a silly name! It's a quiet little inn. Just one room. Only cold cuts to eat, but you can drink what you like. The innkeeper makes money on the drinks, and how! And all thanks to our camp." She nodded. "There are a few pictures of naked girls on the walls, cut out of *Playboy*." (She pronounced the English word correctly.) "And a big juke box. The innkeeper bought it to get people in the right mood...terribly loud...Well, so I left the moor and walked back to the village and then—I thought I'd die—he came tearing around the curve, toward me..."

<h1 style="text-align:center">22</h1>

The truck came silently, without lights. The driver had been in the Skull and Crossbones Tavern only three minutes before and had played one last dice game with camp driver Kuschke, taking his time about it. Only a few motorists and natives had been in the bar, and Kuschke talked for hours about the dramatic and bloody events at the camp that afternoon. His audience drank and shot craps and listened, duly indignant about it all. It had been Kuschke who had suggested they break it up. "It's time I got back," he'd said. He was pretty drunk as he started to go home!

The driver was not drunk, just slightly tipsy. He got into his truck, started the motor, shifted into gear, and was off, too. The moon was shining brightly, which was why he didn't notice that he was driving with no lights. He only realized it when he turned a corner and suddenly saw a shadow ahead of him and then felt he had touched some solid object lightly with his right fender, and could see the shadow being flung to one side. This startled him so that he stalled the truck and it stopped abruptly. He got out, knees shaking, and walked around the truck to a ditch that ran alongside the road. Then he saw what the shadow had been—a little old woman, and she was lying motionless in the rushes.

The driver said hoarsely, "*Ježis Maria, doufám že se staré pani nic nestalo!*" With which he had reached Fräulein Louise.

The fender had sideswiped her; she had fallen on soft ground and was now staring at the driver wide-eyed. Her hat was tilted to one side over her white hair, and she was clutching her bag with both hands.

"What happened?" cried the driver, wide-awake suddenly and cold sober from the shock.

Fräulein Louise just looked at him and said nothing.

"Well?" said the driver.

Fräulein Louise's eyelids fluttered and her lips parted in a smile.

"So what is it?"

Fräulein Louise asked in Czech, "Did you just say, 'Jesus Maria, I hope the old lady's all right?'"

Delighted, the driver answered, also in Czech, "That's what I said, compatriot." Since she had addressed him with the familiar *Du,* he did the same. "So...are you hurt?"

"Not in the least," said Fräulein Louise.

He helped her to her feet. She brushed the dust off her coat, raised her arms, twisted her neck, and stretched. "Anyway, I don't think I'm hurt."

They went on speaking in Czech. "It was my fault. I didn't have my lights on. I was in the tavern, and then, when I drove off—"

"Yes," said Fräulein Louise, "you forgot to turn on your headlights." She put her face up to his and sniffed. "Compatriot, you've been drinking," she said.

"Only three beers."

"Don't lie to me—I can smell schnapps, too."

"Well...a few...."

"Don't you know that's a criminal offense, compatriot?"

The wind from the moor was getting stronger. That was why Fräulein Louise hadn't heard the truck coming. "Were you at the tavern a long time?"

"An hour or so. We were talking about Karel, the boy that got shot this afternoon at the camp."

Suddenly Fräulein Louise's expression was ecstatic. "So you know all about it!" she said breathlessly.

"Sure, I know."

"The poor, poor boy!"

"Yes, the poor kid. Pigs—the ones who did it. Politics are at the bottom of it, shitty politics. Forgive me, compatriot."

Fräulein Louise accepted the apology with a gesture of her

hand. Her head cocked to one side, she said softly and confidentially, "You're my friend, aren't you?"

"Sure I'm your friend," said the driver, limp with relief that the old lady wasn't hurt.

"Yes, I can see it now. Oh, how wonderful! Dear God!" and she looked up at the sky.

"What's up there?" The driver looked, too, then it occurred to him. "Oh. I see. The dear God."

"Yes," said Fräulein Louise.

She's thanking God that she didn't break any bones, thought the driver. I should be doing the same thing, so he looked up again and said aloud, "Thanks!"

"That's all we needed," said Fräulein Louise, "that you run over your Louise, Franticek."

This the driver had to think over. What the hell was she talking about? Franticek? And "your Louise"? And suddenly he remembered the crazy social worker at the camp who spoke to people who weren't there, to dead people, a story Kuschke had told him after making him swear he wouldn't repeat it, ever. The name of the crazy woman was—was Louise! Dear Lord . . . and there she was standing in front of him. Absolutely harmless, a truly good soul according to Kuschke. Well, wasn't *that* something! Here they were, face to face. "I'm sorry, Louise," he said. "Of course I didn't mean to do it. But the damned light—"

"And the damned schnapps and beer," she said, shaking a finger at him. Then both of them laughed.

The driver said, "I am—"

"Oh, I know who you are," said Fräulein Louise, quite sure of herself now.

"Yes?"

"Yes."

"Who am I?" The driver was curious.

"You're my Czech friend."

Careful . . . she's nuts, thought the driver, and said, "Right. And you are my Louise."

Tears of joy welled up in Fräulein Louise's eyes. She leaned her head against his broad chest and said, "Oh, but this is wonderful! Truly wonderful! And you'll really help me?"

"Of course I'll help you," said the driver, who was beginning to feel a little uncomfortable.

"I've got to get to Hamburg," said Fräulein Louise. "But you know all about that. Are you on your way to Hamburg?"

"No. To Bremen. I got some peat, over on the other side of the moor where they're still cutting it."

Fräulein Louise couldn't stop gazing at him, the tears shining in her eyes. "Would you take me to Bremen? To the station? So I can get the train to Hamburg?"

The driver thought this over for a moment, then he decided that the poor crazy old thing could report him and cause him a lot of trouble if he said no, so he said, "Sure I will, Louise."

"Because you're my friend. I knew it! I knew it! So that's how the whole thing starts!"

So that's how what whole thing starts? the driver wondered, but then he thought he'd better not ask and said, "Because I'm your friend, Louise. Get in. I've got to get the truck out of this curve or somebody'll run into me."

"And you're not drunk anymore?"

"Word of honor," said the driver.

Two minutes later the truck, laden with peat moss, was bumping over the miserable road, its headlights on high. Fräulein Louise was sitting beside the driver, her big bag on her knees, her eyes still open wide with excitement and joy. "Where are you from, Franticek?" she asked.

"From Gablonz," said the driver. "It's called Jablonec now," he added. "Not that it matters." And my name is Josef, not Franticek, which doesn't matter either. If the crazy old thing wants to call me Franticek, it's all right by me.

"Which makes you my neighbor!" cried Fräulein Louise. "I'm from Reichenberg."

"Well, of all things!" said the driver. "And we meet up here!"

Fräulein Louise was in a state of bliss. "Did you flee, Franticek?"

"Yes, two months ago. And you, Louise?" And then he added hastily, "What an idiot I am! Of course you didn't flee. You've been here twenty years."

"Twenty years, yes," said Fräulein Louise. It never occurred to her that the driver could have found out all about her at the Skull and Crossbones. This was "her" Czech, her dead friend, her Franticek. Her friends had promised to help her. "You'll take me to Bremen, and from there I'll take the train to Hamburg, and in Hamburg you'll go on helping me, won't you?"

"Of course," said the driver, and thought: In Bremen I'll be rid of the poor nut and I'll never see her again, and she can't report me. God, was I lucky!

He dropped Fräulein Louise at the main station in Bremen at just about the time when an American, supposedly a pharmacist and supposedly called Richard McCormick, was pressing a cloth soaked in some anesthetizing fluid against my nose and mouth, in front of Eppendorfer Baum 187, and everything went black around me.

23

The room was enormous. It didn't have a single window, and everything in it was white: walls, furniture, instruments, floor, and ceiling, with bright fluorescent lighting that gave everything a deathlike hue. The room was dust-free and air-conditioned, and it was a nightmare.

I had to think of George Orwell's 1984. Facing me and sparkling with a thousand little lights that lit up erratically and lightning-fast—red, yellow, green, blue, and white, with magnetic tape reels moving jerkily back and forth behind glass—was the evil spirit of the house, the thing most hated, most feared, cursed by everyone and adored by Herford and his Mama—the computer. There were other machines in the room, among them one that looked like an oversized typewriter. Fat spaghettilike tangles of cables ran on wooden tracks from one instrument to the other. At a white table five young men in white coats were leaning over a long strip of paper and talking to each other softly. A man in white was seated at the strange typewriter, typing on it. You could hear the instruments, and the little colored lights blinked on and off, on and off, nonstop.

The windowless room had two heavy metal sliding doors. The one leading to the passage was secured by many locks and was used by the men who worked here. I had seen it often from the outside. A red flash of lightning was painted on it, and below that, in red letters: Authorized Personnel Only! The second door led to a room next to Herford's office. Here he could rest and take his meals. A car with a warming oven was sent to the Frankfurter Hof for him, and a girl from the cafeteria served. There was a bathroom, too. Herford could spend the night in this little suite when he worked late. He entered his office by a door that was all bookshelves on the other side. It swung back soundlessly when he pressed a button. That was how all of us had entered this inner sanctum, and had proceeded on through the second door, white metal too, but with no flash of lightning on it. It slid to one side without a sound when you pushed a coded number on a control panel, and it closed again by itself. This was Herr Stahlhut's kingdom!

He was standing before us, but he addressed everything he had to say to Herford and Mama, a slender man with fashionable sideburns, cold eyes, a mouth with practically no lips, and a crew cut. He spoke in an unnatural voice, in an aggressive tone that sounded as if it would brook no opposition. So here we had penetrated the heart of the publishing house and the heart of its publisher. What took place here was Kismet, Revelations, and God's will for Herford. And Stahlhut was the interpreter of this magnificent computer, which was as omniscient as God Himself. Perhaps Herford saw God as a computer—anything was possible—in which case, Stahlhut was its high priest.

Stahlhut was standing beside a monitor that looked exactly like the one in Herford's office. He was holding his little lecture in front of the video screen, which didn't show anything yet—only flickered, empty and black. "Our investigation into changing political trends was conducted by our Opinion Finding Institute over widely scattered areas," he said in a tone that sounded like a mixture of pastor, politician, and general. "For once, we had plenty of time. Our questions were aimed at two groups; the program is therefore divided into two parts. On the one hand, we asked people who read *Blitz*, on the other those who don't."

And with that, I thought, we have the first case of manipulation. However the question about a trend toward the left had been expressed, what could those people answer who had no idea how far to the left or right *Blitz* was oriented? Bertie seemed to be thinking along the same lines because he exclaimed, "Just a minute! How can people who don't read *Blitz*—?"

"Quiet!" Herford said angrily. Mama looked hurt.

Hem looked at me and whispered, "Remember what I told you about the good principles and their dreadful realization?"

I nodded.

"Quiet, please!" said Rotaug, pulling at his Hjalmar Schacht collar. Hem grinned across at him. Rotaug turned away.

"Ten thousand people were questioned, all over Germany...."

"What were they asked?" asked Bertie.

"If you would be so good as not to interrupt me," said Stahlhut.

"Quiet, damn it!" shouted Herford.

Bertie looked at him, smiling like a child; then he looked at me and Hem. I shrugged. Hem closed his eyes and shook his head. There was absolutely no point in asking questions here. One might as well have challenged Herford and Mama on the existence of God.

This fellow Stahlhut was a sly customer, I thought, not for the first time. So innocently that they didn't even notice it, he would ask Herford and even more frequently, Mama, what they liked and didn't like in the magazine, because he—and I mean it—a highly intelligent man, had recognized long ago that Herford and his Mama both had the same abysmal taste as millions of their countrymen, the sort of taste that was an absolute guarantee of high circulation. But I must say, on behalf of our people, that many millions did *not* share this taste. With an honest poll, therefore, Stahlhut's minions would have come up with a great many answers that said our magazine was a rag. Stahlhut had to take a very deliberate and selective poll, and to be quite sure of the results, had to formulate his questions in a way that would insure the right answers. These computerized results then miraculously corroborated Herford and Mama's views almost one hundred percent. *Almost* one hundred percent. Because Herr Stahlhut was smart enough to program a few (very few) discrepancy factors into the results.

"Our decision," Stahlhut was saying, in the voice that was used to giving orders and seeing them obeyed, yet with so much heartiness (what an actor he would have been!), "represents the decision of the people. We have taken into consideration all the most common professions and ethnic groups, according to their social and cultural level, according to sex, age, religion, income, occupation. We have also taken the difference between the various provinces into consideration. The south, as we know, reacts differently from the north."

"Aha!" said Hem. Nobody else said anything, and Stahlhut went on in his role as magician.

"The rural districts react differently from the cities. We therefore made certain that the big city, medium-sized city, and

214

small town were all represented. Because of this very wide spectrum, we and the Institute required two weeks for the survey, *gnädige Frau*"—this with a bow. And Mama gazed at him enraptured.

"If you have come to a correct result—" said Mama. "It is so important, all of us realize, that we know exactly how the people feel."

"The result is absolutely correct," said Stahlhut, bowing again. Behind him, on the awesome front of the computer, the little colored lights were flickering with breathtaking rapidity. "A computer, correctly and comprehensively programmed, *cannot* give a wrong answer."

"Isn't that wonderful?" Mama looked up at Herford, who nodded. He also looked strangely moved. For him this room was as hallowed as church.

Mama said, "Bob should see this."

Bob (Robert) was their twenty-two-year-old son, no good, a tramp, girl-crazy, and lazy—Mama's pride and joy and a cause of constant irritation to Herford.

Hem whispered in my ear, "A computer is a whore. You can abuse them both. But Mama and Herford haven't got wise to that yet."

"And they never will," I whispered.

"Psst!" from Rotaug, who was looking at me furiously.

"The important thing was to set up a sensible set of questions that permitted people to answer freely, uninfluenced, and not manipulated," Stahlhut explained.

One always speaks most positively about the things one isn't doing, I thought. You knew exactly what answers you were going to get—the answers your publisher and his Mama wanted. Answers that such a large number of Germans would never have given if they hadn't been manipulated, or we'd have had a social-democratic government long ago and not a coalition government. I looked at Hem and Bertie and they nodded. They were thinking the same thing. Oswald Seerose was looking at me with clinical interest while toying with the handkerchief in his breast pocket. He was the craftiest and coolest customer of them all. I had never heard him give an opinion. "His Excellency"— that was what he was called, and there was something about him that could be compared with Talleyrand, Fouché, and Holstein.

"What did the questionnaire say?" asked Mama.

"Oh, *gnädige Frau*, that can only be summed up," Stahlhut

answered promptly. "First there were general questions: Did the person questioned like *Blitz?* What did he like best? What did he like least?" Mama nodded. "Followed by questions as to what he would like to see in the magazine, what he would like best, what he missed, and why. The main question about the political trend was very cleverly worked into the general questions. The person asked in no way got the impression that he was being questioned about his political views. So many people don't like to talk to strangers about anything like that. Don't you agree?"

"Absolutely!" thundered Herford.

"And then," Stahlut went on, "the questionnaires came to us. A team"— he gestured behind him at the men in white coats who were debating something softly around their white table—"set about programming the results. For that the questionnaires had to be sorted according to the groups questioned; and the general answers were stored in the computer as new information beside the old standard program, which is being constantly revised and which gives us full insight into the magazine. The special question, about the desired political stance *Blitz* should take, was the core question of the program. It was fed into the computer in a new series, separate from the groups already mentioned. We also programmed the answers of those who do not read *Blitz* but know all about it, and who had something to say about the position an illustrated weekly of our dimensions should take in the present national-political situation."

Bertie looked at me, I looked at Hem, Hem looked at Bertie. No comment.

"We were also concerned with the younger generation, those under twenty-four. We know that these young people have never been our regular or potential buyers, but the answers show that *if* the magazine were to move to the left, the chances are excellent of our winning a group of readers we have not reached to date."

"Wonderful!" cried Herford.

Wonderful? I thought. You crafty wretch! You no-good mathematics students! That our young people tend more to the left than the right isn't exactly news.

"And after they had sorted the questionnaires," said Mama, "did they feed them to the computer through this thing here— this typewriter or whatever it is?"

"That's just what it is, *gnädige Frau*," said Stahlhut. "A typewriter with a certain set of controls. Over there they're working on a smaller program. For that we still use this—let's call

216

it a typewriter. But with our ten thousand questionnaires we were able to use a more modern procedure, thanks to Herr Herford's generosity." A deep bow from Stahlhut, a benevolent gesture from Herford. "We now have a computer that can read whole sheets—with their symbols for *yes, no,* and *undecided*—electronically, via photo cells. The impulses are recorded on the magnetic tape, and all we have to do is plug the magnetic tape into the data evaluation box. Since we divided the questionnaires meticulously into separate groups, the computer was able to give absolutely precise answers. Ulli!"

One of the men at the white table looked up. "Yes?"

"Program RX-22, please," said Stahlhut.

The young man called Ulli went over to an instrument that looked like a Wurlitzer organ and began to press buttons. The result was chaos on the computer panel. The colored lights danced wildly, the magnetic tape reels moved even more jerkily, and the first green letters appeared on the monitor.

...LARGE CITY. NORTH GERMANY. MERCHANT CLASS. MALE. AGE: 35–40. MARRIED. 1–2 CHILDREN. OWN HOUSE OR APARTMENT. MONTHLY INCOME: 4000–5000 DM. PROTESTANT. UPPER-MIDDLE CLASS CAR TO EXPENSIVE CAR. RESULT: FOR A LEFT-LIBERAL ORIENTATION FOR BLITZ: 13.2%

Herford and Mama stared at the writing on the screen, entranced. There was a soft rushing sound in the data machine, relays clicked, little lights flickered, the magnetic tapes moved jerkily.

...LARGE CITY. NORTH GERMANY. SELF-EMPLOYED GROUPS. MALE. AGE: 35–40. UNMARRIED. NO CHILDREN. RENTED APARTMENT. MONTHLY INCOME: 1700–2500 DM. PROTESTANT. LOWER MIDDLE CLASS TO MIDDLE CLASS CAR. RESULT: FOR A LEFT-LIBERAL ORIENTATION BY BLITZ: 22.4%.

"Herford! twenty-two point four percent!" cried Mama enthusiastically. Herford nodded solemnly. General manager

217

Seerose stood with his arms crossed, his face expressionless. Dr. Helmut Rotaug was pulling at his stiff collar; then he stood still.

Stahlhut maintained his miracle-man attitude. For half an hour the green words passed across the screen. I was ready to drop; Bertie yawned loudly. Herford threw an angry glance in his direction, then he looked back at the monitor. Mama didn't take her eyes off it. Herford's face was transfigured. That was what Moses must have looked like, I thought, when he saw the Promised Land.

Forty-five minutes later we received the following communication, at last!

FINAL RESULT: ALL THOSE IN FAVOR OF A LEFT-LIBERAL REORIENTATION BY BLITZ: 85.6%.

"Isn't that wonderful!" cried Mama. "Herford, the people feel as we do. Now we know!"

"Yes," said Herford. "We and the people are one."

And I had to admire Stahlhut for the fact that he hadn't brought in a result of eighty-five or eighty-six percent, but eighty-five point six. This six-tenths of a percent suddenly filled me with respect for the man I despised. Quite a personality, this Herr Stahlhut....

24

...FINAL RESULTS: QUESTION: WHICH PO-LITICAL EVENT IN THE LAST MONTHS TOUCHED YOU MOST?...

The green computer words rolled smoothly across the screen in Herford's fantastic office. All of us had come back here, Stahlhut as well, to give further explanations that could interest Herford. Next door, in the windowless room, his colleague, Ulli, was letting the additional questions and answers roll.

...ANSWER: THE OCCUPATION OF CZECHO-SLOVAKIA BY THE WARSAW PACT NATIONS: 82.3%...

"Donnerwetter!" said Herford.
What had he expected?
"Yes, that upset me more than anything else," said Mama, shifting her hunter's hat with the long feather. I looked at Stahlhut sharply, he looked at me expressionlessly. I drank my lemon coffee, which somebody had heated up again for me.

...FINAL RESULTS: QUESTION: DO YOU FEEL THE INTERVENTION WAS JUSTIFIED? ANSWER: NO: 95.4%....

Another idiotic question!

...FINAL RESULTS: QUESTION: DO YOU FEEL SYMPATHY FOR THE CZECH PEOPLE? ANSWER: YES: 97.8%....

"You see," said Stahlhut, "we have also prepared a program for future series and reports."
Yes, we could see that!

...FINAL RESULTS: QUESTION: DO YOU FEEL SORRY FOR THOSE WHO HAD TO FLEE? ANSWER: 98.2%....

That was what questions and answers looked like. I would have liked to know what the 1.8% who had answered "no" or "undecided" looked like.

...FINAL RESULTS: QUESTION: WHO DO YOU FEEL SORRIEST FOR AMONG THE REFUGEES?...A: INTELLECTUALS?...B: POLITICAL REFUGEES?...C: ARTISTS?...D: MEMBERS OF THE LOWER CLASS?...E: MALES?...F: FEMALES?...G: CHILDREN AND JUVENILES?...ANSWER SIGNIFICANT: CHILDREN AND JUVENILES: 97.8%....

"My God, the poor children!" cried Mama, and passed a hand across her eyes.

"Dreadful!" said Rotaug, to no one in particular. It sounded as if he were giving a waiter an order....

...FINAL RESULTS: QUESTION: WOULD YOU LIKE TO KNOW HOW THESE CHILDREN ARE LIVING? ... ANSWER: YES: 85.8%....

Well, at last, there it was. Bertie couldn't keep his mouth shut again. "A computer like that is a wonderful thing," he said. The irony was lost on Herford. "That's right," he said. "Wonderful!"

Stahlhut rose, walked over to the monitor and pressed a button, evidently signaling that the presentation was to stop, because no more green letters passed across the screen, which now was empty and black again. From far away you could hear the noise of the subway construction, all the way up here to the eleventh floor.

Stahlhut said, "The result of the general analysis is that the computer considers a report or a series on the refugee children and juveniles as promising the greatest success, if *Blitz* decides to reorient to a left-liberal course. The theme seems to have the greatest human interest; it appeals to women and men in equal measure, regardless of income, profession, age, and social status."

"Well, then we have our first theme," publisher Herford cried triumphantly. "Herford asked you to come here to demonstrate the results of this survey, just as it was presented to him and his wife for the first time. Does any one of the gentlemen have anything to say against the planned reorientation to the left? We live in a democracy. My publishing house is under democratic leadership. I am a democrat myself." At this point I could have puked. "If a minority can persuade Herford that it's not the right thing to do, Herford is perfectly willing to give up the plan. Well?"

Silence.

"Nobody has anything against it?"

"Nobody," said Lester eagerly. "We think it's wonderful, all of us. Isn't that so, gentlemen?"

"We're all for it," said Rotaug curtly.

"Good, good. Herford asked you, Roland, and you, Engelhardt, to take part in this meeting because you are our best

220

writer and photographer, respectively. Herford wants this first report—or series, or whatever it turns out to be—to be done by Herford's best men. Is that clear?"

"Perfectly clear," I said, and felt a lot better. I preferred working in a house that was oriented to the left rather than to the right, although I realized that was a passing fancy—I mean, on the part of the house.

Bertie said, "I'm honored, Herr Herford. I shall enjoy an assignment with Walter again. And I'm happy about your decision, too. No intelligent person can be anything but a socialist today."

Embarrassed silence. Finally Herford burst out laughing. "You're right, Engelhardt. And it proves that Herford isn't an idiot, doesn't it?" said the man with millions. Then at once he was serious again. "So you two will give us a report on the children and juveniles."

"But what about the sex stories?" said Lester.

"I've sometimes written four series at the same time," I said.

"That's all right. But the article you handed in today...."

Bastard! He'd waited patiently for this.

"What about the article?" said Herford.

"The women had a lot of objections," said Lester, smiling at me. I smiled back.

"For God's sake!" exclaimed Herford, genuinely alarmed. "You'll have to take care of that, Roland. And fast. Today's the last day, isn't it? How did it happen?"

"He was sick," said Hem.

"Aha!" Herford cleared his throat. "Too much you-know-what, eh? Well, then you'll revise it right away, of course...."

Lester looked at me, ready to pounce. Shit! I thought. "Of course," I said. "Right away, Herr Herford." From which you can deduce what a noble person I am.

Lester looked annoyed. He had evidently been looking forward to my refusal and another scene.

"But you must write an article for the next edition, if you're going to go off with Engelhardt," said Herford.

"I'll do it tonight," I said. Accommodating...that's me! But I wanted to write about the children, regardless of what could be made of it. I simply had to write about something beside orgasms, necking, petting, the erogenous zones, or I'd go stark, staring mad!

"Very well," said Herford.

"We're so grateful to have you," said Mama. And I felt sick. "Goodness, he can still blush! Look, Herford!"

"So he can," said Rotaug, sincerely astonished. He looked at me thoughtfully.

"Where are these children, Stahlhut?" asked Herford.

"The juveniles to age eighteen and the children are at Camp Neurode. That's north of Bremen. The adults are in other camps. There are children of all nationalities in Neurode, right now mostly Czechs. But Greeks, too—"

"Greece is a member of NATO," said Rotaug.

". . . Poles and Spaniards . . ."

"Our house in Majorca!" cried Mama, her hand moving nervously to her throat.

"Forget NATO and our house in Majorca," said Herford, rising, his expression grim. "Do we want a left-liberal course or don't we? Well, then we must also have courage. Nothing's going to happen. A lot of our Socis have houses in Spain. And Herford doesn't owe NATO a thing. Anyway, this report will have human appeal and human interest!" He was off, arms spread. "Children, innocent children! A political background, naturally, but everything from a humane perspective. Humane, gentlemen, you understand?"

"Yes," said Bertie.

"Yes," I said. "Humane." And I thought of Klefeld.

"But how you approach it is your business, gentlemen. That's what Herford pays you for, and plenty. I want a shattering protest against the inhumanity of all nations and all regimes. Do you hear, Rotaug? All nations!"

"Neurode, the Golgotha of innocent youth!" said Hem with a straight face.

"Golgotha! Yes, Golgotha! If we could get that into the title," said Mama, passing a hand across her eyes again.

You may think I am exaggerating, creating caricatures out of human beings, but I am not. This is *just* how it happened. What Mama said, if you take into consideration how things worked in this computerized publishing house, may have sounded like colossal cynicism. But Herford and Mama were not cynics. And they weren't bad people either—I mean, they were no worse than many other millionaires. They were simply a part of the society in which we lived. They had our society to thank for their evolution and existence, as all of us did. He who realized this, as

Hem did, was smart. And was to be pitied. Because if he wanted to preserve an ounce of decency, he would have to anesthetize himself constantly to endure this business, anesthetize himself with music and a philosophy that led nowhere. Or anesthetize himself with women and liquor, as I did, Hem's friend and disciple. I'll revise the shitty article right here in the office, I thought, then I'll go home and whip up one for the next edition. Then we can take off, late tonight or early tomorrow morning. I mustn't forget to take my hip flask and a few bottles of Chivas.

"Think up an appropriate title page, gentlemen," said General Manager Oswald Seerose, the English aristocrat. It was only the fourth or fifth time this morning that he'd said anything at all. "We must also stress our political reorientation visually."

Bertie nodded.

Herford walked over to his Bible again. Everyone rose and folded hands—only Hem, Bertie, and I didn't.

"In close Herford will read from the Book of Books again. May it bless our plans and may we succeed," he said, leafing through the thick parchment pages, a lot of them, until he found what he was after. "The Lord is my shepherd; I shall not want," and Mama nodded, deeply moved. "He maketh me to lie down in green pastures; He leadeth me beside the still waters. He restoreth my soul. He leadeth me in the paths of righteousness for His name's sake." Herford was silent, then he added a firm "Amen."

"Amen," said everybody except Hem, Bertie, and myself. A phone rang. Our publisher took a few steps to his desk. "Yes?" He listened. "Very well," he said, and pressed a button on the silver intercom. "Well, Harold?"

You could hear the triumphant voice of the personnel manager. "Some good luck, Tommy! I've looked through the files and found one. Peter Miele. Works in the Readers' Circle group. Has only been with us for two years. A Soci. Holds speeches and incites his audience by telling them what their rights are, union stuff, and so on."

"A Soci, you say? Incites people?" mumbled Herford.

"Yes. He has lots of time till he gets the blue letter. Has a wife and three children and owns his apartment. A lot of debts. Only twenty-nine. He'll accept a settlement and go; I'm sure he will."

"Well, that's first-rate," said Herford, smiling happily. "So fire him. Fire him at once. Herford knew you'd find somebody. So

Herford can bring young Höllering in right away, ha-ha-ha!"

"Ha-ha-ha!" from Harold Viebrock, loud and clear in the receiver. And we were off on a left-liberal course, God love us. On a left-liberal basis. Breasts fully exposed.

3

Composing Room

1

The train to Hamburg was the express from Cologne that stopped in Bremen at 4:30 A.M. and got into Hamburg at 5:49. Fräulein Louise bought a second-class ticket and sat down on a bench beside a column. The station was deserted. On some of the benches men were asleep, curled up, unkempt, as they are in all big stations. Fräulein Louise dozed off a few times, but she always came to when her head began to nod. Her bag! she thought. Her bag with all that money in it! She had wedged it between herself and the column, and it was always there when she woke up.

At 4:00 A.M. Fräulein Louise walked out onto the stormy platform and bought a cup of coffee at a stand. She drank it slowly, then she asked for a second cup and drank that. The man in the stand yawned. He had the early shift and hadn't slept enough. Fräulein Louise, who had slept a bit, felt quite fresh. It's almost a year, she thought, since I've been on a train. And I never went to Hamburg by train, always by car. Three years since I was there last.

Fräulein Louise felt as if she had drunk champagne, not coffee, as if she were in the proverbial seventh heaven. It was, she decided, because of this adventure she had taken upon herself, away from the moor and its loneliness, straight to Hamburg. And then what? She didn't have a plan yet; all she had was a telephone number, two names, and two addresses. And, oh . . . what a sin to forget them! *She had her friends!* They would help her. They had already helped her. She would never have got here so fast without Franticek. She ordered a pair of sausages with mustard, and while she ate she communed silently with God: I thank You for doing all You have done for me and for helping me. Please go on helping me. Let evil be punished and the good thing triumph in the end, as the Herr Pastor always said. With me, please don't let it take too long, because I don't have time to wait. Amen. And with that she scraped together what was left of her second frankfurter, and popped it into her mouth. And paid.

"Was it good, lady?" asked the sleepy attendant.

"Very good," said Fräulein Louise, thought it over for a moment, then added the merciful lie, "Especially the coffee."

"Thank you, lady."

Fräulein Louise carefully counted the change he had given her for a ten-mark bill, then pushed twenty pfennigs across the counter. "For you."

"Thank you, lady."

The train was punctual. The storm was still raging on the empty platform and the arc lights were waving in the wind. A hoarse loudspeaker announced the train. Nobody got out; only two people got in—Fräulein Louise and a big man who looked as if he might be around forty. He had on a thick coat, no hat, and was carrying a red book. The door of the car Fräulein Louise had chosen wouldn't open. "Let me help you," said the man, and smiled at Fräulein Louise.

He had dark eyes, short black wavy hair, and a broad flat face. He fiddled around with the handle and suddenly the door opened. The steps were high and he helped her up just as if he knew she had trouble with her legs, then he got in after her. The corridor was dimly lit for the night. Fräulein Louise went on ahead. Most of the blinds in the second-class compartments were down. "They must all be asleep," said Fräulein Louise. "If we open the door, we'll wake them up."

"Up there," said the man. "I can see light in a compartment." When they got to it, they found the compartment empty.

Fräulein Louise sat down by the window, holding her bag firmly on her knees. The man, who was wearing a dark suit, a pink tie, and a white shirt under his heavy dark-blue coat, sat down opposite her. "Oh," he said at once, "you may want to sleep. I'll put out the light."

"No, no, please," said Fräulein Louise. "I don't want to sleep. I'm wide awake. But you've got a book. You probably want to read."

"Yes, if you don't mind," said the man with the pink tie, taking a pair of gold-rimmed glasses out of his pocket and putting them on. He's farsighted, thought Fräulein Louise. The man smiled at her, she smiled back. When he picked up his book and opened it, Fräulein Louise gasped. She could read what was written in gold letters on the cover: *A New Order: A New Heaven and a New Earth;* and underneath, in smaller letters, *The Watchtower*.

Fräulein Louise's heart beat as fast as the rhythm of the train, which was tearing through the howling storm. The man with the pink tie was reading a book of the Jehovah's Witnesses. *The Watchtower!* That was the name of their publication!

It's unreal, thought Fräulein Louise, like a dream! This man—surely he was here to help her get to Hamburg ... and in Hamburg another friend would be waiting. Oh, how wonderful it all was! Because Fräulein Louise was afraid of the world that she scarcely knew anymore after all the years on the moor. How miraculous it would be if she were accompanied by her friends!

Fräulein Louise said softly to herself: "'And it took place at the beginning of the thousand years of Christ....'"

"What did you say?" The man with the pink tie looked up and over his glasses at Fräulein Louise, and smiled, "Did you say something?"

"Yes," said Fräulein Louise, feeling her way cautiously. "I said, 'And it took place at the beginning of the thousand years of Christ.'"

The man looked astonished. "But that's what I'm just reading! On Judgment Day, it says here, 'Heaven and earth fled from the countenance of the One the Apostle John saw seated on the big white throne.'"

"'And there was found no place any longer for the corrupt heaven and the corrupt earth. That was when they were destroyed forever.' From the Book of Revelation." Fräulein Louise was trembling as she dared to be more bold. "'I saw a great white throne and him that sat on it, from whose face the earth and heaven fled away, and there was found no place for them.'"

"How do you know all that?" the man asked, serious but friendly.

Fräulein Louise felt strangely drawn to him. That was why, sure of herself now, she said in a conspiratorial tone, "But that's what you told me yourself, over and over again, during the years on the moor. Don't you recognize me? I'm Louise."

There was a short silence, then the man nodded and said, "Of course. How stupid of me! You're Louise."

The train roared through the night, the wind howling past it. "And you are my Jehovah's Witness, right?" said Fräulein Louise. "My friend, my dead Witness."

The man was definitely friendly. In a warm soft voice he said, "Your dead friend, the Witness, yes."

"From the moor," said Fräulein Louise.

"From the moor."

"I'm only asking because I have to be careful, you understand? This is a terrible thing we've let ourselves in for. Just between us, sometimes I'm afraid."

"You mustn't be afraid," said the man. "I am with you."

"All of you are with me, aren't you?" Fräulein Louise asked hopefully.

"All of us, yes," said the man.

"What body did you enter?" asked Fräulein Louise. "What's your name? What shall I call you?"

"My name is Wolfgang Erkner," said the man. "But call me Wolfgang and I'll call you Louise, not—" He hesitated.

"Not Fräulein Gottschalk," said Fräulein Louise.

"Louise Gottschalk," the man who called himself Wolfgang Erkner repeated, and nodded.

"I remember everything you told me out there on the moor," Fräulein Louise said proudly. "Everything! You spoke to me so often during all those years, in summer and winter. We're really very old friends, aren't we? You in death and I in life. And when I finally join you—"

"Well, now," said Wolfgang Erkner, "let's not think about that yet!"

"Oh, but we must," said Fräulein Louise. "I'm old and I'm not very well. I know it won't be long now and I'll be with you, my blessed friends. But you're right, let's not talk about it now. We have something important to do first, don't we?"

"Yes," he said.

"Do you want me to tell you the rest of what you said about the new order?" asked Fräulein Louise.

"Please do," said Wolfgang Erkner. He was still looking at her kindly.

"Well, then, that part in Revelation," said Fräulein Louise, "establishes for us the time when this universe will be replaced by a righteous heaven and a new and righteous earth. Have I got it right?"

"You've got it right, Louise."

"But this will not be at the end of the thousand years of Christ, after which all evil on earth and in heaven—" She stopped and laughed a helpless little laugh. "How does the rest go?"

He looked at the book and said quickly, "'After all evil in heaven and on earth has been cast into the lake of fire.'"

"That's it!" cried Fräulein Louise. "My memory's like a sieve these days." She burped and put her hand up to her mouth. "Excuse me, that was the frankfurters."

"What frankfurters?"

"I ate a couple on the platform, too fast. But I was hungry. Now they're making their presence felt. No . . . that isn't the time. The time is the beginning of the thousand years of Christ. And Revelation says it so beautifully." And the wind swept past the train racing through the night, and the air was filled with what sounded like a weeping and a wailing and a vast roaring.

"Dreadful, all this noise, isn't it?" said Fräulein Louise. "That's what the poor souls in the nether regions surely sound like, because it must be dreadful down there."

"In the nether regions?"

"You understand me, don't you?" said Fräulein Louise.

The man nodded.

"That part in Revelation where it says there will be no more death—I never did understand it," said Fräulein Louise. "It sounds beautiful, but all of you, my dear friends, are dead and happy. In life you were unhappy. How will you be when there is no more death?"

"It's too early to think about that," said the dark man.

"Yes, of course. How stupid of me, Wolfgang!" said Fräulein Louise. "That time has yet to come, and it will bring many changes. For you, too."

"It certainly will," said the dark man.

"But long before that I'll be with you," said Fräulein Louise. "Not right away, though. I can't join you right away. I have something to attend to in Hamburg, don't I?"

He nodded. The wind howled, the locomotive whistled, a long, piercing sound. Suddenly the train was hurtling through fog; waves of it swept like clouds past the window.

"The man who murdered little Karel must be found," said Fräulein Louise. "And we must find Irina before something happens to her. Those are the important things, those are the only things that matter. Am I right?"

"Absolutely," said the dark man. Suddenly he leaned forward and took off his glasses. "We have to have a talk, Fräulein Louise."

"But we are having a talk."

"We have to talk about other things. About you."

"But you know all about me," said Fräulein Louise, suddenly uneasy.

231

"I don't know everything yet, Louise. I have to know a lot more," said the dark man. "And you must know all about me. I am not a Jehovah's Witness, and the spirit of your dead friend does not rest in me."

"No?" she cried, startled. "But—"

"Wait," he said. "Nothing is going to happen to you. I shall look after you."

Strangely calm suddenly, Fräulein Louise said, as if she could see into the future, "No. Nothing bad is going to happen to me through you. I believe that, too. With you everything will go well."

He nodded. Then he said, "I must tell you what my profession is. I am a doctor."

"A doctor?" cried Fräulein Louise.

"A psychiatrist."

"Oh, God!" cried Fräulein Louise, just as miserable suddenly as she had been full of hope a moment ago. "But the book? How did you get the book?"

"It was lying on a bench in the station. I picked it up because I was interested in it."

"And what are you doing on the train at this hour? Why aren't you at home in bed?"

"I wish I were." He sighed. "But unfortunately I have to be in Hamburg as soon as possible."

"Why?" Fräulein Louise was trembling. She had made a dreadful mistake. *This was not one of her dead friends!*

"A patient escaped from our clinic last night," Wolfgang Erkner said. "She is very ill. Nobody knows how she managed to get away. The police in Hamburg are holding a woman who they think might be my patient. That's why I must get there fast, to identify her."

"You—you are a psychiatrist?" stammered Fräulein Louise.

"Yes, Louise," he said gently.

"Don't call me Louise!" she cried angrily.

"Whatever you like, Fräulein Gottschalk," he said. "I'm afraid you're not well."

"I'm perfectly well."

"And that's why we must talk about you now," said psychiatrist Dr. Wolfgang Erkner. He got up and stepped over to the door of the compartment to let down the blinds.

A trap! thought Fräulein Louise, in despair. I walked into a trap, idiot that I am! If this doctor gets hold of me, he'll never let me go.

Dr. Erkner drew down the first blind. His back was turned to Fräulein Louise.

2

Just before I lost consciousness I saw Irina open the door on her side and jump out. I only found out later what happened after that.

Irina saw a car coming down Eppendorfer Baum. She ran into the street and waved. Simultaneously, a man jumped out of the olive-green Buick parked behind my car—the friend of the so-called pharmacist who had pressed the wet cloth against my face. This man managed to catch Irina by her coat and began to drag her to his car. She struggled wildly. She kicked him in the shins and screamed, but the wind drowned out her cries. She managed to free one hand and scratched the man down one cheek. Blood spurted; the man cursed and struck Irina in the face. It knocked the breath out of her and she sank to her knees. He grabbed her under the arms and began to drag her to the car again. The man who had chloroformed me ran over to him and the two tried to get Irina into the Buick. They had almost succeeded when the car Irina had seen coming stopped beside the Buick, its tires screeching. A taxi. Two men jumped out—Bertie and the driver. The latter, an elderly man, had a jack handle in his hand. He went for the man who had chloroformed me, aimed at his head, but the jack handle came down on his neck. It worked. McCormick screamed with pain and fell on his knees, clutching his neck, then he collapsed on the ground. Bertie went for the second man, who was still struggling with Irina. He almost had her in the car when Bertie dragged him back by his coat collar and hit him as hard as he could below the chin.

The man must have been a boxer. He shook himself like a wet dog and with a roar charged at Bertie. Bertie went down, and the two rolled over and over in the street. The boxer aimed at Bertie's face; Bertie, who wasn't exactly feeble, punched the man in the side. Irina screamed for help, but again her screams were swallowed up by the storm. Then she saw the jack handle, which the driver had dropped, and ran over to the man who called himself McCormick and who was just trying to get up. She hit him with the jack handle, and he went down again.

At that moment I came to. The first thing I heard was Irina screaming, but I couldn't understand what she was saying. She ran over to me, and now I could understand. "I'm afraid! I'm afraid! They're going to kill us!"

"No, they're not," I said, still feeling shaky. "Get into my car! Fast!"

"But—"

"Get into the car!" I yelled. She got into the front seat, sobbing. Slowly I was able to collect my thoughts. I leaned down, picked up the Colt, which had fallen on the floor of the car, and took a look at McCormick, lying in the street. He'd had it, at least for a while, I decided, and ran over to Bertie and the other man. Bertie wasn't doing so well. He was lying on his back and McCormick's friend was punching him in the head. Bertie's bandage was dirty again. The taxi driver was trying to pull the man off Bertie, but the man turned and swung, hitting the driver in the stomach. After all, he was an older man. Courageous, but old. I stumbled over him to where Bertie was taking a beating, held the Colt against the other man's chest and shouted, "Get off him, or I'll shoot!" and with my free hand I struck him under the chin. He bit his lip and blood began to flow from his mouth.

"Up!" I shouted. "On your feet!"

He got up shakily and staggered back, directly into the arms of the driver, who had managed to get to his feet. The driver swung and struck the boxer under the chin. He was pretty strong after all, this old man. The boxer stumbled backwards, the old driver hit him again, the boxer slammed against the hood of the Buick and went down.

The driver ran to his taxi. "What are you going to do?" I yelled.

"Call the police! Over the radio!"

"No!" I screamed. "No police! By the time they get here, the whole thing will have started all over again, and this time we may not be so lucky." The wind made it almost impossible for us to understand each other.

"You don't think much of the police, do you?" he yelled.

"No!"

"All right, then. So what do you want to do?"

"Get out of here! Fast!" At this point I didn't need the police, and after the way they'd treated Edith after Conny's accident, I didn't even trust them anymore.

"Get out of here fast—sure!" yelled the driver. "But where to?"

Bertie was scrambling to his feet, holding his head but grinning again. What a guy!

"I'll drive behind you," cried the driver.

"That isn't necessary!"

"That's what you think. What if something like this happens again?"

"He's right," said Bertie, standing beside me now. "Let him ride behind us. He's a good fellow. Got here just in time, didn't we? Just like a Western! Wild!" He waved to the driver and yelled, "Follow us!"

The driver nodded and called back, "Take my jack handle with you!" It was lying beside my car.

By now the lights were on in quite a few windows, and I could see the silhouettes of people looking out into the street. One window was open. I couldn't understand what the man in pajamas was shouting. The two so-called American tourists were stretched out on the street. Good! I picked up the jack handle, threw it under my seat, and got behind the wheel. Bertie got in on the other side, I started the car, revved the motor, made a crazy U-turn on screeching tires, and drove off with my foot all the way down on the gas pedal, back the way we had come. In the rearview mirror I could see the taxi's headlights. The old fellow could drive like a young one!

Bertie told me that he had been delayed at the airport. At that time it always took hours to send anything, with only two men on duty at the checking office, and not a taxi to be had but the one that was following us. "He drove like a bat out of hell," said Bertie. "I told him I was in a hurry. I had a feeling you needed me." He clutched his head. "The bastard!" he said. "Hurts like hell. What happened, anyway?"

Suddenly Irina began to tremble, her body shook. Delayed reaction. "They wanted to kidnap me!" she cried. "They wanted to kidnap me! What's going on here! What's—? I can't stand it!" she screamed. "I can't stand anymore! I have to know! I have to—" She grabbed the steering wheel, the car skidded.

"Goddamn it!" I yelled. "Didn't I tell you—?"

Bertie slapped Irina twice, hard. She was quiet at once, staring at him, speechless, but she had let go of the wheel, thank God. I had two wheels on the curb already.

"I'm sorry," said Bertie. "But I had to. All right now?"

She nodded and began to cry again, and I drove more slowly, south this time. She said, "I'm sorry. I really am. But I'm so confused. So utterly confused. What *is* going on?"

"We'll find out," I said. "Didn't you tell me at the camp that you trusted me?"

"Yes."

"Well, do you?"

Very softly, "Yes, Herr Roland."

"Then everything's all right." I looked in the rearview mirror. "Your pal's keeping close behind us," I told Bertie.

"Thank God! I have the file on our gay friend Concon in his taxi." I began picking up speed again. The taxi stayed behind us. "It's quite a drama!" said Bertie. "Not that I believe any of it, but whoever does will have a lot to think about."

"What are you talking about?"

"Your crazy Fräulein Louise and her dead friends." I had told him about my experience with the French antiques dealer, the Polish superintendant, and the Norwegian sailor. "All nonsense, isn't it?"

I shrugged. "I ask myself that often. Not that I could believe in it. I don't believe in anything. But it's strange, no?"

"What?" asked Irina.

"The taxi driver," said Bertie.

"What about him?"

"Well," said Bertie, sounding almost embarrassed. "It's stupid to even mention it, considering...but his name is Ivanov. Vladimir Ivanov. That's what he told me. Came to Germany as a child, with his parents. Has been here ever since. In Hamburg. Speaks without an accent."

"A Russian?" She sounded baffled.

"Yes," said Bertie. "A Russian. They're all such good people, her dead. Isn't that what she said? Well, all I can say is, if that was her American and Norwegian friends back there deciding to stage a comeback, they're anything but good. But this is absolute nonsense! We're normal, Fräulein Louise is crazy, and the dead don't come back!"

"Of course not," I said, and thought of my conversation with Hem. Irina said, "I wonder if the dead can be good only when they're dead and are bad again when they return to life?"

"Irina!" I cried. "Now don't you start with it!"

"I won't," she said. "I've just had too much whiskey and too much of a shock. And I'm so afraid. That's why I'm talking such nonsense."

"We've got to keep our heads clear," said Bertie. "One crazy person in the story is enough. Give me your flask, Walter. Damn it, it feels like he made mincemeat of my face."

"You did all right by him, too," I said.

"Yes," said Bertie, smiling like an angel. "I gave him a few he'll remember."

We had reached the Metropole. I stopped in front of the entrance. The taxi with the Russian driver stopped behind us. A bellboy I knew came out of the hotel. We shook hands. He took care of our luggage and my suits, and our Russian, Vladimir Ivanov, helped him.

Ivanov had a very decent face and he looked friendly. I thanked him and paid him a lot more than he had coming to him. He protested at first, but then of course he took it. He gave me a card with his name and telephone number. "That's the central office," he said. "I'm going home to sleep for a few hours. If you need a taxi tomorrow—I mean today—then, please ask for me. I'll take you anywhere you want to go. You can depend on me."

"I've noticed that," I said.

"And business isn't good right now," he said. "You'll think of me, gentlemen, won't you?"

Why not? I thought, and said, "We will."

3

Nothing could possibly have offered a greater contrast than my suite in the Metropole Hotel and Fräulein Louise's barracks, where I had seen Irina for the first time. The latter had represented all the poverty of the Bundesrepublik, my suite in the Metropole all its wealth. Every window looked out on the park. You entered the salon through an antechamber, and a padded door led from salon to bedroom. Dark blue tiles, baseboard heating, two tubs, and two large washbasins in the bathroom; in bedroom and salon, dark blue silk wall-covering with a lily pattern, blue wall-to-wall carpeting with scatter rugs, stylized furniture, decorative plasterwork ceilings, thick blue velvet drapes. The bed was very large, like the French double beds, the frame cream and gold. Crystal chandeliers in both rooms. Floor lamps with indirect lighting, sconces on the walls. In the salon, old prints of Hamburg; in the bedroom, reproductions of Boucher.

Irina stood in the middle of the room in her simple cloth coat and looked at the splendor around her. "I've never stayed in a hotel like this in my life," she said. "I suppose you have. Always."

"Yes," I said, "since there's nothing better." There was a knock on the door—the bellboy with my luggage and suits, my attaché case and typewriter, and he got much too big a tip, as usual.

"Thank you, Herr Roland. Your car's in the garage."

"Good," I said. It was high time the Lamborghini disappeared. "Do you think I can rent a car?"

"Of course, Herr Roland. We have twenty-four hour service in the garage." He smiled and withdrew. Right after him came a waiter, alert, immaculate, and courteous. All this at 3:25 A.M.! He brought a small silver ice bucket, two glasses, soda, and a bottle of Chivas. "Your bottle, Herr Roland. Herr Heintze notified me at once that you were here."

"Thank you," I said, and the waiter got much too large a tip.

He was followed by a bellboy with toothbrush, toothpaste, nail brush, mouthwash, and a jar of cold cream, all wrapped in cellophane. "With Herr Heintze's compliments. Have a good night, sir."

"Just a minute." I caught up with him at the door. Tip. "Thank you very much, Herr Roland."

But the largest tip had gone to Herr Heintze, the night clerk. He had been alone. Nobody was manning the reception desk at this time of night, and only two bellboys were on duty. I knew all the bell captains and boys here, the day and night shift, knew them by name. This was important. Everybody likes to be remembered by name. I knew the names of dozens of bellboys and captains all over the world. Heintze had assembled the toothpaste and other toilet articles from the hotel stock. Irina had nothing with her but what she was wearing. I must go and shop for her in the morning, I thought, as soon as the stores open.

Heintze was a pale man, with bags under his eyes. He grinned from ear to ear when he saw me come in. I always wonder if these fellows are really pleased to see certain guests, apart from the tips. I think so. They have to deal with so many obnoxious people, they're glad to see someone come in whom they like.

All the lights were on in the lobby. Cleaning women were on the job, working quietly. Even their vacuums didn't seem to make the usual noise. I told Heintze I needed a suite, as high up as possible, and a single for Bertie.

"We have two conventions, Herr Roland, but I'll fix you up, of course, as usual." As usual.

I had stayed here with all kinds of girls. It sufficed if I signed the registration form and simply added "with wife." That's what I did now. Heintze didn't move a muscle. He was very polite to Irina, who was terribly embarrassed. He also pretended not to notice that our clothes were dirty from the street fight. I never had to fill out the form. Heintze, or whatever night clerk was on duty, did that, when I turned up in the early morning hours like this. In the daytime the clerk at reception took care of it. They had all the necessary information. I told Heintze a story of how Irina's luggage had been put on the wrong plane, and he said he'd have everything she needed for the night sent up. We were given Suite 423.

Bertie was given a room on the floor above us; that was the best Heintze could do. He left the desk and came up in the elevator with us and took Irina and me to our suite, where he turned on the lights and checked to see that everything was in order. When he left us, he got his tip. If he got that much from every guest, he'd soon be able to open his own Metropole.

Irina stood in the middle of the salon and looked at the furniture and the prints, and was embarrassed. And dead tired. She could hardly keep her eyes open. I went over to the table with the silver tray, whiskey, and ice bucket on it and opened the bottle of Chivas. I fixed us two stiff drinks and handed Irina her glass. "No, thank you," she said.

"Come on," I told her. "Drink! You'll sleep better."

"I don't want to."

"You've got to!" I made her take the glass. "Please!"

So we both drank, Irina watching me nervously. "I must know where Jan is. I must know who this woman is," she said. "I must—"

"Yes, yes," I said. "We've got to know, too, and we'll find out. But alone. You stay here. It's too dangerous for you."

"Dangerous?"

"Don't you realize what they wanted to do to you? You did a while ago."

"So you really think they wanted to kidnap me."

"What else?" I said, and lit a cigarette.

"But why, Herr Roland? Why?" she cried wildly, and I wondered if I shouldn't slap her, as Bertie had done, because she seemed constantly on the verge of hysteria. I hoped the whiskey would calm her down or knock her out. With what lay ahead for Bertie and me, we didn't need Irina. I was thankful to have her settled here, in the Metropole, where I thought she'd be safe.

"Why, Herr Roland?" Now she was whispering. She was so drunk with sleep that she was swaying.

"Give me time," I said. "A few hours, and I'll be able to tell you."

This startled her. "You're not going to leave me?"

"I have to."

"Where are you going?"

"I don't know yet. We have to find this Concon fellow. When we have him, we'll know why he was going to kidnap you. But we mustn't lose any more time. We've been held up long enough already."

"And I'm to stay here alone?"

"Yes. When I leave, I'll lock you in, and I'll tell the clerk he's to let no one have the key but me. If anyone knocks, you won't hear. I'll close the door to the salon. But you'll hear the telephone beside your bed. I can't have it disconnected because I may want to call you. You talk *only* if you recognize my voice. Or Herr Engelhardt's. You understand?"

"Yes."

"Otherwise you just hang up."

"But why?"

"Because your life is in danger," I said bluntly. "Haven't you grasped that yet?"

She was trembling. She emptied her glass and held it out for more. She was beautiful, very beautiful. I refilled her glass and said, "I want to know if you realize the position you're in."

"Yes," she said. "I do. But why—?"

"No more questions," I said. "I don't have the time. Off to bed with you."

I went into the bedroom where the boy had put my bags on luggage racks, opened one, and took out a dark blue pair of

240

pajamas. "Here," I said. "Put them on. In the morning we'll buy you some things." Her face turned red. "What now?" I asked.

"She pointed to the bed. "When you get back—I mean, you've got to sleep somewhere, and—"

"That's all right," I said, and took the pillows from one side of the bed, and a blanket, walked back into the salon and flung them on the couch. "You sleep in the bed, I sleep here."

I got a second pair of pajamas out of the suitcase for myself, and my toilet kit. "You don't have to worry. I'm not going to make a pass at your pure, democratic little soul," and I marched off into the bathroom and arranged my things. "I don't know when I'll be back. I usually go to the bathroom once in the night. You'll have to excuse me. I've done it for years. I'll be very quiet and make no attempt to rape you."

"You're good to me," said Irina.

"Yes, I am."

"When I think . . . a few hours ago I was in that dreary camp and now . . . in this luxurious hotel . . ."

"Yes."

"It's like a wild dream!"

"Yes," I said again, and thought that all this was anything but a dream, and was going to get a lot wilder. I also thought that I'd have liked very much to sleep with Irina, as I had with all the other girls I had brought to the hotel. But then I decided that actually I didn't want to, and that was a very peculiar realization. I couldn't understand myself. With this girl things were quite different, for the first time in my life, and it infuriated me.

"Come on!" I said harshly. "Into bed with you. I have work to do."

She looked at me, startled; then she shook her head, mumbled something in Czech, walked hesitantly into the bedroom, and closed the door.

I poured myself another drink, a strong one, sat down next to the ivory-colored phone that stood on a pretty low table and called Conny Manners's number. "Yes, sir," said the girl, and I could hear her dialing. The phone rang three times, then I could hear the receiver being picked up at the other end. But no voice answered. All I could hear was breathing.

"Edith? This is Walter Roland," I said. "If you aren't sure it's my voice, I'll understand if you don't answer."

"I recognize your voice," said Edith. She had apparently been drinking since we left and was pretty far gone—that was evident

241

by her slurred speech—but she was still reacting all right.

"Where are you staying, Walter?"

"Where I always stay when I'm in Hamburg," I said. I didn't trust the connection in Conny's apartment.

"Oh—I see—in—I understand."

"Did the hospital call you?"

"Yes."

"And?"

"I was to go there right away. Conny's condition was much worse. It was a man speaking. I called the hospital back and asked if they'd called me." A sob. "They said no. Certainly not. Conny's condition was unchanged. I wouldn't be hearing from them until later in the morning. Walter! Who was trying to get me out of the apartment?"

"No idea," I said, and drank. "But you see what a good thing it was that I told you to call the hospital back."

"Yes. Why didn't you call before? You said—"

"I know. But there wasn't a chance until now. I'm sorry. Did anyone else call?"

"Yes. A man. A stranger. He must have been holding something over the receiver, because his voice sounded muffled."

"What did he say?"

No answer. She was sobbing again.

"Edith!"

"He—he said that Conny would die, even if he survived the operation, that he'd—he'd die if he said one word—"

"To whom?"

"To me. The voice said I should tell him that at once, the minute I see him. One word and the next day he's dead."

"Did the voice put it like that?"

"Just as I've said."

"Tell me exactly what the voice said."

"'One word, and he won't live to see the next day. We can get him in the hospital, too.'"

"'We'? Not 'I'?"

"No! *We, we, we!*"

"Edith!"

"I'm sorry, Walter, but I'm going crazy with fear. You must understand that!"

"I do, I do. But nothing's going to happen to you or Conny," I said, and thought: I hope....

242

"Who was this man, Walter?"

"I'll find out. Give me time. Now stop drinking and try to catch some sleep"

"I can't sleep!"

We argued a while longer, then I gave up. I lit another cigarette and made another call, Hem's private number in Frankfurt. He answered right away.

"So, what's new, Walter?"

I told him everything. He didn't interrupt once. In the end he said, "This is going to be a big thing. I knew it. Herford is ready to give you three or four pages, but I need the advance material by ten."

"Yes, Hem."

"What about this fellow Concon?"

"I don't know anything yet. We're going over there now."

"Nothing's to happen to the girl, Walter! That's more important than anything else. Where is she?"

"In bed. I've locked her in. I can depend on the people in the hotel."

"Good. You'll call me as soon as you can, and at once if anything new turns up. I won't be asleep. I'm much too worked up."

"Not any more than I am. What are you doing for it? Smoking your pipe?"

"Yes. And listening to records."

"Rahmers?"

"Of course."

"Which one?"

"'The Deluge'," said Hem. "And I've been thinking."

"What?"

"How this thing's going to develop. How will it end?"

"And what do you think? Will it be a happy ending?"

Instead of answering, he said, "Good luck, Walter," and hung up. Far, far away—but he had the unfortunate habit of coming close suddenly—I could sense my jackal, so I drained my glass and got up because I wanted to go to the bathroom. And I wanted to see if Irina was asleep yet.

She wasn't asleep. The bedroom was empty, the lights were on in the bathroom, and I could see Irina. Her back was turned to me. She was standing in front of the washbowl, brushing her teeth, and she was naked.

She must have seen me in the mirror over the washbowl,

243

because she turned around, a horrified look on her face, glass and toothbrush in her hands, a ring of toothpaste around her lips. She had beautiful, firm breasts, with brown nipples and large areolae, very narrow hips, long legs, a little rounded stomach, as all beautiful women have, and below it the dark triangle of her pubic hair.

The blood rushed to my head. I had never seen such a beautifully proportioned girl. I forgot completely what I had to do, what had happened, and what still had to happen. I wanted Irina. Right now. At once. I couldn't think of anything else. I walked over to her. She saw me coming, apparently unable to move, panic in her eyes. I didn't care. I wanted this girl. I had to have her. Her skin was clear and white, her nipples were raised. I could feel the blood pulsating wildly in my temples. With every step I came closer. In my thoughts I already had her under me, was inside her....

Irina dropped the glass. It broke into pieces on the tiled floor. The toothbrush fell next. She stood there, motionless, making no effort to cover herself. Now I was beside her, and I touched her shoulders. My hands glided lower, and still she was staring at me, wide-eyed, the ring of toothpaste around her lips....

It was the eyes that did it. Those sad, dark eyes told me what a bastard I'd be if I did it. Only the eyes. I couldn't do it.

I picked up the pajamas I had given her to wear—they were lying on a terrycloth stool—and I thought that I had never behaved like this before, never in my whole life, and I said, "I'm sorry," and then, "Let me help you." And I helped Irina put on my pajamas, which were much too big for her. We folded back the hems of the sleeves and pants, but she still looked slightly ridiculous. Only I didn't find her ridiculous. She never stopped looking at me while this was going on. I wiped the toothpaste from her mouth. "And now off to bed with you," I said. "Be careful of the glass. Wait a minute," and I picked her up and carried her into the bedroom, and put her down on the bed, and covered her. "Good night," I said. And she was still staring at me.

I walked toward the door that led to the salon. When my hands was on the knob, she spoke, so softly I could scarcely understand. "Herr Roland?"

I turned around. "Yes?"

"Come?" she whispered.

I walked over to the bed slowly, hesitantly, and stopped. She made a sign to me to bend down, and I did. And she kissed me lightly on the lips and said, "Thank you." And suddenly I couldn't stand the sight of those eyes any longer—such innocence, such honesty and helplessness.

I left the bedroom fast. In the salon I refilled my flask, took my pad and recorder, and left our suite. I double-locked the door.

4

When I walked into Bertie's room on the fifth floor, he was on the phone. I nodded and walked through the room to the bathroom. As I passed Bertie's bed, I could see the clippings about Karl Concon from the *Blitz* archives spread out on it. In the bathroom I washed up a little and brushed the dirt off my coat. Then I went back to Bertie. He was still on the phone. He wasn't talking, but I got the impression that he wasn't listening, either.

"Who is it?" I asked.

"Motor Vehicle Bureau," he said, smiling. He didn't seem in the least tired.

"Is anybody there? At this hour?" I asked, surprised.

"One man. For emergencies. But I know him. He won five hundred marks off me once at poker, and since then he's felt guilty. My luck that he's on duty tonight. Of course he has no business looking it up for me, but he's doing it. You've got to have friends."

"Of course you let him win."

"Sure," said Bertie. "You can never have too many friends."

"What about headquarters? Did you reach them yet? Hem said we must report to them as soon as possible, remember?"

"What do you think I've been doing all this time? Talking to headquarters. I know the head of the Missing Persons Bureau. I suppose he's the right one to see."

"Yes."

"His name is Hering. He's in Paris right now, at an Interpol conference, will be back early this morning. A man called Nikel is substituting for him. I know him, too, but not so well. I woke him up. He told me his boss was on a night train, on his way back

245

to Hamburg. I told him it was important. No fooling. Fire under his ass. So he gave us an appointment. Eleven o'clock. At headquarters. With Hering."

"How did you get that out of him?"

"Told him it had to do with what happened at the Youth Camp in Neurode," said Bertie, still listening, "and suddenly he was wide awake. We seem to have raised a hornet's nest there. Nikel wanted to know what's up. I didn't say. Told myself, that's for Hering. Nikel was so befuddled, he forgot to ask where I was phoning from. So . . . at eleven. . . ." He grinned. "Did you put the little one to beddy-bye?"

"Shut up!" I said, suddenly furious. But you couldn't shame Bertie. "As if I didn't know it all along," he said, smiling sweetly.

"Know what?"

"That you've taken a fancy to the young lady. Things like that don't escape Bertie, super-psychologist. But psychologist Bertie also told you that the young lady loves her fiancé, even if the fiancé has a second young lady, at least so I hear. Women are funny. With her you'll get your comeuppance, lover boy. When a girl like that loves, the guy can do whatever he likes, and she goes right on loving him." He stopped, because his friend at the other end of the line had come back. "Yes, of course I'm still here. Were you able to find it, Steffens?" He nodded at me, beaming. "Yes? Great! Wonderful! And who does the car belong to?" He listened, still smiling, but now he was rubbing his chin nervously. "Hm," he said finally. "You're sure? You mean the car is licensed to—?" I went over and stood beside him. "Well, all right, then. If that's what it says, it must be right. Thanks a lot, Steffens. What? . . . No, I don't know yet how long I'll be staying in Hamburg. If I have a minute, I'll come by. . . . Oh, I see . . . you have two days off. Well, then we may be able to fit in a game. . . . Don't be silly. You didn't rob me! You just play poker better than I do. And many thanks again." He hung up and went on scratching his chin and smiling.

"Well," I said. "Maybe you'd like to tell me. . . ."

"That's really funny. . . ."

"What is?"

"Damn funny!" said Bertie. "The van that took Michelsen and Bilka and his fiancée—fiancée number two—is licensed to the Municipal Cemetery. It wasn't stolen. *The Municipal Cemetery?*"

246

5

Dr. Wolfgang Erkner, psychiatrist, walked over to the door of the compartment to let down the blinds. A trap, thought Fräulein Louise! I've fallen into a trap. If this doctor ever gets hold of me, he'll never let me go. And I've got to go! I've got to!

Just as Dr. Erkner was pulling down the second blind, Fräulein Louise let out a piercing scream, as if she were in great pain. Dr. Erkner turned, startled. Fräulein Louise had put everything back in her bag, now she charged forward and collided head-on with Dr. Erkner, knocking him down onto one of the seats. Then she slid open the door, rushed out into the corridor, and ran as fast as she could to a compartment at the end. Softly, cautiously, she opened the door, slipped in, and closed it again. The compartment was dark. In the ghostly light from the one dim lamp she could see three people, all asleep. One was snoring softly. Now she could hear steps in the corridor, coming closer, closer ... and going past. The doctor, she thought. He's looking for me. What shall I do now. Oh, dear God, dear God—At that moment she heard the voice of the dead student. "Don't be afraid, Louise. You just met your fate. It has all been ordained."

Fräulein Louise's heart was beating fast. The voice of the dead American spoke next. "We sent you the person who is going to heal you." And the voice of the Pole. "You will see this man again under dreadful earthly circumstances. But all things will turn out well and you will be heard."

My friends, thought Fräulein Louise, deeply moved. They are looking after me. They are not going to let me down. And they say *Du* to me suddenly, for the first time!

The voice of the dead Russian speaking. "Don't be afraid, Louise. There's no reason for it. Get off the train *now!*"

Fräulein Louise didn't take a moment to think it over. She knew her friends were protecting her and nothing could harm her. She got up, left the compartment, and walked down the empty corridor to the door of the car. She intended to get off the train, as she had been told to do, but was surprised to note how fast it was moving. She reached the door and pressed the handle down. The door opened out and she could only open it a crack because the wind was pressing against it. She threw herself against the door in her efforts to open it, determined to get off. Although she could see lights flying by outside, she wasn't in the least afraid. "My friends know what they're doing," she murmured.

Suddenly the train jerked, brakes screeched, the train slowed down. Fräulein Louise could see lighted streets and houses, bright lights on signal posts, and a sign in front of a cement block that looked like a bunker: Signal Box 2. The train was rolling into a station. "Thank you, my friends," said Fräulein Louise.

The train stopped. She got out. About a dozen people got off, about the same number got on. A loudspeaker announced: "Rotenburg! Rotenburg! Expression from Cologne via Bremen on Platform Three. Short stop only. Please get on and off as quickly as possible."

Fräulein Louise remained standing beside the car. She was safe. And happy. So happy! "My friends," she murmured. "My good friends."

She waited for the train to pass by until she could see its rear lights; then, leaning against the wind that threatened to throw her, she walked to an underpass and went down the steps. Not a soul in sight. There were a few benches. Fräulein Louise sat down, her bag close beside her. I won't have to wait long, she thought. There'll be a local soon and it will take me to Hamburg. A clock in the underpass read 4:56 A.M. Yes, she thought, the local will take longer, but that doesn't matter. The important thing is that I got away from Dr. Erkner. She smiled. Then she said softly, "Where I come from nobody knows...and where I'm going everything goes...." She breathed deep and her face was filled with an expression of great peace. "The wind blows, the sea flows, and God knows...."

6

"You know the Marx brothers, of course," said Hem. "American comedians."

He had come into my room just as I was writing the last words of the preceding chapter, and had read it, smoking his pipe and nodding every now and then. His hair was standing on end, as usual. He had put on his metal-rimmed glasses to read.

"Yes," I said. "Four brothers."

"Only one of them's alive now," said Hem. "Groucho. He's seventy-three. What I've just read reminds me of a picture he was in, with one of his brothers. Groucho said, 'You know, there's a treasure buried in the house next door,' and his brother said, 'Look here, there isn't any house next door,' and Groucho said, 'Doesn't matter. So we'll build one.' I can't think of a better definition of parapsychology."

"Parapsychology?"

"What your Fräulein felt down there, in the Rotenburg station. That's the way she told it, isn't it?"

"On my last visit. I always write exactly what she says. I never change a thing."

"What your Fräulein felt then definitely comes under the heading of parapsychology. The brain of a schizophrenic person functions differently. What she experiences is changed. We don't know what causes this different way of experiencing things. It is possible that schizophrenics have capabilities that are exceptionally suited to parapsychology. *Para*, you know, means 'beside' or 'beyond.'"

"You believe in it, Hem?"

"Yes. And I'm not the only one. You'd be surprised who believe in it, who have believed in it. The Russian chemist Mendelyev, the astronomer Friedrich Zöllner, the famous biologist and philosopher Hans Driesch. Madame Curie. Sigmund Freud. Einstein. And many more."

"I've always dismissed it as nonsense," I said, "until—"

"Until you got involved in this," said Hem, puffing on his pipe and nodding. "Every person reaches a point in his life when he decides that parapsychology is either humbug or the fantastic science of the unknown, when he is the Marx brother who believes, or the one who doesn't. All of us are Marx brothers, believers or nonbelievers." He sat down. "Look," he said, "people have believed in that house next door as far back as can be recorded. They positioned their houses next door on stars, in moors, in thickets, in any of nature's eerie landscapes, in deserted castles, and in the brain." He paused. "I said, 'in the brain,' Walter."

"Yes," I said. "In the brain."

"These houses next door were always placed on extraordinary sites. The inexplicable thing needs a dramatic setting. What you write about your mentally ill Fräulein may be described as precognition, if you are willing to rule out coincidence. Pythia, the priestess of Apollo at Delphi, prophesied the future. Dante's son, Jacapo, was clairvoyant. Eight months after his father's death, Dante led him in a dream to the place where the thirteenth stanza of the *Divine Comedy* was hidden. On the following morning, Jacapo went to the place and found the manuscript. Do you remember when a schoolhouse was buried under a landslide in Aberfan, England? After the catastrophe, the English papers got dozens of letters from people living far from Aberfan, some on a different continent, who declared they had seen the catastrophe in their dreams. And they were able to describe the scene precisely, without ever having actually seen it."

"That reminds me of what cosmonaut Gagarin, the first man in outer space, said: something to the effect that on his flight he had seen things that went beyond anything imaginable, and that if he were permitted to tell about it, it would shock all mankind."

"You see?" said Hem. "In our time man is far more willing to accept parapsychological phenomena as part of the world picture, and far better equipped to do so than in the Age of Enlightenment, when reason, reason, nothing but reason counted. Today we again yearn for the miraculous. Fascination with mysterious things is nothing new. I mean that now we need to find a reasonable explanation for everything that happens, to explain fate and to prove logic in coincidence, to believe in life after death and life in the spirit...."

"Like Fräulein Louise."

"And with that find security. The need for security was never as great as it is today. And in the same vein, the readiness to come

250

to grips with parapsychology and its phenomena was never greater," said Hem.

"Well, yes," I said. "And I have an explanation for that. Our times have a Janus head. The one face is Common Sense, the other is Euphoria. A hop in a jumbo jet to New York—with LSD to the world next door. A nod for the computer—and the cry for Aquarius in *Hair*. On the one hand we initiate the most complicated projects, on the other a book like *Memories of the Future* becomes a worldwide best seller."

"So there you are!" said Hem. "Our world is technological to such an extent that it simply has to look for miracles as compensation, if for no other reason. Fifty-five percent of all Europeans read their horoscopes. Half of the population of West Germany believes in a sixth sense. More and more people consult astrologers, if they can afford it. Every fifth adult vows that he has received parapsychological messages from the future. And that's valid for Russia, too. They have a paper called *Technology and Youth*, with a circulation of five million. I have just had an article translated for me about the mysterious disappearance of planes and ships somewhere in the Bermudas. In the article, a Russian scientist vehemently contradicts the shaky rationalization that these disappearances in the so-called Bermuda Triangle are accidents. And as was to be expected, the defense ministries of the great powers are working on it, full speed ahead!"

"You're not serious!"

"Oh, yes, I am," said Hem. "In July 1959, the American atomic submarine *Nautilus* left a port on the east coast of the United States. There was one passenger on board whose name nobody knew, nor why he was there. He was on board for sixteen days. Twice a day he locked himself up in his cabin and wrote lists of numbers and put them in a sealed envelope. At the same time, far far away, a second man from the Westinghouse research center was writing lists of numbers and putting them in sealed envelopes."

"What for?"

"For NASA! The passenger on the *Nautilus* was a medium. The two men were trying to come up with the same numbers, thereby establishing a wireless and energy-less telephonic contact."

"And with what result?"

"Top secret," said Hem. "Meanwhile, the Russians are experimenting in outer space. They've been doing it for such a long time and with such success that, according to NASA director Eugene Konecci, they'll be the first to transmit human thought on an earth-circulatory system."

"Human thought?" I couldn't help being impressed.

"Yes," said Hem. "It's established that the Russians are working on parapsychological projects, sending out human thoughts and receiving them. In a war, such capabilities could be decisive when all other possibilities of communication have failed. The philosopher Tugarinov, again a Russian, has gone farthest in the field of parapsychology. He would like to teach all people the science of telepathy, so that they function just as reliably as, for instance, the telephone. It's almost impossible to keep track of the experiments that are being made today. It is common knowledge that the embryos of hens react to the sun's rising, in spite of equalized temperature and light in the research lab. . . ."

"So how do they get the signal that the sun is rising?"

"That's just it! How? And there's more: Certain bacteria show sunspot activity as much as four days before the finest instruments register an eruption on the sun. Take cats and dogs. Their masters can go as far as two thousand kilometers without leaving a physical trace—the animals find their way back to them. What system of information shows them the way?"

"Yes," I said bitterly. "And when atomic warheads can find their way like that, what a miracle that will be!"

"They've been trying for that for a long time, too," said Hem. "In East and West they're working feverishly on things that would have been laughed at fifty years ago. In Charkov they conditioned a bitch to letting her pups be taken from her from time to time, but when someone inflicted pain on them in a room that was hermetically sealed, she became restless and barked and looked in the direction of the room. The French have established precognition in mice. The animals were put in a cage that was charged by two electric generators, one in each half of the cage, and these generators worked at random. The mouse could escape pain only if she settled on the half that wasn't charged. Neither the scientist nor the mouse knew which half of the cage would be electrified, but the mouse always jumped onto the recharged section in time."

"That's fantastic!"

"And you're writing about something fantastic," said Hem, "only you don't seem to realize it yet. The time has come, Walter, when scientists will want to prove what Paracelsus wrote five hundred years ago. Through the magic power of will, a man on this side of the ocean can let the man on the other side know what he is saying. . . ."

"And you're trying to tell me that Fräulein Louise's sick brain has such magical powers?"

"I don't know. I just want you to think of all these unreal things when you're writing your story about very real things," said Hem. "Today's scientists are talking quite casually about the radio of the brain . . . and synchronicity and reverse causality."

"And what are they?"

"Synchronicity—two people do or think the same thing at the same time. Reverse causality—the effect takes place *before* the cause."

"Like Fräulein Louise's friends, acting on their own before they felt an impetus, because for them there is no such concept as time."

"Something like that, yes," said Hem. "For this knowing ahead of time, Pasqual Jordan gives an exceptionally impressive example. He points to his experimentation with mesons. . . ."

"With what?"

"Mesons: unstable nuclear particles, some of which are neutral while others carry a unit of positive or negative charge. Under certain conditions, they originate and disintegrate in the nucleus of the atom. And it's here that the physicists have observed happenings that can only be interpreted as action or effect—for instance, the splitting of the atomic nucleus— *preceding or coming before* the cause, which in this case is the appearance of mesons in the nucleus of the atom."

"You mean effect preceding cause?"

"Yes. And Jordan calls this reverse causality, and considers it the same procedure as takes place in the minds of those who 'know ahead'—or, in other words, are clairvoyant and see the future."

"The White Queen!" I said.

"What White Queen?"

"In *Through the Looking Glass*. She screamed first and it bled afterwards."

"Exactly," said Hem. "Did you know that Lewis Carroll, the man who wrote *Alice in Wonderland* and *Through the Looking Glass* was a mathematician; and he, too, was fascinated by parapsychology—spiritualism, they called it in those days. The

Alice stories are unique and brilliant compilations of mathematical and parapsychological problems."

"Written for a shy little girl he happened to like."

"Right," said Hem. "And these books for children deal constantly with universal riddles and miracles, recognizable only by adults, naturally. In the universe everything has its own logic. Nothing is coincidental. It was Einstein who said, 'I can't imagine God playing dice with the universe.' Spiritual things have their law and order, too. Visions and thoughts correlate through attraction. The scientists of today are agreed that strong emotional forces of the subconscious—especially all borderline situations affecting life, such as death, illness, danger, risk . . . all of which apply to your Fräulein—serve as 'arrangers' of these visions and ideas."

Hem was silent.

After giving it some thought, I said, "God doesn't play dice with the universe. To go back to your two Marx brothers—this means that the skeptical brother, who says there is no house next door, considers the world and himself as instruments that are not kept in order by any force outside our earth. For him, the throw of the dice is fate. He looks at parapsychological happenings as normal but as things that simply haven't been explored yet."

"That's it! And the other brother, who knows there is a treasure in the house next door, and if there is no house next door, wants to build one so that the treasure can be found, he is the one who can't bear the thought that his life is controlled by coincidence. He doesn't believe in a statistical, physical, throw-of-the-dice existence. He believes that there are still many things between heaven and earth that we know not of. That's what Groucho Marx thinks!"

"And what do you think?"

"I'm a Groucho. In the case of your Fräulein Louise, too. Because there's something neither those for, nor those against, parapsychology can take from us."

"And what's that?"

"The discovery of oneself," said Hem.

7

On Karl Concon, the *Blitz* archives had sent Bertie and me a thick manila envelope full of clippings, newspaper reports, and commentary, and the famous "additional information"—confidential information acquired God knows how. Bertie and I sat on his bed in the Metropole Hotel and looked through the material. We also had the pictures Bertie had taken, but they didn't add much to what we already knew. The daily news accounts of the trial in Hamburg in 1957 gave us a lot more. They told us that Concon had apparently been blackmailing homosexuals for years, forcing them to hand over highly confidential material. But they hadn't been able to prove anything, although there was quite a lot of suspicious circumstantial evidence against him, and they had had to let him go.

The additional information explained that the trial had been conducted behind closed doors when it had become a question of what kind of secrets Concon had been trying to get out of the high-ranking German officer. There it was, black on blue, in small type. I took my cigarette out of my mouth and drank from my flask and handed it to Bertie, who also took a swig.

"Listen to this!" I said, and read a few sentences to Bertie. "'It is clear that Concon was working for West Germany from 1949 to 1953. . . . Frequent visits to East Berlin . . . knew a lot of people there . . . got national, economic, and military information for his West German employers. . . . Was uncovered by the East Zone Internal Security Bureau, but nothing was undertaken against him, at any rate, not noticeably. . . . Returned safely to Hamburg . . . did an about face and began working for the Internal Security Bureau in East Berlin. They succeeded in advising and protecting him so well before the trial, that there was no conviction. . . .'"

"Hm," said Bertie, drinking from my flask.

"'The indictment, which was not made public, was for the attempt to betray top-secret NATO plans . . . preventive measures . . . retaliatory measures. . . .'"

"Donnerwetter!" said Bertie.

"'It is not clear whether Concon switched sides again, resulting in his acquittal, or if he is still working for the East. His place in Sankt Pauli, King Kong, was frequented for years by agents from all camps during the days before the occupation of Czechoslovakia by the Warsaw Pact Nations...many dubious types.'" My voice grew louder. "'Five Czechs visited King Kong every night!'"

Bertie let out a whistle.

"Here!" Now I was really excited. "'September 9, 1968. Raid on King Kong. The Czechs fled. One was hit by a member of the police force. His friends dragged him to a car and drove off without being recognized. Hasn't been seen since.'" I looked at Bertie. "Jan Bilka worked for the Czech Ministry of Defense," I said. "After his flight the Czechs and Russians went crazy, according to Irina. Why?"

"Elementary!" said Bertie. "Bilka decamps with secret documents, seeks out his friend Michelsen in Hamburg, wants to hand over the documents to West German or American agents."

"Or sell them," I said. "Everybody isn't as noble as you."

"Or sell them. Negotiates with them. Feels secure with Michelsen. So Michelsen must be a West German man, right?"

"As far as I can see—right."

"The East wants the documents back—or wants to prevent the West from getting them—but don't know where Bilka is, so they send Concon to the camp to kidnap Irina. She knows where Bilka is, and they'll get it out of her." He coughed. "That stinks, doesn't it?"

"Rather," I said. "If you're right, then East doesn't have a minute to lose. Michelsen was in Prague often. Surely they know in Prague where Michelsen lives and what sort of a customer he is. So they don't have to kidnap Irina to find Bilka."

"Then you tell me what happened, wise guy."

"It could be like this," I said. "Bilka has documents. Wants to sell them to the Germans or Americans. Negotiates price. Is stubborn. Isn't in a hurry. Feels safe with Michelsen. The West lets Concon, who has switched sides again, try to kidnap Irina. Her appearance suddenly endangers everything. When she finds out that Bilka has a girl friend, she'll raise hell." I stopped. "Stinks, too, doesn't it?"

"Yep," said Bertie. "Why should Bilka feel safe with Michelsen when they know in the East where he lives? He'd have to count on their coming to get him any moment."

"Right," I said. "But now Irina turns up, calls Michelsen, Bilka answers the phone. . . ."

"Bilka answers the phone?" Bertie blew his nose. "He's so sure of himself that he answers the phone? Man, that stinks more than my version."

"Yes," I said perplexed. "That won't do, either. But there's definitely something terribly wrong with this fellow Bilka. Right after Irina gets hold of him, they try to kill Conny, who's on his way to Bilka, after which Bilka, fiancée number two, and Michelsen disappear; and servant Notung says that no Bilka ever stayed with Michelsen. But the superintendent and the antiques dealer say he did. Plus a fiancée. Where have they all disappeared to? And why? And why did Notung lie? Why did they almost succeed in killing Conny? Why did they try to kidnap Irina tonight? Twice! What was Concon really after in Neurode?"

Bertie got up and looked at me. "You're thinking the same thing I am, aren't you?"

"Sure."

"So off we go to King Kong," said Bertie.

8

We got the things we needed and went down to the lobby. We gave Heintze our keys, and I told him that under no circumstances was he to let anyone into my suite.

"Yes, of course, Herr Roland," said Heintze. "But if the police come, there's nothing I can do about it."

"When do they send the registration cards over to the police?"

"When I'm relieved," he said. "At seven."

"I'll be back long before then," I said. "So nobody from the police will come. Not tonight. You've known me for twelve years, Heintze. Do you believe me?"

"Yes, sir."

"And do you also believe that I couldn't commit a crime?"

"I know you couldn't commit a crime, Herr Roland."

"Very well, then. I can depend on you."

"You certainly can, Herr Roland," he said, grinning as he

pocketed the hundred-mark bill I had handed him.

"If the young lady—"

"Your wife," Heintze said tactfully.

"If she calls and says she wants to go out, don't open the door, please. Tell her I took the key with me. She mustn't go out."

"Yes, Herr Roland."

"Has my car been taken to the garage?"

"Yes, Herr Roland."

"I need a smaller one. An Opel Rekord would be good."

"I think we have four Rekords. Why don't you take the elevator down to the garage; meanwhile I'll call Herr Croft."

"Who is he?"

"The man who's on duty down there tonight. He'll fill out the forms and give you one of the Rekords."

"What did you say his name was?" asked Bertie. He was still wearing his leather jacket and corduroy pants under his coat. His two cameras were dangling from their straps.

"Wim Croft."

"English?" I asked.

"No," said Heintze. "Dutch. New. Nice fellow. He's only been working for us three weeks."

"You said Dutch?"

"Yes," said Heintze. "From The Hague."

9

The Empress Catherine of Russia was lying on a red velvet cover, her legs spread. The red cover was draped over a wide bed. Various pieces of clothing were scattered around the bed—everything from an embroidered purple royal robe to underpants that could be laced below the knee. The bed stood on a small stage, and she was lying so that the audience could see between her legs, a spotlight on her. The Empress was about twenty-five, voluptuous, beautifully built, and pretending to be sensuous as hell. She squirmed, groaned (a hidden microphone amplified the sound), rubbed her taut breasts, and tossed her head wildly from side to side. The Empress Catherine was evidently a real blond.

258

She was wearing a papier-mâché crown with many glittering stones. A gilded papier-mâché ball and scepter lay on the floor beside the bed. It was 4:15 A.M., but King Kong was still crowded—men, many whores with their clients, and a few couples. They were seated at small tables. Waiters were hurrying back and forth with champagne buckets and drinks. When we got there Bertie said, "There's the place. But where's the hotel? Didn't Concon say he was a hotelier?"

The house in which King Kong was situated was low and very old. The walls were grimy; the windows facing the street were heavily curtained. Beside the entrance there were photographs in lighted display boxes. In red letters I read about this program's sensation: "World Famous Star, Baby Blue from Crazy Horse!" A barker, at least two meters tall, wearing a gold-braided coat down to his feet, clutched my arm and began his spiel. "Come right in, gentlemen! Here you can see something you've never seen anywhere else! Sappho and her playmates! The monk with the whip! Sex, live and original! Two men and one lady! We show everything! We hide nothing! Come right in, gentlemen!" He had already given me a light push toward the entrance. Now he grabbed Bertie and said, "You're just in time for the high point! The famous artiste Baby Blue from the cabaret Crazy Horse in Paris, in her sensational act—Catherine the Great!"

"Listen," I said, grabbing his arm now, "we're looking for Herr Concon. We have to speak to him. It's important."

"Police?"

"No. Is he here?"

"No idea. You'll find out inside. Come right in, gentlemen! You've never seen anything like it! You've never dreamed anything like it! Baby Blue as Catherine the Great!"

In the dimly lit checkroom, two more hands grabbed me and dragged me into the clubroom. Bertie bumped into me, somebody's hand was between my legs. I slapped it hard. "You don't have to get so mad right away, darling," said a woman's voice.

"Man, what a professional! I mean ours," said Bertie a few minutes later when we were sitting, slightly breathless, in the booth somebody had shoved us into. My eyes were growing accustomed to the light, or lack of it, and I could see Baby Blue on the stage and the silhouettes of her audience, facing her. "Somebody managed to unzip my pants. How did you make out?"

"Not much better," I said.

A voice in the loudspeaker, trying desperately to speak elegant German, "What a sad evening for Your Majesty! Not a donkey around, not a rutting stallion, not even a few grenadiers. . . ." Baby Blue's gyrations became more and more agitated; she rolled her eyes, massaged her breasts. . . .

A grand piano stood beside the small stage. A young man in a tuxedo was looking far away into the dark, playing softly. The B-Minor Concerto, Tchaikovsky. My favorite composer. I recognized it at once. There wasn't any of Tchaikovsky's music I didn't recognize.

"Your Majesty is alone and filled with so much desire," the voice in the loudspeaker went on. "If Your Majesty would take the scepter . . ."

Naked Baby Blue picked up the papier-mâché scepter.

"And if Your Majesty would open it . . ."

Baby Blue opened the scepter, lengthwise, like a violin case. A big artificial penis was in it. Baby Blue squealed with delight, dropped the scepter, and kissed the dildo.

"And now, Your Majesty, if you would stroke your most honorable love mound with this instrument of consolation . . ."

Baby Blue did as she was told. The pianist played beautifully. . . .

"And now, if Your Royal Highness would please tickle your divine royal clitoris . . ."

Baby Blue did so, and the microphone gave us her first low moaning and gasping. A waiter came up to our table. "Would you like to order?"

"We want to speak to Herr Concon," I said.

"The young one or the old one?" asked the waiter, as Baby Blue's moans grew louder.

"You mean there are two?" Bertie sounded astonished.

"Why don't you shut up?" cried a fat older woman, sitting in the next booth with a fat older man—a married couple, I decided.

"Father and son," said the waiter. "So, which one do you want?"

"The owner," I whispered.

"And now, if Your Royal Highness would let the tickler slide up and into your vagina . . ."

Baby Blue tucked the dildo up into her vagina and let out a soft cry which the microphone amplified.

"He isn't here," whispered the waiter.

"What about the father?" I asked softly.

"He's here."

"Where?"

"In the men's room."

"When's he coming up?"

"He isn't coming up. He works down there," the waiter whispered, impatient now. "So what do you want?" And I, with my persecution complex, afraid I might be served some lousy liquor, thought: Whiskey, of course. But they wouldn't have Chivas here. And if I ordered drinks, God only knew what they'd serve, and it could make me sick. So I said, "A bottle of whiskey, Black Label. But unopened!"

"That'll cost you a hundred," whispered the waiter, impressed.

Bertie looked irritated. He hated my drinking and I knew what he was thinking: What a fuss!

"And if it's lousy," I told the waiter, "you're in trouble. We're from the press."

"Right away. Yes, sir. Right away," and he went off bowing.

Baby Blue's heavy breathing in the microphone, then the loudspeaker again. "And now, if Your Majesty would please move the tickler in and out in your most magnificent cunt ... and please do not forget from side to side ..."

Baby Blue spread her legs wider, toyed with her nipple, and pushed the dildo energetically in and out. She was going great guns now, rearing up, falling back, whimpering, groaning, trembling. The audience was growing restless.

"What does he mean, 'the father'?" whispered Bertie. "Must be very old."

"Probably," I whispered.

The moaning in the microphone grew louder. A few soft cries.

"The bastard! Lets his father work in the shithouse!" said Bertie, who had strong family feelings.

"I'll go down to him," I said softly.

"Not till the waiter's brought your whiskey," said Bertie. "Or we're in trouble. You pay first. We're behaving conspicuously enough. Concon, Jr., isn't here. You heard the waiter say so. We've got to watch it."

Baby Blue was whimpering. "Oh, oh, I'm coming! Now! I'm dying!"

The waiter came with the bottle on a tray, two glasses, an ice bucket, and soda water. He stuck the bottle under my nose.

"Black Label. Guaranteed unopened. Take a look at the seal, please."

"That's all right," I said. "Thanks."

"A hundred and fifteen marks," he said. "Fifteen percent service charge. Please pay now."

The performance on the stage went on. Baby Blue's moans were ecstatic. She rolled her eyes; her whole body jerked rhythmically.

"Just a minute," I said, opened the bottle, poured some whiskey into one of the glasses and smelled it. Then I tasted it. Perfectly all right. I was the only writer in the house who didn't have to account for his expenses, so I gave the waiter a hundred and fifty marks. "The rest is for you," I said, and he almost fell to his knees. "But now I've gotta go."

"Not till the number's over." The piano concerto was reaching its high point.

"My bladder's about to burst," I said. "Where is it?"

"Just a minute," he said, "and I'll show you."

Baby Blue had reached her climax at last. Her moans had degenerated into a roar. The voice in the loudspeaker said, "Let it lie on your heart, O Catherine, and consider once more the pardon of Count Kropotkin. Be generous!"

Suddenly Baby Blue threw the dildo away and cried imperiously, "To hell with the tickler! I want a man, a real man! Then I'll consider pardoning the count. But not before!"

At that moment three gigantic grenadiers stepped onto the stage out of the dark. They were in full uniform—helmet, sabre, boots. They stood at attention in front of Baby Blue. Only one thing was not in order in their magnificent uniforms. Three enormous, stiff penises protruded from their flies. They can't be real, I told myself. There are none *that* big! But they looked real enough.

The pianist stopped playing. You could have heard a pin drop.

Baby Blue grabbed the most magnificent and largest of the three grenadiers and pulled the man toward her. He fell on her. The lights went on.

10

"Mint-flavored, gentlemen," the old man was saying just as I was walking down the stairs. "A novelty. Selling like hot cakes. They can't keep up with the demand."

Two men were with the old man in the light, blue-tiled room that led to the toilets. There were washbowls and mirrors and a table with a drawer and an assortment of the kind of things one might need down here—paper towels, combs, nail scissors, hairbrushes, clothesbrushes, hair tonic, eau de cologne, and packages of Kleenex. Also a small plate with coins in it. The drawer was open, and I could see porno magazines and boxes of condoms. "If the gentlemen would like to smell..." He was holding an open three-pack up to their noses. The two were drunk. They sniffed obediently.

"*Donnerwetter!*" said one of them. "It really does. What will they think of next? But why mint-flavored?"

"For your breath, idiot," said the other one. "Am I right, old fellow?"

"I guess you are," said Father Concon, who was wearing a clean white jacket. "I guess you are."

I went into the next room and used one of the toilets because I didn't want to attract the two men's attention.

"I'll take a pack," said the first man. "Let's see how it works."

"I'll take one, too," said the second man, throwing the towel he'd used into a wire basket. "A little surprise, he-he-he!"

The two paid and stumbled up the stairs. The pianist was playing "Sunrise Sunset." I went into the washroom, washed my hands, walked over to Karl Concon's father, and said, "Good evening."

"And a very good evening to you, sir," he said, blinking his eyes at me. A bent, pitiful old man. He was holding out a towel, working mechanically like a robot, a servile smile frozen on his lips. "Did you enjoy it, sir?" asked the old man.

"Yes."

"A once-in-a-lifetime program," he babbled. I noticed that he was senile, absentminded, and a little confused. He didn't even look up when Bertie came down the stairs; and that was a good thing, because Bertie had his small Nikon-F with him, ready to shoot.

"Full every night," the old man said proudly. "Until morning."

"Fantastic," I said, while Bertie took pictures. "Herr Concon, right?"

"How—how do you happen to know?"

"Peter Enders," I said.

"Police?"

"No."

"Who are you?"

"A friend of your son's. I'd like to have spoken to him, but he isn't here, is he?"

"No. I don't know where he is," said the old man. "A good son. The best in the world."

"And he lets you work *here?*"

"He doesn't *let* me. I want to. It's lonely at home. I'm all alone. My wife died twelve years ago. Here I have a little distraction. I like the work. Karl wants me to stop, but I tell him, let me have that little bit of pleasure, Karl. Are you really a friend of Karl's?"

"Yes. Why?"

"There have been three here already tonight," said the old man. "Two came together, one came alone."

"What did they want?"

"To speak to Karl. And all of them said it was important. What's going on?" The old man's Adam's apple rose and fell inside his collar, which was much too large for him.

"I had a date with him for this evening," I lied. "I don't know what's the matter. Something must be wrong or he'd be here. What did the three men look like?"

He shrugged helplessly. "I can't remember faces, or voices. I'm perfectly healthy, but I'm not so young anymore. I forget faces. Right away. Dreadful. Three men. That's all I can tell you. The two who came together had hats and coats on. I remember that. The one who came alone was wearing a suit, no coat. All of them were about the same size as you. And that's really all I can tell you."

"Did they speak with an accent?"

"No. Perfectly normal German. And all three wanted to know where Karl was, and I told them I didn't know. But they kept asking as if they didn't believe me." Bertie was still taking pictures from the next room.

"When were the three men here?"

"The two who came together . . . at about nine. And the one who came alone, I guess around ten, right after Karl called."

"He called you?"

"That's what I just said. Before the men came. I had to go upstairs, to the cloakroom, where the phone is. There's a second phone in Karl's office. When he had the hotel in Kastanienallee, I used to work in the office. I used to remember everything then, and I could type, too, you know. . . ."

"How long is it since he gave up the hotel?"

"Six years. It didn't pay. The taxes. And so much annoyance. It's better here. No comparison."

"And what did your son say on the phone?"

"What did he say? Look here, what business is it of yours?" He was getting upset.

"I'm looking for him. I'm his friend."

"He never mentioned your name to me."

"A business friend. Didn't want it to get around."

"What sort of business?"

"Well . . . this and that . . . you understand?"

"I understand." He seemed satisfied. "Well, he said he wouldn't be back tonight, maybe not tomorrow either. He had some important business to attend to. Didn't tell me what. Only said he'd call me tomorrow evening at the same time. And that he was nearby. And I wasn't to worry. Everything was fine. He's always afraid I'm going to worry. When he calls, I'll tell him you were here. Where can I reach you?"

"I can't be reached, unfortunately," I said. "I'm going away. You really have no idea where he might be? It's very important."

"That's what the other gentlemen said, too. By the way, they didn't give me their names like you did. What could be the matter?"

"Yes. I'm wondering, too. But if he called you, it can't be too bad," I said, and tossed a two-mark piece onto the plate.

"Thank you, Herr Enders. Thank you very much." Then something occurred to him. "Do you happen to need some condoms? There are something quite new. Mint-flavored. Selling like hot cakes. Let me show you. They can't keep up with the demand. . . ."

11

At the corner of Detlev and Seilerstrasse there was a post office. I had enough change left and phoned Frankfurt from a booth beside the entrance. Bertie stood guard outside. I called Tutti. It took quite a long time until her sleepy voice answered, "Hello. Yes, this is Tutti Reibeisen. Who is it?" Her voice sounded as if her mouth was full or marbles. Suddenly she said, "Ouch!" Then I heard Max's voice. "What fucking ass is calling us at five o'clock in the morning? Your balls are bursting, maybe?"

"Max, this is Walter Roland. And it's only 4:30." Outside it was pouring.

"Well, that's just great that it's only 4:30. 'Scuse me, Walt*ah*. Didn't know it was you. But I just can't stand this shit phone waking Tutti and me when we've just got to sleep. Man, good old Tutti was doing her stuff until two!"

"Has she recovered from Leichenmüller?"

"Whaddaya mean, 'recovered'? We've got this new co-op apartment. They've gotta help pay for it, kid. But today we really creamed them. Three old guys from the sticks. Two hundred marks a piece, nothin' but French. Now Tutti's mouth hurts. Ain't easy for her to talk."

"I don't get it."

"Walt*ah!* Man...that took time! Old men, all of 'em. But forget it. We're going to the Taunus over the *fiekend*, that'll give her a chance to recover, or she's gonna collapse, bless her. What's the matter? In trouble?"

"No. I just have to ask you something, Max." I told him where I was and roughly what had happened. I ended up with, "You know the area here, Max. Maybe you know Karl Concon, a fag...."

"Sure I know that piece of shit. Fag—OK, that's his private affair. Don't have a thing against it. But the other things he does..."

"I know all about it, Max. Now, listen. Concon used to have a hotel in Kastanienallee. It's quite possible that he knows the owners of some of the hotels around here from way back, and that he's got friends among them who might be willing to hide him if it became necessary. Because he's gone underground. He's afraid of something."

"Because he messed up that business at the camp?"

"Yes. Some men seem to be after him because of that. He didn't get Irina. Do you know the owners of some of the hotels around here that rent rooms by the hour?"

"Sure, I do!" said Max. "I wasn't more than a year in Sankt Pauli, but there's nobody in the business I don't know." I heard him mumbling, "Yes, he's in Hamburg. Needs help. I'll tell you all about it, Tuttilein. . . . What? . . . Yeah. I'm to give you a big wet kiss from Tutti."

"Give her one from me. So what do you think? Where would the guy hide? Somebody who wouldn't talk, so he could stay there awhile."

"Lemme think," said Max. "Really good friends, eh?"

"Yes."

He thought it over for a few seconds, then came up with the names of five hotels in the vicinity of the Reeperbahn and the Grosse Freiheit. I wrote down the names on my pad.

12

Our hopes weren't exactly high. If Karl Concon really wanted to disappear, his friends would protect him and remain silent about it. Our idea was pretty feeble, but we couldn't think of anything better. In the first three hotels we said our names were Carsten and Enders, and that Karl Concon was expecting us. No success. Behind their desks in the indescribably dismal hotels, sleepy night clerks shook their heads and looked at us suspiciously. No Karl Concon in the house. Pleas and threats were useless. The clerks remained taciturn and hostile. One said he had heard the name once, the others had never heard of him.

"Okay, let's get on with it," I said. "Kleine Freiheit next. Paris Hotel."

"That's a dump," said Bertie, "and I'm soaked to the skin."

"So am I," I said, and drove into the Kleine Freiheit. It was quiet here. I parked the car in front of the entrance that had a damaged electric sign: ●OTEL PA●●S, and saw an old man wearing a green apron and a visor cap. He was sweeping the debris the storm had blown up to the entrance. We got out and went into our act of being a couple of gays again, as we had been doing all along. It wasn't easy. We had to be careful not to overdo it.

The man had stopped sweeping and was staring at the Rekord, then at us. His face was careworn, his gray-yellow moustache was poorly trimmed. "Good evening, gentlemen," he said. "What can I do for you?"

"Good morning, good morning," I said jovially, my arm hooked in Bertie's. "We'd like a room. Where's the clerk?"

"Isn't feeling well, sir. Had to lie down. I'll take care of you."

"Very good. A room for an hour," said Bertie, in a deep voice. I was playing the male prostitute; he was the old pederast who had picked me up.

"Come with me, please, gentlemen," said the old man.

He went on ahead. A lamp with a green shade was burning on the counter. A steep flight of stairs led up to the first floor. Behind the counter there was a small room. The door was open. A man, fully dressed, was lying on his back on a cot, snoring loudly. When he exhaled, he whistled, and the stench of cheap liquor issued in a cloud from his mouth. The little lobby stank of schnapps. "Is he ill?" I asked.

"Yes, very," the old man said, his voice expressionless. "Had to drink a lot of schnapps."

"Had to?"

"Because ill," said the old man.

The clerk was dead drunk; not even the explosion of an atom bomb would have roused him. The old man had gone to the key rack that hung on the wall behind the counter. This was the dirtiest hotel we had seen so far. "And please tell our friend, Herr Concon, that we're here."

"Concon?" said the old man.

"Karl Concon," I said irritably, and shivered. "Horrible weather! I'm freezing, Peter."

"We'll soon be warm, sweetie," said Bertie.

"Is no Karl Concon here," said the old man.

"But there must be!" I said. "He asked us to come here. He's throwing a little party. You must know him. How long have you been here?"

"Since seven, sir."

"What are you? Russian?"

"Ukrainian," said the old man, and I felt cold. Hastily I told myself that I still had my feet on the ground, relatively speaking, and that I must *not* let this nonsense drive me crazy. "From Tchaplino. I was prisoner of war." Oh, my God! I thought. "I surrender with friends, then afraid they do something to me if I go home in '45. So I hide. Hear that at home all dead. So I stay."

"Always in Hamburg?"

"Always in Hamburg, yes, sir. Always here. Sankt Pauli. Just the same, don't speak good German. Am all alone. But this not interest gentlemen. I give you number twelve." He handed the key to Bertie, whom he had recognized as the one who would pay. The key had a small wooden ball dangling from it; the number twelve was stamped on it. "Towels and soap upstairs. Twenty mark for hour. Is all right?"

Bertie laid thirty marks on the counter and said, "Karl Concon. A short, dumpy fellow."

"We called him Dumpling," I said, with a silly laugh.

"He's got to be here," said Bertie. "We have a date with him."

The old man looked at us, his eyes half-closed. "Fat?" he said softly, as if he was afraid of waking the night clerk, a quite unnecessary worry.

"Rather," I said, and laughed again.

"Pink shirt, crazy tie, perfume? Smell strong of perfume?"

"That's him," said Bertie.

"But his name not Concon."

"What is his name?"

"I don't know. He came seven, eight hours ago. Speak to Herr Wölfert, the boss. But he not say anything about party. And he not give his name. Must be asleep now."

"I doubt it," I said. "He's expecting us."

"I can't leave here," said the old man.

"Why should you?"

"To tell the gentleman. No phones in room."

"Doesn't matter," said Bertie. "We'll knock. We're old friends." He put another ten-mark bill on the counter. "What's the number of the room?"

"Seventeen. And thank you very much, sir," said the old man, staring at me, his eyes wide.

"What's the matter?" My laugh sounded almost like a giggle.

"Nothing," said the old man seriously. "Nothing, sir."

"Come along, sweetie," said Bertie, and took my arm again.

We walked up the steep stairs and came to a narrow passage. The two dim bulbs that were burning showed that it had been cleaner downstairs. *"Pfui!"* Bertie said softly.

"Shut up!" I said. "We've got him, man. We've got him!"

"Yes. And what if he's not happy about it?"

"He'll love it," I said, and took the Colt out of my coat pocket.

"That being the case, I'd better join in the fun," said Bertie, and got the Hasselblad ready to shoot while we crept slowly along the passage. There was noise behind some of the doors—a girl's shrill cry, a man laughing uproariously, the sounds of a whip and the harsh voice of a woman. "Gee up, gee up, horsey! Let's see you run!"

We passed numbers twelve, thirteen, fourteen, fifteen, sixteen . . . and walked up to seventeen, Bertie with his camera and flash at the ready. I tried the knob. To my surprise, the door opened. Everything was quiet.

"It's me, Concon," I said. "Roland. The reporter from the camp. Engelhardt's with me. The man who photographed you. Don't try anything. The police are here, too. All of us have guns. If you have a weapon, drop it and turn on the light."

No answer.

"You're to turn on the light!"

Not a sound.

As if nothing could possibly harm him, Bertie stood in the doorway and took his first picture. The flash lit up the room for a second. "Good God!" he said, and felt for the light switch. There was one beside the door. He turned it on.

The room was small, the dirty brown wallpaper was peeling, the curtains were drawn. I saw a washbasin, two chairs, a table, and a brass bed. Karl Concon was lying on his back on the bed, fully dressed. Somebody had plunged a knife into his chest, up to the hilt. It was a bloody mess, even though the blood wasn't flowing anymore and rigor mortis had set in.

13

"Yes, I know," said the old man.

We were downstairs, standing in the entrance, sheltered from the rain. The street was deserted, and behind us the sodden night clerk was snoring and whistling. The old man was very nervous—he wanted to be rid of us; but we had told him, as soon as we got downstairs again, that we'd call the police and he'd be in big trouble if he didn't answer our questions. And then we had shown him our press cards. This had scared him to death. He had really taken us for a couple of gays who had come to see Concon. He had told himself that we'd find the mess up there soon enough; he wanted nothing to do with it. He didn't want to talk to us, either, until we said we had to call the police. If he talked, maybe we could help him; otherwise, we'd nail him. There was more money in it for him, I said, and that brought him round.

"How much?"

"Five hundred."

"A thousand," he said. "If you don't mind, sir." A nice old man, our Ukrainian. We settled on eight hundred, and that he'd sign a release. So now we were standing in the hotel entry, freezing and questioning him.

"Well, first two men come," said the old man. "I think is around ten."

"What did they look like?"

"I don't know. I cleaning a room. I only hear voices. And steps in the hall. The voice of boss, too—Herr Wölfert. He go away right after that."

"Do you think Wölfert sent for the two men?"

"I don't know. Herr Concon frightened when he got here, very frightened. Everything happen fast, and secret. Herr Wölfert tell him, 'You be safe with me, Karl.'"

"Not safe enough," said Bertie.

"They friends, Herr Wölfert and Herr Concon."

"Yes," I said. "You can see that." This man Wölfert must have told the two men, whoever they were, of Concon's arrival. For how much? I wondered.

"What did the two men want from Concon?" I asked. "You listened, didn't you?"

"Yes," said the Ukrainian, without a moment's hesitation. "I surely get the eight hundred?"

"Surely. Here is four hundred to start with." I gave him four bills and he began to warm up to his subject.

"So then was big quarrel in Herr Concon's room. Men very mad at him."

"Why?"

"Because he don't get girl out of camp. I not know what camp, what girl."

"That's all right."

"But Herr Concon supposed to do it. Had been given job. Stop her from getting together with man here. This man's name is—is—can't remember right now. They say name several times, the two men who visit Herr Concon, God rest his soul."

"Don't worry about the name," said Bertie.

"Milka. Jan Milka! Now I remember," said the old man. He jumped because the drunken night clerk behind us had groaned and turned on his side, but almost immediately he began to snore and whistle again.

"Jan Milka. Very good," I said. "So this girl was not supposed to get in touch with him. Concon was told to prevent that."

"Yes. The men very, very excited. This man, Milka . . . must be very important person."

"Important for whom?" asked Bertie.

"I understand, for the Amis."

"For the *Americans*?"

"I don't know. Men don't say. Only that Herr Concon have spoiled everything, and things have been going well so far."

"What things?"

"Some business. This Milka have something to sell, that's how I understand. To sell to the Amis. Want more money all the time. Always asking more. Amis mad at Milka, but need him. Lives somewhere, protected."

"Protected by whom?"

"By Amis. Or by man who works for Amis."

"What Amis?"

"I don't know."

"What do you think?"

"Well, Milka Czech, say the men. Refugee. If he has something to sell to Amis, what can be? Political thing, I think. Men say Milka and Amis nearly agree; now Concon spoil everything. Milka must disappear fast, before girl come. Or reporter. That you, yes?"

"Yes," I said. "Where have they taken Milka?"

"Don't know. Men say 'where he safe,' is all. Girl here, reporter here. Men very angry with Concon. Say he must not leave room till they say so. Concon very much afraid. All the time say 'Sorry, forgive me, sorry. . . .' Also say, 'I work for you so often and so well.'"

Just a minute, I said to myself. Something's wrong here. Concon had done a lot for the East, so why were these men from the East reproaching him for ruining the plans of the Amis? I asked, "What language did the men speak?"

"What you mean, sir?"

"Were they foreigners? Did they speak with an accent? Broken German?"

"No. Good German."

Things were getting more and more confused.

"And then?" asked Bertie.

"Then two men go, Concon lock his door. I just have time to hide in next room. Didn't see men. Went on working. Cleaning rooms. Seven rooms. In this time men maybe drink with clerk. One hour, two hours. Was drunk when I come downstairs. Men gone. Clerk asleep."

"You're lying!" I said.

"No. I swear I tell truth."

"You're not trying to tell us that you weren't so curious that you didn't go down once to see who the men were?"

"Don't want to hide anything, please. Was like that. I too afraid, so not go down until men gone."

"It's a lie!"

"Is truth, sir."

"A lie!" said Bertie.

"Leave him alone," I said. "Nothing more we can do about it." And I asked, "What happened next?"

"People come. Men with girls and men with men. I very busy. A lot going on, if you please."

"But Concon was still alive when the two men left. You're sure of that?"

"Yes. Very sure. Hear him cursing."

"Then somebody must have killed him after the two men saw him."

"Yes."

"Who?" asked Bertie.

"Don't know. I swear, gentlemen, I don't know. Could be anybody who come here. At least twelve men come, at least six girls."

"It couldn't have been any of them," I said.

"Why not?"

"Because Concon locked his door. But we found the door open. So he must have opened up for somebody he knew."

"That's right," said the old man, and jumped again when the clerk behind us coughed violently and brought up some phlegm. He coughed for quite a while, but finally he was snoring again.

"You didn't listen at Concon's door anymore?" I asked. "Not once?"

"Not once. Have to be down here. So much going on. Get quiet about hour before you come, gentlemen."

"And *that's* when you went upstairs."

The Ukrainian was silent.

"Well?"

"Yes," he said. "Was upstairs. Listened at door again. Was scary. No sound. Opened door and there he lie, on bed, in his blood. Terrible. . . ."

"And why didn't you tell us that when we asked for him?"

"Didn't want to be mix' up. Didn't know if gentlemen friends or enemies of Herr Concon. Was afraid. You understand? Am afraid now, very afraid."

"Of what?"

"Revenge. Because I tell everything. Men come back and kill me, too. I idiot! For eight hundred marks I risk my life. Idiot!" Now his voice was teary.

"Bertie, take a few pictures of him."

"Okay," said Bertie and took a picture of the Ukrainian, standing in the entrance of the hotel, pale and grimacy with fear. Then we took him along to where our rented car was parked. I made out the release and asked the Ukrainian to show his identification card, so that he wouldn't palm off a false name on me. The dirty card said his name was Panas Myrnyi, age sixty-nine, residing in Sankt Pauli, Schmuckstrasse 89, care of Schwilters. He wrote with difficulty: in fact, he couldn't really write at all. Only sign his name, he told us, and his signature looked like it.

"Where are the other four hundred?" he asked, as soon as he had signed.

"Wonderful people, those friends of your Fräulein," said Bertie, in English.

"Only in death," I said. "Irina thought the same thing."

"Oh, let's drop the nonsense!" said Bertie, still in English.

"That's fine with me," I said. "But you must admit, it *is* rather strange the way all these foreigners cross our path. All right," to Myrnyi, in German, "let's go," and the three of us walked back to the hotel. I called the nearest police station, the Davidswache, and told them to come to the Paris Hotel, Kleine Freiheit—a man had been stabbed.

"Who's speaking?" the officer at the other end of the wire asked, but I hung up. We needed the time now. The police could try to find out who we were from the Ukrainian.

"You stay here and wait for the police," I had told him. "And you tell them everything you told us."

"Also that I tell you everything? That you here?"

"Of course. Whatever you like," I said. Then Bertie and I ran back to our car, I made a U-turn, and drove back on the Reeperbahn. We met a patrol car, its blue light revolving, its siren howling. And according to what we now knew, Irina was still in great danger.

14

Wim Croft, the Dutch garage attendant on duty that night, was a stout man with a rosy, friendly face and funny little eyes. He directed our car onto the elevator platform. 5:40 A.M. The car gleamed in the light, water dripping from it because it was still raining hard outside. We had driven to the airport in Fuhlsbüttel, where Bertie had sent off his latest films. As we drove to the hotel, he was sleeping peacefully beside me.

The underground garage had two floors, and the elevator was on the left side of the hotel, behind a heavy metal door. When it came up, the door slid up, leaving the entry free. Croft was wearing bright yellow overalls. He stood in the light of our headlights after having waved us in, pressed a handle, and the metal door came down again behind us. The platform, shaking a little, took us down to the first subterranean floor. Here Croft showed us the way to a free space. I turned off the motor and the lights; then I picked up my recorder and typewriter, Bertie took his cameras, and we got out. "It's been a long night," I said to Croft.

"I like to work nights," he said. "Prefer it to daytime. So does my colleague. We work the same shift, one week each. Is the car all right?"

"Yes," I said, "everything's okay. No damage."

He didn't seem to hear, but asked, "Have you any idea how long you'll be wanting the car?"

"No," said Bertie.

"Are you here on business?" He was looking at Bertie's cameras and my recorder.

"Yes," said Bertie.

"I was only asking," he said, "because you got the last Rekord. All the others are out. And there's one guest who insists he's got to have a Rekord. So many people want a car right now. We have two conventions and they're driving us crazy, even down here. Tomorrow a third lot's coming in. Heart specialists."

"And the other two?" I asked.

"Stamp collectors and neurosurgeons," said Croft. Friendly fellow. "Doctors from all over the world. I just brought down this Rekord here, beside yours. About half an hour ago. The Herr Professor seems to have had a good time."

He walked into his little office. The only decoration was a Coca-Cola calendar hanging on the wall beside a fire extinguisher. He began checking our car in. "What professor?" asked Bertie.

"From Moscow," said the Dutch car attendant. "Professor Monerov. Well, now...." He was looking at the registration book.

"What?" I asked.

"You have Suite 423, don't you?"

"Yes, and—?"

"And Professor Monerov had number 424," said Croft. "You're neighbors. And both of you rented a Rekord. Funny, isn't it?"

"Very funny," I said.

Apparently he loved to talk and seemed easygoing and utterly harmless, like a child. Many Dutch people are like that. And then, the devil take it, I thought of Fräulein Louise and her dear friends. But it was so late and I was so tired that I suddenly felt an aversion toward Fräulein Louise and her other world, and I thought: I can't—I don't want to believe in this world next door, whatever Hem says. I can only believe what I hear, what I see, what I say. And I know that what I see, say, and hear today—and this holds good for all human beings—is rendered obsolete and reduced *ad absurdum* by the very next moment.

276

15

When Heintze gave Bertie and me our keys, we asked for any messages. There were none. I took the elevator with Bertie, said good night to him, and got out at the fourth floor. A pair of street and a pair of evening shoes had been put out in front of number 424. The evening shoes were very elegant, but very dirty, and they belonged to neurosurgeon Professor Monerov. A Russian: So what! People of many nationalities stayed at big hotels. Stop thinking such nonsense, I told myself. Then I unlocked the door to my suite, took off my shoes before entering and left them in front of the door, locked it, and walked into the salon in my stockinged feet. I turned on the floor lamp beside the couch, where I had thrown a pillow and blanket, hung my jacket over a chair, loosened my tie, then opened the door to the bedroom softly, very softly. I wanted to go to the bathroom, but stopped beside the bed and watched Irina for a while. She was sleeping like a child, lying on her left side, curled up, her fist pressed against her lips.

I thought of her innocence and of myself, until the jackal came close, and I had to drink. A lot. When I finally stopped, I was gasping for breath, but the jackal had withdrawn. I wasn't sure if he would stay away, so I decided I'd leave the bottle on the table beside the couch.

I crept into the bathroom, closed the door softly, and with a towel swept aside the shards of the glass Irina had dropped when I had come upon her naked. I washed fast and went back to the salon, where I undressed, put on my second pair of pajamas, and poured myself a stiff drink, just in case. I listened, but everything was quiet in the bedroom. Then I picked up the receiver. The operator on night duty answered in a low, tired voice. First I asked for Conny Manners's number. It rang for such a long time, I began to worry. At last Edith Herwag answered. She sounded sleepy and exhausted. When she heard who it was, she livened up. "Oh, it's you!"

"I said I'd call up every few hours. How's Conny?"

"The hospital called. They said if there are no further complications, I can see Conny this morning."

"Great! When?"

"Around twelve."

"Okay. I'll call again around 10:30. I'm sorry I woke you."

"It doesn't matter. I—I'm so glad Conny is better. I've been sleeping in the chair beside the phone."

"So now go to bed."

"I will. And . . . Walter?"

"What?"

"Thank you . . . you and Bertie. You—you've been very good to me."

"That's all right, Edith. Good night."

I hung up and suddenly felt very tired. I drank and thanked God, or somebody or other, that Conny was better and would make it. I lifted the receiver again and asked for Frankfurt, Hem's number. He answered at once. I could hear music, a woman's voice singing. "Hello, old boy," said Hem.

"Hello, Hem. What's that? Still playing Schoeck?"

"Yes. *Dürande Castle*. An opera. Maria Cebotari singing. Beautiful, isn't it? So, what's new?"

I told him everything; he listened attentively. Every now and then he asked questions. And all the time I could hear the song and the wonderful music in the background.

"Congratulations," Hem said when I had finished. "Good work. First-rate story we have there. Are the pictures of Concon's body coming with the early plane, too?"

"Yes."

"Good! I asked Lester to let us have four pages, but he said no. So I called the old man, and Herford said of course, four. With a story like *that*! Needless to say, we need photos like *that*, too."

"You're getting them."

"And the text for the advance copy, and the captions. Must be here by ten. Got it? *Must be!* Don't come to me with your jackal now, or anything else, or your story's dead!"

"You'll have everything by ten."

"Herford is beside himself with joy that you've found such a treasure, and that means a lot, because otherwise he's in a foul mood."

"Why?"

"Bob."

Herford's son, playboy, and super-heel-about-town. "What's he done this time?"

"Same thing. Knocked up a girl. Fifteen years old. Herford poured out his heart to me. The girl's a tough customer, no coming to terms with her. Wants the child. Won't have an abortion. No way. Says she'll report Herford if he mentions it again." I laughed. "Yes. Very funny. Doesn't want child support either. Says that's too uncertain. Wants half a million. Cash."

"She must be crazy!"

"Not at all. Idiot Bob raped her."

"That figures."

"Unfortunately she has witnesses. Five. It was one of those mass productions. Nothing to be done about it, says Rotaug. Maybe they can get her down to four hundred thousand, but that's the best they can hope for. Herford gave his offspring more than hell. And he told me that if God really loved him, he'd have given him a son like you."

"You're kidding!"

"No. That's what he said. He's crazy about you. So do me a favor . . . do this thing right, please. It's a big thing, and it's all yours."

"Hem," I said, "I'm going to write this story as I've never written before. I'm only sorry for Irina."

"You're *sorry* for somebody?"

"Yes."

"That's bad."

"No, I really am. Look, she loves this guy Bilka, and according to everything we've been able to find out, he's a bastard. He isn't giving her a thought anymore, and if he does think of her, he's scared to death of her. That fink has plans, big plans."

"That's for sure," said Hem. "Only I haven't figured out yet what plans."

"I haven't either. But whatever—if we go on like this, we're going to collide with the law in some form or other, German or foreign."

"When are you going to the police?"

"At eleven."

"Good. You've got to have the police on your side. I can't say that often enough. Especially since this seems to be a case where foreign elements are involved. I called the office fifteen minutes ago. The newsroom knows nothing. Not a single agency has reported anything over the teletype."

"Bilka? Irina's kidnapping? The shoot-out at the camp?"

"Nothing. I even called our contacts in Bremen and Hamburg. Nothing in Bremen, nothing in Hamburg. And they had nothing extraordinary to report at the Davidswache."

Our contacts were men who had specific talents and connections, and were the first to uncover any sensational items. We had a lot of them, planted all over the place. So the Davidswache had nothing important to report? And I had called them myself, to report a murder.

"Great!" I said.

"Yes, isn't it?" said Hem. "So get some sleep, Walter. It's almost day. Where are you staying anyway? Where are you calling from?" I told him.

"I get the feeling you're smitten."

"Nonsense!"

"When have you ever slept on a couch and a pretty girl in bed in the next room?"

"Way back," I said. "Meanwhile I've become impotent."

"That's a shame," said Hem. "So, sweet dreams, my poor impotent friend. You deliver at ten. 'Bye."

I put down the receiver, got up and drew one of the heavy drapes aside a little and opened the French window. I couldn't sleep otherwise. The window led out onto a small balcony with a wide railing. I went back to the couch, fell onto it, and put out the light. I looked at the illuminated dial of my watch. 6:05. At 10:00 I had to deliver my material. At 11:00 I was due at police headquarters. So I could sleep until 9:00. No, better make it 8:30. Suddenly I saw Irina's beautiful breasts, her lovely body as I had seen it not so long ago, and I was filled with a searing desire for her. You want her, I thought, and Hem said you were smitten. Rubbish! I told myself, and promptly fell asleep. As I was to find out later, this was just about the time Fräulein Louise arrived in Hamburg.

16

I woke up and Irina was sitting on a chair beside me, staring at me. Her eyes were the first thing I saw by the light coming through between the drapes.

"Good morning," I said.

"Good morning, Herr Roland."

I looked at my watch. 8:30. Punctual as usual.

The salon was filled with shadows, the light coming into the room was dim. It fell directly on Irina's beautiful face. "Have you been sitting here a long time?"

"Yes."

"How long?"

"For at least an hour," she replied. "Excuse me, please. You don't seem to like the idea."

"I don't."

"That's what I thought."

"So why did you do it?"

"When I woke up, I looked in here, very quietly, and I could hear you talking in your sleep. And . . ."

"You were curious."

"Yes."

"Did I talk a lot?"

"Yes. And nearly the whole time."

"I do talk in my sleep sometimes, not often. What did I say?"

"A lot of things."

"What things?"

"Disgraceful things," said Irina, "and beautiful things. Very beautiful."

"That's great!" I said, furious suddenly. "And you found them so amusing that you listened to me for a whole hour."

"You didn't only talk during that hour. I mean . . ." She turned her head away.

I got up, walked over to the windows, and pulled back the drapes. The storm had passed, the sky was gray, and it was raining gently. I closed the open window, turned around, and saw that Irina was crying again. She didn't have a handkerchief. I went over to her and gave her mine.

"You know, when somebody talks in his sleep, you mustn't be surprised if—"

"That's all right," she said, but went right on watching me as I collected my clothes and put on my slippers. My suitcases were still in the bedroom. I wanted a different suit and fresh underwear. I wanted to take a bath and shave.

"Will you order breakfast, please?" I asked Irina. "Tell them to send it up in twenty minutes. I'll let the waiter in. I'd like espresso, ham and eggs, orange juice, toast, butter, marmalade. And tell the waiter what you want."

"I also think that Jan is no good," she said.

I threw my things on the bed, then went back into the salon and picked up the blanket and pillow from the couch. "They don't have to know I didn't sleep in the bed."

Irina said, "But is it possible to stop loving a man just like that? Just because one knows he's no-good?"

"Maybe a woman can't. I'm a man, thank God."

She began to cry again. I took the things back into the bedroom and heard her say, "I'm getting your handkerchief all wet. I'm sorry."

"I have others," I said, and found another handkerchief in my suitcase and gave it to her. "Here." Her shoulders were shaking.

She said "Thank you," took it, and gave me back the wet one. "You're welcome," I said.

"If Jan is such a bastard, as you just said—"

"Don't you agree?"

"Yes, I do. And there's something else I must tell you. I wasn't asleep when you came back and looked at me for such a long time on your way to the bathroom."

"You pretended?"

"Yes."

"Why?"

"I thought maybe you'd call your office and find out something about Jan. You did call your office, didn't you?"

"I called my editor," I said. "And you listened to the entire conversation?"

"Yes. I got up and crept to the door and opened it a little, and I heard everything. So now I know what you know about my fiancé, and it's not good."

"No, it isn't," I said, and went into the bathroom and turned on the water for a bath. I unpacked my toilet articles, and as I was switching the voltage on my razor, I looked in the mirror and saw Irina standing in the doorway. She wasn't crying anymore, and her beautiful eyes were open wide. "What do you want?" I asked. The water pouring into the tub made a lot of noise, so I had to raise my voice. She said something I couldn't understand, so I turned off the water. "What did you say?" She was standing very close to me now.

"I said, 'You're going to do all you can today to find Jan?'"

"Naturally. It's my profession."

"Don't," she said.

"Don't what?"

"Don't speak to me like that. Don't be angry with me."

"I'm not angry. I just want to take a bath."

"Yes . . . of course. But, look . . . I've got to have someone I can trust, don't I? A person can't live without somebody they can trust."

"They can try."

"I can't," she said. "I can't even try. I—I have to trust you now, don't I? I don't see what else I can do."

"If you've got to have someone to trust, then you're right, there's nothing else you can do. So . . . are you willing to trust me?"

She nodded.

"Good. And you'll do everything I tell you to do?"

She nodded again.

"And do nothing other people tell you to do?"

"Nothing," she said. "But please, please, Herr Roland, don't let me down. Don't you lie to me, too. Always tell me the truth, please. I couldn't bear it if you lied to me and turned out to be no-good, too."

"What would you do then?"

"I'd run away," she said. "I don't know where, but I'd run away from you. I know that."

"So I'll try not to be a bastard, like Bilka."

"And tell me the truth?"

"And tell you the truth whenever possible."

"Thank you, Herr Roland."

"You're welcome. And now you must tell me the truth."

She started. "I? What truth?"

"What's your shoe size?"

"What do you mean? Why do you—?"

"I have to know," I said. "So? And I want the truth."

"Thirty-nine," she said, and laughed suddenly.

"And your dress size?"

"Thirty-six."

"And your measurements? Let me guess! Eighty-five, sixty-five, eighty-five."

She was wide-eyed again. "But that's absolutely right! How did you know?"

"I'm a genius," I said, "and women are my specialty. Besides, I had the pleasure of seeing you—I'm sorry. That was tactless of me. I need your measurements because I have to buy clothes for you."

283

"No!"

"And shoes."

"No, no! I won't have it!"

"And stockings. And underwear, and don't interrupt all the time. Of course I've got to go shopping for you. You can't run around forever in the clothes you've got on!"

"I—"

"What's your favorite color?"

"Red. But listen to me. This won't do."

"Of course it'll do. You can pay me back from your fee. You have five thousand marks coming to you, remember?"

"Yes—no—oh, I'm so confused! I—forgive me, Herr Roland."

"You may call me Walter."

"Walter."

"Irina." I was still standing there like an idiot with my razor in my hand.

"You're so nice, Walter."

"And you're so beautiful, Irina."

Suddenly she avoided my gaze. "I'll order breakfast now," she said quickly.

"Good. And call Bertie. He's in 512. He's to come down in twenty minutes and breakfast with us. I bet he's still asleep, but he's got to get up."

She nodded.

"And don't forget to order your own breakfast."

"I won't," she said, and turned away. "I'll order tea. Lots of tea."

"And something to eat."

"I'm not hungry."

She came back just as I'd taken off my pajama top. "Now what?"

"Oh, I'm sorry. I was just going to say—I think I am hungry." She blushed. "So I'll order ham and eggs, butter and marmalade for me, too. And I don't think I'll have tea. I've changed my mind. I'll have espresso and orange juice, like you," and she hurried back into the salon.

I took off my wristwatch and saw that it was just 9:00. I turned on the little Japanese transistor radio, got into the hot bath, and listened to the news. Toward the end, local news, but not a word about Camp Neurode, nothing about the murder in Sankt Pauli, nothing related to our case. At the end of the broadcast I was shaving in front of the mirror, naked, and the broadcaster was

284

giving us the weather. Cloudy, with rain. This thing that I was on the track of was even bigger than I had imagined; otherwise, it wouldn't have caused such a total news blackout. And then I remembered suddenly that Irina had said she would have expresso instead of tea, like me, and ham and eggs and orange juice. "At the sound of the gong it will be 9:15," said the broadcaster. And then I knew suddenly that I loved Irina.

This had happened to me only once before in my life, and I wasn't at all sure that it was a cause for rejoicing. The whole thing tended to depress me. My last love lay sixteen years back. It had lasted only a year and a half, and had come to a miserable end.

17

The three of us ate at a table a waiter had rolled in, not a man I knew. I asked him who would be on duty at noon. He told me, and this was a waiter I knew well. His first name was Oscar, and I always called him "Herr Oscar." I was glad to hear that he'd be waiting on us that afternoon and evening.

After I'd eaten my ham and eggs and a lot of toast, I got out paper and pen, and Bertie and I wrote the captions for the photos. Bertie had numbered the rolls of films and made notes. I drank my coffee and smiled at Irina, but she continued to look at me seriously. We asked her if she'd mind if we worked during breakfast, and she'd said no, she wouldn't. After captioning the pictures, I asked Irina if she'd mind if I smoked, and again she said she wouldn't. After three more Gauloises and a lot more coffee, the advance copy was done. Almost 10:00.

I got up, went to the phone and asked the operator to get *Blitz* in Frankfurt. "May I use the phone, too?" asked Bertie. "I'll take the one in the bedroom." He had changed into a flannel suit, blue shirt, a light tie. He looked quite elegant. "Sure," I said. "Go right ahead."

Irina made a helpless gesture. "You can stay here," I told her. "I don't have any secrets from you." And to Bertie, "Whom are you calling?"

"My mother, of course," said Bertie, with his boyish smile.

He called her every day if he could, even when he was traveling. Of course not from South America or Japan. When he was that far away, he cabled. He loved his mother very much, and she loved her son. Bertie said, "This is going to be one crazy day. I won't have a chance later, and I want to send her flowers. There's a Fleurop shop in the lobby. I'm sure they're open already."

"Give her my best," I said as he left the room and my telephone rang. I lit a Gauloise. A woman's voice answered. I was in luck! It was black-haired Olga. She was best at this sort of dictation.

"Good morning, Olga. Roland speaking. I've got something important."

"Machine or steno?" asked Olga.

"Steno."

"Go ahead."

"Okay," I said, and began. As I dictated I looked at Irina. She returned my look sadly and seriously.

18

It was a big city with many people, and it was surrounded by a mighty wall, and the wall had four gigantic towers that rose up high into the sky. And monstrous figures were standing on the towers, calling out in voices that rang in the air. And Fräulein Louise was walking in the streets of this mighty city, at her side her favorite, the dead labor corps man and former philosophy student from Rondorf, near Cologne. And she was happy to have the student with her, because she felt lost and vulnerable in this terribly big city.

And the figure on the first tower cried, "Come to me, all of you who are troubled and burdened! You are all born equal! All of you have the same rights! All of you have the right to protection from hunger, need, and fear! Strive for happiness! Keep faith with the ideals of justice, moderation, abstinence, humility, and virtue!"

But the people hurrying by were not born equal and did not

have equal rights and equal protection from hunger, need, and fear; and there was little evidence of justice or virtue. Poor and rich, blacks and whites, oppressors and oppressed, exploiters and exploited, the brutal and the brutalized, the persecutors and those they persecuted, were much more visible. And Fräulein Louise asked her friend, "Who is that shouting up there on the first tower?" And the student replied, "That is the speaker for democracy."

And the figure on the second tower shouted, "Accursed be all sinners who give in to their lust! May they be forever damned and burn in hellfire, those who in their thoughts and actions succumb to the call of the flesh and all other earthly temptations!"

And the people hurrying by bowed their heads and looked guilty and afraid. And Fräulein Louise asked her friend, "Who is that man shouting on the second tower?" And the student replied, "That is the leader of the Christians."

And the figure on the third tower shouted, "Fight for the dictatorship of the proletariat! Destroy capitalism! Hunt down corruption and immorality! Build a nation of laborers, peasants, and intellectuals!"

And the people shrank away, filled with bitterness and fears, and no one dared to look at Fräulein Louise. And she asked, "Who is that on third tower?" And the student answered, "That is the leader of the communists."

And they walked on through endless streets and heard the gigantic figure on the fourth tower shouting: "Be brave and strong and prepare to give your lives to the fatherland! Destroy the monstrous progeny of the Jewish antichrist! Let purity and honor be your goal for the future of your people and the happiness of your children!"

And the people shrank away further and hurried faster, and their faces expressed terror and fear. And Fräulein Louise asked the student, "Who is that standing on the fourth tower?" And the student answered, "That is the leader of the fascists."

And Fräulein Louise could see that there was great misery in the city, because all the people lived under the pressure of the four mighty figures on the towers and didn't dare object but were confined and in servitude. And Fräulein Louise was filled with a great sadness....

This was what Fräulein Louise was dreaming in an empty compartment of the local that had left Rotenburg for Hamburg three quarters of an hour after she had got out of the Cologne express. The train was almost empty and stopped frequently. Fräulein Louise was determined to stay awake because she knew she had to be very careful now, much more careful than before. But she was too tired, and soon she was asleep and had this strange dream. She told me about it later, and about what happened to her in Hamburg, which I shall relate now. She said, "It was a terrible dream. So eerie. And I don't really know anymore whether I dreamed it or really saw it. Just the same, I am sure it was a blessing bestowed on me...."

"And how did it go on?" I asked.

Fräulein Louise said this she remembered exactly, and that she was sure she had been privileged to look into the future....

Suddenly the people couldn't stand their lack of freedom and the fearful voices of the four men on the towers. The voices grew weaker and were finally drowned out by the cry, "Freedom!" And hundreds of thousands, millions of cries grew out of this one cry: "Freedom! Freedom! Freedom!"

And a revolution broke out in the walled city, and Fräulein Louise and the student experienced it. They saw clusters of people climbing the four high towers like ants. Many fell down, but others came to take their place, and at last they reached the platforms on which the four leaders were standing. And the masses of unarmed people fell on them, and there was wild fighting. Thousands of bodies flew through the air as the tyrants tried to protect themselves, but in the end the desperate ones won, and they pushed the tyrants from their towers and stoned them to death.

And when the tyrants were dead, there was great rejoicing. Millions of people stormed the wall that surrounded the city, and the wall crumbled. And the masses streamed out of the city and their cries resounded to heaven: "Freedom!"

And Fräulein Louise and the student were swept along with the crowd, and they stumbled across the ruined wall, out of the city. And Fräulein Louise thought: Now at last those who have been exploited will get their reward; those trembling with fear will find peace; the oppressed will find justice, the defeated and enslaved, mercy; and the inconsolable will be consoled. But while she was thinking this, she heard cries and saw groups forming among the masses of people, and heard voices shouting, "Now you have your freedom, but do you know what to do with it?"

"You won't!"

"We must help you!"

"We'll show you what you need!"

"We'll create a paradise with your freedom!"

And the millions who had just obtained their freedom forgot all the dreams they had dreamed in the hell of their walled city, and let those who were screaming sell them new dreams. And the ones who were screaming were the dealers.

The dealers extolled what their fellowmen, still helpless and confused, would now allegedly need and what they were allegedly dreaming of—and that, screamed the dealers, was wealth, luxury, beauty, love and lust, career and possessions, fame, success, knowledge, worldliness, power, virility and adventure, and a thousand more things, and away with all inhibitions! And those who had just fled from slavery believed the dealers, and they bought and bought and soon were slaves again. And Fräulein Louise was filled with sorrow as she saw the faces of those who were being misled: how they withered and became ugly, were covered with boils and rotted, as in a pestilence. Now the faces of those to whom the dealers had sold wealth were distorted by greed, and the faces of those to whom the dealers had sold the wildest orgies were hollowed out, and the faces of those who had become addicted were sunken and gray. The faces of those who had sought luxury were devastated, of those who had been made all-powerful were cruel. Those whose only pursuit was their career had stony faces, those who had sought fame—vain, those who had sought property—angry, those who had sought knowledge—arrogant. And the confusion grew wilder all the time. The people bought more and more dreams from the dealers, whose voices were infinitely louder than those of the four previous leaders. "Buy! Everybody, buy, buy, buy!" And the people bought, bought, bought. But everything they bought was worthless. Because the dealers had sold them nothing but dreams.

19

Hem came into my room as I was writing these pages. He read them, then he said, "What a dream!" He puffed on his pipe and blew clouds of smoke into the air, still staring down at the pages. Then he said, "The dealers, the ones who sell dreams ... we're no better. I mean those of us working at *Blitz*. We cater to people who live in their world as if it were a prison behind high walls. And what do we sell them? Dreams of freedom!"

"That was something Fräulein Louise dreamed when she was afraid of the big city of Hamburg and what could happen to her there."

"It was more than that," said Hem. "With your Fräulein it's always more than that. People are still much too immature for absolute freedom. Whoever is aware of this—like the dealers in her dream—can capture people all over again and send them into the slavery of imposed information, of a consumer economy and atrocious taste, and can make his fortune with them. If people were really mature, the first thing they would do would be to free themselves of the dealers! But they are not mature and therefore cannot do it."

I said, "And what do we dream peddlers do? We're no better than Lester, Herford, and Stahlhut. We're just as guilty. We find out how we can write to please the people best; we follow our lowest, most unscrupulous instincts, because they are always the strongest. We know that more than fifty percent of the people prefer the artificial idyll to realistic information. We make idiots of them, systematically. Does it ever cross our minds to make adult, politically oriented human beings of those who swallow our shit on—for instance—the absurd, fictitious problems of the aristocracy?"

"But we have no intention of making adult human beings of them," said Hem. "That's why we dish out shit stories for them. In our age of increasingly perfect communication, the masses are dependent more and more on secondhand information. And *that's* what we manipulate. We explain a complicated world away with horrible simplifications. *Those* are the dreams we sell! We sell the 'simple' man and the 'simple' woman constant flights from reality and console ourselves with the thought that we're doing the right thing by them! Isn't day-by-day life hard and cruel enough? Don't the simple man and the simple woman deserve this escape? And apropos of the absurd fictitious problems of the aristocracy, wasn't the series 'Kings and Emperors' our greatest success, after your sex series? Weren't we able to sell monarchy as the ideal form of government for years?"

"That goes together with our national character," I said. "With that topic our need for subordination and our desire for voluntary slavery were satisfied."

"No," said Hem. "I don't see it like that. We're not satisfying the need for subordination; we're satisfying a genealogical craving. We sell the dream of a still-existent concept: family. Family is great and real and indestructible. We sell the dream of a life of splendor. Farah Diba and Grace Kelly. The marriages of the rich. We auction off heroic dreams—film heroes, sport heroes, prominent people, whoever they may be. With all these stories we lull the buyers of our dreams to sleep. They forget their family worries and the uncertainty of their condition, which are causing more and more apprehension everywhere. We transfer all mass anxieties to symbolic sacrosanct figures—in the course of which, truth goes down the drain. But the reader feels better. He doesn't despair. Yet. We sell anti-despair dreams." Hem laid a hand on my shoulder and said, "And now go on writing, Walter. And hurry up. Time is pressing. And write it all. Everything."

I said, "Yes, Hem," and went on writing.

20

At about the time I fell asleep on the couch in my suite at the Metropole, the local from Rotenburg was rolling slowly into the Hamburg Station. Fräulein Louise had awakened out of her strange dream quite a while ago, but her heart was still beating fast. As the train had crossed several bridges, she had gained a new impression of this monster, this colossus of a city, Hamburg, and her courage had flagged. She had come from the solitude of the moor; she hadn't seen Hamburg in years. At the station before Hamburg, a lot of people had got in, laborers mostly. Now the train was full. The many people frightened Fräulein Louise—even the people in her compartment were too much for her. What will it be like when I have to get out and mill around among thousands of them? Dear God, help me! I am afraid of this city.

When she got off the train she was caught up in a stream of travelers, all surging toward a broad staircase that led up from the platform. They bumped into Fräulein Louise and jostled her; her legs felt swollen and hurt. She staggered, the sweat rolled in little drops down her forehead, and she was breathing with difficulty. The crowd pushed her on mercilessly. She had to think of the dream again. Now she was climbing up a long flight of stairs, not easy, and there were so many sounds, so much noise, so many voices. It all made her dizzy. I must not give up, she thought. It hasn't even begun. I've talked it all over with my friends, and now I have to go through with it.

She reached the main lobby of the station. The newspaper stands and food counters were open already. Three men were standing in front of one, drinking steaming coffee out of mugs and eating frankfurters on rolls. Hot coffee! That would help. Hot coffee always helped.

She steered her way through the crowd to the shop and ordered coffee and a sandwich. Two of the men standing there were laborers, evidently friends, because they were talking and laughing. The third man stood apart. He was tall and thin, had a gaunt, narrow face and steely hair, cut very short. He was wearing an old cloth coat that had obviously been redyed dark blue. Fräulein Louise, who had dealt with redyed clothes for decades, noticed this at once. It was from a uniform, thought Fräulein Louise, sipping her coffee and eyeing the thin man; it was an English officer's coat. The padded shoulders, the cut of the waist, the broad belt at the back . . . yes, the coat had once been worn by an English officer.

Fräulein Louise looked at the man more closely. His trousers weren't blue. Not dyed, she decided, but old. In spite of which they were meticulously creased. The shoes—old, too, cracked black leather, but brightly shined. Heels downtrodden. Fräulein Louise's eyes wandered up—faded tie, out-of-style shirt, but neat. The man was shaved and had the dignified appearance of someone who had seen better days. Gray eyebrows, blue eyes.

The eyes, in contrast to his friendly face, had a cold, aloof look. Very upright posture. How old could he be? Certainly older than I, she thought. Somebody bumped into her in passing, and his elbow knocked her heavy bag out of her hand. It opened when it struck the ground, and at least a dozen hundred-mark bills spilled out. The gaunt man stared at the money as if mesmerized, then he bent down and collided with Fräulein Louise, who had fallen to her knees. "I'm sorry," he said. "May I help you!"

"I—I—oh, but this is—" Fräulein Louise stammered. Her money! All that money! Still on her knees, she watched the gaunt man pick up the money and tuck it into her bag. The bills seemed to want to stick to his long fingers. He closed the bag and gave it back to Fräulein Louise, then he took her arm and helped her up. She said, "Thank you."

"Not at all," said the gaunt man. "But so much money. . . ."

"Yes. Four thousand marks," said Fräulein Louise, and thought immediately: I shouldn't have said that.

"Four thousand? And the bag opens so easily," cried the gaunt man. "You should be more careful."

"I know I should," said Fräulein Louise.

The two laborers hadn't noticed a thing. They paid and went off, still talking and laughing. And more and more people streamed into the station. A loudspeaker began to make announcements. Fräulein Louise couldn't understand a word that was being said. She was still much too excited.

"Reimers," said the gaunt man, introducing himself with a slight bow. "Wilhelm Reimers."

"Pleased to meet you," said Fräulein Louise. "My name is Gottschalk."

"Have you come a long way?"

"Why do you ask?"

"You have an accent. Austrian, isn't it?"

"No. It's Sudeten German. But I've come from Neurode, from the youth camp there, near Bremen."

"Oh, yes," said Reimers. "Neurode. I've heard about it. There's a big moor there, isn't there?"

"Yes."

"It must be a terribly lonely place."

"Yes, it is. And when you come to a big city suddenly, it makes you nervous, you know, Herr Reimers."

"I can imagine." Reimers was a little more animated now. "But I guess you know Hamburg well."

"No, I don't," Fräulein Louise said sadly. "I'm afraid I don't know my way around anymore at all. It's been so long since I was here, and when I think of all the places I've got to go to—"

"Where do you have to go to?"

"To—" Fräulein Louise stopped. Careful, she told herself. I'm talking too much. I talked too much to the Jehovah's Witness who wasn't a Jehovah's Witness but turned out to be a psychiatrist. I must be more careful. "Oh...to all sorts of places."

"If you should happen to need a guide," he said hopefully, "that's what I am."

"A guide? What sort of a guide?"

"A tourist guide," said Reimers. "You can engage me by the hour. I know Hamburg like my own pocket. Herr Fritz here has known me for years." He gestured in the direction of the fat man in a white smock, working behind the lunch counter with two girls.

"Yes, indeed," said Herr Fritz. "Nobody knows Hamburg the way Herr Reimers does. I can recommend him highly if you need a guide."

"I've been breakfasting here for the last three years," said Reimers. "I live just around the corner, so I find it convenient. I get up early and come straight here. Express trains from all over Europe will be arriving soon."

Fräulein Louise looked at Reimers reflectively. She liked him. She would have liked the company of a man, but she didn't know anything about this one. Be careful, she told herself again. Watch what you're doing, Louise!

Reimers had pulled out his identification card and was holding it out to her. "In case you don't think I'm telling the truth."

"He's telling the truth, all right," said Herr Fritz, who was slicing hard rolls. "Herr Reimers has his clients every day, lady, and never any complaints."

But Fräulein Louise was still hesitant. "Do you enjoy doing this?" she asked. "Now, in November? Getting up in the dark? Breakfasting here? Waiting around, so early? In all weathers? Even when it's raining, as it is today?"

"I've risen early all my life," said Reimers, "and always liked it. Fresh air, interesting people, so many foreigners. I speak four languages." He bowed again. "And that's the truth. Besides, I need the money. I'm dependent on what I can earn on the side."

"Don't you have a decent pension?" asked Fräulein Louise. "A man your age—I'm sorry. I shouldn't have said that."

"Why not? 'A man my age'—sixty-nine. No, I don't have a decent pension." He laughed wryly. "Thank God, one can talk about it now, and I usually tell it right away. Then whoever doesn't want me can forget it."

"What do you usually tell right away, Herr Reimers?"

"What's wrong with me ... what *was* wrong with me."

"And what was that?"

"I was an SS leader," said Reimers, still smiling.

Fräulein Louise started. An SS leader! She looked at Reimers sharply; he was looking at her calmly. *Was* this her friend, the SS leader? After what had just happened to her on the train, she couldn't take any chances. She had to be cautious, very cautious.

"Are you horrified or disgusted?" asked Reimers.

"No, no!" said Fräulein Louise. "Only—it's so sudden. And I didn't expect—although—"

"Although?"

"Although you look like an officer. I thought that right away." She hesitated, then she asked, "It must have been difficult for you after the war, no?"

"I'll say it was," he replied. "First I was arrested by the Amis. Prisoner-of-war camp." Fräulein Louise started again. No, she thought then, it could be a trap. "I didn't do anything wrong, not in Russia or France. Nothing. Herr Fritz knows my whole story."

"Herr Reimers was a decent SS man," said Herr Fritz, stuffing sausages in the rolls. Two men in overalls, who looked like dockworkers, were standing at the counter now. One of the girls was waiting on them. "I've seen all his papers. That's why he only had to be in camp two years, and nothing happened to him during the denazification, either."

"No. Nothing at all," said Reimers, with the same wry smile. "But after the denazification I got tuberculosis. I caught it at the camp. So I had to go to a sanatorium, two years more, and another year to convalesce. Before the war I worked quite a long time in a factory. I tried to go back to work there...."

Factory, thought Fräulein Louise. Now all he has to say is that it was a pickle factory. "What kind of a factory?" she asked.

"Paint," said Reimers.

Take it easy, Fräulein Louise told herself. Not a pickle factory. Good sign? Bad sign? Is this my friend? Or isn't it? *I must not take any risks!* But I'm sure it's he!

"Yes. But in the meantime I had passed fifty, and they didn't want to give me the same job I'd had before. I suppose they couldn't. I think what they'd really have liked to do was turn me away. But in the end they gave me a job in the shipping department until I was eligible for a pension at sixty-five. Then I was out. They figured the pension to include the two years I'd been a prisoner-of-war, thank God! But you can imagine that it doesn't begin to suffice." He stopped and looked at her sharply. Herr Fritz was staring at her, too.

Fräulein Louise said, "You know, if I take a taxi, I won't really need a guide."

"That's perfectly all right," said Reimers. "It was just a suggestion."

"But where I have to go . . . I've never been there before. Sankt Pauli."

"Hm," said Reimers.

"Yes. You see? I could do with some protection there." If only I knew he was my friend or not, she thought. If he is, and I don't accept his help, it could be my misfortune. Perhaps . . . on the other hand, what can happen? She asked, "How much do you charge the hour?"

"Ten marks." he said quickly.

"Ten marks?" She looked stunned.

"The official guides charge a lot more, especially those who speak foreign languages."

"But I don't need anyone like that, and you're not an official guide! Five."

"Eight."

"Seven," said Fräulein Louise.

"All right," said Reimers. He couldn't take his eyes off Fräulein Louise's bag, but she didn't notice it, because she was paying for her coffee and sandwiches. At last Reimers was able to look away and paid, too.

Fräulein Louise walked toward the exit with the tall, thin man. She had taken her folded umbrella out of her bag, and as they walked out into the dark and rain, she opened it. Streetcars drove by, their bells clanging; cars passed, long columns with their lights still on; people were hurrying along, pushing their way through the crowded street. Oh God! thought Fräulein Louise. And it's scarcely day! What will it be like later? It's a good thing, after all, that the SS leader turned up. It's going to be just as my friends prophesied.

Reimers hailed a taxi, opened the door, and let Fräulein

296

Louise get in. He got in after her. "Sankt Pauli," he said to the sleepy driver.

"Reeperbahn. Silbersackstrasse. King Kong," said Fräulein Louise. She had written the address and name of the nightclub in her little notebook and had memorized them on the train. The tired driver looked at the strange couple in his rearview mirror. You never know, he thought, and said, "That's closed now."

"We've got to go there anyway," Fräulein Louise said firmly.

"It's all the same to me," said the driver, and he drove off up Mönksbergstrasse, where things were getting quite lively. The streetlights were still on, and so were the glittering neon signs.

"Oh, God, oh, God!" said Fräulein Louise.

"What's the matter?" asked Reimers.

"This city . . . this mysterious city," said Fräulein Louise, and had to think of her dream again, and shivered.

"What's brought you to Hamburg anyway, and to Sankt Pauli?" asked the former SS man.

"A murder," said Fräulein Louise, and the driver almost went into a skid. "But it's a complicated story. Anyway, it's personal."

"Oh, but then I'd like to know it," said Reimers. However, he moved a little away from her. She noticed it.

"Do you think I'm making all this up?"

"I beg your pardon!"

"Or are you afraid you won't get your money?"

"With a lady like you—never!" he cried, and thought what a hard life he was leading. He said so aloud. "It's a hard life I'm leading, at my age. I lied to you before. I like to sleep late. This getting up so early will be the death of me. But I've got to look for clients, don't I?" And the driver thought again that he ought to write a book about his experiences. It would be a best seller.

21

When Fräulein Louise and Wilhelm Reimers got out of the taxi in front of King Kong, it was pouring, and it still hadn't grown light. The street was deserted, the rain drummed on the sidewalk.

"I'm sorry," said Reimers, "but would you mind . . . the taxi?"

He was holding Fräulein Louise's umbrella over her.

"Of course," she said. The driver told her what she owed him, and she gave him a twenty-pfennig tip. "Thank you very much," he said ironically, and drove off so fast that the water at the curb splashed.

Fräulein Louise turned around and saw the glass cases with the photographs to right and left of the entrance. They were still lit. Fräulein Louise walked up to them, and her mouth fell open. "No!" she cried, shocked to the core. "But this—this is—Herr Reimers! How dare they—"

"Don't look at them," he said quickly, and steered her to the entrance. "I'm sure they're closed."

"I don't think so," said Fräulein Louise, with the clairvoyance that so often came to her.

"You'll see I'm right," said Reimers. He had pressed down the handle of the door and it opened. "What did I tell you?" said Fräulein Louise.

He let her go in first and lifted the heavy curtain at the end of the checkroom. Fräulein Louise walked into the nightclub and stopped abruptly. "Oh, dear Jesus!" she whispered.

The ceiling light was burning, cold and ugly in the big room with its many booths and small stage. About thirty men and girls were sitting or lounging on chairs—waiters, the doorman, the bouncer, bar girls, strippers, and their partners. The strippers were wearing bathrobes, but the bar girls were still in evening dress, the waiters and doorman in their uniforms. The latter had on his visor cap and had put his legs up on a table. A few other men had, too—the three grenadiers, for instance, in their fancy uniforms. Fräulein Louise looked at the scene with a total lack of comprehension.

There were full ashtrays, empty soup bowls, and coffee cups on the tables, and many empty bottles and glasses. The blond pianist, still in his tuxedo, was playing softly: "If I Were a Rich Man." Now he stopped. Nobody moved. They looked like figures in a wax museum, everybody staring at Fräulein Louise and her companion.

"Good morning," said Fräulein Louise, summoning up her courage at last. Thank goodness my SS leader came with me, she thought.

"Good morning," said the young man at the piano. Nobody else said a word.

"I would like to speak to Herr Concon," said Fräulein Louise. Nobody answered.

"Didn't you hear me? I want to speak to Herr Concon."

Baby Blue, Catherine the Great a few hours ago, drew her robe tighter around her and said slowly, "Which Herr Concon?"

"What do you mean? I want to speak to Herr Karl Concon," said Fräulein Louise, staring at Baby Blue.

"Father and son are both called Karl, so which one do you want to speak to?"

"I don't know. How old is the father? Around forty?"

"Ha!" said Baby Blue.

A waiter said, "That's the son."

"So, all right. Then I want to speak to the son," said Fräulein Louise.

"You can't speak to him," said Baby Blue. "He's dead."

"*What?*" cried Fräulein Louise.

"*What?*" cried Reimers.

"Dead," said Baby Blue. "Murdered. In the Paris Hotel on the Kleine Freiheit. Sometime in the night. And you can't speak to old Concon either—anyway, not right now. The police took him to the hotel."

"The police?"

"Yes. Homicide," said Baby Blue, while the others sat there, immobile. "They questioned us, too, then they went off with old Concon. To identify the body. They said they'd be back. None of us are supposed to leave. So we're waiting. We thought it was somebody from the police when we heard the door open."

"He has been murdered," Fräulein Louise murmured, and sank down in one of the plush armchairs. Her hat had tipped forward on her forehead. She looked ridiculous. "Murdered. . . . By whom?"

"You're a panic," said Baby Blue. "If the police knew who, we wouldn't be sitting here. Nobody knows. The old man collapsed. It's terrible for him. What a thing to happen! What's the matter with you? Why are you staring at me?"

"You—" Fräulein Louise swallowed hard. "You—"

"What about me?"

"I just saw your picture. Outside. How—how can you do such a thing? Don't you know that you are a dreadful sinner? How could you—?"

"Oh, shut up!" Baby Blue cried angrily.

"Now look here—" Reimers started to say, but Baby Blue didn't let him finish. "And you shut up, too, you dirty old man! Hein, I think it's time you took over."

The tall, lithe bouncer, wearing a sailor's cap and a

horizontally striped short-sleeved shirt, got up slowly and threateningly. "Stop!" cried Fräulein Louise. "Everybody is free to do as he likes with his life, if he doesn't think of later...."

"I think of later," said Baby Blue. "Later I'll have enough money to open a little bar of my own, and then I'm not going to screw anybody for a whole year. Besides, what I'm doing is art. You don't seem to realize that. Erotic theater. I'm an artist. All of us are artists." She waved a hand to include all the strippers.

"Oh, I see. Artists." Fräulein Louise was impressed.

"Yes," said Baby Blue. "And what are you?"

"I'm only a social worker from the youth camp in Neurode." Fräulein Louise didn't notice how the immobile figures came to life suddenly and took their feet off the tables. Some got up and whispered to each other. She was looking at Baby Blue with a friendly expression now. "My name is Louise Gottschalk," she said, "and this Herr Concon, who has been murdered, as you say, was at the camp yesterday afternoon and tried to kidnap somebody."

"Yes," said Baby Blue, appeased. "A young girl."

"You know about it?" Now Fräulein Louise was looking at all of them. The men and girls nodded. "But how do you happen to know?"

"And how do *you* happen to be here?" asked Baby Blue.

"Because I am looking for the girl. And for the murderer of little Karel."

"Of *whom?*" asked Baby Blue.

"*Another* murder?" cried one of the waiters.

"Now listen here!" The SS leader was addressing Fräulein Louise. Suddenly he looked pale. "You should have told me what you were letting me in for!"

"Don't get excited, Herr Reimers," said Fräulein Louise. "I'm not doing anything wrong. On the contrary, I want to see justice done."

"I think I'd better leave."

"No, no. Stay, please. I—" Fräulein Louise was struggling with herself. "I'll pay you ten marks an hour!"

"Ten marks an hour? For what?" asked Baby Blue. "And what about this second murder?"

Fräulein Louise made a tired gesture. "While Herr Concon was at the camp, somebody was shot. A little boy. His name was Karel."

"The police didn't say anything about that," said one of the strippers.

300

"The police didn't say anything," said the doorman. "They just asked questions."

"Then how do you know about the girl Herr Concon tried to kidnap?"

"From Fred."

"Who is Fred?"

"The piano player."

"That young man?"

"Yes."

"Tell Fräulein Gottschalk your story again, Fred," Baby Blue said to the piano player.

He looked at Fräulein Louise. He had beautiful, strangely glassy eyes. Fräulein Louise got up and hurried through the room to where the piano was standing. She took Fred's right hand in hers and shook it vigorously. And suddenly she felt something akin to an electric shock. It prickled through her entire body, as if a current were passing from the frail pianist to her. He sat at the piano, young and shy, and Fräulein Louise had the absolutely positive feeling that this was her dead labor camp friend. My student! she thought. Yes, yes, it is he! This time she was so sure of herself that she said, "You've studied music, haven't you? But not only music. You studied something else, too, didn't you?" She spoke softly. The others couldn't hear.

"Yes," said Fred. "Philosophy. A few semesters. Then I stopped."

"I know all about it, don't I?" said Fräulein Louise.

"You certainly seem to." Fred's voice was gentle and friendly. There he sat, the favorite of all her dead friends! In the body of a living man!

"I'm Fräulein Louise, you know," she said again, with a strange, sweet sensation in her heart. "So tell me—how did you find out?"

The pianist looked down at the piano. Baby Blue came sauntering over. "Go ahead," she said. "Tell it again," and she gave Fräulein Louise a look that was almost friendly. "You told the police, and all of us heard it. It isn't a secret any more, so go ahead. If Frau Gottschalk—"

"Fräulein, please."

"Since Fräulein Gottschalk wants so much to know."

"*Has* to know! Has to!"

"So go ahead, Fred."

"All right," said the frail young man.

Wilhelm Reimers and some of the others had come closer and

were standing around the piano. The pianist passed a hand across his face, then he turned his head toward Fräulein Louise. "Well, you see," he began, "this place doesn't open until 8:00 P.M. In the morning the cleaning women are here until eleven. After that, not a soul. Only Herr Concon and myself. I mean, Herr Concon used to be here. Now he's dead. He always worked in his office. That's behind the stage, and I always came here to play. With his permission. I'd work up new things, arrangements, things of my own. Then, around two, we often went out to eat together. Everybody knew that only the two of us were here. Herr Concon's father was always sleeping at the time."

"And? And?"

Fred was still looking at Fräulein Louise. "And yesterday," he went on, "just before eleven, there was a knock on the door. There'd been a phone call for Herr Concon before that. He was expecting the visitor, and he opened up and let him in."

"Let who in?"

"A man," said Fred. "During the last two or three years he's been here a few times. And always at the same time. They walked past me to Herr Concon's office, and I went on playing. Then I could suddenly hear them talking."

"How could you do that? Can you hear what's being said in—?"

"No. The office is soundproof. But there's a tape recorder in there, for music, and for . . . well, whatever's going on in here, on the stage. Through a microphone. Rather old-fashioned. It isn't transmitted directly. The microphone is independent of the tape, you understand?"

"So when it's turned on, you can hear everything that's being said in the office, in here?" said Wilhelm Reimers. He was getting more and more excited all the time. This was something very different from his ordinary routine!

"That's right, sir," said Fred.

"You mean," asked Fräulein Louise, "that Herr Concon turned on the microphone because he wanted you to hear what went on in his office?"

"That's right," Fred said again.

"Had he ever done that before?"

"No. Never."

"So why did he do it yesterday?"

"Because yesterday he was afraid," said Fred, looking down at the keys again.

302

"How do you know?"

"I know his voice," said Fred.

As he said it, Fräulein Louise was so moved, she wanted to reach out and stroke the hair of the dead student, who, she was sure, was sitting here in front of her. But she didn't do it because she heard a voice which she recognized immediately as that of her dead Russian, saying, "Louise is about to do something she shouldn't do. There is no communication between our realm and the meaningless life of the world."

Fräulein Louise withdrew her hand, which she had already stretched out, and nodded. She had almost made a mistake! But nobody had paid any attention to her, because the student had gone on telling his story.

"And this was corroborated by the conversation I heard now, although I went on playing, so as not to attract attention."

"And what did you hear?"

"The conversation had already begun when Herr Concon turned on the microphone." It was very quiet in the big room. Nobody moved. "Herr Concon said, 'I don't want to! I don't want to! Leave me alone, for God's sake!' And his visitor said, 'I'm afraid you've got to, my good man. You've got to and you will. Because if you don't do as I say, the evidence that the court lacked for your conviction will turn up quite suddenly, and you'll go to jail for the next ten, fifteen, twenty years.'"

"The evidence!" cried Fräulein Louise. "He stood trial, Herr Concon did. I heard about that."

"Yes. In 1957," said Baby Blue.

"For blackmailing a high-ranking officer, right?"

"Yes," said Baby Blue. "It was a big scandal. He was acquitted for lack of evidence."

"And now his visitor was threatening to come up with the missing evidence!" Fräulein Louise shoved her hat back off her forehead.

Reimers said, "If he was blackmailing a West German officer, then Herr Concon must have been working for the East. Then the evidence must be in the East, and the visitor must have come from there."

"That's what it looks like," said Fred. "The visitor said, 'You're coming with me. We've got to get to the camp in Neurode fast. You won't go alone. You'll have protection. A man and a woman will go along with you. You'll take two of our cars.'"

"Two cars!" cried Fräulein Louise, "and a man and a woman

to go with him! What man? That's the man I'm looking for! Do you know anything about him, Herr Fred? Did the visitor say anything about him?"

"Very little. Herr Concon asked, too, who it was going to be. The visitor said it would either be he or somebody else—in any case, an expert."

"Did he say that?"

"Yes. And that the woman would be first-rate. And the cars."

"And the shooting!" said Fräulein Louise. "The shooting was first-rate, too." She wiped her eyes and said, "Go on. So they were blackmailing Herr Concon into kidnapping Irina."

"Irina Indigo. Yes. That's what the visitor called the girl. And then he showed Herr Concon pictures and gave him a description of the girl. Eighteen years old, medium height, black hair—"

"I know what she looks like," Fräulein Louise said impatiently. "But why was Herr Concon to kidnap her? And why right away?"

"Herr Concon asked the same questions," said Fred, "and the visitor said there wasn't a minute to lose. The girl was trying to get to Hamburg, to the man she was engaged to."

"Yes, yes! And—?"

"And this was not to happen, not now, when everything was almost settled."

"That's what the man said? When everything was almost settled?"

"Yes. That's what he said."

"But *what* was almost settled?"

"I don't know. But the visitor went on threatening Herr Concon until he agreed. It was his assignment to kidnap this girl from the camp."

"And then? What was to happen to her then?"

"Herr Concon asked the same thing."

"And?"

"And nothing. The visitor said that was none of his business. As soon as he'd kidnapped the girl, his mission was finished. He would take care of what came next."

"Who? The visitor?"

"Yes. Everything was all set, he said. And Herr Concon should be sure to take his gun along." Fred raised his head again. "Then I could hear the microphone being turned off, and right after that Herr Concon came out of his office with the man, and said he had

304

a business appointment and was sorry but he couldn't lunch with me. I was to lock up and keep the key. His father had a key if he wanted to open up." Fred smiled. "That wasn't true. His father didn't have a key."

"So why did his son say he had?"

"That was something that had been arranged between us years ago. Whenever this man came and Herr Concon left with him, he said that to me about the key. It was a warning. It meant; if I'm not back before midnight, notify the police. He lived in fear . . . poor Herr Concon."

"But you didn't notify the police," said Fräulein Louise.

"No. Around ten, Herr Concon called his father and said everything was all right."

"So what happened then? After Herr Concon said that about the key."

"Then he went off with his visitor."

"And what did the visitor look like?"

"I don't know."

"What do you mean, you don't know? If he passed close by you twice? And had been there several times before, as you said yourself? Or didn't you say that?"

"Yes, I did," said Fred, with a tremulous smile.

"And you don't know what this man looks like?"

"No," said Fred.

"Now you're lying," she cried. "Why are you lying to me? Oh, dear God, I don't understand!"

"I am not lying," said Fred, still with that tremulous smile. "I really don't know what this man looks like."

"But that's impossible! You *must* know!" cried Fräulein Louise, bringing her fist down hard on the piano.

Fred bowed his head. He wasn't smiling anymore. Just then Fräulein Louise felt a firm hand on her arm. She turned around. Baby Blue was standing beside her, looking angry again. "Fred doesn't have to know," she hissed. "Don't tell me you haven't noticed it yet."

"Noticed what?"

"Fred is blind," said Baby Blue.

4

Revision

1

Beim Strohhause 31—that is the address of the police headquarters in Hamburg. It is located at the exit of subway station Berliner Tor and is the only high-rise building in that area, a dark gray cement structure that looks grim in spite of its many windows. Bertie and I walked to the entrance in a drizzly rain.

The Missing Persons Bureau was on the seventh floor. We took the elevator up and walked into a room in which two secretaries were typing. We gave one of them our names and said we had an appointment with Chief Investigator Hering, for eleven o'clock. It was two minutes to eleven. The secretary picked up her phone, dialed a double number, and announced us. Then she said, "Herr Hering will be with you right away." And he really did appear almost at once, a stout man with a bald head. He was wearing glasses and looked miserable. He shook hands heartily with Bertie and said he was glad to see him again; then he shook hands with me and asked us to follow him. We walked behind him into his Spartan office. There was a desk by the window, two flower pots on a gray metal shelf, metal file cabinets, and a huge card index file; in the corner opposite the window—a round table, four chairs, a couch. Couch and chairs were modern and upholstered in blue. Two men were seated on two of the chairs. When we entered, they rose. One was tall and fat, the other was thin and wore strong glasses. The two men were Albert Klein and Wilhelm Rogge from the Internal Security Department, whom we had met in the Youth Camp in Neurode.

2

Our greeting was formal, courteous, and cool. While we had been waiting for Chief Investigator Hering to appear, I had had a premonition and had turned on my recorder. The microphone was also in the case, its small silver tip barely visible, no possibility of its arousing suspicion, and when the recorder was in its case, there was no way of telling if it was turned on. I put it on the table in front of us, and it recorded the following conversation.

Hering seemed embarrassed. I was the first to speak. "Quite a surprise, gentlemen, to find you here. We really came to see Herr Hering."

"Yes, we know," said Herr Klein.

"How do you know?"

"He told us," said Herr Rogge.

"When he came in," said Herr Klein. "We were here before him. We took an early train."

"Why?" asked Bertie. "What are you doing in Hamburg?"

"What are *you* doing in Hamburg?" asked Herr Klein.

He looked as if he were bored with us, as if he found us slightly repulsive. In all probability he shared the opinion of deceased Chancellor Adenauer on how to deal with the press: a cold buffet, withdrawal of advertising, temporary injunction.

"That's what we were just going to tell Herr Hering," I said.

Hering looked more miserable than ever; in fact, now he seemed almost hostile as he said, "This is a case for the gentlemen from the Internal Security Department. They tell me it doesn't concern me, so please answer their questions." He looked at Bertie and said in a more friendly tone, "I'm sorry, Herr Engelhardt."

"It's not your fault," said Bertie, and to the two men, "We came here to report to Criminal Investigator Hering, as head of the Missing Persons Bureau, that we drove to Hamburg last night from the Neurode Youth Camp with Fräulein Irina Indigo, and that she is with us."

"We know that," Klein said again.

"And how do you happen to know that?"

"We know, and that's that. You persuaded Fräulein Indigo, illegally, to leave the camp, and you are staying at the Metropole Hotel with her. And don't ask again how we happen to know. We arrived in Hamburg very early and alerted the various precincts. Where you were staying was reported as soon as you registered at the Metropole. You have locked Fräulein Indigo in your suite so that she can't run away. Is that right, Herr Roland?"

"Yes," I said. "Because she is in danger. And there's something very strange going on in connection with her fiancé. And Karl Concon was—"

"Was murdered. Last night. In Sankt Pauli. Paris Hotel. We know all about it," said Rogge.

"Also that your correspondent, Manners, was hit by a car and badly hurt," said Klein.

"And that Fräulein Gottschalk is somewhere in the city."

"Who said so?"

"A doctor. And because he reported meeting her—but that's not important. As you can see, we know everything you were going to tell Herr Hering."

"And why did you come to Hamburg so fast and make all these investigations?"

"That's our business," said Klein.

A pleasant conversation. . . .

"So if all this is your business, why didn't you see to it that Fräulein Indigo couldn't leave the camp? Why didn't you hold her?"

"Because we had no right to do so," said Rogge. "That would have gone beyond our jurisdiction. This is a law-abiding nation, Herr Roland. We have only been asked to look into the case."

"And besides, we didn't feel it was necessary."

Hering sat there looking miserable again. I had the feeling that he knew a lot and would have liked to tell us about it, if only for Bertie's sake, but he didn't dare.

"Not necessary?" I said. "So you don't think Fräulein Indigo is in danger?"

"Not at all, if she obeys your orders and doesn't leave the hotel or tries to get in touch with anybody. She's obedient, isn't she? We have several forms here, Herr Roland. If you will sign that you are willing to take all responsibility for Fräulein Indigo, then she can stay here and won't have to go back to the camp, where she would be in greater danger. All formalities will be attended to, once you have signed." Klein pushed some papers across to me.

"What's that?" I asked.

"Recommendations," said Klein. "On our letterhead. Asking whomever it may concern to assist you in your journalistic endeavors."

"Just a minute," said Bertie. "You're not going to brush us off? You're not going to report us? You're not going to stop us from going after this matter?"

"We have no legal right to do that," Rogge said again. "You shouldn't always look upon our office as hostile, Herr Engelhardt. We help the press as much as we can, especially in cases like this."

"Like what?"

"Cases that are of public interest."

"And this is such a case?" asked Bertie, playing the idiot.

"Herr Engelhardt, please!" said Klein.

"You must be pretty sure of what you're doing," I said, whereupon both men were silent. Klein just shrugged and went on looking at me, not an iota more friendly.

"Fräulein Indigo told me," I said, "that you questioned her extensively at the camp. She was afraid you'd never let her go. Then the phone rang, you talked to somebody, and that seemed to change the whole picture, and you let her go."

"That's right," said Klein.

"What's right?"

"That this telephone call changed everything."

"Aha!" I said.

"Yes," said Klein. "And we are grateful that you called the Davidswache right after you found Concon's body in the Paris Hotel. After that everything went fast."

"Don't mention it," said Bertie. And to distract them from my recorder he added, "I suppose I'm not allowed to photograph you now?"

"No, Herr Engelhardt, we can't let you do that. Nor may you record this conversation without our permission. But we won't bother about that. We have nothing to hide."

"Well now, how about it?" asked Klein. "Are you going to sign that you will take all responsibility for Fräulein Indigo?"

"Of course," I said, and signed.

"And here are your recommendations," said Rogge, pushing the papers across to me.

"Thank you," I said. "You're doing us a great favor."

"Not at all," said Klein. "You've done us a great favor."

"I don't understand," I said.

"You don't have to," said Klein, and after saying that he smiled for the first time since I had met him. I stared at him, and I could feel my jackal coming closer. I got up, took my recorder, thanked the gentlemen, and said good-bye. So did Bertie. "I'm sorry, Herr Engelhardt," Chief Investigator Hering said sadly. "I would have liked to help you. Well, maybe next time."

"Sure," said Bertie. And then we were out in the hall, Bertie limping along beside me. "Stinks to high heaven, doesn't it?"

"Higher than that," I said, and switched off the recorder.

"That dumb spiel with the recommendations. Caveats, that's what they are! If we present them anywhere they'll be a guarantee of noncooperation. Right?"

"I don't know. Maybe they really want to help us."

"Don't be ridiculous! Why should they want to?"

"For selfish motives. They're using us for—for—" I couldn't go on.

"What's the matter with you? You look green! Don't you—?"

"Yes," I said, and took out my flask and drank. When I stopped drinking, I was struggling for breath. But the jackal was gone. For the present. Until next time.

3

"Now we drive up to the entrance," Bertie said to our friend, taxi driver Vladimir Ivanov, who had helped us a few hours before and begged us to ask for him, which we had done. It was 11:15 A.M. The rain was mixed with sleet and the sky had darkened. The cars had their lights on. We were sitting in the back of the taxi, parked beside a round flower bed—the flowers planted in it were dead—in a small parking area opposite the entrance to the University Hospital on Martinistrasse, not far from Eppendorfer Baum. An enormous complex, this hospital. Various tall buildings housed innumerable clinics. A city within a city.

Tall, blond Edith Herwag was just coming out of one of the buildings as Ivanov drove up to the entrance. We had left our car at police headquarters and telephoned for our Russian from a booth. Before that I had spoken to Irina and Edith. Irina sounded uneasy as she asked us to come back for lunch, however late; being locked in was driving her crazy. I told her we would, so that somebody would be there to let in the cleaning women and she wouldn't be alone when the food was sent up. I told Edith to wait until a taxi stopped in front of her house and either Bertie or I waved up to her, then she should call a taxi and drive to the hospital. We would follow her and bring her home again, but nobody was to see us together.

Our driver, old Russian Father Ivanov, nodded as I explained things to him. All he said was *"Xorosho,"* then he drove like mad through the worst traffic and was at Adolfstrasse in no time flat. From there he followed Edith's taxi without once losing sight of it. Fine. Edith disappeared into the hospital; but now, only twenty minutes later, she was leaving it again. Our taxi stopped near her and she got in. I slid open the glass between us and the driver and said, "Back to Adolfstrasse." Vladimir Ivanov nodded and drove off, and I closed the window again. I leaned back and only then noticed that Edith, who had sat down between us, was weeping.

"Oh God," I said. "Is he—?"

"No," she sobbed, and blew her nose. "He's going to make it. He's all right."

"Wonderful!" said Bertie. "So they're tears of joy?"

She didn't answer but cried harder than ever.

"Was he conscious?" asked Bertie.

"Yes."

"Were you able to speak freely with him?"

"No. There was a guard in the room all the time. Outside his room, too, and another at the entrance to the private wing. He's out of the intensive care unit. He sends greetings to you both—that much he managed to say—and I told him I'd tell you. I may come back this evening, and after tomorrow I can visit him twice a day. Then he wanted to kiss me. I had to bend down and lean over him, and he asked me to loosen my hair and let it fall over him, and I did, and all that with the guard watching us. And Conny kissed me and whispered in my ear, 'The men are from MIB. Tell Bertie.' It happened so fast, I think the guard didn't notice. What's MIB?"

I managed to say calmly, "Oh...Murder Investigation Bureau. A branch of homicide."

"That's what I thought. But why did he want you to know?"

"It's a highly specialized department," said Bertie, who had recovered from the initial shock. "Murder Investigation Bureau. MIB for short. They investigate murders only."

"Really? Are you telling the truth?" Edith was crying again and I knew why—not for joy but in fear. I thought of the threats on the phone—that Conny would die if he said anything. And he had said something....

"He's telling the truth," I said, and could only hope that Edith wouldn't ask anybody else.

"Then that's all right," she said. "Then nobody can get at him and harm him, right?"

"Of course not," I said. "Impossible!"

"But those calls—"

"They can't do a thing to him. I swear they can't."

"Oh, my God, if only I wasn't so afraid!"

Edith sobbed and we let her cry. At last, when we got to Adolfstrasse, she calmed down. We again impressed it on her that she should stay home and let no one in, and I promised I'd call her. And when she went to see Conny that evening, she was to ask for this driver. He had told her that he worked until ten o'clock. I wrote down his name and the telephone number of the taxi office, and his license number. Edith kissed us both before she got out, and as she ran into the house she was crying again.

"Poor woman," said Ivanov. "Is in trouble, yes?"

"Yes," I said.

"God will help her."

"Yes, please," said Bertie.

"Where to next?" asked Ivanov.

"You can let me off at Jungfernstieg," I told him, "and then drive my friend to police headquarters." Bertie had to get our car. As Ivanov drove, I said softly, "So . . . MIB. . . ."

"Yes," said Bertie. "It is a case of public interest, and we have some very nice letters of recommendation, and Conny is being guarded by the MIB. . . ."

MIB is short for the official spy organization of the Bundesrepublik, not *M* for "murder" but *M* for "military"—the Military Investigation Bureau.

4

On Jungfernstieg I went shopping for Irina, and I took my time about it. I had arranged with Bertie that on his way back from police headquarters he should drive around the block until he saw me, because there was no place to park on Jungfernstieg. I went into five stores and bought a lot of things for Irina. I had plenty of money with me and I knew her measurements. I considered the fact that the things should cover what she might need now, so I bought a red silk cocktail dress, sleeveless; a green wool dress with a black patent-leather belt; and an ochre-yellow jersey suit. Then I bought a black coat with mink trim and a mink button-on hood. All the time I kept imagining what Irina would look like in the clothes.

The salesgirls who waited on me were wild about me. That's the sort of man they wanted! I went to another store and bought a robe, underwear, nightgowns, stockings, and so on. I also imagined Irina in the underwear. I bought a gold evening bag to go with the cocktail dress, and then I thought, What the hell! And bought a black alligator bag for twelve-hundred marks. I could always send for more money if I was short. In the bag shop I also bought a black leather suitcase to hold all the things, and as I was going on to the next store I saw Bertie, driving around the block. He waved to me, I waved back, and went into a shoe store where I bought a pair of black patent-leather pumps that Irina could wear with anything, and gold leather shoes for the cocktail dress. Then I went to a cosmetic shop and bought lipsticks, powder, creams, eyeshadow, and mascara; things like that, also a bottle of Estée Lauder perfume and Eau de Toilette. Now the suitcase was full and quite heavy, and I had everything I needed. I walked out into the sleet storm and waited for Bertie to pass by again. He saw me, stopped, and I got in. "To the Metropole," I said. It was 1:25.

"You smell gorgeous, sweetheart," he said.

"Shut up, idiot!" I said, and slapped him on the back.

"I could do with a little Chivas," he said. "As an aperitif."

I unscrewed the flask and handed it to him, and he drank with one hand on the wheel, then I drank. As I look back, this drive to the hotel in the shitty weather, with both of us drinking whiskey and my holding the suitcase on my knees, has remained with me as one of my happiest days in Hamburg.

5

Old Karl Concon wept. He was sitting in the room next to the one in which his son had been stabbed, on the second floor of the Paris Hotel in the Kleine Freiheit. The day was dawning, and the feeble morning light filtered through the filthy windowpanes. All the lights were still burning, and the old man still had on the white coat he wore in the King Kong men's room, because the police had brought him here straight from there. He sobbed; the tears were streaming down his pale face. He was sitting on an unmade bed, and a lot of men were milling around, sporadically talking. There were officers from homicide, from the Identification Bureau, photographers, fingerprint experts. They were working routinely and fast.

When Fräulein Louise arrived with her guide, Wilhelm Reimers, they had just finished, and two men in gray smocks were getting something that looked like a metal bathtub out of a van parked in front of the hotel. They took it up to the second floor, opened it, laid Karl Concon, Jr., in it, closed it, carried it downstairs again, and put it back in the van. And Karl Concon's father sat on a whore's bed and wept.

The corpse in the metal tub was carried past Fräulein Louise just as she was about to go upstairs. Nobody paid any attention to her: The men were too busy, and the desk clerk wasn't drunk anymore, only unshaven, pale and sober, and reeking of schnapps. At that point the Ukrainian servant, Panas Myrnyi, confronted Fräulein Louise and said, "You can't go up there now!"

Fräulein Louise, who had walked from King Kong to the Paris Hotel, looked Myrnyi up and down. She was in a great state of excitement, and this made her forget her good resolutions and caution. She winked at Myrnyi and whispered, "Ukrainian, no?"

He nodded, taken aback, which she didn't notice.

"Were a peasant in your native land, right?"

He nodded again, astonished, which she still didn't notice.

"So here, too," she said. "Why, you're everywhere, just as you promised! So what happened? Tell me."

317

The servant hesitated. "Who are you, please?" he asked.

"You know who I am!" said Fräulein Louise, and Reimers said, "They told us what happened at King Kong. The lady wanted to speak to Herr Concon, but that's impossible now."

"The police upstairs," Myrnyi said hesitantly. "I not supposed to give any information."

"You can tell me," said Fräulein Louise, opening her bag and letting him see her money. "Three hundred for you if you tell me everything," she whispered, taking three bills out of her bag, which she then put down on a chair.

Myrnyi stepped into a hall that led to some cellar stairs. She followed him. Reimers stayed behind. "So take it," she said. "You saw what happened, didn't you?" Suddenly she was again overwhelmed with the feeling that she knew everything that had happened.

"I not exactly see it. . . ."

"Of course not," said Fräulein Louise, and stuck the three one-hundred mark bills into the pocket of his apron. "But you saw everything else that was going on. How did it happen?"

"Two men were here and asked me the same thing. I mean, besides the police. They were here in the night and they saw the dead man and took pictures of him. I can't tell you anything, lady. I've signed a contract, and these two men gave me money for not telling anyone."

"I know those two men," Fräulein Louise said grimly. "An exclusive contract with *Blitz*, isn't that it?"

"Yes," he said, baffled. "How you know—?"

"I know a lot more," said Fräulein Louise, "and you know that I know a lot more." She gave him a piercing look, and suddenly Panas Myrnyi was scared to death, because he had no idea what Fräulein Louise was really referring to and he thought he was caught. She was still staring at him silently. "So," she said at last, "you saw Concon's murderer."

"How you know?"

"That's neither here nor there. Shall I go up to the police and tell them you saw him?"

"No, no! Please don't do that!" he whispered, wringing his hands. "He got away. If I tell the police, what will he do to me?"

As already mentioned, I learned about this conversation and about everything else Fräulein Louise experienced in Hamburg, much later. But it was true. Contrary to what he had told us, the servant had not only heard the murderer arguing with Karl

Concon, he had also seen him running down the stairs. Myrnyi had been standing in this very hall, not daring to move, and he hadn't told the police or us about it, because he feared for his miserable life. And now a totally strange, sopping wet, ridiculous old woman was threatening him and telling him straight to his face that he had seen the murderer. Panas Myrnyi was terrified.

"What did he look like?" Fräulein Louise asked relentlessly. "I have to know. Because it is possible that this murderer also killed my little Karel. Are you going to tell me or do I go to the police? You should be ashamed of yourself! I thought we were friends."

Her last bewildering words didn't register. The Ukrainian was much too frightened. He whispered, "He'll kill me, just the way he killed Concon, if I tell. You can't ask me to tell about him, lady!"

"But I *am* asking you. It's up to you. Either you tell me immediately, or I'll find out from the police!"

The Ukrainian was close to collapse. "So?" hissed Fräulein Louise.

"So...if it must be..." the Ukrainian stammered, "he was a big man. Well dressed. Didn't fit into this place. A blue coat, visor cap—Hey!" he yelled suddenly, shoving Fräulein Louise aside and dashing forward.

"What—?" Fräulein Louise began to say, then she saw what was happening. Her guide, Wilhelm Reimers, had picked up her bag and was about to leave the small hotel lobby. "No!" screamed Fräulein Louise. "Herr Reimers! Herr Reimers!"

The Ukrainian tackled the tall old man from behind and hung onto him. "You dog!" he cried. "Stealing from an old lady!"

"Help! Help!" Reimers screamed in his shrill voice. He had turned pale and seemed to have gone crazy suddenly. When the Ukrainian tore the bag out of his hand he began to howl like a wolf. "Bastard! Pig! Fucking thief!" cried the Ukrainian.

Suddenly there was the sound of feet coming down the stairs, and the little lobby was filled with men in civilian clothes and in uniform. An elderly man in a trench coat, his hat on the back of his head, said in a loud voice, "Quiet!" And it became quiet. "What's going on here?"

"This man here was trying to steal this lady's handbag, if you please, Chief," said Myrnyi. The ex-SS leader was trembling so violently, he had to lean against the wall. He was crying just as hard as old Concon in his filthy room upstairs.

"Is that true?" the chief asked Fräulein Louise, who was

319

terrified suddenly. Police! She couldn't afford to get involved with the police! "No, no—" she stammered.

"What do you mean, 'no, no'?" cried Panas Myrnyi. "I saw it myself! So did you! You screamed, didn't you?" He opened the bag and showed the contents to the chief. "Here you are, Chief. The fellow was trying to get away with all that money!"

"What's your name?" the chief asked Reimers.

"I—I—Reimers. Wilhelm Reimers. My God, this is terrible!" He held his hands up to his face and sobbed so that his whole body shook.

"And yours?" asked the chief.

"Louise Gottschalk," she said fearfully, and thought: What's going to happen now? What next?

"And what are you doing here?" He was addressing Reimers again.

Reimers stopped sobbing and said, "I only brought her here. She's from out of town."

"From where?"

Fräulein Louise was silent.

"Where do you come from, Frau Gottschalk?"

"From Neurode."

"And what do you want here?"

"*I* don't want anything," said Reimers, with the cowardly adroitness of a rat.

"No. Only to steal the woman's handbag with her money," said the chief.

"I only wanted to get some fresh air!"

"A likely story."

"I only came here because the lady asked me to accompany her. We've already been to Sankt Pauli."

Fräulein Louise nodded, looking devastated.

"So will you please tell us what you are doing here?"

Fräulein Louise shook her head.

"You don't want to tell us?"

"I—I—please, Herr *Kommissar*, have mercy upon us. We'll leave. You'll never see us again."

"Oh, no," said the Herr *Kommissar*. "Things aren't as simple as that, Frau Gottschalk. There's been a murder committed here, you must know. Or don't you know?"

"Yes, Herr *Kommissar*," Fräulein Louise said humbly. "I know."

"And is that why you're here?"

"Yes. That's why I'm here," she said, and thought: It's no use. Nothing's any use anymore.

"Officer Lütjens!" cried the chief.

"Yes, sir!" A young police officer in uniform came clattering down the stairs.

"Take these two people to the Davidswache. Take another man with you. I'll be there in half an hour."

"No!" cried Fräulein Louise, in abject misery now. "Not to the police station, please!"

"Where else?" said the chief. "We'll be able to have a quiet little talk there. I'm sure you have quite a few things to tell me."

"But you can't arrest me just like that!" Fräulein Louise cried feebly.

"I am not arresting you. I am just asking you to go to the Davidswache with two officers. You have almost been robbed. We'll arrest your companion for attempted theft."

"Herr *Kommissar*, on my word of honor!" Reimers began, but the chief stopped him and said in a disgusted voice, "On your word of honor? Stealing money from an old woman—that's your honor! Go ahead, Lütjens, take them both."

The young police officer took Louise by the wrist, politely, and pushed her forward gently, while another officer twisted one of Reimers's arms behind his back. The chief gave him Fräulein Louise's bag and said to the ex-SS leader, "Get going!"

"Please, madam," said Officer Lütjens.

Fräulein Louise looked up at him. She had come to the end of the line. She walked out into the rain and got into the patrol car beside Reimers. The car drove off, and the siren wailed, and Fräulein Louise was more desperate than she had even been in her whole life, except for the time of her mother's death.

6

I can't remember a more miserable lunch. One should never look forward to anything. When Bertie and I finally got back to the hotel, it was already two o'clock. Irina was in the salon, staring out at the rain. She had very little to say. I decided to give her her things after lunch, and carried the suitcase into the bedroom. Then I rang for the maid to clean the room.

When we got back I had spoken to an old friend, bell captain Hanslik, and he had said we could take our meals in a free salon on our floor, if we didn't want to eat in the dining room, which I definitely didn't want to do. I was afraid something might happen to Irina. "But you'll have to hurry, Herr Roland," Hanslik had said. "They only serve lunch until 2:30. And if you have room service, it takes longer." "That's all right, Herr Hanslik," I said, but Hem was waiting for news. I had to call him before anything else.

Two maids appeared with a vacuum and their little cart of cleaning stuff and fresh towels. I was nervous. Irina's sadness worried me. It occurred to me, idiot that I was, that I was beginning to be jealous of this bastard Bilka. That was all I needed! I took a swig from my flask, lit a cigarette, and told the girls to start with the bedroom and bathroom. And I told Bertie to take Irina to the salon Hanslik had mentioned and order lunch. I would join them in a minute.

"What do you want?" asked Bertie.

"I don't care. Anything."

After he and Irina had left, I sat down on the couch, took another swig from my flask, and gave central the number of Hem's office in Frankfurt. I could hear the vacuum in the bedroom. It drowned out the voices of the two girls, who were probably chatting, so I could risk speaking freely when Hem answered.

Before I could say anything, Hem exclaimed enthusiastically, "Herford is delighted! He doesn't know what to say! Mama is just as thrilled. Lester has his tail between his legs and is all smiles. You get your four pages. Big spread. They're driving Leichenmüller crazy with the layout."

"And my by-line?"

"Big caps, boy! Don't worry. It's your story. Nobody's going to take it from you. And in the advance publicity they're announcing the 'New Roland'!" He laughed.

"What's so funny?"

"Oh, everything," he said. "Herford has smelled blood, because Lester told him about the objections to your article—you know, more about the man, how to stimulate him—so Herford asked sacred-cow Stahlut to do a quick analysis. The computer just handed it in. Brace yourself! The series you're doing now is going to lead straight into one about the male, his desires and peculiarities. You'll write a connecting article, and then the new series starts. Herford just asked me if you could really handle the two assignments at the same time."

"Of course I can!"

"Herford's going all-out," said Hem. "He's aiming for a number-one rating with your two series: sex and sob stuff. And the switch to the left. The computer prophecies a success *ne plus ultra!*"

"That was to be expected."

"No, it wasn't. And the computer came up with a title for your new sex series: 'Total Man'!"

"What?"

"'Total Man,'" said Hem. "Has been accepted. They're already designing the title. There's going to be a front-page conference this afternoon. We're starting off with your camp story. We'll probably use the boy lying on the floor after he fainted, the one with the trumpet lying beside him. Marvelous picture! Tell Bertie. He'll be pleased. In the next number we start 'Total Man.' They're trying to think up something special for the title page. Listen, you're not a pervert, are you?"

"No."

"Well, for 'Total Man' you're going to have to be. It's going to be a chronicle of all the perversions known to men. Do you have enough material on it? I've sent for everything we can get hold of."

"I have something better," I said. "Tutti. You know— Leichenmüller's super-whore. I'll consult her."

"Great!"

"I'll treat myself to a few happy hours with Tutti," I said, "and now listen: Instead of making a long story of it, I'll just play back what was said at police headquarters." I took my recorder, pushed the play button, and held it up against the phone. Thus Hem was able to listen to our entire conversation with Klein and Rogge, and I heard it for the second time, and again it worried me. What still lay ahead of us? I put the recorder aside and told Hem about the men from MIB who were guarding Conny Manners. In Frankfurt, Hem's secretary, Ruth, was taking everything down in shorthand.

"I'm going to have lunch now," I said, "then Bertie and I will take off to the Hamburg headquarters of MIB. See what we can get out of them."

"It won't be easy," said Hem.

"I know."

"Call me again. And send the new films."

"Okay," I said, and hung up.

The two maids had knocked on the salon door and stuck in their heads. I nodded, and they came in to clean the salon. "You don't have to be too thorough," I said, and gave each of them ten marks. "It looks fine. The hotel's full, isn't it? You must have plenty to do."

"Plenty," said the prettier of the two girls. I took the recorder and put it down beside my typewriter on a bureau.

After this I made four disastrous mistakes. One of them was unavoidable; the other three were not.

After I had laid down the recorder, something occurred to me. The small table on which the telephone was standing had a built-in radio with three knobs. You could get the North German Radio on it, taped music, and music from the bar. I had to find some way to keep Irina amused this afternoon while she was alone—or, as she had said, she'd go crazy. I thought I'd ask one of the disc jockeys in the bar (I knew them all) to play LPs by Peter Nero, Ray Conniff, and Henry Mancini—things like that, while I was away. I also wanted there to be music when Irina was trying on the things I'd bought her, which I intended to get her to do before we left. I pressed the button for the bar, but got no sound. I pressed the two other buttons. They didn't work either. I called central.

"423. Roland. My radio isn't working. Would you please send up the electrician?"

"Right away, Herr Roland."

"Thanks."

The electrician came a few minutes later—a young man, slim, blond, wearing blue overalls and carrying a tool box. A friendly fellow. "Hello," he said. "Your radio isn't working?"

"No. All channels are dead."

He knelt down in front of the radio and opened his toolbox. "We'll soon fix that," he said, and began to unscrew the front panel. And I was thinking of what lay ahead for me—two important series, my comeback as a serious reporter . . . perhaps! I took a drink from my flask.

The two maids finished their work and left with their vacuum, our used towels, and their cleaning cart. "What's wrong with it?" I asked the electrician.

"Nothing much. One bulb and a dirty connection."

"How long will it take you?"

"About half an hour."

"I have to go and eat. My friends are waiting for me. We'll be in salon 436. Lock up when you leave and bring me the key, please." I gave him twenty marks.

"Thank you very much," he said. "I'll bring the key to you when I'm done."

He busied himself with a screwdriver. I watched him for a few minutes, then I said, "All right. I'm off," and hurried to join Irina and Bertie, who were waiting for me. With which I had made three of my four mistakes.

7

It should never have happened to me after so many years in the business, but it did. I was too elated and too presumptuous and too damned sure of myself. In spite of all my experience, I trusted the wrong people and thought I was on the track of the truth. I had lost sight of the fact that all things are only partially true, the other part false, that truth and lies, justice and injustice interplay, and that those one trusts can betray and those one mistrusts can be one's salvation.

Mistake number one: That the radio wasn't functioning should have aroused my suspicion. In my situation, I should have looked at it myself and seen to it that it *couldn't* function, instead of calling in an electrician I didn't know.

Mistake number two: I should never have left the suite while the electrician was working on the radio. No employee or stranger should have been allowed to be in the suite unless one of us—Irina, Bertie, or I—was present.

Mistake number three: I was so excited, like a goddamned beginner, that I left the recorder on when I put it down beside my typewriter. I had been fiddling with the buttons while our conversation with the two men from Security was running for Hem, after which I had absentmindedly left it on *Play*. So far this was not a mistake, but when I picked up the recorder later and saw that it was off, I didn't think anything of it; I thought it had just turned itself off when the tape had run out, and *that* was when I bungled it. Again I was in a hurry. Thinking that the tape was full, I took it out, put it away, and inserted a new one. When I finally listened to the tape that had run out and heard what was on it at the end, it was too late. The tragedy had already taken place.

8

This is what I heard: The sound of the radio being turned on. The sound of the vacuum. My voice: "423. Roland. My radio isn't working. Would you please send up the electrician?"

That was the first thing the recorder picked up after our conversation with the security men at police headquarters. This was followed by my conversation with the electrician and my leaving. Then a pause, interspersed by the sounds of the work being done on the radio. Then the voice of the electrician: "It's the microphone. It's come loose," and a furious voice, no accent: "Idiot! Too dumb to install a microphone! What would I have done if Herr Roland hadn't called you in?"

The electrician: "I'm sorry. I can't help it. Two screws came loose."

The strange voice: "Because you didn't tighten them properly! If Roland hadn't fiddled around with the radio and seen it didn't work, it would have been a disaster!"

The electrician: "It won't happen again. I'll do anything you want, if only you'll keep your promise."

The strange voice: "I'll keep my promise if everything turns out all right and nothing goes wrong that's your fault. Otherwise, you can forget my promise, you idiot!"

The electrician: "Listen! I'm risking everything for you—my job, getting caught, jail!"

The strange voice: "For *me*? For your *father* is what you mean, isn't it?"

The electrician: "Yes, yes . . . of course. . . ." And in between, the sound of filing, scraping, tapping; and then the voice of the

326

electrician again: "Testing . . . one, two, three, four, five. . . . How does that sound to you?"

The strange voice: "Sounds fine. Beats me! To plant a microphone is too much for the young man!"

The electrician: "I can only say again, *I'm sorry.*"

"You deliver good work, we deliver the goods." A short laugh. "Or perhaps I should say we *don't* deliver the goods."

More noises of the men working, about five minutes, then: "Now it's in again."

"Pack up and take the key to Roland."

"Yes. And—and thank you again."

After that the tape ran out without recording anything more except the steps of the electrician and the opening and closing of the door.

I made my fourth mistake right after that—but, as already mentioned, this was one I couldn't have avoided.

I walked into the salon where Irina and Bertie were sitting. They *had* waited for me and I was touched. "We've ordered," said Bertie. "Lady Curzon soup. Sole Walenska. Peach Melba. Moselle wine, Spätlese. The waiter recommended it. All right with you?"

"Sounds great," I said, smiling happily at Irina. She looked at me solemnly, but said nothing. She had on very little makeup and was still wearing her light blue skirt and matching pullover and her flat shoes. Bertie had rung for the floor waiter. Now there was a knock and the door opened.

By now it was afternoon, and according to the morning waiter, my friend Oscar should have been on duty. But he wasn't. The man who rolled in the table with its damask cloth, hot plates, wine, and the soup wasn't Herr Oscar. It was a waiter I had never seen before.

"Good afternoon, monsieur," he said to me, as he started to serve. He spoke with a French accent.

"Good afternoon," I said. "I thought Herr Oscar was on duty after two."

"And he was, monsieur," said the strange waiter. "But tomorrow I have something I must do, so we switched."

"And what is your name?"

"Jules, monsieur. Jules Cassin." He had served the mock turtle soup; now he poured a little white wine into my glass. I tasted it. The wine was excellent, and I told him so. He said, "*Merci*, monsieur," and withdrew after filling our glasses.

"Well, cheers!" I said, emphasizing just that, and we began to eat. Nobody spoke. It was as if we were sitting at a table with three persons missing. Finally I asked, "What's the matter with you two?"

"Well," said Bertie, "Fräulein Indigo is alone all the time, worrying. She told me a little about it. It's understandable."

"Of course it's understandable," I said.

And then both of us started trying to console her. Bertie cracked jokes, nothing rough, and all I could think of was that I was in love with Irina, no doubt about it. I stroked her hand and assured her that in a few hours we would know a lot more. Waiter Jules came with the sole, and served us elegantly. He was an older man—over fifty, I decided—and had all the charm and lithe facility of a French waiter. The sole was marvelous. My spirits rose rapidly. I wasn't nervous anymore, and I told Bertie that we were getting four pages and everybody thought his pictures were terrific. Irina ate slowly, her head bowed. She didn't say a word.

Jules Cassin came in with the Peach Melba and asked if we wanted coffee. "Yes," I said, "and cognac. Remy Martin. But in our suite, please."

"Very well, monsieur. Here is your key. The house electrician gave it to me. Your radio is working again."

"Thank you, Jules."

One of the chandeliers was lit. Because of the steady rain outside, it grew dark very early. The weather was abominable and we soon had to go out in it. We ate our dessert, and I told Irina, "I've brought you some things. I want you to wait here until I've had time to unpack everything and arrange it in the bedroom."

Suddenly she smiled. "Oh, yes," she said. "That will be fun." And Bertie and I smiled at each other because Irina was smiling, and I was as delighted with her smile as if it had been a sunrise I had been waiting for in the cold for a long, long time. I rang, and when Jules came, I told him that we were going back to our suite.

"Very well, monsieur." I noticed that he was trying to give me some sort of message, something he didn't want to mention in front of the others, so I gave Bertie the key and said, while I was pretending to look in my wallet for a tip, "Go on ahead. I'll be right with you," and Bertie and Irina left the room.

"So what is it, Herr Jules?" I asked, and gave him twenty marks.

"Thank you, monsieur." He looked at his wristwatch. "It is just nine minutes before 3:30. At exactly 3:30 your publisher will call you."

"What do you mean? How do you know?"

"Later. He will explain everything to you; that is to say, he won't but Herr Seerose will."

"How do you know his name?"

He laughed. "How do I know his name?" But then he was serious again. "The call won't come here, monsieur, but at Club 88."

"And where is that?"

"Opposite the hotel. The doorman will give you an umbrella. All you have to do is cross the street."

"And why doesn't my publisher call me here at the hotel?"

"He'll tell you why; that is to say, Herr Seerose will. It is very important. Please be sure to go."

"Is the club open now?"

"It is not a club, it is a bar. It opens at three. When you get back, you will know a lot more and understand everything much better. Now please go, monsieur. In five minutes—"

So I started back to my suite, and this was when my fourth mistake began, the worst one, but I suppose it was a mistake anyone could have made.

"And, oh, yes! Most important!" I was already at the door when Jules came hurrying after me and pressed a folded piece of paper in my hand. "Here . . . take this. . . ."

"What is it?"

"Take it with you to the bar. You'll need it."

10

Club 88 really was directly opposite the hotel, in an old patrician house. Small, intimate, decorated in red and almost empty. Two couples, very much in love, sat at small tables, whispering. I checked my borrowed umbrella in the cloakroom, sat down, and ordered a double Chivas, neat. The waitress, a pretty girl in a black minidress, pink apron, and pink cap, had just brought me my drink when she came back to my table. "Herr Roland?"

"Yes."

"You're wanted on the phone, Herr Roland."

I looked at my watch. It was exactly 3:30.

The waitress walked ahead of me, past the bar, and opened a mahogany door that led into a lighted passage. The passage led to the rest rooms; the telephone booth was near the door. The receiver was lying on a shelf under the phone. I walked into the booth, picked up the receiver, and said, "Roland."

"*Blitz* Publishing House. Frankfurt calling, Herr Roland." I recognized Marion's voice.

"Yes," I said. "Hi, sweetheart! What's the matter with you people? Why don't you call me at the hotel?"

"I'll connect you, Herr Roland." Click, and she was gone.

"Roland? This is Herford."

"Good afternoon, Herr Herford. Why—"

"No questions, please. We have to move fast. You'll soon know why. But first, from the Bible: Romans twelve, verse twelve. 'Rejoicing in hope; patient in tribulation; continuing instant in prayer.' Do you believe in prayer, Roland?"

"Certainly, Herr Herford."

"Good. And now—congratulations, Roland."

"Thank you."

"Great stuff, what you're doing. Herford is delighted. Frau Herford is also delighted. This is going to be the best thing we've ever done."

"Knock on wood."

"Now Herr Seerose wants to speak to you. We're in my

studio." And the next thing I heard was the cultured voice of our general manager, the well-dressed gentleman with the impeccable manners. "Hello, Roland."

"Hello," I said.

"What sort of a booth are you in? A perfectly ordinary one?"

"Yes."

"Good. Jules seems to have done the right thing. No one can hear us."

"Are you sure?"

"Yes." His tone was curt. "That's why I'm calling you there and not at the hotel."

"You mean to say that in the hotel—?"

"Jules will explain everything. Just to be safe, describe him, please."

"I'd say fifty-three, my height, gray hair, slim, green eyes, speaks with a strong French accent."

"What kind of a watch is he wearing?"

"Gold band, narrow, square."

"Black dial?"

"Yes. But—"

"He has the watch from me. Did he give you a note?"

"Yes."

"Read the names to me."

I took the note out of my pocket and read, "Patrick Mezerette. François Tellier. Robert de Bresson. Michel Moreau. Charles Rabaudy. Philippe Fournier. Bernard Apis."

"Very good. No doubt about it, that's my Jules Cassin."

"*Your* Jules Cassin?"

"He'll explain everything. And please—hereafter if we need to contact each other, we will do so through Jules. Don't forget. But now *I* have to explain what you must do, and what this Jan Bilka business is all about."

"Why must *you* explain it to me?"

A pause, then, "Because I know more about it than you do. I am—hm—on very good terms with certain American services, and I have been in touch with one in Hamburg about Herr Bilka and the whole story you've dug up. I take it you are also of the opinion that Herr Bilka is trying to sell something?"

"Yes. That's what Engelhardt and I think."

"And do you know what this thing is that Bilka has to sell?"

"No."

"But I do," said Oswald Seerose with dignity and amiability, as usual. "It is a complete set of plans of the Warsaw Pact Nations, in case war should break out in Europe."

I gasped. "The Warsaw Pact Nations?" Suddenly it was terribly hot in the booth. I broke out in a sweat.

"Yes," said Seerose. "And what's more, he has already sold them!"

11

Five minutes later I was back in my suite. Bertie was there, and Jules Cassin, Chef d'Étage. He was setting the table elaborately, for coffee this time, and a real table. "So, what happened?"

"I'll tell you in a minute," I said. "Where's Irina?"

"In the bedroom. Celebrating Christmas."

And it really looked like that. I peeked into the bedroom and there was Irina, standing in front of the bed on which Bertie had spread the things I had bought for her. They were all still in their wrappings, and Irina was staring at them. "So go ahead!" I said. "Get going! Open them!"

"You're crazy!" she said. "You *must* be crazy, Herr Roland."

"Of course I'm crazy! Take your time. Look at everything. Try it on. Everything can be exchanged. And then join us in the salon. But I want to see you with makeup on and in a new dress, understand?"

She was smiling as she nodded, and I thought how simple it was to make people happy. And then I thought that, being a woman, it would take Irina a little while to absorb what I'd bought, and that suited me, because I needed a little time, too.

I went back into the salon and said to Bertie, "I talked to Seerose on the phone. He is in direct contact with the Americans and knows a lot more than we do. He knows what we're racking our brains over—what Bilka has sold."

"What?"

"The complete plans of the Warsaw Pact Nations in case of a European war," I said. "To the Amis."

Jules's face was expressionless, Bertie was speechless. Finally he managed to say, "The Warsaw Pact Nations' plans? Fantastic! Fantastic!"

"I didn't know," said Jules. "But it was certainly good that you went over to Club 88."

"Damn' good!" I said. "But why, Jules? Why did you have to send me over there? Why couldn't I have taken the call here?"

The French waiter shrugged. "You know Herr Hanslik, the bell captain, don't you?" he said. "Well, he's a good friend of mine. Today was my day off, but Herr Hanslik called me and said I should come to the hotel at once. You were here, and some men had been there and fooled around with the switchboard, and he was sure they had installed a wiretap for this suite. He called the main office, of course. They said the work the men had done was all right; something had been out of order. But Herr Hanslik didn't believe them. He thinks they tapped you."

"Wouldn't be all that illogical," said Bertie. I could see him taking Jules's picture as I walked over and picked up my recorder. Jules noticed nothing. I was still so excited, it didn't occur to me that our conversation at police headquarters had not filled the whole tape—all that registered was that the tape had run out. Mechanically, I took the cassette out of the recorder, put in a new one, and turned the recorder on again. It was that simple. Unfortunately. "So? What next?" I asked Jules.

"I came here immediately and called Herr Seerose from a booth on the street, and he told me to take care of it. And was very grateful. And I am very grateful to him. That is why I am doing all this. That is why I changed places with Oscar. To be here today. All conversation must go through me. Isn't that what Herr Seerose said?"

"Yes. That's what he said."

"If anything happens, I'll telephone from the bar over there. I can always get away for a few minutes. And I owe this to Herr Seerose, that I help him now. Him and you."

"How do you happen to know Herr Seerose?" asked Bertie.

"Just a minute," I said. "Can we be heard in the bedroom?"

"Impossible, monsieur. The walls are thick, the doors are padded. They were separate rooms once. You speak as loud as you like—you can even scream—nobody can hear anything in the next room."

"Just the same," I said, and went over to the bedroom door and opened it. Irina, dressed only in one of the new bras and bikini panties, screamed. She was just going to try on the green wool dress with the patent leather belt.

"I'm sorry," I said. "I only wanted to see if the things fit."

"They fit perfectly!" she cried. Her eyes were sparkling. "I just need a little more time, then I'll come in and model them for you."

"Fine," I said, and closed the door again. I looked at Jules, who had finished setting the table with our coffee and cognac. "Herr Seerose saved your life, am I right?"

"Yes, monsieur. And that is why I would do anything for him."

"When did he save your life?" And the tape was recording everything—this I knew. And the microphone in the radio was picking up everything, but this I didn't know.

Jules Cassin said, "Monsieur Seerose was an officer in France. I was with the Maquis. Blowing up bridges with my comrades. The Germans caught me and all the men whose names I wrote down on that note I gave you. Monsieur Seerose was the commanding officer. He let us escape, risked his life to save ours."

"A true friend of mankind," said Bertie.

"Please don't joke about it, monsieur. Monsieur Seerose is a wonderful man. In 1945 I reported to the French military government and told them what he had done for our group. That's why he was given one of the first newspaper licenses. Then he got together with Herr Herford and found money and *voilà*—Blitz was born!"

"So *that's* how it was! Seerose got the license, not Herford."

"That is right, monsieur. We were friends, Monsieur Seerose and I, good friends."

"*Were?*"

"Still are. In France I lost everything, so monsieur Seerose said, 'Jules . . . would you like to be my butler?' He already had a big house. I worked for him for eight years. Before that I was a waiter. It's always been my profession. In Paris, at the Ritz, before the war—"

"And why did you leave Herr Seerose?" asked Bertie.

"Oh . . . I wanted my own business. A bar. But . . . no good."

"Why not?"

Jules gestured with his hands. "Not interesting. I do very well here. I am satisfied. And I still owe Monsieur Seerose so much."

"Did you know he was in touch with the Americans?"

"Yes. Many Americans come to his house."

"What sort of Americans?"

"Oh . . . specialists. Long talks in the library, political talk." He stopped because the bedroom door had opened. Irina walked in, wearing her new green dress, her new shoes, makeup on—very alluring. "Beautiful!" I said.

334

"Lovely," said Jules, "if I may say so."

Irina was radiant. She turned slowly. "You like it?" To Bertie. "And how!"

"And the perfume, Walter! I love it! It's marvelous."

"I'm glad. And now try on the suit."

"Right away. What's going on here? What are you talking about?"

"Herr Jules knows somebody from our firm," I said. "That's what we were talking about."

"Oh, I see. Then I don't want to disturb. I'll try on the suit. But our coffee..."

"On the hot plate, madame. It won't get cold."

"Thank you, Jules," she said, and smiled at him.

She went back into the bedroom. I had a thought, went over to the phone, and asked central to connect me with the bar. Charlie was on duty, and I asked him to give us some music and told him what records I wanted. Then I pressed the bar button on the radio and sat down.

"So what did Seerose say?" asked Bertie.

"According to Seerose," I said, "it's like this: Jan Bilka managed to get photocopies, microfilm of the plans of the Warsaw Pact Nations in the event of war. He got out of the country and went straight to his friend Michelsen, whom he has known for years as an American agent. There he felt he would be secure. A big mistake. Because his good friend Michelsen isn't an American agent at all but is working for the Russians. Has been for years."

"So Bilka fled to a *Russian* agent?" said Bertie.

"But that is a disaster!" said Jules.

"Wait," I said.

Just then the music began to come in from the bar. "October in Connecticut." The James Marck orchestra.

12

"Michelsen is working for the East," I went on. "And Bilka is greedy—that's been established. And unscrupulous. As you can

335

see in his behavior toward Irina. He fled with this other girl to Michelsen, offered him his plans, and left it up to him to deal with the Americans. Which is just what Michelsen wanted. He proceeded to behave like a double agent, and actually offered the plans to the Americans. Besides an enormous sum of money, he made other demands, which the Americans couldn't possibly meet: the freeing of two convicted agents in the United States, the extradition of a top Soviet agent from Saigon and a Soviet advisor to the Egyptians taken prisoner by the Israelis, a reduction of NATO rocket bases in Europe. Because, as Michelsen told it, Bilka is an idealist. And he's a moralist as well, because the final demand is the public exposure of a sex scandal in American government circles. All this without any knowledge on Bilka's part. Michelsen's purpose is to prevent the Americans from buying. He needs time for his Russian employers to find out where Bilka has put the plans."

"What do you mean," said Bertie, "'where Bilka has put the plans'?"

"Well, he doesn't exactly carry them around with him," I said. "He's not an idiot. All one would have to do, if he did, is knock him off and steal the plans."

"Of course," said Jules. "So where are the plans?"

"Seerose says the Americans told him that Bilka had sent some of the films to a friend in Helsinki, the rest to a friend in New York. Nobody knows who these friends are. Bilka demands that he and his girl friend be flown to Helsinki first—under heavy guard, naturally—then to New York. His final goal is the U.S.A. In Helsinki he'll hand over the first batch of film and receive his first installment; in New York he'll hand over the second batch and get his second payment."

"Nice thinking," said Bertie.

"The Gardens were on fire with Autumn Leaves...." somebody sang. Not Sinatra.

"Not so good thinking," I said. "According to Seerose, Michelsen deliberately let the negotiations drag on and on. And Bilka and his girl friend were not allowed to leave the apartment. They were completely dependent on Michelsen, who told them he was still negotiating with the Americans and dragged things out so that the East would have time to make their preparations for the return of Bilka and the films to his native land. Because, of course, Michelsen told his employers first about the location of the films. And the Russians could have pretended to be

336

Americans, and flown Bilka to Helsinki and New York, and gotten the films that way, if—"

"If Irina hadn't turned up and created a highly unwelcome disturbance," said Bertie.

"Exactly." The *Rhapsody in Blue* next. . . . "Irina endangered everything. They couldn't let her get in touch with Bilka. So Michelsen or someone on his side of the fence sent Concon to kidnap her."

"For what purpose?"

"For no good purpose," I said. "That's for sure. She had to be eliminated. Concon was murdered because he made a mess of the assignment and we found out about it."

"Who murdered him?"

"His own people, naturally. And now listen: When Michelsen found out that the kidnapping had failed, he really distinguished himself! He switched sides again! He called the Americans and had himself, Bilka, and the girl picked up and taken to safety. So now he's a good American agent in the process of delivering the goods. All this according to Seerose. That's what the Americans told him. They also told him that the Russians made one final attempt to get Irina after we got to Hamburg."

"The Norwegian sailor!"

"Yes. But the Americans wanted Irina out of the way, too, because they didn't know what our intentions were. So there you have our pharmacist and his friend. But now the Americans have calmed down because we've got Irina in safekeeping."

"And the men from Security have calmed down, too. Nice going," said Bertie. "Where is Bilka now? And his girl friend, and Michelsen?"

"Safe with the Amis."

"And where is that?"

"I don't know. Seerose didn't say. I figure the Amis didn't tell him. They don't want any more complications."

"But we have to know."

"Of course," I said. "Funny . . ."

"What's funny?"

"That they didn't tell Seerose where they've hidden Bilka and the others. Because they did tell him something much more important."

"What?"

"When they're flying to Helsinki. But that may not be true. That may just be a little distraction."

"Or they want to be absolutely sure that nothing interferes with their plans from here on and still want maximum publicity. Don't forget what we've found out to date, and the photos *Blitz* has."

"I know the Americans," said Jules, "and I think Herr Engelhardt is right. Publicity before anything else. World sensations. The defense plans of the East now useless against the indomitable Americans. That's it."

"I wonder," I said. "I don't know...."

"And that's why we must find out where they're holding Bilka," said Bertie. "Once we know that, I'll keep an eye on him. So when are they taking off for Helsinki?"

I took the note on which Jules had jotted down the names of his Maquis comrades out of my pocket; I had scribbled my notes on the back. "Tonight," I said, with no idea that a microphone had been planted in the radio, poor fool! "Under guard, of course. Seerose says they're flying Pan Am, leaving Fuhlsbüttel at 7:40 P.M., arriving in Helsinki at 10:30. The plane to New York leaves at midnight, so they have enough time. I'm to stay with Irina tonight, Seerose insisted, to be sure nothing happens to her. If I have any news or need information, Jules is to go to the bar across the street and phone for me. Seerose doesn't trust anyone as he trusts you, Jules. I was to tell you that."

"*Merci*, monsieur. Very kind of Monsieur Seerose. I will not disappoint him."

"And one of us must fly to Helsinki. Am I right?" said Bertie, and got up. "And since only one of us three isn't occupied, we'll buy a plane ticket for good old Bertie, fast. To Helsinki–New York. A good thing I have a warm coat with me."

"You're to remain in the background, naturally, but you're to follow the party and take as many pictures as possible."

"Nothing could be simpler," said Bertie. "We'll do just fine, as usual, once I know where Bilka and company are hiding out."

"The plans of the Warsaw Pact nations, *mon Dieu!*" said Jules.

"Yes," said Bertie, "which leaves us with a nice bit of history to report, doesn't it?" He turned to me. "And when you consider that the Russians aren't just sitting back through all this and twiddling their thumbs, I wouldn't mind at all if I had a gun."

I walked over to the hall closet, took the Colt out of my coat, and gave it to Bertie, who put it in the pocket of his jacket, where it was a plainly visible bulge. "You'll have to find a better place for it," I said, "or they'll never let you on the plane."

338

"My thick coat," said Bertie.

We heard a noise and turned around. Irina was standing in the doorway to the bedroom. She was wearing the yellow jersey suit and the patent leather pumps, and she walked toward us like a model, one hand on her hips. She was smiling. "Rhapsody in Blue" was coming to an end. Irina stopped and asked Jules, "You're still talking? Doesn't anyone else ever ring for you?"

"I have two colleagues working with me, madame," said Jules, with a bow. "Bewitching, madame! *Vraiment* bewitching! And now, if you will excuse me—" I unlocked the door to the suite, let him out, and locked it again. I did this for everyone who came and went. I was very cautious—oh, yes . . . very.

"You really look ravishing, Irina," I said.

Bertie whistled. "The woman of my dreams!"

"Of *my* dreams! Irina, may I give you just one little kiss?" But that's as far as I got, because she froze suddenly, and paled. Her smile was gone. She burst into tears and ran back into the bedroom. "What on earth—?" Bertie sounded flabbergasted.

"The music," I said, turning the radio off. "It's the goddamn' music! Why did it have to happen right now? It's her song, hers and Bilka's." Violins had started playing "Remembering," sweetly, sadly, yearningly. . . .

"For God's sake!" said Bertie. "What do you want me to do?" he asked.

"Nothing. Just stay here and wait. I'll try. . . ."

I went into the bedroom and closed the door. Irina was lying on the bed, face down, and she was crying all over the gold bedspread. Open boxes and torn wrappings were scattered on the spread and carpet. I sat down on the edge of the bed and stroked her shoulder. "Don't cry," I said. "Please, don't cry. It's nobody's fault that they played just that song. I ordered the music for you . . . to cheer you up. . . ."

"Our—our song," she cried, her body racked by sobs.

"Yes. I know. But you know that your fiancé deceived you with another woman and that—"

"And what?" She sat up suddenly. Her face was close to mine, her eyes were glittering with anger. "And what? He deceived me. Do I hate him? No! I'll love him till I die, do you hear? Until I die I shall love this man who deceived me."

"All right," I said, and felt ill suddenly, ill and cold. The happy excitement of the last few hours was gone. "Go right ahead."

She tore at the jacket of her suit, unbuttoned it, took it off, and sat in front of me with nothing on above the waist but her brassiere. She threw the jacket on the floor. "You can have it back! Everything you bought for me! I don't want any part of it!" The last words were a scream.

I remembered that Jules had said you could scream as loud as you liked in this room and nobody would hear you. But I also thought that I couldn't leave Irina in this condition. So I said, "I had a telephone conversation with someone. Your fiancé has done something dreadful."

"What?"

It was all the same to me now. I had to calm her down. "He is a traitor, Irina. He betrayed your country, yours and his. Don't try to contradict me. I know that's just as true as that you are the most beautiful woman I have ever known. We have to find him, Irina. It's our job. He is not the Jan of your dreams. He is an avaricious, thoroughly low character, an unscrupulous bastard...."

She struck me in the face so hard my head was jerked to one side. Then she paled. "Forgive me."

"But of course," I said. The place where she had hit me stung. I took a swig out of my flask.

"I'm sorry."

"That's all right."

"I—I have to thank you for so much," she stammered. "My safety, probably my life, and then—then I go and—I'm not sane, you see? I'm not sane!"

"You're perfectly sane," I said. "If I were in your position, I would probably react the same way. It must be wonderful to be loved as much as you love Jan Bilka. Only that Jan Bilka doesn't give a damn. Your love is a burden to him. Don't you realize that?"

"Yes," she said softly. "I do. You must forgive me."

"I've already done that."

"And be patient with me. I really am a bit crazy...."

"I'm a bit crazy, too," I said. And not only where you are concerned, I thought.

"Walter." A whisper.

"What?"

"I'm sorry for everything I said. Don't be angry with me. I loved all the new things. They made me so happy. I never had such beautiful things. And nothing like this will ever happen again. I swear it won't."

"And it mustn't happen again," I said. "Because we have to

340

leave you alone now, and we must be sure you won't do anything silly."

"I just told you . . . I swear—" She stopped. "You don't believe me!"

I said nothing.

"You don't believe me!" she cried again.

I shook my head. And then she took my head in both hands and drew my face down close to hers and kissed me on the mouth. And with the sweetness of that kiss, all my fears and anxieties were gone, all my restlessness and depression. "Now do you believe me?" she whispered.

"Yes," I said, and put my arms around her and kissed her again. Her lips were soft, her tongue was between my teeth, our tongues touched. I thought that I surely smelled of cigarettes and whiskey and was ashamed; still, the kiss couldn't seem to end. The rain beat against the panes, the light in the bedroom was dim, and whoever could have seen us would have thought that here was a pair of true lovers.

I have already written that during this time I didn't realize how everything in life—every action, yes, even every kiss—is only a half-truth, the other half is a lie. We live alone on this earth, every one of us—more than three and a half billion people, in the night of their existence, in the jungle of their lives, and by the laws of that jungle. As I held Irina in my arms and kissed her, I thought of something Bertie had said when he had come back from Vietnam. There had been this GI, a Negro in an army hospital, sitting in a wheelchair. Suddenly he had pitched forward and fallen on the floor. The man had had both legs amputated above the knee. Bertie had hurried forward to help him, but the Negro had beaten him off, yelling, "Take your hands off me, you goddamn' son of a bitch! Leave me alone! Everybody's got to fight his own battles!"

Bertie had said, "But all I want to do is help you," and the Negro had replied, "Alone! He has to fight his battles alone! Every time! Every one!"

13

The first thing Fräulein Louise heard when she woke up were voices, many voices, male and female, and the *rat-tat-tatting* of typewriters. She opened her eyes and sat up. What had happened? She saw that she had slept on an old leather sofa in a sparsely furnished room, covered by her winter coat. An aerial photo of Lübeck hung on the wall, and a bulletin board with "Wanted" posters. There was a big window, covered by a green curtain.

A door fell shut with a bang and Fräulein Louise could hear steps coming closer. "Hello!" she called out in a hoarse voice, and then cleared her throat. "Hello! Please!"

A police officer came into the room. Fräulein Louise recognized him. That was her policeman! What was his name? Lütjens, of course. The one who had escorted her from the Paris Hotel.

"Well," said the tall young police officer in a friendly voice. "How are you? Sleep well?"

"Where am I?" Fräulein Louise hadn't really come to.

"At the Davidswache," said Lütjens. "Don't you remember?"

"Not a thing! What on earth happened to me?" Then she screamed, "Where is my bag?"

"Don't worry. We've taken good care of it. It's in the dispatcher's room."

"The dispatcher's room? Davidswache? How did I get here?"

"But Fräulein Gottschalk, don't you remember?"

"I just told you—I don't remember a thing!"

"You don't remember how Chief Sievers from homicide talked to you? In the Interrogation Room?"

"*Who* talked to me?"

"Chief Sievers, from homicide. About Herr Concon. The murder in the Paris Hotel."

"Now I'm beginning to remember," said Fräulein Louise. "So he talked to me? About what?"

"About everything you knew, and you gave him a very detailed account."

What did I tell him? Fräulein Louise tried to remember. Dear heaven . . . *what?* Suddenly she heard the voice of the American pilot. It came from where Lütjens was standing. "Louise is confused. Louise can't remember. But she has betrayed none of our secrets. She can't do that because we are always with her."

"Thank God!" said Fräulein Louise, aloud.

"Did you say anything?" asked Lütjens.

"Nothing, nothing," Fräulein Louise said hastily. "And the chief was pleased?"

"Very."

"Where is he now?"

"Oh, he's been gone a long time. He must be at headquarters by now."

"Gone a long time?" Fräulein Louise brushed her coat aside and got up, staggering. Lütjens jumped forward to help her. "Gone a long time?" she said again. "When was—what's the time?"

The officer looked at his watch. "3:00 P.M."

"*What?*" Fräulein Louise was startled. "But you brought me here in the early morning. It's—it's that long ago?"

Lütjens said calmly, "The important thing is that you feel better. I've fixed tea for you in the kitchen next door."

Fräulein Louise sank down on the old sofa again. The springs squeaked. "So I've been lying here for hours!"

"Yes," said Lütjens, walking into the little kitchen. He came back with a tray. "Now drink some of this."

"But what happened?"

"At the end of your conversation with the chief, you collapsed. Just a weak spell, according to the doctor. Fortunately you were still here. He gave you a needle and said you were exhausted; we should let you sleep till you woke up. So we put you in here. This is one of our waiting rooms. There's so much going on up front, and it's not exactly restful in the cellblock. You slept like a baby. I looked in on you every once in a while." He poured her tea. "So now, Fräulein Gottschalk, have some tea."

Fräulein Louise found she was thirsty. She asked, "And Herr Reimers?"

"He's in the basement. The cells are in the basement."

"But why did you lock him up?"

"I beg your pardon!" Lütjens laughed. "What were we supposed to do with him? He'll be held and jailed pending trial, until we can bring him before a judge. That was attempted theft."

Fräulein Louise put down her cup. "No!" she cried. "No! Please, Officer, I don't want that! I—I don't want you to lock up Herr Reimers. I'll declare that he did me no harm. I forgive him. He's just a poor, confused man. And he didn't steal my bag!"

"Because he was stopped at the last minute. No, no, Fräulein Gottschalk, don't get all excited again. The whole thing doesn't concern you anymore. Now it's a case for the court. We have to hold Reimers."

"But that's dreadful!" cried Fräulein Louise. "The poor SS—poor Herr Reimers!"

"What do you mean, 'poor'?" said Lütjens. "He's an old crook." Somebody was calling his name. "Now you rest a bit longer, Fräulein Gottschalk. That's the most important thing." And he went off, after giving her a friendly nod.

14

About fifteen minutes later, Fräulein Louise got up. She saw that there were closed doors here and open corridors. Passing through one of the doors, she found herself in a passageway. On her right there was a cigarette machine. A staircase led down to the basement. She could hear a hoarse voice singing, "A drunk fell off a roof; his sodden neck he broke; police came right along and took away the bloke!"

"Shut up!" The screeching voice of a woman.

Fräulein Louise walked past several rooms. There were signs on the door: Female Protection Squad. Interview Room 3. Interview Room 2. Interview Room 1. There was a wide opening, and Fräulein Louise found herself in a big room, swarming with male and female officers, detectives, and persons awaiting to be booked. Clerks sat at desks and were typing. Men and women sat on chairs beside them and were being questioned. There was a wooden barrier that divided the room, and shelves with small compartments in which objects were lying, which she presumed had been taken from persons arrested. A row of light buttons below the compartments and above each one, the number of a cell. The flag of the

Bundesrepublik hung diagonally into the room. There were city maps on the walls, and two photographs of police officers in black frames. Probably died in the line of duty, she decided. An opening in the wall led to a second big room, from which calling police cars could be heard. A young officer sat in front of a radio console. Then suddenly she saw her "guide." He was being brought into the room, a policeman on each side. He wasn't wearing a coat, and the expression in his blue eyes was pitiful. His face was gray, his body was trembling visibly. "Herr Reimers!" cried Fräulein Louise.

He saw her and burst out crying. She wanted to rush over to him, but a policeman stopped her. "No," he said, in a friendly tone. "Please, Fräulein Gottschalk, go back to the room you were in and rest a little longer."

"But I want to help Herr Reimers!"

"You can't do that."

"Why not?"

"Please!" Officer Lütjens had joined them. "Please, Fräulein Louise. I explained it all to you, didn't I? You can't do anything about it. You—"

"But I don't want Herr Reimers locked up! Please, please, let him go! And I have to go, too! I have so much to do. But please promise me first that you won't harm Herr Reimers. I forgive him! I forgive him for everything!"

"Not so loud, please," said a broad-shouldered clerk, sitting at one of the desks. "Calm down, Fräulein Louise. You have nothing to say anymore about happens to Herr Reimers. And you have to wait for a while, too."

"Why?"

"For the court-appointed doctor."

"What court-appointed doctor?"

"The one we've just called. He'll be here any minute. He's a very busy man."

"Why do you need a court doctor?"

"Well, we can't just send someone to the psychiatric ward just like that," said Lütjens. "That wouldn't do. A psychiatrist has to examine the person first. He's the one who decides if there are indications of insanity, or general, or self-destructive elements. Now please go back to your room, Fräulein Gottschalk."

A psychiatrist! Commitment to an insane asylum. Oh, dear God in heaven, thought Fräulein Louise. Why am I being so sorely tried? Perhaps I am to join my friends soon?

15

A quarter of an hour later, sitting on the old leather sofa again, Fräulein Louise heard steps and voices. She recognized the voices of Wilhelm Reimers and Officer Lütjens. He was saying, "If you would please go in there, *Herr Doktor*. Interview Room 1, is free."

A door was opened and closed. The steps faded away. Just a minute! thought Fräulein Louise, clutching her head. What is this? The doctor isn't coming to me? He's seeing Herr Reimers? Has everyone gone crazy?

She got up and crept through the deserted passage to the door of Interview Room 1, laid her ear against the wood, and listened breathlessly. A conversation was going on inside. Reimers was saying, "Rays. Yes, *Herr Doktor*."

"What sort of rays?"

"Electromagnetic," said Reimers. "They radiate from various centers planted all over the city."

"Ah," said the doctor. "Go on."

"And these rays are always directed at me, *Herr Doktor*. Wherever I am, wherever I go, day and night. All the time. So the men in the central station can hear everything I say, even when I whisper."

"Even when you whisper. Ah!" said the doctor.

Oh, my God! thought Fräulein Louise, and had to close her eyes for a minute.

"And the men at central are hearing everything right now," said Reimers, in Interview Room 1, his voice hurried and fearful. "I'm telling you all this, *Herr Doktor*, because I just can't stand it anymore. This constant persecution! This constant fear! I can't go on. I just can't go on! That was why I wanted to steal the lady's bag."

"Why?"

"Because there's a lot of money in it. I thought I could flee with it, to another country. But that would have been useless. The rays would have followed me. They wouldn't have left me in peace, those men."

This is impossible! thought Fräulein Louise. Things like this don't happen! And then she heard the voice of the dead American again. "It *is* possible! And much more is possible. And everything has its reason. Even if the poor earthbound creature can't fathom it."

Fräulein Louise folded her hands and swallowed hard. Meanwhile, behind the closed door, the doctor was asking, "What sort of men are they, Herr Reimers?"

"They belong to an organization. You understand?"

"I understand."

"And this organization is watching me, has been watching me for years!"

"For years, Herr Reimers?"

"And a lot of cars from central follow me, too," said Reimers. "At night they signal to each other. Light signals. I can see it all. Don't you believe me, *Herr Doktor?*"

"Certainly I believe you, Herr Reimers. Have you—have you ever told this story to anyone else?"

"I should say not! One never knows who one's talking to. I'm telling you now because I want you to understand my situation. I want you to know why I need money. Perhaps you can save me, after all."

"I shall certainly try. Why do these men persecute you?"

"Unfortunately, I have told you everything I can. Please understand . . . if I said anything more, my life would be in danger."

"I understand," said the doctor. "If you don't mind staying here, please—I'll be back."

Fräulein Louise could hear a chair being moved, and she ran forward quickly, to the room that was filled with people. She went and stood in a corner, beside a basin installed for arrested drunks to vomit in. The court-appointed doctor, a fat little man with a nervous expression, was right behind her. Without paying any attention to her, he walked up to the desk where the broad-shouldered clerk was sitting. "Well?" asked the clerk. "How about him?"

"You were right," said the doctor. "A persecution complex with hallucinations. I'll fill out the commitment forms right away." He sat down and took some papers out of his briefcase. Now the dead American pilot was standing behind the doctor. Fräulein Louise knew he was there although she couldn't see him, and she said to him, "Thank you. You have given me courage again."

"Louise must trust us," said the dead American.

Fräulein Louise stepped forward bravely. The broad-shouldered clerk looked up. "Please," said Fräulein Louise. "I am in a hurry. I would like my bag now. I have to leave."

"Are you sure you're all right now?" said the clerk.

"Perfectly all right," said Fräulein Louise. The doctor looked up at her for a moment, then went on filling out the commitment papers.

"Well, on your responsibility, then," said the broad-shouldered clerk. "Lütjens, give the lady her bag."

The young officer got Fräulein Louise's bag out of its compartment. "Everything's here," he said. "I'll count the money for you."

"That isn't necessary," said Fräulein Louise. "I'm sure nothing could disappear here." She hesitated, then she said, "*Herr Doktor*, please . . ."

"Yes?" The doctor looked up at her again.

"Herr Reimers . . ."

"What about him?"

"That's what I'd like to know, *Herr Doktor*. Is he going to be sent to the psychiatric ward?"

"Certainly."

"And the charge of theft?"

"That's no longer valid. He'll stay in the hospital, I'm sure."

"That's what I thought," said Fräulein Louise. "That's why I'm asking. He doesn't have any money. And I can't bear the thought of that." She rummaged around in her bag. "I would like to give him something, so that he can buy a few things for himself, if he has to be in a long time. Cigarettes, soap, something extra to eat—that sort of thing." She laid a few bills on the desk. "Here. I'd like him to have this."

"*Four hundred marks?*" The clerk was stunned.

"It's my money. And he's such a poor fellow. I heard what the *Herr Doktor* said. Persecution complex. God knows what that is."

"Now listen, Fräulein Gottschalk. This man was going to steal your money," said Lütjens, but Fräulein Louise wouldn't let him go on.

"And I want to give him something because I'm sorry for him."

"Well, all right, then," said the broad-shouldered clerk. "We can't forbid you to give the man something. I'll make out a receipt."

"I don't need a receipt," said Fräulein Louise.

"But we need our copy," said the clerk, who had already started to write. "Or they'll be saying we kept your money."

"I would never think anything like that!" cried Fräulein Louise.

"Nothing like being sure," said the broad-shouldered clerk, and gave Fräulein Louise her receipt, which he had stamped.

"Thank you," she said. "And now may I leave?"

"Of course, Fräulein Louise. We have your address if anything comes up. But do you really feel well enough?"

"I feel fine," said Fräulein Louise, nodding. "Thank you very much, gentlemen—especially you, Herr Lütjens. The tea was wonderful."

"Was glad to help."

"So I'll be off," she said. "*Grüss Gott*, gentlemen." She shook hands with every one of them, with the doctor, too. Lütjens escorted her through the swinging door in the barrier, to the top of the stairs. "*Auf Wiedersehen*, Fräulein Louise," he said. "All the best. And take good care of your money!"

"I'll do that," said Fräulein Louise, and walked down the nine steps to the exit. At the bottom she turned around once more and waved. Lütjens waved back. Fräulein Louise opened her umbrella and walked out into the street. She hailed a taxi, got in, and told the driver, "Eppendorfer Baum 187, please."

"Yes, ma'am," said the driver, and drove up the Reeperbahn in a drizzly rain. Fräulein Louise sat in the back, her bag on her knees, a peaceful smile playing about her lips.

In the Davidswache the officer in charge, an elderly man, came out of his office. He walked over to the desk where the doctor was still writing, and read over his shoulder.

Well, there you are," he said. "I thought right away: That man isn't sane. Lütjens, take a look at Reimers. He's liable to do something to himself."

"Yes, sir!" Lütjens went off.

The young officer in charge of the radio equipment that transmitted and received messages from the patrol cars came into the room. He was holding a piece of paper in his hand. "What is it, Friedrichs?" asked the commanding officer.

"This woman . . . Fräulein Gottschalk . . . she was here, wasn't she?"

"Yes, but she's gone. Why?" asked the broad-shouldered clerk.

"Gone? Well, that's great!" Friedrichs slapped the paper he was holding. "This got mixed up with other teletype messages. I just found it."

"What does it say?"

"'To all precincts from police headquarters,'" Friedrichs read. "'According to a psychiatrist from the Ludwigskrankenhaus in Bremen, a certain Dr. Erkner, a mentally disturbed woman, Louise Gottschalk, has apparently escaped from a mental institution, and was last seen on a train to Hamburg....'"

16

That day it never stopped raining. I drove with Bertie, in our rented Rekord, quite a distance northwest. At 4:30 it was already night and the cars had their lights on. Raindrops glistened on the windshield. Bertie sat beside me. His duffel bag and suitcase with his films, Hasselblad, and Nikon-F were in the back. I had called Edith from the hotel and told her I'd be waiting in front of the hospital again when she visited Conny, then I had looked in on Irina. I had given her ten milligrams of Valium, and since she wasn't used to it, the effect on her was strong. She was lying on the bed and just nodded sleepily as I said good-bye.

In the Metropole travel bureau we bought a plane ticket to Helsinki, 7:40 P.M. with Pan Am, and a flight from Helsinki to New York, also Pan Am, leaving at midnight. There were seats left on both flights. The tickets were ready for us at the Pan Am desk in Fuhlsbüttel, and Bertie paid for them. He was so accustomed to flying all over the world at a moment's notice, he didn't even comment on the trip. He wasn't particularly pleased about it, but he didn't complain; he had only stopped to say a hurried good-bye to his mother from the telephone booth in Club 88.

While he was packing his things, I had taken another look at the material from the *Blitz* files on Karl Concon. According to them, the headquarters of MIB were in Von-Hutten-Strasse, far to the west, near Luther Park and the Ottensener Cemetery. There were a lot of cemeteries west of the city—a Jewish one, too. I had put a note with the address in my pocket, and a photograph of Jan Bilka, the one Irina had given to us on our arrival in Hamburg. I should say "lent" to us. In the picture Bilka was in civilian clothes, and he didn't look happy. Something in Czech was written on the back. "With love, your Jan," according to Irina's translation.

The drive to MIB headquarters was a tedious one and made me think again what a huge city Hamburg was. I let myself be guided by the steady stream of traffic and saw hordes of pedestrians hurrying along the sidewalks. "Such a lot of people," I said, and Bertie agreed. "An awful lot of people." We finally arrived at Von-Hutten-Strasse. I parked behind the Regerstrasse crossing and we proceeded on foot from there, through the dark and the rain, past old houses and villas built at the turn of the century. They stood behind gardens. It smelled good here—of wet leaves, trees, and grass.

Bertie had both cameras strung around his neck under his coat. By now it was completely dark. "Did you leave the binoculars in the car?"

"No," I said. They were dangling from a leather strap around my neck. They had a very sharp lens. We had used them often when we were doing research together. You could see clearly over a fantastic distance with them.

We came to a high iron fence and walked alongside it until we reached a large, neglected garden in front of a brick building. So this was where MIB functioned, according to the information in our files. It was our intention to play the idiot and simply ask why MIB was guarding Conny in the hospital. If they let us in at all. And then we were going to—

"God lives!" said a soft voice.

A thin little man was huddled against the fence under the bare, drooping branches of an old tree. He was shabbily dressed, had deep hollows in his cheeks and a kindly expression on his face. He was holding a plastic bag with about a dozen pamphlets in it and I could read the title of the one on top: *The Watchtower*.

"What is it?" asked Bertie.

"God lives!" the little man said again, quietly, politely.

"Of course He lives," said Bertie.

"How much?" I asked.

"One mark a copy."

"Let me have five."

He got them out of the plastic bag awkwardly, and handed

351

them to me. I gave him ten marks and said he should keep the change.

"Thank you, sir. I shall give it to the poor."

"You'd better buy yourself something substantial to eat," said Bertie. "You look starved."

"I *am* hungry," said the little Jehovah's Witness.

I am not making up anything, nor am I lying. This is just how it happened. We met all of them, one after the other, men who had the same nationality or faith as Fräulein Louise's dead friends.

"Well, if you're hungry, why don't you go and get yourself something to eat?"

"I can't go away until I've sold all my copies."

"Who says so?" asked Bert.

"I say so. I have made a vow."

"But very few people are going to come by here tonight," said Bertie. "How many copies have you sold so far?"

"You bought the first ones," said the Jehovah's Witness. "I've been standing here since eleven this morning. But you bought five. Now I only have five left. That's never happened to me before."

"What hasn't?" I was looking at the big brick house. All the curtains were drawn—very thick curtains, I decided. I could see only two rays of light filtering through where they hadn't been closed properly.

"That somebody buys that many," the Jehovah's Witness was saying. "You see, I'm living on a pension. I always stand here, in front of this house. It's not a bad place. Many who go in or come out buy a copy. And I live near here. I made my vow two years ago, but I haven't always been able to keep it. Most of the time I feel weak and dizzy before I've sold them all, and can't stand any longer."

"God will forgive you," said Bertie.

"He forgives all sinners," said the old man. "I'm very happy you came. In the rain nobody buys anything. When it rains, people aren't good."

"Why don't you look at it like this?" I said. "You got ten marks from me instead of five, so practically speaking you've sold ten copies. So you could go home."

"Oh, no, sir! If I did that, I would be deceiving God, and the Lord Almighty won't let you deceive Him."

"I see," said Bertie. "Have you any idea who lives in that house?"

"Oh . . . a lot of gentlemen."

"What kind of gentlemen?"

"I don't know. They come and go all day. Some are in uniform. And many cars. Then the gate opens automatically, and closes the same way."

"Did you ever speak to any of the gentlemen?"

"Oh, yes. Often. When they buy a copy from me. Very polite gentlemen, all of them. A few times they bought all my copies in one day. And there are young girls, too. Secretaries, I suppose. They sometimes buy a copy. Yes, this is a good spot." He sounded lost and now he sneezed—a cold, hungry old man.

"What sort of cars?" asked Bertie.

"Oh, all kinds. Last night, at around half past eight, for instance, it was really strange."

"What was strange?"

"Three cars drove up—two were full of men, but the third was a big, closed, black car. The kind you move a dead body in, you know what I mean?"

"A hearse?" I asked.

"Not exactly. A van, I'd say. I thought somebody must have died and they were coming to get the body."

"And did they get the body?"

"Well, first all the cars drove through the garden and around to the back, and I couldn't see them anymore. But right after that, just a few minutes later, the cars came back, and the van stopped right beside me, because the car in front had stopped, and the driver got out. He came over to the driver of the van—stood right there where you're standing now—and said, 'Niendorferstrasse 333. You know how to get there?' And the driver of the van said something strange."

"What?"

"He said, 'To the Amis. Of course I know how to get there. I know the street, so let's get going.' And they they all drove off. I don't understand. Why were they taking the body to the Amis?"

"You said Niendorferstrasse 333?"

"Yes."

"You're sure?"

"Absolutely sure. That's a number you don't forget. What are they going to do with the body at Niendorferstrasse 333?"

"Listen here," I said. "I'm going to buy the other five copies from you, and here's five more marks for your poor."

"Oh!" He gave me the remaining five copies. His hands were

353

trembling, and he looked at me with an ecstatic expression on his face. "Thank you, gentlemen. Now I have kept my vow. I haven't been able to do that for a long time." He shook my hand. "I'll sleep well tonight because I have had a blessed day. May God the Almighty protect you and make your day blessed, too."

"Yes," I said. "That would be nice," and I watched the old man walk away on stiff legs, but with dignity. His coat was stained by the rain and his shoes were downtrodden. I watched him for quite some time, until Bertie said, "Come on. Let's go. Niendorferstrasse 333. Such luck! Incredible!"

"Yes," I said, and thought of Fräulein Louise. "Incredible!"

And I thought of the antiques dealer, Garnot, and the superintendent, Kubitsky, and of Fräulein Louise's Frenchman and her Pole, and of the car belonging to the Municipal Cemetery and its license, which Garnot had written down.

17

Niendorferstrasse 333 was surrounded by a long iron fence with pointed palings. A big garden lay behind the fence, and a broad driveway led to a large villa. It was lit up as light as day by strong floodlights. We came to an iron gate. Behind it big German shepherds began to bark crazily and jumped up against the fence. Bertie raised his fist at them, and they barked louder.

The villa had a balcony on the second floor, supported by white columns. In the bright light of the illuminated front (the floodlights were evidently installed in the grass and shrubbery), two men in dark suits walked out onto the terrace. I took my binoculars and looked through them and could see the two men clearly. Square shoulders, heavyset, boxer figures. One was holding a gun. They stared in the direction of the gate. The sight of the gun startled me, and involuntarily my binoculars moved up. And then I saw them, behind the window on the left side of the balcony. "Bertie! Up there!"

"I see them," he said, the Hasselblad up to his face already. He was taking pictures, and I thought: If we're lucky and they turn out, we've got something. The front was so brilliantly lit that it might be possible to enlarge the window, or a part of the window. Even if the result was coarse-grained, one might be able to make out the man and the woman. Because that's what was visible behind the window—a man and a woman. They, too, were looking in the direction of the gate. The man was much taller than the woman, who was young, pretty, and blond. The man was wearing a brown suit, not old; he could have been thirty, and looked strong. His hair was blond, too, a military crew cut; his face was long. I fiddled with the binoculars in an effort to get a still clearer picture and saw the scar on his tanned face, to the right of his chin. It was the man whose face I knew from the picture Irina had given me.

"I'll be damned!" said Bertie, who was still taking pictures.

"That's enough," I said. "Let's get out of here." I had to yell because the dogs were going crazy. "This way," I said, pulling him to one side. "It's going to get hellishly light here in a minute."

He limped along behind me, and almost right away two bright floodlights in the trees in front of the entrance lit up the entire area. But we were out of its range. I could see the men on the terrace looking as if they didn't know what to do next.

"We've got him!" I said. "Bertie, we've got him!"

"I don't know...."

"What do you mean?"

"I don't know," Bertie repeated. "Things are moving too smoothly for my taste. Too damn' smoothly."

"Oh, go on!" I said. "Let's get off the street." I pointed to a bar on the other side. "To that dive over there. From there we can watch the entrance."

We crossed the street. A car came driving up. It splashed mud all over us, then it swerved and stopped in front of the iron gate, in the floodlights, its engine throbbing. A man wearing a hat and coat got out and stood quietly for a moment, so that the men on the terrace could see him. They came running across the gravel driveway and opened the gate. The men shook hands with both of them, got back into the Citroën he had been driving, drove into the garden, and stopped just behind the gate. The men locked the gate again and got into the Citroën, which drove up to the villa, where everybody got out and disappeared into the house.

"I don't believe it!" I said, almost too amazed to speak.

"I do," said Bertie.

"But I just spoke to him!"

"When? Two hours ago. Longer. If he went to the airport right after your talk and there was a plane free, he could have managed it easily. The airfield isn't so far from here, and he rented the car."

"Well, I can see that it's possible *Blitz* has two corporate planes. One of them could have been ready to take off."

"There you are," said Bertie. "And can you understand now why I say I don't like it? Can you tell me why just this man has to come to Hamburg to see the Amis and Herr Bilka? And is in such a hurry about it?"

The man we had just seen was our immaculately groomed and always impeccably mannered general manager—Herr Oswald Seerose.

18

The "dive" across the street turned out to be an elegant restaurant. Three steps led up to the entrance. There was a shiny dark-wood bar, the floor and wall paneling was also in dark wood. There were booths with small tables, a small lamp on every table, three on the bar, and a fire burning in the fireplace. A few old men were sitting in some of the booths, playing cards or chess and drinking beer.

A waiter in black pants and a green jacket came over and greeted us. There was a large menu. They even had Chivas! I ordered some, Bertie ordered a beer and schnapps, then we pushed aside the heavy curtain over the window a little and could see the lit-up villa in its garden. We couldn't have asked for a better location.

The waiter brought our drinks and wanted to know if we were going to have dinner. I said no, but Bertie wanted something to eat. "Well, then, I'll leave you," I said, after the waiter had gone away. "I have to go to the hospital to meet Edith. Then I must go back to the hotel. You take the car. Here are the keys. When Bilka and the rest come out to go to the airport, you drive behind them. The car can stay at the airfield. Give the keys to the attendant, with the registration, in an envelope addressed to me. I have the receipt for the car. I'll pick it up tomorrow. If you can, call me from Helsinki. At Club 88."

"Will do."

"And from New York, call Hem. At the office or at home. I don't know where I'll be tomorrow. Depends on what happens tonight. As soon as I'm finished here I want to get Irina to Frankfurt. Fast. That's where she's going to have to stay. I need her available when I write."

"Do you have any more ammo for the Colt?"

"Yes." I had seen two clips in Conny's apartment and had taken them with me. Now I gave them to Bertie. "If you have any difficulties, call Club 88 and ask for Jules. I'll be back at the hotel in an hour, and be staying there. Be careful what you say over the phone. Jules can read you."

"Incidentally," said Bertie. "Let me have three thousand marks. After paying for the tickets, I don't have much left."

I gave him the money. Fortunately, I had taken quite a lot with me. But the 15,000 from *Blitz* weren't going to be enough, not the way things were going.

Bertie was incredibly calm and relaxed—one might almost say bored. To Helsinki, to New York, on the trail of a man who had stolen vital top-secret papers from his country—Bertie wasn't impressed. He was studying the menu. "They recommend pot roast with dumplings. Specialty of the house." Good old Bertie!

I went out into the rain to our Rekord and drove it a little nearer the restaurant so that Bertie wouldn't have to walk too far on his lame leg. Then I went back in and gave Bertie the keys to the car and the registration, also my binoculars. "Good luck," I said.

"The same to you. 'Bye, old fellow." He had pushed the curtain back far enough so that he could keep a constant eye on the villa. "And all the best to Irina. She's a nice girl."

"Yes," I said, and shook hands with him, and asked the waiter to call a taxi. When it came, I nodded to Bertie once more and he smiled back like a boy.

"Where to?" asked the driver.

"The University Hospital in Martinistrasse."

We got into the late-afternoon traffic and it took a long time to get to the hospital. The driver, a nervous little man, cursed constantly. He damned all car drivers, but he drove badly himself, and a few times I thought we'd surely have an accident. I was thankful when he finally stopped opposite the hospital entrance, and I paid fast and got out.

Little driver Ivanov would be waiting in the parking area, beside the circular bed of dead flowers, opposite the entrance of the University Hospital. It was my intention to get into Ivanov's car and wait for Edith with him. That was the way we had arranged it. I reached the circular flower bed. Six private cars were parked there, and I could see Ivanov's taxi, a black Mercedes 220. I had memorized the license number. I remember numbers easily. The parking lights of Ivanov's taxi were on, the motor was running. I opened the back door and got in. "Here I am," I said.

One side of the glass that separated passenger from driver was open and I could hear the voice of a girl. It came from Ivanov's two-way radio, which he used to keep in touch with his dispatcher. The voice said, "Car 3-1-9. Please, call in. Car 3-1-9," and it sounded as if she wasn't saying it for the first time.

The old Russian was sitting behind the wheel, staring out at the rain. He seemed to be watching for Edith. "Car 3-1-9, please call in! Car 3-1-9." The rain was drumming on the roof of the car and you could hear the roar of the traffic even here, and the driver of Car 319 wasn't responding, although the girl tried again.

"What's the matter with him?" I asked Ivanov in a loud voice, leaning forward so that I could talk through the window.

He didn't answer. I was going to repeat my question when I saw a small enamel sign on the dashboard. In black lettering it read: Taxi 319.

I jumped out of the car. Ivanov had let down the window on his side. His left sleeve, the whole left side of his black leather coat gleamed wet. He was still looking straight ahead. The noise of the traffic was deafening. I could barely hear the voice of the girl from central, "Car 3-1-9 call in please! Car 3-1-9."

I leaned forward and could see a small hole in Ivanov's left temple. A little blood had seeped out of it. Very little. The bullet must have passed through his skull without tearing any blood vessels. The gray hair around the hole looked charred. Somebody must have held a small-caliber gun directly against Ivanov's head, and pulled the trigger.

I stood on the rim of a sea of lights and noise, and the rain fell on me and on the left side of Vladimir Ivanov. He hadn't been dead long. His hands, still holding the steering wheel, were warm. I touched them, and the streak of blood on his head glistened in the light of a passing car. "Car 3-1-9. Please call in right away! Car 3-1-9...."

19

I took the elevator up to Conny's room on the surgical floor. Edith had told me the number. I ran down a passage; the room lay at the end behind a closed door. Two men stood in front of it. "Stop!" said one of them. "You can't go in!" said the other.

"There's a taxi downstairs," I said. "The driver's been shot dead." I showed them my press card.

"Oh ... Herr Roland from *Blitz*."

"Yes."

"Come with me to the taxi," said the second man. And to his colleague, "Don't let the woman leave yet."

"Very good."

The second man was already running down the corridor with me close behind. We took the elevator down together. He said, "My name is Wilke."

"Pleased to meet you," I said. "The driver's name was Ivanov. Vladimir Ivanov."

"You knew him?"

"Yes," I said, and told him how I had met Ivanov. It would all come out now, anyway. As we left the elevator I felt sick suddenly, and knew that the jackal was near. Delayed reaction. I got out my flask and drank, then I ran after Wilke, out into the dark and the rain, across the hospital grounds to the parking lot and the taxi with its motor still running and its parking lights still on. Ivanov had slipped to one side a little, his jaw was sagging, his eyes were open wide. Since he had slumped down against the lower window, the rain was falling into his open eyes.

20

Edith Herwag walked through the small garden in front of her house, Adolfstrasse 22-A, to the taxi waiting for her. Vladimir Ivanov was holding the door open for her. He greeted her. "I'll sit in front with you," she told Ivanov. She had on a fur coat and a scarf tied around her head, no umbrella.

"Very well," said Ivanov, opening the front door. "To the University Hospital?"

"Yes."

There was a lot of traffic and he had to drive carefully. From time to time the voice of a girl could be heard coming from the radio, calling other taxis. Ivanov had reported right away that he was on his way to the University Hospital; after that he was silent. But once they had crossed the Lombardsbrücke, he said cautiously, "You won't be upset if I tell you something?"

"Upset?"

"You mustn't get upset, or I can't tell you." He let down the window on his side. "The glass fogs over in this weather. Will this be too much for you?"

"No," said Edith.

The Russian said, "Your friend's name is Conrad Manners."

"Yes. How do you—?"

"I'll tell you. He was hit while crossing the street on a zebra stripe, early last night. Eppendorfer Baum. Am I right? By a big black car."

"Right."

"Well, after your friend was hit, one of our drivers, who happened to be driving down Eppendorfer Baum, reported it to his dispatcher. He got the license number of the car and reported it, too. HH-CV 541."

"Yes, and—?"

"And my friend followed the car. A crazy drive. Farther and farther out of the city. All the way to Lake Krupunder. You don't know where it is? Doesn't matter. It's in Relingen. My friend could barely keep up with the car. It's very lonely out there. He got scared. Understandably. Because the chauffeur let the big black car roll into the lake."

"*What?*"

"Yes. And my friend thought that was very strange. That's why he called his dispatcher and said he'd lost sight of the car. But he hadn't. He saw a big Ford waiting there, at Lake Krupunder. The driver of the car got into it and the Ford drove off with him. Now my friend followed the Ford, back to the city. To Niendorferstrasse 333. A big villa, all lit up by floodlights. A high iron fence, vicious dogs, says my friend. The Ford drove through the gate to behind the villa. My friend waited, some distance away, because he was afraid. Then, an hour later, a taxi drove up, and the driver of the black car came to the gate with two men. They said good-bye, and the driver went off in the taxi. My friend followed the taxi to where the man lived."

"And where was that?"

"At the other end of Hamburg. A big new apartment house. Lots of tenants."

"And the address?"

"I can't tell you."

"Why not?"

"I had to promise my friend not to tell the address to anybody. My friend is very afraid. Doesn't want to have anything to do with it. Didn't tell anyone at the office either, or any of his colleagues. Only me. The police are acting very funny in this case. But I am not afraid; and tonight, when I'm through, I'll drive to where the man lives. My friend gave me a description. I'll find him and then I'll call the police. Then they'll *have* to do something!"

"Did your office at least give the number of the car to the police?"

"Yes, of course."

"And—?"

"Nothing. I'm telling you, the police are behaving very strangely."

"What's your friend's name?"

"I can't tell you that, either. I really can't. Because he's so afraid. He won't do anything, I assure you. But I will. Tonight. Ah, here we are. I'll be waiting where I waited at noon, yes?"

"Yes. My friend will come here to fetch me. He'll wait for me in your taxi, if I haven't come out yet."

21

"'And he'll wait for me,' I told Herr Ivanov," said Edith Herwag.

She was telling her story for the second time, in the office of a doctor on emergency duty. The doctor wasn't there, but two men from MIB were, and the chief of homicide with two of his men. One of them was taking everything down in shorthand.

The first time Edith told her story, she and I had been alone amid the general confusion that had accompanied the arrival of the car from homicide. I had managed to get hold of her in front of the doctor's office. Wilke, the second MIB man, was on the phone. He didn't pay any attention to us. Edith got over the shock of Ivanov's death fast, thank God, but she was terribly frightened. "On the phone...last night...that voice! It said Conny would die if he told anything. But he didn't say anything...although he may know the license of the car, too, and more. But the Russian talked, and they killed him."

"What a pleasant surprise, Herr Roland!" A man's voice behind me. I turned and found myself facing Herr Klein and Herr Rogge from Security. They had come up very quietly.

"It's my pleasure to see you again," I said.

"You found the murdered man," asked Rogge.

"You know I did."

More men got out of the elevator and came toward us, officers from homicide, and the chief. We greeted each other.

"They've given us a doctor's office," said the chief, a sad old man. "I have to question you, Fräulein Herwag, and you, Herr Roland. Just a matter of routine. One after the other...if you don't mind waiting here while I question Fräulein Herwag."

"I have already told Herr Roland everything I know," said Edith. "I was so happy that Conny was feeling better, and now—now the Russian is dead, just because he told me this story."

"What story?" asked the sad chief.

"A very strange story," I said.

The chief looked at me broodingly. Rogge said, "I think we

can all go into the doctor's office together. Herr Roland is working on this case, too. We shouldn't keep anything from him."

No...I'm sure none of you want to do that, I thought. "Besides," Rogge went on, "Fräulein Herwag has already told him everything."

So all of us walked into the small, white emergency office, with a bed, a cupboard, a desk, and a few chairs in it, and Edith told her story again. The man listened to her without interrupting her. I walked over to the window. We were very high up here, in the surgery wing; and between the orthopedic clinic and the administration building, I could see across Martinistrasse to the little parking area on the other side. Vladimir Ivanov's taxi was standing there in the beams from the headlights of several police cars. Police officers were walking back and forth, photographers were taking pictures, a crowd had collected behind a barricade. From up here they all looked like toys. I could see them take the dead man out of the car, put him on a stretcher, roll it into an ambulance, and drive away. Policemen formed a chain to hold back the curious people who were pressing forward. And it was raining hard on all of them. They can't cover this thing up, I thought. This will make the papers. But in what form? A taxi driver murdered. Yes. And what else? Nothing.

"You don't know the name of Ivanov's friend?" the chief asked when Edith had told her story.

"No. I told you, he wouldn't give me his name. What sort of an address is that—Niendorferstrasse 333? What sort of villa is that, in a big garden? Who lives there?"

Rogge and Klein, and Wilke, the man from MIB, all stared at me. Rogge's thick glasses glittered. Their looks said quite clearly that if I said who lived there and what purpose the villa served, I was finished. They would see to it that I left Hamburg fast.

"We don't know, Fräulein Herwag," said the sad chief with a perfectly straight face. "We'll find out right away, of course." He looked at Edith, bit his lip....

"And you, Walter?" asked Edith.

I said, "I have no idea." What else could I say?

"Under the circumstances," said Klein, "I think Fräulein Herwag should be taken into protective custody right away. Until further notice. It's much too dangerous for her to be alone in her apartment."

"The room next to Herr Manners is free," said the first man from MIB. "Fräulein Herwag could stay there until this case is cleared up and she can no longer be considered in danger. And she would be close to her fiancé. Would you like that, Fräulein Herwag?"

"Yes. Yes, please," said Edith. She was trembling.

"Well, then a police car will drive you to Adolfstrasse, where you can pack what you need, and bring you right back," said Klein. "Is that all right with you, Chief?"

He nodded. He was still biting his lip.

Edith looked at us, from one to the other. "It's all so—so strange. So incomprehensible," she said. We looked at her stonily. "Can't anyone here tell me what's going on?"

"Right now, no," said Rogge.

"This friend of Ivanov's gave the number of the car to a taxi dispatcher yesterday. Didn't the company pass on the number to the police?"

"Of course," said the chief.

"And?"

"We couldn't find the car. How were we to know that it was at the bottom of Lake Krupunder?"

"Yes," I said. "That was something nobody could guess."

There was a pause and every man in the room was looking at me, and I knew: If I got fresh once more, my work here was finished.

"And now may we drive you home, Fräulein Herwag?" asked the officer who had been taking down everything in shorthand.

Edith was startled out of her thoughts. "Yes, of course. May I—?"

"What?"

"May Herr Roland come along? I know him and I'd feel safer if—"

"Certainly," said the chief, after a look at Klein, who nodded.

I looked at my watch. 7:11. If everything went according to plan in Niendorferstrasse, Bertie should be on the trail of Bilka, his fiancée, Michelsen, and God knew who else, on their way to the airport. Should have been for quite some time. Hopefully, nothing had gone wrong. If something had gone wrong and Bertie had called Club 88, Jules was supposed to let me know immediately, but he didn't know where I was and I couldn't call the Metropole and ask to speak to him. And I had to comply with Edith's wishes. She was close to hysteria, and I didn't want her to break down completely. "Of course I'll come with you," I said.

There was a knock on the door. A policeman came in and

without a word laid something that looked like a large button in the chief's hand. "Where did you find that?" he asked.

"Stuck under the dashboard beside the steering wheel."

"Well, that explains everything," said Klein.

"What is it?"

"A bug."

"A *what*?"

"That's what we call it," said Klein. "A tiny transmitter with microphone. Its range is a thousand or two thousand meters. In a car that was undoubtedly following Ivanov without his noticing it, there was a receiver for this transmitter."

"You mean—" Edith drew a deep breath. "You mean that whoever sat in that car could hear everything Ivanov was telling me?"

"Yes. That's exactly what I mean," said Klein.

"And that's why Ivanov is dead," said the chief, and his look as he gazed out the window was more melancholy than ever. The raindrops were running down the dark pane like tears.

5

Page Proof

1

"*Bon soir, monsieur,*" said the *chef d'étage*, Jules Cassin. He had knocked, and when I opened the door, there he was with a silver tray, soda, an ice bucket, a bottle of Chivas, and glasses.

"Good evening, Jules," I said as I let him in. The floor lamps and sconces were lit, the radio on the little table was playing the theme song from the film *The Apartment*. I had got back to the Metropole a half hour ago. It was now 8:20.

"How is the young lady?" asked Jules. "Everything all right?"

"Everything's fine. She's just changing for dinner. I talked her into it." I had changed, too. I was wearing a dark blue suit, a white shirt, and a red and blue bow tie.

"Good," said Jules. "And how is she feeling?"

"Better."

She really was. I had found her calm. She had even met me with a smile. All hysteria seemed gone. To avoid any further scenes, I had lied and said that we hadn't found Bilka yet—only a trace—and that Bertie was following it up. Bertie was coming later, and later I would have to tell Irina the truth. But not now. I was tired. Ivanov's death, getting Edith safely to her apartment, then back to the hospital with her things, had unnerved me. It would pass; I just needed some Chivas. I poured myself a strong drink and a weaker one for Irina.

"The night shift is on," said Jules. "Herr Heintze has taken over from Herr Hanslik. I spoke to Herr Engelhardt. He called Club 88 and asked for me."

"When?"

"At 7:45, monsieur."

"But the plane was to leave at 7:40!"

"A slight delay. Only fifteen minutes. They must have taken off by now. Monsieur Engelhardt said everything was going according to plan. Bilka, his girl, Michelsen, and seven men left the house in Niendorferstrasse in two cars. Monsieur Engelhardt recognized Bilka and the girl and Michelsen, according to the description of a resident on Eppendorfer Baum. He followed

369

them to the airport, didn't let them out of sight. They were all perfectly calm and not—how do you say—*wöhnisch?*"

"*Argwöhnisch . . .* suspicious."

"That's the word! And not suspicious. Your friend looked at the passenger list on the counter. Bilka is flying under an assumed name. All the others, too. With forged passports. What is the matter, monsieur?"

"It's terribly hot in here," I said, tugging at my collar. It *was* very warm in the salon, but I was very excited again—that was why I was so hot.

"Then I'll open the window a little," said Jules.

"Yes, please do."

Jules disappeared behind the heavy blue drapes and opened one of the French windows that looked out on the park. He emerged again. "I also spoke to Herr Seerose."

That meant Seerose couldn't have spent more than half an hour with the Americans. What had they talked about in that half hour? Something so important that our general manager had had to fly to Hamburg? Evidently Bertie hadn't told Jules that we had seen Seerose at Niendorferstrasse 333, so I said nothing about it. I asked, "And—?"

"Monsieur Seerose is very pleased. He is in your publisher's office. They're waiting for what happens next; the whole house is waiting."

He was right about that. Before going back to the hotel, I had phoned Frankfurt from Club 88 and told Hem everything that had happened since my last call. He had said, "We live in an age of patents. We invent things to kill bodies and save souls, and spread them around with the noblest intentions."

"You're absolutely right, Hem."

"That's not by me. Somebody said it a long time ago."

"Who?"

"Lord Byron. By the way, I've found out that Seerose wasn't in his office this afternoon. Only came back just now."

"What could that mean?"

"I don't know. Everything seems A-OK so far. He really is on very good terms with the Amis, always has been. I've found that out, too. Now he's upstairs with Herford and Mama. Lester and I are supposed to stay here until we know Bertie has left Helsinki for New York with Bilka and the others. At least that long, says Herford. He's absolutely beside himself with enthusiasm."

I had left the bar and crossed the street in the rain, back to the

Metropole. I had changed, and now I was in the salon, fixing two drinks, which I carried into the bedroom. A scream from Irina! She was standing in front of the mirror, half-naked, holding the robe I had bought in front of her. "I'm sorry, my darling," I said, closing the door all but a crack through which I handed her her glass. "Thank you," she said. I stuck my other hand with my glass in it through the door, and she clinked her glass against mine. "Chin-chin!" I said.

"Chin-chin. You're nice."

"I'm the nicest man in the world, my darling," I said. "I want to order our dinner. Are you hungry?"

"Yes." I could hear her drinking.

"That's good," I said. "So what would you like to eat?"

"Oh...I don't know. Ask Monsieur Jules. He should recommend something."

I turned around. "Monsieur Jules?"

He was smiling. He said in a loud voice, "We have very fine chicken today. Here in Hamburg we call them *Hamburger Kücken*. Very little chickens. I can recommend highly."

"Did you hear him, darling?" From the bar, over the radio, came the melody of "The Wayward Wind." "Strange," she said.

"What's strange?"

"How you can get used to whiskey. Yesterday I hated it, today it tastes wonderful."

"Yes," I said. "That happens fast. So...two *Hamburger Kücken*, Monsieur Jules."

"Very good. And before that? Lobster cocktail?"

"Fine. Let's not spare the expense account."

"And for dessert?"

"We'll see."

"And to drink?"

"Champagne, of course. What did you think?"

Jules was smiling. "Then I would recommend Pommery Demi-Sec. Not too dry. We have some '51 bottles left. A very good year."

"How does that strike you, darling?" I asked.

"Wonderful!"

"Very well, then," I said, and closed the bedroom door.

Before Jules had come, I had sat at the beautiful antique desk and written on pieces of hotel paper, folded them, and stuck them in envelopes. Now I began to hide them—under my typewriter, under the couch, behind the drapes. Jules watched me, amused. "What are you doing, monsieur?"

"It's a surprise."

"Oh." He smiled as only a Frenchman can smile in such a situation. "I understand—you have to console the little lady."

"Yes."

"*Très charmante* . . . the mademoiselle. It is touching how she always pretends to be your wife. But be careful, monsieur. Mademoiselle is not from the West. She comes from the East, and the ladies from the East are not so easily—"

"It'll work out all right," I said, and hid another envelope.

He smiled, but then he was serious again. "Just the same," he said, "Mademoiselle impresses me as being very innocent. . . ."

"Innocent?" I said, and nodded grimly. "For two years she was the mistress of this man Bilka. He's thirty-two, she's eighteen. Innocent?"

Jules said, "Last night you slept here in the salon. The maid told me."

"Well, yes," I said, irritated suddenly. "I wanted to be a little discreet about it."

"I understand," said Jules.

"You do?" He was looking at me intently. "What's the matter?"

"If you have fallen in love with Mademoiselle, that is good."

"Now, listen," I began.

But he went on, "Because Monsieur Seerose said you must watch over Mademoiselle tonight very carefully. This is very important. Look after Mademoiselle, nothing else. She must not be allowed to disturb what is going on. Besides—"

"Besides what?"

"If you want to find out everything about Mademoiselle—her life, her fate—that you must really *faire l'amour* . . . not sleep on the couch."

"I think I know what I have to do."

Just then the bedroom door opened and Irina walked in. I stuck the rest of the envelopes in my pocket, and stared at her and had to swallow hard. Out of the corner of my eye I could see that Jules was staring at her, too, just as astonished.

Irina was a beautiful girl. I knew that. What I didn't know was how this girl could be transformed. It was fantastic! I had known a lot of girls who could transform themselves, but I had never seen anything like this.

She stood there in the sleeveless cocktail dress, in the

372

high-heeled gold shoes, one hand on her hip. She had on silk stockings, she was wearing makeup. Her mouth was bright red and big, her skin was smooth and pink. She wore mascara and velvety blue shadow on her big black eyes. Her thick black hair, which she wore in a pageboy cut, was brushed smooth. The dress made her look provocative; you could see the cleft of her breasts. I emptied my glass and could feel my heart beating fast. She was so beautiful . . . so beautiful. . . . "Oh, mademoiselle!" said Jules.

I went up to her and put my arms around her, and could smell her fresh skin and the Estée Lauder perfume. I drew her close and kissed her on the mouth, then I let her go and said, "You look enchanting."

She reddened under her makeup; Jules noticed it, too. He bowed and left us.

"Walter!" said Irina. Her eyes were shining.

"Yes?"

"That was—that was—you ought to be ashamed of yourself! You took advantage of me!"

"I did. Can you forgive me?"

She looked at me, then she nodded, and the trace of a smile played about her lips.

"Wonderful!" I said. "And now, so that you can say I took advantage of you twice," I drew her close and put my lips to hers again.

She resisted at first, but then her body yielded. Her lips parted, she pressed her body against mine and responded to my kiss. And I thought that perhaps there *was* that thing about which so much is written in novels, which I had often described and cheapened, which everyone on this earth longs for and dreams of—love.

2

At last she pushed me away. She was breathing heavily. I mixed us two more drinks and handed her her glass. Her black eyes were blazing. "*Another* whiskey?" she said.

"Yes."

"No."

"Yes," I said. "You must. To our friendship."

"Our friendship?" She laughed, a strange, brittle laugh.

"Yes," I said. "Please."

She raised her glass. "All right, then. To our friendship." She drank and handed me her empty glass. I filled it again. The radio was playing "Let's take a trip into the land of loving." Irina leaned against the bedroom door and hummed the old song. I walked past her and hid the rest of the envelopes around the bedroom and the bathroom, all the time chatting with her. She had walked into the salon and pushed aside one of the drapes.

"So many lights," I could hear her say. "On the water and on the other side of the water. And such a marvelous hotel!"

"You like it?"

"I love it. Chin-chin, Walter."

"Chin-chin, Irina."

I walked back into the salon and put my arm around her shoulders, and both of us looked out into the night with its many lights and glittering rain.

"This is the first German hotel I've ever been in," said Irina. "No—the second."

"What was the first?" I asked, and drank. She drank, too.

"Oh, I was with the Young Pioneers, a good ten years ago, and we went on a trip to East Berlin. That's when I saw a German hotel. But it was horrible—shabby, cold, dirty—practically a ruin."

"What was it called?"

"The Adlon."

I laughed. "That was once the finest and most famous hotel in Germany."

"You're kidding me!"

"No, I'm not. The Adlon was—" I got no further, because the radio was playing a different song, sad and filled with longing—"Remembering."

"Goddamn it! I told them—" I was about to hurry over to the radio to turn it off, but Irina stopped me.

"Don't!" she whispered.

"Don't what?"

"Don't turn it off." Her eyes were sparkling. "I called the bar and asked them to play the song. I *want* to hear it. Yes . . . I want to! Because it doesn't matter anymore—see?" She laughed. "Now it's my song again, my beautiful song that I've always

374

loved. Things couldn't go on the way they were."

I looked at her meditatively. "You mean it?"

She nodded and put down her glass. Then she took mine out of my hand and put it down beside hers. "Wouldn't you like to dance with me?" she said softly.

I took her in my arms. Our bodies were close, she laid her head on my shoulder, my cheek touched hers, and we began to move to the sweet music. Irina recited the first words of the text: "Remember, love; remember, love—how you and I were dancing . . . my heart beat against your heart . . . how can I help remembering . . ." She stopped and pressed her body closer. I kissed her cheek, she smiled, and we went on dancing slowly, slowly, to the melancholy melody, without saying a word. Suddenly I stopped and let Irina go abruptly.

"*You!*" I said. "How did *you* get in here?"

"Through the door," said Fräulein Louise. "It was open."

Damn it! I had forgotten to lock it after Jules left. And there was Fräulein Louise in an old, black, very wet coat, a ridiculous hat on her white hair, carrying a large bag and quite evidently very excited—Fräulein Louise Gottschalk! The soles of her cracked boots had left their dirty imprint on the light velour carpeting.

3

Fräulein Louise pressed the button of the door with the name Michelsen on it. She was doing so with a feeling of hopelessness, because she had been trying to get an answer for ten minutes. Nobody seemed to be in the apartment, or else they had no intention of opening. Fräulein Louise was discouraged. The feeling had overwhelmed her in the taxi that had brought her from the Davidswache to Eppendorfer Baum. I haven't gotten a step farther, she thought. I don't know who murdered little Karel. The whole thing grows more mysterious and confusing all the time. What bad thing have I done that everything I try to do seems to fail? Have I sinned, and is that why my friends are misleading me? The young pianist—blind; the Ukrainian servant in the hotel; the Czech...what are they really planning? Why can't I understand them? All I wanted was to do the right thing, and this is where I am! Why do I make such terrible mistakes all the time? The doctor in the train who I thought was my dead Jehovah's Witness, the SS leader who wasn't my SS friend at all. How can what I'm doing possibly be right if my friends aren't helping me? What did I do wrong? Or have evil spirits entered into the picture and managed it so that my friends *can't* help me?

For the first time Fräulein Louise was beset by the feeling that she and her friends weren't seeing eye to eye. She was bewildered by the chaos of the big city, her feet hurt, and she was growing more and more hopeless all the time. And now nobody was answering at this man Michelsen's apartment! It was a plot, a plot against her! What point was there in going on?

She gave up and walked across the red carpet, down the elegant staircase with its marble steps and walls, the way she had come. She was afraid of cage elevators—not of any others, only of the cages that moved on wire cables. She walked out of the house into the rain. What next? She didn't know. It was almost dark now, the street and shop lights were on, and a warm, golden light streamed down on the wet pavement from an antique shop beside the house entrance. Fräulein Louise walked slowly up to the window. What wonderful things there were on display there! Fräulein Louise smiled when she saw the ivory elephants, the opium pipes, the Japanese roll prints with their delicate watercolors, the demon masks, the coral jewelry, the carved objects. She read the name of the owner beside the entrance: André Garnot. And suddenly she froze. Because beyond the display, in the shop itself, she could see a slender man with short gray hair, twisting and turning in an armchair...and beside him a second man, older, wearing glasses, with a fringe of thin gray hair on his otherwise completely bald head. The older man was holding something over the other man's mouth and supporting him at the same time. The man in the chair was evidently having trouble breathing. His face was purple.

Fräulein Louise's heart was beating wildly. André Garnot! A French name...the man in there was having difficulty breathing...the older man was holding something over his mouth—an atomizer, surely! The man who was having difficulty breathing had asthma!

My dead Frenchman had asthma, thought Fräulein Louise. Perhaps—no, surely it is he! And she was already opening the door of the shop. I am not alone, she thought, I am not alone!

She remained standing in the doorway and gestured to the two men that she would wait until the attack was over, which didn't take long. Then the two men introduced themselves, so did Fräulein Louise. "You must excuse me," said André Garnot, "but I always have these attacks in this kind of weather."

"I know, I know," she said, and added hastily, "it's the worst kind of weather for asthma."

"I was helping Herr Garnot unpack a crate of Chinese bronzes; that's when it happened. A good thing I was here. It was a nasty attack," said the older man.

"But now I'm all right again," said Garnot. As usual, he was elegantly dressed and moved with grace and dignity.

"And you are Polish," Fräulein Louise said to Kubitzky.

"Yes, Fräulein Gottschalk."

"Would you like me to guess where you're from?" asked Fräulein Louise, her discouragement miraculously gone. Now she was actually happy. "You come from Warsaw, right?"

"How did you know?" asked Kubitzky, thoroughly perplexed.

"Yes . . . how?" said Fräulein Louise, smiling at him. He was smiling, too, a little helplessly, but this was lost on Fräulein Louise. All she saw was the smile.

"And I'm from Neurode, from the Youth Camp there," she said.

"Ah, yes," said Garnot. "You're a social worker."

Fräulein Louise nodded blissfully. She didn't ask how Garnot knew. She didn't know that he had his information from Irina and me.

"Your name is Louise, isn't it?" said Garnot.

Fräulein Louise suddenly felt young and not at all weary, and her feet didn't hurt anymore. "Louise," she said. "Of course! Oh, how lucky! Thank you. Thank you very much!"

"What for?"

"Well, that you two are here. You'll be able to help me, I'm sure. I was upstairs at the Michelsen apartment, but nobody answered."

"Nobody's home there, not even the servant. He left two hours ago," said Kubitzky. "What did you want?"

"You know what I wanted," she said, winking at him. "I am looking for Irina Indigo and this reporter, Herr Roland. It's very important."

"Very important?" said Kubitzky.

"Of course, very important," said Garnot, "after all that's happened." And Fräulein Louise looked at him gratefully.

"Yes, after all that's happened," she said. "They were here, weren't they?"

"Yes."

"And they talked to you," she said in a sudden burst of clairvoyance.

"In great detail," said Garnot.

"About what?"

"About Herr Bilka and his fiancée and everything that concerned them."

"What did they say?"

Garnot and Kubitzky took turns telling the story. It seemed perfectly all right to them that they should give the social worker I had mentioned the information she wanted. Fräulein Louise also found it perfectly natural that her dear friends should be filling her in. So all of them talked at cross-purposes without realizing it, and Fräulein Louise found out everything that had happened.

"And where are they now—Fräulein Indigo and Herr Roland?" she asked. "I must find them!"

"Herr Roland gave me an address," said Garnot. "In case anybody asks for him or we have something new to tell. That's where you can reach him."

"And where is that?" asked Fräulein Louise.

"At the Metropole Hotel," said André Garnot.

4

"Yes, *meine Dame*," said night clerk Eugene Hanslik, leaning forward as he answered Fräulein Louise's question. "Herr Roland is staying here."

"With a young girl?"

"With his wife," said Hanslik, looking at the poorly dressed old woman with a mixture of curiosity and sympathy.

"Of course... with his wife," said Fräulein Louise. "Would

you please tell them I am here. I must speak to them." And now I have them, she thought. Now I have them!

Hanslik, who had my instructions, got out of the dilemma elegantly. He gestured in the direction of the key board. "The key is here."

"That means they're not here?"

"Yes."

"Have they gone away?"

"No, no. They're just out."

"When are they coming back?"

"They didn't say. Thank you, sir," he said unexpectedly, in English. An English guest, or an American, had just put his room key on the desk. "I have no idea when Herr and Frau Roland will be back. They may be gone quite a while."

"May I—may I wait?" asked Fräulein Louise. She was very impressed and at the same time oppressed by the glitter and luxury of the Metropole Hotel.

"Certainly, *meine Dame*. Please take a seat in the lobby. As soon as Herr Roland comes back—" He took another tack. "Herr Roland will see you, I'm sure. You know each other, don't you?"

"We certainly do," said Fräulein Louise. "Thank you, sir."

"Front!" cried Hanslik. A boy in uniform came running. "Check the lady's coat." "Yes, sir," said the boy, going up to Fräulein Louise. "May I?"

Absently she began to unbutton her shabby coat, then she thought, Oh, dear Lord! I'm still wearing my old gray skirt and my old brown cardigan. I can't go in looking like that! They'd throw me out! So she told the boy, "No, thank you. I'll keep on my coat. I'm—I'm a little cold."

"Very well, ma'am," he said with a slight bow.

Fräulein Louise walked into the lobby on a cloud. She'd never seen anything like it. The crystal chandeliers, the carpets—each one must have cost a fortune! The walls—pink marble! The old paintings! The flowers in priceless vases! The elegant furniture and—oh, the elegant gentlemen and the beautiful women with their colorful dresses and dazzling jewelry. How it glittered! And me in my shabby coat, she thought. It's embarrassing. I'd like to run away. But I mustn't. I must wait here until Irina and Herr Roland come....

She remained standing hesitantly in the entrance to the lobby. A waiter in tails came up to her. "Would madame like to sit down?"

A pretty little table with swung legs, three chairs around it with turned arms, upholstered in brocade. The waiter drew back one of the chairs. Things were beginning to swim in front of Fräulein Louise's eyes. She sat down with a sigh. This is a terrible experience, she thought, all of a sudden depressed again; and she tried to hide her ugly boots under the table. "Would madame like to order anything?" asked the waiter.

All around her people were talking and laughing, and she could hear many languages. Perhaps I'm still at the Davidswache and dreaming all this, she thought. . . . The waiter's voice seemed to come from far away.

Order anything? I must drink something, she thought, or they won't let me go on sitting here. "I'd like a schnapps," she said courageously.

The waiter managed to keep a straight face. "Very good. Cognac. Whiskey? Gin and tonic?"

"Something sweet," said Fräulein Louise.

"A Benedictine? Cointreau? Grand Marnier?"

"Yes."

"Which one, please?"

"The one you said first."

"A Benedictine?"

"Yes."

"Right away." And the waiter in tails went off.

Oh, dear God, please help me to stick it out here, she prayed. Please! All these people—they're staring at me. . . . They're whispering about me . . .

Nobody was looking at Fräulein Louise, nobody was whispering about her. She gritted her teeth and sat up very straight, her big bag on her knees, and stared out at the reception desk so as to be sure not to miss Irina's return. She began to feel very warm in her coat, in the overheated lobby, but she would not remove it. I can't take off my coat, she thought. Impossible!

The swallow-tailed waiter came back with a silver tray, a glass on it, a light brown liquid in the glass. "A Benedictine, *meine Dame.*"

He put down the tray in front of her and was about to go away when Fräulein Louise cried, "Just a minute!" and thought, Oh, God, now I'm shouting!

"Yes, *gnädige Frau?*" said the waiter, coming back.

"I'd like to pay now."

"Certainly. Six marks fifty."

"Six marks fif—" Fräulein Louise was speechless. For a little schnapps like that? Six marks fifty! That was insane! But she mustn't show her dismay.

She opened her big bag. The waiter couldn't control a slight start as he saw the bundles of money in it. But Fräulein Louise didn't notice. She handed him a hundred-mark bill. "I'm sorry, but I don't have anything smaller."

"Thank you very much, *gnädige Frau*," said the waiter as he hurried off.

Fräulein Louise looked after him, horrified. There he goes with my hundred marks! she thought, as she saw him disappear behind a red silk screen. They can't just walk off with my hundred marks in a fine hotel like this! She raised her glass and drank quickly. The light-brown liquid was sweet, but it burned. I don't care, she thought. I'll go to the nice man at the desk and tell him that this fellow has gone off with my hundred marks. I don't have to put up with—

"Here you are, *gnädige Frau*, if you please."

The swallow-tailed waiter was back with a small plate. Her receipt and change were on it. So he wasn't a thief, thought Fräulein Louise. One shouldn't think the worst of people right away....

"Just a minute," she said, and fished around in the change until she found fifty pfennigs. She handed it to the waiter with a smile. "And this is for you."

"Thank you, *gnädige Frau*," said the waiter, also smiling. He bowed and withdrew again. Fräulein Louise emptied her glass in one swallow, whereupon she was suddenly very hot and felt sick. Air! I must go outdoors for a minute, she thought, or I'll throw up right here on their fine carpet. Oh, dear God, you are testing me hard. I can't go on like this much longer....

She rose uncertainly and hurried out of the lobby, past reception and the bell captain's desk. Nobody paid any attention to her. A bell boy turned the revolving door for her and she was outside in the cool evening air. She breathed deeply. Slowly she began to feel better.

A limousine turned into the driveway and stopped under the marquee at the entrance. The chauffeur helped two ladies in mink coats to get out. Fräulein Louise shrank into a dark corner. She heard one of the ladies say, "Take the car to the underground garage, Emile. We'll need you again at ten. I'll call."

The chauffeur bowed, cap in hand, got into the limousine

again, and drove along the front of the hotel and around a corner. It gave Fräulein Louise an idea. So they have an underground garage here, she thought. What if Herr Roland brought his car into the garage? And there was an elevator there that led up to the rooms? Perhaps one could have the key to the room brought down? In which case she was waiting up here for nothing. She wouldn't even see them when they came back.

The underground garage, she thought. I must take a look at it. She opened her Knirps and hurried along the front of the hotel on her painful feet, looking for the entrance to the garage.

5

For about ten minutes she stood in front of the big steel door to the underground garage in the dark and the rain. There was a circular staircase beside it, but Fräulein Louise didn't dare go down it, not all alone. That would be more conspicuous, she thought, than if I went down with somebody. I'll wait for the next car.

The next car was a Rekord. It drove up very close to Fräulein Louise and its headlights blinded her. A man in a raincoat got out and rang the bell for the elevator, a thin man. You could see white hair underneath his hat. He had a fine, narrow, cultured face. He stood beside Louise as he waited for the elevator to come up. Then he raised his hat and said, "Good evening."

"Good evening," said Fräulein Louise.

"Is anything wrong? Do you need any help?"

"No, thank you." Fräulein Louise had already thought of a story for whoever was down in the garage. "Very good of you."

"Here's the elevator," said the man, and got back into his car. A rattling noise got louder and louder and finally stopped. The metal door slid up, startling Fräulein Louise. She was afraid she might fall down the shaft, but there was no shaft, only the elevator platform and a stout, rosy-cheeked man with a friendly face and laughing eyes standing on it. The attendant, Wim Croft, had come on the night shift at seven. He was wearing bright yellow overalls, and he beckoned to the man at the wheel. To

Fräulein Louise he said, "Good evening. You want to go down?"

"Yes, please," said Fräulein Louise.

"Come in and stand way back there. I have to get the car in," said Croft.

Fräulein Louise nodded and walked into the elevator ahead of the Rekord which Croft was directing. Then all of them went down together. The elevator made a lot of noise, and talking was impossible. Croft smiled at Fräulein Louise and she smiled back. A friendly man, she thought. The elevator stopped. Croft waved the car onto the floor area and into a parking space. Fräulein Louise followed slowly. Fluorescent lighting lit up the entire floor. One had gone out, and a young man on a high ladder was replacing it.

Fräulein Louise looked around and saw the driver of the Rekord coming toward her with the attendant. She heard the driver say, "Bad weather doesn't bother me. I've just heard it's snowing hard in Moscow." He gave the attendant his car keys and walked past Fräulein Louise into the little office beside the elevator where a bare bulb was burning and a Coca-Cola calendar was hanging on the wall beside a fire extinguisher. The attendant registered the Rekord in his book and hung the keys on the rack.

"You're from Moscow?" Fräulein Louise asked timidly of the man wearing a homburg and carrying an attaché case. Her blood was pulsating wildly in her temples.

"Yes, madam. From Moscow," said the man with the silvery hair. He spoke without an accent. He had taken off his hat to her and bowed. "My name is Jossif Monerov."

"Louise Gottschalk," said Fräulein Louise. "You're from Moscow?" She couldn't say anything more. All she could think was: The Russian! The Russian!

"Herr Professor Monerov is in Hamburg to attend a convention," said Croft. "He is a famous doctor."

"Oh, come now," said Monerov, unbuttoning his coat and fumbling for change in his trousers pocket, and Fräulein Louise could see that he was wearing a tuxedo. "Convention! One reception after the other! I can't eat or drink another thing! And there are still so many things to do tonight. But I've got to lie down and take a little rest first."

"So much still to do?" said Fräulein Louise. She thought she had seen Monerov wink at her. The Russian, she thought. The Russian is here!

"Yes, my good lady, a lot still to do," said Monerov. "If my friend here, Wim Croft, hadn't rented me a car, I wouldn't have been able to manage at all."

"You are friends?" asked Fräulein Louise. It sounded naive, but in her excitement her face had narrowed shrewdly. This conversation meant everything to her.

Monerov sounded good-natured as he said, "Very good friends. Isn't that so, Herr Croft? Herr Croft is from Holland. I love Holland. I've been there often."

Oh, dear God, thought Fräulein Louise. The Dutchman, too. So at last, at last!

"I have a Russian and a Dutch friend," said Fräulein Louise, staring at the two men.

"That's an honor," said Croft. "We like to have friends."

"Yes," said Monerov. "We're glad when somebody likes us," and he shook hands with Croft before he tipped him.

"See you later, Herr Professor," said Croft, and he and Fräulein Louise watched the professor walk over to an opaque door and press the button on the brass plate beside it. A hotel elevator came down. Monerov opened the door, waved to them, got in, and the elevator ascended again. And that's just as I imagined it would be, thought Fräulein Louise.

"And what can I do for you, lady?" asked Croft.

Fräulein Louise looked at him as if they were conspirators. "It concerns Herr Roland," she said.

"Aha!" said Herr Croft. "Herr Roland." He smiled. Fräulein Louise smiled back, filled with childish faith.

"Yes," she said, and thought: Now I must lie. It's a sin, but I can't help it. "You see," she said. "I must speak to Herr Roland. I forgot a book in his big white car, and I need it. Herr Roland isn't in. I asked at the desk. So I thought perhaps I could wait for him here until he comes. So that I don't miss him. I really need that book."

"Your book's in the big car?" asked Croft.

"You mean he has a small one, too?"

"He's rented a Rekord. Like Professor Monerov's. Herr Roland's big car is over there. Can you see it?" He pointed to the Lamborghini, parked between two columns.

"Yes, yes! That's his car," cried Fräulein Louise, recognizing the Lamborghini which she had seen at the camp entrance. Now she was worried. The car's there, she thought. If this Dutchman unlocks it for me to look for my book, what do I do then? The Dutchman said hesitantly, "Yes, that's Herr Roland's Lamborghini. He gave me the keys. But—but you must understand, lady—I mean, I can't unlock the car and let you get your book without his permission, you understand?"

"Of course I understand," said Fräulein Louise. (Thank you, dear God!) "Then—then would you mind if I waited down here until Herr Roland comes?"

"Of course not. But I have no idea when he'll be back."

"I have time," said Fräulein Louise. "But he will bring the car down here when he gets back, won't he?"

"Certainly. Just like the Herr Professor." Croft looked at the keyboard. "Hm. . . ."

"What?" asked Fräulein Louise.

"I noticed last night, when Herr Roland asked for a car. He and his wife," said Croft, looking at the room plan, which he received daily from reception with all the new registrations, "—they live in Suite 423."

"He and his wife," Fräulein Louise said softly.

"I beg your pardon."

"Nothing. Nothing. So?"

"And Professor Monerov lives in Suite 424, next to them. And both of them rented a Rekord."

"Well!" said Fräulein Louise, and thought: Now I have reached my goal. At least one of them. And my friends are here. Oh, dear God, I was so close to despair, but now I'm moving right along again.

"Why don't you wait in my office?" said Croft.

"That's very good of you," said Fräulein Louise. She walked into the little room and sat down on a chair under the calendar; Croft sat down on his desk. They chatted. There was an awful lot going on right now, Croft told her. The hotel was full. And Professor Monerov was a very high-class gentleman. "He's been in Holland very often." Croft was homesick. He began to talk about his native land, and he talked until the garage bell rang again. "Perhaps that's Herr Roland," he said. But it wasn't.

Croft came back and sat back down on the desk and went on talking. The young man who had been repairing the lights came into the office. He was young, slim, and blond, and he was wearing blue overalls. "Everything's OK now," he said. "Please sign in my time."

Croft signed his book. Meanwhile the young man looked at Fräulein Louise and smiled. She smiled, too. A nice young man, she thought.

"There you are, Jürgen," said Croft. "And thanks."

"*Wiedersehen*," said Jürgen. He nodded at Fräulein Louise and left.

"Nice young man," said Fräulein Louise.

"He is," said Croft. "And such lousy luck!"

"Lousy luck?"

"Well, yes. His name is Jürgen Felmar. Do you recognize it?"

Fräulein Louise thought hard. "Felmar ... Felmar.... I've heard the name somewhere but right now ..."

"Ludwig Felmar. The biggest war criminal of them all. They've just caught up with him in Brazil. The former SS leader."

"SS Leader Felmar?" Fräulein Louise was stunned.

"Yes. And that young man is his son," said Croft. "They're going to try his father. If he doesn't get life—He certainly deserves it, no question of that. But the boy—it isn't his fault. What do you think's going on inside him? He's doing his best not to show it, poor devil."

Fräulein Louise heard his last words distantly. She was thinking: so I have met the Frenchman, the Pole, the Czech, the Ukrainian, the Russian, the Dutchman ... and now the SS leader! Or the son of the SS leader. Shouldn't make any difference. They're here! All of them. She thought, with the clarity that so often overwhelmed her: The judgment will fall here, in this hotel, tonight!

The bell rang again. Again Croft took the elevator up and came back with a dripping wet car, and still it wasn't the car Fräulein Louise was waiting for. Doesn't matter, she thought patiently. Nothing matters. I have time. I can wait.

She waited for half an hour, an hour, an hour and a half. Croft was very busy now; he didn't have time to pay any attention to her. Cars were called for and brought back, finally a rented one that had been involved in an accident. Croft had to examine the extent of the damage. He got a dolly, lay down on it, and rolled under the car.

Apartment 423, thought Fräulein Louise, coming to a sudden decision. Perhaps Herr Roland *had* come back ... and had not put his car in the garage because he wanted to go out again. Yes, she told herself, he's back. I know he is!

She left the little office and walked over to the opaque glass elevator door. She pressed the Up button. The elevator came down. Nobody noticed her opening the door and getting in. She pressed the button for the fourth floor. The elevator was fast and soon stopped. Fräulein Louise got out. The long, wide hall was carpeted; antique chests and dark chairs stood against the wall. Not a soul in sight. Arrows and numbers on signs opposite the elevator indicated where the rooms lay. Fräulein Louise found her way easily. She walked down the hall, past old prints and large oil paintings. 427 ... 426 ... 425 ... 424 ... that was where the Russian lived ... 423....

A white door with a gold handle. Fräulein Louise took a deep breath. "God be with me," she said, and pressed the handle down. The door opened. She could hear soft music....

6

"How on earth did you get here?"

I was standing beside Irina, staring at Fräulein Louise.

"From the garage. With the elevator. Nobody saw me," she said.

"And what do you want?"

"I want the girl. She must come back to the camp with me. At once! I won't have it!"

Irina grabbed my arm. I held on to her. "What won't you have?"

Fräulein Louise marched up to Irina. "I've been looking for you all over the city without finding you. Then, at last, my friends showed me the way." She glared at me. "You are a wicked man. You betrayed your trust!" She grabbed Irina by the arm and tried to pull her away. "And now you come along!"

"No!" she cried. "I'm not going back to your filthy camp. Never!"

I said softly, "Fräulein Louise, this is my suite. You had no right to enter it. If you don't get out immediately, then—I'm sorry, but I'll have to have you thrown out."

Fräulein Louise pushed back her hat. "Is that so!" she said angrily. "And you know what I'll do then? I'll bring charges against you. For kidnapping. Irina isn't even twenty-one. She has no permit yet! She hasn't even been vaccinated!"

"Herr Roland has signed for me!" cried Irina. "If somebody's signed for me, I don't have to go back to the camp. Herr Roland has accepted all responsibility for me in writing! *In writing*, you understand?"

Apparently this made no impression on Fräulein Louise, because she cried, "Fools! That's what you are! Fools! One worse than the other. He has signed for you. He has taken all responsibility. For how long? Until he's had enough of you, then he'll throw you out!"

"Just a minute—" I began, but Fräulein Louise wouldn't let me finish. Turning to Irina she said, "And look at you! Dressed up like a—like a—you know what! Aren't you ashamed of yourself? Look what he's done to you *in one day!*" And to me again: "You're no better than the rogues on the Reeperbahn, the ones who come and get girls from the camp! You want to have your fun with her, that's all."

I walked up to Fräulein Louise and said, "Now that's enough!" I got no farther than that when the telephone rang. I picked up the receiver. "Yes!"

"Why are you shouting?" asked a voice I knew but for the moment couldn't place.

"Who is it? What do you want?" I asked in a normal voice.

"This is Victor Largent." Of course, damn it! And it was all I needed right now. "And what do I want? To speak to you. It's important."

"Where are you?"

"In the lobby. I'm talking from a booth. I'll be right up. So long."

"You're not coming up!" I shouted. "If you want anything from me, call me tomorrow morning."

"Tomorrow morning's too late. It has to be now."

"It doesn't have to be now! I don't have the time! Do not come up!" And I slammed down the receiver.

"Who was that?" asked Irina.

"Victor Largent," I said. "An agent."

"An agent?" cried Irina.

"Not what you're thinking," I said, trying to smile. "A literary agent. Deals with authors, novels, films." I looked at Fräulein Louise, blind suddenly with fury. "And you get out! This minute!"

Fräulein Louise's voice was soft, almost a whisper. She said, "Irina is still a child. Can't you see that, Herr Roland? Are you so depraved that you can't see she's still a child?"

"I am not a child!" cried Irina. "What do you know about me? You don't know me! You don't know anything about me!"

With great dignity Fräulein Louise said, "I know all about you. You are still a child, and I know all about children. I never gave birth to one and I was never married, and still I have had children, more than any mother in the world. Hundreds! Thousands! I have taken care of them and protected them all my life. I have sat beside their beds at night when they were ill. I have defended them and protected them from evil. Just like a real mother. Better than a real mother! I have had thousands of children and they have loved me. All of them." She swayed, and fell into a chair.

I couldn't have cared less. I walked over to her and did something incredibly cruel. I said, "If you don't get out of here right away, Fräulein Louise, I'm going to have a little talk with someone."

"A talk with someone? With whom?" She looked up at me. There were tears in her kind eyes.

"I know the director of the Mental Health Institute in Bremen—" I began, but was interrupted by a loud, jovial voice.

"Hello, everybody! I'm not intruding, am I? The door was open so I walked in. Ladies, dear friend Roland. . . ."

The man who had just walked in was tall, and stocky and didn't have a hair on his head. He was wearing rimless glasses, looked sly, and was a shining example of colossal nerve and bad manners. When I saw him, I was so enraged I even forgot Fräulein Louise. "I told you I didn't want to see you!"

"And I told the desk you were expecting me," the man said, grinning. "You have a visitor. Charming! Charming! Don't you want to introduce me?"

"No!" I said. "Get out!"

My visitor bowed to Fräulein Louise and Irina. "Largent. Victor Largent. A pleasure to meet you ladies. Herr Roland and I are old friends."

"Friends!" I shouted, enraged. "I said, 'Get out!' What's the matter with you? Are you deaf?"

"I have something very important to discuss with you," said Largent. "So, do be more polite. Offer me something to drink. No . . . don't bother. I see you're not in the mood, so I'll fix one for myself." And he waltzed across the room and actually did pour whiskey into a glass, added water and ice, toasted all of us, and drank, after which he grunted contentedly.

"You are a literary agent?" asked Irina, still slightly stunned.

"That's me, beautiful lady. Victor Largent." He spoke German fluently, with a strong American accent. I had known him for years. He had a big agency in New York with branches in Hollywood, Paris, London and Rome; his clients were authors, film writers, and actors. He sold series, documentaries, and novels, and was a legend in his field. Not fifty yet, but looked older because of his bald head. He wore ready-to-wear suits that were always creased, nylon shirts, and cheap ties; but everybody knew that he was a wealthy bachelor. He owned a famous collection of old clocks and traveled all over the world. Until now, our business had been indirect. He had sold my sex stories in many countries, but all transactions had gone through the house—I had merely collected my percentage.

Largent sat down, sighed happily, drank, looked us over with his little pig eyes, and seemed very pleased with himself. I got more and more furious. "Listen, Largent," I shouted, "I'll have you thrown out if you don't get out!"

He merely grunted.

"Isn't he an idiot?" he said to Irina. "Always bashing his head against a wall. A stormy character. And he knows me. You don't know me yet, ladies. I have a proposal to make to Herr Roland. Right away. And I'm not a man to take no for an answer." He stretched his legs out on a low coffee table, drank, and turned to Irina again.

"What's your name, child?"

"Irina Indigo." She still looked baffled.

"A pretty name." Largent nodded. I realized I couldn't throw him out myself—he was too big. "And you, madame?" Largent took his feet off the table.

Fräulein Louise hadn't taken her eyes off the American ever since he had entered; obviously he fascinated her. She looked ecstatic. She got up and walked over to him. "Gottschalk. Louise Gottschalk. But you know that...."

This strange greeting—she had addressed him with the *Du*—didn't seem to bother Largent. He grinned. "Of course I know you, Fräulein Louise Gottschalk. I meet so many people. You must forgive me if I didn't recognize you right away."

Fräulein Louise beamed at him. "Now everything will turn out all right," she said.

Largent gave me a look. In his profession he met up with weirdos all the time, so nothing surprised him anymore. And as he had always told me, he loved freaks.

"Everything will turn out all right. Absolutely, Fräulein Louise. You can relax. Largent is here. Nothing can go wrong now."

"Wonderful," whispered Fräulein Louise. "Oh, how wonderful! Everything is going to happen just as I wished."

"No doubt about it," Largent said calmly. "Never despair, just call in Largent."

"My American!" whispered Fräulein Louise.

"At your service, madame. America is always at your service!"

"Thank you, dear God," whispered Fräulein Louise.

They couldn't have done better in a madhouse!

I said to Fräulein Louise, "Now that's enough. Either you leave or I call the desk."

"No, no! You mustn't do that!" cried Fräulein Louise. "It's too important that Herr Largent came just now."

"I'll say it is, Fräulein Gottschalk!" cried my unwelcome visitor. "Or may I say Louise?"

"Of course you may!" cried Fräulein Louise, delighted.

Just then the door opened and waiter Jules walked in with the first course of our dinner on a table—damask cloth, silver, the lobster cocktail, an ice bucket with champagne. He stopped, perplexed. "*Pardon*... I didn't mean to disturb. The dinner—" He looked at Largent sharply.

The latter gave him a broad smile. "Hello," he said.

"Monsieur," said Jules. And to me, "Should I bring in the table now?"

"Yes, please," I said. "Our guests are just leaving."

"That's what you think," said Largent, winking at Fräulein Louise. She was still staring at him, wide-eyed; then her gaze wandered over to Jules. "French, yes?"

"Yes, madame," Jules was busy arranging the table.

"If you only knew how happy that makes me," said Fräulein Louise. "You're looking after things, too, aren't you?"

Jules looked at Fräulein Louise nervously. "I'm doing what, madame?"

"Looking after things."

"I don't understand, madame—" Jules began to say, but just then Largent tapped a finger against his forehead and shrugged. Jules raised his eyebrows but didn't exactly look relieved. "Should I open the bottle, monsieur?" he asked me.

"Yes, please. We're going to eat now. *Alone!* I'm going to get these people out of here," I said, while Jules picked up a damask napkin and took the bottle of champagne out of the bucket. Fräulein Louise went over to him. "Just a minute," she said.

"I beg your pardon, madame." Jules was nervous again.

Fräulein Louise looked at him sternly. "You know very well—" Again she used the intimate *Du*.

"*Pardon*, madame," said Jules, overcome with embarrassment. "I really have no idea—"

"Aha!" said Fräulein Louise, sounding threatening now. "So that's how it is! I thought so! But just wait a minute. I have a message for you."

Jules stared at her. Largent laughed. For him it was great fun. "Part of your story?" he whispered to me. "What a type! Jee-sus!"

"A message for me? What message, madame?" asked Jules.

Fräulein Louise's eyes looked faraway. She said slowly, "You must pause a minute and listen to what those two up there say to you."

Jules reddened with embarrassment. "Those two . . . up there, madame?"

"Yes." Fräulein Louise was obviously listening. There wasn't a sound except for the radio playing "A Wonderland by Night." Now she addressed herself directly to Jules. "What you are about to do is evil. You will bring misfortune upon people." Her voice was monotone. "And you will share in their misfortune."

Jules grew pale. I could see he was shocked. "Madame— really—I—"

"Quiet!" said Fräulein Louise, while Largent laughed and Irina grasped my arm. "You will have to atone for it for a long time."

"Walter, please!" whispered Irina.

"Yes," I said. "Enough!" I walked up to Fräulein Louise and barked at her, "You interrupted me a few minutes ago!"

"Interrupted you? When?"

"When I said that I knew the director of the Mental Health Institute in Bremen. If you don't leave this minute—"

"But I have to—"

"You don't have to anything. All you have to do is get out! At once! I've had enough. If you don't leave right away, or if you turn up again, I shall speak to the director of the institute."

Fräulein Louise looked agitatedly at the smiling American and the perturbed Frenchman, then back at me, and stammered, "Speak to—"

"Yes," I said angrily. "And you know what about. It seems to me that it's really high time you were pensioned."

"Pensioned?" cried Fräulein Louise.

"No, no!" said Largent smoothly. "But really, you've got to behave, Louise. I'll see to it that everything here turns out all right. You can depend on me."

"I can? Really?"

"Really. I am a friend. Everything is going to have a happy ending. Don't worry."

"That—that—" She was still struggling for breath. "That's wonderful. You're here now and—and so are the others." She glared at Jules. "Only you've got to watch this one. He wants to do evil! He *is* evil!"

"Of course we'll keep an eye on him," said Largent, and again gave Jules a sign which Fräulein Louise didn't notice. "And I know Herr Roland. A wonderful man. You can trust him."

"But Irina—"

"Is in the best of hands. Everything will turn out all right, you'll see. But now you must go, Louise."

She stood there indecisively. Largent smiled. "So long, my dear. And good luck!"

"I interfered," said Fräulein Louise. "I shouldn't have done that. I must trust my friends." Suddenly she was close to tears. "Forgive me. But watch this Frenchman, please."

"We will," said Largent, imperturbably.

Jules stood there like an idiot, the champagne bottle in his hand.

"He is not a friend," said Fräulein Louise. "But you know that, don't you?"

"Of course I do," said Largent.

"Well, then, I'll go now. And pray that it all turns out all right." She nodded to Largent, Irina, and me; she didn't look at Jules again. Tiny, shabby, and ridiculous, she left the room. For a moment there was silence; then Irina said, "Thank God!" But Jules hadn't calmed down. "Who was that? How did she get in here?"

"I forgot to lock the door."

"Yes, but how did she get up here?"

"Don't worry about it," said Largent. "Crazy people always find a way."

"Crazy?"

"Of course she's crazy," said Largent. "But harmless. If you've dealt with crazy people all your life, you get to know the difference. Now calm down, man, and open that bottle."

Jules removed the wire cap and began to twist the cork. He was still so confused that the cork came out too fast and some champagne spilled onto the carpet. "*Pardon*, madame, monsieur. I—I—this woman—"

"Well, now she's gone," I said, and tasted the champagne. "Excellent!"

Jules filled our glasses after I had led Irina to the table and sat her down in one of the brocade chairs. I sat down, too.

"I shall see to it that she doesn't come back," said Jules. "Who was she, monsieur? Somebody you know?"

"Yes. Somebody I know. With eleven dead friends. They talk to her. Sometimes she sees them."

"But that really is crazy!" said Jules, offering us toast from a lined basket.

"It certainly is," I said.

"Saw one of her dead friends in me," said Largent. "Ha-ha-ha! Charming old dear! I had an author in Hollywood who saw elephants. Not the little pink ones drunks see—no, big ones! Everywhere! And once, when I went to see him—"

"Largent," I said. "Please! We want to eat. You've finished your drink. Will you please get out, too?"

"Certainly not," said Largent. "I've finished my drink, true, but I'll fix myself another. No, no, don't bother, Jules. I'll do it myself." He got up clumsily and actually did pour himself another drink. To Jules he said, "You may go now. Everything looks fine. You can attend to the next course."

"Very well, monsieur," said Jules, and withdrew. He was still pale. "I'll bring the entrée in fifteen minutes. Is that all right, Monsieur Roland?"

"Fine," I said, raising my glass to Irina. "*Prosit!*" She raised her glass and we drank. Jules withdrew. Largent followed him to the door and locked it. Then he dropped like a log on the couch and said with a deep sigh, "There! And now to us, my boy."

I had started to eat; so had Irina. I knew Largent was a leech, no shaking him off. "Go to hell!" I said.

"I will, I will. All of us will," he said. "Don't let my presence bother you, Fräulein. I'm here on business, and no time to lose."

"I told you—"

"Yes, yes," said Largent. "And now you listen to me, you sodden genius." He took a pad out of his pocket, wrote something on it, tore off the sheet, and laid it down beside my glass. I looked at him, nonplussed. On it he had written the name of the largest and most prestigious illustrated magazine in the United States.

7

"That's where you can start," said Largent, swizzling the ice in his glass, and my Chivas. "They want you. As far as they're concerned, you can fly to New York tomorrow and start the day after."

Irina, who couldn't follow what was going on, looked at me. I ate a large piece of lobster and toast with butter, and drank some Pommery Demi-Sec, 1951—a very good year for champagne, according to Jules. "Our waiter has taken you to his heart," I said to Irina. "I never got this much lobster in a cocktail in my life. Wonderful, isn't it?"

Irina nodded uneasily.

"Oh, come off it now," said Largent. "You're not going to get more money that way. They're offering you an outrageous salary anyway."

"How much?" I asked. I wanted to see how long he'd last.

He took back his note, wrote a figure on it, and laid it on the table again. "Guarantee per month," he said. "Whether you make it or not. You realize, of course, that you can't possibly meet such a sum."

The sum he had written down was four times as much as the guarantee I had with *Blitz*, and that was the highest in Germany.

"Impressive, no?" said Largent, the man who juggled daily with people and millions. He tugged at his cheap tie and fingered the collar of his creased nylon shirt. "They pay my percentage. You don't have to give me a cent. It's the biggest thing I've ever experienced in the magazine business, and I've been around. I've experienced plenty. But this is the biggest bonanza of them all!"

I went on eating my lobster and drinking Pommery, and didn't answer. The paper was tops, the salary was fantastic. But of course this bonanza had a flaw. In our business every bonanza had a flaw.

"They've sent me out just for you," said Largent. "In Frankfurt they told me you were in Hamburg. Hamburg—Metropole, I told myself. Came straight here. You'll say yes, of course. I'm at the Atlantic. Tomorrow morning at 8:30 I'll bring over the contract and a bank check for the first six months."

"I have an exclusive contract with *Blitz*," I said, "and you know it."

"Sure I know it. You can give notice—"

"You mean break it."

"Or break it. They'll take it to court. These guys"—he pointed to the note—"will look after it for you. With the best lawyers money can buy. And pay your debts."

"What debts?" asked Irina.

"Oh, he has a two-hundred-and-ten-thousand mark advance," said Largent. "They'll pay it, of course. Incidentally, *Blitz* won't sue. I can assure you, Roland, they won't sue."

"I heard you," I said. "That's what *you* think. Why do they want me? And why right away?" I could guess, but I was anxious to hear how he would put it.

"Your name. They're crazy about your name. It takes time for a name to get through to the Americans. I've been telling them for years: *Get that boy!* And now they're ready. Of course they want Walter Roland, ace reporter, not that hack writer, Curt Corell. They don't need any more porno sex over there. On the contrary. They want serious stuff, as serious as you like. The first thing they want from you is the moon landing. From *A* to *Z*. They'll send you straight to Houston. After that the world is your oyster. Political articles? Nobody will try to influence you. You can dish out science, history, essays . . . the best, the biggest themes—"

"And the story I'm after now—do they want that?"

"No. Not that one, Roland. You've got to learn to think on an international scale. What's with this story, anyway? Can you charm Germany with it? Maybe. But these people here—he pointed to his note again—"are read worldwide. Nine different editions. Circulation five million. Forget your crappy story. It's for the birds."

So that's where we were heading, I thought. *There* was the flaw in my bonanza. "Doesn't interest a soul," Largent went on. "Walter Roland—that's who they want to build up into a man the whole world knows. And what they're willing to let it cost them isn't chicken shit!"

396

Again, I said nothing but went on eating. Irina was looking at me nervously. I smiled at her.

"And you get away from this stinking continent. See the world! Hear the world! Experience the world!"

"Yes," I said. "The stench of the whole wide world!"

But you couldn't shake him. "You said it! So it's settled! Tomorrow contract and check. So glad we were able to—"

"Largent," I said. "*Blitz* wants this story."

"Have you been happy there?"

I said nothing.

"Wasn't it the pits, what they made you write? Haven't they taken advantage of you, shamelessly? So you simply give them notice, as of right away. Because you can't stand it in that cesspool a moment longer! In that computer stable!" He laughed.

I don't think sharks can laugh, but if they can, that's how Largent laughed. "If you want to, little girl, you come right along. I was to invite you, too. Almost forgot."

"To New York?" asked Irina.

"Sure."

"But—but I have something I must attend to here; so has Herr Roland."

"This story!" Largent took a big swallow of his drink as if to wash down his contempt for it. "This fucking story. It'll never see the light of day!"

"I have given Herr Roland a signed release, for *Blitz*," said Irina.

"Really," said Largent, and laughed. "You don't know the meaning of the word, child. A release!"

"Would you like some more toast, Irina? Here's the butter. She knows what a release is, Largent, and I have contracted for releases from quite a few other people."

"*Blitz* can do you-know-what with those releases," said Largent, grinning.

"I have tapes, and we've sent in a lot of photos already."

"Engelhardt?"

"Yes."

"I don't care. Your story won't appear."

"That's what you think. They're already working on the advance publicity. They've already announced it."

"And they'll never print it!"

"What *are* you talking about?"

"Not a line," said Largent. "You can bet your sweet life on it. Advance publicity—maybe. So they'll recant. So what? It won't be the first time it's happened."

"How come you're so sure they won't print it?" I asked. I began to feel a little uncomfortable about the way the conversation was going.

"The nice old gentleman in Cologne."

I laid down my knife and fork. "That's not true!"

"May I drop dead if it isn't," said Largent. "The nice old gentleman in Cologne will have a nice little telephone conversation with your publisher. That should do it. Always did, didn't it?"

I said nothing. Yes, it had always "done it." Damn it all anyway, what sort of intrigue had I got myself into here? In order to explain briefly: "The nice old gentleman in Cologne," as he was called, was one of the richest men in the Bundesrepublik, the great father of the troubled and burdened millionaires of our country. He looked after them all. He was the chief of the clan, with the power of his billions. He helped make marriages and speed divorces; he covered up munitions scandals and prevented industrial bankruptcies. He also helped foreigners—French, English, Italians, but most of all, Americans. Only if they were members of the clan, naturally. The clan of the super-rich. The nice old gentleman of Cologne had a soft voice, he never raised it, and he knew everything. In the course of the years he had called up Thomas Herford several times when we were starting a series that didn't suit the clan. The nice old gentleman in Cologne then asked Herford, pleasantly, not to publish the series. Nobody in Germany would have dared cross the nice old gentleman in Cologne—because if he did, he was as good as dead. The nice old gentleman in Cologne could ruin bigger and better firms than *Blitz*, if he considered it necessary. If anyone at *Blitz* should happen to protest, it sufficed if suddenly there was no advertising from big industry, national and international, and from various other clients. *Blitz* would go broke. That's how things were done—amiably and with velvet gloves. Until now Herford had always given in.

Would he give in this time? And if he didn't, should I wait until he had to close shop and the Americans decided they could do without me? Smart rats don't stay on a sinking ship. One thing was certainly clear: There was a very good chance that the story would not appear.

But then why had the Amis told Seerose that they were taking Bilka to Helsinki and New York? Why had they given us so much information, so that Bertie was now on his way to Helsinki? First all smiles, and then, suddenly, the threat of the nice old gentleman in Cologne? Was Largent bluffing? I wouldn't have put it past him. I wouldn't have put anything past him!

"You'll bring the tapes with you to New York, of course," he said. "Or—better still—give them to me when I come with the contract tomorrow morning."

"Oh, no!" I said.

"Oh, yes, Roland, man of character!" He laughed like a shark again. I looked at the figure on the paper. Four times what I was making now. The nice old gentleman from Cologne. . . . I got the feeling that Largent wasn't bluffing. But I couldn't fathom the whole thing. Just the same—no more Herford, no more Mama, no more Lester, no more sex shit. Instead—freedom to write what I wanted to write. In another country. With Irina.

There was a knock on the door. I jumped up and unlocked it. It was Jules with the entree. He rolled in a second table, pushed the first one aside, and got ready to serve. "I'll see to that," I said. He looked at Largent for a moment; then he nodded, an exemplary, discreet *chef d'étage*.

"If I may, madame?" he said, filled our glasses again, and opened another bottle. "Have you thought what you'd like for dessert, madame, monsieur?"

"I won't be able to eat anything after this," said Irina.

"No dessert," I said. "But another bottle of champagne, please."

"Very good, monsieur. I'll be back in twenty minutes." He wheeled out the first table and I locked the door after him.

"What a life!" said Largent. "But just think what it's going to be like in New York!" Suddenly his voice was cold, harsh. "Wake up, man!" I was just putting the chicken on my plate and had my back turned to him. "Wake up! It's your last chance!"

"What do you mean, 'last chance'?" Irina was startled.

"Look at his hands, young lady. They're trembling, the old lush."

"So if I'm an old lush, why do they want me? And for such an insane price!"

"Because they believe in you!"

"Aha!" I said. "And you believe in me, too, Largent?"

"And how! Haven't I been trying to get you for years? All

right, all right, I'm on my way. You don't have to say yes now. Tomorrow will do." He got up. "Those are the tapes?"

"Hands off!" I said. "Don't you dare touch them!"

"Don't shit in your pants," he said. "Nobody's going to take anything from you. You'll come to New York. It's written all over your face. Don't try to tell me anything about German loyalty and all that jazz. I know my man. Tomorrow morning you'll sign. It's the best thing for you anyway, in my opinion, to get out of Europe. Oh, come on, don't look sheepish. Good old Uncle Largent is right, isn't he?"

Well...he wasn't all wrong, either. "Wonderful chicken—isn't it, Irina?"

She didn't answer, just stabbed at the food on her plate. I gave her *pommes frites* and green peas and noticed that my hands were really shaking, and the other two noticed it, too. But it wasn't the liquor, it was tension. Suddenly I thought of the jackal. I didn't feel him, I only had to think of him, and I quickly emptied my glass.

"So that's that," said Largent. "Now you can let me out. I'll send a cable that you've agreed." I said nothing. "And tomorrow morning I'll be back. With the contract and money." He kissed Irina's hand and gave me a hard look.

I said nothing as I escorted him to the door. "So that's settled," he said. I said, "Good night," and opened the door for him. Then I went back to Irina, but suddenly everything I was eating had no taste. That was because—and I'd only just realized this—it was very easy to make a rat of me. Very easy.

8

Ten minutes later. "Some more chicken?" I asked Irina.

We hadn't spoken since Largent had left. Drunk? Yes, especially I. Irina had drunk quite a lot, too. The radio was still playing soft music. "I can't eat another thing. Walter, you can't do that."

"Do what?"

"Walk out on *Blitz*, just like that."

"No," I said. "Of course I can't."

Under her dress I could see her breasts rise and fall agitatedly, "But then why didn't you tell Mr. Largent right away?"

I poured more champagne into our glasses. "You know," I said, "the Americans are really offering me a horrendous sum of money. Don't you think I should at least give it a try?" I drank again. With the way my jackal was behaving, I couldn't be too careful.

"*Pfui Teufel!*" said Irina, and hastily covered her mouth with her hand. "Excuse me."

"Certainly."

After a while, during which she hadn't taken her eyes off me, she asked, "Is it true that you owe *Blitz* two hundred and ten thousand marks?"

"Yes," I said. "Why? A while ago it was three hundred thousand."

"But that big white car—it belongs to you, doesn't it?"

"Yes, it belongs to me. I—what's the matter? Why are you looking at me like that?"

She was tipsy, and she laughed tipsily. "I have a contract with you," she said, "according to which I am to receive five thousand marks."

"And?"

"And you've bought me a lot of things to wear, but you haven't given me any money yet."

"But I have!"

"No, you haven't."

"Yes, I have," I said, thinking suddenly of Bertie on his way to Helsinki. "You just don't pay enough attention. Take a look under the couch, at the top end."

Irina stood up, swaying a little, and knelt in front of the couch. After fishing around under it for a while, she brought out an envelope. She tore it open and bills fell out of it. "Seven hundred marks!" she cried.

"Don't be so materialistic, Comrade," I said. "There's a letter in it, too." And now the game with the letters I had hidden began. And I had meant it to begin now. It was all part of my plan. I had had such a beautiful plan for every hour of this night during which I was supposed to look after Irina, during which the Americans were flying Jan Bilka to New York with the first batch of microfilm of the plans of the Warsaw Pact Nations in case of war. . . .

Still kneeling in front of the chaise, Irina read aloud what I had written: "'Enchantingly beautiful lady! The man writing these lines is the poorest creature of all the creatures on this earth. If you want to know why, look behind the curtain on the wide window in the salon....'"

Irina got up, none too steadily, and laughing, ran over to the curtain, and found the second envelope. When she opened it, two large bills fell out. "Two thousand marks!"

"Read the letter."

She read the letter. "'He is the poorest of all living creatures because he has had to spend fifty hours with you without being allowed to kiss and caress....' No, really, Herr Roland! This is too much!" She was red with embarrassment.

"Go on," I said, and drank Pommery.

"'... to kiss and caress your hair, your throat, your beautiful big eyes, because he ... To be continued in the bathroom behind my shaving kit.'"

Now she was laughing again. With the envelopes, the letters, and the money in her hands, she ran into the bedroom. Just then there was a knock on the door. Jules, with an ice bucket and a new bottle. "Let's have it," I said, and started to open the bottle. There was very little left in the second one.

Jules arranged the dishes on the table he was about to remove. "Everything's going well, monsieur. I just spoke to Monsieur Seerose. He is in close contact with the Americans, and you are getting additional information from him."

What the hell's going on? I wondered. *Was* Largent bluffing after all? Or are the Americans bluffing? Do they really want to rock the boat, and have they managed to hoodwink ultrasmart Monsieur Seerose? We had covered quite a lot of ground and found a lot before the Amis had suddenly decided to be so helpful. Are they being so helpful because they're afraid that in the end we might spoil everything? And is it their intention to fuck us up afterwards? Largent had implied this, indirectly. But if so, then he was the biggest fucker-up of all! But what reason could he have for bringing me to New York? His percentage! Of course! And yet—I had to put off thinking about this thing for a while.

"And what about the big news agencies?" I asked.

"They won't be allowed to touch it."

A joyous scream from Irina in the bathroom. "What's that?" asked Jules.

"A little money from my publisher, a few kind words from me, just as you prescribed. You see, things are in best order here, too."

Jules laughed. "*Bonne chance*, monsieur." He had set down a tray with fresh champagne glasses. Now he rolled the table out. I waved good night and locked the door after him, then I filled the two clean glasses with champagne.

Irina came out of the bedroom. She had another letter, another envelope, and more money in her hands, and she looked flushed. Her eyes were blazing. "You're fresh!" she said.

"Don't you want to read it aloud?" I asked.

"You know very well that this is nothing that can be read aloud!"

I walked up to her. "Has nobody ever told you anything like that?"

"Anything like *that*, and put just that way? No! Never! No one."

"But may I say so?" I took her arms, but she freed herself wildly. "Let me go! I have to look under your typewriter for the next one!"

"But first—" and I handed her her glass.

She looked at me with her black, restless eyes. "You want to make me, drunk, don't you? Shall I get drunk? Really drunk?"

"Yes, please," I said, and thought of Bertie, and Largent and his office, and then I thought that I wanted Irina very much, wanted her now!

"Well, then, I'll get drunk—roaring drunk. Why not?" She drained her glass and handed it back to me. Then she ran over to the typewriter and found the envelope under it, tore it open, and again money fell out.

"But that's too much!" she stammered. "Two thousand *again*? That's more, much more than five thousand altogether." She read the letter aloud. "'Not all the banks in the world have the amount of money I would like to give you. Just as all the men in the world—'" She stopped. "Oh, my God! If anybody ever read this! I must tear this letter up and burn it right away!" But she didn't tear it up and burn it; she read on. "'Continued under the cushion on your bed.'" She smiled at me, very tipsy now, and ran off into the bedroom. I picked up the receiver and asked for the bar. Charlie answered, and I spoke quickly. "Very good, Herr Roland," he said.

I put down the receiver and walked into the bedroom, taking

two full glasses of champagne with me. There was a radio in the bedroom, too, built into one of the bedside tables. In the bar they were playing "I'm Always Chasing Rainbows."

Irina was standing beside the bed in a great state of excitement. She had dropped all the envelopes and letters and money on the bed and was staring at me. "You're out of your mind!"

"Of course," I said. "And it's all your fault."

"Two hundred and ten thousand marks in debt . . . and then to do a thing like this! Oh, dear God, I've never seen so much money in my life! *Why* did you do it?"

"It's all in the letter," I said. "Because . . . well, why?"

She read obediently, "'Because I love you!' Such nonsense!"

I gave her her glass and both of us drank. Then I took her glass from her and put it down beside mine on the table, and took her in my arms again. "It's not nonsense," I said. "It's the truth." And as I said it, it was the truth. I had done many reprehensible things in my life, but this was really true.

"We don't know each other at all!" said Irina, in my arms now but no longer protesting. "We don't know anything about each other."

"I know all I want to know about you," I said, holding her close. "I fell in love with you when you walked into Fräulein Louise's room in the camp. I fell in love with your eyes and your black hair, which actually is blue-black, like your eyes . . . and with your voice. . . ." And at that moment the music began what I had asked Charlie to play . . . "Reigen." I let Irina go and swept money and paper off the bed onto the carpet. Then I took her in my arms and tried to get her to lie down. "No," she said. "No . . . please!"

"Yes," I said. "Yes, my darling . . . please!"

Her knees gave way, she sank down on the bed, and I sank down upon her and kissed her lips, her forehead, her throat . . . and began to undo the zipper on her dress. "If somebody comes. . . ."

"The door is locked," I said, and found the light switch beside the bed and put out the ceiling light. Now only the bedside lamp with its red silk shade was on.

We didn't say anything more. She twisted and turned in my arms, and I took off her dress, her brassiere, and her white panties, and she moved under me like a snake and moaned softly. Her gold shoes fell on the floor and she lay naked under me,

404

nothing on but her garter belt and stockings, and she was beautiful . . . so beautiful.

I got up and undressed quickly. I threw my clothes on the floor and lay down beside her and caressed her and kissed her—her throat, her eyes, her ears, her breasts, her stomach. My lips moved lower, her moans grew louder, and now she was lying motionless. Her legs parted as I reached the place I was seeking, and I pressed my face against it and was as gentle as I could be. Irina's fingers gripped my hair, I could feel her excitement growing, and I was excited as never before in my life. But I went on kissing her and waited until she had had enough and cried out to me. She did so suddenly, and with a little sob, "Come—come into me quick—now, now—come!"

I lay on top of her and it seemed to me that the music of "Reigen" grew louder and louder, as if the beautiful melody was sweeping everything away, all restlessness and insecurity, all grief, tension, doubt, and anxiety. And the jackal. Yes . . . him, too.

9

The "Reigen" was over. I was sitting on the edge of the bed, naked. Now they were playing the theme song from the motion picture *Laura*. Irina was sitting on the bed, naked, her knees drawn up to her chest, her hair tousled, the tears streaming down her cheeks. She was very unhappy and I was furious. I looked in the pocket of my jacket, lying on the carpet in front of me, for my cigarettes and lighter, and found both; but the lighter wouldn't work, and I threw away the cigarette I'd already put in my mouth, cursing, and dropped the lighter. "Now you're mad," said Irina.

"Not at all." I began to dress.

"Yes, you are. And I can understand it, and it's all my fault."

I took a swallow of the champagne and shook myself. It was lukewarm. I put on my pants, my loafers, and my jacket. With my tie in my hand I walked toward the door that led to the salon. "Where are you going?"

"To drink whiskey," I said. "I've had as much champagne as I can take. Stay where you are. I'll take my blanket and pillow back to the salon."

"Walter!" She sounded distraught.

"Yes, yes," I said.

"Don't—don't go away like that. Sit down here again."

"What for?"

"Please!"

So I sat down on the edge of the bed again and asked, "So ... what?" I didn't sound friendly.

"I'm so sorry," she said, and now she began to cry again, but this time I didn't give her my handkerchief. "You don't have to be sorry," I said. "I'm evidently not your type."

"No!" she cried. "That's got nothing to do with it. I think you're awfully nice...."

"Yes," I said. "I'm sure."

"I really do. And I'd made up my mind to—to—well, that's why I got drunk."

"Aha!"

"I kept telling myself: I'll do it! This time I'll do it. I was determined to, Walter, but then ..."

"Hm."

"Then I was suddenly so terribly ashamed, and I just couldn't."

This was too much for me. I got up and began pacing up and down. "You were determined to. And what do you mean by that? Why were you determined to? Out of gratitude?"

"No," she whispered, but it didn't register with me.

"And if you were determined out of gratitude, why get yourself and me all excited and then push me away and start behaving like somebody crazy?" Which was what she had done. Nothing like this had ever happened to me before.

"It wasn't out of gratitude," she said, still hugging her knees. "It didn't have anything whatsoever to do with gratitude."

"Then, why—"

"Because of Jan."

That was all I needed. "*What* did you say?"

"Because of Jan. Yes. I was—I was drunk. I had something absolutely crazy in mind."

"What?" I was putting on my tie.

"I—I thought that if I gave in to you, you'd tell me the truth."

"The truth?"

406

"About Jan."

"I see. Practicing psychology. Now I understand. Psychology 101. I should have thought of that. Not very experienced yet. After all, it's only the first semester."

"Please, Walter! Please! You're lying to me. All of you. Even Bertie. All this whispering...that French waiter...Mr. Largent....Where is Bertie now? Why are you so nervous?"

"Nervous?" I couldn't even knot my tie properly, my hands were trembling so. If I didn't drink a full glass of Chivas right away, the jackal would be there. "I've never been less nervous in my life!" I said, fumbling with my tie.

"I'm so terribly worried about Jan. Walter, I can't help it. Please, please, tell me what's really going on. Where is he? What are they doing to him? Take back your money. All of it. I don't want it. You can write whatever you like about me—but please, please, tell me the truth!"

I was stunned. "So you still love him so much?"

She didn't answer. Our eyes met. A few seconds of silence, then the phone beside the bed rang. I sat down and lifted the receiver. It was Heintze. He only said a few words, but I could feel my stomach heaving. It was all I could do to give a sensible reply. "Yes," I said dully. "Yes. Tell him to come up," and I hung up. I looked down at my shoes and nothing made sense anymore. To Irina I said, "He is here."

"Who?"

I'm no better than Fräulein Louise, I thought. What sort of a trap was this? And Bertie had the Colt. My head was swimming.

"Who?" Irina asked again.

I turned to face her and said, "Bilka."

"Jan?" she screamed. All I could do was nod. "He's here, in the hotel?"

"Here in the hotel," I said, and pressed both hands against my temples.

"How can he be here? That's impossible! But he *is* here ... and he's coming up!"

She jumped out of bed, slipped into the robe I'd bought her, and the slippers, ran her fingers through her hair to smooth it down, and went to the bedroom door and opened it. I rose and followed her. But in the doorway she suddenly stopped dead and screamed: "Walter!"

I had already seen him. He was sitting in one of the low armchairs, his legs crossed, a man of about fifty, with a high forehead, silvery hair, and a pale face. He was wearing a smartly tailored tuxedo and the elegant evening shoes I had admired once... in front of the suite next to ours.

10

Irina spoke in a whisper. "Who—who are you?"

"Call me Monerov," said the Russian, who spoke without an accent. "Jossif Monerov. One false name is as good as any other."

"And whether one is a neurosurgeon or not," I said, and he smiled.

"That's right, Herr Roland." He noticed where I was looking and explained without my asking. "Yes. I came through the window. It's not closed. The balconies run all along the front, and we're neighbors, aren't we?"

"What are you doing here?" I asked, and had to think of Fräulein Louise and wondered where she was, and if she had suspected or known what was going to happen here tonight.

"I am waiting for Herr Bilka," said Monerov. "I've been waiting for him for quite some time. But now I guess he's on his way."

"How do you know that?" Irina was swaying on her feet as she clung to me.

"Well," Monerov said amiably, "your excitement. The way you came rushing in here. The telephone call a moment ago. I take it Herr Bilka had himself announced. We arranged to meet here."

"You—what?" stammered Irina.

Meanwhile I had started to walk over to the phone. Suddenly, Monerov—or whatever his name was—had a gun in his hand. A small gun. The metal gleamed in the light from the chandelier. He gestured with the weapon.

"Away from the telephone, Herr Roland. Over to the door, please. When he knocks, open and let him in. If you do anything else, I shoot. I'm sorry to have to do this, but you've caused us a lot of trouble," and he gestured with the gun again.

408

I am not a hero; I never wanted to be. I walked to the door. Monerov came over and stood a little behind me, so that anyone coming in wouldn't see him from the small entrance hall. "And don't lock the door behind him," said Monerov.

I nodded. After that nobody said anything. The radio was playing "Night and Day." About twenty seconds passed. They seemed like twenty hours. Then there was a knock on the door. Monerov had the gun aimed at my back. "Who is it?" I asked.

"Bilka," said a voice.

I unlocked and opened the door.

A man of about forty came in. He was ashen and looked desperate. He was wearing a wet raincoat and he was drunk.

"Come in," I said, and can't remember ever having been so bewildered.

The man who had said he was Bilka walked into the salon. Then he stopped. Rainwater was dripping from his coat. He wasn't wearing a hat; his hair was thin. He saw the Russian, bowed low, and almost fell. He was very drunk.

Irina screamed hysterically, "You are not Jan Bilka! I never saw you before in my life!"

The Russian waved to her with his gun to be silent. Then he turned to the drunken man. "What's your name?"

"Bilka." The man sounded miserable. Raindrops were running down his face.

"That's not true!" cried Irina.

"Vaslav Bilka," said the man. "I am Jan's brother."

Irina came and stood beside me and grasped my arm, a helpless expression on her face. "His brother," she whispered. "Jan never told me he had a brother."

"Jan didn't tell you a lot of things," I said, and to the drunken man: "Where have you come from?"

"From Munich. I've been living there for the last twenty years. My wife is dead. I'm all alone. Have a picture-framing shop. Used to do good business. Now it brings in nothing." He seemed to be trying to collect his thoughts, then he said, "And I have very beautiful frames. But perhaps nobody wants them anymore. I make them myself."

"Where is Jan?" cried Irina. "What do you know about him? Tell me, please!"

"Just a minute," Monerov said harshly. He looked at Bilka. "Why are you so late?"

"My train was late."

"Your train got in an hour ago," Monerov snapped. "You stink of schnapps."

Bilka's brother raised a defiant fist. "Yes," he said. "I drank. I hate you!"

"That breaks my heart," said Monerov.

"Herr Bilka," I said, "why did you come here?"

He looked at me with his bleary eyes. "Early this morning," he said, speaking with difficulty, "two men came to see me. In my Munich apartment. Sent by him." He pointed to Monerov. "They ordered me to."

"Ordered you to come here?"

Vaslav nodded.

"How can anybody order you to come here?" I asked.

Bilka wanted to answer, swayed, saw the bottle of Chivas and asked, "What's that? It doesn't matter . . . let me have some."

I poured a glass half full; he drank it all, then he sank down on one of the armchairs, wheezing, with all of us staring at him.

"Yes, yes. . . . How can anybody order me around like that?" But he was calming down. "You see, I love my brother. Only living relative. My wife loved him, too. Jan used to visit us in Vienna, or we visited him in Prague. He seduced my wife, goddamn him! But what could I do? I love him, the bastard!"

"Don't say that!" cried Irina.

Bilka looked up at her. "Well, wouldn't you say it was a lousy, filthy thing—running away?"

"He fled because he had to!" cried Irina. "You, as his brother, should understand that! But nobody here in the West understands it because they're all spoiled rotten!"

"Fled," said Jan Bilka's brother, and laughed angrily. "For years he let his country educate him, advance him, pay him, place him in the Defense Ministry—" He belched loudly. "And then he photographs the Warsaw Pact Nations' plans and runs and sells the plans to the Amis. . . ."

"That isn't true!" cried Irina. She looked at me. "Is it?"

I nodded. So now she knew. All right. Meanwhile, I had been trying to get to the recorder to turn it on. I stretched out my hand. "Don't touch it," said Monerov. "You're not going to turn it on. And you, Fräulein, listen carefully and you'll find out all there is to know about your fiancé."

"Yes," I said bitterly. "Now you'll find out, and we could have spared ourselves a lot." I looked in the direction of the bedroom.

Bilka's brother was looking at Irina. Now he said, "Your opinion, please, lady. Isn't my brother a bastard?"

Irina said nothing. Her lips trembled, her hands were fists.

"These two men, this morning in Munich—they told me everything. Showed me proof. No doubt about it. They told me, 'Go to Hamburg, Metropole Hotel. Talk to Herr Roland. Then we'll put your brother behind bars for twenty, thirty years. We'll jail him, but we won't kill him, which is what he deserves.'"

I opened my mouth to speak but closed it again.

"You were going to say, 'First we must have him,' weren't you, Herr Roland?" said Monerov.

I said nothing.

"You prefer to remain silent?" I looked at my watch. "You're looking at your watch. You're thinking: Jan Bilka arrived in Helsinki long ago. In half an hour he'll be on his way to New York. The Americans are protecting him and his second fiancée. Sorry, Fräulein Indigo."

"What do you mean? Helsinki? New York? For God's sake, tell me what it all means!" cried Irina.

Monerov smiled. "In a minute." He turned to me. "You are wondering how I know all this, aren't you?"

"Yes."

He looked at the table with the built-in radio. I ran over to it. With a pocket knife I ripped off the grill cloth, revealing the inside of the radio. The music went on playing. Then I saw it. "A microphone," I said idiotically. "So you know everything."

"Everything, Herr Roland," said Monerov. "Of course I wasn't in my suite all the time. I had a lot of other business in the city to attend to, as you can imagine. After all, we can't permit Herr Bilka to hand over our most important defense plans to the Americans after he steals them. I mean, that's understandable, surely. But when I wasn't there, somebody else was, listening to everything said here. And taping it. We're not stupid, Herr Roland. And we're not villains. Like Herr Jan Bilka. We can understand the Americans. They would understand us if the situation were reversed. As a matter of fact, I think even you understand us, Herr Roland."

"Yes," I said, in a low, hoarse voice.

"Well, I'm glad of that," said Monerov.

"Oh, God!" Irina sat down. Her robe fell open, baring her

thighs. She didn't notice it. She was crying softly.

"Who built in the—?" I interrupted myself. "The young electrician!"

"Yes, Herr Roland. The microphone wasn't working. Fortunately, the radio wasn't working either. And you yourself called in the electrician. Funny, isn't it? For a moment we in the next room thought all was lost. But then Felmar was able to repair it."

"Felmar?" The jackal suddenly was there. I picked up the bottle of Chivas and drank from it, drank a lot.

"Who is Felmar?" asked Irina.

"Ask Herr Roland," said Monerov. "I think he knows."

Yes. I knew.

"Felmar," I said, and noticed that my voice sounded dead. "Ludwig Felmar. War criminal. Responsible for the annihilation of the population of entire cities in Russia. Fled to Brazil. But he was found. You are talking about that Felmar, aren't you?"

"That's Papa Felmar," said Monerov. "But go on, Herr Roland. What else do you know?"

"That Felmar is to be extradited. The German government has asked for it, and Brazil has agreed . . . if the Bundesrepublik can produce sufficient evidence incriminating Felmar. So far the Bundesrepublik hasn't been able to do that. So Felmar is still in Brazil. I knew he had a son. Jürgen. His wife is dead. Committed suicide years ago."

"Jürgen grew up in various homes," says Monerov. "He's a good boy." He said it sincerely, without cynicism. "He's had a rough time—because he loves his father, just as Herr Vaslav Bilka here loves his brother Jan. That's the dreadful thing about love. Dostoevksy writes—"

"And you knew that young Felmar was working here in the Metropole?"

"Yes. A happy coincidence. We could have found someone else, but this was exceptionally favorable. Because you see, the incriminating material that your government lacks to get Papa Felmar extradited is in Moscow. We have it. And we've been asked to hand it over. So far we haven't done so. We're often asked, but we don't often give. You never know, do you? So we told Jürgen we'd keep the material and hand over nothing if he would help us. If he didn't help us, it was curtains for his father."

The drunken framemaker from Munich sprang to his feet suddenly and rushed over to me, grabbing me by both arms, and

I could smell his foul breath. "Don't write your story!" he cried. "That's what I'm supposed to tell you! That's what I've got to get out of you! If you write your story, my brother is a dead man! If you don't write your story—"

"And give us the tapes," said Monerov.

"—then all that will happen to Jan is that he'll go to jail. But he won't have to die! He'll be alive!"

I pushed Bilka away, because I couldn't stand the stench of his breath, and he fell back on his chair. I said, "You are the second person who insists that I shouldn't write this story. I take it you know all about that, too, Professor Monerov."

"Of course," said the Russian, friendly, friendly. "I heard what Mr. Largent had to say. And what he offered you. Herr Roland, you are an intelligent man. You can't believe that Largent was speaking only on behalf of this New York illustrated magazine." He turned to Irina and Bilka, who were staring at him, wide-eyed. "Everything depends on Herr Roland now. The Americans are offering him an incredible position if he doesn't write it. We are offering him nothing. We are merely promising that Jan Bilka will not die. In our case, the decision will therefore be a humane one." I had to laugh. "Don't laugh, Herr Roland. At a time like this, laughter is foolish. Is it the word *humane* that amuses you?"

"Yes," I said. "I find it very funny."

"That only goes to show how little humaneness you have left," said the Russian.

"For God's sake!" Bilka jumped up, but I managed to hold him at arm's length because he was trying to grab me again. "I implore you. I beg of you. I am ready to go down on my knees," and he actually did fall on his knees in front of me, wringing his hands. "Don't write it, Herr Roland! You will be responsible for the death of a man. Herr Roland! Herr Roland!"

He was clutching my knees now. I reached down and tore his hands away. He fell over and remained lying on the carpet, dead drunk and drooling. The radio was playing "Blue Skies."

"Why is it so important to you that this story isn't written?" asked Irina, who seemed utterly confused.

"Well, you see," said Monerov, "there are things that have an upsetting effect on people. And that isn't good. It's bad for peace. A story like this, if it reaches people who know nothing about it—" He stopped because the telephone rang. I stared but I didn't move. "Take the call," said Monerov.

I walked over to the phone like a marionette, a robot, and picked up the receiver. Just as clearly as if he had been standing beside me I heard Bertie's voice. "Walter, is that you?"

"Yes," I said. "But why are you calling here? You're not supposed—where are you?"

"Helsinki!" He sounded out of breath.

"And?"

"So wait a minute. I'm calling to tell you about it. Listen!"

I listened. After the first sentence I had the feeling that Muhammed Ali—at least—had hit me full force below the belt. I couldn't stand; I actually doubled up and sank down on the couch. The receiver slipped from my hand onto the carpet. I could hear Bertie, still talking. Slowly, laboriously, I picked up the receiver and held it to my ear. "What's the matter? Are you still there, Walter?"

"Yes," I said. "I'm here. Go on, Bertie."

And he went on talking.

11

The Pan Am flight had made up its earlier delay and was arriving on time, at 10:30 P.M. Bertie was traveling first class, and Jan Bilka, his blond girl friend, and Michelsen were sitting five rows ahead of him. Seven men were sitting beside him and in the rows in front and back. These seven men had brought Bilka and his girl friend to the airport, a solid bodyguard. In Fuhlsbüttel they had walked as closely as possible to Bilka and the girl, forming a tight circle around them. A few had their right hands in the opening of their jackets. Bertie was sure they were wearing shoulder holsters and were equipped to shoot at the least sign of interference.

But there was no interference, neither in Fuhlsbüttel nor during the flight. The men didn't speak to Bilka and his girl friend, nor to Michelsen; and the three didn't have much to say to each other, either. Nobody wanted dinner. The members of the bodyguard kept looking around and took turns walking slowly through the plane, including tourist class. The plane was three-quarters full. Couples. Young people. Various foreigners. Nobody Bertie knew.

The plane landed on the runway and taxied slowly up to the airport building. Both exit doors were opened, the gangways were let down, the passengers left the plane. Bertie saw that Bilka, the girl, Michelsen, and the seven men remained seated. They evidently wanted to be the last to leave the plane. He walked to the first-class exit and down the gangway. A strong, cold north wind was blowing. A big black car was parked next to the plane with two men in the front seats.

What I am about to write was told to me by Bertie that night, on the plane—not in such detail, of course; that came later. And he didn't experience all of what he told personally; some of the information came from third persons. For instance, he knew when he called me, but not at the time, that the big limousine was armored and its windows were bulletproof. And it had running boards, like the cars of prominent statesmen, for the use of security officers.

Bertie walked slowly toward the main building, looking carefully around him all the way. But Bilka and his entourage still hadn't left the plane. Several planes were standing in front of the building, also in front of hangars and farther off, on the runways that led to the various takeoff points. Bertie saw a huge cargo plane that had just been unloaded. Heavy pieces of agricultural equipment were standing around it. They had been carried in the belly of the plane and been rolled out on a wide metal ramp. Bertie noted that the cargo plane belonged to a Polish airline. A Yugoslav Boeing was just taking off on one of the runways.

Bertie turned around again and saw Bilka, the girl, and Michelsen in the doorway of the plane, about to exit. The seven men were ahead of and behind them. Now all of them had their hands in their jackets and were looking cautiously all around them, but nothing untoward happened.

Bertie, who was familiar with the Helsinki airport, knew that the exit for cars with permission to drive up to a plane was situated beside the cargo area. He limped to the main building, shouldered his way rudely through the passengers waiting in line, showed his passport, didn't bother to claim his duffel bag—he could do that later—ran out of the building, and hailed a taxi. It drove up, Bertie got in beside the driver. "Do you speak German?"

"Yes," said the driver, a big fellow with blond hair and very white skin. He was wearing a leather jacket. Bertie handed him two one-hundred mark bills. "What's that for?"

"Drive over to the cargo area. A big black car is going to drive out of the gate any minute now. I have to follow it. But you've got to be clever about it. They're not to notice."

"Police?" asked the driver.

"Press," said Bertie, and showed his card.

"I don't usually ask questions," said the driver. "If I'm paid well, I'll do anything I'm asked to do, as long as it's not illegal."

"Nothing illegal about this," said Bertie, and wondered what the man would consider illegal and refuse to do. What luck to have found him!

He turned out to be an excellent driver. He parked beside the gate but behind a truck, and turned off his lights. A few minutes later Bertie could hear the big gate being opened. The armored car emerged. Five men were standing on the running boards; the other two were in the limousine with Bilka, the girl, Michelsen, and the two men who had been in the car originally. The limousine stopped.

Two smaller cars now emerged from an open warehouse building. The men on the running boards got into them, three into the first car, two into the second, and the small convoy began to move, the limousine between the two cars.

"Wait a minute!" said Bertie.

"Of course. I'm not an idiot!"

Bertie took a picture of the three cars as they drove around the rotary in front of the airport building and from there turned into a street that led to the city. "Now!" said Bertie.

A few other taxis and private cars that had been parked in front of the main building began to move, too. There was quite a lot of traffic. But the taxi driver turned out to be a genius. He soon caught up with the small convoy, which was driving faster now on the highway to the city, always managing to keep a car or two between them and himself. And he really didn't ask any questions.

They drove past stretches of water, with the moon reflected in them, and some woodland. The highway led to the center of Helsinki—Bertie recognized it—but the convoy evidently didn't want to enter the city, because the three cars suddenly turned right into the Eläintarhantie. To the right were woods; to the left, the sea. The night was so bright that Bertie's driver turned off his lights. "Pretty lonely out here," he said. "They might notice us."

"Here," said Bertie, handing the driver another hundred-mark bill.

Now they were driving along Runeberginkatu. To Bertie's

surprise, the three-car column turned sharply onto a street that led to the Hietaranto Beach. Here very wealthy people owned bungalows or houses set far apart. "Stop here!" Bertie told the driver. "Wait for me. It's too desolate. I'll have to do the rest on foot."

"That's all right with me," said the driver. He had been chewing gum all the time and couldn't have been calmer.

Bertie got out. The north wind hit him full force as he limped down Eteläinen Hesperiankatu, the street that led to the beach. He could see the three cars driving on a narrow lane between the dunes in the direction of a row of elegant bungalows, and he threw himself on the ground behind some thick, windblown bushes. He took out his binoculars.

The convoy stopped in front of a dark-wood bungalow standing on fenced-in property. For a while nothing happened. Finally all the occupants of the cars, except Michelsen and the girl, got out. The men guarding Bilka stood in a circle around him. Bertie could see that they were holding automatics in their hands; this included the two men who had been waiting in the limousine. They took Bilka between them. Bertie decided they had to be the American colleagues of the men in Hamburg, stationed in Helsinki, where they probably knew their way around.

A light was on over the entrance to the bungalow. The garden gate opened automatically. Bilka, the two men from the limousine and two of the men from Hamburg, walked across the sand and stone to the bungalow. The remaining men stood motionless in the moonlight. They looked around them constantly, standing back to back, and all of them held their weapons ready. Bertie took a few pictures but didn't think he'd get anything.

The door of the bungalow opened. A man stood in the doorway. He wore his hair long, like a hippie. Everybody walked into the bungalow and the door was closed. The wind changed suddenly, and Bertie could hear the noise of the surf. He waited five minutes.

Of course, he had no idea at the time of what was going on in the bungalow during those five minutes. However, since he found out about it just before he called me, I can record it here.

The man with the long hair greeted Bilka. This was his friend in Helsinki—a painter. He led his visitors through a large living room with a fire burning in the fireplace, into a big studio. He

417

knelt down and opened the bottom drawer of a bureau with prints, lithographs, and watercolor sketches in it. The scene was grotesque—easels everywhere, finished and unfinished paintings leaning against the walls, palettes, tubes of paint, brushes, bottles of turpentine, stretched canvases—chaos! And standing in the middle of it all, four silent men with automatic pistols, a pale Czech, and a nervous painter rummaging around in a bureau drawer. At last he found what he had hidden—two aluminum containers, the kind microfilm is stored in. They were about as long as a little finger and were three centimeters in diameter. The painter handed them to Bilka.

Bilka gave them to one of the men from the armored car. With his colleague he walked over to a strong light that was hanging from the ceiling. Together they opened the containers, took the films out of them one at a time, and held them up to the light. With a magnifying glass, they examined the films; what they saw seemed to satisfy them. The driver of the armored car, who apparently was in charge of the expedition, sat down for a moment and carefully put the films back into their containers. Then he gave them to his colleague. Bilka shook the painter's hand. The latter accompanied his visitors to the door.

Bertie, lying in the wildly windswept bushes, saw the door of the bungalow open again and a man come out, holding his gun. A second man followed him, a third, a fourth, finally Bilka. The men surrounded him and they all walked through the garden again, to their cars. Bertie jumped to his feet and ran as fast as he could to his waiting taxi. "They'll be here any minute," he said.

The driver nodded, started his car, backed into a dark driveway, and stopped. A few minutes later the three cars drove past them, moving fast. The driver waited a moment, then followed the convoy, his lights out.

They drove back to the airport the way they had come. Soon they were joined by other cars and got into some heavy traffic. Bertie's driver put on his lights; when they reached the airport rotary, he put them out again. The three cars drove up to the cargo area, the gate was opened again, and the three cars passed through. The gate closed behind them.

"Stop!" said Bertie. The driver stopped, Bertie got out and limped through the wind to the gate and stared at the airfield. What were they going to do now? Wait out there until the midnight plane left for New York? Evidently, thought Bertie, and then, alarmed suddenly: Evidently not!

What happened next, happened fast.

The armored car, which had been driving between the other two, suddenly broke away and sped in the direction of the takeoff runway. Bertie could see the men in the smaller cars chasing after it. Again and again Bertie could see the fire from their pistols. Not very effective, he thought, to shoot at an armored car. The limousine drove on at high speed without returning fire.

The two chasing cars streaked across the runways. Suddenly they collided. One of the gas tanks exploded. A gigantic orange flame shot up into the sky. Bertie saw the men staggering out of their cars and running to safety.

Immediately all the floodlights outside the airport building were turned on. Sirens howled, firetrucks roared, and all in brilliant lighting. Bertie took pictures. Meanwhile the armored car had sped on. Where was it going? Then Bertie saw where it was heading. The huge Polish cargo plane was standing on the takeoff runway, its navigation lights blinking, its engines running, ready to take off. As the car came closer, the loading ramp was lowered, the car drove up the ramp and disappeared in the belly of the plane, and the jet engines began to whine. There'll be men in there, thought Bertie, anchoring the car.... Slowly, then faster and faster, the heavy plane took off. Now it was airborne and the pilot began the ascent. The jet's exhaust spewed out a black cloud as the plane rose higher and higher, until it was very small and banking to the left.

The first fire truck had reached the burning car. They began to smother it with foam. The men who had jumped out of the cars were screaming at each other and gesticulating wildly; then they all ran over to the control tower.

12

Bertie, limping badly, got out of the elevator and walked down a passage to the main office in the control tower. The area was closed to unauthorized people; but in the general panic following the explosion, Bertie managed to get through.

The passage was empty. There were a lot of doors. He heard a noise and turned around fast. He was standing beside a toilet. He opened the door, walked into one of the booths, and locked himself in. Almost immediately he heard the voices of two men, talking excitedly in Finnish as they passed by the toilet door. And after that—Bertie always was a lucky guy, especially when he was working—he could distinctly hear voices through the toilet wall. He pressed his ear against it. A loud conversation was going on in the next room. Several men—Bertie was able to distinguish five voices—were talking in English. American English. They must be four of the Amis I followed, he decided, and one more, somebody with a deep voice—who must have stayed behind, because now he was letting the others tell him what had happened.

"Jim . . . over in the control room. He's going crazy. Telephoning to everyone he can think of. Insisting that they've got to send up fighters to stop the transport!"

The deep voice: "I know. Take it easy. I told him to do it."

"But he needs Defense Department permission for that, Pete."

So Pete was the one with the deep voice. Now he said, "Yes. So?"

"And Defense isn't going to go along with us. An East bloc plane! In Finland!"

"We've got to do everything we possibly can," said Pete. "It's only a hundred and fifty kilometers to the Russian border. Even if we got the order, it'd be much too late."

"But what's driving me up the wall, Pete—what are the chances we have a Judas?"

"What makes you think that?"

"Well, look: There aren't only Bilka and Michelsen and his girl in that armored car. Four of our boys are in it, too. Two from here and two from Hamburg. All of them rats? What do you suppose they got paid for it? What do you—?"

"Idiot!" Pete's voice, harsh now. Then friendly again: "Sorry, Wally. I forgot you weren't there when they announced it."

"Announced what?"

"Some Finnish motorist found two men, bound and gagged, behind a hedge alongside the road. They were your two friends from Helsinki."

"Shit!"

"Yes, shit! They were the original drivers of the armored car."

"But how—?"

"They say they suddenly saw a child lying in the road on their way to the airport. They'd been sent out alone because more cars might have attracted too much attention. So . . . they saw the child and got out. . . ."

"Idiotic!"

"Criminal negligence!"

"Don't be unreasonable. They thought it was an accident. And of course that was just what the Russians were waiting for."

"Naturally."

"They say the men were Russians. Brilliantly selected to pass as Americans. Not a trace of an accent. Dressed like Americans and fully briefed. Knocked our men unconscious, took their papers, guns, ID cards. Tied them up, hid them behind the hedge, and drove to the airport in our limousine."

"And the child?"

"The child's fine. Had been told to lie there. A car took him away."

"Those goddamn' bastards!"

"It's fantastic! Simply fantastic! And we never noticed a thing! Never doubted them for a moment! I spoke to both of them."

"So did I!"

"So did I!"

"Well, there you are," said Pete. "You didn't know each other. That was our mistake. Somebody must have told the Russians what plane you were taking, how many of you there would be, that Bilka was going to lead you to the place—everything."

"So those were two *Russians* who drove the car onto the plane!"

"Don't tell me you've just caught on!"

"Just a minute! Besides the two Russians and Bilka and his girl and this guy Michelsen two of our men from Hamburg were in that car, too. What about them?"

Pete's voice: "The captain of the cargo plane radioed right after takeoff that nothing was going to happen to them. The Russians overpowered them, the crew helped. They're being taken along as hostages."

"But then what Jim's trying to do is nonsense! To force them to land with fighter planes."

"He has to try. You know what's at stake."

"But they'll kill our men!"

"The Russian captain's threatened us with just that. As soon as he sights the first fighter. Otherwise they'll send our two men

421

back as soon as they've landed. On the condition that nobody tries to stop them. A shitty situation, granted. But headquarters has told us to try—"

The noise of a door opening and a new voice, raging, "It's all over! Finished! Finished, fuck it!"

"Calm down, Joe. What's finished?"

"Here. Take a look at these films. Here! And here! One of the Russians took the containers from the painter, and gave them to me. But he took them back to put the films inside again. That's when he must have switched films!"

"Oh, God!"

"I'll be damned!"

"These films are from a report on the last NATO maneuvers!"

"I can't believe it!"

"And Bilka's films?"

"With the Russians, of course. In the transport."

"God Almighty! We've made asses of ourselves!"

"Let's take this again," said Pete, "and more slowly this time. Now what exactly took place in the bungalow? How did this exchange of films take place? Slowly, please. And in detail...."

13

"So they told Pete the whole story all over again, in detail this time, and I listened. That's why I can tell you all about it now."

Bertie's voice in my ear. I was seated on the couch, listening to his report. Monerov, Bilka's brother, and Irina were standing motionlessly around me, like figures from Madame Toussaud's. The man who called himself Monerov was smiling. And he was still holding his gun.

I had taken several drinks from the bottle while Bertie was telling his story, now I drank again. "Go on," I told Bertie.

"Well, I got away as fast as I could. And telephoned you. I still have the same driver. He'll do anything for me. Says he'll drive me to the first early-morning plane to Hamburg. By the way, this is for laughs: The driver isn't a Finn. He's Norwegian. A Norwegian communist. Your dear Fräulein Louise—"

"Shut up!" I said. A Norwegian. A Norwegian communist in Helsinki! "Come back as fast as you can," I said. The receiver almost slipped out of my hands, they were sweating so.

"The Russians have Jan?" Irina's voice was a whisper.

"Yes. And his girl. And Michelsen."

Bilka's brother groaned.

"You see—" Monerov began, when suddenly the door was opened and Jules Cassin came tearing into the room. He was wearing a hat and coat over his uniform. He didn't look at any of us, only at Monerov. "Everything's in order, Jossif," he cried. "The plane must be over Soviet territory now. Will be landing in a few minutes. There's nothing more we can do here. Let's go!"

Monerov gave him the gun. "I'll pack my things. Be back in a minute," and he ran out of the room.

I got up and walked over to Jules. "You bastard!" I said. "You're working for the Russians!"

"Oh . . . you've caught on! Didn't take you long," said Jules Cassin, raising his gun as I approached. "Stay where you are. Don't think for a moment that I wouldn't put a bullet through you."

"You—you—" But I stood still. "You were assigned to sound me out for—for that!" I pointed to the microphone in the radio, which was still playing soft music. "You were given the assignment to keep me here—"

"Clever, clever!" said Jules. "Congratulations!"

"And Seerose? Who saved your life? Or isn't that true either?"

"Saved my life?" Jules spat and swore in French. "*Merde!* Repayment, that's all! I got him out of a prisoner-of-war camp in '45. And got him his license. But my family—all of them—died in that damn' war! Bombed. Or in the Resistance. Or in concentration camps. I hate all Germans!"

"Forever and a day, yes?"

"Forever and a day—yes!" His face was filled with rage. "You asked me why I was still a waiter at my age. Why I don't have the bar of my own I wanted."

"Yes."

"*Alors* . . . I married a German woman. Thought there should be an end to all this hatred. So what did she do, my sweet little German wife? Deceived me! Lied to me! Said I was too old! And then, when I'd saved enough money to buy a bar, she stole it and ran off with another man. An American. Good friends today—the Americans and the French. But not of mine!" His eyes

423

were blazing. "I'm going to leave this country and find work somewhere else, and I'm never coming back! Never!"

"I understand."

Monerov came back with a small suitcase. He had on a hat and coat now, too. "You won't get far," I told him. "You'll be arrested."

"Oh, no," said Monerov. "In five minutes we'll have disappeared and nobody will find us." He picked up a heavy candlestick and smashed the telephone with it, and the panel with the buttons to call for the waiter, maid, and valet. He went into the bedroom and bathroom and smashed every means of outside communication. At last he came back.

Bilka ran up to him. He had been drinking steadily all the time I had been telephoning and by now was out of his mind. He babbled, "My brother, my brother! What will happen to him now? I don't believe you! I don't believe you'll let my brother live if Herr Roland doesn't write his story!"

"You don't have to," said Monerov.

"What—what do you mean?"

"Now that we have Bilka, Herr Roland can do whatever he likes. Write . . . not write . . . we don't care. That was only a little precautionary measure, in case we didn't succeed in kidnapping your brother. But we succeeded."

"So . . . are you going to kill Jan?"

"Not yet. We need him to get the rest of the film, in New York."

"And when he has told you where they are . . . when you have them, too . . . what—what will you do with Jan then?"

"What do you suppose we'll do?"

Bilka went for him. Jules Cassin struck the drunken man with the butt of his gun, and he sank to the floor, groaning.

"So," said Monerov. "I'm sorry about having to lock you in here, but I'm sure they'll find you soon. Pound on the door. Shout. All we need is time to get out of the hotel, and that won't take long." He ran out of the suite; Jules Cassin followed him, walking backwards. Then we heard him double-lock the door.

When they were gone, nobody moved. It was as if all of us had died. And then, very slowly at first but growing louder, we heard the melody of "Reigen" again, coming from the damaged radio.

At that moment Vaslav Bilka shrieked wildly and staggered across to the French window that led out onto the balcony. It all happened so fast, there was nothing I could do. He tore aside the

424

curtain; the glass door behind it was ajar. He opened it wide. I saw him walk out onto the balcony, teeter on the balustrade; then I heard him shout, "Jan!" as he let himself fall from my balcony on the fourth floor into the depths below.

Irina turned her back and buried her face on my shoulder. We could hear Bilka's body landing at the bottom with a sickening thud. Irina's fingers were clutching my jacket like claws. I could feel her nails go through the material, sharp on my skin. And the "Reigen" sounded sad, yet so beautiful....

6

Imprimatur

1

"She is a traitor ... a traitor...."

"She is a sinner ... a sinner...."

"She has betrayed us ... betrayed us...."

Voices, loud threatening voices, coming from every side of the dark night in Alster Park, voices Fräulein Louise didn't recognize. Male and female. Yes, female, too. What was going on? What was going to happen to her? She hurried back and forth between the paths, across the wet grass, panting, panic-stricken, holding her umbrella over her head.

"Disaster ... disaster...."

"Misery ... more and more misery...."

"It's her fault ... her fault ... her fault...."

"Because she betrayed us ... betrayed us...."

"Because she was arrogant ... arrogant...."

"Corrupt ... corrupt...."

"Because she doesn't know love ... love ... love...."

"Because she interfered ... interfered ... interfered...."

"Who are you?" Fräulein Louise cried. "I don't know you. I never heard your voices before! Go away! Come to me, my friends!"

But the dreadful voices only grew louder. They seemed to come from the treetops, from behind every bush. "False friends!" The strident voice of a woman.

"False friends ... false friends...." A chorus of men's voices. "Revenge!" A male voice, bellowing. Fräulein Louise began to tremble.

"Retribution!" shouted another.

"Death!" screeched a woman's voice.

"Damnation ... damnation...."

Fräulein Louise leaned against the trunk of a tree. She was utterly exhausted. Rain and tears were pouring down her face. Her boots sank into the wet grass. Terrified of me, she had left our suite, hurried to the elevator, and gone down to the lobby, her one thought to get away from the hotel.

Everything had gone wrong. She hadn't found Karel's

murderer; she hadn't been able to persuade Irina to come with her. She had failed. Failedfailedfailed! The fragile net of faith in her friends, which had prevented her from breaking down for years, was tearing . . . here. . . .

She knew that my suite faced the Alster. She wanted to look up at my window and pray, pray that there might still be a miracle and that her friends would help her, at least to bring back Irina. She stumbled through the dark. She looked up at the hotel with its many windows and balconies. Which was my window? My balcony? She didn't know. Most of the curtains were drawn, only a few windows showed light. She stood in the rain, staring up at the facade and was desperate. And that was when she began to hear these strange voices all around her.

"There she is. . . ."

"It's all over . . . all over. . . ."

"Doesn't know what to do . . . do . . . do. . . ."

"They threw her out . . . out . . . out. . . ."

The voices were scornful, malicious, and cruel, cruel, cruel! And they grew worse. They began to berate her, insult her, threaten her. "Liar! Liar!" And as she cried out to her friends, she could hear a new chorus of voices, male and female.

"We're not your friends . . . not your friends. . . ."

"Because you blasphemed . . . blasphemed. . . ."

It barely registered with Fräulein Louise that these voices were speaking to her in the third and second person. Everything was all mixed up. The systems of thought in her brain collapsed, bit by bit. She began to run across the wet grass to the street. But the voices accompanied her wherever she went.

"Now she's running . . . running. . . ."

"Chase her! Chase her!"

"We're behind you . . . behind you. . . ."

"See her runrunrun . . . she's going to fall!"

Fräulein Louise stumbled over the root of a tree and fell.

"There she lies. . . ."

"In the dirt. . . ."

"Where she belongs. . . ."

"Get up!" A man's voice.

Fräulein Louise struggled to her feet and fled on.

"Now she's fleeing . . . fleeing. . . ."

"But we'll get her . . . get her. . . ."

"Destroy her . . . destroy her. . . ."

And then, a monstrous voice, like thunder from heaven: "Revenge is mine!"

430

Fräulein Louise fell on her knees and folded her hands. "The dear Lord," she whispered, "is speaking to me."

"No!" screamed a woman's voice. "It isn't the dear Lord! The dear Lord doesn't speak to sinners!"

Fräulein Louise jumped to her feet and hurried on, dragging her umbrella behind her, her heavy bag dangling from her arm, wet through now, and dirty. And then a wonderfully gentle voice said, "God's mercy is everywhere...."

But there was no respite. Three voices bellowed in unison, "Now we've got her!"

Fräulein Louise ran as fast as she could to the street with its lights, but the voices were after her. "We shall follow you... follow you...."

"We shall punish you... punish you...."

"Away! Away from here... back to the moor... the moor...."

"It's your fault... your fault...."

"You interfered in our plans... our plans...."

I betrayed my friends, I trusted false friends.... Thoughts like this were coursing through Fräulein Louise's tortured brain. And the voices continued to torment her, even when she got to Harvestehuder Weg, where there were people and cars and normal voices and sounds. They only served to frighten Fräulein Louise even more, because they mingled with the terrifying voices from the park and created an uproar in which she could make out single voices.... "Now! The time has come...."

Without realizing what she was doing, she ran across the street. A car just missed her, the driver blowing his horn wildly. The cars, she thought, shaking with fright. They're hunting me with cars. They're signaling with strange lights and their signals are aimed at me. At me....

The cars drove by, their tires swishing in the rain. Fräulein Louise stumbled on, bumped into pedestrians, almost fell, caught herself. And then she heard a voice, a voice she knew: "I shall protect you!"

It was the voice of the former SS leader Wilhelm Reimers. Involuntarily she raised one arm. A car stopped. "Where do you want to go, lady?" asked a man, leaning out of the car window. A taxi.

"To—to the train station," stammered Fräulein Louise, opened the back door, and fell into the seat. The taxi drove off.

2

In the taxi the misery went on.

"She thinks she can get away from us!"

"She'll never get away from us...never...."

A glass window separated her from the driver. He couldn't hear a thing. "Who are you?" groaned Fräulein Louise. "I don't know you."

"You know us...."

"But we don't want you anymore."

"We're abandoning you...abandoning you...."

The taxi arrived at the station. Fräulein Louise handed the driver a bill through the opening in the glass and jumped out of the car. "Just a minute! That's much too much!" yelled the driver. But Fräulein Louise didn't hear him. She hurried into the station where she had met the former SS man. A lot of people. Standing around and walking back and forth. A loudspeaker. She only caught a word here and there. "Train...leaves for Bremen...a few minutes...track four...." And there they were again, the dreadful voices! But now they were the voices of the people in the station. Everybody was staring at her, talking about her, calling out to her.

"There she goes! The old lady—"

"—who did everything wrong!"

"—who sinned!"

Fräulein Louise held one hand over her face, and people finally were staring at her as she ran, as if hunted—dirty, disoriented, her white hair disheveled. She had lost her little hat.

"Look at her run!"

"Because she wanted to do everything herself!"

"Because she betrayed God...betrayed God...."

"She is an outcast...an outcast...."

Fräulein Louise had bought a return ticket. Miraculously her crazed eyes and trembling fingers found it in her bag. She handed it to the conductor at the gate and hurried down the stairs. Below her she could see a train coming in. And now she could hear voices again, but this time voices she knew . . . oh, what bliss! What incredible relief! The voice of the Russian. "Louise . . . come to us in the moor. . . ."

The voice of the Jehovah's Witness: "Come quickly . . . quickly . . . before it is too late!"

And then again, the strident voice of a woman: "There she is! Running down the steps! Go after her . . . after her. . . ."

Louise ran down the steps as fast as she could. She was at the end of her strength.

"She tried to play God . . . play God. . . ."

"She must be humbled . . . humbled. . . ."

"But you told me yourselves that I should do it!" she screamed, as she finally reached the platform . . . and people turned around to stare at her.

The voices answered scornfully, "We didn't . . . we didn't. . . ."

"The false ones did that . . . the false ones. . . ."

Fräulein Louise didn't know how she got on the train to Bremen. Her memory failed her. The next thing she remembered was that the train was moving past many lights, and over bridges and silver-gray water with the rain beating down on it. She came to her senses slowly. The voices, the dreadful voices were silent. For the present.

A pretty, heavily made-up, rather vulgar young woman in a fur coat was sitting opposite her, watching her curiously. Fräulein Louise looked at her, her eyes still full of fear.

3

"Why are you trembling?" asked the pretty young woman in the fur coat. She had a high voice that sounded as if she were astonished; she seemed to be good-natured and simpleminded. "Are you cold?"

"No," said Fräulein Louise.

She was exhausted, her feet hurt, she felt like someone who had just had a serious heart attack. These voices . . . those terrible voices. . . . At least they were quiet now. But they could come back any minute. She shivered.

"What's the matter?" asked the pretty young woman in the fur coat in her baby voice.

"Nothing . . . nothing. . . ." mumbled Fräulein Louise.

"But you're so excited!"

The train was moving fast now, the lights had been left behind, the rain was beating against the window. Fräulein Louise had passed a hand across her forehead and saw that she was dirty. With trembling fingers she opened her heavy bag to find a handkerchief. The pretty woman stared at the bundles of money. She watched Fräulein Louise clean her face and run a comb through her hair. "Excited?" said Fräulein Louise. "Yes. I am excited."

"But why?"

"Oh . . . I've been through a lot. Horrible things. And it's not over yet."

"What's not over yet?" asked the pretty woman. "By the way, my name is Flaxenberg. Inge Flaxenberg. But everybody calls me Bunny. You don't want to tell me your name?"

"Oh, yes," said Fräulein Louise. "I don't mind. My name is Gottschalk. Louise. Everybody calls me Fräulein Louise."

"So what's not over yet, Fräulein Louise?" asked Bunny Flaxenberg.

"They're after me," Fräulein Louise said simply and still somewhat stupefied. "They're pursuing me."

Bunny half closed her eyes. "The police—right?"

Fräulein Louise didn't answer. Bunny took this to be assent. "The pigs! Just because one's managed to do a little business on the side, right?"

"I must get to my friends," mumbled Fräulein Louise.

And so each went on talking. . . .

"They raised us tonight, too," said Bunny. "The bandits!"

"They'll protect me," murmured Fräulein Louise.

"Came tearing into the casino and behaved like animals," said Bunny. "I worked in a casino. Small place. About thirty kilometers from Hamburg." She gave its name. "Was a dive, but Herr Olbers rebuilt it and arranged for bus service, so people from Hamburg could come. They came in their own cars, too . . . roulette."

"If I can just get home . . . I still have a chance."

"Just roulette. Everything worked out fine. For two years. I worked at the bar. Made good money. Lived there, too. My home is in Zeven. Sometimes I'd go there for a visit. Or my fiancé came to see me."

"Once I get there, maybe they'll leave me in peace and my friends will help me," murmured Fräulein Louise.

"And then the pigs had to come! Said the game was rigged. Magnets under one table."

"What?" asked Fräulein Louise, startled suddenly.

"Magnets. Under the wheel. To manipulate the ball, you understand?"

"No."

"Confiscated everything. Arrested Herr Olbers. Closed the casino. The damn' cops. Just because they found a magnet under one wheel. And in spite of the fact that Herr Olbers swore by the life of his mother that he'd known nothing about it. What do you think of that?"

"They're after me," mumbled Fräulein Louise, who was on the verge of falling asleep from exhaustion.

"My fiancé is meeting me in Bremen with his car. Where are you going?"

"To Neurode."

"*That's* where you have friends?"

"Yes."

"You know what—my fiancé will drive you there. It's no distance from Zeven. And you've got to disappear fast, right?"

"Yes. Fast." Fräulein Louise was half-asleep.

"Well, then that's settled. We'll get you there. Must stick together, mustn't we?" said Bunny Flaxenberg. "Against the goddamn' pigs! The other wheel was perfectly all right. Somebody who had it in for Herr Olbers must have installed that magnet. Somebody who wanted to bust him. Some bastard! That's what I told the police. Do you think they believed me? They laughed at me! The business was doing *so* well, too. Herr Olbers would have been crazy to put in a magnet. But you can't reason with those guys. They're pigs, dumb pigs!"

She could see that Fräulein Louise's head was dropping forward and that the old woman was asleep. Quietly Bunny Flaxenberg closed Fräulein Louise's bag with all that money in it. "And now I can look for another job," she said. Fräulein Louise heard the words in her sleep. The train was moving fast.

4

"Nobody knows where I . . ." Fräulein Louise hesitated. How did it go—the beautiful poem? She couldn't remember. "Under the stars, under the moon." No, that was wrong. She sought desperately for the right words. They didn't come. And that was sad. Step by step she made her way along the narrow path that led onto the moor between bulrushes and water holes, to the knoll with the fog swirling around it. She felt dreadful and so weak. Her feet were smarting. She was short of breath and very unsteady. Every now and then she swayed. Never before had she found it so difficult to walk along this path. But she had to! She had to get to the little knoll out there. She had to get to her friends. That was the only place on earth where she would be safe. . . .

She had fallen asleep in the train. Just before reaching Bremen the nice young woman who had said everybody called her Bunny had wakened her. Bunny's fiancé had been waiting on the platform—a silent, tall, very good-looking man. He had taken Bunny's suitcase and introduced himself as Armin Kienholz, and been very cordial after Bunny had told him about Fräulein Louise's trouble and the danger she was in.

"Of course you may come with us," said Kienholz. "And you can trust us. We won't say a word. We never saw you. Have no idea who you are if anybody asks us."

"Thank you very much," said Fräulein Louise.

Kienholz drove an American car. He drove fast and well. Fräulein Louise sat in the back and dozed, while Bunny, sitting in the front beside her fiancé, went on and on about the goddamned pigs who had closed down the casino. And Fräulein Louise kept hearing the word "magnet," and didn't know what they were talking about. What kind of magnet? Didn't matter. She had met two friendly people, and the dreadful voices that had tortured her were silent. Fräulein Louise felt faint. There was only one thing on her mind: to get out on the moor, to the knoll, to her friends. . . .

They passed through Zeven, and Kienholz proceeded on the

miserable road to Neurode. Just before they got there, Fräulein Louise asked him to stop. "I'd like to get out here, please."

"Very good, Fräulein Louise," Kienholz said politely, and stopped. He and Bunny shook hands with Fräulein Louise. "Are they reliable friends, the ones you've got here?" asked Bunny.

"The best."

"Well, then, good luck," said handsome Herr Kienholz.

He drove into the village to make the turn to go back and his car came by again almost immediately. As he passed Fräulein Louise he blew his horn three times; she waved.

She watched the car until its red taillight had disappeared; then she walked carefully out into the reeds to where the narrow path began, the path she was balancing on now. The moon was shining brightly, the cloud ceiling had broken up, and it wasn't raining anymore. The bare birches were silvery in the moonlight and a lone swamp owl cried, "*Bu-bu-bu-bu. . . .*"

Fräulein Louise slipped. She almost fell into the swamp but managed to regain her balance and hurried on, on her swollen feet. She couldn't wait to get to the knoll, which she could see dimly now, as if floating in fog. There lay her salvation—there she would be safe from the cruel, horrifying voices. Her friends would have to help her now, protect her, and explain everything to her, because she didn't understand anything anymore. She was utterly confused, desperate, and totally discouraged.

The knoll came nearer . . . nearer . . . a few ducks whirred up out of the water. "I'm coming!" cried Fräulein Louise. "I'm coming to you!" Then she stopped dead—because for a few seconds the wind had blown the clouds of fog away, and she could see the knoll clearly. And her eleven friends weren't standing on it, as they always had been. All she could see was eleven ugly, gnarled osier willows.

She rubbed her eyes. That's impossible! she thought. I'm not seeing properly! She looked at the knoll again, and again saw only the eleven osier willows.

"Oh, dear Savior!" whispered Fräulein Louise. "What does this mean?" But she hurried on, stumbling every now and then, teetering precariously, and it was a miracle that she managed to stay on the path. Now the knoll was shrouded in fog again.

"Dear God, dear God," she whispered. "Let them be there! Let my friends be there! They told me to come, didn't they? I heard them clearly. Please, please, Almighty God, let my friends be there!"

But Almighty God didn't hear her prayer, and when she was finally standing on the knoll, she found herself surrounded by eleven osier willows and wisps of fog.

"Where are you?" she cried, stumbling back and forth between the willows. "Where are you? Come! I beg of you—come to me!"

But her friends didn't come.

Fräulein Louise was panic-stricken. She screamed, "For the love of Jesus, come to me! I need you! I need you so much!" But all she could feel was the wind, and all she could see was the billowing fog, and all she could hear was the swamp owl's cry. And her friends didn't come, not one.

Now she was standing on the edge of the knoll, which sloped down here, to the moor. I don't understand, she thought. I don't understand anything anymore. Why don't they come? What has happened? And just then she heard it, coming out of the fog, again the strident voice of a woman. "There she stands, the accursed one!" And a murmur of men's voices, "Now we've got her!"

"No!" screamed Fräulein Louise, and stepped back in horror, and slipped. This time she lost her balance and fell into a deep dark water hole beside the knoll. Her bag sank with her.

She tried desperately to keep her head above the water, managed to grasp a root, lost it. Her head went under, came up again. She swallowed water, coughed, spat out what she could; and as she could feel mysterious forces trying to drag her down into the depths, down, down . . . as she fought for her life, flailing with her arms, trying to reach the root that could save her, she began to scream at the top of her lungs, "Help! Help! Where are you? Come to me! Help me! Help me!" But there they were again, the unbearable voices, roaring at her out of the fog, sounding like thunder in her ears, unendurable, horrible beyond belief. . . .

"Revenge!"

"Death!"

"Annihilation!"

"Help!" screamed Fräulein Louise, spitting out a mouthful of swamp water. "Help! Help!"

5

Chauffeur Kuschke sat up in bed, torn out of a dream he had often. It was early 1948 in his dream. He was living in Berlin and playing with his little girl, Helga; and his wife Frieda was sitting beside them in the courtyard of their apartment house, in the sun, knitting. Kuschke and Helga were putting on a great show and making Frieda laugh, little Helga was chortling with pleasure, and the three of them were so happy in the desolate, bombed-out city of Berlin, and Kuschke knew he was never going to be so happy again....

"Help! Help!"

"That—that's—" Kuschke jumped out of bed and into his slippers. He had recognized the voice at once. So now it's happened at last, damn it! He zipped up his overalls as he ran out the door of his room, and could see camp doctor Schiemann at the other end of the dimly lit passage, in a training suit, running toward her.

"Those screams—"

"Yes, *Herr Doktor*. It's our Fräulein, *Herr Doktor!*"

"Come on! Hurry!"

Both men rushed out into the night. They hadn't gone far when every floodlight in the camp was turned on. Two guards came running out of the barracks by the gate. The lights went on in several barracks, children in their nightclothes appeared, and some of the young people, boys and girls. They looked frightened and curious. Fräulein Louise's cries could be heard, coming from the moor, carried by the wind. "Help! Help!"

Pastor Demel came running out of his barracks. He had on a black suit, no tie, his shirt was open. "Our Fräulein!" he panted.

"Yes. But where?"

"I know where. On the little knoll with the eleven willows!" he yelled.

Camp director Dr. Horst Schall, in pants and shirt, his jacket still slung over his arm, came running. "We've got to get her!"

"How? There's no way out there!"

"Get ladders, boards, long poles! Quick!" cried Demel.

The men ran off and came back carrying ladders, dragging planks and poles to the northeast corner of the camp. Kuschke was helping the pastor with a long ladder. Now the young people left their barracks, their coats over their shoulders, calling out to each other excitedly—all of them running to the corner where the cement post had been torn up the night before. "We're coming! We're coming!" cried the camp director. "Hang on, Fräulein Louise! We're coming!"

"Help!" answered Fräulein Louise, but it sounded weaker.

Kuschke and the pastor reached the broken post. They tossed the ladder across the tilted fence and climbed up on it. The moon lit up the night. In the diffuse light caused by the fog, they could see the knoll every now and then, and something flailing around in the water below it. "There she is! Fallen in! Oh, good God. . . ."

Other men came running. "One of the poles! Quick!" cried Demel.

He jumped in first and sank fast, up to his waist, but he was able to shove the long ladder ahead of him. Then he pulled himself up and laid down on it and with the pole began to punt. The ladder with the man lying on it glided out into the moor in the direction of the knoll. Kuschke followed on a broad plank. He was punting, too, and cursing, and praying loudly. "Shit! Goddamn, shit! Save our poor Fräulein, Almighty God!"

Now there were five men in the swamp . . . six . . . eight . . . ten, all of them stretched out on ladders or planks, moving forward between the reeds and the water poles. "Help!" A soft cry now.

Kuschke turned around and saw the many people—social workers, young camp inmates—standing by the fence, watching the men floating forward on the moor. "Call for an ambulance," Kuschke shouted. "Call Zeven! They're to send an ambulance, fast! Just in case. I have the feeling—" And he could see one of the social workers run off.

Kuschke went on punting. His plank rocked under him, his legs were submerged. He swore, then prayed aloud again.

He and Pastor Demel reached the knoll at almost the same time, and Kuschke was horrified when he saw Fräulein Louise. Her face was distorted and she was deathly pale. She was clinging to a root, but her fingers were letting go and she was starting to sink, down, down. Kuschke jumped up on the knoll, the pastor after him, but he slipped and fell into the brackish water and swallowed quite a lot of it. He was dripping wet as

Kuschke—strong as a bear—fished him out. They lifted the ladder and Kuschke's plank half out of the water and laid them up against the knoll, their poles beside them. The camp director and the doctor were coming nearer. Kuschke and the pastor ran over to the water hole that Fräulein Louise had fallen into. Kuschke knelt down and said to the pastor, "Hang onto my feet." The pastor did. Kuschke, soaked through now, too, stretched out on his stomach and grabbed Fräulein Louise's hands. "Keep calm now, Fräulein Louise," he said. "Just try to keep calm. We're here."

He was shocked beyond belief when she shrieked in response, "Here they are! My tormentors! Here they are! Help! Help! Help!" and tried to wiggle out of his grasp.

Now the camp director stretched out beside Kuschke; Dr. Schiemann was holding onto his feet. Together the two men tried to drag Fräulein Louise out of the water by her hands, but she screamed as if demented, "Leave me! Leave me! Go away! You are the false ones, too!"

"But Fräulein Louise—"

"It's no use," said Schiemann, "she doesn't know us anymore."

"Doesn't know *me?*" from a thoroughly bewildered Kuschke.

"She doesn't know any of us," said Schiemann.

"Dear Jesus!" said Kuschke, "now she's really cracked up."

"Get ready—at three we pull her up," said Schiemann, between clenched teeth. He counted. When they got to three they used every ounce of strength they had to pull the waterlogged woman out, and succeeded, Fräulein Louise screaming at the top of her lungs and trying desperately to free herself. They dragged her, raving, up the knoll, her clothes, her hair, all dripping wet. Once on land she fought tooth and nail, literally. She kicked and bit and scratched and screamed. "Criminals! Murderers! Keep away from me! Help! Help!"

Kuschke grabbed her by the arms and turned her around, her back to him, and held her in an iron grip. The pastor came up to her. "Come to your senses, Fräulein Louise. Please, please *try*—" But he got no farther. With the face of a demon she looked at him out of crazed eyes, kicked him, and spat in the face of the man she had liked so much but whom she didn't recognize. "Monster!" she screamed. "Miserable persecutor!"

"Fräulein Louise—" stammered Demel, her saliva running down his face. But she only screamed louder, "They who take my name in vain shall be the first to be judged!"

"Oh, Lord, Lord, she thinks she's Jesus," said Kuschke, thoroughly unnerved now. He laid a hand over her mouth. To do that he had to let go of one of her arms. Immediately she struck out behind her and hit him in the stomach and bit his hand. "Ow!" Kuschke yelled. At that Fräulein Louise suddenly sank to the ground without uttering another sound. She had fainted.

6

She heard something whining. She didn't know that it was the siren of an ambulance in which she was lying. In the dim light she could see the shadowy figures of two big men. There they were! Now they had her! Now they were taking her to hell! "No!" she screamed. "I don't want to go to hell!"

"We can't do a thing," Dr. Schiemann explained to Pastor Demel. "It's no use. She's in a paranoiac state. Nothing to be done about it."

"Can't she be given something? I mean—"

"Not till we get to the clinic," said one of the orderlies, who was sitting behind Fräulein Louise. "We might do the wrong thing."

Fräulein Louise didn't hear these words right either. To her they sounded like, "There she lies. Now she can't get away from us anymore. . . . Now we shall pass judgment on her. . . ."

"Away! Away! I want to get away!" shouted Fräulein Louise, and tried to get up, until she realized she couldn't. Her hands and feet were strapped to the stretcher on which she was lying. "Lost! I'm lost! I am damned!"

The siren went on wailing and the ambulance sped through the night. It left the autobahn and soon after that arrived at the Ludwigskrankenhaus in Bremen. Fräulein Louise screamed and struggled against the restraints, she screamed until she had no more strength left, then she was quiet, but only for moments, after which she began to howl again, shouting, cursing, blaspheming.

The ambulance stopped in the courtyard of the psychiatric

442

clinic. The doors opened; two orderlies lifted the stretcher off the ambulance and wheeled it across the yard to Admissions and from there into a brightly lit room in which two night nurses and an intern were on duty. Here they finally put it down. Pastor Demel and Dr. Schiemann went along with them.

"Let me go, you devils, you dogs! Let me go! Help! Murder! Criminals!" screamed Fräulein Louise in a voice that no longer sounded like hers. The young doctor knelt beside the stretcher and tried to touch her, but she began to howl like an animal. He hesitated, afraid. He had only been here a few weeks. One of the nurses phoned. Pastor Demel also knelt down beside Fräulein Louise and tried again. "Everything will be all right, dear Fräulein Louise. Everything—"

"Go away!" yelled Fräulein Louise, her voice breaking. "Leave me, Satan! Satan! Satan!" And she spat in his face again. "Untie me! Let me go!"

"We can't do that," said the young doctor, addressing the others. "It's impossible. She'd attack us."

"Remove the straps," said a deep, calm, man's voice.

Fräulein Louise was silent abruptly. She stared at the man in the white coat who had just come into the room. He was big and looked strong, and he had dark eyes. "Well, now," he said, smiling, "at last, Fräulein Louise. Good evening."

He gave the young doctor a sign and he undid the straps. Fräulein Louise sat up. There was complete silence in the room. Slowly, eerily, Fräulein Louise got to her feet and stood there in her wet clothes. The blanket that had covered her fell to the ground. She walked up to the big man who was still smiling at her. The pastor held his breath. "You . . ." said Fräulein Louise, in her normal voice, and using the intimate *Du*, "I know you."

The man in the white coat closed his eyes for a moment, then he opened them again and looked at Fräulein Louise.

"Of course I know you," said Fräulein Louise. Now she was standing in front of him. "You—" She paused, he nodded. "You are going to be my salvation."

The psychiatrist, Dr. Wolfgang Erkner, nodded again. And suddenly Fräulein Louise embraced him and clung to him, and at last, at last, she began to cry.

7

"'The lines are fallen unto me in pleasant places; yea, I have a goodly heritage,'" Thomas Herford read in an emotional voice from the big open Bible on his lectern. His hairy hands were folded, the diamond on his finger sparkled in the indirect ceiling lighting. He looked at his text and added, "From the sixteenth Psalm. One of David's little treasures."

"Amen," said Mama, lawyer Rotaug, manager Seerose, editor-in-chief Lester, picture-editor Kurt Ziller (back at last from the U.S.A.), and Heinrich Leidenmüller, our top layout man. Hem, Bertie, Irina, and I said nothing. Irina was overcome by the splendor of Herford's office—like everyone who saw it for the first time—and she was exhausted by everything that had happened, and the drive from Hamburg to Frankfurt. I had driven the 495 kilometers on the autobahn at suicidal speed, with only one short stop. The long period of rain and the high wind had cooled down everything to prewinter temperature; the dark forests and fields on either side of the autobahn had looked as desolate as the innumerable black crows, flocks of them, which we had seen from time to time.

I had driven straight to *Blitz*, and Herford had asked us to come in at once, together with Lester and Hem, and this time Leidenmüller was included because he was to play an important part in what lay ahead. He stammered a little in his excitement over the honor, and there were beads of perspiration on his forehead. He was carrying press sheets under his arm—big sheets of thick, shiny paper.

After Mama had said "Amen," she rushed over to Irina—who, startled, stepped back a little; which didn't faze Mama—who embraced her, drew her head down, and kissed her on the cheek. "Oh my child, my child!" she cried. "We are all so happy to have you with us—aren't we, Herford?"

"Very happy, indeed," said her husband, bowing and smiling; and the gentlemen Seerose, Rotaug, Ziller, and Lester were smiling, too. Mama was dressed as outlandishly as ever—a blue knit suit with a sleeveless knit jacket that hung down below her rear (blue with her shocking violet hair!), innumerable strings of pearls, and a brown, mannish hat with a wide brim. On the top, in the middle, the hat had a deep crease.

"Well," said Herford. "We haven't been idle here either. Show what you've got, Leidenmüller."

The cadaverous old whore-fucker spread his sheets on the conference table. He got more and more excited. His hour had come! Everybody went over to the table; and Leidenmüller, bowing and scraping, began to explain. "The—these sheets have already been approved by Herr Lester and Herr Ziller. I have—"

"We can see what you've done," said Lester, short and sharp, our little Caesar, and we certainly did see. Leidenmüller had enlarged the negatives Bertie had sent and had had prints made in the various sizes he had in mind, and had pasted them on the sheets. Headings and captions—all there. He had photocopied them and pasted them where he wanted them.

They had been working feverishly since yesterday on this issue. Color printing is very complicated and takes time. It can take four or five days. But Herford had decided to go ahead with it for the story, my story!

"This issue was to come out on Thursday," he said. "Can't be done, they told me. Would have to one day later. So Herford decided to go along with it. General astonishment when *Blitz* isn't on the stands on Thursday. Big mystery! No ads announcing the delay. Then, a day later—bang! The bomb!"

"The atom bomb!" said Mama.

"The hydrogen bomb!" said Lester.

"Knock on wood," said Dr. Helmut Rotaug, tugging at his Hjalmar Schacht collar.

Next Friday? In exactly one week? I admit I was excited as I leaned over the press sheets. So was Bertie. This time it was our—it was *my* story that was being announced! The headline on the left side read:

TREASON!

in wild, ragged, bright yellow script which Leidenmüller had designed, and running across the whole page at the top, in typewriter face, the word

On the right, in the same script and color as TREASON:

THE NEW ROLAND

THE STORY OF AN INTERNATIONAL SCANDAL

THIS MOST EXCITING FACTUAL ACCOUNT IN THE HISTORY OF OUR PUBLISHING HOUSE STARTS IN THE NEXT ISSUE!

And below this:

PHOTOS—BERT ENGELHARDT

The photo I had hoped would come out well Leidenmüller had used to cover both pages—the moment when the volley had hit the boy Karel and catapulted him up in the air. It was a fantastic picture. You got the feeling that the boy was really flying across the pages—his face facing death, his body hurtling by ... the gold, glittering trumpet that had slipped from his hand, almost too bright, too clear, flying right along with him. Trees and shrubs black against the flaming sunset, a fiery red wall under a stormy sky. And the many people, adults and children, who had thrown themselves on the ground, panic on their faces. I had never seen a photo like it.

"Herford would like to congratulate you on this picture," said Herford, and shook Bertie's hands. "Herford congratulates you on every one of them, Engelhardt. Best thing you've ever done."

"Well, now ... " said Bertie, with an embarrassed smile. "I was lucky."

"And Herford wants to congratulate you, Roland, for the research you've done," said Herford, and shook my hand. "Gentlemen!" Whereupon Mama and the other men, except Hem and Bertie, shook my hand, too. Rotaug's felt like leather, Lester's like a cold fish; Seerose's hurt as he pressed mine. He was dressed more elegantly then ever, and his eyes—as he looked at me—sparkled.

"This is going to be the super-success of all time," said

Herford. "Herford can feel it in his balls. Excuse me, Mama. Is going to raise the circulation by a hundred thousand."

"Two hundred thousand!" cried ass-kisser Lester.

"Amen," said Mama.

"Not so high, please," said Herford. "A hundred and fifty thousand will do nicely. Think of the advertising!" he grunted. "But I want to be *numero uno* with this, and with 'Total Man.' Show the bastards what Herford can do."

Bertie and I looked at the other two pages. Here there was room for captions and a short teaser: "Continued on page 96." On page 96—the text I'd dictated over the phone. And the pictures! Karl Concon, dead on his bed in the Paris Hotel. Irina (big). Irina and Fräulein Louise screaming at each other in the barracks. Very coarse-grained but still recognizable—the window in the lit-up front of Niendorferstrasse 333, and behind it the face of Jan Bilka and his girl. The two cars tearing away from the area in front of the camp. Fräulein Louise, her arms raised imploringly to heaven—front and back view. The two phony Americans sprawled on the street in front of Eppendorfer Baum 187. I hadn't even noticed that Bertie had taken pictures after he'd been beaten up... and so on. Four wild pages.

"Elegant job!" I told Leidenmüller, and Bertie, grinning, slapped him on the back.

"Th—thanks," stammered Leidenmüller.

"Your attention, please!" Herford had stepped in front of a big board lying on a table. We turned and looked at him. He was pointing with a stick—the field marshal in front of his map at the start of a battle. "So this is how things look today. We've just sent out number 46. Next Wednesday, November twentieth, is Day of Atonement. Herford does not intend to come out with number 47 on the twenty-first, as just mentioned, but on Friday, the twenty-second. In number 47, Herford has the racial unrest article and these four switched pages. A week later, on November twenty-eight, in number 48, Herford will feature the first part of 'Treason.' You're going to have to pull yourself together, Roland! All of us are going to have to! Herford is making you personally responsible, Leidenmüller, for the title page with the unconscious boy being ready on time."

"Yes, Herr Herford. Of course, of course...."

"In number 48, Roland will give us a transition from the current sex series to 'Total Man.'" I nodded. "'Total Man' will start in number 48, and again, a week later, on December fifth.

we've got to have that title page as soon as possible, too. Herr Ziller has a great idea, which we're going to have to discuss in detail. It's going to be a long night, gentlemen."

I noticed suddenly that Irina was staring straight ahead. She looked tired and pale. Nobody paid any attention to her. None of us had anything on our minds but the issues being discussed. One of the four telephones on Herford's huge desk rang a few times before anybody noticed it. Herford hurried across his vast carpet and picked up the phone that was allegedly gold. He said, "Herford," then waved me over. "It's for you."

"Who wants to speak to me?"

"Herford doesn't know. Didn't understand the name. Somebody in Neurode."

I took the receiver from him. I said, "Roland," and heard a calm voice. "This is Pastor Demel. I didn't know where I could reach you in Hamburg. I've called your publishing house several times. They told me they expected you this evening."

"What is it, Herr Pastor?"

"Fräulein Louise—"

"What's the matter with her?"

He told me. His voice wasn't calm anymore. He talked fast, sounding harassed. He had a lot to tell. Herford was still holding forth at the conference table. I could hear him and the pastor at the same time. "What's the matter, Roland? What are you talking about? What's happened?"

"Fräulein Louise," I said, covering the receiver with my hand. "She's in the psychiatric clinic, Ludwigskrankenhaus, Bremen."

"Who?"

"Fräulein Louise Gottschalk."

"Who's that?"

"The social worker who—"

"Oh, I see. Damn it. Had to be committed at last, right?"

"Yes, Herr Herford."

"Shit! Had to happen right now. Tell them to put her in a private room, at our expense, of course. Lester, attend to that right away. Call the hospital."

"Yes, Herr Herford."

"Can one visit her? Question her further? Photograph her?"

Pastor Demel was still talking. I put my hand over the receiver again. "Not right away, Herr Herford."

"Herr Roland? Herr Roland? Are you there?"

I took my hand off the receiver. "Yes, I'm here, Herr Pastor.

448

Go on, please. I'm listening," and I put my hand over the receiver again.

"Why not right away?"

"Because her doctor, a certain Dr. Erkner, has put her under heavy sedation. She's in a half-sleep. Then he says they're going to try electric shock treatments."

"Goddamn it!"

"Herford, please!"

"I can start to write without her, Herr Herford. I have enough material to tide me over until she can receive visitors."

The pastor's voice in my ear. "Dear, unfortunate Fräulein Louise. Isn't it shocking to see how hard Almighty God tries those who should be His favorites?"

And the voice of my publisher. "Shit! Miserable goddamn' shit! Enough material for the first article! What if she's in shock for weeks and can't have visitors? What do we do then, Roland? Isn't it the damndest thing that the old bag has to lose what little sanity she had left right now?"

I took my hand off the receiver. "Yes," I replied to my publisher and to Pastor Demel simultaneously.

8

Vaslav Bilka fell on the stone terrace under my suite. He had jumped out of the fourth-floor window, landed on his head, and was killed instantly.

The terrace was directly outside the bar. Charlie the bartender heard the loud thud outside. He didn't show it. He waited a second or two to see if anyone else had heard it. The bar was fairly full, a small combo was playing "Blue Velvet," and Charlie withdrew unobtrusively. He walked through an anteroom and a small door, out onto the terrace, saw what had happened, and at once informed Heintze. Ten minutes later the homicide squad was there.

They went to work quietly and efficiently. I was standing on the balcony of my suite in the rain and called down to the men. They played one of their spotlights on me, then three of them, with Heintze, came up to us and opened the door, and I told them what had happened and how. That Monerov and Jules Cassin had disappeared, had already been established. The officers wanted to know what it was all about, and just before I began to lie, the two men I had been expecting all along turned up—tall Herr Klein and Herr Rogge with the strong glasses, from Security. They looked tired and disgusted. I could imagine that they were thoroughly sick of this assignment, which didn't even belong in their jurisdiction.

In the meantime Heintze had called in the icily polite hotel manager. Irina, exhausted, was dozing in the bedroom; the rest of us were in the salon; and once, when I looked out of the window, I could see that the men on the terrace had evidently finished photographing and searching for clues, and were shoving Bilka's body into a van. The people in the bar hadn't noticed a thing. The little radio in the salon was playing "Stranger in Paradise."

"So what happened, Herr Roland?" asked Klein, looking at me as if I were a bad smell.

"I'm as happy to see you again as you are to see me," I said.

"Let's not get fresh, OK?" said Rogge.

"Who's fresh?"

"You are. And God knows you've got no excuse for it."

"Frankly, I don't understand. What concern is it of mine—"

"Shut up!" said Rogge; then he evidently decided to be less hostile and explained that he had nerves, too, and let me say all I had to say. I interrupted my story once with, "I'm sure you know what happened in Helsinki."

"Yes, yes," said Rogge. "We know. What we don't know is what happened here."

"Of course not," I said. "The only thing you were able to listen in on was my conversation with Engelhardt in Helsinki. You tapped my phone, didn't you?"

"Yes," said Klein, amiably.

"If you'd built in a microphone like the Russian," I said, "you'd know a lot more."

"Our mistake, granted," said Rogge. "By the way, young Felmar gave himself up and confessed everything."

"What are you going to do with him?"

"We don't know. Right now we're holding him. He'll go before a judge tomorrow—that is, this morning, and it will be up to him."

450

"Poor devil," I said.

"We're all poor devils," said Klein. "And now, go on."

I went on, they listened; so did the men from homicide, to whom Klein had explained that all this was top secret. Nothing was to go to the press or news agencies. Klein and Rogge demanded that the whole thing be suppressed. Case of suicide by jumping out of a fourth-floor window would have to suffice for the general public. The officers shrugged. To which I would like to add that not a newspaper, radio station, or television broadcast even mentioned the event, not on the following day, not ever, and the big news agencies evidently found the item that a hotel guest had jumped out of a fourth-floor window uninteresting. In such respects, we still have law and order in the Fatherland!

After they had got all there was to get out of me, Klein and Rogge asked what I intended to do next. I said, "I'll wait until Engelhardt gets back from Helsinki, then I'll go to Frankfurt and start working. You're against it, aren't you?" I asked. I was sure they were going to forbid me to write about it, and that they would demand that I hand over my tapes and Bertie the pictures he had taken in Helsinki. But I was wrong. They nodded and smiled and said they were only doing their duty on a job that wasn't theirs to begin with. And they sympathized with me....

"So I may leave? Take the girl with me? Write about it?"

"As far as we're concerned, certainly," said Klein. "Didn't we tell you that we are not your enemies and have no intention of preventing you from writing about this? It's a case of great public interest. Go ahead, Herr Roland. Write. But it must not be backed up by any official elucidations," said Klein.

I found all this pretty mysterious, and I had to think of Victor Largent, who had said that not a line of this story would ever see the light of day and that he was going to bring me the contract and check from the American illustrated magazine in the morning. And I also thought of the nice old gentleman in Cologne. And then I thought I'd better get in touch with my publishing house right away.

It took me another hour to get rid of everybody. I looked in the bedroom. Irina had fallen asleep with the light on. She looked peaceful; her breathing was slow and regular. I turned out the light, took my coat, and left the suite. I locked the door and took the elevator down to the lobby. I could hear the music from the bar all the way to Heintze's desk.

I didn't want to show myself in Club 88 again and asked Heintze to call a taxi. He was formal to the point of hostility, this man whom I had known for such a long time. "What's the matter, Herr Heintze?" I asked.

He was looking through some papers as he answered, his voice flat. "I'm sorry, Herr Roland, but after everything that's happened, the manager would like you to vacate your suite by tomorrow noon, you and your . . . wife."

"I was going to leave anyway," I said, "but listen, Herr Heintze . . . I can't help it if somebody chooses to jump out of a window in my suite."

He shrugged. "It's not for me to say anything about that, Herr Roland. I'm very sorry that I have to be the one to tell you this, but the manager would appreciate it if you did not stop at the Metropole in the future. If you do come, there won't be a room for you."

"I understand," I said, "and I can understand the manager. But we can remain friends, can't we?" and I pushed a hundred-mark bill across the desk. He pushed it back and said, his face expressionless, "I'd rather not accept that, Herr Roland."

"Well, then there's nothing I can do about it, is there?" I said, took my money back, and walked outside. A taxi was just driving up to the entrance. I got in, a bellboy closed the door for me. "To the train station and back," I said.

"Yes, sir," said the driver. It was raining hard.

9

At the station I changed a twenty-mark bill for coins and went to the booth from which I had phoned Hem before. This time I called the house direct and had them connect me with Herford. He answered at once.

"Good evening, Roland. Herford is pleased to hear your voice."

"Good evening, Herr Herford," I said. "Something has—"

"Where are you speaking from?"

"The train station. A booth. A lot has happened during these past hours—"

452

"Herford knows all about it!" he said in his complacent voice.

"You know—?"

"Everything!" He laughed. "That surprises you, doesn't it?"

"Oh, I see," I said. "Herr Seerose has heard from his friends."

"Smart boy. Yes, he has. A rotten mess, isn't it? But first-rate for the story. First-rate. Seerose says so. They all say so. They're all here with me. Your friend Kramer, too. Herford has turned on the loudspeaker system. Everybody can hear you."

"But I don't think you know yet that Bilka jumped out of a window of my suite and bashed his brains out," I said angrily, and could hear Herford gasp.

"Are you drunk, Roland?"

"No, Herr Herford."

"But how could Bilka—?" He was speechless.

I threw in another coin and said, "Let me explain. Also a thing or two which I doubt very much that Herr Seerose's friends told him."

After that he let me talk, and I went on throwing in coins, and the booth still stank of urine and perfume, the urine stronger, and I felt sick and had to take a swig out of my flask. I told everything that had taken place in my suite, not leaving out Victor Largent's visit, but I did *not* mention the fact that he had told me they would never print my story. As a final bombshell I asked, "So where do we stand now, Herr Herford? Do we print the story or not?"

"Of course we print the story!" he thundered. "Have you gone crazy? We've never had anything like it! Why do you ask such a damn' fool question? You want to leave us, maybe? Sell the whole thing somewhere else? I'm warning you, Roland—don't try anything on us! I'll take you to every court in the country! This is Herford's baby! Of course Herford's going to print it. You can have Herford's word of honor on that. Herford swears that—oh—wait a minute! You're thinking of the nice old gentleman in Cologne maybe?"

"Yes."

"He's got nothing against it. We've found that out in the meantime, too, ha-ha-ha!"

"Have you spoken to him?"

"Wait a minute! I'd rather Oswald explained that to you. Oswald, come here."

Our general manager came and the next thing I heard was his impressive, resonant voice. "Hello, Herr Roland."

"Hello, Herr Seerose."

"It's just as Herr Herford said, my friend. We're going to press. No protest from the nice old gentleman in Cologne, not from the Americans. On the contrary."

"What do you mean, on the contrary?"

"The Americans *want* the story to appear. They've already briefed the gentleman in Cologne to this effect. He just told me. I've been on the phone with them both several times."

"The Americans want—but Herr Seerose, they don't come off very well in it."

"That's just why. Besides, it's only halftime."

"I don't understand." I lit a Gauloise because I couldn't stand the stench and couldn't open the door.

"Well, the other half of the film is still in New York, isn't it?"

"If the Russians work on Bilka hard enough, it won't be there long."

"Nobody knows what's going to happen next," said Seerose. "The Americans will continue to keep us informed; they've promised that. They're not blind optimists, but they're diplomatic. But look here—let's say the East gets the other half of the film, too . . . anything's possible. But in that case we've *got* to run our series."

"I don't get it. A series that describes a defeat of the Amis?"

"Yes. But with a little retouching."

"And what'll that be?"

"Namely that Bilka gave the Americans *copies* of the microfilms when he was in Niendorferstrasse, and that they arranged the flight to Helsinki and everything else to mislead the East," said Oswald Seerose.

"But that isn't true!" I said. "Or is it?"

"What do you think?"

"Well, that isn't true . . . of course. . . ."

"Hm. That's what *you* think. But when you write—and we print it after it could have happened, so that it hits like a bomb—and imply (very delicately, of course) that that is why we are printing the story, then millions are going to believe it, right? And the Russians will have the same doubts you're having right now. They'll ask Bilka, if he's still alive. And what can he say?"

"That he didn't hand over any copies."

"Exactly. And the Russians won't believe him. That's why it's so lucky that we come out with our version later. Altogether, we're lucky."

"In what way?"

"Well"—Seerose sounded downright cheerful—"brother Bilka is dead, you say. So you don't have to have any more qualms about writing and making him unhappy. Vaslav Bilka—may he rest in peace."

"Listen," I said, "and I'm serious about this. You're not just stringing me along, are you?"

"My dear young friend, why are you so suspicious?"

"I saw you in Hamburg, going into Niendorferstrasse 333," I said. Now I had to have absolute assurance. And Herford had turned on the loudspeaker so everybody could hear me.

"Yes, certainly," Seerose said cheerfully. No shaking him. "The Americans asked me to come as quickly as possible."

"Why?"

"To discuss just what has become so acute now," he answered, sounding a little arrogant. "Now listen to me, Roland, the Americans *need* your story. Would you like to call them at Niendorferstrasse? I'll give you the number. It's unlisted, of course."

"Yes."

He actually gave me the number. I wrote it down.

"One of the lead men will answer, but he won't talk until you give him the code word for this operation."

"And what's that?"

"*Satisfaction*. When you've said that, he'll say *Red Mountain*. There's a phone beside his bed. His name is Ronald Patterson. Ask him if he gave us the green light to go ahead and print."

"I'll do that," I said, "and call right back."

I hung up, dialed the number he'd given me, and when I could hear the receiver being lifted at the other end, I said, "Satisfaction."

"Red Mountain," said a man's voice, and the conversation was conducted in English, American English.

"Mr. Patterson?"

"Who is it?"

"The *Blitz* reporter. What's my name?"

"Walter Roland. I was expecting your call."

I asked him if he had three or four dogs and if they were terriers. He said he had two German shepherds. And then I asked him what Bilka looked like, and his girl, and where they'd been taken in Helsinki, and a few more things like that. I had to be quite sure that Seerose hadn't given me a bum steer. In the end I was satisfied.

"And you are agreed that we publish the story?"

"Under the conditions Mr. Seerose mentioned to you."

"And is it true?"

"That is an idiotic question, Mr. Roland. Do you expect me to say we lied?"

And so on. Everything really seemed to be in order. I was pretty sure that the Americans *didn't* have copies of the films, but it was a clever idea to make the Russians feel insecure.

"And the old gentleman in Cologne?"

"Has been informed. Won't undertake a thing against it. That is to say, he will if the story *doesn't* appear."

I thought the thing over but couldn't think of a single reason to doubt it. I said good night to Mr. Patterson, called Frankfurt again, asked for Seerose, and told him I felt everything was all right.

"Well, we're pleased about that," said Seerose, and I could hear Herford laughing.

"And if we hadn't succeeded in calming you down, Herr Roland, what would you have done?"

"What would you have done in my place?"

"I would have accepted Victor Largent's offer and let us sue," he said happily. "Everybody has to look after himself. I have great understanding for that. Take Herr Notung—"

"Notung?"

"Olaf Notung. Michelsen's servant."

"Oh, yes." For a moment I hadn't known who Notung was. "What about him?"

"He looked after himself."

"What do you mean?"

"Well, he would have become a target for attacks from the East as soon as it got out that Michelsen had changed sides, wouldn't he?"

"Yes. So?"

"So that's why he left the apartment on Eppendorfer Baum that afternoon and drove to Niendorferstrasse and asked the Americans to protect him. He's there now, with the Americans. Safe. When are you coming back?"

"Tomorrow. Just as soon as Bertie gets back and I've settled everything with the police, and seen Conny Manners's girl friend."

"Very good, Herr Roland." And an aside: "What did you say? . . . Oh, yes. Herr Kramer sends greetings."

"Give him my best," I said. "Good night all."

"Good night, dear friend," said Seerose. "Oh, just a minute. Herr Herford wants to speak to you."

"I only have two marks left."

"It won't take a minute." And Herford was on the wire.

"A word from the Book of Books, Roland," he said. "Herford is speaking from memory. One of his favorite verses, from the 56th Psalm. 'In God will I praise his word, in God I have put my trust; I will not fear what flesh can do unto me.' Wonderful, isn't it, Roland?"

"Yes, Herr Herford."

"Praise God's word, Roland!"

"I shall praise God's word, Herr Herford."

"And remember, Rotaug will put you behind bars if you try to sell the story anywhere else."

"I get it, Herr Herford." The light signal on the phone lit up. I had no more coins, so I hung up and walked out of the booth.

"Good evening, Herr Roland," said an elderly man who had evidently been waiting for me outside the booth. He was tall, was wearing a trench coat, and tipped the brim of his hat which he had shoved back on his head.

10

"Chief Sievers," said the elderly man. "Homicide."

"What can I do for you?"

He hesitated, his expression solemn.

"Well?"

"Well, I really only wanted to see you for a moment and ask a few questions." He showed me his ID card.

"What did you want to ask me? How did you know I was here, anyway?"

"I got to the Metropole just as you drove off. One of the boys heard you tell the driver to go to the train station. He's waiting outside. He said you had gone into the station for a moment and wanted to drive back to the hotel with him. So, I came in here. My car's parked outside, too." He took my arm lightly and we

457

strolled through the station like old friends.

"You see," he said, "I'm working on the Concon case. You know that he was stabbed?"

"Yes. Any clues yet?"

"Not a trace." He shook his head, let go of my arm, took a cigar out of his vest pocket, and smelled it as we walked along slowly.

"Did you hear my conversation?"

"Yes," he said. "But don't worry. I won't mention it to anybody. I thought you'd be leaving Hamburg soon—that's why I came here now. To catch you before you left. And to ask you something."

He lit the cigar and leaned against the window of one of the many closed stores.

"What do you want to ask me, Chief Sievers?"

"Well, you see," he said, "I've been listening to everything that's come up about the case at headquarters. I know everything that happened at Camp Neurode. I know that this little boy, Karel, was killed, and that the taxi driver, Vladimir Ivanov, was shot in front of the University Hospital. I have been informed of Vaslav Bilka's death and everything that took place in your suite at the Metropole—at any rate, as much as they'd reveal to me."

"Why did you do that?"

"Because I am convinced that all these things hang together. All I have to do is find Concon's murderer. I think Concon was only a link in a series of events. One has to see all these things as connected, beginning with little Karel."

Suddenly I had to think of Fräulein Louise. Where was she now, I wondered?

"You don't happen to know where Fräulein Gottschalk is, do you?" he asked promptly, which I found rather weird.

"No idea. Why?"

"I think she could have helped me," said Sievers. "I questioned her at the Davidswache. But at the time I didn't know—" He stopped.

'What didn't you know?"

"That she was insane."

"And since you know that, you think she could help you?"

"Definitely."

"A madwoman? How?"

"She knew Karel. She loved the boy. She told me so.

Everything starts with Karel. She could have told me a lot about him."

"She'll turn up again," I said. "Then you can ask her."

"I hope so," said Sievers.

"What do you mean?"

"I meant that I hope I'll still be able to question her when she turns up again."

"I began to feel uncomfortable. He noticed it. "Don't worry, he said, smiling. "*I'm* not insane. But I could have done with the Fräulein's help right now. She is mentally disturbed, but she knows a lot of mysteries. Well . . . I'll get to the bottom of it without her. After speaking to her I am absolutely sure that I shall find Concon's murderer." He moved his face close to mine and lowered his voice. "And I am absolutely sure that Concon's murderer and the murderer of little Karel are one and the same person."

"How did you come to that conclusion?" I asked, baffled.

"I've given this case a great deal of thought," he said, "and I know what I have to do to find this person."

"What?"

"That's my secret. May I always count on your help, Herr Roland?"

Something I couldn't explain touched me about this elderly, soaking-wet police chief with the sallow complexion. "Always," I said.

"That's wonderful," he said. "Thank you," and he touched the brim of his hat again and walked away fast. I looked after him, more perplexed than ever. Even the way he left was mysterious. For a second I could see him at the exit, then he was gone, vanished.

I walked slowly to the exit and my taxi. At the time I didn't know that we had stood and talked in front of the delicatessen where Fräulein Louise had met the former SS man, Wilhelm Reimers. I thought, confused suddenly, that here a circle had closed. And now, as I write these lines, I remember something Fräulein Louise said to me later, on one of my visits. "And if there is really no end and no beginning, or if both are the same thing—then our end is always our beginning, and that's true also when we die, isn't it? The end is the beginning . . ." And Fräulein Louise traced a big circle in the air with her finger.

11

Bertie came back from Helsinki on a plane that arrived in Fuhlsbüttel at 8:35 A.M. When he got to the Metropole at 9:30, Irina and I had already had breakfast. (I had slept on the couch again!) We went to Bertie's room with him and had more coffee to keep him company. He was very hungry. Before the flight he had slept a little in the taxi of his Norwegian driver friend, and then on the flight, from start to finish. Bertie could sleep anywhere.

I told him everything that had happened. He grinned and said, "I noticed that I wasn't being given the red-carpet treatment when I came in. The hell with it! Wait till you see the pictures I've brought with me. Man, oh, man!" Then he went over to the phone, his cup in his hand, egg yolk in the corner of his mouth, and called his mother in Frankfurt and said good morning and told her he loved her. During the night I had been very restless, but now that Bertie was back, I was perfectly calm again.

"You know what?" he said, after the call. "Considering everything that's happened, I think the time has come for us to say *Du* to each other, what do you say?" And he looked at Irina with the most disarming smile. His smile was contagious—Irina had to smile, too.

She nodded and got up, and Bertie embraced her and got a kiss on the cheek. Then I got a kiss on the cheek, and Irina said, "All right, *Du*. It really is high time—you're quite right, Bertie."

"I'm always right," said Bertie. Good old Bertie.... "Here's your minicannon," he said, handing me the Colt. "God, but the damn' thing's heavy! No complaints, though. I was glad to have it."

The sight of the weapon gave me an idea. "Largent!" I said. "What about him?"

"He was coming with the contract and the check." Irina looked at me, startled. "Don't worry," I said. "I'm not going to accept. I'd just like to find out how he's feeling this morning."

I asked for a connection to the Hotel Atlantic. The telephone operator there said, "Just a minute, please," then the voice of the man at reception: "You wanted to speak to Mr. Largent?"

"Yes."

"I'm sorry, but Mr. Largent isn't with us anymore."

"Is that so? I had an appointment with him. When did he leave?"

"Very early. He had to get to the airport to catch the first plane to New York."

"My name is Roland," I said. "Walter Roland. Did Mr. Largent leave any message for me?"

"No, Herr Roland. Mr. Largent didn't leave a message for anybody."

"Thank you," I said, and hung up. "Well, there you are," I said, "—fair-weather friends. So that's that."

"I get the feeling they'd like us out of here as soon as possible," said Bertie. "Even the guy in the garage was nasty."

"Yes," I said. "Let's pack. Irina and I have to go to police headquarters once more to sign the statement we made last night, and then I want to see Conny and Edith."

"I don't have to pack," said Bertie, "because I didn't unpack anything. So get going, you two. I'll have the car filled up."

So Irina and I went down to our suite with all the telephones ripped out, and got ready to leave. Then they came for our things and I paid at reception, where everyone was icily polite. I looked around once more. Sad, to be thrown out like this. I had always been especially fond of the Metropole.

The manager, who had put in an appearance during the night, walked past me without a glance in my direction, whereupon I said in a loud voice, "I shall recommend this hotel in which the waiters and guests are foreign agents!" A sorry revenge. The manager pretended not to hear me.

Irina and I took the elevator down to the garage, where Bertie was standing beside the Lamborghini, supervising the stowing away of our luggage. I paid for the rental of the Rekord and the gas and oil for the Lamborghini, and the Dutch fellow didn't look at me once. He didn't get a tip. I'd had it. At last.

We drove to police headquarters, Irina between us, and Bertie waited outside for us. It took quite a while. Then we drove to the hospital to see Conny and Edith. Two MIB men were standing at the door of his room, but Edith came out of her room, next to his, and was so pleased to see us. "He's better! Much better!" she cried.

"That's fine, Edith," I said. "We'll keep in touch. Through *Blitz*. Don't worry. Nothing's going to happen to you anymore."

"We're looking after her," said one of the MIB men.

Then, at last, we drove out of the city. When we got to the autobahn at Veddel, I turned on the heat because there was an icy wind. I stepped on the gas and had been driving for about ten minutes when I heard Irina say softly, "Oh...you two..."

"What about us?"

She said, "I—I'm so glad you're both with me." Bertie didn't hear her. He'd fallen asleep again.

12

Tchaikovsky's *Pathétique* was still on the record player when we got to my penthouse apartment at Lerchesberg, after leaving *Blitz*. I showed Irina all the rooms, including the guest room, which she was to use. Now that I was going to begin to write, I needed her near me. The cleaning woman had been there, the apartment sparkled, nothing was left to remind me of the two whores who had still been there on Monday morning.

We had interrupted the conference with Herford so that I could take Irina home. She was exhausted. On the way from Hamburg she had accepted the idea that she stay in my apartment. I had told Hem of her decision when I had phoned him during our short stop for a rest, and in Herford's preposterous office on the eleventh floor, the latter had said, "Take the young lady home, Roland. Get something to eat, both of you. We'll stop now, too, for a meal. Mama will go home. Then we'll meet again, here. We've got to settle on exactly what's to be done with 'Total Man,' too. Today. You don't have to worry, Fräulein Indigo. You'll be well guarded at Roland's apartment."

"Guarded?"

"Two police officers will be parked at the entrance around the clock. Oswald arranged it."

"The Americans want it," said Oswald Seerose. "And it's really for the best. All of us will feel better about it, Fräulein."

"Yes, yes," said Irina, sounding lost.

"And tomorrow I'll send you Leo," said Mama. "Leo is the best salesman in the salon where I have my things made. You'll need clothes. You can rely on Leo, my dear. He'll look after you. He has fantastic taste!"

Oh, God! I thought, and looked at Hem who looked at me, his face blank. I could only hope that Leo's taste was really fantastic. Going by the way Mama dressed, it wasn't likely.

"Of course, I never let him influence me," said Mama, and I felt better.

When we got to my apartment house I saw the car with the two plainclothesmen sitting in it. They nodded and waved while I was taking our things out of the Lamborghini. In the apartment, I unpacked and carried my typewriter and tapes to the desk in my workroom. I noticed that I had left the recorder in the car. I could get it later.

I wasn't hungry, but I asked Irina if she would like to eat something, but she said, too, that she wasn't in the least hungry. I'm just so tired...overtired, really. You know what I mean?"

"Oh, yes," I said, and fixed us two whiskeys and took Irina into my bedroom because the record player was there and Irina had said she loved Tchaikovsky, too. We sat on my king-sized bed and listened to the *Pathétique*, and everything was peaceful.

"In my workroom there's a record cabinet. Lots more Tchaikovsky. If you can't sleep after you've had a bath, play some of the records. And have another drink. You know now where everything is."

"Yes, Walter."

"And then go to bed. I'll be back late. I'll lock you in, but you have a second set of keys. Don't open the door for anyone. Answer the phone only when I call. I'll let it ring three times and hang up. The next time I'll let it ring till you answer. OK?"

She nodded. Suddenly I saw tears in her beautiful eyes. "What is it, Irina?"

She grasped my hand and held it to her wet cheek and whispered, "Thank you. Thank you for everything."

"Oh...skip it."

"No, really. I mean it. What would have happened to me without you?"

"Without me? You know I've done all this only because I want your story."

"And that's a lie," said Irina, smiling.

"Yes," I said. "It's a lie, my darling."

She kissed the palm of my hand, then she let my hand fall abruptly and drank, a lot. "What now?"

"I—I thought of him. Forgive me...."

"Of course," I said. "It will pass...until nothing is left."

"Yes," she said. "I want it that way. Nothing should be left. Nothing!"

I didn't understand her at the time, but I was to understand her very soon.

A jet flew over the house, just after takeoff. The noise was dreadful. We said nothing because we couldn't have heard each other. I smiled, but Irina's dark eyes remained serious, sad, and veiled. The noise of the plane receded. We could hear Tchaikovsky again, the wonderful *Pathétique* with its minor mood and the eastern mystique of eternal suffering, interrupted every now and then by the sweet cantilenas of western sentiment. We looked at each other. The music played on, and I went over to the table with the bottle of Chivas on it and fixed myself a stiff drink, and this time it had nothing whatsoever to do with my jackal....

13

"Now listen, Max," I said, "according to Tutti, you've got a pecker like an elephant."

"He has! He has!" Tutti assured me. "Man, Walt*ah*, Max's got the biggest cock I've seen in my life, and I've seen plenty. Professionally speaking, of course."

"Well...it ain't the smallest one around," said Max, smiling with a possessor's pride. "But why're you so interested, Walt*ah?* You ain't no fag, he-he-he!"

"He-he-he, you idiot!" I said. "I'm interested in your prick because we want it for the title page in *Blitz*."

"Walt*ah!* Dear Jesus, you can't mean it!" cried Tutti.

"I'll be damned," said Max. "You been drinking, Walt*ah*, yeah?"

"I'm sober as a judge," I said, "and I mean it seriously. They want your prick, Max. I've just come from a conference, as I told you on the phone."

"In the middle of the night?"

"And still going on. We're working on two very important series. I need you both."

"Max! Your pecker on the front page! You'll be famous! They'll put you in the movies!" cried Tutti.

It was 10:30 P.M., and I was in Tutti and Max's living room in a brand-new apartment house in Herbartstrasse. A covered bird cage stood by the window, I presumed with Tutti's darling and Max's archenemy, the canary, sleeping in it. I knew the apartment; I'd been here several times. Twenty-eight-year-old Tutti Reibeisen, whose real name was Gertrude which she found ugly, had very bright blue eyes and a big mouth. Even when she wasn't smiling, the right corner was always a little upturned. She was wearing high-heeled shoes and a salmon pink miniskirt, and she sat in a way that showed off her blue underwear. Her pimp, Max Knipper, a great fellow, was tall, slim, and muscular, and he was built like a Greek god. Looked like a Greek god, too. Noble, a truly noble-looking guy. Only his hands were three sizes too big for him.

"You see," I said, "I knew I'd come to the right place. But we've got to work fast. I've got to be finished by middle of next week."

"Max!" Tutti sounded startled. "Poor Wal*tah's* gone bonkers! Oh, Lord, Lord... I've always begged you to come to my love bed, Wal*tah*, but now you say you've gotta be finished by middle of next week? Today's only Thursday! Wal*tah*, you ain't got all your marbles! Compared to you, Leichenmüller was a dodo!"

"No, no," I said hastily to my friend Tutti with the big heart and the small brain. "That's not what I mean. I mean finished with what I have to write for *Blitz*. With my first article. And for the next one I need all sorts of information from you. But right now I need Max's cock."

"Oh, my God," said Max. "What's the world coming to?"

Beer, schnapps, and glasses were standing in front of us on the table. For once I was doing without my Chivas because I didn't want to embarrass my friends. Max was wearing a blue suit with broad white stripes, a yellow shirt, and a wildly colorful tie. He was sitting against a wall with a lot of framed photographs on it. Some were family pictures, yellowed by age, a little out of place in this modern apartment, but Tutti was sentimental. You could recognize her in every picture—little Tutti holding her mother's hand in front of the polar bear cage at the Berlin Zoo. Little Tutti holding her father's hand at a fair. Little Tutti with her mother at a spa, on a pony, under the Christmas tree, always with relatives—parents, aunts, uncles, grandparents—all of them dead long ago, according to Tutti. All she had now was Max. There were no pictures of him on the wall.

I had called them from Herford's office and asked if I could come over. Max answered the phone. "Can't come now," he said. "In an hour's OK. Tutti has a john. Mr. Moneybags. Doesn't want to be seen. Didn't park his car in front of the house. A little farther along. But you can't miss it. A red Alfa. If you come in an hour and it's still there, you gotta wait. Drive around the block a bit. Okay?"

"Okay, Max."

The other men in the office looked at me expectantly. "Well?" said Herford.

"Everything's set," I said. "I'll talk to him tonight. He's the ideal man for it. Can we take the pictures tomorrow?"

"You, Engelhardt," said Herford.

Bertie laughed.

"What's so funny?" Lester's tone was sharp. Lester, the worm. Bertie gave him a look but said nothing.

"Let's keep it peaceful, boys," said Herford. "Herford isn't going to tolerate any display of animosities."

The air in the room was blue. Everybody was smoking. Herford had taken off his jacket—the boss's privilege; the rest of us couldn't. But we were allowed to smoke. And bottles of beer stood on the conference table. Stag party. Mama had been taken home long ago.

During the conference I experienced again the beauty of my profession in all its grandeur. The decision on the title page with the unconscious boy had taken only fifteen minutes. How the series was to begin was left entirely to me, whereas "Total Man" absorbed the gentlemen endlessly. They had ideas, brainstorms; they all talked at once, interrupted each other, were full of admiration for themselves and each other, and were just crazy about this shit series.

"The man must be in profile! The whole figure in profile!"

"Well, I don't know. I think I'd prefer it full front."

"Are you crazy? The penis must show up against a black background!"

"And in erection, of course!"

"Right! In all its glory!"

"It should be a lulu!"

"It will be, it will be!"

"The women will be dazzled!" crowed Ziller.

"Herford doesn't like the tone, gentlemen," said Herford. "What our women are getting here is life-saving advice!"

"Of course, Herr Herford!"

"Naturally, Herr Herford!"

"Life-saving advice!" He actually said it!

"This series is a serious thing," said Hem. (The thing was getting the better of him.)

"You said it, Kramer." Herford was impervious to irony. He didn't know the meaning of irony. "*Two* series at once with serious impact. In 'Total Man' you mustn't lose sight of the humane element, Roland. You'll be sure not to, won't you?"

"I shall not lose sight of the humane element, Herr Herford."

"Then you can be as explicit as you like. You know what I mean?"

"I know what you mean, Herr Herford. I shall be *very* explicit."

"No inhibitions! Not this time. We mean business. Serious business. I think even the church will give us her blessing. And don't neglect the sociocritical viewpoint, Roland. The retardation and denigration of women in the late capitalist era. Keep our new course in mind!"

"I shall, Herr Herford. I'll keep our new course in mind." He evidently also wanted the blessing of the labor unions for this shit-and-fuck series!

Photo-editor Ziller said, "The studio must be ready."

Blitz had a huge photography studio with all the most modern equipment in a house on the Zeil. "What do you mean, 'ready'?" asked Lester.

"We need naked girls."

"What for?" Lester was a prude, in spite of everything else. And he had no imagination.

"Well, if the man's to have an erection, we've got to spread out a few naked girls," Ziller said impatiently. "Where can we get them on such short notice?"

"I'm sure Herr Roland can help us out with that." Lester's tone was malicious. He hadn't recovered from our scandalous little scene on Monday.

"Certainly, Herr Lester," I said. "It's only a question of money. If I'm allowed to spend a lot of money, I can get you the most beautiful girls in Frankfurt."

"Money is no object in this case, you know that," said Herford. He was very excited and took his little gold pill box out of his vest pocket again and swallowed five pills—red, yellow, blue. He washed them down with beer. "This is going to be *the* sensation of the year, if we can bring it off! This and your other series, Roland. And we'll be on top! Herford is predicting!"

"Or we'll be censored," said elegant general manager Seerose.

"We will not be censored, Oswald," said Herford. "You and Ziller weren't there when Rotaug approved the whole thing. Please, *Docktor*, explain it again."

The human turtle blinked his eyes, tugged at his collar, fingered the pearl in his stickpin, and spoke. "We will not be censored, we will not be banned or confiscated, we won't even be chastized. All we have to do is put a band over the controversial section, to hide it."

"What controversial section?" asked poor benighted Ziller.

"The member, of course!" shouted Herford.

Oh, yes, of course," said Ziller.

"What did you think? The nose?" Lester couldn't stand Ziller either.

"Be quiet, Lester. The *Doktor's* speaking."

"I'm sorry, Herr Herford."

Oh, yes, it was a great session!

"The band can, of course, be removed," said Rotaug.

"Naturally!"

"Of course!"

"Will the little girls ever be stunned!"

"Quiet!" shouted Herford. "Are we in a brothel or in the office of a publisher?"

It was quiet. Rotaug was tugging at his collar again. "The band will suffice to quell any public protest against indecency and pornography. I base my contention on a ruling of the county courts in Münster and Lübeck in 1964 and 1967, according to which..." and he proceeded to describe the tenor of these decisions and gave a legal explanation that lasted ten minutes. "Well, that seems to be the solution," said Seerose, finally impressed.

"Marvelous idea, Oswald, isn't it, with the band?"

"Yes, Tommy."

"Herford's idea," Herford said proudly. "Rotaug just mentioned something about a band—and Herford had the idea!"

"Amazing, Herr Herford!" said Lester worshipfully.

"You're not saying anything, Herr Kramer." Herford sounded annoyed. "Is anything wrong? Don't you like Herford's idea?"

"I think the idea is great," Hem said amiably, puffing on his pipe. "I would go so far as to say nobody else could have thought of it."

Herford beamed. "Yes. Herford has a good head on his shoulders. Sometimes I wonder what you'd do without me, you jerks!"

Lester, Rotaug, Leidenmüller, and Ziller laughed dutifully; Seerose looked at Herford sharply, but Herford returned his manager's look all-innocence. Then followed the debate on how 'Total Man' was to be handled graphically, and this was again one of Leidenmüller's splendid hours. He presented designs, lectured on the layout and headings, and everybody listened to the poor old whore-fucker, because he was an expert.

Three quarters of an hour later I left and drove through the night to Herbartstrasse. A red Alfa Romeo was parked five houses away from where Tutti lived. I stopped, turned off the motor and my headlights, and waited. For twenty minutes. Then a man came down the street, looking to right and left cautiously, got into the Alfa quickly, and drove off fast. I thought I had seen a ghost!

14

"That was young Herford, all right," said Max Knipper. "But you'll keep your mouth shut, won't you?"

"Bob was *here?*" I couldn't get over it.

"With Tutti. Sure. For two hours—four hundred marks. Never knew her to ask so much, but he paid, pronto! But that's peanuts compared with the others he screws. Nothing else he can do, though."

"What do you mean—nothing else he can do?"

"Knocked up another girl. Does it every time," Tutti explained. We were sitting in their living room. "And the last one wants half a million. Because he raped her, sez she. And she's a minor. And she don't want to get rid of the child. All I can say is, I believe her—that he raped her. Here he carried on like a bull, tore me apart. . . ."

"How did he get your address?"

"Got it out of Leichenmüll*ah*. Gave him money and pestered the old goat till he got it out of him." ·

"*Donnerwetter!*" I said. "Leichenmüller!"

"Was satisfied," said Max. "I mean young Herford now. Told me so when he was leaving. So we have a new steady customer. Not bad, eh? We can do with the do-re-mi. . . ." And he was off on his pet subject. "This co-op apartment . . . whaddaya think we still owe the bank? And the interest! But we had to have it. Needed a—whaddaya call it? Headquarters. Big enough. A room for me, a room for Tutti to work in, a bedroom for the two of us, and the *salon* here. Kitchen, bath, oil, heat—and all the furniture's new! The built-in kitchen's a jewel! Tutti's pride and joy! We've been wanting this for a long time, ya know, Wal*tah*. Tutti's had to work for it."

Faithful Tutti said, "Wasn't a bed of roses, but now we're safe from the rent gougers. And we're our own bosses. Ownership is ownership."

The two had come to Frankfurt from Berlin three years ago. I'd known them that long. At first they'd lived in a hotel that rented rooms by the hour. When I was writing my article on prostitution in Frankfurt, I'd asked them why they left Berlin.

"Because we couldn't live decently there anymore," Tutti had explained. "You see, Berlin—it's a two-bit town. Either you get the young people, students who've come there because they don't want to go into the army. They don't have enough to eat! You can't do business with them. On the other hand—the old people? Living on pensions? It's a sad thing when an old Berliner like me has to say something like this, but that city's had it, and it gets worse and worse. Those old guys don't have any money either. And the tourists? The traveling salesmen? They're stingy as hell. And then the competition. You get that in Frankfurt, too, but here it's swarming with well-heeled gents and they pay . . . whee! How they pay. And then there was Max."

"What about Max?"

"He was with the sanitation department," said Tutti.

"Yeah," gorgeous Max corroborated. "I earned my money the hard way, Herr Roland. With garbage you work till your asshole splits. Like a dog. Like ten dogs!"

"I can imagine."

470

"And do you think it's appreciated when you collect other people's crud?" Max was red with fury. "No! They look down on you. And the pay stinks more than the crap you're collecting!" Max had pounded on the table with his fist. "They need workers—and how! No unemployment in garbage. But nobody wants it. And they're right! Ya see"—he was warming up to his theme—"when them asshole teachers tell their dumb kids, 'If you don't work hard you'll never be anything but a garbageman,' all I can say is: If that's *pedajogik*, then they shouldn't be surprised if nobody wants to work in garbage anymore. Am I right?"

"Absolutely, Herr Knipper."

"Just take a look at *Nyu Jork*. Right now they've got their crud on the street. The garbagemen are on strike. And in the heat! Bravo, I sez! Right on, I sez! In *Nyu Jork* you can see the rats running across *Fifs Evenyu*, that's what I've read. Let 'em run over to *Vall* Street and the stock market and eat up all them stocks and bonds. *Nah*, Herr Roland, who knows what would have become of Tutti if life hadn't thrown us together!"

"And what are you doing now, in Frankfurt?" I asked.

"Oh...I got a few things going...ain't going too well. Nuthin's movin'...."

15

Unfortunately, Max wasn't doing too well three years later either, because he now put up a fierce fight for the amount to be paid him for the title page. He asked for five thousand. That was outrageous, and I managed to bring him down to two thousand.

"OK, OK, shit on me, you bloody capitalists! You're a capitalist stooge, Walt*ah*, and I thought you were my friend."

"I am your friend, Max, but be reasonable!"

"He is, he is!" Tutti tried to calm him down. "He didn't mean that about a capitalist stooge, did you, Max?"

"All right, all right," mumbled Max.

"There you are. We know you're a guy who goes along with us socialists, Walt*ah*, and when you say there's nuthin' more to be got out of it, then there's nuthin' more to be got out of it. Still, I gotta admit, two thousand marks—that's peanuts for Max's super body. That shitty publisher of yours is gonna earn himself silly with Max's super cock. And that's why we've gotta have communism. We can't go on like this with these vultures! So . . . when's Max gotta be in the studio?"

"Tomorrow at eleven."

"I'll be there," said Max.

"We'll be ready for you, girls and all."

Max made a derogatory gesture with his hand. "Don't need 'em. I can get it up without girls. But now let's get on with it. You want information, right? About the funny stuff, sixty-nine an' so on. What the woman's got to do to get the guy up. Let Tutti put you wise to that. What's in it for her?"

"Two hundred marks per article."

"*Two hundred marks?*" Max roared scornfully. "Did you hear that, Tuttilein? Wal*tah*, if all the gents was as generous as your publisher, Tutti could have her box tightened."

"Max, be reasonable! It's going to be a series with a lot of articles. You've got to add it all up together!"

"Not a scrap of information under five hundred," said Max. He said it very loud; all of us were loud, with the result that canary Hänschen, who should have been asleep long ago, began to sing.

Max was furious. "Now the goddamn' canary's gotta start singing," he shouted. "That goddamn' bird's gonna drive me crazy! Shut up, you fuckin' bird, d'ya hear?" He had walked over to the cage and was yelling at the cloth covering it. Hänschen paid no attention. "You miserable animal! I'll kill you! I'll choke the life out of you!" The veins over his temples were swelling with rage.

"Just try it," cried Tutti, jumping to her feet, "and you've humped me for the last time!"

She took a lettuce leaf out of a bowl that hung beside the cage, lifted the cover, and pushed the leaf between the bars. "There, there, dear heart, my sweetie, my pet. . . . Come on . . . eat the nice leaf . . . so . . . so. . . . That's the way. . . . Mama loves you. . . ."

Max watched the performance, still trembling with fury, but he said nothing. Tutti had glared at him. At last she was finished, Hänschen settled down, and the two came back to me.

"We must speak quietly," said Tutti. "Hänschen is a light sleeper." Max wanted to say something, but Tutti glared at him again, and he settled for some incomprehensible mumbling. In the end we agreed on three hundred marks per article for Tutti's information. Max shook hands with me to show that the financial end of the transaction was settled. He almost crushed my fingers in the process.

"So may I start now, lover boy?" asked Tutti.

"You can start now," said gorgeous Max.

Tutti took a deep breath and began to reveal some of the treasures of her experience.

16

I didn't get back to the apartment until midnight. Two different men were parked outside the house now, in a different car. I recognized them at once as police, and they didn't try to hide it from me. I nodded to them, they nodded back. This time I took the recorder up with me, and as I walked into the apartment I could hear music. The Second Piano Concerto in D-Minor, Tchaikovsky.

The door to the bedroom was ajar. Light fell through the crack. I threw my coat over a chair in the hall and hurried into the bedroom. Irina was sitting on the floor beside the record player. She had taken a bath and washed her hair—a towel was wrapped like a turban around it—and she was wearing a pair of the pajamas and the robe I had bought for her. Records were spread on the floor all around her—Tchaikovsky, Rachmaninoff, Smetana. An ashtray and a bottle of Chivas and soda stood beside her. She was sitting propped up against the wall, smoking and holding a glass of whiskey in her hand. She gestured toward the record. "Beautiful, isn't it?"

"I know. I can't sleep. I wanted to sit here and smoke and drink a little, and listen to the music. Do you mind?"

"Of course not."

She gestured toward the Chivas. "Have a drink and sit down with me."

She seemed to have drunk a lot more than I'd realized at first. I got a glass and ice cubes in the kitchen, went back to the bedroom, and sat down beside her on the floor.

473

"I know one shouldn't smoke in the bedroom," she said.

"That's right." I lit a Gauloise, fixed my drink, and raised my glass. "Chin-chin!"

"Chin-chin!" said Irina, and we drank. "Where were you?" she asked.

"At the office. And then I went to see a prostitute and her pimp. I've told you about the two."

"Your friends?"

"Did everything go all right?"

"Perfect."

A pause. No sound but the concerto. Then: "Walter?"

"Yes."

"It's awfully nice up here."

"Yes, isn't it? Wait, I'll fix you another drink." I took her glass. Another pause. Nothing to be heard but the music and the tinkling of the ice in the glass. "Thank you," she said as I handed it to her. She took a big swallow. "Walter?"

"Yes?"

"I've been thinking it over for a long time . . . whether I should tell you or not. But I can't manage it alone. I don't know anybody in Germany. And it's a criminal offense. I don't want to go to prison."

"What *are* you talking about?"

"I told you that I fled from Prague because the police kept summoning me and questioning me, and I couldn't stand it anymore, right?"

"Yes. And—?"

"And it's not true. Or anyway, it's not entirely true. They did question me again and again, but it wasn't as bad as I made it out to be. I didn't flee because of that. Jan's friends were arrested quite a bit earlier than I told you, not just before my decision to leave. Their arrest isn't what did it. They wouldn't have arrested me. They saw that I didn't know anything."

"So why did you leave?"

She looked at me for a long time. Now the piano was playing solo. "Because I'm pregnant, Walter," she said. "With Jan's child. In my third month."

17

She finished her drink and I finished mine, then I made two more drinks for us, very slowly, and Irina turned off the record player, and two minutes passed like that without our looking at each other. At last, when each of us had a glass in our hands again, I looked into her big sad eyes and said, "You wanted to get to Jan and tell him you were expecting his child."

"Naturally," she said. "And that I wanted to stay with him and go with him wherever he was going. And marry him. And have our child." She laughed.

"Don't laugh!" I said, and she stopped.

"Of course, now everything's different," she said. "Entirely different. Everything—did you say something?"

"No."

"I thought you—"

"Not a word."

"I don't want the child. Not now. I don't want a child by—by this—by Jan. Can you understand that?"

"Yes."

"And—and will you help me?"

I said nothing.

"You know Frankfurt. Have you never helped a girl out?"

"Oh, yes." I had helped three.

"Well, there you are," said Irina. "So you must know a doctor."

I was silent.

"Please!" said Irina. "You do know a doctor, don't you?"

I nodded.

"A good one?"

I nodded again.

"Who'd do it?"

"Yes."

"And he's reliable?"

"Absolutely. Anybody in Frankfurt with money and in your kind of trouble would go to him."

"So . . . will you take me to him, Walter? There's just time.

Three months. I'm healthy, my heart and and all that, so there's no danger. Will you, Walter?"

"But it can't go into the story," I said.

"That means you will?"

"If you're sure you want that."

She drank. "I'm sure I want that."

"Well, then—"

"What do you mean, 'well, then'? It's the only sensible solution, and we've got to be sensible, don't we?"

"Yes," I said. "We've got to be sensible. I'll get in touch with the doctor tomorrow so that we get an appointment as soon as possible. He's a very busy man."

Suddenly she began to cry, soundlessly. The tears rolled down her face onto her robe. "But—but you said you wanted it!" I said, startled.

"And I do, I do," she sobbed. "I'm only crying because I'm so happy . . . and so relieved . . . and because I'm so grateful to you, Walter, so very, very grateful! I'll never forget it, never!"

I gave her a handkerchief again, and she dried her tears. "So," I said, "now everything's all right." She nodded. "And now we can sleep." She nodded again. "Then come," I said, and lifted her up and held her in my arms. She cried out, but I held her firmly. She was astonishingly light. As I carried her into the spare room, she nestled her cheek against mine. I took her to bed like a child, and put a glass of water on her bedside table, and two sleeping pills. "Take one. If it doesn't work, take another."

"I don't need anything," she said. "I'm going to sleep like a log, now that I know you're going to call the doctor. You really will? First thing in the morning?"

"First thing in the morning. We'll have to watch it, though, because the police are guarding you."

"Oh, God!"

"But don't worry about it. The house has three entrances, and one in the cellar. This whole business of guarding you is ridiculous. They won't see us leave or come back. And now go to sleep."

I covered her as one covers a child, although I thought that now, with such a golden opportunity, I could try it. But I didn't.

"Lean down," she whispered. I did, and she kissed me on the mouth. "Thank you, Walter."

"Don't mention it."

"Are you going to sleep now?"

"Yes," I said, and got up from where I was sitting on the side of the bed. But I didn't go to sleep.

I left Irina, got my bottle of Chivas, my glass and soda and ice, and carried everything to my office. I put it all on my desk and closed the door so as not to disturb Irina. I looked in my leather bag for the cassette I wanted, found it, and inserted it in my recorder. Although I hadn't slept for such a long time, I felt wide awake. I took off my jacket, loosened my collar, and rolled up my sleeves. Then I inserted paper in my machine, with a carbon copy, and began to type.

ROLAND / TREASON / PART ONE

I let the recorder play a while and listened. Then I turned it off. It was wonderfully quiet in the apartment, and I thought about how I would begin. Once I knew that, the whole story would write itself. I didn't have to think long. I soon knew where the story had to start. Of course, this was before I visited Fräulein Louise in the Ludwigskrankenhaus in Bremen, and spoke to her. That came later. And so I didn't begin as I have done in this, my second draft; that is, not with the dialogue between Fräulein Louise and me which opens it. That night this scene still lay ahead of me.

I drank, lit a Gauloise, and began to hammer away at the typewriter, and these were the first lines I wrote: "He heard seven shots, then he heard his father's voice. It seemed to come from far away. The shots didn't frighten him, there was so much shooting in his dream, but his father's voice woke him.

"'What's the matter?' He rubbed his eyes. His heart was beating fast and his lips were dry.

"'You must get up, Karel,' said his father...."

The third girl had tits that could drive you crazy and an ass that was out of this world, and she did a striptease that topped

477

everything the other two girls had produced. A redhead. Not dyed. You could see that. And all the gentlemen present in the *Blitz* photo studio reacted in a way that was quite natural. Bertie was wiping the sweat off his forehead, the two assistants in charge of lighting were mumbling something to themselves, their faces scarlet. Gentle little photo-editor Ziller kept licking his lips, and my cigarette fell out of my mouth when the redhead began swinging her boobs around. Only poor old Max wasn't reacting! There he stood, on a small dais in front of a black background, naked from top to toe, and he'd been looking at the three naked women, the most beautiful ones I'd been able to find, for half an hour, limp, not a move, not a rise out of him! He apologized for the *n*th time. He was terribly embarrassed.

The redhead, naked now and still gyrating, gave up. "After all, I've not been hired to cure a totally impotent man!"

"Shut up!" I said.

"Well, isn't it the truth?" she whined. "I've never seen anything like it! Monroe couldn't have upped him! And pills ain't going to do it either. He's hopeless. I've had enough!"

"Do the bridge once more," said Bertie. "Please. Do it for me. And spread your legs wide!"

"For you, darling," said the redhead, and did the bridge, legs spread wide.

It was quiet in the studio, the lights made it frightfully hot, and everybody was looking at Max's limp cock. "Nix," he said. "It's just dead. Absolutely dead!"

"Well, that does it," said the redhead. "I'm through!"

"And this is the sort of thing you bring us," said photo-editor Ziller. He was a small, humble man and really quite nice, and he didn't say it reproachfully.

"If you want to give me two hundred more, I'll try a blow job on him," said the redhead. "Maybe that'll do it."

"No, no!" Max was crushed. "Thank you, *Frollein*, but I know myself. My *dschonni*'s got an obstruction. Blowing an' tooting ain't gonna help one bit. Damn it all, anyway!"

"Get dressed," I told the redhead.

The three other girls in the studio were sitting on low stools and were aghast about the whole thing. Two had already put on their show, also without success. Now we were going to try number four. A blond. The girls really were beautiful. My choice. I had written until five, then slept until nine, bathed, breakfasted, said a hasty good-bye to Irina—after bringing her breakfast in bed—and promised to get hold of the doctor. Then I'd driven to an agency for film and stage extras and models. It was actually a cover for a call-girl operation and terribly expensive. I knew the woman who ran it, something in her own right. Not quite thirty and a specialist in wall jobs. I'd tried her. That's how I happened to know the place. The girls cost a small fortune, but you were assured of the best merchandise. I chose four beauties from a catalogue and ordered them to come to the studio punctually at eleven. They were punctual, and three of them had already done their best, to no avail.

"Come on," I said to the fourth girl. "It's your turn."

She got up. "Nah, Walt*ah*," said Max, up on his dais. "Don't bother. It's no use. The broad don't have to take the trouble to get undressed. Won't do any good." Whereupon the blond began to cry, bitterly and loudly.

"And what about my money?" she sobbed. "My fee? The others get paid, I don't? That's not fair. And I won't put up with it. I'll tell the boss!"

"For heaven's sake!" Gentle Herr Ziller already had his wallet out. "Of course you'll get your fee, just like the other ladies. How could anybody know this would happen?"

He opened his wallet and a lot of bills became visible. Max was looking at Ziller, and I saw it the same time Bertie did. He gestured with his chin. I nodded. Both of us had noticed it. At the sight of the money, Max's *dschonni* had twitched.

"Herr Ziller!" I cried. He looked up. To the girls I said, "Stand aside for a moment," and to Ziller, "Go stand in front of Herr Knipper, where he can see you better. In the light. Yes, like that. And hold five hundred-mark bills in the air."

"I'm to—but why?"

"Go ahead, do it," said Bertie.

Ziller did as he was told, uncomprehending at first, but in a few seconds he comprehended. "Oh! I see!"

And, indeed, he saw! With Max things began to move...not very much yet, not by a long shot, just the same, everything was by no means dead!

"Add another five hundred!" cried Bertie. He was standing behind a large Linhof camera on a tripod, working with film packs.

Ziller was holding ten hundred-mark bills in his hand now. Max was at half mast. The girls were astounded. They were all talking at once. "They could have saved us all this!" "I've never seen anything like it!" "*Voilà*, look at that thing go!"

"Quiet!" shouted Bertie. "You're doing all right, Herr Knipper. Just fine. Now try hard. Do your best. Look at the money. Concentrate on the money!"

"That's what I'm doing!" groaned Max. "Don't you have maybe another thousand?"

"Yes, yes," said Ziller.

"Then, please, be so good as to hold up two thousand?"

Ziller held two thousand in one-hundred-mark bills over his head and up went *dschonni!*

"Oooh!" moaned the redhead, overcome. And it was an impressive sight. Bertie was grinning with delight. "There, you see? Just like that. Nothing to it. Can you hold it, Herr Knipper?"

"As long as the gentleman holds up the two thousand!"

Bertie took one picture after the other. A Greek god was nothing compared to Max Knipper. You could have heard a pin drop in the studio. Everybody was speechless. Bertie worked as fast as he could. One of the assistants had put a spot on our gentle photo editor, and he stood opposite Max, flooded by light, holding the two thousand marks over his head. And Max kept his promise. He stood motionless and rigid. When Bertie was finished at last, everybody present applauded, and Max, flattered, bowed to all sides. Then he got off the dais and put on a robe. "*Donnerwetter*, Max!" I said.

"Yeah," he said. "That's the way it goes. My *dschonni* has a mind of his own."

Suddenly Bertie yawned. "Don't tell me you're tired," I said.

"Dog-tired. Tonight I'm going to bed early and really sleep."

"So am I," I said. And so we did, deeply and dreamlessly, both of us, ten thousand meters over the Atlantic.

19

A lot of planes were ahead of us, waiting to land at Kennedy. We had to circle the airport for three quarters of an hour, and the control tower let us descend one at a time. I had only been in New York three times before, Bertie at least a dozen, and he explained the city to me lovingly and showed me its five boroughs from the

480

air—Manhattan, the Bronx, Brooklyn, Staten Island, and Queens. I could see the straight avenues form a geometric pattern with the cross streets of Manhattan, the skyscrapers, and the monumental bridges. A weak sun was shining and, oddly enough, I felt as if I'd had enough sleep in spite of the past crazy nights.

We had caught the plane just in time after Herford's alarming call had reached us—me, while I was typing my story, and Bertie, developing his photos of Max. Leo the Magnificent had turned up as arranged and was showing Irina a collection of dresses, suits, and coats. I had called the doctor on my way back from the studio and said that my wife would like a routine examination. That was the expression for it. He recognized my voice and said he was terribly busy, but perhaps he could see Irina at around 1:30, during the midday break. He would have to examine her before the minor operation, and he would do that then. I said that would be fine, and drove home, leaving the Lamborghini in front of the entrance, and waved to the police officers in their Mercedes on the other side of the street. It was the third shift. Again new faces.

When Irina had dressed, we took the elevator down to the main floor and went out the garden entrance. This led to another street, with no police on guard. We walked a short way, then I hailed a taxi. I had the driver stop near the doctor's office, and we went the rest of the way on foot. We were not about to take any risks.

Nobody was in the waiting room. The door was opened for us by the doctor's wife. She was young and pretty and had once been his nurse. Now she assisted him when he did abortions. He looked like a film star, but he was a clever doctor just the same. And avaricious. Irina had scarcely spoken all the way there. She looked very serious and calm as she walked into the doctor's office. I stayed outside in the empty waiting room that smelled faintly of cosmetics and a delicate disinfectant.

I sat there thinking of Irina, stretched out on the examination table in the next room, in the obligatory undignified position with the doctor fumbling around inside her. To distract myself I read a long article about ants. It didn't help very much. When Irina came back into the waiting room with the doctor, she looked as serious as ever and the doctor looked cheerful. "Everything's fine," he said. "Your wife is in excellent condition, Herr Roland. I have assured her there will be no complications. But we don't want to lose any more time. Would Tuesday at six P.M. suit you?"

I looked at Irina; she nodded, and I said it would be all right.

"Good, good," said the cheerful doctor. "You'll bring your wife here? But I'm afraid you won't be able to wait for her, you understand?"

"Yes, doctor."

"My wife will assist me. After that your wife should rest for two or three hours. But you must come for her at ten, at the latest, please. She can't spend the night here."

The girls were never allowed to spend the night there. I had always had to come and get them. "Very well, doctor," I said.

"When she gets home, she should lie down. If anything doesn't seem right, you must call at once, and I'll come immediately. But you know that."

I did. One of the girls had run a high temperature and he had come right away and attended to her, effectively.

"Thank you, *Herr Doktor*," said Irina. "I trust you implicitly. You are being a great help."

"One has to help wherever one can," the doctor said kindly, and took us to the door. On the way there he said softly to me that on Tuesday I should please bring a check, payable to cash, and he gave me the outrageous price. I'd expected this because I'd paid it before. I nodded. I'd always paid him like this. He was a very good and a very cautious doctor.

I went out into the street again with Irina. The sky was gray and it was very cold. Irina walked slowly, looking down at the sidewalk all the time, and when we were sitting in the taxi I had hailed, she laid her cold hand in mine and said, "Now I'm completely happy and reassured. And I have you to thank for it. I'll never be able to thank you enough, Walter."

"No," I said. "I know you won't. But in me you've got a shining example. They should print a big poster of me with the inscription 'Mothers, you can entrust your daughters to this man!'"

That made her laugh. It sounded a little hysterical and she didn't stop for quite a while—the driver looked around curiously—but at least she was laughing. That's what I'd been aiming for.

When we got back to the apartment and had just taken off our coats, the downstairs bell rang. It was Herr Leo, announcing his arrival on the intercom. I asked him to come up; he stayed for hours, during which time I sat in my room, typing "Treason," until the moment when Herford called.

That had been Friday afternoon; and now, as we were circling over New York, it was Saturday morning; and I hoped I'd be back in Frankfurt by Tuesday, November 19, for Irina's sake. That was the day I had to take her to the doctor and bring her home again. I hoped very much to be back in time. Herford had said on the phone, "It's terribly important, Roland. Herford has just spoken to Oswald Seerose. Oswald has news for you. You'd better sit down. Oswald, come here."

So general manager Seerose came to the phone and greeted me in his usual formal, dignified fashion. Then he came straight to the point. "News from my friends, Herr Roland. You and Engelhardt are to proceed straight to New York. Things are going to happen there."

"How do you know?"

"They're no idiots, our friends over there. Since the business in Hamburg, they're in a state of alarm. Radio experts have intercepted communications between a short-wave transmitter in New York and a Soviet trawler in the Atlantic. In code, of course. Can't break the code. But it concerns the films. My friends are positive about that."

"How can they be?"

"They didn't tell me. They'll tell you when you get there. The thing can't wait. It's to take place tomorrow. They'll explain everything to you in New York. When you get there, go to the Lufthansa counter. They'll be expecting you. The man's name is Cooley. Marvin Cooley. He'll fill you in."

"OK, Herr Seerose," I said. Then I told Irina that I had to fly off somewhere—not for long—and that she wasn't to let anyone into the apartment, nor should she go out or answer the phone. Suddenly her arms were around me. "What's the matter?"

"You'll really come back soon, Walter? Please, please, come back soon!"

"Of course I will," I said. "As quickly as I can. In the meantime, be a good girl. Promise?"

She was smiling and crying at the same time. . . .

At last we got permission to land. At the Lufthansa counter a tall, lanky man who reminded me of Jimmy Stewart spoke to us. He was wearing a gray coat and carrying a gray hat. "Mr. Engelhardt and Mr. Roland?"

"Yes."

"Pleased to meet you. My name is Marvin Cooley. Please

come with me. I see you have your baggage already. My car is parked outside."

His car was a silvery-gray Chevrolet. Cooley drove, I sat beside him, Bertie in the back. Cooley filled us in. "Our people have been especially interested in all radio communications during the last two days and night, ever since we found out that one of the transmitters is on a Soviet trawler. We've tried to locate the transmitter. Not easy. Luckily, there was a lot of communication going on..." Cooley drove past Aqueduct Raceway under the IND subway, and approached Brooklyn. He went on talking. "Well, our boys were lucky. They found the block. *And* the house. In Flatbush. Near the Holy Cross Cemetery. Troy Avenue."

Spring Creek Park next, its trees already bare. The parkway passed through it. To the left I could see water and the islands of Jamaica Bay. Small children were still playing in the weak sunshine, and people were walking.

"We sent two men to the house, into every apartment. Said they were from the telephone company, checking out the phones. They worked their way from floor to floor. In the end it was quite simple. A certain Floyd Turner has a radio shop on the ground floor. Radios and record players. Lives in the house. Fourth floor. He has his workshop in his apartment. Our boys didn't have to look long before they found the transmitter. Very modern, very sensitive. Turner said he was a ham operator. Showed us his license."

"Maybe he's really only a ham operator," said Bertie, "and the man you're looking for has found a better way to hide his transmitter."

"I doubt it," said Cooley.

At the end of Spring Creek Park there was another cloverleaf. Here Cooley left the parkway and took Pennsylvania Avenue north, crossing one street after the other—Schroeders, Vandalia, and broad Flatlands Avenue. "After our boys had been there, Turner's radio activity became hectic, and for tonight, 2:00 A.M., he has reserved a seat on a plane to Los Angeles. In his own name. Our people have his phone tapped, of course. We're using an empty apartment in an old house across the street."

Linden Boulevard. Cooley turned left and drove quite a long way west. The Chevy had a two-way radio, and Cooley kept calling in his position and asking if there was any news. There wasn't, his colleagues in the apartment told him. The radio technician was in his workshop upstairs, and he hadn't left the house. We passed Kings Highway, Rockaway and Utica Avenues, and at last reached Troy Avenue. The block that lay between Linden Boulevard and Church Avenue was long. Cooley parked two blocks away. We went back to Troy on foot. We saw Turner's radio shop, also two employees waiting on customers. It was Saturday afternoon.

We entered the old house opposite and walked up some dirty stairs to the fourth floor. Cooley knocked in a certain rhythm against a dilapidated door. It was opened. The apartment beyond it was unfurnished, the paper was peeling off the walls. Two young men were on duty here. They were sitting in the apartment's biggest room, looking out at the street, and greeted us when Cooley explained who we were. They were seated at a table with two field telephones beside them. Wires led from the phones all the way to the ceiling. There was a third, normal phone and a large tape recorder, connected to the field phone that was tapped into Turner's. A gray metal box was a short-wave transmitter, with which the men could call cruising cars. Every now and then calls came in. Quite a lot of cars were apparently on duty, certainly most of them unmarked, like Cooley's. I saw thermos bottles and sandwiches, and against a wall, two army cots. The men also had binoculars, one a special instrument for use at night. "What's Turner doing?" asked Cooley.

"Repairing a television set," said one of the men, and gave Cooley his binoculars. Cooley handed them to Bertie, who gave them to me. I could see into Turner's workshop. The window of the empty apartment we were in had a thin curtain over it. You could see out, but not in. Floyd Turner *was* in his workshop, doing something to a television set. He had a very big head, a large nose, short black hair, and very fine hands. The hands fascinated me. Beautiful—woman's hands.

"Of course it *is* possible," said Cooley, "that we're on the wrong track." He sat down and put his feet on the table.

"It is that," said Bertie, and smiled his boyish smile. "Entirely possible. You never know."

Well, yes.... And after that we waited for eleven goddamned hours for Turner to leave the house. But he didn't do us the favor. He worked, then he walked into the next room and stretched out on the couch and slept, then he worked again and when it got dark he turned on every light in the place and went on working on a TV set. The two young men had, meanwhile, been replaced

485

by two others; Cooley had left and come back; only Bertie and I sat on two old chairs like idiots, waiting for something to happen. But nothing happened. Turner didn't use the phone once, nor did anyone call him. At eight a third young man brought us sandwiches and hot coffee, and we ate and drank in the dark, and then Bertie said he was going to take a nap. He'd taken pictures of Turner through the window on arrival. Now he lay down on one of the army cots and next moment was asleep. And then, at last, at 10:05 p.m., something happened.

20

One of the field telephones rang. The tape began to roll automatically; one of the men at the window picked up the receiver. Nobody was in the brightly lit rooms of Turner's apartment at the time. The telephone conversation was short. The man hung up and said, "Turner's called a taxi. Troy Avenue. In front of his house."

"Let's go," said Cooley.

We grabbed our coats—Bertie, his cameras...I, my binoculars—and tore down the steps. We left the house by a back entrance that led to a dirty yard and from there to a side street. We ran to Cooley's Chevy and jumped in. Cooley turned on the two-way radio, took an automatic pistol from under his seat, and tossed it to the back, where I was sitting now. "Are you armed?" he asked.

"No," I said. "They wouldn't have let us through customs if we had been."

"Then stay in the background as much as possible," said Cooley. "I have another gun, but I need that myself." He reported to control that he was ready. We heard other cars reporting, at least a dozen. Now the radio was working nonstop. The men in the upstairs apartment could see the taxi drive up. "Yellow Cab just drew up. Suspect is getting in. Driving away. Turning into Linden Boulevard, west. Car 12 follow first. OK?"

"Roger," said Cooley. As he said it, we saw the yellow taxi pass by.

The traffic wasn't heavy. We followed at a discreet distance.

Now Cooley began to direct the other cars by reporting constantly where Turner's Yellow Cab was heading, at first the entire length of Linden Boulevard to Flatbush Avenue. Here it turned right into Flatbush and proceeded north.

Flatbush Avenue veers northwest and passes through Prospect Park, pitch dark now. I knew from a former visit to New York that a branch of the BMT subway ran under it, and on our right were the Botanical Gardens, lit up by very few lights and barely visible in the dark. After we passed the big central library building at the end of the park, there was a rotary around Grand Army Plaza. The Yellow Cab drove almost all the way around it and proceeded south past Prospect Park again. "Now why the hell did he do that?" said Cooley. "He's making a detour. He could have crossed the park at the south end."

"Perhaps he's noticed you." A voice from control. "Fall back. Let Car 18 take over."

We drove slower, quite a few cars passed us, then, after a while, control again: "Attention! Yellow Cab turning into Prospect Avenue, direction northwest to Fifth."

To our left, behind a block or two of houses, lay the vast Greenwood Cemetery. I could see the wall and some trees behind it. We passed Avenues Five and Four. Control reported that the Yellow Cab was traveling southwest now, on Third Avenue. We crossed beneath the Gowanus Expressway, turned left on its service road, and continued south, paralleling the highway.

"Yellow taxi turning into Second Avenue. Seems headed for the harbor."

The harbor, in this case, was the Brooklyn pier, warehouse, and dock area in the Upper Bay of New York Harbor. "Proceed south, direction Bush Terminal Docks. Don't follow too closely. Surround the block. Cars 1, 2, 3, and 7 approach from the playground; Cars 5, 9, 10, and 11 proceed to Sanitation Department and Brooklyn Union Gas Company. Car 12 follow Yellow Cab cautiously. Yellow Cab slowing down near Pier 3."

Cooley drove slowly through a maze of bad or totally unlit streets, down to the harbor. There was a smell of water and oil. Suddenly the huge piers lay ahead of us, with their ships, cranes, freighters, and warehouses. There were barricades in front of the piers. Turner evidently wasn't headed for the ships. We saw the yellow taxi drive past Pier 3, the docking area and storage houses of American Hemisphere, Marine Agencies, and American Star Line. The street narrowed. Railroad tracks ran into the Bush

Terminal. Here gigantic trucks were parked, fortunately also several cars. The Yellow Cab stopped in front of what looked like a seaman's dive. Light from it fell out onto the street and we could hear a radio. Turner got out and went into the place. He was wearing a dark raincoat and a hat. Cooley reported that Turner had gone into the pub.

"When he comes out," said the voice from control, "follow him, cautiously."

"Will do," said Cooley.

Five minutes later Turner came out of the pub. He was carrying two bottles of liquor and was about to get back into the taxi when the driver stuck his head out of the window and talked to Turner and gestured behind him, at us. He had evidently noticed that we were watching him, and was apparently refusing to take Turner on again. We saw Turner toss the bottles in the back of the taxi, then he had a gun in his hand, with which he hit the taxi driver over the head. The man collapsed. Turner dragged him out of the car and let him drop on the sidewalk, then he jumped behind the wheel and began to drive away. Bertie was taking pictures, Cooley was informing control about what was going on.

"Follow him! Turner's got to be stopped. Take him in!" The voice at control was raised to a shout. "Cars 1, 2, 3, move two blocks closer. . . . Cars 8, 4, 5, 6—" We didn't hear the rest because Cooley let the motor race and we shot forward. I was thrown back.

We raced over the narrow, cobblestoned street past the unconscious taxi driver and alongside the warehouses, when suddenly Turner, just ahead of us, turned around, still driving, and shot. The bullet hit the Chevy's left headlight. Cooley swore. He took his gun, stuck his arm out of the window, and shot at the taxi. He hit a tire—or that's what it looked like, because the taxi swerved wildly, turned around and almost tipped over, but a cement pillar stopped it, after which it skidded into an alleyway between two warehouses.

Suddenly there were cars—from the Brooklyn Union Gas Company and from elsewhere—and the sound of sirens howling. Cooley's Chevy had a strong spotlight. He turned it on and up. Other spotlights on other cars flared up. Now the whole area was brightly lit. Men came running out of the pub and from the pier, but they kept their distance. Cooley drove the Chevy up to the alley between two high red-brick warehouses. When the taxi had skidded into it, it had rammed into a row of open crates, toppling them. Pieces of wood and wood shavings obstructed the entrance.

Sirens howled, spotlights and headlights blazed, and the first cars slowly approached the devastated driveway. The front of our Chevy was just inching forward into the entrance when a second shot was fired, hitting our second headlight. Cooley stopped the car, grabbed his gun, and jumped out. "You stay here," he told Bertie. "It's much too dangerous without a weapon."

"Sure," said Bertie, readying his Hasselblad. Cooley had barely left the car when we jumped out, too.

Cooley was standing at the corner of the warehouse, protected by it, and was shooting into the driveway. Police behind the corner of the other warehouse, were doing the same thing. Their fire was answered. Bertie and I threw ourselves on the ground and crawled forward until we had a full view of the driveway—a narrow yard, actually, between high walls, dimly lit by two lamps. The taxi had turned around completely and stood now with its headlights facing us. The door next to the driver's seat was open and Turner was crouched behind it, shooting.

"It's a dead end," said Bertie, who was taking pictures.

The sirens were quiet suddenly, and a voice on a bullhorn was saying, "Give up, Turner! You don't have a chance."

Turner's answer was three shots.

Now the plainclothesmen threw themselves on the ground. "Come out, Turner! Hands up!" said the voice on the bullhorn.

Again three shots.

A lot of shots answered Turner's attack. They hit the taxi, some ricocheted wildly through the yard. Turner shot back. One of the plainclothesmen's car inched forward a little, enough to light up the yard. Turner shot at it but failed to hit it. We could see his knee under the open door of the car. As long as he had ammunition—and he seemed to have plenty—it would be extremely dangerous, if not impossible, to go in and get him. Suddenly something was flowing across the pavement under the taxi. "What's that? Blood? Did they get him?" asked Bertie.

"I don't know."

They didn't seem to have hit him, because next Turner shot out the lights of the other plainclothesmen's car. Now only the two street lamps lit up the yard. Suddenly I saw a shadow move under the hood of the taxi. Everybody saw it, but nobody did anything about it. We were all too astounded. *What* was Turner up to now?

Something glittered.

"He's put the bottle under the motor," said Bertie.

The shadow moved a little. There was a sound of grinding metal. "He's screwing something under there—good God!" cried Bertie. "Do you know what he's doing?"

"What?"

"He's unscrewing the gas pipe from the pump!"

"What for?" I asked, as the bullhorn voice shouted that in a minute everybody would open fire on Turner if he didn't give himself up.

"And that wasn't blood—that was alcohol he poured out."

"Why?"

"You'll see. Now he'll start the car. . . ." And almost at once you could hear sputtering of the starter, for quite a while, only the car didn't start.

"He's gone crazy," I said.

"He's normal as hell," said Bertie, taking pictures.

Again Turner's shadow could be seen under the hood, then, for a split second, the top part of his body was clearly visible above the door. The police shot but failed to hit him. And a small flame flared up in the yard. Then something came flying—the liquor bottle. It hit the wall beside Cooley and broke. In the next moment, itss contents sprayed in every direction and caught fire. Cooley fell, screaming. His clothes, his hair were on fire. His colleagues ran up to him and began beating out the flames with their jacket and coats. Others caught fire. At the same time, quick as lightning, like a lawn sprinkler, a curtain went up in front of the entire entrance—not water, but fire. The wooden crates and wood shavings had ignited, too. Men came running up with fire extinguishers and tried to help their friends. Others wanted to get through the flames and into the yard. . . . Impossible! "When he started the car, it pumped gas into the bottle, then he stuck his handkerchief or his tie into it and lit it and threw the bottle!" cried Bertie. "I knew it! I knew it!"

Now he was photographing standing up, as if nothing could happen to him. Those are going to be pictures, I thought . . . fantastic! Then I saw Turner climbing a fire-escape ladder up the side of the left warehouse. "There!" I screamed. "There he is!"

Two, three, six automatics began to shoot. Another car moved forward, a new spotlight flared up and tried to follow Turner. Got him. Followed him. The automatics hammered away. I saw shards of brick flying into the air where the bullets hit, very close to Turner. The man was unbelievably lucky. The ladder angled and disappeared to the back of the house. You couldn't see Turner anymore.

Cooley limped to his car and shouted into the microphone, his face distorted with pain. He explained the situation to control and told them to alert the cars at the back of the warehouse. They should be able to see Turner from there. Precious time went by until Cooley had made the situation clear. More time until control was able to notify the other cars. All we could hear was gunfire beyond the walls. But then we heard something else—the rotor of a helicopter.

I looked up and couldn't believe my eyes. A roaring sound from the roof of the warehouse and then, above our heads, a helicopter. The men shot at it—in vain. The helicopter made a wide turn over the Upper Bay, then rose up straight and disappeared in the clouds. We stood there, staring up at the sky, and at our feet the fire crackled cheerfully.

21

They arrested the owner of the pub, a certain Joe Bradshaw, who admitted at once that he had given Turner a box with two aluminum containers. He had received the box some time ago, as a small package from Prague. The sender? A certain Jan Bilka. Bradshaw had met Bilka three years ago when he had been on a tourist trip in Europe. At the time he and Bilka had met quite by chance in a museum. Bilka had arranged this "accidental" meeting, no doubt about it. Bradshaw and Bilka had become friends and had corresponded for years. Bradshaw showed a lot of letters received from Bilka. He lived in the same house as his pub, and his wife corroborated his story. Then this small package had arrived, together with a letter. In the letter Bilka asked his friend to look after the package until he arrived in New York, which would be very soon. If he didn't come, he would write and tell Bradshaw to whom he should give the package. Early that evening an airmail special delivery letter had arrived from Bilka, in Prague, saying that for the moment he wasn't able to make the trip, but late that evening a certain Floyd Turner would come and Bradshaw was to give the package to him. ("They must have started working on Bilka already in the Polish cargo plane," said Bertie, as we listened to Bradshaw. "Man, do they work fast!")

In Bilka's letter Turner was described exactly—his address, even his Social Security number. Bradshaw had therefore had no qualms about giving him the package, which he had never opened. Turner had opened it and the containers. According to Bradshaw there had been films inside. What kind of films? Bradshaw didn't know. Turner had thanked him, bought two bottles of bourbon, and left. Bradshaw had no idea what it was all about. Cooley's men took him along, just the same; his wife, too. And although a dozen police helicopters were sent up at once, they were unable to locate the one in which Floyd Turner now sat with the microfilms. The radar airwatch New York, which was on high alert that night, suffered from interference for seven crucial minutes for reasons that were never explained—with the result that Turner's helicopter was never even spotted, and there was a near collision of two police helicopters. Turner's machine was found later by security police, abandoned on a lonely football field in Staten Island. And that was that, on Saturday, around midnight, November 16. . . .

22

"I knew you'd come, Herr Roland," said Fräulein Louise.

Her white hair was combed straight back, the little knot at the nape of her neck was neat and tight, her little face no longer expressed exhaustion, and she wasn't pale anymore. Her blue eyes looked rested and she seemed completely at ease.

She was very pleased to see me. She talked slowly; the fear, the sense of being driven, and the occasional outbursts of temper seemed to have disappeared. She looked small and fragile, lying in a bed that also seemed small and fragile, although it was standard size. She lay alone, in a big private room, in the Psychiatric Clinic of the Ludwigskrankenhaus in Bremen. The windows of her room looked out on a courtyard with bare chestnut trees. They were not barred, and the door had handles on both sides.

492

"How are you, Fräulein Louise?" I asked. I know I sounded worried.

"Oh, I'm very well. Really. You have no idea how much I sleep. The food's not very good, but I never was very particular about what I ate. Hospital food from a big kitchen.... I know all about if from the camps I've been in."

The door opened and a fat jolly nurse carried in a vase with the flowers in it that I'd brought for Fräulein Louise. "Flowers!" she cried. "Flowers are always beautiful. You are a good man, and I see that you're not angry with me."

"Angry? *Me?*"

"Well, yes. That's why I asked them to let you visit me right away."

"Why?"

"I kept thinking: You behaved dreadfully to Herr Roland. You must apologize to him. And that's what I'm doing right now. Thank you, nurse." The nurse nodded and left us. "I'm saying it and and I mean every word of it. Don't be angry with me anymore, Herr Roland, please!"

"But why should I be angry with you?"

"Well," said Fräulein Louise, looking down at her hands, "the way I forced myself into your hotel room and screamed and yelled and behaved badly in front of the other gentlemen..."

"Nonsense. You were just terribly excited, that's all."

"Well, yes, I was. Because I wanted to bring Irina back with me." She smiled. "Meanwhile, *Herr Doktor* Erkner has told me she's with you and you're looking after her and she's better, much better than she was in the camp. And you've taken over the responsibility for her, and all formalities will be attended to. I did you an injustice, Herr Roland. I thought you were going to—harm her, and I'm very ashamed of that. So now there's peace between us again, Herr Roland, isn't there?"

"Yes, Fräulein Louise."

She took a deep breath. "Now I feel free," she said. "It's a load off my mind. I had very bad thoughts about you and Herr Engelhardt. He isn't angry with me either, is he?"

"Not at all. He sends greetings. So does Irina."

"Oh, God be thanked!" she cried. "Now I can go on carrying my burden. Now I may even find peace here."

"That's what you're here for," I said.

"And I will, I will, Herr Roland. Everybody is so worried about me. I should just get well. First *Herr Doktor* Erkner gave me something and I slept for two days, then he spoke to me and

493

said he'd like to give me electric shock treatments, one after the other, every other day, and he also wanted to give me medicine and injections. I really can't complain."

"Electric shock treatments"—she had said the words without a trace of emotion.

"When will they begin the treatment?"

"I had the first one yesterday."

"You *did?*"

"Yes. And tomorrow I'll have the second one. Always early in the morning. Then there'll be four more. No, no, Herr Roland, I'm very well taken care of. This is the private sector, first class. I've been told you're paying for it. Of course I'm going to pay it back. I have plenty of money. And I'm so glad to be in a room by myself. It's really best for me." And I thought how Demel had told me on the phone that Fräulein Louise's bag with all her money had fallen into the moor.

"My publisher is paying for it, Fräulein Louise," I said. "And you don't have to pay it back. He's a millionaire. And I'm going to write about you and the children—remember?"

"Yes. And if your publisher is really a millionaire, then all I can do is say thank you and accept. My children—if only I knew why I'm here and not with them."

"You don't know why?"

"I have no idea."

"But you know where you are."

"Well, of course. In the Ludwigskrankenhaus in Bremen. *Herr Doktor* Erkner told me that. But *why* am I here? He said to recover my health. But what does he mean by that? I'm not sick. What's supposed to be wrong with me? And in my *head?*" She sounded truly puzzled, but not the least aggressive—just surprised.

Before going in to see her I had spoken to Dr. Erkner. He took me into his office and told me that Fräulein Louise was doing very well; he was most gratified. Pastor Demel had told him about Fräulein Louise's dead friends.

"All that disturbed world of hers is momentarily in the background," said Dr. Erkner. "The healthy aspect of her personality predominates. The insane happenings are obscured. If you were to speak to her about her dead friends now, she wouldn't know what you were talking about. She remembers all the realities, but in between there are gaps."

"Will they close? Will that disturbed world return?"

"I don't know," he said. "It's a common schizophrenic

condition. Symptoms may appear again later." And now I was sitting opposite Fräulein Louise. I had been afraid she would ask me questions about all the things she couldn't understand or where her memory failed her, but she didn't. The way she saw it, she was perfectly healthy: She knew where she was, she knew that Dr. Erkner was her friend and meant to do only what was best for her. She felt well.

"You must get back to your work," she said. "You were in such a hurry."

"I still am!" I said.

"You see? That's why I begged Dr. Erkner to call you up and tell you to come. But mainly because you were always so good, and I didn't want you to be angry with me anymore."

"Yes. I got back yesterday and found the message from Dr. Erkner, and flew straight here."

"There are such gaps in my memory," Fräulein Louise said sadly. "Of course I know what happened in the camp: that they shot poor little Karel, and you took Irina to Hamburg. First a truck driver took me to Bremen, and from there I took the train. In Hamburg a lot of things happened to me. I took a guide at the station, poor Herr Reimers, and it turned out that he was sick. And I was at King Kong and in the Paris Hotel, where they murdered this man, Concon. And I remember Eppendorfer Baum, where I met a French antiques dealer, and the superintendent was a Pole. They told me where you and Irina were. So then I drove to the Metropole, but it seems to me that there's much more to it, and and that's what I can't remember."

"It doesn't matter, Fräulein Louise. You remember enough. And you told me such a lot at the camp. I have it all down on tape. I'll manage all right."

"Does that mean you're not coming to see me anymore? That there's nothing more I can do for you?"

"But of course I'll come to see you again," I said, and thought that perhaps she would remember her dead friends again, and I would be able to write in much greater detail. "I'll come often."

"Well, I won't always be here," she said.

"Of course not. Then I'll come to the camp in Neurode. With the plane it won't take long."

"I've never flown," she said; and then, with no connection whatsoever: "I was in the park, too, behind your hotel, and that was where I was so terribly afraid."

"Of what?"

"I don't know, Herr Roland. I only remember that I took the

495

train back to Bremen with a very friendly young woman. Her name was Inge Flaxenberg. She said everybody called her Bunny. The way everybody calls me Fräulein Louise. She said she'd worked in a gaming casino, but they'd closed it down because there were magnets under the roulette table. Now you see? I can remember all that exactly. And that her fiancé drove me to Neurode in his car. But after that I can't remember anything. The next thing I remember is talking to *Herr Doktor* Erkner here in the clinic."

She had scarcely mentioned his name when the door opened and he came in, tall, in his white coat. He looked happy. "Have you enjoyed your visitor, Fräulein Louise?"

"Oh, yes. Very much. Herr Roland isn't angry with me."

"Didn't I tell you that?"

"Yes, you did, *Herr Doktor*."

"So there you are!" And to me, "I'm afraid you'll have to leave now, Herr Roland. Fräulein Louise needs a lot of rest."

"Yes," she said. "That's true. I do need rest. And it's so quiet here. I could sleep all the time."

"I'll come again," I said, and stood up. "Whenever you like. You can call me, or I'll call you. Don't worry about our story. I'll soon have it all done."

"Yes, yes," said Fräulein Louise. "Come whenever you like. You don't have to ask, does he, *Doktor?*"

"No," said Erkner, "you can come anytime, Herr Roland."

"Only not in the early morning for the next few days," Fräulein Louise said seriously. "Because that's when I get my shock treatments, and after them I always sleep for a while, very deeply."

23

On Tuesday, November 19, ten minutes before six o'clock in the evening, I was again walking with Irina on that street in northwest Frankfurt where the doctor had his office. We had come here the same way as last time, leaving my apartment house by the garden entrance. Traffic was heavy, and the sidewalks were crowded with pedestrians. We had to walk slowly. It was dark already, and a thin, cold rain was falling.

"So," I said, "in a few hours you'll be home again and it will be all over."

"Yes," said Irina.

"You mustn't be afraid," I said. "He's the best doctor in Frankfurt for this sort of thing."

"I'm not in the least afraid," said Irina. "What are you going to do during these few hours?"

"Oh . . . I'll have a drink. Perhaps I'll take in a movie."

"What movie?"

"I don't know yet."

"I'd like to go to a movie with you someday, Walter."

"Yes," I said. "That's something we'll do."

"When?"

"When it's all over and you're feeling perfectly well again."

"And when you have time."

"Yes."

"Because right now you're terribly busy." She pressed my arm. "That's why I'm doubly grateful to you for coming with me."

"But that goes without saying. Of course I wanted to go with you."

"I knew you'd help me," said Irina. "From the very first time I saw you, I knew it."

"Well, now, you weren't exactly friendly then," I said.

She said nothing. But after a while she said, "You've taken other girls to this doctor, haven't you?"

"Yes."

"And everything's always turned out all right?"

"Always. You really have nothing to worry about."

"I'm not worrying. I'm perfectly calm. Really I am. I'm already looking forward to when you'll be picking me up in a few hours. And it's not going to hurt, is it? He's going to give me an anesthetic, isn't he?"

"No!" I said.

"He's *not?*"

"No!" I said again in a loud voice, and stopped walking.

I don't know if you've ever had this feeling. You're convinced that something's going to happen, no getting around it. You tell yourself you can't influence it in any way (which is a lie), that the course of life takes care of everything (which is stupid), that you still have time, that the right moment hasn't come, and so on. And suddenly, in an absurdly short passage of time and without warning—you hadn't even been thinking about it—your conscience or your mind or your heart—whatever—gives you a jolt, and it happens! Without any volition on your part. It just happens, that which had been ordained anyway.

"But that's crazy!" cried Irina. "Without an anesthetic—"

"Stop talking about the anesthetic," I said, and suddenly everything was simple and obvious. "I'm not talking about the anesthetic."

"But you said, 'No!'"

"Yes."

"I don't understand you! No what?"

"No, we're not going to the doctor."

"But we have an appointment! I've got to be there in a few minutes!"

"We're not going," I said calmly and filled suddenly with happiness, if you want to call it happiness, what I felt there, on the street, under the streetlights, in the rain. "We're not going to him. You're not going to have it done."

"But—but that's crazy!" she cried.

"It's not crazy," I said. "It's the right thing to do. It's taken me long enough to realize that. You must have your child, Irina. Anything else would be a crime."

Somebody walked into me and cursed, and I took Irina's arm and drew her into a doorway where we were protected from the rain and the many pedestrians.

"Walter!" Irina was breathless. "You're out of your mind! We were agreed on everything, and the doctor's waiting."

"I'll phone him and call it off!"

"But you can't do that! It's impossible! I can't give birth to Bilka's child! Walter, I'm only eighteen! And in a strange country! And I don't even know what's going to happen to me, much less a child—"

"Irina!" I interrupted her. "Will you marry me?"

"*What?*"

"I'm asking: Will you marry me?"

She stared at me, her mouth open, and couldn't utter a word. "What's the matter?" I said. "Don't you like me? I'm too cynical—is that it? Or is it that I smoke too much and drink too much? I'll see what I can do about that, but believe me, the core of me's all right. So . . . will you marry me?"

"The child," she whispered. "The child. I can't—"

"Why not?"

"It's Bilka's child, Walter."

"I know," I said. "But it's you I want to marry, not Bilka. And the child is just as much yours as his. More yours than his because you're going to give birth to it. And then it will be our child."

"You're saying that now, because—because you're so kind... because you're so—so wonderful!"

"I'm not."

"But later—later it may grow to be like him...."

"You can't say that. Criminals have sired saints, benefactors of mankind, geniuses. Of course we may be unlucky, but from the moment it's born, it's *my* child. Not Bilka's. And whatever I can do to make a decent human being of it, I—" I stopped. "Nonsense!" I said. "As if I were a decent human being. We'll just have to risk it. And do you know why? Do you know why I want us to have this child?"

"Us," she whispered. "You said 'us.'"

"Of course—*us!* You and I. You'll be my wife then. There was a moment in Hamburg when I wished so much that you would love me and not Bilka. Don't laugh, but I thought then how wonderful it would be to have a child by you. Don't laugh, damn it!"

"I'm not laughing," she whispered.

"This child," I said, "you wanted it, didn't you, before you knew all about Bilka?"

She nodded.

"You see, Irina, you are eighteen. I—I'm thirty-six. I want so much for you to be my wife, and I want a child. But I wouldn't dare to give you a child. I've drunk too much. With all the whiskey I've consumed, the poor thing would probably be a cretin. And I want a child! Ever since I've known you, I've wanted *your* child. And now I can have it. Not the child of an alcoholic. Bilka didn't drink, did he?"

"No."

"So there you are! See how well it all works out? And now you may laugh!"

"I—I can't."

"Then say that you'll marry me. Say it now. Because I'm not going to let you go to that doctor, whatever you decide. So... what's it going to be?"

She laid her cheek against mine and whispered, "Yes, Walter, yes. I want to be your wife. And I'll do everything I can to be the best wife in the world. Oh, I'm so happy. I wanted it so much!"

"Me or the child?"

"Both of you," she whispered.

"My God, why didn't you say so sooner? We could have saved ourselves a lot of trouble, and I could have been working! So let's get married just as quickly as we can."

"Yes, Walter. Please! Oh, hold me! Hold me close!"

So I held her close and kissed her, many, many little kisses on her rain-wet face and for the first time since I'd known her, her eyes weren't sad but filled with joy. "Thank you," she said, "thank you, Walter."

"You're welcome," I said. "And now let's get out of here, fast. Let's go home."

I took her hand and we walked out of the house entrance into the rain, and became part of the stream of people hurrying along the sidewalk. Every now and then Irina leaned her head against my shoulder and we strolled along like that till we reached a bar. I drank a double Chivas and Irina drank orange juice. I called the doctor and said we'd changed our minds; he was furious and hung up, although I assured him I'd pay for the examination.

When I told Irina, both of us laughed like children. We hailed a taxi, and when we got home, I went on working and Irina busied herself in the kitchen, preparing dinner. I felt as if we were already married, and it was a good feeling. The rain drummed against my windows, and I wrote what Bertie and I had experienced with Fräulein Louise at the camp, and I felt the way one feels after a relaxing bath.

Our dinner was a happy event. Irina cooked well. I told her so and she was delighted. After dinner we cleared the dishes together and put them in the dishwasher. We went to the bedroom and I drank Chivas and Irina drank orange juice again because she was going to have a baby and therefore shouldn't drink alcohol. We sat there and played Tchaikovsky, a lot of records, then Irina retired to the bathroom. Later I went to the guest room to say good night to Irina. She had fallen asleep with the light on. She was breathing slowly and evenly, and she was smiling. On her face there was an expression of great peace.

7

We Go to Press

1

"One case of Gordon's gin, please...."

"Coburg ham, five hundred grams...."

"I want caviar. Four of the large glasses. No—the ones with the blue lids...."

The voices penetrated through the Kniefall Market all the way to the area at the back, with the bar and small tables. I was seated at one of them. In here the noise of the subway construction was muted. The day was gloomy, although it wasn't raining. A strong wind was driving black clouds across the gray sky, and the lights were on in the store. In all office buildings, too.

Blond, dark-eyed Lucie had greeted me with a shy, bright smile. It was 8:30 A.M., Thursday, November 21. I had been here last on Monday morning, November 11. To me the days in between seemed like ten years. So much had happened....

The night before I had completed Part Two of the "Treason" article. Part One was surely in print by now. I had put it on Hem's desk before my flight to the U.S.A., and high time, too, if it was to meet the deadline for the issue that was to be on the stands a week from today. I handed in Part Two this morning. The series wasn't going to cause me any trouble. I was writing it fast because I was enjoying every minute of it. Now I had to settle down to the first article of "Total Man," but I wasn't worried about it. I'd get that out of the typewriter in no time because I had *my* story!

I had written in every free moment, even at night, with Irina sleeping peacefully in the spare-room bed. But I had had nightmares. That was because I was in such a state of excitement. I had got up at seven. It was still dark. I had let Irina sleep and listened to the news as usual while shaving, and drunk a lot of black coffee. I hadn't eaten anything, but that had nothing to do with the alcohol I'd consumed the night before, although, watching television with Irina, happy in the thought that a lot of the groundwork lay behind me, I'd drunk quite a lot. But I wasn't drunk when I went to bed, and in the morning I felt fine. I just wasn't hungry. Excitement—that's what it was. Today, as agreed before my trip to New York, I had handed in the second part of my story, like the first—in a sealed envelope on Hem's desk. Original and one copy. There was to be public reading. The first two articles, at any rate, were to remain top secret, to be read only by Hem, Lester, and the management. When the gentlemen had finished reading Part Two, they would call me.

"Here you are, Herr Roland!"

I looked up. Lucie was standing in front of me, looking worried. She put a glass, a bottle of soda, and a bowl of ice cubes in front of me, and poured Chivas into the glass out of "my" bottle. I took the Gauloise I was smoking out of my mouth, looked at Lucie, and then I don't know what possessed me, but I threw the half-smoked cigarette into the whiskey. "What—what *are* you doing, Herr Roland?" stammered Lucie.

"I don't know," I said, just as astounded. The cigarette smoked and smoldered in the drink. I pushed the glass away. "I guess it means that I don't want any whiskey. And I don't seem to want to smoke either. At any rate, not in the morning."

"Herr Roland!"

"I know. It's peculiar. But suddenly I don't want to. As a matter of fact, I find the idea of whiskey repulsive. Please take it away, Fräulein Lucie."

"Are you ill?"

"I'm perfectly well." I laughed, and she laughed, too. She sounded happy and relieved, and she took everything away again fast.

"You know what?" I told her. "I'm hungry. And I have time. Could you give me breakfast? Two soft-boiled eggs, fresh rolls, tomato juice, and black coffee."

"Of course, Herr Roland! I'd love to!" She was still smiling, but there were tears in her eyes. "Oh, but that makes me feel good! Whatever's come over you? The last time you were here—"

"Oh, last time!" I made a derogatory gesture with my hand. "A lot has happened since then, Fräulein Lucie. I'll tell you all about it. But first get me breakfast."

"Yes, yes," she said, and ran off.

I was sitting with my back to the store. Now I looked at myself in the mirror behind the bar, and decided that my face had changed. It wasn't gray and old and debauched any more. It was a different face. But one couldn't have a different face in ten days. Or could one? I listened to the voices in the store and wondered what it would be like when Herford called me in and told me the two articles were great! Because they were. I was positive about that. Anyway, he'd have complained about the first one by now if he hadn't approved. He and Hem and Lester had read it, and nobody had had a word to say against it on my return from New York.

Lucie brought my breakfast. I downed the tomato juice in one go, then I ate the eggs, and the fresh rolls with butter, and drank coffee and felt marvelous. Chewing all the time, I told Lucie that in these ten days I'd found a story, a terrific story that was going to come out under my name. And she listened, all excited, her cheeks red.

"After all these years, at last, a story under my real name!"

"It's wonderful!" said Lucie. "Just wonderful! I've been so worried about you. But now everything's going to be all right, isn't it?"

I nodded, my mouth full.

"You have no idea how happy that makes me," said Lucie.

"And me, Fräulein Lucie! And me!"

Of course I couldn't tell her what the story was about—she understood that; but after I'd finished my breakfast, I asked her a few things about her home life, her plans, and she talked about her parents—they were peasants—and about her brother, who was in the army, and about her village, Brandoberndorf. And I was genuinely interested. It had been such a long time, I thought, since I had listened to anybody talk about himself unless I had to write about him or needed him in some way or other. Then, at ten, much earlier than I had expected, the phone rang. Lucie answered it, then turned to me. "You're to go over."

"Fine," I said happily.

I paid, gave Lucie a large tip, as usual, and she thanked me and said again how happy she was about the change in me. We shook hands. As I left the market, I turned back once. Lucie was standing behind the counter, still smiling, and she waved. I waved back, and a fat woman in a mink coat was saying, "Goose liver, Herr Kniefall. Three large cans."

2

People were hurrying across the plank bridge over the Kaiserstrasse subway excavation, jostling each other. I had my hands in my pockets—I'd left my coat in the office—and I was whistling. It was cold, and I turned up the collar of my jacket. The international "army" was working as usual in the tunneling below. Giant cranes were moving steel beams into position, drills were *rat-tat-tatting*, bulldozers were scooping up dirt. It was all just as it had been ten days before, yet it was all quite different. I took my pack of cigarettes out of my pocket and threw it down into the excavation. A little Italian caught it, looked up, saw me, and grinned as he raised his yellow hard hat. *"Grazie, signore, grazie...."*

"Molti auguri!" I shouted back. This time I felt one with the men working below, a fine feeling.

I took the VIP elevator up, first to the seventh floor where I went to my glass office and got another pack of Gauloise out of my coat pocket. I didn't want to be entirely without cigarettes. You don't become a saint in a day!

Everybody was already working in their offices and I greeted everybody in sight and they greeted me, a friendly atmosphere all round. As I was about to leave, my old friend Angela Flanders came in. She had on a navy-blue suit, her chestnut-brown hair was as beautifully groomed as ever, so was she, and she, too, was smiling. It seemed to be a day on which everybody smiled at me!

"Hello, Angela!"

"Good morning, Walter." She blushed a little. "You're going in to see Herford, aren't you?"

"Yes."

"Herr Kramer and Herr Lester are with him already. It's about your new story, isn't it?"

"Yes, Angela."

"Well, I guess I'll be getting to read it soon. Herr Kramer says you haven't written anything as good in years."

"Really?"

"Yes. I—you see, Walter—we've known each other for such a long time, we've been through a lot together. I know how desperate you've been, often, and now—now you have a great story again, and it's your own. . . . " She became more and more confused. "And—and that makes me very happy I—I do like you a lot, Walter. But you know that, don't you?"

"Yes, Angela," I said, "I know. And I'm very fond of you . . . very. But you know that, too, don't you?"

Now she flushed scarlet. "Because—because we're such good friends, Walter . . . I'm so happy for you. And I do wish you the best of luck in every way, for your writing, especially, and a *big* success with the story. I've been hoping and hoping that you'd write under your own name again."

"And I've been hoping for the same thing."

"Then up you go to Herford," said Angela. "I'll be thinking of you. Oh, sometimes you can get desperate in this profession, can't you? And then, when you least expect it, something good turns up. One's just got to believe that the good Lord's watching over us, don't you think so?"

"Absolutely," I said. "Anyway, today and right now I believe in Him firmly, Angela."

3

Old Schmeidle, Herford's number one secretary, told me I could go right in. The gentlemen were waiting for me. As I walked into the huge room, I could see Hem, Bertie, Lester, and photo-editor Ziller. They were sitting in a corner, opposite the computer monitor, in front of one of the windows. Although we were on the eleventh floor, the light was dim and wintery, the indirect lighting was on, over the bookshelves, too. The effect was a horrible, unreal atmosphere, a middle-earth effect, as if between life and death.

"Good morning, good morning," I said cheerfully.

The others murmured something; Hem smiled, Bertie nodded. "What's the matter?" I asked.

"We're waiting." Bertie was grinning.

"For Herr and Frau Herford and Dr. Rotaug," said Lester.

"Why aren't they here yet? Schmeidle said—"

"They *are* here," said Lester.

"Aha!"

He was looking at me as if the very sight of me irritated him. He hadn't forgiven me for my behavior ten days ago.

"They're in Herford's private office," Ziller explained. "They've been there quite a while. When we arrived, there was no one here."

"What are they up to?"

"No idea," said Bertie. "We've been waiting half an hour."

"Yes," said Lester, glaring at me.

Just then there was a noise, and a section in the wall of bookshelves swung open. In marched Mama, Rotaug, and Herford, slowly, solemnly, ceremonially. The men who had been seated stood up, the bookshelf door swung back and clicked shut.

Herford went straight to the lectern and began to leaf through the Bible. At last he found the place he'd been looking for and read softly, a little hoarsely, "From the Book of Job. Chapter One. 'Then Job arose, and rent his mantle, and shaved his head, and fell down upon the ground, and worshipped, and said, Naked came I out of my mother's womb, and naked shall I return thither; the Lord gave and the Lord hath taken away; blessed be the name of the Lord.'"

As some said Amen and others didn't, I looked at Bertie and Hem, and both of them raised their eyebrows and nodded. Things were starting off strangely. And things continued to take a strange course. Mama sat down. All of us sat down except Herford. Nobody said a word. Herford took his old pillbox out of his waistcoat pocket and took out an assortment of pills—blue, red, white. He tossed the whole lot into his mouth and drank some water. He didn't put the pillbox back in his pocket but laid it down in front of him on his desk, and *that* wasn't a good sign.

"Gentlemen," he said, and began to pace up and down his monstrous office. "What Herford is about to tell you is top secret. Not a word is to go beyond the walls of this room. Whoever may decide to be indiscreet will not only have to answer to Herford for it, but will also face punishment from the state."

So that was how it began. We stared at him like idiots and Mama murmured, "Oh, God. Oh, God...."

"Be brave, *gnädige Frau*," said Rotaug. It must have been the weird light, but today the liver spots on his bald head seemed darker than ever.

Herford, still pacing, went on. "We fought to the bitter end. We just hung up on the last phone call, and it's all over. We lost. Nothing more to be done about it. For the first time since the founding of *Blitz*, an issue will not come out, the one that was to go on the stands tomorrow."

Silence.

"It is the issue with the four pages of illustrations announcing the series 'Treason,'" Rotaug added, as if that had been necessary!

"But—but—" (Lester, shaken and stammering.)

"I know you are horrified, gentlemen," said Herford. "But not any more than I am, believe me. We can't come out. We were ordered to destroy the entire issue already on Monday morning, but we decided not to pass on this information to you at the time because we didn't want to upset you unnecessarily. Dr. Rotaug thought we still had a chance. He did what he could. He negotiated day and night, up to the last minute."

"With whom?" asked Hem.

"With the old gentleman in Cologne," said Herford. "Speaking on behalf of the Americans. It was he who begged—and you know what *that* means—that the issue be stopped."

"But at first he didn't have anything against it, nor did the Americans," said Bertie, smiling.

"At first the situation was quite different," said Herford. "The first time the old gentleman called, on Monday, we stopped all distribution and had the whole edition put under seal in its various trucks, trains, on airports, wherever. If we could have prevailed, the magazine could have gone straight to the wholesaler without delay. Because, until the thing was decided, nobody was to see the edition. That the people who had produced it had seen it was, of course, unavoidable. So we were faced with recalling two million copies and destroying them."

"But why?" I asked.

Herford looked at me like a stricken animal. "Because of your new series, Roland."

"I don't get it!" I said. "I don't understand a word of what's going on! Before I flew to New York with Bertie, the new series was the best thing we'd ever done. Have you read Part Two?"

"No!"

"You haven't *read* it?"

"No!" Herford shouted like a madman.

"Herford," whispered Mama. "Please. Your heart. . . . Things are bad enough already."

"Herr Herford," said Hem. "Please come to the point. *I* have read both parts and I think they are excellent. I therefore can't understand—"

"Excellent—shit!" shouted Herford. "And if Goethe had written them! Have none of the gentlemen noticed that one member of our family is missing?"

To be honest, I hadn't noticed it; neither, apparently, had any of the others. "Herr Seerose," said Lester, almost inaudibly, and Mama mumbled, "Oh, God. Oh God. . . ."

"Yes," said Herford. "Herr Seerose. My friend Oswald Seerose, who got the license for *Blitz* for me in 1946. My good old friend Oswald Seerose, who, since Monday noon, has settled down happily in East Berlin!"

"Who *what?*" Ziller jumped up, so did Lester, and, "You heard me," said Herford, his hand over his heart. "He crossed over so fast that neither the Security Police, nor the men at the border, nor the Amis had a chance to stop him."

"Stop him? Why?"

"Because my dear old friend Oswald Seerose has been one of the most important and successful agents for the East for the last twenty years," said Thomas Herford.

4

For a few moments there was complete silence. We were all more or less in a state of shock. I looked at Mama; she had collapsed. Rotaug was looking at me with undisguised animosity. Why? What did I have to do with the fact that Seerose had turned out to be a double agent? He noticed me watching him.

"Don't look at me like that!" Rotaug said angrily. "I can't help it that you couldn't see through Seerose."

"I?" Now I was furious. "How about you?"

"You were in constant communication with him, you carried

out his orders, you saw him enter Niendorferstrasse 333 in Hamburg—"

"You're crazy!" I shouted. "This is grotesque! He flew to Hamburg in a corporate plane. You knew where he was going! He told me on the phone that night, in front of all of you, that he'd spoken to the Americans!"

"*You're* not going to shout here!" shouted Herford.

"Herford . . . your heart. . . ."

"Goddamn my heart! He's not going to raise his voice here! Not he!"

"What do you mean, 'not he'?" asked Hem, his tone sharp.

"He and Seerose got us into this mess," said Rotaug.

"That's right," said Lester, fast. At last he had his sweet revenge for the embarrassment I'd caused him.

"And Herr Engelhardt," said Rotaug coldly, and Bertie laughed aloud. "Go ahead, laugh! Very funny, isn't it? A whole edition destroyed. Our losses in the millions. Every secret service agency in the Bundesrepublik on our necks. A scandal, when this thing with Seerose gets out. And the effect of all this on the magazine. Very funny, Herr Engelhardt!"

"Terribly funny, Herr *Doktor*," said Bertie, and laughed again. "It's my fault and Walter's! I'm going to laugh myself sick!"

"I wish you would," said Rotaug.

"Well, I don't understand anything," said photo-editor Ziller. "Herr Seerose and the Americans were friends, good friends. He flew to Hamburg to discuss certain details with them. They revealed their secrets to him. Otherwise Roland and Engelhardt wouldn't have been able to work on the project."

"Yes," said Rotaug. "Yes, my poor dear Herr Ziller. But in the same way the Russians were able to work, too."

"How—oh, I see!" Ziller was visibly shocked as he finally grasped the situation. "The waiter, the microphone, and everything. . . . " And, I thought, Jules Cassin! So he *had* been an accomplice of Seerose's from the start and had fooled me with his final outpouring of hatred for his former boss and all Germans. . . .

"Yes, Herr Ziller. And what the Russians didn't know: for instance, what was to take place in Helsinki. And Seerose was able to find out something even more important—the business with the copies of the microfilm."

"What about them?" asked Lester.

"Seerose told us that night, as you may recall, that the

Americans wanted the story printed on condition that we state that they had copies of the films—right? Which would have been possible. But when he visited them in Hamburg, he found out that they did *not* have any copies of the film, and this he passed on to the Russians, too. Naturally. A fine gentleman."

"Horrible!" said Ziller.

"And it's going to be a lot more horrible," said Rotaug. "Now comes the investigation. How much did Herr Roland and Herr Engelhardt really know about Herr Seerose's activities? To what extent were they perhaps working with him? How deeply were—"

"Herr *Doktor*," I said, "if you dare to mention one more infamous suspicion like that, I'll haul you into court."

"Let us hope that you won't be the one to be hauled into court!"

"That was a very uncalled-for comment, Herr *Doktor*," said Hem.

"That's what you think," said this human toad. "Interesting, very interesting. They will, of course, investigate you, too. They will investigate all of us. We are faced with the most serious crisis since the founding of the magazine. Let us pray that we survive it."

"Amen," said Mama in a broken voice.

"So," said Herford. "The story is dead. No point in wasting another minute on it. The old gentleman in Cologne has just told Rotaug that if one word, one picture, is printed on the subject, all advertising will stop and the magazine will be boycotted. American advertisers will follow suit. A boycott in every possible way. We've already thrown out the title page with the picture of this goddamn' Czech boy. Will be replaced by a bikini girl. Thank God, we have plenty of them in reserve. Kramer, you'll find something to replace the 'Treason' story, but you'll have to work fast. Lester will help you. A fine mess you got us into there, Roland."

Lester said, "When the jackass is feeling too good, he goes dancing on the ice."

"Shut up!" I told my editor-in-chief.

Lester jumped to his feet. "This is monstrous!" he screamed. "All of you gentlemen heard it. I demand that this—this man apologize to me. At once!"

"Oh, sit down, Lester," said Herford. "Apologize, Roland."

"No."

"You're to apologize, goddamn it!"

I said, "I will not apologize!" Because, you see, I had suddenly reached the end of my rope. Finally.

In moments like this, the strangest memories go through one's mind. I had to think of a children's poem that I'd heard on an assignment in London, while visiting a school. It went like this: "I think I am an elephant who is looking for an elephant who is looking for an elephant, who isn't really there." And that's what I thought of before anything else during that moment. For many years I had been an elephant, looking for an elephant, looking for an elephant, and *thinking I would find him!* And because of that, I'd put up with all the crap I'd had to write because one day, yes, one day I would find that elephant. And then I thought I'd found him in my story. But they weren't going to print my story. They weren't allowed to print it. I could see that. But I could see something else with blinding clarity: In this business you could look and look and look for the elephant, but you'd never find him. *Because he wasn't there!*

"You don't intend to apologize?" shouted Herford, and I shouted back, "No!"

Herford stepped up to me and remained standing in front of me. I was looking at his feet and saw him raise himself on tiptoe. And suddenly I was filled with a blind rage such as I had never experienced before in my life. I was clutching the arms of my chair so hard my knuckles were white, because I was afraid I might punch Herford or Lester in the face. Herford must have noticed it, because he stepped back and began pacing the room again.

"All right, then," he said. "A blow of fate. It won't kill us. God will help us. Now we must all pull together, gentlemen. Full capacity. 'Total Man' will get us out of this mess. The pictures are fantastic. Roland will do his best to make up for what's happened and will write something superlative. Right away. We have no time to lose. That's the most important thing on our agenda now. The show must go on. Herford will write a letter, addressed to our readers, explaining why the issue didn't appear. Rotaug will write it for Herford. He's good at that sort of thing."

"Very good of you to say so, Herr Herford," said the toad.

I got up and said, "Herr Herford, I am not going to write 'Total Man.'" I was on the verge of breaking down, but only Hem noticed it.

"You are going to write 'Total Man,' Roland! And *how* you are going to write it!" Herford was shouting again. He took some pills out of his pillbox without even looking at them and swallowed them without water. He choked on them for a second, but then he went on shouting. "You're under contract! Herford made you what you are today! *Blitz* taught you everything you know! So I don't want to hear another word!"

"Right," I said. "Not another word. I'm not writing the series."

He glanced at me, his lips tight. My smile, I knew, was a grimace.

He said softly, "You owe us a good deal more than two hundred thousand marks."

"Yes."

"You live in an apartment that belongs to *Blitz*."

"Yes."

"You draw an insane salary. Don't say yes again or Herford won't answer for what he'll do. Roland, you miserable jerk, you will write 'Total Man' and you'll write better than you've ever written, or—by God, Herford will—Herford will—"

"Yes?" I asked. "You were going to say, 'or Herford will fire you.' So fire me, Herr Herford. Come on, get it over with."

Herford was trembling with rage. "You miserable, filthy son of a bitch, you stinking animal!" He was panting. "Who do you think you are? If Herford fires you, you think you'll find work somewhere else? You do? Ha-ha-ha!"

"Herford, please—"

"Ha-ha-ha!" Herford couldn't be stopped. "If Herford throws you out, every illustrated magazine—what am I saying? Every newspaper in the country, down to the most insignificant local rag, will hear things about you so that nobody would *dare*, I say *dare* give you a job! Women! Alcohol! What a two-faced creature you are politically! If Herford fires you, you can starve! *Herford will destroy you!* Did you hear that?"

"I heard you, Herr Herford," I said. "It was loud enough. You will destroy me. Well, I intend to risk it."

My heart was beating wildly. I had to get this thing over with or I would never be able to look Irina in the face again. "I shall never write another line for you, Herr Herford."

"You ungrateful wretch!" cried Mama.

Rotaug said icily, "You recall, perhaps, Herr Herford, what I told you years ago...."

I didn't know if Herford remembered, but I did: "A great fellow," Rotaug had said. "But mark my words, one day this

514

great fellow is going to involve us in the biggest scandal of our publishing history." Rotaug knew his man, and at last we had reached the point.

"Now I've had it!" Herford raged. "Roland, in consideration of your attitude—"

I looked at Bertie and Hem. Bertie looked at me. He wasn't smiling; Hem closed his eyes for a moment. I took it to mean he approved of what I was doing. And it *was* the right thing, in fact it was the only thing to do at this point. I interrupted Herford. "You don't have to finish your sentence, Herr Herford. *I* am leaving. Without giving notice. Sue me, slander me, do whatever you like. I, too, have had it. To here." I made the appropriate gesture. "Good-bye. No, that's wrong. I don't wish you anything good!" And I began to walk to the door. Herford yelled, "Roland!" but I went right on walking.

"Roland! Stop! At once!" yelled Herford. I didn't stop.

"Roland, you're to stop!"

I stopped. I turned around. He was standing in front of his desk, panting, one hand pressed against his chest, pale as a ghost. He was feeling for his pillbox again. Mama hurried over to him and clung to his arm. "Herford demands that you—that you—"

But I interrupted him again. "Herr Herford?"

"Yes. What—what is it?"

"You can kiss my ass!" I said, and walked briskly out of the office. And it seemed to me that with every step the fury and guilt and unworthiness of years fell from me, the fourteen years spent in this cesspool, in this phony "dream factory," in these luxurious halls, in the service of mass stupefaction. Yes, I felt great. And with every step I felt better and better. The only thing I didn't believe in anymore was the existence of a dear Lord in heaven.

5

The termination papers arrived the same day, special delivery, registered mail, signed by Dr. Rotaug and demanding that I appear in his office the following day at 10:00 A.M. Irina was upset, but I calmed her down. I was still in a state of euphoria. No more *Blitz!* No more *Blitz!* Everything else would resolve itself, I thought. And it did. And how!

When I got to our office building the next morning, I greeted our massive doorman, Kluge. I'd known him for years, and he'd received a small fortune from me in tips; Herr Kluge, however, didn't seem to remember me and kept me waiting while he chatted with some other visitors. Then he said, "Oh, Herr Roland," and looked at a list, then at me, indifferently. "I see you are no longer with us, Herr Roland," he said. "May I please have the key to the elevator?"

"Now look here, Kluge—"

"Herr Roland, please—the key."

I gave him the key for the VIP elevator. He didn't even say thank you but turned to speak to a young lady who said she wanted a job as a volunteer. I walked over to the Plebian Cage where seven people were waiting patiently, and waited with them until the miserable elevator came, four minutes later. We crowded into it, it stank, and that's how I got to Dr. Rotaug's department. Everybody in the elevator avoided looking at me. Nobody spoke.

Rotaug kept me waiting half an hour, then at last he had time for me. He was standing stiffly in his mahogany-paneled office, looking hostile. We didn't shake hands. He pointed to the least comfortable chair, and after I had sat down, he began to pace up and down on stiff legs, tugging every now and then at his stiff collar or his beautiful pearl stickpin, while the following conversation took place.

Rotaug demanded that I pay the two hundred and ten thousand marks I owed them, and that I leave my apartment at once. "I don't have two hundred and ten thousand marks," I said, "and you know it."

"Of course I know it, Herr Roland." He stepped in front of me every now and then, rocking back and forth on his feet. "I don't have much time for you. I'm very busy. Now—there are two possibilities," and he went on to explain them.

The first one was that the publishing house sue me. I was living in an apartment provided by the house, our working relationship had ceased because of my "shameless behavior," so I had no further right to the apartment. The court would order me to hand over everything I owed, except for the legal minimum, thereby paying my debts to the house at least in part. I would then have to declare bankruptcy and would be subject to investigation at any time by the court sheriff, who would have the right to seize any money I might earn in the meantime, again excepting the legal minimum.

"Since you can hardly expect to be in command of any substantial sums of money in the near future," said Rotaug, "I would advise you to accept the second possibility, a possibility that demonstrates the greatest benevolence of your former employer."

"And that is—?"

"You agree to the following demands: You leave the apartment within the next ten days. All furnishings remain in our possession. This applies also to your bank accounts and your car. However, this will not cover the two hundred and ten thousand marks." He rocked up and down. The conversation was giving him almost orgiastic pleasure. "You sign an acknowledgment of debt, notarized by us. The things you hand over to us will be appraised, you will sign a promissory note for the remaining debt. Under these conditions—and I can't understand why— Herford is willing to let you keep your clothes, your typewriter, a small part of your library, etcetera. I advise you to accept his generosity—which, in my opinion, you don't deserve. Please come to a decision. I'm in a hurry."

I said, "I accept Herr Herford's generous conditions."

"Good. One more thing. We would be willing to pay a substantial sum—substantial in consideration of your deplorable situation—if you would be willing to let *Blitz* continue to use your pseudonym, Curt Corell."

My hands were fists. I said nothing.

"Well?" He rocked back and forth.

"So that you can enhance 'Total Man' with it?"

"Naturally. Corell is a concept, and we are the ones who made it famous, as you know only too well. Without us and the promotion we gave you, you could never have made it to the top. So, how about it?"

"No."

"You won't let us use the name?"

"No."

"Under any circumstances?"

"Under any circumstances."

I was furious. The name Corell *had* to disappear. Forever! Had to!

"You won't consider any amount?"

"I won't consider any amount," I said. "Forget it. The name belongs to me and disappears with me. If you use it in spite of my specific refusal—"

"Yes, yes, yes," said Rotaug. "That's all you need now to get on your high horse. We'll survive without Curt Corell; whether *you* can is a different story. I doubt it. And now, please, the papers and keys for your car. The Lamborghini stays here. I'll see you this afternoon at your apartment, with qualified appraisers, and we'll find out what your property's worth. You will, of course, then hand over to me all the tapes that are in any way connected with your last assignment, also all your research material and notes. Do you have your checkbook with you?"

"Yes."

"Call your bank and have them give you the amount in your account as of now. I'll listen on the other phone."

I phoned. The girl in the bookkeeping department recognized my voice and gave me the information—approximately twenty-nine thousand marks were still in my account. (I had just paid a large amount in back taxes.) Dr. Rotaug had me write a check for twenty thousand marks. I was allowed to keep the remaining nine thousand thanks to his 'generosity.'

"You have no other accounts?"

"No."

"I'm warning you, if you're lying and we find out that you have any other accounts, we'll sue. You'll have to sign a declaration anyway, under oath." I nodded. It had been Bertie's idea to make duplicate copies of all the tapes. He had spent the whole night on it. Hem had photocopied my notes.

"As soon as we have appraised your belongings, we'll see the notary. Tomorrow morning. It's Saturday, but he'll see us. That's all. I'll be at the apartment with the appraisers at 3:00 p.m." And with that he walked out of his office.

I got up and left. None of the secretaries responded to my greeting, and in the elevator everybody again avoided looking at me. I went all the way down to the basement and took one last look at the Lamborghini. I stroked the hood and walked away fast then. I walked all the way home. It was a cold day and the fresh air did me good. And another thought gave me satisfaction. In the apartment that had once been mine there was a wall safe. I had always kept money in it and three unset clear diamonds, a little over four carats in weight. I had given them and twelve thousand marks to Bertie for safekeeping.

518

Irina had prepared veal cutlets and pretended to be cheerful, so did I. And I really was! I was also hungry.

Punctually at three Rotaug came with two appraisers, stoical fellows. They worked fast. I wasn't surprised when everything they appraised was worth only a fraction of what it had cost. A third appraiser had meanwhile evaluated the Lamborghini at fifteen thousand, which was shameless. The car had cost fifty-eight thousand. Nothing I could do about it.

Rotaug and the appraisers made an inventory of the apartment's contents, then they spent a while figuring, and after subtracting what was left of my debt, I still owed *Blitz* a hundred and twenty-five thousand marks. Rotaug took the tapes and notes (Hem and Bertie had got them back to me in time, thank God!). Next morning I went to the notary and dutifully signed a declaration of debt and the promissory note, also a sworn statement to the effect that I had no hidden properties or had put anything away. I signed this declaration with an especially light heart.

Rotaug and I received a copy each of every document, and the notary kept one. Of course I was allowed to foot the bill. Two more things must be noted: The clothes Mama had let Irina choose were not confiscated, the house paid that bill without a murmur; they also went on paying Fräulein Louise's expenses in the psychiatric clinic. In a huge enterprise like *Blitz*, once a minor employee has been told to attend to something and the powers that be forget to rescind the order, the minor employee goes on doing as he has been told....

The notary's office was on the second floor of an office building, and in the end Dr. Rotaug and I walked down the one flight of stairs together. Outside the building Rotaug turned left without a word and walked to where his chauffeured car was parked; I turned right and walked to the nearest streetcar stop. And that was how my fourteen years as star reporter and writer for *Blitz* ended. In my opinion, it was a thoroughly dignified end.

I reached my apartment, which was mine for only ten days more. Again I put on a show of being cheerful, so did Irina, and we pretended to be confident and carefree. Everything would turn out all right. Ridiculous to contemplate anything else. That's what I thought, until the afternoon mail came.

In the Bundesrepublik there is a *Press Bulletin* that prints the inside news and gossip of the profession. All of us subscribe to it. The afternoon mail brought the latest edition. Herford worked fast. Two pages were attached to the issue, and under the headline "Latest News" there was an article about me. "The End of Walter Roland?" was the heading, and the whole article was as sly, legally, as the question mark after my name. It was peppered with phrases such as "it seems that...," "it appears to be true...," "according to what we hear..."; in other words, every sentence was legally safe and infamous beyond anything I could possibly have dreamed up, and there was very little in this business that I considered impossible. Rotaug had written a masterpiece!

Because of recent events at *Blitz*, what had been suspected for a long time had finally to be acknowledged: that alcohol had written finis to a brilliant career. I was nothing more now than an irresponsible, disloyal, amoral alcoholic on the brink of total collapse and without the capacity to write as I had once written. I had insulted my publisher in the most shameful fashion when he had dared to give me some well-meant advice. He had therefore been forced to dismiss the man who had been his star writer but was nothing now but a liability and a threat to the magazine. And so on and so forth, two pages of it. I read it through again, and drank, and thought that now I'd have to sue the *Press Bulletin* and *Blitz*, but then I thought: What was there to gain with such a suit? The *Bulletin* and *Blitz* must have counted on the possibility, and *Blitz* must have treated the *Bulletin* to a hefty sum of money and promised them all support if I did bring suit. I was sure, after all the experience I'd had with similar slander campaigns during my years with *Blitz*, that Herford was even counting on such a suit and having to recant. But months could go by before such a suit was concluded, months during which the assertions in the article would remain uncontested. And that was the main objective of Herford's revenge. He wouldn't give a damn if he had to pay stiff damages (I owed him enough anyway)—or perhaps *Blitz* wouldn't lose, because some of the things that were expressed in such a devilishly clever way were true. And even if I won and the denial was printed, what use would it be to me after so many months? Who took denials seriously, anyway, in my profession? I had been fired; that was fact, no getting around it. Nothing else was of interest—because there must have been a damned good reason for Herford to fire his top writer. And it was clear to me now suddenly why none of the rival houses, why nobody in the business, had called me yet to ask me to work for them. Herford's people must have spread the accusations that were in the *Press Bulletin* by phone also, I thought, and for the first time felt uneasy. And then, in a flash, it attacked me. I couldn't breathe. My hands flew to my throat and I felt fear, deadly fear, utter helplessness, and a terrifying weakness. He had come without warning—the jackal.

6

I shall never forget what followed. It started as it always did—I undressed fast and took 20 mgs. of Valium, went to bed, lay quietly on my back, and tried to breathe deep. I tried to control my fear by recalling the many similar situations when this had helped. Irina was shocked. She hurried over to me and I explained as best I could, in clipped, halting words, that this happened to me sometimes. It came from drinking, and that was why she shouldn't call a doctor, because that was what everybody was talking about, the fact that I was a heavy drinker. And a doctor might insist that I go to a clinic, probably quite unnecessarily, and then it would really be out and everyone would say, "There. You see?"—and I'd never get another job. She was terribly worried but promised not to call a doctor, and then I tried to sleep.

But I didn't have a chance. My accelerated pulse, the difficulty I had breathing, the dreadful sense of weakness and the nausea that went with it, grew worse. I began to sweat—this hadn't happened to me before, especially the palms of my hands, my head and my chest—and my sweaty hands began to tremble. But I was stubborn and determined. I didn't drink whiskey, but took another 20 mgs. of Valium, then another 20, after which I slept, a deep sleep with terrifying nightmares. I can't remember them, only that in them I nearly died of fright. When I woke up, Irina was sitting beside my bed, wiping the sweat off my forehead. She gave me fruit juice to drink. And I had slept three hours. Three hours, with 60 mgs. of Valium!

I wanted to get up but almost fell. Irina had to support me. In the bathroom I vomited, although I had eaten nothing. I wanted to take more Valium, but the small glass vial slipped out of my hand and broke. Irina collected the little blue bills and handed them to me, and took me back to my bed, which she had made up fresh in the meantime, because I had soaked the sheets. Irina. . . .

Whenever I woke out of my frightful dreams, she was sitting beside me. She brought me something to drink, tried to make me eat, insisted that I eat and drink even if I threw it all up again. She led me—no, by now she was dragging me to the bathroom and back again, and always she'd made up my bed fresh in the meantime. She didn't speak, but she smiled although I could see the tears in her eyes. Irina. . . .

I don't know how she managed to stay awake, but she was awake every time I opened my eyes. She had brought the mattress and bedding out of the guest room and made a bed for herself on the floor beside mine, and she was always sitting up in it, near me, when I came to. Irina. . . .

I came to, but I wasn't really awake. I became more and more confused and when I was awake I relived the horrors of my dreams. My dreams pursued me, ever present, waking or sleeping. They got mixed up with reality, and occasionally I would scream at Irina and curse her and tell her I hated her. She should get out! Go away! She never took me seriously. Irina. . . .

Besides the Valium, which I was taking in dangerously big doses, because I told myself the damned stuff had always sent the jackal away, I took all sorts of sleeping pills. But my dreams only grew worse, so did the perspiring, the trembling, the fear. I couldn't focus properly. My room was tiny, suddenly, then it was large again; my bed was in the wrong position and everything changed shape, color, even Irina's face.

"Don't you think you'd better try some whiskey?" she asked once—I think it was on the second day.

"No," I said, the saliva running down my chin. "No, no. I've got to manage without it. The jackal's got to go away without it. Give me some more Valium."

She did, but the jackal didn't go away and my condition worsened hourly. I dreamed a hell of Breughels and Dantes, and when I came to, my waking hell was worse. I couldn't move without Irina's help. She had to hold me and support me, even in the bath. I was deeply ashamed, but she showed nothing but worry and compassion, never impatience or revulsion, not even when I had diarrhea and vomited and soiled everything I touched. She cleaned up after me. Irina. . . .

My dreams became unbearable. I could smell the stench of the jackal's breath. The animal was lying beside me, in my bed,

522

licking my face, and I retched and retched. Then Irina was there again with fruit juice or soup or white bread with butter and honey, insisting that I eat and drink, no matter what happened afterwards. I couldn't tell the difference anymore between artificial light and daylight; I didn't know whether it was day or night and had to ask Irina.

At the end of the second day, my heart stopped beating. Of course it didn't really stop beating, or I would have died, but it felt as if it had, and it was the most gruesome experience I have ever had. Everything went black around me, and with my mouth open wide, I struggled for air, air, air, and couldn't breathe. I pressed my sweating hands against my sweating chest and—this I do remember—my body curled up and I panted, "Help! Help! Help!" Then I collapsed and was at peace.

7

I have no memory of the next two days. I survived them, but all I know about them is what Irina told me. She watched at my bedside and never left me. She told me that during those two days and nights I slept, but I screamed in my sleep and tossed from side to side. Occasionally I awakened. Then she took me to the bathroom or fed me. I even sat up in a chair once and shaved. But when I finally came to on the fourth day, I knew nothing of all this. She must have been right, because I was clean-shaved and had on clean pajamas, the bed was freshly made, and I saw Irina lying on the mattress beside my bed, fully dressed. She had fallen asleep, exhausted. The light was on. The minute I moved she woke up, and her smile was there. "What—what is it?"

"Better," I said, sounding as surprised as I felt. "I—I think I'm better."

She uttered a cry of joy and ran off into the kitchen. She came back soon with a light meal. When I sat up in bed and ate, I realized how weak I was. My hands started to tremble again and I began to sweat. But the jackal was gone, no doubt about that.

It had been 1:00 A.M. when I had awakened; now I took some more Valium and slept until the following morning, and for the first time could go to the bathroom alone, although I had to feel my way along the walls and stop every now and then. My knees were shaking, the sweat was pouring down my body; but I managed to shave standing, and to wash myself. Then I stumbled back to bed and without taking anything, fell into a deep, dreamless sleep. This time I slept around the clock, and when I woke up it was the morning of November 28, 1968, a Thursday, a day I shall never forget.

Gray light was filtering through the window, the light was on in the room, Irina had fallen asleep on her mattress, and she didn't wake up when I got up. And then—it was miraculous—my legs felt steady, I could stand and walk. I didn't feel sick, I wasn't sweating, my heart was beating normally, and I could breathe. And I was hungry!

I went to the kitchen and prepared a big breakfast for Irina and me. While I was waiting for the water to boil, I thought of something. I went to the bar and the pantry, got what I could find in the way of whiskey and liquor, then I took a heavy hammer and smashed every bottle. When I was done I swept up all the glass shards and dumped them. That was the last time I had to vomit, when I smelled the alcohol as I washed the stuff down the drain. In the bathroom I cleaned my teeth. It was then I noticed that someone was watching me. Irina.

"It's over," I said.

She ran to me and threw her arms around me and kissed me over and over again. "Thank you, thank you, thank you...." Nothing else. I asked her whom she was thanking. Whoever it was, I thanked him, too.

We breakfasted in the kitchen. I was very hungry. We laughed and were silly, and the five worst days of my life were over.

Some time later, I asked Dr. Wolfgang Erkner if such a thing was possible. He said indeed it was—when profound psychological disturbances occurred during a certain stage of alcoholism, or if the alcoholic was torn out of his accustomed milieu, but also if he was freed from a profound sense of oppression; but such conditions, if treated at home, rarely led to recovery.

What I am about to write now is not told to moralize, nor to sound like a preacher, but because something important would be missing if it were left out: From that twenty-eighth of November to the present day, I have not touched alcohol in any form whatsoever. And the jackal never came back.

8

Hem took Irina and me into his big apartment. He gave us two rooms, one for us to sleep in, the other for me to work in. When we left my apartment in the penthouse, two employees from *Blitz* watched that we didn't take anything with us that was on Rotaug's list, so we took very little. It fitted easily into two large suitcases. We moved them, and my suits and Irina's clothes and the books I was allowed to take, in Bertie's Mercedes. We only had to make three trips. I gave the keys to the men from *Blitz*, Hem had given me the keys to his apartment. We moved on the Monday after Advent, and it snowed for the first time that year.

Hem's apartment was furnished with antiques. The big double bed he and his wife had slept in was in the bedroom he had assigned to us. He slept at the other end of the apartment.

Irina and I were alone on that first Monday because it was closing day, and Hem and Bertie had a lot to do. I knew Hem would be home late.

Toward evening I grew uneasy because I realized I would now have to sleep in the same bed with Irina, and this worried me. I told myself that we loved each other; it was perfectly natural, therefore, for us to sleep together; but then I had to think that the child she was carrying wasn't mine, but another man's. I wanted desperately to sleep with her, but couldn't help thinking of everything that had happened. In the end I decided to tell her that I could control myself and wait until the child was born, even if it meant waiting half a year. I didn't know whether I could stand it, night after night, but if things became unbearable, there was a couch in the room I worked in.

When I went to her finally she had put out all the lights except the one beside the bed, and she was lying on the bed, naked. She opened her arms wide and said, "Come, Walter." And after that everything was so simple, so good, and so right. It was as if I had never loved before. We made love again and again, and I was in ecstasy, so was she. That which I had dreaded was wonderful, the most wonderful experience of my life. Once, as I ejaculated, I

525

had the feeling that all life was flowing from me, and I thought that I would have liked to die now, like this. But that wouldn't do—we had a child.

In the end Irina fell asleep in my arms. I lay awake for a long time in the dark and was happy. Then I must have fallen asleep because I felt something move. I opened my eyes. The clock read three. Irina was sitting up in bed beside me, her hands folded. I asked, "What is it, darling? Aren't you feeling well?"

"I feel wonderful," she said.

I sat up, too. The city lights lit up the window. The curtains weren't drawn, and I could see little white snowflakes drifting down. "What are you doing?" I asked, my arm across her shoulders.

"I was praying," she said, and added quickly, "but I don't know what for."

"No. Of course not."

We were silent for a while, then Irina said, "It isn't true."

"What isn't true?"

"What you said in Hamburg. That there's nothing but meanness on this earth."

"Did I say that?"

"Yes. And it isn't true. There are also such things as friendship and decency and love. No . . . don't say anything!" And then she whispered, "Because if there was nothing but meanness on this earth, there wouldn't be any people on it. Not one. And there are so many people. . . ."

After that we were silent. My arm was around her shoulders and we looked at the window and watched the snow falling outside, silently, inexhaustibly.

9

"Herr Roland!" Fräulein Louise greeted me with a smile. "How good of you to come! I've missed you."

"I couldn't come earlier. I was ill for a few days."

"Ill?"

"Nothing serious. But after that I had such a lot to do, or I'd have come earlier."

I was sitting at a table, opposite Fräulein Louise, in a large room. She was wearing an old gray suit and bedroom slippers. A thin, hard crust of snow lay on the branches of the chestnut trees in the yard. It was too cold to snow again. "Hasn't anyone from the camp visited you in the meantime?" I asked.

"Oh, yes. Herr Pastor Demel and Herr Kuschke, the bus driver—they were here. Once. Each of them. They brought me some of my clothes. So nice of them. But they couldn't stay long. I was sorry about that. I'm lonely here. Nobody really cares for me, and I have no relatives, and no friends." I looked at her sharply as she said the last word, but her face expressed no emotion. She had undoubtedly said it without the meaning it had had for her before. "And that's why I'm glad you're here." She laid her little old hand on mine and smiled.

"How are you feeling, Fräulein Louise?"

"Oh, I'm very well. I really am." And she did look well, and rested. "And I'm so happy to be so well taken care of." She leaned forward and lowered her voice to a confidential tone. "Although things here are not all they seem to be."

This was in the afternoon, on December 9, a Monday. Bertie had let me use his car and I had driven to Bremen in it. I had really been very busy the last few days. First Irina and I had gone to the registry office, where we were told we could marry only after Irina had declared before a notary that she had never been married before and after she had presented an *Ehefähigkeitszeugnis*, or Marriage Fitness Certificate. Since this was a document she could not produce under present circumstances, we had to go to the Provincial Court to fill out the form for an exemption. We were told it would take a month before we could expect an answer to our request.

It turned out that Hem knew someone at the court, and he asked the man to put in a word for us to hasten the reply to our petition. Hem was crazy about Irina. In the evening they sat together, telling each other stories, or Hem played the cello or the stereo for her; Schoeck, of course. He showed her color prints of madonnas, paintings, and sculptures in his voluminous art books. He did this, he said, so that Irina's child might be as beautiful as the Christ Child on the Madonna's lap. He seemed to believe that it would have that effect.

Meanwhile, Irina was working from nine to six for a child psychologist as a sort of Girl Friday. He couldn't employ her as a full assistant, but he needed help for his paper work and he paid well. Irina had declared she wanted to work. When the child came, she would stop for a while; after that she would like to complete her studies. "But right now we need every mark," she said, "until you get a job."

It didn't look as if I was going to get a job. I didn't hear from a soul. Herford and company had done a thorough job. As far as the press was concerned, I was a dead man. But I wasn't dead. On the contrary, I was very much alive. I was writing my story like someone possessed, every day from morning to night. I had no idea what I was going to do with it, but something impelled me to get it down on paper as fast as I could. I had my photocopied notes and the tapes Bertie had duplicated. The recorder stood beside my typewriter on a big table in front of the window, the tapes piled high on it. Whenever Bertie had time, he came and sat with me and read what I had written, filled in when necessary, and edited it according to his experiences and memories. It became routine.

The first number of *Blitz*, with "Total Man" in it, was on the stands on December 5, with the picture of Max with a removable band over his *dschonni*. Herford had ordered an extra printing of a hundred thousand copies, and it was sold out the first morning. They printed another fifty thousand. The article was a sensation. Lester had hastily bought three American standard works and one Swedish book on the subject. Four authors—two men and two women—had formed a team and were writing the series under the byline "Olaf Kingstrom." Hem told me they copied whole pages—choosing the most lascivious references they could find—and they used every suitable picture they could get from the library's archives.

"The article is the greatest shit we've ever printed," said Hem. "Pieced together, some of it miserably translated from the English. The Swedish stuff's even worse. The transitional passages and the parts the team has written are infantile. But what can you do? The women's conference adored it, our readers evidently do, too. It only proves how right I was when I said style doesn't count. A thing can be written abysmally—if the content is popular, nothing else matters." And the whole thing reminded me of something I'd said once: "Nobody is indispensable."

The picture of Max naturally stirred up a lot of excitement in his circles. He told me that since Friday, the day the issue had come out, the telephone had never stopped ringing. He'd heard from people all over Germany, even from some he hadn't seen in years. There were telegrams, too. He was being congratulated constantly on his new profession.

"Tutti keeps havin' to cry," he said. "She says she never thought she'd be living with anybody famous. But she don't want me to be getting any big ideas when the women come running in droves and the movies want me, and what-else-all! But she don't know her Max. This ain't gonna ruffle me! I ain't gonna lose my cool! No. I can't help it that my *dschonni's* so big. I didn't do nuthin' to make it that big. It's just a gift from God, that's what it is. Ain't that so?"

As I wrote, I was coming closer all the time to what Fräulein Louise had experienced. I had already left blank spaces to be filled in later, but now I simply had to see her and find out more, if I could. And what I heard was this strange sentence, "Things here are not all what they seem. . . ."

"What do you mean?" I asked. "Is it the nursing care? Or the doctors? Aren't they nice to you?"

Fräulein Louise said, "Shh . . . yes, they're nice to me. To *me*. But during the last days I've noticed that the nurses and orderlies don't speak very nicely about their patients. Who knows, perhaps about me, too, only I just don't happen to hear it."

"I can't believe it," I said, whispering too.

"Who knows? Who knows?" Fräulein Louise shook her white head slowly. "And another thing I've noticed, Herr Roland: There's no real friendship between these people. And they don't know anything about the laws of the other life. They're just people of our earth," she shrugged sadly.

"Of our miserable little earth," I said.

She nodded.

"Yes. Alas. But," she whispered, "there's something else going on, Herr Roland."

"There is?" And: Oh, God, I thought, it's starting again!

"Yes, yes," she whispered eagerly. "Last night I could hear a loud murmuring among the employees out in the hall. And then, in the night, some of them were talking in their little lounge. I could hear them through the wall. I got up and crept out into the hall and listened at the door. I know that wasn't right, but I simply had to know what they were being so secretive about."

"And what were they talking about?"

"About Dr. Erkner," whispered Fräulein Louise, looking troubled. "Always about Dr. Erkner."

"What about him?"

"Well," she said hesitantly, "some of them said that Dr. Erkner was not a real psychiatrist, that he isn't the real Dr. Erkner."

"But that's—what else?"

"I couldn't understand anything else, but I'm sure it wasn't good. I think Dr. Erkner is in great danger."

"Oh, no!" I said.

"Oh, yes," said Fräulein Louise. "And Sister Veronica said the same thing this morning. I couldn't stand it any longer, so I spoke to her about it. She's my favorite. I told her what I'd overheard and what I was afraid of."

"And—?"

"She said, 'Oh, no!' Just like you, Herr Roland. But then she said something else."

"What?"

"She said I wasn't to tell Dr. Erkner anything about it because that would only make matters worse. Now I'm asking you, what did she mean, 'make matters worse'? So Herr *Doktor* Erkner must be in some sort of danger."

The whole thing depressed me. I had hoped to find Fräulein Louise in better condition. "I'm sure you're wrong, Fräulein Louise," I said. "You didn't hear right."

"Do you really think so?"

"Yes. You haven't mentioned any of this to the doctor, have you?"

"No. I—I didn't dare."

Thank God, I thought. And Sister Veronica must have thought the same thing. She probably wanted to prevent Fräulein Louise from having to stay here endlessly, even if she had chosen a strange way to do it.

"No. I only told you," said Fräulein Louise. "Because I know I can trust you. You won't betray me. And you're right. I may have got things wrong. But there's something I know I'm not wrong about."

"And what is that?"

"That the people here have no idea whatsoever of the higher things in life. You can't shake me on that." She nodded emphatically, and there was silence. Finally I decided to try again, without much hope. "And my work, the story I'm writing—that doesn't interest you anymore, Fräulein Louise?"

Still immersed in her worries, she made a tired gesture with her hand. "Oh . . . your story. . . ."

530

"Yes."

"That happened so long ago, Herr Roland. All that has sunk down into eternity. The relationship between things that happen—we'll never really grasp them, not as long as we're on this earth. I mean, what all these things portend. That's why I think it isn't such a good thing to occupy oneself with things that have happened and are over and done with. Don't you think so, too?"

"Yes. You may be right."

Nothing to be got out of her anymore. I chatted with her a while longer, about trivial things, then I got up to leave. "But you'll come again, Herr Roland, won't you? Please come again!"

I felt sorry for her, so I nodded.

"When, Herr Roland? Soon? Come soon, please. I may have something new and interesting to tell you."

I doubted it, and with that was quite wrong.

10

He lived in a big villa in Königstein, not very far out of the city. There were many elegant villas here, standing in parklike gardens. A section for the very rich. Joachim Vandenberg evidently had more money than I had thought. As I got out of the car, the front door opened and a man in a blue suit appeared—tall, heavyset, with black hair, a prominent nose, and shifty eyes. "Herr Roland! I'm so glad yov came. Please come in." We shook hands. "Nobody followed you, I hope?"

"No, Herr Vandenberg. I watched. I didn't notice anything."

"Good. Everybody doesn't have to know about our meeting, do they? That's why I asked you to come to my home, and so late. The servants have already left." He walked into the villa ahead of me. He didn't seem to have a wife—anyway, he didn't mention one—and no children.

The villa was full of treasures: wonderful furniture, carpets, paintings, Gobelins, vases and buddhas. Vandenberg evidently collected buddhas. He led me into a large room with a great many buddhas and a fireplace. A fire was burning in it, the curtains were drawn, lamps with silk shades shed a gentle light. We sat down in front of the fireplace in big leather club chairs.

Vandenberg rolled a little cart with bottles out of a wall closet that seemed to be the bar. "You drink Chivas, don't you?" he said.

"How do you know?"

He laughed. "Things like that get around."

"Well, in this case something wrong got around," I said. "I don't drink Chivas. In fact, I don't drink at all."

He looked astonished and slightly suspicious, then he shrugged and asked what I'd like to drink. I told him soda, and he gave it to me. He drank Chivas, and it didn't bother me in the slightest. He offered me Havana cigars, lit mine for me, and waited until it was burning properly and I'd drunk some of the soda, all the time watching me intently. An amber-colored cat came strolling out of a corner and jumped on his lap. During our entire conversation, he scratched the animal behind the ear and it purred softly. He said, "You have left *Blitz.*"

"So that's got around, too."

"Naturally. Although why you left *Blitz* hasn't reached me yet."

"It will."

"No," he said, stroking the cat, "I don't think it will."

"But you know?"

"Yes, I know." He laughed again. "I'm sure you haven't forgotten Herr Seerose."

"What about him?"

"He lived in Königstein, too," Vandenberg said amiably. "Not far from here. We were friends—at least, I thought we were," he added quickly. "Actually I knew nothing about him. That he's gone, for reasons both of us know . . . well, I had no idea. I would have laughed at anyone who told me Seerose was an agent for the East. An absolutely absurd idea."

I said nothing.

"You find it absurd, too, I'm sure. But then, who can look into the heart of a human being?" And who can look into yours? I thought.

"Seerose and I played golf together, even in November when—when you were in Hamburg. Seerose implied that you were onto something very important." I didn't believe him, but next minute I had to. "The plans of the Warsaw Pack Nations in case of war. It was going to be the biggest story in the history of *Blitz.*"

"He told you that?"

532

"Yes. He trusted me. I told you we were friends, and for so many years—neighbors. He gave me Frankie."

"Frankie?"

"My cat. My darling."

"Aha."

"Herr Roland, listen to me. I was Seerose's friend. I am horrified, naturally, by what he did, but I don't pass judgment on my fellow men. I never liked your publisher, after the way he tried to ruin my publishing house so that he could buy it cheap."

"Why?"

"Because he wanted to publish books."

That was true, only I hadn't know that it was Vandenberg's publishing house that Herford wanted.

"Today I'm much too big," said Vandenberg. "He can't touch me. But there were times when his good lawyer, Rotaug, had me by the throat. Right after the currency reforms. He hasn't forgotten that." Suddenly Vandenberg seemed to have no lips. "I haven't forgotten it either. I'm still not a friend of Herr Herford. I live according to the principle, 'An eye for an eye, a tooth for a tooth.' You understand?"

"Yes," I said, and took a sip of the soda water. The fire crackled.

"To make a long story short, I have heard—don't ask me how, because I can't tell you—that you are still writing the story. Am I right?" He exhaled a cloud of blue smoke.

"Yes." I puffed on my Havana. "I am. So?"

"Don't be so touchy, Herr Roland. I'm not going to do you any harm. What's the matter with you? Are you nervous?"

"A little," I said. "I don't like it when there are things people can't tell me."

That made him laugh. "Now look here, you shrinking violet. You're not writing for the wastepaper basket, are you? You want to see your story in print, don't you?"

"Right now I'm writing it because I feel impelled to put down what happened. I haven't thought beyond that."

"But I have," said Vandenberg. "I want to see the story published. Do you want to write a book for me?"

"I—you want me to—"

"Yes. For our fall '69 list. I'd like to come out early with it—let's say in August. Can you be done in time?"

"If I go on writing the way I'm writing now, I could have a first draft in two months."

"Fine. And then we'll work on the final draft. I know your

books. I've kept an eye on what you've done for *Blitz*. You're a hellishly talented fellow. I have confidence in you. Of course, the whole thing must remain absolutely secret, as long as possible. I don't even want any of my colleagues to know about it. An explosion—that's what I'd like it to be. Time enough when you give us the manuscript to sign the contract and publicize the thing."

"Oh, I see."

He laughed again. He seemed to like to laugh. "You don't think I'm serious? You think I'm stringing you along? Well, I'm not. The contract is just a formality. We'll discuss the terms now and I'll give them to you in writing. And the advance . . . since it's you, let's say twenty thousand marks now and another twenty thousand when you hand in the manuscript. Is that all right with you?"

"Herr Vandenberg," I said. "I researched that story while I was still under contract to *Blitz*. *Blitz* paid for it. A *Blitz* photographer worked with me. We were in New York together. *Blitz* has all rights to the story. So it's impossible."

"Yes, he said," "and that's why you're to go on writing."

"What do you mean?"

"You can't tell me that the thought that *Blitz* had all rights to your story and that therefore you can't sell it elsewhere never occurred to me."

"No," I said slowly.

"But you thought—"

"I thought—I don't know—I thought—"

"Well, there you are," Vandenberg said. He smiled. "So why make a fuss? Do you want a bigger advance?"

"No . . . only . . . I don't know how you can get the rights from *Blitz*. They don't want the story to appear. Under any circumstances."

"And I want it to appear, under all circumstances. Now listen to me. I don't want you to give the legal aspect a thought. Write your story as fast as you can. I'll get permission to publish from Herford, either by mutual agreement or in court."

"And if you lose the case?"

"I won't lose it."

"Herr Vandenberg, if you know what the story's about, then you must also know with whom you're going to conflict, besides, Herford."

"I know."

"And you're not afraid?"

"That's something I've never been in my entire life," said Joachim Vandenberg.

I must say, I was impressed. He said it so calmly, smiling, and I believed him. Then he added, still calm and smiling, "But I'm going to have the decency to tell you why I'm so confident about it. You see, I know a thing or two about Herford and his colleagues, the ones who want to keep your story from seeing the light of day." He shrugged. "So there it is. Take it or leave it. I doubt if you'll get an offer from anyone else. I am ninety-nine percent sure that I can publish the story, but I'm only human. If I'm unlucky, I'll have to cancel the contract. But if that happens, you can forget about the story for good. Because then it really is unpublishable. But I doubt that will happen. Does that satisfy you?"

I said, "Yes."

After that we talked about the contract and Vandenberg really did write everything down and both of us signed. Then he copied the whole thing out again and we signed again. Thus each of us had a copy. It was past midnight when I left.

I was waiting next morning in front of the bank on which the check was drawn, for it to open. I was the first at the teller's booth. I handed in the check, signed on the back with a false name, as Vandenberg had suggested. A little later, after the teller had verified the check, the money was paid out to me. I had to sit down on a leather armchair in the lobby because I suddenly felt weak in the knees. I had money. I had a publisher. I was lucky again. Yes, I thought, from now on I'll be lucky!

11

"Something wonderful has happened," said Fräulein Louise. She looked happy, almost ecstatic, as she walked beside me through the hospital park. She was wearing her old boots, her old black coat, a shawl, a little black hat on her white hair, and black woolen gloves. A light snow had fallen and glittered on the ground. The trees in the park were black, the air was very clear

535

and sharp. Fräulein Louise had asked me to go out in the park with her. She was allowed to do that. She had in the meantime become a trusted patient; besides, I had been told she had been given something to do. "Something wonderful?" I said. "What?"

For some inexplicable reason I still felt drawn to Fräulein Louise, and in spite of the fact that my last visit had revealed nothing, here I was again, a week later.

"Right away, right away!" said Fräulein Louise. "I've got to tell it chronologically, Herr Roland. Isn't the park beautiful?"

"Beautiful," I said.

This time I had come by plane. It was eleven o'clock in the morning.

"The Herr Professor thinks it is, too," she said, striding along vigorously beside me.

"What Herr Professor?"

"His name is Leglund. Oh, Herr Roland, what a wonderful man!" She lowered her voice confidentially. "You know what? He has been blessed with the power to live in the other world *in his lifetime!*"

"Aha!"

"Yes. He is an old man, will be seventy-six on his next birthday. He's not very strong and he doesn't see well; his legs give out on him every now and then. His daughter was here a few days ago. She's married and lives in Baden Baden. The Herr Professor introduced us and told her that we get along so well. That made me very proud, because the Herr Professor was a famous doctor once—a psychiatrist, Herr Roland—and I can talk so beautifully to him. He's different from all the others here. He's a truly good man; I could see that at once, the first time I met him. It may sound stupid and overweening for me to say this, but I really believe that Herr Professor Leglund is one of the blessed."

"What do you mean?" Big black birds flew cawing above us and away.

"The Herr Professor understands me when I speak my thoughts aloud. He knows that human existence is many-faceted, and that here on earth we experience only a poor little example of the infinite universe. He is so clever. Some of the things he tells me I can't even understand!"

"For instance?"

"Well, when he talks about an ego, and a superego." Fräulein Louise laughed. "I'm only an ignorant woman, but such a great man speaks to me, such a blessed man who knows all about that other life, that magnificent life that awaits us."

As we walked along the path, Fräulein Louise went on eulogizing Professor Leglund. He loved the park, I found out, and he liked the pond best. Formerly he had always gone there alone, but now he couldn't anymore. "He's too unsteady on his feet, you see. . . ." So Fräulein Louise had offered to take the old man out for a walk every afternoon, to his beloved pond. The doctors, the employees, but above all the professor's daughter were delighted. At last somebody was willing to do something for the old man!

"The daughter gives me money for taking the Herr Professor for a walk," Fräulein Louise explained. "Isn't that wonderful? My money disappeared, didn't it? Well, now the professor's daughter is bringing it back to me. And you know what? I'm saving every bit of it. The professor has a birthday in March, and I'm going to buy him a beautiful present. Look, there's the pond."

It was a quite large body of water, with dead leaves floating on it. A narrow plank bridge led to a small island in the middle. Fräulein Louise walked quickly across it, ahead of me. The little island was overgrown with bushes, and at the top there was a bench. "This is the Herr Professor's favorite spot," she said. "He's always happy here. We take most of our walks to this island and have such good talks here." She was looking straight at me with sparkling eyes.

"What is it, Fräulein Louise?"

"Yesterday afternoon the Herr Professor wasn't feeling well so I came by myself, around four, maybe later. It was already getting dark. And such a marvelous thing happened to me, Herr Roland." She grasped my arm and spoke very intensely. "But I don't want anybody but you to know about it. You mustn't tell a living soul! Because they told me not to talk about it. If I did, I would have to atone for it."

"Who told you not to tell anyone?" I asked, and could feel my heart beating faster.

"Well . . . my friends, of course," she said "You see, Herr Roland, only the dead are faithful."

12

"Louise...."

"Louise...."

"Louise...."

Fräulein Louise could hear voices, wafted to her from far away, then coming clearer. She was standing on the little island, between the bushes, looking out into the twilight.

"Greetings, Little Mother...." That's the Russian, thought Fräulein Louise, and was filled with a feeling of bliss. Her friends! Her friends! She couldn't see them, but she could hear them. Her friends had returned.

"Oh, how marvelous!" whispered Fräulein Louise, "and I greet you, too, all of you, all of you loved ones. And I thank you for coming back to me."

"Yes, we are with you again, Louise." And that's the Frenchman, thought Fräulein Louise.

"We had to come back." The voice of the Pole. "Because Louise belongs to us. She must trust us."

"Us...."

"Us...."

"Us...."

Three voices said it—the American, the Dutchman, and the SS leader.

"I trust you," whispered Fräulein Louise, "not the doctors here."

"And that's right." The voice of the Czech. "The doctors here mean well, but they are only living creatures. They can't see things clearly. All they see is limited, in spite of their good intentions."

The voice of the Jehovah's Witness: "We have a loftier vision. Louise must join us. And she should obey us."

"Obey us...."

"Obey us...."

"Obey us...."

"And that's what I want to do," said Fräulein Louise, tears in

538

her eyes. "There's nothing else I want to do, my dear friends."

The voice of the Frenchman: "We pity the poor doctors here. Their knowledge is so limited."

The voice of the student: "You don't belong here, Louise."

"I know, I know," said Fräulein Louise, and her heart beat fast as she heard the voice of her favorite, who now went on speaking.

"You belong to us, Louise. You are one of the chosen."

"Chosen? I?" stammered Fräulein Louise.

"Yes." The voice of the student again. "You are one of us and soon you will be with us, completely!"

The voice of the Dutchman: "Louise should listen to us. We stand closest to the godly creatures. Therefore she should believe us and follow us... and not the earthly creatures."

The voice of the Russian: "Little Mother must believe that what we do is right, and that what we did was right."

The voice of the Ukrainian: "Louise has experienced dreadful things...."

"... and it seems to her that everything has come to a dreadful end," the voice of the Norwegian went on. "But it only seems so to the living. In reality everything turned out well."

"It did? Really? But—" Fräulein Louise couldn't go on.

"And if things went wrong for Louise, then only because she allowed herself to be misled by false friends," said the voice of the American.

"False friends," said Fräulein Louise with a deep sigh. "Yes, that was it. False friends...."

"You are still confused." The voice of the student. "Where we are, everything is clear. When you are with us you will see that everything turned out right...."

13

"So that's what my friends told me," said Fräulein Louise, standing beside me on the little island in the middle of the pond. "We went on talking for a long time, until it was quite dark and I had to go back to the house. But they're here again, Herr Roland."

"Yes," I said. "And that must be a great joy to you." I felt happy and sad at the same time—happy because now I could expect Fräulein Louise to recall everything she had experienced and tell me about it, sad because it was now quite clear that she had reverted to her former schizophrenic condition.

A bell rang in the main house. "That means lunch," said Fräulein Louise. "I've got to go back." She was already crossing the narrow plank bridge. I followed her. We walked quickly through the park. The pond wasn't far from the clinic.

Fräulein Louise said good-bye to me at the entrance to the private sector. She opened the door with the handle outside and showed me how it could be opened on the inside also, by turning a small knob. "Whoever knows that can always get out," she said, with a short laugh. "The poor, deranged people we have here sometimes don't know that the knob can be turned. They just shake it and can't open the door. But I can go back and forth as I please. They've let me do that for quite a long time now." The bell rang again. "I must go to the dining hall, Herr Roland," she said. "They don't like us to be late, and after lunch there's a rest period."

"I have to leave, too."

"But come again soon, please. Because very soon now I'm going to have a lot of important things to tell you."

"I'll come again in a few days," I told her. Then we said good-bye, and she walked down the corridor of the private sector, happy and graceful suddenly, like a young girl. She turned around every now and then and waved until she was out of sight.

I told myself that it was my duty, and with a heavy heart went to Dr. Erkner's office. A few people were waiting outside. Before I had a chance to sit down, the door to the office opened and a young doctor came out. He had long blond hair with a beard. "You want to see Dr. Erkner?"

He had an arrogant voice—everything about him was arrogant, vigorous and overbearing. He was tall and slender, had blue eyes, and wore gold-rimmed glasses. I said, "Yes."

"Dr. Erkner is very busy, as you can see." He gestured in the direction of the people waiting. "Can I help you? What do you want to see him about?"

A doctor is a doctor, I thought, and said, "It concerns one of your patients in the private sector."

"I am in charge of the private sector," said the long-haired doctor. He had a rasping voice. "Germela. Doctor Germela." He took my arm and led me to a window niche. "To what patient are you referring? You can talk to me. I am responsible for that department."

An exaggeration, I couldn't help thinking. The man couldn't be older than I. He was probably on duty in the private sector at this time, nothing more than that. But he was a doctor.

I controlled my aversion to the man and told him what I had just experienced with Fräulein Louise. He listened, nodding every now and then and smiling, a smile that was more like a sneer. In the end he was looking out of the window, at the park. Once or twice he hummed.

"Is that all?" he asked when I had finished.

"Yes. I'd say it was enough."

"Dear Herr Roland," said Dr. Germela, "I also think it's enough, although we see things differently."

"So how do you see it?"

"Well," he said, "no offense intended, dear Herr Roland, and with all due respect for your concern about Fräulein Gottschalk, but don't you think we know better than you how to treat our patients and judge their condition?"

"I only wanted to let you know—"

"Don't you believe that every one of us should attend to his own field of activity? I don't try to write for illustrated magazines, ha-ha-ha! So my suggestion is that you don't try to do our work. Leave Fräulein Gottschalk to us. She is one of our best patients."

"Best patients?" I was furious. "What about the voices she hears?"

He answered sharply. "Now listen to me, dear Herr Roland. You've been here quite a few times. You are a reporter. You question Fräulein Gottschalk about her past because you want to know more about it—"

"That isn't true!"

"—and confuse her and provoke hallucinations that left her long ago, and cause them to reappear." Germela had no intention of letting me interrupt him. "And when the patient is sufficiently aroused to think the wrong thing, you come to me, all excited about it, and tell me that her condition is worse!"

"Now look here," I began, but there was no stopping him.

"Fräulein Gottschalk has adapted splendidly," he went on, "and is well integrated in our therapeutic community; there can be no question whatsoever of a relapse!"

The young idiot! I thought, and then I had to think of what Fräulein Louise's friends had told her about the well-meaning but fortunately limited doctors, and was filled with admiration for her mind, which could absorb and produce such knowledge through her friends and their voices. I said rudely, "What do you mean, 'therapeutic community'?"

Germela ran his fingers through his long blond hair in a desperate gesture, as if he thought I was an idiot, too. "Seriously speaking now, Herr Roland," he said, "haven't you ever heard anything about the democracy of psychiatry?"

"No."

"Well, that surprises me. A man versed in public opinion, of all people! It is a reform that was long overdue. Patients, personnel, and doctors form a democratic community in which everyone has the same rights, duties, and responsibilities. We doctors have to get used to the fact that we don't have more rights than our patients. That's perfectly understandable, don't you agree?"

I said nothing.

"You don't agree?"

I shrugged.

"I see you don't. Well, there are quite a few people around who don't agree, either. That's why the younger generation has to start the ball rolling. I see it all the time. The times change, Herr Roland. You know what we're contemplating in this clinic? A patients' parliament, in which everyone has a voice and equal influence, and decisions are made by a majority—by patients, head doctor, nursing personnel, and the last cleaning woman in the place." I shuddered, I hope imperceptibly. *Blitz* hadn't been all that backward, I thought.

"Yes," said Dr. Germela, who misunderstood my silence. "That impresses you, doesn't it? We've living in the twentieth century, Herr Roland. A new era with new methods! We must have the courage to put ourselves on the same level as our patients. Of course there are some who don't want to go along with this, in this clinic, too, as I just said. But we'll convince them, you'll see!" He patted me on the shoulder. "Don't worry. You have no idea how well Fräulein Gottschalk is doing with all these innovations: for instance; this old gentleman she's looking after."

"Professor Leglund?"

"Yes. Leglund. You can't imagine how he helps her and how she helps him, and us, with her participation."

What he said made me feel sick, but it was beginning to make an impression. After all, he wasn't telling me fairy tales. Perhaps I really was old-fashioned and they were practicing new methods here which were beneficial.

"You mean because she looks after him?"

"Exactly. Professor Leglund was a famous psychiatrist. In Breslau. Demented now. Absolutely demented. Thinks we're still living under the Kaiser. Has no idea where he is. Gets time and space all mixed up. Remembers only scraps of his scientific knowledge. If we'd let him walk alone to his beloved pond, he's never find his way back. And when you take him there he thinks twenty years have passed on his way back. And Fräulein Gottschalk looks after this unfortunate, pitiful ruin of what was once a great mind, and it's not only the walks. It's what they talk about, her admiration and sympathy for him, her blithe spirit and courage and optimism, that help the patient. The sick woman takes the hand of the sick man—a beautiful picture, isn't it?"

I was silent and thought that it really was a beautiful picture. And after all, a lot of men ran around with long hair and beards. Perhaps it had been stupid of me to feel such a strong aversion to Dr. Germela. The young man evidently knew what he was talking about. Perhaps I had really aroused the past in Fräulein Gottschalk's mind by my mere presence—who could tell? What I had felt was a relapse and what Germela didn't see as such was possibly my fault. Perhaps Fräulein Louise *was* doing very well, or at least making the best progress possible after such a stubborn schizophrenic condition.

"Well, now!" Germela was smiling smugly. "Are we convinced and reassured?"

I smiled, too, reluctantly.

"You see," he said, "now we can be friends. You have your work, we have ours. We don't interfere with your writing; you don't get mixed up in our psychiatric methods. You don't disturb Fräulein Gottschalk, and you may visit her as often and as long as you like. Otherwise—no, dear Herr Roland—otherwise, I'm afraid I'll have to stop your visits. Have I made myself clear?"

"Absolutely."

"And you agree?"

"I agree." After all, these men had to know what they were doing. They'd studied it!

14

We were married on Friday, December 20, at 11:00 A.M. in a registry office. The Provincial Court had granted permission and with Hem's intercession had dispensed with the *Ehefähigkeitszeugniss* for Irina in record time. After that our banns had been posted for a week, and our time had finally come. Bertie picked us up in the Mercedes. It was a cold, sunny day. There was frost on the grass in Grüneburg Park. We men wore dark suits, Irina had on a black suit, one of Leo's creations, and her black coat with the mink trim, black pumps, and the alligator bag I'd bought for her in Hamburg.

Irina's psychologist had given her the day off. Bertie brought her flowers, and we drove off. We had to wait a little; there were two couples ahead of us. Irina was very pale and very beautiful, and her hands, which I was trying to warm with mine as we waited in the hall, were ice cold. At last it was our turn. The clerk, an elderly man, nodded encouragingly at Irina because she looked frightened. He spoke briefly and simply, just a few appropriate and beautiful words. I remember the gist of what he said, and feel like including it here.

"When I say that I wish you happiness in your life together, then I must add that happiness, true inner happiness, is a gift of fate and does not come from outside. If happiness is to last, one must fight for it again and again. Which is not necessarily cause for mourning. Because every human being can fight for his happiness, and this is made so much easier if he has someone to help him. That is why the union of two people can add value to their lives." Irina felt for my hand, and I tried to warm hers again. The clerk went on.

"One should realize that no one can be completely happy, and that realization may be the best way to come as close as possible to complete happiness. He who recognizes himself truly and values himself correctly will soon recognize his partner and all the people the same way. It is all a question of mutual radiance, and that is why, my dear people, happiness can be found only in sincerity."

544

We signed the marriage certificate, and Bertie and Hem signed as witnesses, and I put my hand in my pocket and took out a little etui with the ring, a narrow platinum band with tiny diamond baguettes. Irina stared at me, speechless, when I placed the ring on her finger, because we had agreed that there would be no ring, and she had none for me. I didn't want to wear a ring, but I had noticed how much she wanted one. So I had gone to a jeweler and sold my gold cigarette lighter and bought this ring with the money. Hem knew about it. I didn't smoke much anymore, so matches would do.

"Where did you get the ring?" Irina whispered.

"Shh," I said. "I stole it. Don't let anybody notice anything, for God's sake."

In the car, driving to the Frankfurter Hof, I told Irina the truth and she cried a little, but with joy, because I said, "And I gave the jeweler the whiskey flask, too," which Bertie and Hem knew was a lie. Actually, I had thrown the flask into the dirty Main River from the Friedensbrücke, on the day before our wedding. It was an attempt of sorts to bribe the dear Lord. I am very superstitious, and I thought if I didn't drink anymore and threw the damned flask away, Irina would have an easy birth and a beautiful child, and we would be happy ever after.

In the Frankfurter Hof we were received by the doorman, bell captain, receptionist, and all the waiters with broad smiles. They knew I wasn't working for *Blitz* anymore, but they didn't know why, and I was such a good old customer. Hem had reserved a table in the French restaurant, and the hotel had decorated it with flowers. We were Hem's guests. The waiters came and congratulated us and served the stupendous meal Hem had ordered. Irina and I drank orange juice, he and Bertie had champagne. After the meal they had to go straight back to the office. Before Christmas all hell always broke loose. I walked hand in hand with Irina back to Hem's apartment and we undressed and got under the covers of the big bed and made love, and then we fell asleep and slept for a long time.

I woke up to hear the bell ringing. I put on my robe and opened the door. A boy, with an enormous bouquet of flowers from Tutti and Max. They called soon after that and wished us all the luck in the world and gave us their blessing. Max said, "We just felt we had to do it, dear Wal*tah*. After all, you're our best friend, and your little wife's gonna be our best friend, too, now. Where is she?"

"She's asleep."

"Well, then give her a kiss from me and Tuttilein when she wakes up. And you're gonna come and see us, aren't you?"

"We certainly are. Soon. I'm awfully busy...."

"I know, I know. And you can't imagine what's going on here right now! Tutti's working herself to death. I don't understand it. The city's gone crazy!"

"How come?"

"It's before the Holy Days. They all wanna get in as much screwing as they can. I reckon because the guys have to stay home with their families during the holidays. Leichenmüller's tanking in advance. And young Herford ditto."

Tutti, sobbing softly, "My dear Walt*ah*, I'm so happy for you. You know, Max and I, we want to get married, too, but right now we can't. Max has such—whaddaya call 'em—moral scruples. Says we've got to have a little more stashed away first. Then, when we've got enough and his business is going properly, I'll retire, and we'll get married, and you'll be our witnesses, agreed?"

"Agreed!"

I walked into the bedroom with the flowers. Irina was awake, and I told her about Max's call and that all the men were crazy for a loving before the Holy Days.

"You, too?"

"Certainly, me, too," I said. "Come, sweetheart, I've got to love you again."

"Yes, yes, yes," she said. "Love me!"

When Hem got back with Bertie we had bathed and dressed. Hem and Bertie brought salads and cold cuts and we ate in Hem's big kitchen, and Bertie and Hem drank a lot of beer and Irina and I drank red currant juice. We went over to Hem's room and he got out his cello and played compositions by Helmuth Rahmers. It was an infinitely peaceful evening. In the end Hem said, "Rahmers set many poems to music—Eichendorff, Lenau, Hesse, Gottfried Keller, Matthias, Claudius....I'm going to play you one of my favorite songs, composed to a poem by Karl Weller. 'Homecoming.'"

The sound of the cello was lilting and the melody full of confidence and joy, and Hem spoke the words softly as he played. "This is the place where I belong; my hand is on the key. The lark and cuckoo sing my song and every flower blooms for me...."

Irina and I sat side by side and held hands, and Bertie was looking at us and smiling, and I felt calm, and every flower bloomed for me.

> I walked upon the mountains
> I strolled along the shore
> I drank from sparkling fountains
> But now I'll wander no more.
> Although the world so wide, so wide
> Beguiled my heart in seasons past.
> Here is the realm where I'll abide
> I have come home at last.

Hem was silent, the music faded away. Nobody spoke. Then, suddenly, Irina said, "Fräulein Louise. . . ."

We looked at her and at each other. "I was just thinking of her, too," said Bertie.

"So was I," said Hem.

"And I," I said. "Strange. . . ."

"Very strange," said Bertie.

Fräulein Louise," said Irina, laying her head on my shoulder. "She brought us together. It all began with her."

15

"So now my friends will kill this person," said Fräulein Louise. This was on December 27, and it was raining hard in Bremen. The branches of the bare old chestnut trees in the yard glistened. "They will kill this person," she repeated, smiling happily. "Nothing can stop them."

A strange compulsion had made me fly to Bremen right after Christmas. In Fräulein Louise's room there was an arrangement of fir branches with a red candle, and a bowl of nuts and cookies. She had just lit the candle. She looked better every time I saw her. My visit today had made her very happy. She told me that her friends now spoke to her regularly, and I saw a chance to at last find out more about her experiences, most of which were

547

revealed to me only on this day. I decided to ignore the directives of democratic reformer, Dr. Germela. I could see that Fräulein Louise's memory was restored when in the course of our conversation, I mentioned Karel.

"Poor Karel, with his trumpet, yes," she said. "Little Karel and his murderer. I talked a lot about both of them with my friends." And then she began to tell much of what I have described earlier in this story, in its rightful place. And while she spoke I was wondering if she was creating what she was saying as she went along, inspired by my mention of Karel, if what she was saying and obviously believed was only taking shape in her mind now, as she spoke, and she was simply arranging it into the past from recent conversations with her friends. Who could tell? She told me she had "outwitted" her friends, and went on, "I also told them that more terrible things could happen if we didn't find the murderer, if we didn't unite the murderer and his victim, so that they might be reconciled in a higher sphere. You understand me, don't you?"

"Yes."

"Have another lebkuchen, Herr Roland, do. They're very good."

The rain was washing so hard against the pane, you could scarcely see the trees outside. I said, "I met a police chief in Hamburg. His name is Sievers. This happened weeks ago. He told me he was determined to find the murderer, and he said he had a plan."

"Yes," said Fräulein Louise without a moment's hesitation. "That's my student. I know."

"But—"

"But what? Didn't I explain to you once that there is no 'time,' no yesterday and no today and no tomorrow for my friends. Surely you remember."

"Yes, I do."

"And that my friends have to find a living human being if they want to come back. So now you can see how it works. My student, the darling, chose a chief of police. That's quite clear, isn't it?"

"Quite clear."

Fräulein Louise was nibbling on a cookie. "What I couldn't understand at first was why they've only started looking for the murderer now. But they explained it to me. By the way, now, all of a sudden, they say *du* to me. Yes, well . . . they told me, 'You were sick, Louise. You were confused. You are still a human being whose thoughts can be disturbed. Nothing can disturb us. And because you were confused, you chose the wrong friends—" Suddenly she stopped speaking and looked at me fearfully.

"What's the matter?" I asked.

She said very seriously, "There were so many false friends. Herr Roland, please, please assure me on your word of honor that you are not a false friend! Because that would be horrible! You see, I'm not really clever enough to cope with all this, and if you—" She stopped again, then, after looking at me searchingly, she said firmly, "No. You are not a false friend. I am sure. A while ago I couldn't tell exactly. Such a lot of things happened that I couldn't fathom, and that's why things haven't come to a good end. Yet. That's what my friends tell me." She was getting quite excited. "I never spoke to you so clearly, Herr Roland, but my voices were so clear. Of course I didn't see my friends, but it was as if they were speaking into my ears." She looked far away and said nothing for a while, then she said softly, hesitantly, "And still . . . I keep wondering if I didn't do something wrong."

"Something wrong?"

"Because I got so terribly confused. I keep asking my friends, 'Did I? Did I?'"

"And what do they say?"

"They don't say anything. I keep begging them to tell me, 'What does it all mean?' And they say, 'It has meaning. All of it has meaning, Louise, and is concerned in a higher sense, but we can't explain it to you. Be patient.' That's what my friends say. 'Wait a little and you will know the answer to this great riddle. Very soon now.' That's what they say. . . ."

Again she looked far away, then she said, "When I think of all the things that have happened to me, Herr Roland . . . suddenly I can remember it all so clearly." And then, without my having to ask anything, she went on recounting her experiences. She told about her conversation with her friends on the moor after Karel's death, of her trip to Hamburg, and how she had fled from Dr. Erkner, of her strange dream about the city with the high wall, and the four towers with the four tyrants, of her adventures in Hamburg—everything.

I took a room in Bremen, in a small boarding house, and visited Fräulein Louise every day until New Year's Day. I had my recorder with me, and this time I captured her entire odyssey on it. And I found out other things from her, too, very strange things.

549

The first thing she said to me one day was, "I have a message for you and Herr Engelhardt, from my friends. I'm to tell you because you're a good man." And she went on to speak, in her symbolic, cryptic way, about Bertie's and my future. On my last visit she said something I would like to insert here, because it made a deep impression on me. "I am stupid, I am uneducated, I am weak and old, but I keep having to imagine something...."

"What, Fräulein Louise?"

She looked at me earnestly. "I have a feeling," she said, "that the whole world is mirrored in what we have experienced. The errors of humankind... we have come to their center. I felt this from the beginning. That's why I was always so excited and restless. Look, Herr Roland... of course we have to reconcile the murderer and his victim so that everyone can see that there is a higher justice. Of course that is important. But it isn't everything. It is no longer a case of the murderer and his victim—it is a case of peace on earth. It is a case of making clear to mankind that everything man suffers he suffers only because he has such primitive instincts, because he is earthbound, although his misery is only a partial misery. Because it *could* serve everyone as an opportunity for purification and exaltation. But—isn't it true?— people expend most of their strength and energies in tearing themselves to pieces, in senseless struggles on ridiculous problems. And why? Because they are blind. That's why! If only they could be made seeing and grasp that this other, wonderful world holds our miserable world in its hand... just think, Herr Roland! Then people could at last turn to the higher things of life. Beauty! Religion! Wouldn't that be wonderful? I can only feel it. I really don't know the way. But wouldn't it be miraculous?"

"Yes, Fräulein Louise," I said. "It would be miraculous."

16

REWARD: 20,000 MARKS
A Desperate Mother Needs Help!

On November 12, 1968, my eleven-year-old Karel was shot to death in Youth Camp Neurode, near Bremen. There is no trace of the killer. But it is a fact that three people know what happened. The murderer fired the shots that killed Karel from a black Dodge and fled in the same car. A second man, who was apprehended in the camp, escaped and fled in a black Buick that was parked in front of the camp. A woman was at the wheel of the Buick. She cried to the man, "Karl! Run! Run, Karl, run!" With the help of this woman, the man was able to escape in the Buick. The woman's function was only that of accomplice. I am beseeching her to contact me and I promise to respect her anonymity and to give her a

Reward of 20,000 Marks

for any information leading to an arrest of the killer. A desperate mother is appealing to the conscience of a woman! No. AH-453291.

"Well," said Max Knipper. "How does it read? Elegant, no?" He was beaming at me.

"Your idea?"

"Sure!"

The ad was printed in a prominent spot in every Hamburg morning paper. They were laid out in the office of King Kong, the little room behind the stage. Besides Max, the stripper Baby Blue and old Father Concon were present. It was around noon on January 10, 1969, a Friday. I had taken a night train and arrived in Hamburg a short while ago.

"In an hour, the Hamburg *Evening News* will be out," said Max. "The ad's in that, too. You're just in time, Walt*ah*. My nose tells me tonight's the night, and my nose's never been wrong yet."

"What's with tonight?" I asked. "What's this all about anyway? Where is the boy's mother? She's not supposed to be in Germany anymore. The police have looked for her and never come up with anything."

"And that's just what's so good about it," said Max.

"I don't get it."

Tutti had called me the day before. Bertie had been with me, as he was so often these days, editing and filling in my first draft, over three hundred pages by now. "What's up, Tutti?" I asked.

"I just spoke to Max on the phone. He says you should take the night train to Hamburg."

"Max is in Hamburg?"

"Yeah. His pals called a few days ago, asked him to come and give them a hand. They got a problem, Walt*ah*, an' you know Max. He's got a good head on his shoulders."

"What sort of a problem?"

"Something to do with a murder. They're all nutty as fruitcakes. Max says be sure to come. He's had an idea. Will you go?"

"Of course!" I was beginning to feel excited. "*Donnerwetter*, Tutti! Your Max!"

"Yeah. My bull." She sounded dreamy. "A jewel, that's what he is. I'm telling you, any bitch who tries to take him away from me gets kicked in the ass *and* you know where! He loves me just as much as I love him. *Ach*, Walt*ah*, I'm so happy!"

That was the telephone conversation. I told Bertie I had to go to Hamburg and why, and he said he'd work on the manuscript while I was away. He had some time. And he had access to the apartment with Hem's key. . . .

So now I was in Hamburg and had just read the ad and couldn't make head or tail of it.

"Why is it a good thing that the boy's mother is nonexistent?" I asked. "Who's going to pay the reward if this woman really turns up and sings?"

"We pay," said Baby Blue.

She was wearing a minidress and a mink coat over it, although it was warm in the little office. Father Concon had on the white jacket he wore in the men's room.

"And how do you happen to have twenty thousand marks?" I asked.

"Donations," said old Concon.

"Donations from whom?"

"From everybody," said Baby Blue, with her Swabian accent. "The Intimate Bar, Lolita, Cockatoo, Eldorado, Lido, Show Ranch."

Max interrupted her and filled me in. His colleagues had asked him to come to Hamburg and help them in their darkest hour. Disaster had struck Sankt Pauli. Police from the

Davidswache, under the leadership of a certain Chief Sievers, were combing the entire amusement area night after night, mercilessly. They had appeared in Eros Center, Palais d'Amour, every strip joint, in boardinghouses and hotels that rented by the hour. They forced scared family men to show their ID cards and wrote down their names. The whores were just as scared as the pimps, the nightclub and boardinghouse owners, and the strippers. People were reluctant to come to Sankt Pauli. If things went on like this much longer, some of the night spots were going to have to close down.

"And they don't skip the porn movie houses either," said Max. "And they're the best thing going, from nine in the morning till midnight. They had a hit—a gal, horny as a bitch in heat—had to stop showing it. At every performance the lights went up at least twice and the fuzz marched through the place and asked for ID cards. In the end nobody wanted to see the horny bitch anymore and the place had to close."

"If things go on like this," said Father Concon, "we can all close." He was wearing a black band around one sleeve of his white jacket.

"They raided the Sex Shop, the Casino, the San Francisco Strip Center," said Baby Blue. "Who can put up with that sort of thing night after night? It's getting on everybody's nerves. Every night when I shove that dildo up my twat I'm afraid I'll hear: 'Stop! Lights! Identification!'"

"We're losing a fortune," said Father Concon. "Our turnover's down sixty percent. A catastrophe, that's what it is!"

I thought of my meeting with the strange chief of homicide, and how he had said he thought that young Concon and the boy Karel had been murdered by one and the same person, and that he knew how he would find the man. So this was his plan: to bring chaos and panic to Sankt Pauli, so that all those working and making money there would get together and start hunting for the murderer out of sheer self-preservation. And Sievers's plan was beginning to work!

"This is a community project," explained Baby Blue, "because we're all in the same trouble. The murderer *must* be found. Karel's mother doesn't seem to exist, at least not in Germany. You say so, Herr Roland. But does the murderer know it? No."

"Maybe he does," said old Concon. "But that doesn't matter. The important thing is that he reads his ad today...."

"He can think Karel's mother really put it in or that it's a trap.

553

In any case, he must begin to worry that the woman who was in Neurode that time reads the ad, too, and falls flat on her face because of the fat reward!" said Baby Blue.

"And answers it," said Father Concon. "And he can't let it come to that!"

I nodded.

"So everybody was glad to donate—all the ones I just mentioned. A lot of others, too—Saint Tropez, In Sahara, Lobster Lobster, Steel Net, Ellis Elliot, the Sex Theater, even Schroeder's Wieners, the hot dog stand. Nobody wanted to be left out."

"And we already have results!" Father Concon cried triumphantly.

"An hour ago," said Baby Blue.

"What happened an hour ago?" I asked.

"She came to Baby Blue's apartment, shitting in her pants, and begged her to help."

"Who?"

"Tamara Skinner," said Father Concon.

"Who is Tamara Skinner?"

"A hooker, of course," said Max.

"But a very special hooker," said Father Concon.

"What's so special about her?"

"She's the woman we're looking for," said Max. "She was the woman at the wheel of the car in Neurode."

"*Donnerwetter!*"

"Yeah! You're surprised," said Max. "And she told Baby Blue everything."

"She doesn't know me all that well," said the sensation from Crazy Horse in Paris, "but she doesn't have any friends."

"What did she have to say, Max?"

"That on the day this happened at the camp, she'd had a john in the morning already—a funny guy, a comedian. All he'd wanted from her was that she drive a car. With young Concon. Tamara knew him, of course. She was to drive him to the camp. Offered her two thousand marks for the trip. Gave it to her, too, later. Just to drive Concon to the camp and wait for him and drive them back to Hamburg, him and the girl."

"Irina."

"Right. But things didn't go according to plan. She was glad to get away with Concon in one piece. Then, when they knocked him off, she was scared to death. Prayed day and night that they should leave her alone and that she'd never see the guy again who got her into this. Never did see him again. And now she doesn't know what to do with herself, she's so scared. All she can think of is that he'll come back and knock her off. Because of the ad." Max was beaming. "We're doing all right, ain't we?"

"Yes," I said. "You certainly are."

"After this ad," said Baby Blue, "the murderer won't know a moment's peace. He's got to be afraid that Tamara will answer it or go to the police or a friend, which is what she did. And tell everything—that she was at the camp, what the man looked like who hired her, the man who drove the second car and shot the boy."

"Did she tell you the man's name?"

"No. She didn't know his name, but she described him."

"And what did he look like?"

"A big man. Well dressed. Spoke good German," said Baby Blue. "He was wearing a blue coat and a visor cap." Vaguely I remembered that the Ukranian servant from the Paris Hotel had described the man who had been looking for Karl Concon to Fräulein Louise in much the same way. "Long face, narrow lips, black hair, sideburns. Tamara said she would recognize him again anywhere."

"My God, Max!"

"Ha!" he said proudly. "Now they'll begin to talk about Max's brain again, not just his *dschonni!*"

"We gave Tamara the twenty thousand marks already," said Father Concon. "We know how to do things!"

"And what happens next?" I asked. "The woman's really in danger."

"She sure is," said Baby Blue. "Lives near here, on Hans-Albers-Platz. Is afraid to go out."

"Of course we're keeping an eye on her," said Max. "Don't let her out of our sight. We and the police."

"You notified the police?"

"Sure," said old Concon. "The Davidswache. Chief Sievers. Tamara may get a fine because she didn't come forward sooner, but they won't be too hard on her, said the chief. They've got men from the Davidswache over there, and from headquarters, and then there are our people, all keeping an eye on Tamara and waiting for the guy to turn up . . . and he will! You can bet on it."

"What do you mean, 'your people'?"

"Oh, you name it, we've got it. A real international group."

"International group?"

"Two bartenders," said Baby Blue. "One's French, the other's an Ami, both left over from the war."

"Three bouncers. We need strong guys," said Concon. "A German, a Pole, and a Dutchman."

"And then there's Panas Myrnyi," said Baby Blue, "from the Paris Hotel. He's Ukrainian. An old man. But he insisted on being in on it. He's watching the entrance of Tamara's house."

"And who else? Oh, yes. A boss from one of the night spots. In person. Heavyweight guy. Used to wrestle. He'll smash the guy to pulp. He's from here. Hamburg."

"A German?"

"Sure. What else? That was an intelligent question, Walt*ah*!"

"And then there's the young Russian," said Baby Blue. "A gas station attendant from around here. Tamara and he are crazy about each other. Have known each other for a while."

"Where's the Russian from?" I asked, unable to get Fräulein Louise out of my mind.

"He's the son of a Soviet officer who collaborated with the Germans in the war. The father fled to West Germany with the boy in '45. Stayed. Died here. The boys' name is Sergei. He's in Tamara's apartment, guarding her."

"The others are stationed all over the place—on the roof, in the halls, on the stairs, on Hans-Albers-Platz."

"And then there's Jiri," said Baby Blue.

"Who is Jiri?"

"My sweetheart. He's been here for four months. Fled from Brünn. He lives with me. He's watching, too."

And Chief Sievers, I thought, who had started the whole ball rolling. A German. Eleven men watching over Tamara Skinner besides the police and Max. Eleven men, with the nationalities of Fräulein Louise's eleven friends. . . .

17

"If I survive," whispered Tamara Skinner, "I'm going to buy the gas station with the money. For Sergei. An old man owns it. He wants to retire. And I'll be able to live a decent life."

She was about thirty years old, blond, very pretty, with a rosy complexion. She chain-smoked. Her friend Sergei spoke German fluently and softly as he tried to calm her down. Chief Sievers and I had been sitting in Tamara's living room since 7:00 P.M. Now it was almost midnight. The house in which Tamara lived was old and ugly and badly in need of repair. Poor people and a few prostitutes lived in it. The night was cold, yet a lot of girls were still loitering in house entrances around the square, and in nearby Gerhardstrasse in front of taverns and bars, trying to compete with Herbartstrasse, the street where brothels were legal. Tamara was brewing coffee for us for the third time.

The police and Tamara's private protectors were scattered all over the place, had been for hours. We spoke very little and softly because one could hear every word outside in the dank hall with its window at one end. Tamara's apartment was on the third floor. This whispering and walking on tiptoe for hours was getting on my nerves. Tamara never stopped trembling. Sergei and Chief Sievers were calm as Tamara filled our cups again. Sievers whispered to me, "You'll see. I'll be proved right. The man who comes has Concon and Karel on his conscience."

"How are you going to know that?"

"If Tamara recognizes him and Panas Myrnyi recognizes him, then he's the same man." Sievers nodded his thanks for the coffee and poured milk into it. "But the man didn't shoot the taxi driver, Vladimir Ivanov. I've found that out in the meantime."

"Then who did?"

"Amis. Somebody from Niendorferstrasse 333. We have all sorts of proof. The Amis had to kill Ivanov because of the car that was run into the lake, after Ivanov said he was going to find the driver and report him. Very good coffee, Tamara. Gets better every time. Maybe we'll stay the night and come again."

Tamara tried to smile. Sergei whispered comforting words in his deep, throaty voice.

"So one murder may remain unpunished," said the chief, "but not these two. I've sworn to that."

"Sworn to it?" I recalled what Fräulein Louise had told me and was startled. "To whom?"

"To myself," he said softly, smiling a little as if he were having his own private bit of fun.

To sound him out, I said, "By the way, Fräulein Louise is much better."

"I know."

"How do you know?"

"I spoke to her."

"You *did*?"

"Well, now why does that excite you? I called the clinic and they let me speak to her yesterday." He added softly, "She'll soon be leaving the clinic."

At that moment Sergei gestured that we be silent. He had heard something. Now we could hear it, too. Somebody was tiptoeing up the stairs. They were wooden stairs; impossible to walk up them without a step creaking.

Tamara pressed both hands to her chest, her lips were trembling. The steps came nearer . . . nearer . . . the wood creaked. Chief Sievers whispered to Tamara to be absolutely quiet, then he gave me and Sergei a look. We slipped out of the living room into the small entrance hallway and stood behind the bathroom door. It was beside the entrance. Very narrow quarters; we had to stand close. Chief Sievers suddenly had a gun in his hand. I wished I had one, too, but the gentlemen from *Blitz* had taken the Colt from me weeks ago, together with so many other things.

The steps stopped in front of the door. It was an old door. A ray of light from under it could surely be seen in the passage outside. There was a knock. Sievers gestured to Tamara to open it. She walked uncertainly to the door and asked, "Who's there?"

"Come on, open up, sweetie," said the voice of a man. I knew that voice, but where—where had I heard it before?

Tamara took the chain off and opened the door a crack, then she stepped back. I was standing in the rear of the bathroom and therefore couldn't see the man who came in, but the man could see Sievers's gun because he was standing nearest the door. He turned immediately and we could hear him running down the hall. "It's him! It's him!" screamed Tamara.

The chief, Sergei, and I ran out into the hall. I could see the man vault onto the sill of the window at the end of the hall, which he had opened. Air flowed into the hall, ice cold. Then he jumped.

We tore over to the window. There was a flat roof about a meter and a half below. The man ran—all we could see was a shadow—to the edge of the roof where there was a fire escape ladder, and disappeared. "Goddamn it!" said Sievers. He blew his whistle three times, then he jumped down on the roof. Sergei and I followed him. There was snow on the roof, and I slipped and almost fell over the edge. Sergei just managed to catch me. I had scraped my hand, and it bled. Panting, we followed Sievers to the ladder. The rungs were iced over. We stumbled down into an abandoned lot full of junk. There was a narrow alley, a light in front of it. We ran on, and at the end of the alley found ourselves on Hans-Albers-Platz.

Chief Sievers and I saw the shadow of the man at the same time, running into Gerhardstrasse, in the direction of Mary's Treff. Men came running out of house entrances, down ladders from rooftops, out of courtyards—the chief's men and Tamara's guards. I saw Max and the old servant, Panas Myrnyi, who was screaming hoarsely, "That's the man! That's the man from the hotel!"

"So there you have it!" said Sievers, grinning, as his men chased the man over the thin snow, down Gerhardstrasse, past panic-stricken prostitutes, pedestrians, and pimps. Suddenly the man turned, there was a flash. A shot. The men who were pursuing him scattered against the walls of houses. "After him!" yelled Sievers, running on, with Max, Sergei, and I following him. I kept slipping on my leather soles.

Gerhardstrasse ran into Erichstrasse. The man stopped. His pursuers were apparently approaching now also from the left, because he shot again and turned right and disappeared behind the corner of Mary's Treff. The houses on Erichstrasse were old and dilapidated. When we reached it, we collided with three officers from the Davidswache, one in uniform, a gun in his hand. "Which way did he go, Lütjens?" yelled Sievers.

"Down the street, then left into Balduinstrasse," cried Lütjens.

We ran on—two dozen men at least, and one woman, because Tamara had come tearing after us. We ran into Balduinstrasse, past Bernhard-Nocht-Strasse, past the famous tavern, Onkel Max. Here the street ended in a staircase that led down to Sankt-Pauli-Hafenstrasse. I saw the shadow of the fleeing man again.

Now several officers were shooting, and the man was returning fire. He hit one officer in the thigh. The man collapsed. Another stayed behind to look after him; the rest of us ran on, slipping over the ice on the steps. I fell once, but got up again immediately. Down below there were piles of gravel covered with snow. This was the car strip. Girls scattered, screaming. Drivers stepped on the gas and drove off fast as we came running up. I slipped again, this time on a condom. I knew Hamburg, I knew the car strip. In the morning following a lively night you could find anywhere from twenty to thirty condoms to the square meter here. I got up, cursing. Beside me I saw the River Kasematten, the elegant little harbor nightclub where famous stars entertained and famous people dined. "Over there!" yelled a man.

I could see the shadow, on the other side of the car strip now, running down some stone steps to the water, turning around all the time and firing. And reloading. You could hear him inserting the clips. At the bottom of the steps, in the water, there was a long cement dock on concrete pillars, a pontoon dock, with transverse floor planking below. It led to the fish market. Max was at my side, breathing hard. "If we lose him there...."

Yes. That would be hopeless. He could hide behind any of the pillars. It was pitch dark down there, no thought of aiming a shot from the outside, but from the inside—yes, as I was to find out seconds later when a bullet whizzed past my head. "Look out!" yelled Sievers.

He threw himself down on his stomach and shot four times, fast. There were a lot more shots after that, and the click of the man reloading. No one could tell if there had been a hit, but then, suddenly, all of us heard a scream, then a whimper, then silence.

Slowly, almost soundlessly, the men approached from all sides. Now Tamara and Myrnyi were talking beside me. The police and Officer Lütjens were carrying their guns at the ready—they weren't taking any risks.

"Come out!" cried Sievers.

No answer.

"Come out at once or we're coming to get you!"

No answer.

"Well, in that case," said Sievers, feeling his way down the steps, pressed against the stair wall. He put his hand in his pocket. In the next moment a flashlight flared up. I had followed Sievers and could see, beyond the second pillar, a man lying face down on one of the floor planks, arms spread—our man.

Lütjens stopped the man who wanted to follow us down the steps. They stood still, panting, armed and unarmed—officers and civilians, Germans and foreigners. "Take it easy! Stay where you are!"

I sat down on one of the lower steps and saw Chief Sievers bending over the motionless figure. The beam of his flashlight

560

fell on a motor boat, tied to the third pillar. "He must have come in the boat," said Lütjens, "and that's how he wanted to get away."

"Fräulein Skinner, Herr Myrnyi, come here!" shouted Sievers.

Lütjens let them pass through. They clambered over the floor planks to Sievers. I followed them.

The man's light coat was slowly being dyed red. The blood flowed out of his back, above the heart. Tamara, Myrnyi, and I were quite close now; the water splashed and flowed over our shoes. The planks were slippery and I held onto one of the pillars.

"Now," said Sievers, kneeling beside the dead man. "Let's see your face."

He turned the body slowly on its back and I looked into the face of the servant, Olaf Notung.

18

Next morning, at 7:15, I arrived at the Bremen Main Station. Pastor Demel was waiting for me on the platform. We shook hands and walked silently to his Volkswagen. Demel looked exhausted and shocked. He didn't speak for a long time either as we drove off.

His call had reached me at 3:00 A.M. in the Davidswache, where I happened to be at the time. Hem had advised him to try there when the pastor had called him in a great state of excitement. I was to take the first train to Bremen, which I had done, terribly upset myself after what Demel had told me on the phone.

We reached the autobahn. Here there was fresh snow, the day was gray, the cloud ceiling was low.

"You'll want to know how it all happened," Demel said at last.

"Naturally."

"I can tell it more or less chronologically, and with very little missing, according to the information we have received in the meantime from various quarters," he explained. "So... chronologically..."

Last night, at 9:30, Fräulein Louise, in hat and coat, had

appeared at the gatehouse of the Ludwigskrankenhaus. The gatekeeper, who, like all the employees and doctors, by now knew Fräulein Louise very well, noticed that she looked happier than he had ever seen her—radiant, in fact—and she didn't seem to be in a hurry.

"I must go out for a moment," she told him. "The Herr Professor asked me to. You know, he doesn't sleep very well, and when he can't sleep, he smokes, and he's all out of his favorite cigarettes. I'm going to get him a couple of packs."

"Very well, Fräulein Louise."

"How is Elizabeth? With mumps you've got to be careful."

"She's a lot better, Fräulein Louise. The doctor says she'll be all over it soon."

"I'm glad to hear that. You know, once I had a child..." and she told him about a very bad case of mumps; then she chatted with him about his other two children. Finally she hurried off into the dark street. It was snowing quite heavily at the time.

A half hour later, when she hadn't returned, the gatekeeper had called the private sector and reported the incident to the night nurse in charge. The nurse woke the doctor on duty—by coincidence it happened to be Dr. Germela. He berated the gatekeeper for letting Fräulein Louise go out at such a late hour.

"I'm sorry, *Herr Doktor*," said the gatekeeper with a false show of politeness, "but I thought since we now have a democratization of psychiatry and are supposed to be getting a patients' parliament soon and all that, that there wasn't much sense in—" with which he wanted to show Dr. Germela, whom he disliked just as much as the rest of the young arrogant "revolutionary" doctors, just what he thought of them. Later that night, when the whole clinic was in an uproar, he was, of course, severely reprimanded.

The first thing Germela did was to hurry to Fräulein Louise's room, where he saw that she had taken with her her shawl, gloves, hat and coat, and what she had saved from the money Professor Leglund's daughter had given her. Hoping to find out something from the professor, Germela had stormed into his room. The old man was not asleep. "Fräulein Louise?" he asked, astonished. "What do you mean, 'Where is she?' She died twelve years ago."

Now Germela was nervous and rang the alarm. By this time Fräulein Louise was already riding in the autobahn in a taxi. She had chosen one of the taxis that were always parked near the entrance of the hospital. The driver came back to the clinic after this fare, and when the gatekeeper told him what had happened, he told all about his encounter with Fräulein Louise.

"She was very nice," he told Dr. Erkner, who was now conducting the search for Fräulein Louise. "I thought she belonged to some sort of sect."

"What made you think that?"

"Because..."

"Well! A man your age! You should be ashamed!" Fräulein Louise had exclaimed a few minutes after they had driven off. She was pointing to a copy of *Playboy* magazine lying between them—open, unfortunately. "Stop all this sinning!" she had told him. "When you reach the other world you'll find out how stupidly you've behaved. You'd do better to prepare yourself for that other world...." ("Really a nice old lady," the driver observed, "but very religious.")

It had stopped snowing, the cloud ceiling had parted, the moon was up.

"Please, could you drive faster?" Fräulein Louise had asked the driver.

"Sure can, lady."

"You see, I'm in a great hurry."

"In a hurry? Why?"

"Well, you know, I've had a simply terrible evening. They kept calling me, my friends did. I was to come. I was to come to them right away. Something really big must be going on."

"You have friends in Neurode?" the driver had asked, because Fräulein Louise had told him that was where she was heading.

"Yes. Good friends. The best. I must hurry. Could we drive still faster?"

"Sure thing," said the driver.

On the miserable road, however, he couldn't drive fast, but just before they came to Neurode, the Fräulein had asked him to stop. "But we still have a little way to go."

"I know. But—but I'd like to go the rest of the way on foot. I need some fresh air. What do I owe you?"

He told her and she paid him from money out of a small paper bag, which he thought odd, and she gave him five marks for a tip. "Thank you, lady. Good luck."

"The same to you," Fräulein Louise had cried happily as she walked out into the fresh snow. "And sin no more, right?"

The driver had laughed and driven into the village to turn around. When he had come back, he hadn't seen Fräulein Louise anymore, but then he hadn't been looking for her.

Dr. Erkner found out about all this at 11:45 P.M., when the driver reported it. He called the Youth Camp at once. At night, camp director Dr. Schall answered the phone. He had one in his bedroom, there was no one at the switchboard.

He got out of bed at once when he heard what Dr. Erkner had to say, and woke Dr. Schiemann and driver Kuschke and Pastor Demel. Together they ran to the entrance gate and asked the guard there if he'd seen Fräulein Louise. Of course he hadn't. Then, without much hope, they ran to her office, and finally they began calling her name aloud. Grown-ups and young people were awakened by their cries. A Spanish girl came up to them. She was still fully dressed and very excited. Schall spoke Spanish. He talked to her, then he translated for the others. "Juanita says she was in the Skull and Crossbones Tavern today for quite a long time, with a man who wanted to give her a job as a dancer, in Hamburg. The man gave her something to drink—quite a lot, as you can see." The beautiful girl really was tipsy. "Juanita said she got frightened and ran away from the man, back to the camp. She says she looked around all the time to see if he was following her."

"So?" From Kuschke.

"He didn't follow her," said Schall. "But a car drove up and turned around in the village—a taxi—and after that Juanita saw a figure in the moonlight. She can tell us exactly where. She isn't sure that it was Fräulein Louise, but she thinks it was. She says whoever it was walked into the reeds just below the village, out toward the moor."

"Jesus, Maria, and Joseph," groaned Kuschke.

"And then, Juanita says, the figure walked *out onto* the moor. It looked as if she were floating on it," said Schall. "She floated like that for quite a while, then suddenly she was gone."

"And now let's hurry!" said Kuschke.

"I'm afraid we can't hurry enough," said the pastor, after which there was a heavy silence. Nobody said a word. The moon shone on the little group. Juanita began to sob. Schall said, "I'll call the fire department. Perhaps they—" He didn't finish the sentence but ran to his barracks.

19

"The fire department responded quickly," said Pastor Demel. "Three trucks from neighboring villages, with all their equipment and floodlights. They worked all night. They're still working."

"Did they find the right place?"

"Yes. Juanita showed us before they came. Fräulein Louise walked from the village out onto the moor on the narrow path she always used when she went to see her friends. We found her footprints. That's where they're looking."

"And they've found nothing?"

"Nothing," the pastor said softly.

After that we didn't speak. We came to the dreadful road with its potholes and passed through the miserable little villages. They looked even more dismal than when I had seen them the first time. The whole area looked eerie. There was snow on the firm ground, but the moor was a black expanse of water except for a few white mounds and hillocks. The branches of the birches and alders were covered with snow, and the bulrushes were powdered with it. The reeds stood alongside the road, straight and stiff, like lances; the moor was shrouded in a miasma of fog. At last we arrived.

Red fire trucks blocked the way. I saw men with ladders and on planks, far out on the moor; others were sitting on the running boards of their trucks, drinking hot coffee out of paper cups. I spotted Camp Director Dr. Schall, Camp Doctor Schiemann, driver Kuschke, and Dr. Erkner. They were drinking coffee, too. Demel stopped the car and we got out. I greeted the gentlemen. They were pale and unshaven, and looked exhausted. The camp director said, "I think the men will give up soon. They've combed every inch of the moor where she could have possibly sunk. They can't find a trace of her. Nor her clothing. Nothing. She has simply disappeared."

"Without leaving a trace," said Kuschke, staring down at his big hands.

Dr. Erkner said softly and bitterly, "This is the second time in three months that a patient has managed to escape. And this time I'm going to do something about it. I'm not going to put up with what's going on at the clinic any longer. And Fräulein Gottschalk was doing so well."

"She was?"

"Yes. Why? Don't you agree?"

I told him that when I had seen her last, she had obviously reverted to her former condition and had evidently managed to keep it secret from the doctors. He asked me, "Why didn't you report it?"

"I did," I said. "Quite some time ago when I noticed the first signs. I wanted to see you, but Dr. Germela stopped me. So I told him all about it. He told me to mind my own business, said that Fräulein Gottschalk was very well integrated in your therapeutic community, and gave me a lecture on the democratization of psychiatry—"

"Stop!" Dr. Erkner was furious. "I don't want to hear any more. So it was Germela, damn him! God knows I don't have anything against long hair and beards and new ideas, but I'm going to set that young man straight when I get back. You can depend on it!"

"Unfortunately, that won't bring Fräulein Louise back to life," I said. The pastor and Dr. Schall joined us. "Happy and gay as never before in her life—that's how Fräulein Louise hurried by, because her friends had summoned her," I said slowly.

"Yes," said Demel. "That's what the few witnesses say." He thought for a moment, then he spoke as if to himself, "'Let me take leave of it all, not complaining but singing like a swan....' Who wrote that?"

Nobody knew.

"I'd like to go out there," I said.

They gave me a rubber suit like the ones the men with the ladders had on, and a pole to punt with, and I lay down on a ladder and pushed myself out onto the moor beside the narrow, snow-covered path. The snow on it clearly showed the imprint of a woman's pointed shoes, close together, as if Fräulein Louise had hurried across it. Another meter. Another. And then, without warning, the footprints ended. Nothing visible but the untouched snow. I lay on the ladder and stared at that last footprint. A fireman drew up alongside me and watched me for a while, silently, then he said, "This is where she fell in. But we've looked and looked. She's not under here."

"But she must be!"

"You'd think so, but she isn't. We'll never find her." And he floated away. I watched him go, but I stayed on a while longer beside the path and that last footpath, and thought of Fräulein Louise. Then I began to feel cold and hurried back to the shore. I took off the rubber suit and put on my coat and asked the pastor if I could go back to the camp and see Fräulein Louise's room once more. He nodded and accompanied me.

The barracks at the end of the camp, where the fog was collecting again over the moor, looked deserted; there were no voices, no sounds whatsoever coming from the rooms. We entered Fräulein Louise's office. It was bitter cold, and everything looked exactly as it had that afternoon when I had come for the first time. I looked around me—the ugly furniture, the files, the papers on the desk; somebody had cleaned the room a long time ago, and the dust had collected again, covering everything. The three cactuses on the windowsill were frozen. Ice flowers covered the window panes. I saw the hot plate which the pastor had repaired.

I walked slowly into the bedroom. It was cold here, too. There was the braided rug, the floor lamp, the wardrobe, the bookshelf, the wall with the six pictures painted by children, and on the bedside table the radio and the book I had leafed through. The bed had been made up again after Fräulein Louise had got up, on a night that now seemed very far away, and hurried to her friends on the moor before taking off for Hamburg.

"Why did you want to come back here once more?" asked Demel.

"I want to know what's left of such a human life," I said.

"Well," he said sadly, "now you know. Not much."

"I don't know about that," I said.

I picked up the book on the bedside table. It lay open between the alarm clock and a vial of sleeping pills, the book with the passage marked in red that I had begun to read once. Shakespeare, *Collected Works*, Volume III. This time I wanted to read the entire passage she had marked. *The Tempest*, Act IV, Scene 1. Prospero speaks: "Our revels now are ended. . . ." I read, then I handed Demel the book. He took it, and in the icy room, in a soft voice, he read the lines that might have been a necrologue for Fräulein Louise.

"Our revels now are ended, these our actors,
As I foretold you, were all spirits, and

Are melted into air, into thin air;
And, like the baseless fabric of this vision
The cloud-capped towers, the gorgeous palaces,
The solemn temples, the great globe itself,
Yea, all which it inherit, shall dissolve,
And, like this insubstantial pageant faded,
Leave not a rack behind. We are such stuff
As dreams are made on, and our little life
Is rounded with a sleep...."

20

"We are such stuff as dreams are made on...."

Again and again I had to think of the line as I sat in the train from Bremen to Frankfurt crossing the snow-clad countryside. And in my thoughts I said farewell to Fräulein Louise, who had touched me in a way no one had ever touched me before. At the time I didn't know that I was never really to say farewell to Fräulein Louise, that she was always going to be with me, around me, in me....

From the station I took the streetcar to Hem's apartment in the old house on Fürstenberger Strasse, beside Grüneberg Park. I took the elevator. As I unlocked the door, the lock seemed unusually loose, as if it was worn out, but I paid no attention to it at the time.

It was warm in the apartment. I knew Hem was at the office and Irina at her job, and that Bertie was working on my manuscript. I called out to him, but there was no answer. I walked through the long, dim passage to the two rooms Hem had given Irina and me, and opened the door to the one in which I worked. On the desk, beside the window I saw Bertie's body, slumped over, his head on the desk, his arms hanging down on either side. He had taken off his jacket. The back of his shirt was bloody. Blood had dripped on the floor, a lot of blood. Shuddering with horror, I walked over to him. At least five bullets had been fired into his back. The murderer must have worked fast. Bertie doubtlessly had suspected nothing, had heard the door open and thought it was me coming home. He probably hadn't even turned around. So there he sat; a pencil that had slipped out of his hand was lying in a pool of blood on the floor; his head lay sideways on the desk. His eyes were open, his face was white, but his lips were upturned in a smile. He had died smiling.

The entire apartment had been ransacked, drawers torn out of the desk and cupboards, their contents scattered on the floor. My entire manuscript, with copy, was gone. I couldn't see any of the tapes, nor the recorder, and none of my copied notes. In a panic, I searched for them but found nothing. I called the police and told them to come at once. It was all clear to me, and I was filled with helpless rage and indescribable sorrow.

"What's the matter?" asked the officer on the phone.

"There's been a murder," I said. "My friend Bertie—my good friend Bertie is dead."

"*Who* has been murdered, Herr Roland?"

"I have been murdered," I said, beside myself with grief, because it was absolutely clear to me—Bertie had been shot by mistake. The one whom they had meant to silence was myself!

"You—you have been murdered? Are you crazy?"

I couldn't speak and hung up. Five minutes later the first car from homicide arrived.

21

The police agreed with me—Bertie had been shot by mistake; I was the one they were after. After all, the manuscript and tapes were gone. The investigation of the case was carried on in as great secrecy as possible. When Irina and Hem came home, Bertie's body had already been removed, and I had washed away all traces of blood.

Irina wept when I told her what happened. Hem said only, "The pigs! The goddamn' pigs! Who do you suppose did it?"

"Anyone who is interested in the story not appearing," I said, "or all of them together. They may have hired a hit man—who can tell? The story is not to be published. Herford doesn't want it, the Amis don't want it, the Russians don't want it, and—who knows? Vandenberg may not want it either."

"But he told you to write the book!" cried Irina.

"Yes, he did," I said. "But perhaps on order or with the complicity of others. So that they could be sure I was writing the book for Vandenberg and not letting anyone else in on it. Only, they did away with the wrong man! I'll sue them all: Herford, the Amis, the Russians, *and* Vandenberg! From here on in I don't trust anybody. You'll see—they'll never find the murderer!"

And I was right—they never did.

"One of us has to go and speak to Bertie's mother," said Hem. "I will, if you want me to, Walter."

"No," I said, "that's something I want to do myself."

Bertie's mother lived not far away from Hem in a section of the city called Bockenheim on Leipzigerstrasse. A maid, her eyes red-rimmed from crying, said Frau Engelhardt had collapsed after the police had informed her of her son's death, but I was to come in; she was expecting me. I had phoned that I was coming.

The maid led me into a large, beautifully furnished room. Frau Engelhardt was sitting very upright on a sofa, wearing a black dress. To my knowledge, she was eighty-four years old. She was slender and tall, her hair was gray, and her fine features gave her face an effect of transparency.

"Sit down, please, Herr Roland," she said, and her voice, the voice of an old woman, was firm and calm. "I am glad you came and not anyone else. Bertie's publisher and editor-in-chief and so many others have called—reporters from the newspapers, too—so an hour ago I took the receiver off the hook."

I sat down and looked at the old lady whom I had known for so many years, and found I couldn't utter a word. There were a lot of flowers in vases on various tables. Bertie's mother gestured in their direction. "They just came. Bertie had so many friends. He was a good boy, wasn't he?"

"Yes," I said. "He was my friend. We worked together for many years. I—I—"

"I know," said Bertie's mother. "He was very fond of you, you know. He admired you."

"*Ach....*"

"He really did. And he was always happy when he could work with you." She looked at me, a gentle expression in her eyes. I was silent. I still didn't know what to say. Everything that came to me seemed banal. "God's ways are strange," she said. "I have been waiting for death for a long time, yet I am alive, and my Bertie is dead. Now I am all alone. He wasn't home much, but we always kept in touch. He called me whenever he could, or sent a wire or wrote, and sent flowers. Perhaps God will be merciful and let me die soon, too. What is there left for me to do on this earth?"

"Dear Frau Engelhardt—"

"No, don't say anything. I know how you feel. This is a moment when the best thing we can do is be silent and think of Bertie. Would you like to be silent with me?"

I nodded, and for quite a long time neither of us said anything, and I thought of the many adventures I had shared with Bertie, of his blithe spirit, of how often he had laughed and of how even in death he had been smiling. At last his mother rose and walked over to a chest, which she opened. She motioned to me to join her, and I did. The chest was three-quarters full of letters and telegrams. There must have been hundreds. "All from him," she said. "In all these years he wrote me these letters and sent me these telegrams. He is not altogether gone. I still have a lot left, don't I? I can read these letters and wires, can't I?"

"Yes, Frau Engelhardt."

"And that is a great consolation to me."

"I'm sure it is," I said, and thought, surprised and depressed at the same time: What can be a comfort to one in one's misery! She showed me a few of his letters, from Tokyo, Hollywood, Saigon, Johannesburg, and as she did so she forgot more and more that I was present. She was so old, so tired of life, and finally, as I said good-bye, all she did was nod vaguely, without getting up. The last thing I saw was her reading a letter of Bertie's, a letter he had written to his beloved mother from some faraway place on this earth. I closed the door of the room softly and felt absolutely miserable.

The cremation took place two days later. Bertie had expressed the wish to be cremated, and the ceremony took place at the crematorium. A lot of people came: Bertie's colleagues, and from *Blitz*, everybody who could possibly have been present—Herford to the fore, of course, with Mama. Hem was there. Irina and I didn't go, and Hem told us that Herford held a long speech, in execrable taste, listing all that Bertie had done for *Blitz*. "I loved him like a son," Herford had said, sobbing. There were wreaths and flowers and everything was pompous to the nth degree, and Bertie's mother had sat through the entire ceremony in the first row, motionless. She had looked at no one, spoken to no one; and when the urn had finally been lowered into the grave, she had simply walked away.

That evening—it was Tuesday, January 14, 1969—Hem said

to me, "You know what it means, don't you? That they shot the wrong man and that you're still alive."

"Yes," I said. "I know."

"And you have a wife now, and your wife is expecting a child."

"What are you talking about?" asked Irina.

"Nothing, my darling," I said. "Nothing. Don't get excited. But there's something I have to do now, Hem, isn't there? Right away."

"Yes," said Hem. "As fast as you can."

"Oh, I see," said Irina. "Yes, Walter. Of course. That's what you must do." And suddenly I remembered something Fräulein Louise had said to me in the Ludwigskrankenhaus in Bremen. "It is a message from my friends, for you and Herr Engelhardt. I am to pass it on to you because you are good people. You are going to be happy, Herr Roland—that is my friends' message, but you still will have a long way to go until you reach a state of bliss, and you will have to overcome many trials and be patient. But for your friend Engelhardt it will be easier, and more beautiful. He has always had it easier, hasn't he? And he will soon attain everything that is desirable. . . ."

22

His name was Peter Blenheim. He was a graphics artist, in his late forties, and he had a shy charm and a habit of placing the tips of his beautiful fingers together when he spoke. He was tall and tanned, looked happy, and had thick brown hair, a long face, and the blank, dark eyes of a squirrel. In spite of his height, there was something about him that reminded you of the speed and comic playfulness of a squirrel.

But of course he wasn't like a squirrel at all. He wasn't tall, nor did he look happy. He didn't place the tips of his beautiful fingers together when he spoke, he didn't have a sly charm nor was he a graphics artist. But he *was* near fifty. His name certainly wasn't Peter Blenheim. It is obvious, I am sure, that I have had to give him a different name and persona.

"Any friend of Max Knipper's is a friend of mine," was his greeting. Then he asked Irina and me to come into his mansard apartment and led us into a big studio, where he worked. Posters and designs for advertisements were attached to the walls with thumbtacks—big ones, little ones, colored, and black and white. Crayons, pens, brushes, and templates were scattered across a table. There was an easel with a canvas on it.

He asked us to sit down on a couch with a low table in front of it. The couch had no feet and was covered with a colorful blanket. He sat down opposite us on a red-leather Oriental hassock. He made a good impression on Irina and me right away—reliable, capable, a man who could be trusted, and that he was.

"You can't get a better man," Max had said, when I had told him our problem. "Wait. I'll call him and tell him you're coming."

"Is he so busy?"

"Naw...but he'll only see you if a good friend has recommended you. And he's right. He's been doing this all his life, and he's never had any trouble with the police."

Peter Blenheim forged papers—passports, citizenship papers, birth and baptismal certificates, whatever you needed. For any country, in any language. Any original documents that he couldn't dig up didn't exist. We soon found that out when he asked us what country we intended to reside in and what we wanted our names to be.

"I work fast and well, and I'm expensive," he said. "I've never had an unsatisfied customer, and nothing's ever gone wrong."

A pity that I can't identify Peter Blenheim and recommend him highly to whoever might be interested. He looked after us fabulously. And he wasn't all that expensive in the end. I still had the diamonds. I was able to pay for everything else easily—the flight tickets and what we needed when we finally reached our destination. We managed the whole first difficult time on the money I was able to get for the diamonds.

All this seems to lie an eternity behind me. Naturally, I can't reveal our names and where we have found a new home on this earth. We are well. I don't write anymore but have a completely different profession, and I'm making good money. And there are three of us. Irina gave birth to a girl, whose name I shall also not reveal. I adore the child. Sometimes I think Irina is a little jealous. The work I am doing is honest and decent, a far cry from my past. And I have changed, too, to the extraordinary extent that I

573

paid off my debts to *Blitz* and my tax arrears—complicated transactions, but I managed them. And to this day I haven't drunk a drop.

We were with Peter Blenheim a long time that day because we had no time to lose, and he set to work right away. He took our passport pictures and we looked through two collections of printed forms with him and composed two new lives, one for Irina and one for me, with names, dates, and places.

"You must learn these dates and places by heart," said Peter Blenheim. "If anybody wakes you out of your sleep and yells at you with your former name, you mustn't give the slightest sign that it means anything to you. Your new life must be in your blood. Practice it! Try it! Let one of you wake the other in the middle of the night and ask him when he was born, and where, and what his mother's name is. That's just as important as the papers."

"Yes," I said, and we actually did practice these nightly alarms for a long time after our flight.

"I always say," said Blenheim, "that one hundred percent perfect papers are no use if the person himself isn't one hundred percent forged."

I looked at Irina, then at him again. "What's the matter?" he asked.

"You speak with an accent," I said. "A slight dialect. You're not from Frankfurt, are you?"

"No," he said, pressing the tips of his fingers together and smiling. "I'm not from here, although I've been living here for many years. But it's a funny thing—I don't seem to lose my accent."

"Where are you from?" I asked slowly. "Austria?"

"A little farther away. Bohemia. That's where I come from. My parents were born there, all my family from way back. We had a small farm in Spindlermühle."

"Spindlermühle...where's that?" asked Irina.

"In the Riesengebirge. Not far from the White Meadow," he said. "There's a high moor there. You won't believe it, but after I graduated from high school, I went to the University of Vienna. Studied philosophy. That startles you, does it?"

"Yes," I said, and looked at Irina, and she looked at me.

"Well, that didn't last long. I got together with some people doing—well, this kind of work, and I gave up my studies. Soon after that my parents died, and I sold the farm." His eyes looked far away. "But those were good days, at the university. I always went home for my vacations, to Spindlermühle and the White Meadow. Was there every summer." His smile broadened. "Even fell in love. Lasted for a whole summer. With a girl who'd come from Vienna. She worked in a children's home. Social worker. A pretty girl and a beautiful love. Well . . . and since then so much time has gone by."

"Your friend was a social worker?" asked Irina.

"Isn't that what I said?" said Peter Blenheim. "There were a lot of them around at the time. Young. Pretty. But I liked this one best. Only lasted a few months, then we had to part. But it was true love, and for her, the first, even though she was a little older than I . . . ." He nodded nostalgically, a middle-aged man recalling his youth. "I often dream of her and that wonderful summer, and the wide expanse of moor. But—" He stopped.

"But?" I asked.

"But however hard I try to remember—I've even tried searching for her. . . ." He shook his head. "Nothing to be done about it. After all, it's almost forty years ago. Frankly, I don't even recall the exact year it happened. As for the name of the girl—"

"Yes?" asked Irina.

"I've forgotten it," he said, with a shy smile, fingertips touching, a man with brown hair, tanned, reminding one of a squirrel. In his clear dark eyes there was an expression of wonder, veiled by sadness over the fact that in our world we forget everything. We forget what was painful and terrible, but also what was beautiful and lovely . . . after a time.